OPERATION SNOWSHOE

TOM ERICKSON

DURBAN HOUSE

Printed in the United States of America.

For information address:

Durban House Press, Inc.
Two Galleria Tower
13455 Noel Road, Suite 1000
Dallas, Texas 75240

Library of Congress Cataloging-in-Publication Data

Erickson, Tom

Operation Snowshoe/Tom Erickson

Library of Congress Control Number: 2008934976

p. cm.

ISBN: 978-0-9818486-0-0

First Edition

10 9 8 7 6 5 4 3 2 1

Visit our Web site at
http://www.durbanhouse.com

To Patricia with love

ACKNOWLEDGEMENTS

Many people, including Jane and Bill, read my manuscript and offered insightful suggestions. Three others did much more.

Carol Scott tutored me from the beginning, encouraging a struggling writer to find his voice.

Robert Middlemiss shared his considerable talents and, like all great teachers, gave me valuable instruction without trying to change my perspective or style.

John Lewis believed in my work and allowed a first-time author to live the ultimate dream of being published.

To all, my heartfelt thanks.

CHAPTER ONE

Thomas L. Kempner, Jr., walked into a courtroom on the fourth floor of the Everett M. Dirksen Building, a Chicago high-rise where those accused of felonies were put on trial. He draped his winter overcoat over the rail behind the defense counsel's table, sat down, and opened his satchel-style briefcase. His three clients were seated beside him. The young men were part of Mr. Gary Barbera's Mafia family. Each of the gentleman don's soldiers was facing a charge of first degree murder.

Kempner waited a few moments, then pushed back his chair. With a legal pad in hand, he glanced at the polished granite floor. While the gallery of TV pundits and print journalists settled in, he stood up, remembering how Mr. Barbera's mobsters had moaned when he insisted they leave their sharkskin sport coats and bright silk ties in the closet.

Tom Kempner was born a year before the end of World War II. He was an amateur bicyclist whose physique suited his sport. At just under six feet and one-seventy, he was fit and lean. His hazel eyes, sandy hair, and smooth complexion made Tom look much younger than his age, an asset he used to temper the idea that all mob attorneys were unprincipled, cold-hearted shysters.

He wore a three-piece, dark gray suit, a pin-striped, French-cuffed shirt, and a Hermes tie. Had he been standing in an office instead of a courtroom, he might have passed for a high-powered investment banker. But Tom Kempner was no Wall Street wheeler-dealer. He was Mr. Barbera's savvy trial lawyer and *consigliere*.

Years before, he'd kept his composure when asked by a reporter why a Jewish guy with a law degree from Harvard worked for the ruling don of the Chicago Mafia:

"Mr. Barbera wants a winner who plays by the rules. I fit that bill."

Tom's answer, like his style, had been direct. Of course, he knew the makeup of the boss's business empire. That was why it was important to play by the rules. Some called it ethical misconduct when a lawyer made the system work for his client. He called it being clever.

The courtroom quieted. Tom Kempner stared at the bullet points he'd written on the legal pad. Once the judge called for order and told him to proceed, he looked up. He knew the pitfalls of playing to the media. Instead of embarrassing the federal prosecutor with a grandstand speech, he made eye contact with the judge.

"Your Honor, our system of criminal justice embraces the presumption of innocence." Tom paused to allow the simplicity of his words to resonate. "In America, guilt must be proven beyond any reasonable doubt."

Using his free hand, he pointed toward his three young clients. On cue, the men turned toward the jury. Each had a Princeton-style haircut and was clean-shaven. And each was dressed in a blue suit with a white shirt and bland rep tie.

"The district attorney has not met his burden," Tom went on. "His witnesses have told inconsistent and in some instances, contradictory stories. To prevent a miscarriage of justice, I ask this court for a directed verdict."

William Pavin, the Chicago Federal District Attorney, jumped to his feet and began citing case law. Tom listened, then placed his legal pad on the defense counsel's table. Why take notes? He knew Mr. Barbera's mob soldiers were guilty. He also knew the DA was a tough, capable prosecutor. But on this day, those facts wouldn't be relevant. Unknown influences, from sources he didn't control, had turned the trial to his advantage. A courtroom battle that had received national publicity was about to end with a whimper.

Tom ignored Pavin's ranting. Instead, he stared straight ahead and let his facial muscles relax. He wanted to appear confident, but his composure hid deep concerns. Why had the DA's case fallen apart? Who had made that happen? And for what reason?

The trial had begun yesterday morning. Bill Pavin had opened by parading two men to the stand. Each swore the defendants had beaten a reputed drug dealer to death. Their testimony appeared solid, but after the noon recess, when Tom had begun his cross-examination, the witnesses had changed their stories. Of course, he'd been pleased, but mostly, he'd wondered how the DA's stoolies could have been eyewitnesses in the morning and blind witnesses in the afternoon.

Tom rocked back on his heels and stared at the ceiling. While the prosecutor shouted and waved his arms, Tom touched his Hermes tie, using his thumb and index finger to make sure the knot was centered. Only on the rarest of occasions did he raise his voice or use hand gestures to emphasize a point. In fact, Tom had reminded himself to stay calm when he'd entered the courtroom a little less than ten minutes ago. He was baffled by the recantations of the prior afternoon, but since the Fed's witnesses had discredited themselves, he decided to scrap his opening statement. A smart lawyer didn't try a case that was likely to be dismissed.

"Mr. Pavin," the judge said, eying the DA. "I've heard Mr. Kempner's motion and listened to your objection. This is an important capital case. Before I rule, I want to review the transcripts."

His Honor banged down the gavel and left the bench for chambers. With the court temporarily in recess, Tom stuffed his legal pads into his briefcase, then he and his three young clients grabbed their winter overcoats.

As the bailiff led the way, they walked out a side door, into a hallway, and down the back stairs. They hoped to outflank the press, but when they entered the lobby, TV floodlights popped on and he and Mr. Barbera's mob soldiers were engulfed by a swarm of media personnel.

Using "No comment," to answer every question, Tom shepherded his clients through a small army of shouting reporters. On any other winter day, the gale force winds and subzero temperatures might have deterred them. But not today.

With scarves pulled up to shield their faces, they walked briskly along one of the snowplowed paths that crisscrossed Daley Plaza. Once at the corner, they turned onto Dearborn Street and headed for the top floor in the Security Chicago National Bank building. Minutes later, Tom herded his clients into a boardroom stocked with doughnuts and hot coffee.

While Mr. Barbera's three men lounged—their ties loosened and their feet on the mahogany conference table—Tom headed down the hall to his office. The day was cloudless and brilliant. Sunlight glistened off the steel and glass high-rises, but when he dropped down onto his leather chair and looked eastward past the business and residential towers, the recanted testimony of Bill Pavin's witnesses stayed with him. Why, he wondered, had they crumbled?

Out a short distance from the shoreline, patches of swirling vapor rose off Lake Michigan. More than three decades ago, he'd seen the same phenomenon. On that bright day in late December, Tom had signed on as a junior attorney for Holly Corporation, Gary Barbera's giant construction company. Since then, the showpiece of the crime boss's legitimate business empire had gotten much bigger. Of course, Tom's stature in the organization had grown too. As *consigliere*, he was now part of the inner circle and had the gentleman don's ear.

Tom looked up and saw his secretary, Debbie Nyko, standing in the doorway.

"It's your wife, Mr. Kempner," she said, mouthing her words. "The missus sounds angry."

As his secretary turned and left, he groaned, then hit the speakerphone button. "Hello, Katherine. Busy as hell. What can I do for you?"

"Plenty," she snapped, her voice filling his office. "But for openers, hold your bloody tongue and listen."

Tom tensed, his wife's cockney slang getting his attention. Katherine was born and raised in the fashionable West End of London, but shortly after moving to America, she'd dropped the elegant tones spoken in Hyde Park and mixed her English colloquialisms with a Midwest accent.

"Your nickel, Katherine. Let's have it."

"MI-6 got their act together. Grandfather's documents arrived at ten this morning."

Tom sat back in his chair. He was still baffled by her earthy inflection, but at least he knew the source of her distress. For the past several months, his wife had been frustrated by MI-6, the British Secret Service. Her initial attempt to obtain her grandfather's World War II diaries and memoirs had been stonewalled. Of course, that hadn't lasted very long. Katherine's mother and father were descended from royalty. At first chance, she'd dropped a few family names to make sure MI-6 realized they weren't dealing with an ordinary Brit.

"Glad the limey bureaucrats finally made good on their word," Tom said, turning toward the speakerphone. "Did they gift-wrap General Cunningham's documents as a way to make amends?"

"Not funny, Tommy. For your information, Grandfather Cunningham's documents came in a crate. A big wooden crate."

"Really," he said, faking enthusiasm. "With that much to choose from, you're bound to find something useful. Even money says your grandfather's papers will give you some insights."

Initially, Tom wondered why the delivery of General Cunningham's wartime papers hadn't made Katherine happy. Now, as his response was greeted with silence, he felt his stomach churn. It never failed. It was best to take Katherine's bullying and keep a low profile when the subject matter concerned her grandfather's papers and the reason she'd sent for them.

Of course, he hadn't been so passive when she'd proposed the idea of digging into the British archives. Back then, he'd encouraged her. Katherine had reacted badly to the recent death of her father.

Her guilt stemmed from her inability to gain closure on a nearly life-long estrangement, a situation Tom believed was the result of the man's aristocratic snobbery.

The alienation had come to a head when she was fourteen. Over her mother's objections, her father had contacted his sister, Harriet, then shipped Katherine off to America. To be sure, she'd been a rebellious free spirit; and certainly, she hadn't been interested in learning the feminine graces or taking her rightful place in the Court of St. James. But did that justify banishing her to a Chicago suburb to live with her Aunt Harriet and Uncle Sean?

Tom knew Katherine had flourished during her teenage years and thereafter, thriving in the more free and easy American culture. He also knew her achievements had gone unnoticed. Her father had refused to attend any of her graduations, even when she excelled in high school, college, and medical school.

"What's with the attitude?" Tom asked. "Your grandfather's documents are here. Dig in and you'll get answers. Sure, it's been a struggle, but you prevailed."

"Wrong on at least one count," she replied. "My struggle isn't over. It's just beginning."

Tom picked up a pencil and let his mind mull over the facts: The papers had arrived at 10 AM. Since then, Katherine had been examining them. She had hoped—and still had a right to hope—that her grandfather would use his World War II diaries and military journals as a platform to express family sentiments. If that happened and General Alan Cunningham wrote of his own frustrations in dealing with his son (Katherine's father), she would not only know she hadn't been alone, but perhaps gain a new perspective—some reason to help her understand why her father had abandoned her—some excuse for her to love him again.

Tom checked his watch. 12:15 PM. Katherine—his bride for more than three decades and the mother of his son—was brimming with anticipation when he'd kissed her and left for the courthouse. Since then her attitude had undergone a significant change. Granted, the death of her father had left her with many unresolved emotional frustrations, but two hours was hardly enough time to pass judgment on a crateload of documents.

"Sorry you're upset," he said, doodling on the notepad. "Guess the general's memoirs never touched on his son."

"You're slipping," she replied, her tone sarcastic. "Lawyers aren't supposed to draw conclusions from incomplete facts."

"Guilty as charged," he agreed. "You've got the answers. Set the record straight."

"With pleasure. Your statement assumes I had a chance to dig into the material. That didn't happen. Grandfather's documents arrived with strings attached."

"Strings?" Tom asked. "What kind of strings?"

"The human kind," she replied, her voice rising again. "Our neighbor started pounding on the front door a few minutes after the UPS guy dropped the crate off."

Tom knew Katherine's anger was back, and once again he was bewildered by her reaction. Throughout his wife's negotiation with MI-6, she had sought their neighbor's advice. Now Katherine was upset. But why treat Joanna Gaylani as a confidante before the delivery of the general's papers and as an obstructionist afterward? Her best friend couldn't control the content of the documents. It wasn't her fault if the general hadn't dwelled on his relationship with his son.

"Joanna's a sweetheart," Tom said. "I'm sure she just stopped by to help."

"It wasn't Joanna!" Katherine scoffed, her acrimony more apparent than ever. "Remember our dinner with the Gaylanis the other night? Tony—the pious Italian Catholic—was the only one interested in Grandfather's memoirs."

"Now that you mention it, I do remember."

Tom's heartbeat increased. He tried to sound casual, but the tone of his wife's comment disturbed him. They'd been dining at the club with Dr. R. Anthony and Joanna Myerson Gaylani. During cocktails, Tony had expressed interest in Katherine's grandfather, wanting to know specifics about General Alan Cunningham's career. When his wife said the general had been stationed in Palestine during and after World War II, Dr. Tony Gaylani really bored in. For the next several minutes, the obnoxious half of the duo living next door wouldn't let the subject alone.

Normally, the doctor's interest would have gone unnoticed. The Middle East was a hot topic. People of all races and religions debated Arab-Israeli politics. But Dr. R. Anthony Gaylani wasn't a Midwesterner caught up in world affairs. Tony also wasn't an Italian Catholic.

Tom knew he had his facts right. Back in the mid-sixties, US Army Lieutenant Thomas Kempner had spoken to the nurses as he recuperated from battlefield wounds in an Army hospital outside Da Nang, Vietnam. Those nurses told him that the man who'd saved his life—Army Captain Dr. R. Anthony Gaylani—had made a great effort to hide his true nationality.

"Wednesday is Tony's day off," Tom said, touching the knot of his tie. "What did he want?"

"Everything," his wife complained, her voice echoing through the speakerphone. "At our tree trim party, I mentioned Grandfather's papers and my problems with MI-6. Since then, our Wop neighbor has had an insatiable appetite for the written commentary of World War II British generals stationed in the Middle East."

Again, he was taken aback, this time by her use of the term *wop*. Katherine abhorred any form of prejudice. Even if livid, she would never debase ethnicity. Yet just now, Tom knew her slur was intentional.

He dropped the pencil on the notepad and looked at the ceiling. His wife must have come across some eye-openers in her grandfather's memoirs. No other explanation made sense. In Italy, Gaylani was a name found in the phone directory. In the Muslim world, the surname was in all the Iraqi schoolbooks.

"Guess Dr. Tony Gaylani shares your opinion," Tom said. "You've always told me that your grandfather was a fascinating guy."

"Fascinating, but plainspoken. Tony is more complicated. Based on a few glimpses of Grandfather's memos, I'd say the Catholic choirboy is two-faced."

"World War II was pivotal for Europe and the Middle East," he said, hoping a sweeping statement would elicit a specific response. "The general had to witness many telling events."

"He did," she acknowledged, "but unfortunately for me, Grandfather wrote more about other families than his own. A handwritten note, paper-clipped to a typed memo, identified a notorious Arab father who had plans for his young son."

Tom's face steeled. He wanted to understand the depth of Katherine's knowledge, especially if her grandfather's memoranda had made reference to Rashid Ali el-Gaylani.

Decades before, shortly after being shipped back to the US for recovery and rehab, Tom had gone to a library to verify the Army nurse's claim. His research produced results. Rashid Ali el Gaylani— a firebrand Iraqi right-winger who had sought political power in the late thirties and early forties—was married to a woman named Ziyara and had fathered a young son.

"You mentioned an Arab father and his son. Did the memo refer to anyone we know?"

Tom chose his words with care. He would control the dialogue by employing a lawyer's tactic. *Never ask a question you can't answer yourself.*

"An Iraqi named Rashid Ali el-Gaylani was featured," Katherine answered. "From what I saw, the guy harbored some nasty ideas."

"Like what?"

"According to Grandfather Cunningham's memo, this man, Rashid, traveled to Nazi Germany and met with Hitler. He wanted the Axis powers to back his attempt to overthrow the pro-British government in Iraq."

"What about his son? Can you be more specific?"

"I know he was a young boy in the early 1940s," Katherine replied, "but that's about it. Tony hovered so much, I couldn't do serious reading."

Tom picked up the pencil. He'd done the math once before, and he did it again. A young boy during the time of World War II would be about Tony Gaylani's age today.

"I'm confused by the word *hovered*. Are you telling me our neighbor was aggressive? That he wanted to prevent you from looking at the general's papers?"

"He was everywhere. Peering over my shoulder. Creepy, so damned creepy." Katherine spoke softly, but a thread of fear ran through her voice. "And that's not all. Aside from keeping tabs on me, the doctor did his own rummaging. Call me paranoid, but I see danger."

His wife continued her account, saying that documents were strewn around the crate. By any definition, Tony's behavior was outrageous. But for a time she put up with it. The doctor seemed frantic, and she was worried their neighbor's compulsion to skim through her grandfather's papers might have ramifications for Joanna, her best friend. Katherine wanted to unmask Dr. R. Anthony Gaylani for what he was, but if their neighbor had been trained in a second less-visible career, she also wanted to alert Tony's wife, Joanna Gaylani.

"I figured out one thing for sure. Our neighbor didn't learn all his trade secrets in medical school. A cover letter from my grandfather to MI-6 made reference to a tutorial. As I read it, Rashid Ali el-Gaylani set up a plan for his son and wife to leave the country for America. His motives were dual purposed: Rashid wanted his family to come back in triumph if his coup was successful, or stay and build a subversive network if it wasn't."

Tom took a deep breath, shocked and caught completely off guard. Katherine had just upped the ante. Aside from suggesting that Tony was Rashid Ali el-Gaylani's son, she'd branded him as a spy. None of his research had even hinted at that possibility.

"Create a spy network in America?" Tom questioned. "Sounds a little farfetched. By your own admission, Rashid's son came to the US as a boy, not a man schooled in espionage."

"Grandfather Cunningham wrote that his evidence wasn't iron-clad, but his sources had claimed that Rashid's wife was in charge of implementing her husband's agenda."

"Is Tony still hanging around?" Tom asked.

"Just threw him out. When he stuffed one of Grandfather's memoranda into his sport coat, I told him I had to leave for a nail appointment and he had to go too."

Tom tried to assimilate Katherine's allegations with an event that had occurred yesterday. Just before he'd entered the courtroom, Admiral Eric Weiss, Deputy Director of the CIA, had contacted him. Since he and the admiral had worked on the QT before, Tom thought it was business as usual. But this time Eric Weiss didn't want mob informants to dig up dirt on Hispanic-American trucking executives. This time the admiral asked about his neighbor, Dr. R. Anthony Gay-lani.

"I'm glad you told Tony to leave," Tom said. "Think he'll come back?"

"Not likely. He's gone and good riddance."

As his wife reassured him, Tom was distracted when his secretary knocked on his door and poked her head inside.

"Hold on, Katherine."

He waved Debbie over and read the note she laid on his desk.

"Sorry, I have to go. His Honor just called us back."

"Damn it, Tommy, there's more to tell."

"Already late," he replied, "but I'll phone when I know something."

"Does that mean an hour... two... maybe more?"

"Please, Katherine. Don't make me hang up."

He hated being short with the woman he loved, but Tom knew he had to get off the phone. Katherine couldn't know his reasons, but he was boxed in and had already said too much. CIA rules were clear. Once Admiral Eric Weiss had made contact and verbalized his request, Tom Kempner wasn't allowed to discuss anything about their neighbor or his past.

He stood up, but as he prepared to return to the courthouse, his thoughts kept going back to his wife's phone call and her plaintive words: *"Call me paranoid, but I see danger."*

CHAPTER TWO

Tom Kempner picked up his winter overcoat and grabbed his briefcase. Duty called, but instead of rounding up his clients and getting back to the courthouse, he stopped and allowed his mind to focus on the first day of the trial. Someone had influenced the testimony of Bill Pavin's prosecution witnesses. But who? And why?

He crumpled his secretary's note and tossed it in the wastebasket. Regrettably, that bizarre flip-flop wasn't the only thing giving him a nervous stomach. Tom had also been disturbed by his wife's phone call and her depiction of their neighbor's bold intrusion.

Of course, he didn't think Katherine was in any immediate danger. Tony Gaylani had no reason to fear any allegations made by General Allan Cunningham. Sure, his diaries and documents named Rashid Ali el-Gaylani and his son. And yes, Tom believed Tony Gaylani was the boy in question, but the sins of the father are not the sins of the son.

Tom lowered his head. He knew none of General Cunningham's written opinions were admissible in a court of law, and yet one of his wife's statements continued to echo in his ears:

"A handwritten note, paper-clipped to a typed memo, identified a notorious Arab father who had plans for his young son."

Katherine's reference to a tutorial was, in all likelihood, a low probability event. But what if Rashid Ali el-Gaylani had designed a scheme? What if his wife had carried it out? What if Tony Gaylani was engaged in some kind of clandestine undertaking?

Tom's stomach knotted. He dropped his satchel-style briefcase on the floor and threw his overcoat across his desk. The courthouse could wait. A new thought had his brain buzzing.

A little over twenty-four hours ago, Eric Weiss, Deputy Director of the CIA, had called. Today, minutes after declassified wartime papers were delivered to his house, Dr. R. Anthony Gaylani had made a beeline to his front door. Coincidental? Maybe, but maybe not.

He sank back into his chair but couldn't get comfortable. As he picked up a pencil and felt his grip tighten, he stared out the window. Earlier, the shocking about-face of the DA's witnesses had bugged him. Now he couldn't get the admiral's call out of his head.

It had happened yesterday morning. He'd been standing outside the courtroom when his very private cell phone rang. He'd expected to hear Mr. Barbera's quiet voice. He'd been wrong.

"Morning, buddy-boy."

"Admiral, what a pleasant surprise."

He and Eric Weiss had grown up in a poor Jewish neighborhood in Brooklyn. Each had excelled academically and gotten scholarships. Since college, they'd gone their separate ways. But over the last twenty-five years, they'd talked more than a few times.

"Drop the smooth talk, buddy-boy. We both know you hate hearing from me."

"On the contrary, Admiral, I'm all ears. What's on your mind?"

"I need to talk to your boss."

The admiral despised the Mafia. Calling him "buddy-boy" underscored the man's particular disdain for those who defended their constitutional freedoms. But Eric Weiss was a pragmatist. While joint ventures between the Mafia and CIA were rare, they did happen. And why not? When the Company couldn't use regular channels to get the job done, the CIA looked to an innovator. Since the spies at Langley had a unique way of showing their appreciation, the mob was anxious to find creative solutions to sticky problems.

"Mr. Barbera is always happy to cooperate. Any chance I can tell him what it's about?"

"Why so nosy?" the admiral asked. "Don't you trust me?"

"Our roots go back to the old neighborhood. Trust has never been an issue with us."

"I suppose you're right. Remember when the rabbi called our temple the Wailing Wall of Brooklyn? Back then, we stood back-to-back and defended our turf. Right now, I need your help again. We're Jews. We respect each other. Why wouldn't you lend a hand?"

Tom pondered the admiral's words: cordial, reasonable, and false. While that wasn't cause for alarm, something else annoyed him. Weiss had just put a new slant on the procedure. In the past, as *consigliere*, he'd been the liaison between his boss and the deputy director. Now, Admiral Eric Weiss wanted to talk directly to Mr. Gary Barbera.

"Like you, Admiral, the boss is a busy man. If your business is urgent, knowing the subject might expedite the process."

"You disappoint me, buddy-boy. Don't all my demands get high-priority treatment?"

"Without question," Tom agreed.

"Then stamp this one life or death."

Tom wondered why his role had gotten scrapped, but he knew he still had to cooperate. He'd pass along the request and caution the gentleman don to choose his words carefully.

"I'll ask the boss to call on your private line, but you should know that Mr. Barbera doesn't get involved in surveillance activities. If the person of interest is another trucker..."

"Calm down, buddy-boy. This isn't about a trucker. It's about your neighbor. I believe you and Dr. R. Anthony Gaylani have a history almost as long as ours."

"Figured the Company kept an eye on me, but... but..." Tom felt his face flush. "Looking for skeletons in my neighbor's closet... Isn't that a stretch?"

"You haven't changed. Even as a kid, you had to have the last word."

"Just joking, Admiral."

"Maybe you are, but I'm not. Cut the damn lawyering. Get Barbera on the line."

The chessmen were on the board, and Admiral Weiss had just made his first move. Tom hoped to be a worthy opponent, but feared the admiral had heard the quaver in his voice. When Weiss had said, "You and Dr. R. Anthony Gaylani have a history almost as long as ours," Tom realized he was dealing with a man who'd done his homework. The Company must have checked his military record and knew how it intersected with Tony Gaylani's.

"Shall I assemble the usual stuff," Tom asked, "or is there a special area we should look into?"

"Look, buddy-boy, I know you're about to argue a very important case. Why don't you concentrate on your opening statement and let me speak with your boss."

Tom gazed out his office window. His recollection complete, he began drawing concentric circles on a legal pad. Yesterday morning, Eric Weiss had ended their courthouse phone conversation without saying good-bye. That hadn't been surprising. Over the last two-plus decades, on more than a dozen occasions, Tom had been through the same drill before. But this time there was a difference. This time the CIA wanted information on Dr. R. Anthony Gaylani.

In past years, Weiss's person of interest had always been a bilingual Hispanic-American male—an executive with a trucking firm that shipped heavy machinery between the US and South America. And that wasn't all. Each trucking honcho purportedly had a squeaky-clean record—no indictments or convictions, not even a parking ticket. Of course, that hadn't deterred Gary Barbera's intelligence gatherers. The mob moles had ignored the laws of privacy and uncovered one very dirty secret. Each person of interest had used his trucking fleet to smuggle cocaine into America. And each had been rewarded for taking the risk. Payments from the Cali and Medellin cartels had been deposited into their numbered Swiss bank accounts.

Tom's brow felt moist, but he didn't wipe it. Instead, he sat frozen in place and let his brain sort things out. Yesterday, he'd had tunnel vision. When the admiral had asked for information on Dr.

Tony Gaylani, Tom had wondered how his neighbor figured into the CIA's profile to target high-level drug traffickers. Now, as he relived the conversation and factored in his wife's panicked call, Tom had a new perspective. Weiss's inquiry wasn't about drugs at all.

His grip on the pencil tightened and the lead point broke. All at once, Eric Weiss's strategy became clear. The admiral wanted to get the boss's attention. Of course. Anything that positively influenced the outcome of the trial would have made Mr. Barbera happy.

Tom bit his lip. Why hadn't he seen the obvious connection? Yesterday morning, the Fed's witnesses had had clear recollections. After the noon recess, they'd had amnesia. All very sensible if Eric Weiss, the Deputy Director of the CIA, had canceled his lunch plans to phone James Fitzgerald, the Director of the FBI.

Everyone knew law enforcement didn't give a damn about getting justice for a murdered drug dealer. To polish their image and harass the mob, the Feds had rounded up a couple pushers who were willing to finger Mr. Barbera's hoods. But if Weiss had pressed the director of the FBI for a favor, and if the admiral had made his request an issue of national security, Fitzgerald would have told his witnesses to change their stories.

Tom pushed away from his desk and stood, staring blindly through the window at Lake Michigan. Being slow to recognize the admiral's intent had been a mistake, but not a fatal one. There was time to devise a new plan. But first things first. He'd get his clients back to the courthouse, then he'd deal with Admiral Eric Weiss and Dr. Tony Gaylani.

Tom Kempner's victory was bittersweet. Once the judge dismissed the charges, his clients wanted to celebrate. Initially Tom had declined, but after weighing his options, he agreed.

Unwritten CIA rules were clear. When the Mafia and the Company cooperated, no one opened his mouth. Going home meant facing Katherine. Since he couldn't tell her about Eric Weiss's demands, taking the coward's way out seemed reasonable.

About an hour into the drinking, he got a call on his cell phone. Tom was caught off balance when Dr. Tony Gaylani applauded his courtroom win. He was even more stunned when his neighbor asked if he and Katherine would stop by for a celebratory wine tasting. In the past, Tony had either ignored his legal accomplishments or used debasing terms to describe them.

Naturally, Tom suspected the doctor had ulterior motives. To find out for sure, he thanked Tony for his kind words, but remained noncommittal. He wanted to see how hard the doctor pressed. When Tony persisted, Tom decided to play along and accept.

He knew Katherine would pooh-pooh the invitation, but he saw the wine tasting as an opportunity to see if his wife had pegged Dr. Gaylani right. Still, Tom needed to insert one caveat: To make sure Katherine couldn't say no, he agreed on condition the event was staged at his house, not Tony's.

Tom clicked off his cell phone, then returned to the barroom and told his clients he'd been summoned home by the little woman. As they snickered, he suggested they continue their bash in Mr. Barbera's stretch limousine.

They traveled northwest for nearly forty miles, then exited the tollway. During the trip out of Chicago, he'd sat next to the chauffeur in front of the open glass partition. Behind him, the young mobsters took swigs from a fifth of single-malt Scotch.

Tom called out directions as the limo cruised along winding country roads. Once through the village of Barrington, the scenery changed. Instead of spacious houses on five-acre sites, fenced-in mansions dotted the wooded and rolling countryside.

On most days, traveling around Barrington had a soothing effect. Even in winter, the affluent equestrian enclave was his oasis. But today was different. The late afternoon sun shimmered off a thick mantle of snow, but Tom saw none of the beauty.

The tires vibrated on the icy cobblestones as the limo sped past outcroppings of ponderosa pines and blue spruces. When his two-story Tudor mansion came into view, one of the gentleman don's soldiers reached through the partition and draped the whiskey bottle over his shoulder.

"No thanks," Tom said, shaking his head. "Right now I need a cup of black coffee."

The limo stopped in the circular turnaround. As Tom stared at his oak and stucco-faced manor, impulses of fear spread throughout his body. Suddenly, he began asking himself the same questions he'd dismissed during his earlier conversation with Katherine.

What if the man who'd roamed around in his house had been tutored by his mother? What if Dr. R. Anthony Gaylani had participated in clandestine undertakings? What if he was a spy?

Tom breathed in deeply, happy he'd accepted Tony's invitation. Going forward, he'd scrutinize his neighbor during the wine tasting, check out the MI-6 documents after the Gaylanis left, then figure out what to do. But one thing was certain. His plan would protect Katherine.

He looked at the dashboard clock. 5 PM. In an hour a new kind of battle would begin. He didn't want to subject Katherine to another encounter, but more than ever he understood the benefit of getting back in the loop. Admiral Weiss's witness tampering might have kept the mob's soldiers out of jail, but Tom was convinced the deputy director had a secret agenda. From the moment he'd received Katherine's call and heard about Tony Gaylani's roguish behavior, he'd wrestled with one thought. Eric Weiss must have known the Brits had released General Alan Cunningham's memoirs.

"Enjoyed your company," Tom said, looking back at his clients, "but let's not make this habit-forming. The boss liked the verdict, but tomorrow, when he sees your mugs plastered on the front page of the *Tribune*, he may reevaluate his position."

He stepped out of the black Cadillac and flipped up the collar of his overcoat. Standing on the cobblestone turnaround, he slammed the door and rapped his gloved fist on the roof. When the limo drove away, he turned. In that second, he saw her. The wind howled out of the north, but his wife stood just outside the front entrance, crossarmed, without a coat.

Tom moved quickly to Katherine's side, but when he leaned in to kiss her cheek, she turned away without saying a word. She didn't have to.

He followed her inside, feeling more worried than snubbed. Tom knew Admiral Eric Weiss suspected Dr. Tony Gaylani of something. He assumed the admiral had been briefed by MI-6 and knew the contents of General Cunningham's memoirs. Since the admiral must have cleared the documents for delivery, it followed that he knew the papers contained explosive information. While he felt betrayed that Weiss had withheld material facts, there was no evidence to suggest that the admiral had leaked the information to the doctor. That was Katherine's doing. Last night, during dinner with the Gaylanis, she'd confirmed the delivery of her grandfather's papers.

"You have every right to be mad." He slammed the front door behind him, then massaged his thigh to ease the pain from a wound he'd suffered in Vietnam. "I goofed big time."

"Tell me about it," Katherine said.

When he tossed his overcoat over a peg on the hall tree, the pain in his thigh sharpened. It happened like clockwork every winter. Whenever the temperature dropped, the nerves in his leg muscles became ultra sensitive, possibly a reaction between the frigid air and the titanium plates, pins, and screws that held the once-shattered bone together.

"I'm sorry," he said, trying to look contrite. "Not getting back to you was an oversight, not a premeditated act. Once the judge dismissed the charges, the boys wanted to celebrate."

"Fine, Tommy. Call me, then meet your pals."

"Clients, Katherine. Not pals."

"Goddamn it. You haven't heard a word I said."

Tom stiffened. Ever since he'd gotten the phone call and passed the admiral's demands along to Mr. Barbera, he'd felt like a man exiled to a deserted island. Not only had Eric Weiss made it clear that he only wanted to talk to the boss, but his boss had acted distant and boycotted him too. The twice-daily discussions with Mr. Barbera had stopped.

"Give it a rest, Katherine. You've made each of your allegations perfectly clear."

Glaring, she leaned in. "And…?"

"And what?"

She inched closer. "Don't you get it? Our neighbor is a fraud. After we hung up, I loaded Grandfather's papers in the elevator and took them up to my office. I know what I saw."

"No one's disputing that."

"Then why aren't you doing something?" she asked, her face flushing red. "The man could be dangerous. It's all there in black and white. Either the documents are a crock, or there's something very scary going on next door."

He shrugged. "So you say."

"The papers are in my office. Let's go up and take a look."

"Not right this second."

"Why, Kempner?" As veins bulged around her temples, she used both hands and shoved him in the chest. "You're a considerate guy. Why are you blowing me off?"

"I forgot to call. That's not the same as blowing you off."

She eyed him, stared down at the floor, then jerked her head up and eyed him again. "God knows, I never question your business, but this situation is different. Give me a little credit."

He looked away. Katherine had just swirled her neck-length auburn hair and turned her blazing emerald eyes into lasers, both clear signs that she was very upset. His wife was petite—only five-two and just over a hundred pounds. But she was no shrinking violet.

"Katherine, please. This is hardly the time or the place…"

"Will there ever be a right time and place?" She snatched his coat off the hall tree and threw it in his direction. "After you put this in its proper place, check for hangers. In case it slipped your mind, your secretary called and said you invited the jerk over for drinks."

"I agreed to the wine tasting," he conceded, moving toward the closet. "Tony did the inviting, not me."

Tom hung his coat, then glanced over his shoulder. Katherine was angry, but as she stood with her feet spread and her hands on her hips, he only saw the woman he'd adored throughout their thirty-five-year marriage. To him, Katherine was an accomplished physician who had a wonderful bedside manner—a fun-loving romantic who loved to snuggle and sip brandy on the couch in front of the fire—and a devoted mother and wife who had not only taken him to task and smoothed some of his rough edges, but had raised their son to be a gentleman too.

"I don't care who invited whom," she fired back, her cheeks crimson. "When you accepted, guess who became the patsy? Around here, I get steamrolled whenever it suits you."

They faced each other, and for a long second, neither moved. Then Katherine turned, crossed the foyer, and stared at their huge Christmas tree.

Had his wife signaled a truce? If so, he was thankful. Katherine had pressed him to look at her grandfather's documents. He'd resisted, offering irrational excuses. Now he was running out of explanations, even lame ones.

"The Gaylanis will be here in a half hour," he said. "Let's try to be civil."

"Civil people communicate," she responded, snapping out her words. "I'd have a better chance talking to a stone."

As hostilities resumed, Tom tried to keep his inner rage in check. He was boiling mad, but not at his wife. Katherine's summation of her English grandfather's claims had made one thing clear: Two people he'd trusted—Mr. Gary Barbera, the don of the Chicago Mafia, and Admiral Eric Weiss, the Deputy Director of the CIA—had cut him out of their conversations. Was this also a coincidence, or did he have reason to fear both men?

He walked past Katherine's Christmas tree toward the sweeping staircase that led to the second floor. After climbing a few steps, he stopped and massaged his thigh.

"You have my word. Once the wine tasting is over, I'll look at the papers. If there's something in Dr. Gaylani's background, we'll get to the bottom of it."

"Is that a promise?" she asked, gently touching one of her antique ornaments. "My concern is for Joanna. If Grandfather's diaries are right, she's living with an Arab spy."

He gripped the banister and squeezed hard. "Slow down. Tony is a respected professional. Even if your accusations are right, the doctor is not about to do something stupid."

"Pillar of the community or not, the man is a bloody traitor. Tony Gaylani should be reported to the CIA or FBI."

"And if you're wrong?" He grabbed his lapels, then reached up and touched the knot of his tie. "Insinuations coming from a deceased man's diaries are hearsay. Face facts. Without collaborations, your allegations aren't admissible. It's not the fifties and you're not McCarthy."

Until Katherine mentioned officialdom, Tom hadn't realized his other predicament. He was totally isolated. Whom would he call if he dug into General Alan Cunningham's papers and decided to disregard the mob's gag rule? The FBI had tampered with the prosecution's witnesses, the CIA was in secret negotiations with his boss, and the local constable was on the mob's dole.

He resumed climbing the stairs, feeling his wife's gaze on his back. Once safe behind the bathroom door, he peeled off his clothes. Since he'd had a few drinks, he turned on the faucet, then stood under the shower and let cool jets beat against his body.

Minutes later, he slipped on a terrycloth robe, shivering but clear-headed. After running a straight razor over stubble that had barely grown out, he towel-dried and finger-combed his hair.

Tom tried to put his wife's charges in perspective, but as he stared at his boyish reflection, he knew he had to reserve judgment on his neighbor until he saw how the man interacted with Katherine. Still, two facts were certain. Dr. Gaylani wasn't Italian and he wasn't Catholic.

Years before, when their paths had crossed in Vietnam, Army helicopter medics had left his bloody body on the doctor's operating table. Back then, there hadn't been a formal introduction. Near death, Lt. Thomas L. Kempner had only moaned when Dr. R. Anthony Gaylani went to work.

The doctor was accustomed to treating the critically wounded and had made a quick but thorough diagnosis. Using a scalpel to cut and sutures to paste, Dr. Gaylani patched up the bullet holes in his chest, then reconstructed his leg. Once stabilized, Tom left the OR for a stint in recovery and rehab.

The first week hadn't been pleasant. But after the pain subsided, he asked to see his doctor. Informed that the nurses monitored patient recovery, he switched his focus and queried them about the surgeon who'd brought him back from death's door.

Their response had been unanimous. The RNs were in awe of Dr. Gaylani's surgical skills, but not his aptitude for convincing people that he was an Italian Catholic.

All the medical personnel knew of R.A.'s insistence at being addressed by his first two initials. The doctor told everyone who would listen that "Raffaello Anthony Gaylani was too Catholic, too Italian, and too difficult to remember." But while they obliged him, not all were believers.

One day, the RNs told Tom how they'd snuck into the hospital's administrative office and scanned Tony's 201 file. The official record had said it all. US Army Captain Dr. R. Anthony Gaylani was the son of Rashid Ali el-Gaylani and his wife, Ziyara. From then on, without ever mentioning their reconnaissance, the Army nurses had referred to him as the Roman Allah.

Tom slapped on a light dose of aftershave and stared into the mirror. He looked tired, but he didn't care. As he rubbed his hands together, now a lawyer's hands and no longer rough from combat, the Vietnam hospital memories came back.

Years before, an Army lieutenant hadn't cared about the scuttlebutt. R.A. may have been the Roman Allah to the nurses, but to him the doctor was a miracle worker. As a Jew, he knew all about culture-based biases. If the guy who'd saved his life wanted to hide his ancestry, far be it from him to blow the whistle.

He peered down, avoiding the mirror. Usually he could look himself in the eye and be satisfied with the finished product. Not today. Almost two decades ago, the Gaylanis had moved next door. Back then, he realized Tony hadn't remembered their OR encounter. At the time, he saw no harm in leaving well enough alone. But what about now? Joanna was Jewish, and Katherine was concerned for her best friend's safety. He hadn't shared the nurses' gossip with his wife for fear the RNs' claim would add credence to General Cunningham's memoirs. But once the wine tasting was over, once he saw how Dr. Gaylani conducted himself, he'd know what to do to make sure nobody was in danger.

He was putting his razor away when the doorbell rang. The Gaylanis' arrival was his cue to finish getting dressed. He felt like a turncoat cloaked in a new uniform—turtleneck, alpaca sweater, and slacks —but once he started downstairs, his mood changed. Suddenly, he was on edge and fearful.

When he reached the landing, his wife turned her back. Without commenting, Tom smiled at Joanna, a five-seven blonde who looked more like a woman in her forties than her sixties.

"Don't tell me," he said. "Your ugly better half is out popping corks in the kitchen."

Joanna nodded. "That he is. Come join us. Let the *vino maestro* get his act together."

Tom followed them into the living room, but when Katherine gave him a steely glare, he detoured around the coffee table. Only after his wife and Joanna were seated on one end of the curved sectional did he edge past the fieldstone fireplace and sit on the other.

"Tommy, dear," Katherine said, "tell Joanna she and Tony aren't imposing."

"For Pete's sake," Joanna scolded, "don't put the poor man on the spot. First Tony drops by, now he drags me over. Enough is enough."

"Happy to accommodate," Katherine said, fiddling with her wedding band. "Around this neck of the woods, every man with a corkscrew thinks he's a Napa Valley wine judge."

"You've pegged my hubby to a T," Joanna replied, undoing the top button of her cashmere cardigan. "Of course, Tony's real passion is Middle East history."

"That much I can vouch for," Katherine agreed. "Grandpa's stuff was pretty boring, but that doctor of yours… Wow. Once R. Anthony started going through the general's papers, he forgot his Boy Scout manners."

"He's always looking for obscure information," Joanna said, her smile wry. "Who knows? Being married to a history buff may pay off. A man with a head full of minutiae could make a big splash on *Millionaire.*"

"The concept works," Katherine agreed, "but Tony doesn't strike me as a guy who shares."

Tom listened stone-faced, then got up and tossed a hickory log on the dying embers. As sparks danced upward, he wondered about his predicament. Could he be in denial? Weren't the facts simple? The CIA only poked around when they smelled a covert foreign operation. Even if he discounted the general's writings, simple logic pointed to concerns next door. Why, then, couldn't he accept that the gentleman don, Mr. Gary Barbera, and the CIA Deputy Director, Admiral Eric Weiss, might have let him dangle on a string?

Joanna smiled. "Enough about your grandpa. Tonight there'll be no discussions of the general's diaries."

"Don't be so dogmatic," Katherine replied, still twisting her wedding band. "If the boys want to talk about wartime documents, we'll ditch them and make it a girls' night out."

Tom stared out the window at the snow-covered pines. Why did he have to be so pigheaded? Why hadn't he just broken the rules and told her everything?

His anxiety building, Tom watched Tony Gaylani come into the living room and set a tray of four half-filled wineglasses on the coffee table. Until today's disturbing events, he hadn't paid much attention to their neighbor's appearance.

About six feet tall, heavyset, probably in the two-hundred-and-fifteen-pound range. Tortoiseshell glasses, dark-complected. Steely eyes, black hair. A mustache.

He kept watching Tony, this time comparing him to his boss, the gentleman don. Mr. Barbera had dark hair, groomed, not unruly. His mustache was thin and shaped, not thick and bushy. And of course, the boss had piercing eyes. But again, there was a dissimilarity. While Mr. Barbera's eyes could be menacing, they could also be warm. Arab eyes seemed deeper set, darker, and far more serious.

"Attention, ladies," Tony said, "and you, too, Mr. Kempner."

Tom eyed the doctor as Tony smiled and picked up one of the wineglasses.

"Please take note of the color and bouquet. After we taste this wonderful chardonnay, I'll fill you in on the winery."

The doctor handed glasses to Joanna and Katherine, then signaled him to move closer.

"What's the verdict?" Tony asked, swirling his wine and taking a sip. "Thumbs up or down?"

"Great flavor, darling," Joanna said, lifting her glass. "What do you think, Tom?"

He picked the lone glass off the tray, took a sip, then sat down next to his wife. "As usual, the doc has outdone himself."

"Drink up, Kitty." Tony's voice sounded solicitous, but his eyes stayed hard. "I'm always beholden to your opinion."

"Sorry, neighbor, too bitter for me." Katherine mocked the tasting, first gulping down her wine, then setting her glass upside-down on the tray. "The activity around here seems to have killed my zeal for flawless fermentation."

Tony stared at her before taking a second sip. "You make a good point. It does have a bit of a bite."

Tom watched the doctor collect the wineglasses, surprised a self-appointed connoisseur like Tony Gaylani would accept Katherine's taunting.

"Give me a sec to open another bottle," Tony said, picking up the tray. "With the next one, I'll bet the vote is unanimous."

When the doctor left, Joanna swung around. "Tom, you're so quiet. Feeling okay?"

"Don't mind my little sweetie-pie," Katherine said. "He's all tuckered out. Defending the constitutional freedoms of Mafia bottom feeders can be so exhausting."

When Katherine patted his knee, Tom looked out the living room window, getting her message. But a moment later, when her hand clutched his thigh, his head snapped around. In that instant, as her nails dug into his leg, Tom watched her face drain of blood.

"Katherine! My God, what's wrong?"

He was petrified as she slumped over and rolled off the sofa.

CHAPTER THREE

Gary T. Barbera, Jr., ruling don of the Chicago Mafia, stared through the dark-tinted windows of a rented limousine. He'd left his armor-plated Cadillac in the garage of his suburban Lake Forest estate. He missed the comfort of riding in his own vehicle, but his car and especially his license plate—FALCON 1—were well know to the authorities. To preserve his anonymity, he'd sent one of his underlings to Hertz. Gary needed to be in a limo rented to someone else.

He leaned against the back seat, then glanced through the open partition at Danny Finn, his chauffeur, bodyguard, and most trusted lieutenant. Well before Katherine Kempner's burial service had begun, he'd instructed Finn to drive to the highest point in the cemetery. The Irishman had obliged, and once at the hilltop location had pulled alongside a window-high snow bank. As a further precaution, Finn had turned off the engine. They didn't want the exhaust fumes to telegraph their presence.

"I should have ignored Admiral Weiss's dictate," Gary snapped, knowing he had no choice but to obey. "Tommy is a friend and my *consigliere*. I belong at the gravesite."

"You made the right call," Finn replied. "Admiral Weiss doesn't want anything to spook Doc Gaylani. If you cross Sailor-boy, the CIA will be on our case."

Gary didn't reply. Instead, he adjusted his powerful binoculars, continuing to observe Mrs. Kempner's service. He hadn't known

Tommy's wife would be targeted, but he also hadn't warned his *consigliere* of the impending dangers. Now, he felt alternating emotions—pangs of guilt and urges for revenge, unfitting thoughts for a man known as the gentleman don.

Well over six decades ago, Irv Kupcinet, a noted Chicago newspaper columnist, had written, "The Windy City Mafia is no longer ruled by a crime boss or thug. Since the Feds put Al Capone in jail, Gary Barbera, Sr., and his son, Gary, Jr., have reinvented how enlightened mobsters conduct business. Both of the gentleman dons speak like Billy Graham, look like Rudolph Valentino, and dress like Cary Grant."

In 1941, Kup's analysis had been correct. He and his father had been gentlemen dons. Then the unexpected had happened. It had occurred during a trip his father made to Hawaii.

Gary Barbera, Sr., had concluded that hostilities were inevitable once President Franklin Delano Roosevelt cut off oil to the Japanese. Seeing Pearl Harbor as vulnerable, he'd gone to the Department of the Navy and pledged that Holly Corporation, his world-wide construction company, would bid all contracts at cost. The Admiralty hadn't refused, but ironically, on the Day of Infamy, as he stood with flagship officers discussing needed changes to the harbor facilities at Pearl, a Japanese bomb had ended his father's life.

That startling event had changed everything. Suddenly, he—Gary T. Barbera, Jr.—was recognized by the other mob families as the new ruling don of the Chicago Mafia. Alone at the helm—twenty-three, recently married, and a college grad—he had felt a host of new pressures.

With no one to advise him, he'd developed a list of priorities. First and foremost, he had to solidify his position, but in doing so, he wanted to make sure the mob lieutenants not only recognized his right to rule, but respected it as well.

His father had been in his forties when he inherited the top spot in the Capone crime family. To be sure, Gary Barbera, Sr., had been a modern-thinking man, but he also embraced the past and was a stickler for titles and protocol, enjoying the honor of being addressed as *the Godfather* and *the don*.

Gary understood his father's thinking, but believed his transition to power would be smoother if he relaxed some of the Sicilian traditions. He never wanted any man to kneel down before him, and very early in his tenure he told older and more seasoned subordinates to call him Mr. Barbera or the boss or even Mr. B.

Today, he wasn't an untrained kid, but in spite of having gained the confidence to successfully lead a crime family, more than ever he saw the advantages of a less formal working environment.

Gary wanted the Chicago Mafia to be faceless. He shunned any form of publicity and encouraged his associates to do the same. Flamboyance was gone. Mobsters were businessmen who made profits, not headlines.

"Damnation," Gary said, looking down at Katherine Kempner's casket. "Why did I ever get involved with the CIA?"

He didn't expect or wait for Danny Finn to answer. Instead, Gary placed his field glasses on the seat beside him and tried to imagine how his father would have reacted.

Born in 1892 and christened Geraldo Taliaferro Barbera, his father never had to battle with anger management. As his dad often said, "My even disposition is the result of my upbringing. I wasn't bred in an atmosphere of violence. I wasn't the male offspring of a Mafia don. I was the son of a shopkeeper."

For as long as anyone could remember, Gary's father, like all the Barbera fathers before him, had been a butcher in Palermo. As the eldest son, he had been raised to take over the family business. Early on, he'd learned how to turn the hindquarter of a slaughtered animal into chops and steaks. He'd also been taught to be well-mannered, law-abiding, and respectful of women. But in spite of his good grooming and on-the-job training, he seemed ill suited for the meat markets. In short, Gary's father wasn't like other Barbera males. He had a deep-seated curiosity, a quick intellect, and a steadfast ambition to achieve.

In 1910, Gary's father left Palermo to attend a university in Rome —the first Barbera to be awarded a full college scholarship. After graduating *magna cum laude* with a joint degree in accounting and the new science of aerodynamic engineering, he came home and married his high school sweetheart. He had a yearning to start a family, but was also bent on using his education. Armed with a college transcript replete with A's, he looked toward the Continent for a job.

Shortly after World War I broke out, he accepted a position with *Luftschiffan Zeppelin*. Originally founded by Count Ferdinand von Zeppelin, the company built rigid frame aircraft (dirigibles). After 1914, they began to design and manufacture warplanes as well.

As Gary's father often told him, "Working under the pressures of a wartime economy not only crammed twenty years of experience into a fifty-four month stint, but forever shaped my business philosophy." Then he'd winked at his son. "That's the good news. But there's a downside. I picked the wrong side."

His father was right. The Great War had ravaged Germany and the German economy. Job prospects were bleak after the signing of the Treaty of Versailles. That was particularly true for foreign nationals who had sided with Kaiser Wilhelm II.

To escape post-war prejudice, Gary's father booked passage for his family on a boat to New York. Once he, his wife, and his infant son cleared immigration on Ellis Island, they traveled overland and settled in Chicago. His father was an innovator. Not only had he read about Samuel Insull and the utility empire the financier had created in the Midwest, but he'd done his homework on America too. He knew the United States was a melting pot, where successful people embraced new ideas, not old traditions.

To showcase his talents and stay in step with the times, Geraldo Taliaferro Barbera Americanized his name. Going forward, his résumé would have a fresh look. He would be known as Gary Thomas Barbera, Sr., and his son would be Gary Thomas Barbera, Jr.

Gary lifted his binoculars and his reverie disappeared. He enjoyed thinking about his father, but he knew he needed to refocus on the funeral service, an event worse than a bad dream.

He scanned the large group that encircled Mrs. Kempner's casket. As the burial ceremony continued and the hundred and fifty or so mourners huddled together, Gary dropped his binoculars on the seat beside him and looked through the open partition at Danny Finn. His trusted lieutenant sat behind the steering wheel, his Donegal cap tipped rakishly over one eye.

Irv Kupcinet had never written about Finn, but not because the man didn't strike a commanding pose. In his late fifties, the carrot-top Irishman stood six-two and weighed two-thirty. He also had a cherub's face and the physique of an NFL linebacker.

"By all that's holy, we shouldn't be here," Gary said, closing his eyes. "Tommy's wife died for all the wrong reasons."

"No argument, boss," the Irishman replied. "Only a coward targets a man's old lady."

Gary sat back in the limo seat and watched Finn lower his field glasses. The temperature had fallen to below zero, but Gary wasn't cold. He and Finn peered past the snow embankments and stared down on the gathered assemblage. Common decency required that he watch. The rules of smart business were equally demanding. Of course, Gary ached to send out a carload of hit men to avenge Mrs. Kempner's murder. But he remembered his father's unwavering advice: "Before a modern Mafioso crime boss adopts machine gun tactics, he considers the consequences."

As his emotions quieted, he thought back to last Tuesday. The initial request from Admiral Eric Weiss, the Deputy Director of the CIA, had come through his *consigliere*. Once Tommy Kempner had passed along Eric Weiss's special cell phone number, Gary had placed the call.

His talks with the admiral had been businesslike. Eric Weiss wanted biographical information on a Dr. Tony Gaylani and his deceased mother and father. Most of the admiral's demands had been straightforward, but one in particular had alarmed him.

In the past, Tommy Kempner's role had been dual-purposed. He'd acted as the mediator between himself and Admiral Weiss. He also oversaw the investigations. This time, the admiral didn't want Tommy involved.

Gary reached his gloved hand inside the sleeve of his over-coat and touched one of the solid gold cufflinks his father had given him on the eve of his wedding. The miniature replica of a peregrine in flight had been designed and commissioned by his father to cele-brate his love for falconry and to honor a bird that he'd used for drawings of an aircraft with a sweptback wing.

Gary took a deep breath. He often thought about his father—a man he had revered in life and mourned in death. Gary Barbera, Sr., had made a profound impact in two very different lines of work. As a World War I aviation engineer, he'd pioneered a new swept-wing design. As a crime boss, he'd tempered machine gun diplomacy. In both instances, he'd altered stodgy thinking by bringing a busi-nessman's perspective to bear. And in both instances, he'd instituted a healing process by welcoming his detractors back into the fold.

One event—a high-profile marriage he'd arranged between two rival Mafia families—epitomized his father's ability as a forward thinker and diplomat. Gary knew all the details firsthand. His father had only manipulated the parties involved. Gary had been one of the principal players.

It began in 1937. He was enrolled at the University of Chicago and had just completed his sophomore year. During the summer recess, his father asked him to transfer to Northwestern so he could study under an aging economics professor who had just agreed to come to the university and discuss his book, *The General Theory of Employment, Interest, and Money.*

He knew his father was a devotee of John Maynard Keynes. Gary hadn't realized his father also had made an anonymous dona-tion to Cambridge as a way to persuade Keynes to spend a year at Northwestern. To his regret, that wasn't the only thing his father had kept to himself.

In the fall of '37, Gary remembered being surprised when his father insisted they both attend an upcoming production of *Romeo and Juliet.* The Saturday night event was a Northwestern University Drama Department presentation starring Maria Nostromo, the most popular co-ed on campus.

Maria, like himself, was part of the class of '39. But that was where the similarities ended. He was a numbers geek, and she was an icon. She hung with the movers and shakers; he worked part time keeping the books for a local pizzeria.

Romeo and Juliet played for five nights to a packed auditorium and rave reviews. He and his father attended the final performance and were both impressed by Maria's thespian skills. As they stood and gave the cast a standing ovation, he thought they'd both head home. He had no idea his father had arranged for them to meet the star actress backstage.

Only he had been intimidated by the get-together. Almost tongue-tied, he rarely entered the conversation, preferring to avoid eye contact and stare at the floor. Of course, Maria lived up to her billing. She was beautiful, personable, and charming. Not to be outdone, his father was engaging too. He'd kept the conversation going by not only doting on Maria's every word, but praising her avant-garde interpretation of Juliet Capulet.

Unbeknownst to Gary, early the next morning, his father had flown to Italy to visit Maria's father. Following the meeting, Antonio Nostromo, the ruling don in Florence, had come to an agreement with the ruling don in Chicago. A marriage between their children would promote better relations between the American and European families.

Not surprisingly, the union had been a political success, but a failure on all other fronts. Maria had been in love with another man. In the end they'd both been victims. When she gave in and accepted her father's dictate, Gary became the unloved husband of a vivacious Italian woman. But he'd never blamed Maria. She had given him a son and had been a good mother and faithful companion.

"God damn that Weiss," Finn muttered, lowering his binoculars and looking back through the open partition. "I hate the fucker's guts."

"Tell me something new," Gary said, his recollection cut short.

"Sorry, boss. I just can't believe Sailor-boy will deep-six the burial."

Gary didn't comment. Instead of feeling the weight of an unhappy remembrance or the discomfort of a plan he knew Admiral Weiss was about to implement, he thought about Danny Finn.

It never failed. If he stripped away the Irishman's barroom vernacular and concentrated on his message, Finn made thoughtful observations. Content over form. Why, then, did a man who spent his spare time reading classic literature find it necessary to brace his sentences with salty colloquialisms and raw profanity?

"Pay close attention," Gary said, using his gloved hand as a pointer. "Our people tell me the admiral's men did some rewiring. We're about to see an electrical fire."

"Talk about a bullshit stunt," Finn moaned. "When that casket motor starts smoking, your boy Kempner is going to feel like somebody's out to get him."

"That's the problem," Gary replied. "Someone is out to get him, and we can't stop it."

Finn turned in his seat and straightened his Donegal cap. "One question, boss. If the motor conks out, won't they crank her casket down manually?"

Gary's jaw muscles tensed. "The handle will spin, but nothing will happen. The admiral hires resourceful men. Earlier, they came by and stripped all the gears."

Tight-lipped, he kept looking through his binoculars. Gary saw blank faces, wind-chapped lips, and intermittent puffs of frosted breath, but mostly, he saw Tommy. His *consigliere's* tormented expression was as real as the red rose he'd just placed atop his wife's walnut coffin.

"Why didn't I keep Tommy posted?" he grumbled. "Maybe he would have seen it coming."

"We're dealing with a new breed," Finn said, pulling a wool scarf higher around his bull neck. "Ever since 9/11, nobody plays by the rules."

"Honorable men still have a place in this world. Don't ever forget it."

"Honorable men will always have a place," Finn replied, "but right now I'm pissed at Sailor-boy's lackeys. How do they rate? Those bastards are warm."

"The admiral's men have an advantage," Gary conceded. "They're riding in a vehicle that makes them look like they belong."

He swung his binoculars and zeroed in on a panel truck parked, motor idling, on an access road not far from where his *consigliere*'s wife would be laid to rest. From his network of informants, Gary knew that the white-painted van with the cemetery logo painted on the side had been sent by Admiral Eric Weiss, Deputy Director of the CIA.

Finn whistled. "Jesus, you were right. That casket motor is smoking like a chimney."

Gary nodded. "They're a collection of devious humans, but the CIA can pull off a covert operation."

He and Finn watched as a mortuary mechanic with the cemetery name stenciled on his parka rushed over and unplugged the smoldering electrical motor. While the mourners backed away, another man wearing a stenciled parka began turning the manual crank. As predicted, nothing happened. Mrs. Kempner's casket stayed above ground.

Finn put down his field glasses. "Looks like the show's over."

"Except for Tommy. His ordeal is just beginning."

He watched the Anglican priest presiding over the ceremony come to Tommy Kempner's side. As if to salvage the dignity of the burial, the priest murmured something in his *consigliere*'s ear, then blessed the crowd.

When the mourners lowered their heads and began to move away, Gary put his binoculars aside. He didn't need to watch the chesterfield and mink coat convocation ditch all piety and hurry for the warmth of their cars. The naked eye could see that the gentry from the country village of Barrington had left their neighbor alone with his grief.

Gary noted the contradiction as his Jewish attorney knelt like a Christian child saying prayers before bedtime. Tommy had his palms clasped together and his lips were moving, but Gary knew he wasn't asking for divine guidance. No, indeed. The new widower had to be taking more than one person's name in vain.

"Never trusted lawyers, but always liked your mouthpiece," Finn said, his voice showing a hint of emotion. "Right now, I know how he feels."

Gary avoided the Irishman's eyes. "We both know, my friend."

During his long reign as Godfather, he'd attended many funerals. Burying Family members was difficult, but witnessing the interment of people he cared for affected him more deeply. In that regard, Mrs. Kempner's death stood out, as did the long-ago murders of Danny Finn's wife and only daughter.

Gary's fingers touched one of his gold peregrine cufflinks, the movement comforting, almost a ritual.

He'd first met Daniel Kevin Finn in the summer of 1967. He needed a new chauffeur, and after attending a meeting at Holly Corporation, Gary had gone to the loading docks to check out a man who'd been highly recommended.

"*Canterbury Tales*," Gary had said, noting the title on a paperback a man was reading in the cab of a Holly Corporation truck. "All my drivers should make such productive use of their breaks."

"Mr. Barbera," the Irishman had replied, scrambling out to meet him. "Didn't see you."

"Is Chaucer one of your favorites?" Gary asked, extending his hand.

"He's a damn good poet. When it comes to versification, the fucker was ahead of his time. It took four centuries for most scholars to understand his metrical technique." Danny shrugged, then eyed his paperback. "This is a masterpiece and Chaucer was a genius, but Micks like me are more in tune with the philosophers. Guys like John Locke and John Stuart Mill created ideas, not soppy stories."

Gary had come away from their first meeting shaking his head.

The man was respectful, his clothes were pressed, and his shoes were shined. If dressed in a coat and tie, the Irishman's clean cut and hulking physical appearance would fit the image of a Mafia don's chauffeur and bodyguard. But what to do about his language?

In the end, he'd hired him. No one questioned Finn's driving ability or his heart. And there was a bonus too. Finn's commitment to classic literature made him an interesting and eclectic conversationalist.

Gary knew he'd done the right thing after the Irishman's first day on the job. Of course, he had no idea he'd begun a process that would develop into a strong working partnership. But it had happened. Finn didn't mince words or make any attempt to clean up his vernacular, but he understood his role as protector and confidant. Whether in the car or dining at a fine restaurant, Danny Finn had never taken liberties with their friendship.

Nothing had tested the strength of their relationship more than the events on the day Danny's daughter had celebrated her eighth birthday. The killers had meant to target Gary and the Irishman. But fate had intervened. He and Danny had gotten stuck in traffic, and the delay made them late getting to the Irishman's house.

The men had been sent by a loan shark that Gary had run out of Chicago several months before. Samuel Shylock had made a career preying on old indigent people. He'd also issued brutal orders. When his killers couldn't locate their targets, they eliminated the loved ones. Kathleen Finn, Danny's wife, and Meagan Finn, his young daughter, were shot several times with automatic weapons. From that day forward, a unique bond had united them—the gentleman don and the Irishman.

As Gary breathed in, he closed his eyes and sat back in the rear seat in the limo. He was aware that survival in his profession meant hardening oneself to barbarity at its worst. His remembrance of Meagan Finn's birthday was difficult, but no more so than this current killing.

He took a deep breath and picked up his binoculars, observing a husband pay final tribute. At that moment, he felt more than just remorse for Tommy Kempner's loss. When the panel truck moved into view, his own complicity burdened him. No one could accuse him of not telling the truth, but Gary knew he'd withheld vital details. Why, he wondered, had he acquiesced to Eric Weiss's demands and kept his loyal friend in the dark?

"Son of a bitch," Finn said, "those bastards have no respect for the dead."

Gary watched the van pull up and park near the grave. Three men got out. The one holding a clipboard looked toward Tommy Kempner, then motioned the others to wait. The man playing the role of foreman wanted his presence felt, but couldn't risk close-quarters contact. If his *consigliere* got a good look, he might have become suspicious. Gravediggers rarely went to work in Bogner ski parkas, woolen pants, and Gucci loafers.

"Jesus," Finn said, "Sailor-boy's guys are hanging around like hungry vultures."

"Admiral Weiss's men have good reason to be antsy." Gary swallowed hard when Tommy touched the rose on his wife's casket. "They're on a tight schedule."

When Tommy Kempner walked to his vehicle, the well-dressed men closed in on the casket. Gary watched, glancing at his watch, knowing the real gravediggers were slated to arrive shortly. The impostors—a coroner and two forensic experts—had been sent on an early morning flight from Dulles to O'Hare. Admiral Weiss had ordered them to check Katherine Kempner's neck and throat for bruising and damage to her larynx.

Gary didn't reach for the binoculars when the men opened her casket. He knew the examination would be brief and non-invasive. While he wouldn't witness the medical team's postmortem, he did have a keen interest in the results. Too many things failed to add up. After Tommy had prepped Gary, Eric Weiss had called with a proposal. The face-to-face Mafia/CIA meeting had never taken place, but a series of preliminary phone exchanges between himself and the Company deputy director had occurred. Those secret calls had made him edgy. He'd expected to negotiate the ground rules, but hadn't anticipated the bizarre questions concerning Dr. Gaylani's wife and her rich uncle, Lawrence Magel.

The outside air slowly chilled the rented limousine. When Finn put his field glasses in a leather case, Gary didn't tell him to start the engine. He wanted to leave Barrington and go home, but if a delay protected the health of his business, he would wait until the CIA departed.

"Might have been a bit hasty about this cloak and dagger racket," Gary said, watching the Irishman's eyes light up. "You're always looking for a new challenge. If we beat the CIA at their game, I'll put another gold star on your résumé."

"Just made my day," Finn replied, grinning. "When do we start ripping Sailor-boy a new asshole?"

CHAPTER FOUR

Patricia Zwilling Shaver stood in the country kitchen of her five-room renovated caretaker's cottage. She placed her coffee mug on the L-shaped granite counter next to one of her prized possessions—a 5"x7" framed photograph. The picture had been taken on the courtyard outside her house many years ago. She and her surrogate mother, Ellen Eichler, wore bikinis and were holding Snowshoe, an eight-week-old yellow Labrador puppy.

Pat smiled. Back then, they were both tan, trim, and kind of sexy. Today, they were still trim and maybe a little sexy, but when she glanced through one of the picture windows, the prospect of wearing a bikini seemed far away. The snowfall last night had added several inches to an already record accumulation that had piled up on the wooden swing hanging from the rafters in the open-air porch.

She walked toward the front hall closet and eyed her two yellow Labrador retrievers curled up on the hard wood floor. Snowshoe was now a senior citizen. Shoe-Too, her adolescent sidekick, had recently joined their household, a rescued animal from an abusive pet owner.

Pat watched the dogs lift their heads as she zipped up her parka and pulled on fur-lined gloves. Labs loved to play even when the weather was freezing.

She hadn't always lived in the caretaker's cottage. More than four decades ago, she'd taken her first breath just an eighth of a mile away. Amongst doctors, nurses, and a cadre of servants, Patricia Z. Shaver came into the world in one of the upstairs bedrooms in her family's country manor. Honeymead, the name Grandpa Zwilling gave to his mansion, had been built on a hill in the wooded section of a five-hundred acre Barrington horse farm overlooking Honey Lake.

She yanked a wool stocking cap down over her ears, remembering that a long-ago fire had incinerated Honeymead and many of the surrounding trees. Only a favorable wind had spared the caretaker's cottage and stables. That bit of good fortune had allowed her to reclaim part of her legacy. Fifteen years ago, after being awarded a Ph.D. in literature, she'd decided to move back onto the estate.

The five-room caretaker's cottage had survived, but it needed a woman's touch. After she had the inside gutted and remodeled, Pat turned her architects loose to convert the stables into an office. In the end, she'd found simple country living easier and more to her liking.

"All right, you two, let's move it."

Snowshoe and Shoe-Too scrambled to their feet and loped to the front door. She wrapped an alpaca scarf around her neck, then looked into the living room and checked to be sure the hearth screen was closed and the fire was out. She had reason to be cautious. The 1977 inferno that had consumed Honeymead had been a human tragedy as well. Her mother and father were in the house when the arsonist set the fire.

"What's the deal… and where are your door manners?"

The dogs heeded her stern tone. They stopped pressing forward and sat.

"Just so there's no confusion, we're not going out to play Frisbee."

With the Labs leading the way, Pat left her cozy home and endured the short scamper across the courtyard to her office and most private refuge.

"Okay, okay," she said, hanging her parka on the coat rack. "Message received."

Prodded by gentle head butts, she reached into the dog biscuit jar and tossed them treats. While they munched, she grabbed a couple of logs and banked the hearth in the floor-to-ceiling fieldstone fireplace, the latest addition to her ongoing renovation.

"Lie down, girls. I've got work to do."

She put a match to the gas jet, then walked to the kitchenette. After grinding her favorite beans, she hit the brew button. When a trickle of Kona coffee dripped into the glass pot, she went to her desk.

Her foundation books needed balancing, but she could only muster enough energy to sit. Normally, when she settled into the task at hand, her brain stayed focused. But not today. As the oak logs caught fire and crackled, she squirmed, tweaking an errant lock of ash-blonde hair. Seconds later, she stared at the beamed ceiling, pulling back her shoulder-length mane and tying it into a ponytail.

"Damn you, Grandfather."

Her words hung in the air, alive with sounds of burning wood and percolating coffee. Agitated by a remembrance, she walked to one of the oblong windows that flanked the hearth. Whether she liked it or not, her mind kept digging up the past, recreating images of the Barrington countryside and especially Honeymead, the estate where it had all begun.

In the 1930s, her grandfather, William F. Zwilling, Chairman of Security Chicago National Bank, had damn near stolen a five-hundred-acre, distressed-sale parcel abutting Honey Lake. To celebrate his entry into the unofficial club of America's country gentlemen, Bill Zwilling built a thirty-room manor and adjoining horse farm that had made him look like he belonged.

Pat pressed her forehead against the pane. She blinked a couple times as she focused on a cluster of junipers near the icy shoreline. Her recurring nightmare shaped itself, an ugly film flickering behind her eyes.

Last May, quite by accident, she'd unearthed a dossier. The date of the cover letter—Spring 1976—convinced her that the multi-paged document had been hidden on the grounds of Honeymead for more than three decades. While that surprised her, it was the content that had put her on edge. On one page, her grandfather and father were included amongst a larger group of judges, politicians, and industrialists, each juxtaposed to a numbered Swiss bank account. On another page, they were listed as part of a secret Mafia payroll administered by Gary Barbera, Jr. Could there be any doubt? Along with all these other prominent men, the male icons in her family had mortgaged their souls.

She stepped back from the window, but couldn't stop the disquieting reverie. In late 1976, Bill Zwilling had passed away in his sleep. Ten months later, his daughter met her maker in a far less natural way. Pat knew that Grandfather's heart would have broken to discover that the crown jewel of his life had committed suicide. But would the hard-nosed banker have accepted some responsibility for her mother's death?

More than a quarter century after the fact, only two things were certain. Patricia was her family's only living heir, and all that remained of Honeymead was the land, the reconfigured stable, and the renovated caretaker's cottage she now called home. Everything else had burned.

Pat turned toward the sound of a loud noise. "Girls, did you hear that?"

Snowshoe and Shoe-Too had already jumped up and run to the door. They knew who was outside. The backfire from Ellen Eichler's pickup truck announced her visits.

Pat smiled as her best friend and surrogate mother walked in and petted the Labs.

"Hi," she said, hugging Ellen. "You skipped the gathering at his house?"

"The burial service was tough enough," her friend replied, shedding a heavy black coat and wool scarf. "Couldn't bear going back to Tommy Kempner's house with a game face."

"Wouldn't have been my bag either," Pat agreed. "Always difficult losing a friend, especially one like Katherine Kempner."

"I'll be okay, but I'm not so sure about Tommy. In spite of the brave front, he's devastated."

Ellen turned her attention back to the dogs and gave them each a between-the-eyes forehead kiss, a gesture indicating her upbeat personality was just temporarily on hold.

"Ladies," Ellen said, snapping her fingers. "Why aren't you two outside doing your thing?"

"Jeez, Ellie, don't encourage them. They prefer sub-zero wind chills to sitting with me."

"No wonder," Ellen replied, pointing toward the account ledgers. "Watching a doodler isn't a Lab's cup of tea."

"I'm not doodling," Pat protested. "This is important stuff."

As the sole beneficiary to a king's ransom, she never worried about paying the rent. Her concerns centered on which worthy cause would get mega-buck funding from the Patricia Z. Shaver Foundation. But charitable work wasn't the only thing keeping her deskbound. Since receiving her doctorate from Northwestern, she'd been employed as a print journalist who researched and wrote articles dealing with topics ranging from politics to gangster crime.

"To each his own," Ellen said, moving toward the hearth. "Me, I'd rather nestle near a warm fire than sit in a swivel chair and juggle numbers."

"Sounds like a cup of coffee would go well with your laziness."

"An appealing idea," Ellen said, sitting on the Moroccan rug, "but who besides you can attest to the flavor?"

Pat eyed her friend, then walked toward the kitchenette. "Bought the beans at Starbucks, and the water came out of a Hinkley & Schmidt jug. What could possibly go wrong?"

"With you mixing the ingredients?" Ellen asked. "Sticklers like me prefer stirring our coffee to cutting it with a knife and fork."

Pat poured a mug and delivered the brew without comment. She was heartened. When her friend got feisty, it signaled a return of her resiliency.

At fifty-nine, Ellen Eichler was a grandmother twice over who hardly looked the part. Her five-four, small-figured frame was trim, and her long, French-braided brunette hair had only a trace of gray

to betray her age. Her eyes, bright and intelligent, drew in any listener. An attractive face and an olive complexion added to the package. But there was much more to Ellen than her stately appearance.
She had a quick mind and a sarcastic tongue.

"Did this fall out of your coat?" Pat asked, picking up the church
program from Katherine Kempner's funeral service.

Ellen looked up and nodded.

"What a pity," Pat went on, scanning the two-page brochure.
"Gosh, Ellie. She wasn't that much older than you."

"And way too young to die."

"Isn't that strange," Pat said, still reading. "She had two middle
names."

"Quite common for the English," Ellen replied. "Kitty was born
Katherine Balfour Cunningham. When she married Tommy Kempner, she kept both her mother's maiden and her own last name."

"Did she and Kempner meet overseas?" Pat asked, engrossed
in the text.

"Kitty came here as a teenager. It's a long story."

Pat knelt down on the Moroccan next to her friend, then leaned
against a couple of large floor pillows piled on top of each other.
"Bore me, Ellie. Got nothing but time."

"Well… let's see…"

Pat listened… and listened… Then she got impatient. "The
stuff about her parents is interesting, but could you pick up the pace?
How Katherine got to America… that sort of thing."

Ellen nodded and went on, saying that Kitty's straight-laced
father had been aghast at his offspring. For generations, Cunninghams had commingled with other bluebloods without ever producing a misbehaved tomboy. Kitty changed all that. Her rebelliousness
not only dashed her parents' hope for a marriage into the queen's
extended family, but became a springboard for regrettable report
cards too. While her grades were exemplary, her stay at any academy
never exceeded a couple of years, sometimes only a term. One head-
mistress had followed the other, each dialing Lord Cunningham to
suggest his daughter move on.

Pat frowned. "Did she get tossed out of school, or was she deported?"

"Both," Ellen said. "As Kitty leapfrogged from boarding school to boarding school, her father's frustration grew. In the mid-fifties, angry and disgruntled, he lowered himself and prevailed on his baby sister to enroll his daughter in an American school."

"I'm confused," Pat replied, sitting up straight. "If Lord Cunningham thought his sister didn't measure up, why did he ask for help?"

"Ever hear of a court of last resort?" Ellen asked. "When he ran out of options in England, his sister got the nod. But make no mistake. Harriet Cunningham O'Banyon wasn't on her brother's hit parade either."

"How so?"

"She defied her mother," Ellen answered. "After World War II, Harriet married an American GI and moved to Chicago. It's a story unto itself."

"And one I'd like to hear. The name O'Banyon interests me."

Pat remembered researching a piece she'd done on the Chicago mob. During one fact-finding trip to the library she'd come across a reference to an Irishman named Sean O'Banyon.

While she wanted to explore that angle, first she needed more information on the Kempners.

"I'm curious about one thing. After Katherine married Tom Kempner, did she ever convert to Judaism?"

Ellen grabbed her shins and pulled herself into a sitting position. "What?"

"Isn't Kempner a Jewish name?"

"Yes, but... Lord in heaven. Don't you ever stop digging?"

Pat looked away. Ellen viewed Tom Kempner's religious heritage and his deceased wife's preference for in-between monikers as none of her business. In most instances, she would have agreed. But right now she had a good reason to dig. She was in the final stages of a research project. Her upcoming article—a treatise dealing with the birth of Zionism, the creation of the State of Israel, and the roots of the present-day Arab-Israeli conflict—contained many biographical sketches. While it was a stretch to link the key players in her manuscript to the surnames listed in the Episcopal funeral program, some coincidences couldn't be ignored.

"You've got me all wrong," Pat protested. "I'd never snoop on one of your friends."

"Of course you wouldn't," Ellen said, her voice etched in sarcasm. "You're just passing the time of day."

"Since we're on the same wavelength… I mean… because we agree…"

"Have you no shame?" Ellen asked. "If you must know. Yes. Kempner is a Jewish name. And no. She never converted. Anything else, or can Kitty stay buried in peace?"

Pat rechecked the names of the honorary pallbearers. She knew her probing had upset Ellen, but in spite of being on a short leash, her reporter's instincts demanded she dig deeper.

"Dr. R. Anthony and Joanna Myerson Gaylani are listed as pallbearers. I don't know them. Who are they?"

"Aside from being their dearest friends, Joanna and Tony are godparents to the Kempners' son." Ellen leaned over and looked at the funeral program. "Before you ask, Tony is Italian… and he didn't convert either."

Pat half-smiled, silently applauding her friend's intuition. As Ellen surmised, Joanna Myerson Gaylani's maiden name was probably Jewish. From her research, Pat knew that former Israeli Prime Minister Golda Meir had once taught school in Milwaukee as Golda Myerson. But when it came to Tony Gaylani, Ellen's nationality designation was off base. Joanna's spouse might be Mediterranean-skinned, but his last name sure wasn't Italian. In fact, if she dropped the doctor tag and substituted Rashid for the initial, R, and Ali for Anthony, the name Rashid Ali el-Gaylani matched the identity of a one-time Iraqi right-winger who'd sucked up to Hitler.

"Correct me if I'm wrong, but you did say Dr. Tony Gaylani is an Italian Catholic?"

"Why are we playing twenty questions?" Ellen asked. "You're acting like a reporter whiffing a fresh scent. Play it straight and tell me what's on your mind."

Pat readily agreed, anxious to make her case. After locking eyes, she spent the next half hour briefing her friend on the key players in the early Zionist movement. Then she provided thumbnail biographies on Arthur Balfour, General Alan Cunningham, and other individuals who'd played pivotal roles in the post-World War II formation of the state of Israel. Finally, to further pique Ellen's interest, she drew word pictures of Rashid Ali el-Gaylani and other Arab troublemakers who had roamed the Middle East deserts during the same period.

"Get real," Ellen said, getting up and pulling up her pant legs. "The horse manure in here is ankle deep."

"Are you second-guessing my research?"

"No, my dear, just your inferences."

"When did I say they were related to the historical figures?" Pat asked. "I just brought up the possibility."

"Balfour, Cunningham, Myerson, Gaylani." Ellen ticked off the names with her fingers. "There must be tons of listings for each. And that's just Chicago. Nationwide, there have to be zillions."

"The names may be common, but what's the probability of finding them on adjoining mailboxes?"

Ellen threw up her hands. "Oh, for heaven's sake!"

Pat looked away. Maybe she'd pushed too hard. Maybe her gut was wrong. Maybe a Jew and an Arab had gotten married and ended up being neighbors with a descendant of English royalty and a mob attorney.

She knew a mathematician could compute the probability of such events. But she also remembered what her college statistics professor had said: "The laws of probability do not lie, except when they run counter to feminine intuition."

Back then, she and her classmates had laughed. Today she wasn't laughing. Today her feminine intuition told her that the honorary pallbearers—Dr. R. Anthony and Joanna Myerson Gaylani—hadn't moved into the neighborhood by chance.

"Ellie… are you leaving?"

"Unless you've got more names to trash, I'm going home to pack." Ellen reached for her coat, letting her eyes soften into a motherly twinkle. "Another thing, my dear. You and your Labs are due at our place at six sharp. I hope that hasn't slipped your mind."

"You know it hasn't."

Every Christmas Eve since Snowshoe's birth, Pat had eaten dinner at the Eichlers'. This year the tradition had been pulled back a day. Due to circumstances, some happy and some not so happy, they all planned to fly out of O'Hare tomorrow night.

Pat was leaving for Rome and a rendezvous with Ken Dale. Years before, she'd worked for Ken at the *Chicago Tribune*. They'd also dated, but like her career at the *Trib*, that hadn't worked out. Then last spring, a quirk of fate had brought them together again. Now, she and her onetime boss and now long-distance lover were more passionate than ever.

Ellen and her husband were far less sanguine about their destination. They were scheduled to see their daughter and grandchildren, but for reasons Pat understood, they dreaded going to Lexington, Kentucky.

"Think about it, Ellie. Since Snowy was a puppy, this is the first Christmas we won't be together."

Pat knew Ellen said something, but she didn't listen to her friend's reply. Her mind was still focused on the Gaylanis and Kempners… and their adjoining mailboxes.

CHAPTER FIVE

Tom Kempner stood beside his wife's casket, alone and drained by his ordeal. He wiped his eyes and bid Katherine a silent good-bye, but just as he started walking toward his car, he paused. Something seemed odd about the men near the white panel truck.

He eyed them again, then dismissed his concern and continued to trudge through the snow. He'd made it through the sermon… endured the eulogies… led the overflow crowd in a motorized caravan to the cemetery… and survived the freezing temperatures. But he still faced another test.

Tom drove home, clutching the steering wheel. When he turned his four-wheel-drive vehicle into the driveway, he clamped down even harder. The gathering was well under way. The tree-lined lane leading to his Tudor mansion looked like a snow-banked showroom for pricey foreign sedans.

He pulled into the garage, got out, and stared back at the turn-around, a circular cobblestone space jam-packed with luxury automobiles. Tom hit the garage door button and went inside. In the courtroom, he faked the required emotions. Today, all he cared about was hiding his guilt and despair.

His postmortem began when he strode into the kitchen over-crowded with Katherine's friends. He thanked the women for preparing the huge buffet luncheon, then begged off and slipped into the dining room. Tom had thought he'd find some relief, but everywhere, he was waylaid by more forced smiles.

He moved to the foyer and stared at Katherine's Christmas tree. Hundreds of ornaments offered their glitter and seasonal joy. Most were gifts from their friends. Now, as he struggled out of his overcoat, Tom wondered if he'd ever use them again.

Ten days before her sudden death, he and Katherine had hosted their annual tree-trim brunch. In preparation, she'd put up her extensive collection of Christmas decorations. Festively-clad Santas, snowmen, angels, and reindeer had been tucked, hung, or placed throughout the house. No space had been overlooked, except the spot in the foyer in front of the curved walnut staircase.

Katherine's Christmas tree had always been the showpiece. This year, as in all others, deliverymen had muscled the seventeen-foot Douglas fir into its enormous cast-iron stand. And this year, as in all others, Tom had climbed an extra-tall stepladder and painstakingly entwined countless strings of Italian lights around every short-needled bough.

"You okay, Tom?"

He turned, feeling Dr. Tony Gaylani's hand on his shoulder. "Oh, hi, Tony. I'm fine. Just daydreaming."

"Need help finding a hanger?"

Rather than answer, Tom hung his coat. Then, to keep up appearances, he shook hands with his neighbor.

"Let's head this way," Tony suggested. "We can join your son."

"He's here?" Tom asked. "Trevor decided to come after all?"

"Came alone. The babysitter canceled at the last minute." Tony pointed past the makeshift bar set up in the living room. "Why don't we grab a drink on the way?"

"Sure... but give me a second."

After Dr. Tony Gaylani left, Tom looked down at the hairline crack in the slate floor. During a carefree moment less than a fortnight ago, he and Katherine had stood on that very spot. Back then, they'd giggled and carried on like lovesick teenagers. Back then, they'd reveled in each other's company. Back then, he'd felt alive. But now, the *back thens* were over.

Amongst all the faces, he spotted his son chatting with Harriet O'Banyon. He walked toward them, hoping Katherine's adopted mother would act as a buffer. Trevor had said otherwise, but Tom suspected his son's quick exit from the cemetery hadn't been to get the family out of the cold. Trevor's abhorrence for the Mafia was well known.

Tom Kempner carted two garbage bags into the open garage. He'd been something less than an engaging host, but had managed to hold it together. Take the last forty minutes, for example. As people filed out, he'd stood alone by the front door and said good-bye. He'd even gotten Katherine's best friend, Joanna, to put on her coat. At first she didn't want to leave, but after he had assured her he'd be fine, the Gaylanis had agreed to go home.

Tom looked skyward. When pain contracted the muscles in his thigh, he winced and began rubbing the old scar. As he separated the recyclables into bins, Tom wished he could relive the afternoon his wife had died. If only last Wednesday hadn't come and gone. If only… If only…

On that day, he'd behaved badly. Instead of making Katherine understand his precarious position, he'd allowed a cycle of events to escalate. Instead of being sympathetic to his wife's concerns, he'd taken Katherine's noontime call and pretended to ignore the danger signs. Even now, as he stood in the garage, he could hear the distress in her voice.

"Damn it, Tommy, listen to me! There's something off about this guy."

"I'm sure you're right, dear, but I can't discuss it now."

"Can't or won't?"

"Please, Katherine."

"Don't *please* me. Just answer the question."

"My God, woman! The judge is about to rule on my motion to dismiss. You have my word. I'll call you back the first chance I get."

Scanning the darkening horizon, he recalled how his decision to hide out with his clients had allowed Dr. Tony Gaylani enough time to arrange the wine tasting. But while that lapse had compounded itself and led to a tragedy, he'd still had chances to reverse his mistakes and gain control.

Once back home, he could have taken Katherine aside and told her the truth. Instead, he'd withheld much of his thinking and acted like the loyal *consigliere*.

Later, at the wine tasting, he should have confronted Tony and told the Iraqi sonofabitch that he knew all about his Muslim ancestry. But again, he'd just observed the doctor's behavior and decided not to bring up the subject. Talk about a bump on a log. He'd sat still after Tony's tasting ritual began. Even when Katherine panned Gaylani's choice of wine, Tom hadn't moved a muscle. Not a word. Not a hard stare. Nothing.

Of course, he'd also been victimized by circumstances. Admiral Weiss was a master tactician. Instead of stressing the unwritten code of silence, the admiral had lulled him into complacency. How well he remembered how his old neighborhood chum had used his *buddy-boy* condescension to make it seem like they were working as a team.

"Listen, buddy-boy. Set this up and there'll be something in it for you. Right now I need to talk directly to your boss. But don't worry. It's nothing personal. We're friends, and I'll prove it. In a day or two, you and I will sit down and discuss the big picture."

Then Admiral Weiss had underscored another point:

"It goes without saying I want you to keep this under your hat. And one other thing, buddy-boy. Don't make it obvious, but when you're around your neighbor, keep your eyes and ears open. Some of us at the Company think Dr. Gaylani is a very intriguing figure."

Since Katherine's death, he'd had forty-eight hours to mull over Eric Weiss's words. There was no concrete proof Katherine hadn't died naturally, but when he coupled the admiral's message with his wife's panicked call, he realized foul play was involved.

Tom stared at the darkened sky, but when cold air and swirling snow lashed at his face, he looked down and recalled the wine tasting, still baffled that Tony Gaylani was a spy and murderer. My God... not only had the doctor acted quickly, but the man had targeted Katherine in her own home. Tony Gaylani had killed Tom's wife while Tom and Joanna looked on.

Tom stepped out of the garage and out onto the cobblestone turnaround, unnerved by the finality of the truth. An unforgivable calculation had proved wrong. Dead wrong. But it was only one of many mistakes he'd made.

When Katherine had slumped off the couch, Joanna had jumped up and screamed. Seconds later, as he knelt by his wife's side, Tony had rushed in and pushed him away.

He remembered moving closer as the doctor checked Katherine's pulse. He'd said nothing, but was taken by the troubled look on Dr. Gaylani's face. Of course, Tom had no idea he was abetting a crime. He just acted like a good soldier and listened to Tony's command:

"Tom, get my medical bag from the car. Joanna, go to the kitchen and dial 911!"

He'd sprinted to Tony's car. By the time he found the black bag in the trunk and got back, the situation had worsened. Dr. Gaylani continued to administer mouth-to-mouth resuscitation, but Katherine wasn't breathing. He wanted to help, but when paramedics rushed in and set up their equipment, he was shoved aside.

The second Tony activated the shock paddles and Katherine's upper torso bowed off the carpet, he'd looked at the non-beeping monitor. When all attempts failed to restart her heart, he shouted his fear and moved closer.

The rest blurred. After the paramedics placed Katherine's body in the ambulance, Dr. Gaylani climbed in. Joanna shoved him into Tony's car, then followed the blue and red flashing lights in a race to

Good Shepherd Hospital. Once they'd arrived and he ran down a long corridor, the nightmare became more vivid. The moment he pushed open the emergency room doors, he knew something had gone radically wrong. The organized bedlam he'd watched on TV wasn't in evidence. Only Tony stood by the gurney, and once his neighbor lifted the sheet, his whole world had come crashing down.

Tom looked around the garage, thinking he could still detect the sanitized smell of the hospital. When he took a deep breath and regained his bearings, he knew one thing for sure. The smell wasn't there, but the memory of Katherine lying in the ER was forever imprinted in his brain.

Looking at her had been awful. It was Katherine, all right, but she didn't resemble the woman who'd stood outside without a coat and argued with him at their front door.

Her eyes, always steadfast, stared unseeing at the ceiling. Her high-collared silk blouse, pinned at the top by Lady Harriet's brooch, was ripped open and torn to make room for the heart paddles. Her neck-length auburn hair, never out of place and perpetually shimmering, looked greasy and matted around her head. Her mouth, once soft to the touch, was locked half-open, her lipstick smeared from Dr. Tony Gaylani's grandstand attempt to breathe life into lungs that had already collapsed and died.

Katherine's death mask had drawn him closer, but in spite of knowing she was gone, he'd refused to process the truth. Even when Tony replaced the sheet and transformed her back to an eerie body profile, he'd stayed by his wife's side. Only after the doctor turned off the overhead lights had reality begun to sink in. That was when Tony grabbed his upper arm and tugged gently. That was when tears were streaking his cheeks. That was when he'd consented to leave.

Tom's memory vanished when another blast of arctic wind stung his face. Rather than turn away, he stood his ground just outside the garage door, closed his eyes, and bowed his head. For several seconds, he didn't move. Then, as he prayed for a sign that Katherine could hear his apology, his hand was nudged by something wet and cold.

"Jesus!" Tom jumped back.

His alarm was short-lived. When he stared down, he realized there was no reason for concern. A dog's cold nose had touched his hand. As a former Lab owner, he recognized the breed. The sad-eyed stray only wanted a handout.

"Old girl, you picked the wrong house. All I have are pop cans and wine bottles."

The yellow Labrador retriever wore no collar or tags. She also appeared unafraid. But her ice-covered fur pointed to prolonged exposure to the bitterly cold weather.

He bent down as the dog did a slow, weary spin and lay beside his feet. His uninvited guest responded to his gentle touch, and he took solace that the dog wasn't in any pain.

"Did God send you to watch over me… or is it the other way around?"

Years before, after their son left for college, he and Katherine had bought two yellow Lab puppies. Both had lived a full life and brought them so much happiness that last month, they'd been united in their desire to have another dog.

Seven weeks ago he'd called Ellen Eichler. When the breeder promised him a female from a recent litter, Tom knew he'd found the perfect Christmas present.

Earlier, he'd listened to the radio and heard the blizzard storm warnings. Now, more swirling snow blew on his face.

"Girl, let's go someplace warm. Wager Katherine's girlfriends left us plenty to eat."

He turned, ignoring the burning sensation in his thigh. The Lab followed, and once they went inside and he opened the refrigerator, her interest really perked up. As he massaged his old Nam bullet wound, she sat in front of the shelves packed with containers and casseroles, her nose twitching with anticipation.

"How 'bout it, Blizzard? You hungry?"

Suitably christened, Tom fixed her a bowl of leftovers. Then he found a blanket and folded it into a temporary bed. When Blizzard chowed down in one breath and fell asleep during the next, he doused the kitchen lights and headed for the living room.

Tom stood by the flagstone hearth. After stacking hickory logs on the white-hot embers, he grabbed two snifters from under the liquor cart. But when he splashed a generous dose of brandy into one, he remembered his new status as a widower. Tight-lipped, he replaced the empty glass, the one he usually fixed for Katherine. Then he slumped back onto the sofa.

Hours before, he'd felt alone in the company of their friends. Now he just felt alone. Even a healthy sip of brandy didn't help. Like it or not, a new form of imprisonment began to close around him.

As the fire flamed anew, Tom looked straight ahead and took a deep breath. Others were involved in Katherine's murder, but they hadn't forced him to act like a timid fool. He had no excuse. His conduct had been reprehensible. And unless he avenged his wife's death, he'd go to his grave with an unshakable feeling of blame.

Tom stood up, his eyes glistening and riveted on the fireplace. Notions he'd once thought outrageous began to take hold. Admiral Weiss's phone call had seemed like business as usual. But it wasn't. When he had agreed to pass on the admiral's request, Tom had sealed Katherine's fate.

He used both hands to steady the snifter. The cognac burned his throat, but it still gave him no relief. He slumped down, certain Tony Gaylani had sedated his wife, then finished the job by strangling her while Tom ran for the doctor's bag and Joanna went into the kitchen to dial 911. Of course, the death certificate read differently. According to Dr. Gaylani, Katherine had succumbed to a   cerebral thrombosis. But medical jargon aside, he had no way of proving a blood clot hadn't lodged in her brain and caused a massive stroke.

How ironic. For years he'd used courtroom skills and constitutional guarantees to keep Mr. Barbera and his mob soldiers out of jail. Now he was the one on the wrong side of the American legal system. His wife had fallen to a premeditated act, but the evidence was circumstantial. Plain and simple, there wasn't a lawful way to punish the murderer.

The brandy snifter warmed in the palm of his hand. Again he brought it to his lips, and as more thoughts crowded his brain, he looked into the fire.

When Admiral Weiss had asked for an introduction to Mr. Barbera, he'd obliged and arranged a meeting. He suspected the admiral was trying to cut him out of the negotiation, but he didn't complain. Instead, he briefed the boss on what to expect.

Normally, such an inquiry would have prompted the gentleman don to call a summit. Even if Admiral Weiss had demanded that all conversations be private, why hadn't the boss talked to him on the QT? He was the *consigliere*. Hadn't he defended the man who ran Chicago's Mafia? Hadn't the mobster sought his counsel for the last twenty-five years? When the CIA came calling with an under-the-table request, why had the boss suddenly acted standoffish? Was it because Mr. Barbera knew he and Admiral Eric Weiss had grown up in the same neighborhood? Had the don, who'd treated him like one of the Family, been worried that he and the deputy director of the CIA might have had their own private discussions? But hadn't he always handled the mob's delicate situations? Wouldn't Mr. Barbera know that he'd never disclose confidences to the admiral?

He put his brandy snifter on the coffee table, but as a new recollection crossed his mind, the knot in his stomach intensified. On the night his wife had died, he'd come home from the hospital and talked with the boss.

"Tommy, I'm so sorry for your loss. Danny Finn and my wife, Maria, also send their condolences."

"Thank you, Mr. Barbera."

"What a shock… and so sudden."

"My neighbor thinks it was a massive stroke. Probably a brain clot."

"Was Dr. Gaylani there?"

"Yes, Mr. Barbera. Katherine was stricken while he and Joanna were at our house for a wine tasting."

"Did the doctor try to save her?"

"He did, but nothing worked. Even the paramedics couldn't bring her back."

"Did she die in the hospital?"

"Yes," he replied. "Tony signed the death certificate in the emergency room."

"It's terrible. If there's anything I can do. Please, Tommy, don't hesitate to ask."

"Thank you, Mr. Barbera. Tony has already seen to the arrangements. With Christmas falling on Sunday, we've decided to have the wake tomorrow and the burial on Friday."

"Makes sense, Tommy."

"I suppose… but my gut tells me I should ask the hospital to do an autopsy."

"Is that normal?"

"Optional, Mr. Barbera. When I brought up the subject, Tony checked it out. According to him, the State of Illinois won't require an autopsy."

"Sounds like a needless delay to me too… and with Christmas right around the corner…"

"You're right, of course, but—"

"No buts, Tommy. Not a good idea."

Tom picked up his brandy snifter and took a sip. Late Wednesday night, Mr. Barbera had discouraged him in no uncertain terms. The boss claimed the admiral would be upset if anything disrupted the Mafia/CIA cooperation. At the time Tom was too numb to disagree, or for that matter, to comment on the boss's request to be a no-show at Katherine's wake and funeral.

Tom's face tensed. Back then, he hadn't thought about Mr. Barbera's call. But just now, after reliving the conversation, he had new doubts. What if the boss knew his wife had been murdered? That would explain why Mr. Barbera had nixed the idea of an autopsy. My God! Maybe he and Katherine were expendable. Maybe the boss and Eric Weiss had conspired.

He stood and walked toward his office. Once inside, he pushed his chair away from the desk and got down on his knees. After lifting a corner of the area rug, he pulled open a small trap door that had been cut into the oak floor.

The safe was welded onto some I-beams that crisscrossed the crawl space under his office. After entering the combination, he opened the door and removed a manila folder entitled Kempner/Weiss. His work done, he locked the safe, closed the trap door, and smoothed the area rug back in place.

Seated at his desk, Tom took a sip of brandy and opened the folder.

Back in the eighties and nineties, when Admiral Weiss wanted bios on Hispanic-American trucking executives, Tom had handled the request and seen it through to fruition. At first he had suppressed his suspicions and followed the admiral's orders to the letter. But after delivering several bios over a number of years, he began to wonder why the CIA sought information on people they never prosecuted.

Back then, Tom had been as cynical as he was today. That proved to be beneficial. He'd made a startling discovery when he tested his theory that Admiral Weiss was pushing the boundaries of his authority.

Year in and year out, the same thing had happened. The targeted executive disappeared hours after Tom had delivered a report to the admiral. And that wasn't all. According to the Mafia's informants, none had died or packed up and fled the country. They'd vanished, and no one knew how or why. Their wives, families, and co-workers had been united in their responses: "The man was here one minute and gone the next."

The conclusion was obvious. The Company wanted to disrupt drug traffic into America. Since they couldn't get the Columbian government to wage war on the cartels and they had no admissible evidence against the persons of interest, they'd done the next best thing. The CIA had attacked the delivery system, and in so doing had put other trucking executives on notice.

Tom thumbed through the manila folder, scanning the more than a dozen dossiers. He recalled that Admiral Weiss had found compelling ways to pay for the information he received, but the mysterious disappearances had created one unintended consequence. Important mobsters from Families around the country had heard rumors. Time and again, they'd called, wanting to know what the boss had done for the deputy director of the CIA and what he'd gotten for his efforts.

Their reasoning had been sound. Within the hierarchy of the American Mafia, Mr. Barbera's stance was well known. The boss thought making cocaine available on a wide scale would be a corruptive influence on teenagers, college students, and young working men and women.

Mafia dons paid lip service to Mr. Barbera's concerns, but rejected his position. The drug business generated huge profits. Money trumped morals. Underworld crime bosses went to great lengths to increase their share of the market. That translated into one certainty. Anyone who inhibited the flow of illegal substances was a dead man. Mob families disagreed on many procedural matters, but if word had gotten out that Mr. Barbera's moles had helped the CIA close down the flow of cocaine, the vote would have been unanimous. And a bloody war would have begun.

Admiral Weiss's first request for a dossier on a person of interest had coincided with Tom's appointment as Mr. Barbera's *consigliere*. His elevation into the inner circle had given Tom more authority and more operating discretion. But autonomy notwithstanding, once he realized that the requests for dossiers would be ongoing, he'd decided to get the gentleman don into the loop.

After Mr. Barbera approved his proposal, Tom had instituted a plan that had not only shielded the crime boss from his Mafia brethren, but from the Company too. Going forward, Tom would violate one of Admiral Weiss's direct orders. Instead of shredding the information the mob's informants had collected, he'd keep a copy of each dossier.

Years ago, at the boss's Lake Forest estate, Tom had laid out his plan over a brandy:

"We need an insurance policy. If one of the CIA's stings ever goes bad, we could be drawn in as an accessory to their plots to kidnap and murder trucking execs."

He remembered how Mr. Barbera had looked at his brandy snifter, rotating the stem, catching firelight. With a small smile that he had grown to fear, the boss said, "Any thoughts?"

Tom had swallowed hard and replied. "The Kempner/Weiss file won't give us legal immunity, but if I say I acted without your knowledge, it will minimize the pressure on you. Furthermore, if I threaten to leak the dossiers to the press, the admiral will be in a bind. The CIA can mount covert operations, but they're not supposed to eliminate US citizens without a trial. Even Hispanic-American drug runners are entitled to due process."

At the time, he'd been sincere about shielding the boss. He'd not only told Gary Barbera that he'd keep the Kempner/Weiss file in his secret safe under the rug, but he'd given the boss the combination too. He kept it at home because a safety deposit box was too secure. If anything happened to him, the contents of his box would be administered by the courts.

Tom opened his desk drawer and put the Kempner/Weiss file in a plain folder. The material in that file was explosive, and if given to the right reporter it would cause his boss and the deputy director of the CIA a lot of trouble. Of course, he wouldn't take such drastic action right now. But he would call Barbera and Weiss and tell them that he'd taken two precautionary moves:

First, he would put the file in his safety deposit box with a note attached: "In the event of my death, deliver these dossiers to the editor of the *Chicago Tribune*."

Second, he would deliver duplicate copies to a friend with a similar note, instructing the unnamed friend to give the packet to the editor of the city's other leading paper, the *Chicago Sun Times*.

Of course, Admiral Weiss and Mr. Barbera would be livid, but their anger would never escalate into any action against him. Threatening to use the Kempner/Weiss File would keep both men at bay while he formulated a plan to make sure Katherine's killer got his due.

CHAPTER SIX

Patricia Shaver looked out one of her office windows. The winter sun was low on the horizon, a reminder it was time to close the foundation books. She was due at Ellen Eichler's in less than two hours.

Pat dropped her pencil, pushed away from her desk and walked toward the coat rack. In the summertime, the large brick courtyard that separated her home and office was easy to navigate. She'd stroll amongst the ceramic pots planted with daisies, lilies, and ornamental grasses. But in December, there were no colors to enjoy. Everything, including the perennial beds and flowerboxes, was encrusted in a thick layer of snow.

Snowshoe and Shoe-Too rushed out when she tossed her parka over her shoulders and opened the door. She followed, glad to be leaving the paperwork behind. The short run was exhilarating, but once inside her home the gnawing uneasiness returned.

Why, she wondered, did her mind keep recreating frightful remembrances? First she envisioned the long-ago fire—the inferno that had incinerated Honeymead and burned her parents' bodies beyond recognition. And next, she pictured herself thumbing through the multi-page file she'd unearthed—a dossier that proved her grandfather and father were among a group of public figures who'd gotten rich after making secret alliances with the Chicago Mafia.

Pat climbed the stairs to her second-story bedroom and stepped into the large walk-in closet. Packing a suitcase and boarding an airplane didn't excite her, but seeing Ken Dale did. She didn't understand how a gut-wrenching probe into her family's ties with the Mafia had rekindled their long-distance romance. But when her old boss and lover had helped guide the investigation in the aftermath of last May's discovery, Ken had also awakened her heart. Since then, she'd experienced a sensation she'd always thought was reserved for others.

Still, doubts prevailed. She was certain she was in love. But she'd also watched her parents. Witnessing their troubled marriage made her question whether she'd ever be able to make an unconditional commitment to anyone.

Instead of getting her warm-weather clothes together, she picked up what was left of last night's sleeping pill. With the half-empty wine glass in hand, she sat on her king-sized bed, gazing through a large window at the hardwood and pine trees that surrounded Honey Lake.

Fifty miles northwest of the flat ground buttressing Chicago's skyscrapers was the hilly and forested topography of Barrington. To blue-collar Windy Cityites, the village was a place where the elite with big incomes, big houses, big cars, and big egos beat their chests. She'd lived in the equestrian community all of her life, but had never considered herself a country gentlewoman. Sure, Grandfather had deeded Honeymead to her mother as a wedding present. And yes, she'd grown up in a palatial mansion. But after her last graduation— a Northwestern University ceremony where she'd received a Ph.D. in journalism—she'd been happy to move back on the estate and assume a no-frills existence in the caretaker's cabin.

She sipped more Chianti and walked to the window. Leafless oak and maple trees contrasted with outcroppings of ponderosa pines, Douglas firs, and blue spruces. As she looked down at ice-covered Honey Lake, snow began falling and twilight gave way to darkness.

Instead of seeing the beauty, she was intrigued by another phenomenon. The back lighting from the bedroom lamps reflected off the thermal pane and created a mirrored image of her face. Like an animal mesmerized by its own shadow, she brought the wineglass to her lips.

Professionally, she was a freelance investigative reporter. Physically, she was ash-blonde, blue-eyed, five-seven, less than one twenty-five, and in the eyes of some admirers, not tough to look at. She'd never gotten to know Katherine Kempner, but based on Ellen's description, they were cut from the same mold. Both had been born to wealth, had a curious intellect, and possessed an unquenchable desire to help the underdog.

She took another sip, all the while staring at her reflection. Of course, she'd hated growing up in the lap of luxury. From her earliest remembrances, she'd either been supervised by the servants or pawned off on boarding school teachers. As the unwanted byproduct of a loveless union, she'd rarely seen her parents. Mother was a party animal. She had Hollywood looks and a jet-setting style. With her credentials, Elizabeth Louise Shaver had been welcome at chic shindigs from Beverly Hills to Paris. Father was more of a stay-put guy with a blinding obsession to make money. Robert Douglas Shaver's one-track mind had kept him at the bank, living his business every waking hour, seven days a week.

Pat moved her hand, then watched her reflection wipe away tears. Dysfunctional behavior had run rampant at Honeymead. Early on, her parents had engaged in verbal intimidation. Later, the shouting was accompanied by physical abuse, climaxing just before her eighteenth birthday, while she was away for freshman orientation.

She looked away and took quick breaths. Two things had happened after her mother had shot her father, then taken her own life. Those involved in the cover-up had set Honeymead ablaze, and a first semester college student had become the sole heir to Grandfather Zwilling's financial empire.

She tried to calm down, but even when the setting sun cast an orange tint on ice-covered Honey Lake, she held the wine glass tightly.

Before being eligible to vote, she'd been left to fend for herself. Of course, she'd completed her undergraduate and graduate education. Along the way, she also established a half-billion dollar foundation. But her scholastic effort and philanthropy had gone for nothing. Last May, when she'd unearthed the secret dossier and read the names of politicians and other notables lined up alongside numbered Swiss bank accounts, she realized that much of the monetary base that underpinned her wealth had come from gambling, drugs, and prostitution.

Pat stepped back from the window and her image disappeared. That discovery had killed her enthusiasm. She still gave away a sizable amount of her staggering riches, but funding worthy causes didn't fulfill her. She was the caretaker of an estate brimming with felonious cash.

Pat gripped the wine glass until her knuckles turned white. Once she'd unearthed the file, she'd given the bribe lists to the Chicago federal district attorney. Unfortunately, death and a lack of talkative informants made it difficult to build a case. But there was an upside. Bill Pavin wouldn't guarantee an indictment, but he had made one promise. If she took the stand and testified about the events surrounding the discovery of the dossier, Gary Barbera, Jr., and his son, G.T., would be exposed to damaging publicity.

She brought the wine glass to her lips. Did the gnawing feeling in her stomach stem from the prospect of admitting that Grandfather and Father had been white-collar criminals? Or was it from the shame of pointing a guilty finger without seeing herself in the mirror?

After the Honeymead fire, she'd kept her head in the sand. To avoid a tabloid feeding frenzy, she'd bought into Senator Scott Sheppard's cover-up. Today she knew her parents hadn't died from smoke inhalation. Back then she hadn't challenged the glaring inconsistencies in Uncle Scott's story. Back then, she'd cried as the senator told the press that her mother had fallen asleep smoking a cigarette. Back then, it was easier to blame an alcoholic mother and an uncaring father for the inadequacies in her life.

Pat finished her wine. She needed to get ready to go over to Ellen's, but instead of heading for the shower, she sat on her bed and lifted a framed photo from the nightstand. The picture of herself and Ken Dale had been taken as they sipped wine at an outdoor café in Paris, one of the two cities they'd visited after she turned over the bribe lists to the district attorney, Bill Pavin.

She rubbed her fingers over the glass protecting the photograph. Why wasn't her house full of snapshots and memorabilia? The bikini picture with Ellen and Snowshoe was in the kitchen, along with a few dog shots held to the refrigerator by magnets. Upstairs, photographic displays were equally sparse. There was the Hawaii album in the drawer that only reminded her of what could have been, and the Paris photograph.

No doubt countless images of her family existed. Her grandfather had been a financier to reckon with, and her grandmother had rubbed elbows with all the names on Chicago's social register. As for her parents… her mother had admirers in every major city in the free world, and her father had hung out with Senator Scott Sheppard, the chairman of the Judiciary Committee and a man who lost his party's nomination to Bob Dole the year Bill Clinton won re-election.

Once again, she glanced at the Paris photo, focusing on the wine glasses she and Ken held. In that instant, her mind flashed back to a different scene.

She was a young girl, finished with another year of boarding school and home for the summer. Joining her on the marble terrace overlooking Honey Lake were her parents and grandparents. They'd all just gone riding on the estate grounds. But once her mother headed for the liquor cart, the tension had begun.

Pat closed her eyes. How she had ached to be a normal kid— one who'd lived with normal parents in a normal neighborhood.

She set the Paris picture back on the nightstand and picked up the phone. Ken Dale always worked late. As CNN's Southern Europe and Middle East bureau chief, he stayed in his Rome office until the end of the US evening broadcasts.

"Hey, big guy," she gushed, smiling into the phone, "do you miss me?"

"Is this the breathtaking blonde from Barrington?" he asked.

"More breath-stopping than breathtaking. I'm packing. What's your weather like?"

"Pleasant nights and sunny days, but you know that. Is everything okay?"

She listened to Ken's deep voice and visualized his six-one frame, dark hair, and rugged good looks. "Everything on this end is fine. I just like hearing that you're in love with me and my body."

"How much time do you have?"

"As a matter of fact, none. Tonight I'm going to Ellie's to celebrate an early Christmas."

"Boy… I'm about to get sentimental and you give me the brush-off." He laughed. "Say hello to the Eichlers, and don't forget to hug the other two blondes in my life."

"I'll give them each a cookie. Snowshoe and Shoe-Too love you too." She stared at the Paris photo. "Counting the hours. The sooner I get my arms around you, the sooner I'll feel safe."

CHAPTER SEVEN

Tom Kempner awoke on Christmas Eve morning well after the sun had come up. He'd consumed too much brandy and his head hurt, but after energizing himself with cold and hot showers, he got dressed and came down to greet his new boarder.

Blizzard still looked at him with a Lab's sad eyes, but her body language told a different story. She held her head high and wagged her tail. She also gobbled down more leftovers.

Tom hit the brew button on the coffee maker and looked through the kitchen window. The overnight storm had left eight inches of new snow, and the outside thermometer read ten degrees. But there was a plus side. The sun was shining and the air was clear.

He had two cups of black coffee, then took Blizzard for a short walk. Back inside at 10 AM, Tom went to his office, grabbed the Kempner/Weiss file from the drawer, and set it on his desk. Aware of the bank's closing hours—noon on Saturdays—he placed a call. When Ellen Eichler assured him the roads were plowed, he left his office, put on his down-filled parka, and loaded Blizzard into the front seat of his Chevy Blazer.

Tom navigated seven miles of country roads, parked, and headed toward the Eichlers' barn. The Shamrock Acres sign—a wooden placard painted with a white background and kelly green printing—paid homage to Ellen's maiden name of McCarthy.

"The place looks great," he said. "Last time your kennel was in the garage."

"Business is good. Nowadays, everyone wants a puppy."

Ellen embraced him and he hugged her back, but when her eyes began to tear, she let go and so did he.

"Tommy, I'm so sorry."

He nodded. "One life taken, another put on my doorstep. Who can figure?"

"Isn't that's why we have faith?" she asked, turning and heading toward her office. "Give me a sec to grab my medical bag. I'm no vet, but I can check to see if her heart's ticking."

Tom watched her leave, then walked to a window. From conversations with Katherine, he knew that some thirty-five years ago, the Eichlers had bought a half-section corn and soybean farm to escape the confines of urban life. His wife had also said that from her newlywed days on, Ellen had juggled her time between managing the household and keeping the books for her husband's feed-lot business. That lasted until Lauren, their only child, eloped. After that Ellen had started to breed Labrador retrievers and German shepherds.

Tom heard the sounds of file cabinet drawers being opened and closed. The clanging reminded him of the activity he and Katherine had enjoyed when they'd met Ellen in her garage/kennel almost fourteen years ago. They'd stopped by after their only child had gone off to Yale. With Trevor away, the house felt empty.

From the beginning, Tom had liked Ellen's no-nonsense style. Katherine had also been intrigued by their cross-town neighbor. In fact, after a brief collaboration with Ellen, his wife decided the Kempner household needed two Labs.

As with most things, Katherine had viewed puppy rearing as something she could handle by herself. From the outset, she focused on the task, not the people who could help her out. Of course, she never viewed Ellen as another name on the Rolodex. Katherine just figured that her store-bought manuals would cover every aspect of canine care.

But almost immediately, his wife's systematic approach had crumbled. The two puppies were cute and rambunctious. They wanted no part of Katherine's by-the-numbers regimen. Before long, a frustrated Lab owner called their breeder. It never occurred to her that Ellen's unique brand of country charm would be impossible to ignore.

"Sorry it took so long," Ellen said, walking back in. "The medical bag wasn't in the medical cabinet. It was in a drawer marked Medical Files."

"You're like me. I mismatch things all the time."

She nodded, pointing toward Blizzard. "Like bringing in a senior citizen on the day you plan to pick up a puppy?"

"Exactly," he replied, "and it worries me too. Can an eight-week-old dog be boarded with an old girl like Blizzard?"

"Is this a prelude to a sales pitch?" Ellen asked. "I sell puppies, but don't accept trade-ins."

"Didn't mean it that way," he said, smiling. "If you say they're compatible, I'll give them both a new home."

"No reason it can't work." Ellen opened her doctor's satchel and frowned. "Nuts."

"What now? Wrong bag?"

"Got the right bag, but the wrong tools are in it. The stethoscope and other junk must be in the house."

Ellen excused herself, then hurried across the driveway. As her braided hair bounced off her back, she vaulted the porch stairs and ducked into her two-story Victorian farmhouse.

Tom could only shake his head and grin. No wonder Katherine had found their breeder's enthusiasm so engaging. Ellen had done much more than teach their puppies some manners. Shortly after instruction began, his wife's calls became fewer and her excursions to Shamrock Acres more frequent. Both women were headstrong and from very different backgrounds, but the teacher-student alliance grew, and so did their friendship.

Katherine's willingness to get back in the saddle exemplified their mutual trust. For English families like the Cunninghams, fox hunting was a way of life. Katherine had spent weekends at the country house in Surrey and had given in to her father's demands to participate in the hunt. But she'd never accepted his lifestyle. Her velvet-covered hat and scarlet coat had become symbols of a social hierarchy she despised.

That vehemence had stayed in place for several decades. But Katherine's mindset changed once Ellen began helping with the puppies. He'd watched it happen. Somehow Ellen Eichler had reversed Katherine's teenage vow to hang up her spurs.

How many times had he seen them mount up and head out on the trails around their estate? Often, Joanna Gaylani joined them, as did other horsewomen from the hunt club. But whenever Katherine and Ellen rode alone, he knew they traded soul-searching confidences.

Tom gazed through the window. Just as Ellen scooted out the front door and across the covered porch, he heard three short yips.

He turned toward the sound and looked at a small dog cage with a puppy inside. For a moment, he was fine. Then he saw a tag marked SOLD KEMPNER hanging off the wire door.

Tom wiped the corners of his eyes before Ellen walked over. He also kept his head down as she opened a different medical bag and began to examine Blizzard.

"What's your read?" he asked. "Will she be okay?"

Ellen held up one finger and continued to feel Blizzard's body, checking for signs of discomfort. Moments later, she used a stethoscope to listen to the dog's heart and lungs.

"Her eyes look a little listless and she's underweight, but this Lab is no stray." Ellen looked up. "She's been abandoned."

"What's with people?" Tom asked, petting Blizzard's head. "Any idea how long she's been wandering?"

"She's got the winter coat of a dog who's accustomed to sleeping indoors," Ellen replied, picking up Blizzard's front paw. "By the looks of her pad, I'd say at least one day, maybe two."

"Should Dr. Nordlund check her out?"

Ellen nodded, then crossed the room, opened the cage with the SOLD KEMPNER sign, and handed him an eleven-pound Labrador puppy.

"This one's had all her shots, but it never hurts to get her acquainted with a vet." Ellen stepped back, grabbed a camera off a nearby table, and took their picture. "Why not make it a double introduction? Let them both meet their new doctor."

"It's Christmas Eve," he said. "It's bad enough I'm imposing."

"Nonsense," she replied, taking another picture. "While you say hello to your new boarder, I'll give Dr. Nordlund a call."

He looked into the puppy's eyes, but before he could slip back into his pervasive despair, Ellen reappeared and the puppy licked his nose.

"All set," she said, "he's expecting you to pop over."

Tom wished Ellen Eichler a Merry Christmas, then took his dogs to see Dr. Ray Nordlund. The vet met him at his office. After spending the next hour developing X-rays, taking blood samples, and performing other diagnostic tests, the doctor pronounced the puppy fit. He said Blizzard was weak, but also in good shape.

Tom thanked Dr. Nordlund, loaded up the dogs, then glanced at the clock on the dashboard. That was when he remembered he'd left the Kempner/Weiss File on his desk. That was when he also concluded that fifteen minutes wasn't enough time to go home and still get back to the safety deposit vault before the bank closed.

He was annoyed with himself, but when the puppy rose up on her hind legs and tried to dog kiss his face, he forgot about the bank and turned the ignition key.

The drive back to his house went smoothly. The new puppy fell asleep in his lap, never stirring, not even after he parked in the garage and opened the driver's-side door.

"We're home. Which one of you girls wants to get—"

He spoke too soon. Without warning, the puppy popped up, used his lap as a stepping stone, and leaped to the floor.

"Hey, where the devil are you going?"

He watched her scamper diagonally across the cobblestone turnaround and head for a snowdrift alongside the heated walkway to his front door.

"Slow down, young lady."

Keeping both eyes on the puppy, he got out and opened the hatchback.

"Okay, Blizzard. It's your turn."

Just as Blizzard jumped down and sat by his side, Tom heard the sound of a car coming down the driveway. He didn't bother to close the hatchback. Waving both arms, he ran toward the puppy and the heated walkway.

CHAPTER EIGHT

Patricia Shaver awoke and eyed the nightstand clock. 10:30 AM. Her dinner with the Eichlers had been grand, but she still had last-minute packing to do and errands to run.

After a trip to the bathroom to brush teeth and primp, Pat got dressed, then fed and walked the dogs. With her Starbucks thermos in hand, she drove to Walgreens for a travel mirror. Back in the Mercedes, she went to see the owners of her favorite boutiques—Karen at Satin Filly and Donna at Barry Bricken. By noon, after making a few purchases, she returned home, parked in her garage, then climbed the icy porch stairs.

"All right, you two."

She saw her dogs looking out the window, their eyes glowing with excitement. To protect herself from a stampede, Pat dropped her shopping bags, opened the front door, and stood aside.

"Knock yourselves out."

As the dogs raced around in the snow, she put her packages inside. Seconds later, she came out, followed the shoveled path across the courtyard, then unlocked her office door and arm-waved Snowy and Shoe-Too inside.

While they munched on a dog bone, she put a log on the andiron, turned on the gas jet, and restarted the remnants of yesterday's fire. Rather than make fresh, she heated up day-old coffee in the microwave. Armed with everything but a pencil, she pulled out her foundation ledgers. Before her Christmas Eve flight, she needed to make a few adjustments.

It took an hour to balance the books. Then she got waylaid. The moment she reached for her parka, the Labs ran to their toy box and each grabbed a Frisbee.

"Girls, just once, can we go home?"

She knew the answer. When the dogs whiffed the numbing air, they burst outside. Instantly she became the designated missile launcher, and her driveway turned into an aerial playground.

"Are you two slow learners? It's cold."

Moments later, as Shoe-Too made a leaping catch, Pat looked up and noticed a wisp of smoke coming from her office chimney. With a vision of the Honeymead fire alive in her memories, she went back inside and checked the fireplace. The dying embers posed no danger, but she still felt ill at ease. For her, the image had never gone away. The red-orange ashes glowing in the hearth brought back a recollection of a blaze that hadn't been so tame.

More than three decades ago, a college freshman had gotten out of a limo, shaken and scared. As she stood amongst the fire trucks, squad cars, and media vans, Pat had viewed Honeymead's two soot-blackened chimneys and the charred aftereffects of a now cooled-down inferno.

Over the years, her scars had hardened. Then last spring, the discovery of the secret file had awakened an old question: Was there a rationale for the insanity that had brought deadly confrontation to her parents' doorstep?

Last May, in an attempt to get answers, she'd placed a call to Senator Scott Sheppard. After some arm-twisting, her father's World War II Navy pal had invited her to the nation's capital.

Pat moved toward her desk and closed her eyes. She recalled the trip to Washington, but mostly she remembered the last night of her stay at the senator's Georgetown residence. She and Uncle Scott had sat in his library. They'd each sipped brandy. It was late in the evening when her family's oldest and dearest friend relayed the story of how it had all begun.

Ten months before the '29 crash, her grandfather, William F.

Zwilling, became president of Security Chicago National Bank. After assuming operating control, Bill Zwilling instituted new rules and regulations. With some luck and considerable skill, he positioned the bank to weather, then prosper, during the Great Depression.

As the panic deepened, Bill scavenged amongst the wreckage. While other firms reorganized, he'd purchased delinquent paper and enticing properties for pennies on the dollar. Before long, his knack for buying bargain-basement values paid off. Rich people noticed, and as the recovery got underway, Security Chicago began to out-shine other lenders.

The growth of Bill's bank had been spectacular. From Black Friday in 1929 to the Day of Infamy and Pearl Harbor in 1941, Se-curity Chicago went from a second-tier player to the fourth largest bank in the state. Profits soared. But for her grandfather, the achieve-ment had come up short. He needed more. He needed to quench an insatiable thirst. He needed to branch out.

Before long, Bill Zwilling had begun viewing most of his busi-ness opportunities for their return, not their righteousness. As greed enveloped him, he formed networks with other robber barons and never looked back. Bill Zwilling had championed a new breed of capitalist.

It worked. Her grandfather accumulated more money than he could spend in a lifetime. But it still hadn't been enough. No matter how big the pot or how many hands he won, he'd always managed to look around and see someone with a higher stack of chips.

Pat leaned back in her chair, remembering how the senator had been a master narrator. To keep her attention focused, he'd occa-sionally interrupted his story or stood up and walked behind the claw-footed wingback. One time, she recalled, he'd seemed to stop altogether.

"Uncle Scott," she had asked, "is that it?"

"Not quite," he'd said, sipping his brandy. "I just don't want to keep broaching painful topics."

"I'm a big girl, Uncle Scott. Let me be the judge."

She remembered how he'd eyed her, then continued, saying that Gary Barbera, Sr., the father of the current don of the Chicago Mafia, was also a man with the Midas touch. Years before the Great Depression, her grandfather had known the dapper Sicilian who ran Holly Corporation, the largest construction company in the city. As the lead man on the Holly account, Bill Zwilling negotiated the covenants for all kinds of loans. But that was just business. Once the economic recovery had gotten underway and Bill did some sleuthing, he'd found out that Gary, Sr., also had an uncanny gift for buying commercial real estate at the bottom and kicking it out at the top.

Her grandfather hadn't been a man who let an opportunity pass. At a private dinner, Bill suggested that being a cooperative banker was foremost among his many talents. He had reason to be bold. He'd suspected that Gary Barbera, Sr., had an equally impressive list of secret aptitudes.

Bill Zwilling's guesswork ended once they'd formed an alliance. Gary Barbera, Sr., was open with the men he trusted. The dapper Sicilian freely admitted that Holly Corporation was not only a construction company, but doubled as a front, laundering the cash the Capone organization generated from its speakeasies.

Initially, Bill had been uncomfortable, but not because of any ethical problem. He regularly entered into business arrangements that drove companies into bankruptcy. Bill Zwilling just couldn't get used to the idea that his bank had become inexorably linked to the mob.

Gary Barbera, Sr., had sensed Bill's reticence and dealt with it. At a meeting in the bank's boardroom, the dapper Sicilian laid out a set of ground rules:

"You and I are businessmen, not friends. We'll never see each other socially. Our interaction will be limited to a handshake after the terms of each deal are negotiated."

That get-together had turned the tide. Bill Zwilling already knew Al Capone's right-hand man was a master at finding unique ways to reward a banker who knew the combination to the vault. When he found out that Gary, Sr., would also be mindful of his standing in the community, Bill had swallowed his pride and watched his money multiply.

Pat remembered being poised on the edge of her chair when Senator Scott Sheppard had stopped speaking, put his snifter on the mantel, and added another log to the fire. Back on that cool night last spring, she'd thought his story was over. But again, she was wrong.

After Uncle Scott closed the hearth screen, he'd gone on, saying that the deposits from organized crime had fueled rapid growth in Security Chicago's assets. But the real bonanza came later. In 1932, shortly after Scarface Al Capone was convicted of income tax evasion, Gary Barbera, Sr., took over the Windy City mob.

An accountant by trade, Gary, Sr. reorganized the Chicago Mafia into units. He believed financial coercion, not muscle, produced the best results. Accordingly, he searched the ranks of his criminal brethren and appointed the shrewdest and smartest businessmen to be lieutenants in charge of prostitution, extortion, speakeasy operations, and gambling. Each reported back to him much the way a corporate VP reported back to the CEO.

Senator Scott Sheppard went on to amplify this point, telling Pat about a cocktail-hour chat he'd had with her grandfather—during which Bill Zwilling had described Gary Barbera, Sr.'s philosophy:

"That Godforsaken Sicilian had a straightforward style. When he found a business he liked, he bought it. To mold the operation to his way of thinking, he hired hardworking and resourceful people. He always paid top dollar for talent, often using signing bonuses as a way to strip competitors of their key people. And except for drug trafficking, he always let a product's profit potential determine the amount of time and assets he committed to develop the market. In that vein, he never ran away from a price war. He'd supplement his prostitutes and bootleggers until his rivals went under. Like that wop bastard used to say, 'a bankrupted mob boss can only ask his men to beg, borrow, and steal, but a don with resources can reward his Family with high wages and a safe working environment.' "

Pat stared at the beamed ceiling in her office, recalling how the senator had finished the anecdote, then taken another sip of brandy. Last May, she'd been startled by Uncle Scott's candor. Of course, she knew the senator and her grandfather had been close. During their evening in Georgetown, she'd also learned that Bill Zwilling had gotten in bed with the man who had changed the face of American racketeering.

Pat got up and sat on the corner of her desk. She remembered watching the senator pause, then continue his narration, explaining that as the years wore on and her grandfather's nest egg got bigger and bigger, even Bill Zwilling began to tire of the grind. But a banking empire with Mafia connections wasn't easy to walk away from.

Gary Barbera, Jr., told her grandfather to choose a well-qualified successor. To satisfy the current mob chieftain and also to ensure that the wealth stayed in his family, Bill Zwilling had to find someone he could trust. Fortunately for him, he did just that. His son-in-law fit everyone's requirements. From the onset, her father, Robert Douglas Shaver, had exceeded all expectations.

Pat lowered her head, weighted down by her recollection. She knew her father had had a flair for international banking. When the senator described how R.D. had arbitraged the mob's greenbacks in the world's currency markets, Pat realized that her father had added a new wrinkle to the art of being a white-collar crook.

Gary Barbera, Jr., had good reason to welcome R.D. Like his father, he was a renaissance man who embraced a businessman's mentality and also abhorred violence for violence's sake. And like his father, he needed to launder enormous amounts of money to keep the mob machine growing.

Pat stared blankly out one of her office windows. Her grandfather had epitomized St. Paul's most notable axiom—*money is the root of all evil*. But the other male icon in her family hadn't been a slouch. She found it painful to admit, but as financial filchers went, her father had taken Bill Zwilling's lead and created his own share of smoke and fire.

The muscles in her body stiffened. Discovering the file last spring had knocked her off a self-imposed treadmill. It also forced her to confront reality. But it hadn't prepared her for everything.

Dirty money alone hadn't made her an heiress. On the night her parents died and Honeymead burned to the ground, the love triangle involving her mother, father, and the senator had gotten entangled with Gary Barbera, Jr.

Today, she knew that Gary Barbera, Jr., had come to Honeymead to solve a problem, not witness two shootings. He was a businessman who didn't care that her parents' marriage was a disaster or that her mother had been carrying on with the senator. But the gentleman don was also a realist who had an obsession to shield his Family from the microscope of public scrutiny. He might not have been involved in any misdeeds, but horrific crimes had been committed in his presence. Considering his line of work, it was not an ideal situation for him to be in.

Last spring, she'd been surprised by Senator Scott Sheppard's forthrightness. At the time she didn't realize that Gary Barbera, Jr., had been behind the senator's loose lips. The mobster had ordered Uncle Scott to dispense damning information about her grandfather and father as a way to discourage her from becoming a witness for Bill Pavin, the Chicago Federal District Attorney.

Pat wiped beads of sweat from her brow. Her face felt flushed, but not from the radiant heat of the fireplace. When she stared at the dying embers, they were gray, not red-orange.

She continued to sit on the corner of the desk. She wanted to move, but found it difficult to get her body to respond. Why, she wondered, did she keep conjuring up the past? Why couldn't she stop triggering a remembrance of the Honeymead fire?

She looked up and stared out the window. Until she'd ended the therapy sessions several years ago, her shrinks had been unanimous in their pronouncements: *Don't repress your memories.*

Easy for them to say. The psychiatrists hadn't lived with her anguish. They didn't know how much she wanted to forget the past and get on with her life.

CHAPTER NINE

Tom Kempner watched the Mercedes SUV come down his cobblestone driveway. Without losing sight of the puppy, he ran out of the garage and began waving his arms.

The vehicle slowed down. Tom was enraged when he saw Dr. R. Anthony Gaylani behind the wheel, but he knew he had to keep his emotions in check.

"Careful, the puppy is loose."

The doctor's car crept forward, stopping near the heated walkway to Tom's front entrance.

"Well, well," Tony said, hanging his head out of the driver's side window. "I see you went through with it after all."

"How could I say no?"

"Guess you couldn't, but I thought you just bought one." Tony pointed as Blizzard sauntered up. "Who's this? The version that got steroids mixed with the Puppy Chow?"

"That's Blizzard. She stopped by yesterday."

Tony got out of his Mercedes SUV. Just as he squatted down and petted Blizzard, the puppy bounded over a snow bank and slid next to his feet.

"If the big one is Blizzard, this Jezebel must be Snowflake."

"Actually…" Faking a smile, he picked up his puppy. "Not bad, doc. Snowflake it is."

With Blizzard at heel, Tom walked through the garage and led everyone inside. He hated inviting Katherine's murderer into his house, but he wanted revenge, and that meant making the doctor think they were on neighborly terms.

"Snowflake," Tom said, depositing the puppy on the tile floor in the laundry room. "Take a look around. For now, this is your back yard."

He watched Snowflake sniff her dog nest and toys. Satisfied she would amuse herself, he turned to Gaylani. "Can I interest you in a drink?"

"A bit early," the doctor answered, tossing his parka on a breakfast nook chair, "but what the hell. If you're joining me, I'll have a light Bloody Mary."

"Two Bloody Marys, coming up."

Tom started mixing the drinks, keeping an eye on Snowflake. The puppy had come out of the laundry room and was examining a lattice-style gate he'd installed in the doorway between the kitchen and dining room.

"Your version of an invisible fence?" the doctor asked, pointing to the barrier that kept the puppy from the carpeted areas in the house.

Tom nodded. "Until she's trained, Snowflake will be walking on tile."

He stood with his back to Gaylani, cutting a celery stalk into two swizzle sticks. He wanted to turn and bury the knife in his neighbor's heart. Instead, he just turned.

"Unless you object, I'm loading this up with garlic salt, Tabasco, and all the trimmings."

"Why not? It's Christmas Eve and I'm not on call." The doctor eyed him. "By the way, old man, you look like an unmade bed. Are you holding up all right?"

"Last night I changed prescriptions," he answered. "Left those sleeping pills you gave me in the medicine cabinet and switched to an alcohol-based sedative."

"That's not the answer," Gaylani warned.

"Yes, Mother. Next time, I'll follow doctor's orders."

"I'm serious," the doctor continued, his tone unforgiving. "Kitty's death should never have happened. Don't compound matters by doing something stupid."

"Appreciate your concern. Now do me a favor. Fill the pooches' water bowls and let me finish the drinks." Tom looked up. "One other thing. The jug in the water cooler is empty. The full bottles are in the garage."

He watched Dr. Tony Gaylani's face muscles tighten, a reaction to being ordered around. That pleased Tom, but it also brought back a painful memory.

Last Wednesday night, he'd been in a state of shock. He was aware that Katherine was lying on a gurney, but the sight of her body draped in a white sheet haunted him.

When Joanna Gaylani escorted him out of the ER to a remote part of the waiting room, he was unable to cope with his new reality. Each time the image of his dead wife came back, Tom became glassy-eyed and hysterical.

Thankfully, Joanna had been there. No matter how much he cried, she'd never wavered or left his side. Her husband hadn't been so understanding. Dr. R. Anthony Gaylani brought in reams of papers, placed a pen in his hand, and pointed to the X's.

When Tom told the doctor he'd handle the paperwork on another day, Gaylani had stared him in the eye. "Trust me on this one, Tom. None of the arrangements can be made until you sign the medical releases. If it wasn't important, I wouldn't insist."

Time and again, Tom had inked his name. Back then, he hadn't realized he'd signed more than just medical releases. The doctor must have feared that someone would ask about an autopsy. To minimize that possibility, Tony had wanted Katherine's body released to the morticians so they could drain his wife's blood before anyone thought to test it for barbiturates.

"Jesus," the doctor said, slamming the door behind him. "You might have mentioned the water bottles are hidden under those horse blankets."

"Sorry, you docs can afford heated garages. Guys like me have to improvise."

He watched Gaylani struggle with the five-gallon plastic jug. Going forward, he'd change his tactics and be pleasant. But it would be tough. He didn't want to make small talk with the man who'd sent his wife to the undertaker before her body had gone cold.

"Anything else I can do?" Tony asked, his acrimony obvious. "Now that Kitty isn't around to pander to your whims…"

Tom glared, his focus riveted on the doctor's face.

"My fault," Gaylani said, holding his hands up in a submissive position. "Didn't mean to be a jerk. My attempt to lighten the mood came out wrong."

Tony joined him at the table in the solarium-style nook. Tom sensed his neighbor had intended to be hurtful, but even if the doctor had just spoken out of turn, it didn't matter. Last night, Tom had vowed to do two things: Find out why his wife had been murdered, then take his revenge. He wasn't sure how Dr. R. Anthony Gaylani would react to an old nickname, but he figured it was a good way to start the process.

"R.A., old buddy, I'm a lucky man. No guy could have a better guardian angel."

Gaylani's eyes went cold. "Lieutenant Kempner. Lots of things got buried in Vietnam. Maybe we should leave it that way."

Tom shrugged, his expression deadpan. During the years they'd been neighbors, Gaylani had never referred to Vietnam. But just now, when challenged, the doctor had called him Lt. Kempner.

His discovery that Gaylani remembered their OR meeting in Da Nang was enlightening. But what did it prove? He still wondered why the doctor had killed Katherine. If General Cunningham's papers had unmasked a spy, Dr. Tony Gaylani should have run to the Iraqi Embassy. In America, foreign agents got deported, not executed.

"We've been pals since you moved next door," Tom said, lifting his glass in a mock salute. "I only called you R.A. because back in Nam, like right now, you took special care of me."

Gaylani's eyes watched him, calculating. "Didn't I just ask you to let it drop?"

Rather than apologize, Tom stood up, hands raised. All in all, he was pleased. The Roman Allah had reacted to the initials, giving greater credence to Katherine's accusations.

As he planned his next verbal assault, another light went on. If Gaylani was a spy, he had taken his orders from the old Iraqi régime. When Saddam Hussein got toppled, his intelligence agency must have gone underground too. That meant Gaylani had no place to run. The embassy was no longer a haven for Ba'athists. The doctor was a man without a country.

"How 'bout a truce?" Tom suggested. "Nobody wants to forget Nam more than me."

"Then do it, old man… and while you're at it, do something about the phone." Gaylani pointed to a wall-mounted telephone. "In case you hadn't noticed, it's ringing."

Tom ignored the doctor's request. He'd heard the muted ring and saw the flashing signal light. The phone panel consisted of a hand-held receiver, two push-button connectors, and three flashers. Two of the push buttons and their corresponding flashers signaled use on the incoming lines that rang in the kitchen and throughout the house. The third flasher—the one that had lit up and was ringing—did not have a connector button. That was in accordance with his wishes. Tom always wanted to know when someone was calling on his very private telephone line. But he didn't want it answered anywhere but in his very private office.

"Don't feel much like talking," he said. "The recorder will pick it up on the fourth ring."

"Not this time," the doctor replied. "Call me a nit-picker, but the last one was the fourth."

Daniel Kevin Finn, Gary Barbera's bodyguard, chauffeur, and most trusted lieutenant, stepped out of the elevator and into the mahogany-paneled library in the boss's suburban Lake Forest mansion. It was early afternoon, Christmas Eve. He'd taken the lift from the three-room basement apartment Mr. Barbera had built for him after his wife and daughter had been murdered. Danny still owned a house in the old Irish neighborhood, but over the years, he'd slept there less and less.

"Great fire, boss, but it still seems a little nippy in here." Danny walked in front of the hearth and reached down toward a metal lever. "Maybe if I close the flue a smidge…"

"Don't touch it," the boss grumbled. "You tend to your business; I'll tend to the fire."

Danny smiled. Mr. Barbera had his fetishes. And ever since they'd been together, two had stood out. The first redefined proper golf etiquette. When they played, no one offered advice. Even Tiger Woods wouldn't be allowed to help the boss read a putt. The second dealt with the flue. When a fire burned in the library hearth, no one but the boss monitored the flow of air.

"Sorry, boss," Danny said, taking his hands off the flue. "Just trying to be helpful."

"Then do your thing and let me do mine. If it gets cold, I'll put on my Irish knit."

Danny nodded dutifully. Fixations aside, the boss—his Godfather—was a man to behold. While other Mafia chieftains demanded respect, the gentleman don earned it by being a strong, even-handed leader. And that wasn't all. In spite of being in his eighties, he was fit, looked great, and could still shoot his age, a feat most golfers never accomplish.

"Another thing," the boss barked. "Why do you stay in the basement and page through those paperbacks? What's wrong with the books up here?"

"We both know the answer to that one," Danny said, his voice pleading forgiveness. "Nobody underlines first edition books. Those suckers can't be replaced."

The Irishman scanned the bookshelves in the boss's library—

his eyes aglow with adulation for a collection including monastery-scribed pages from St. Thomas Aquinas' *Summa Theologica* as well as a Gutenberg release of Niccolo Machiavelli's *The Prince*.

Danny revered the written word and never tired of rereading the classics. But since his wife's death, he got a lump in his throat every time he picked up one of his paperbacks. They had shared many passionate moments, not all of them in the bedroom. Discussing the classics during a candlelit meal had also been a stimulating, almost sensual experience.

He and Kathleen had first met near his home on the northwest side. She had recently graduated from college and was starting a new job at a branch of the Chicago Public Library. He had grabbed Dante's *Divine Comedy* from the shelves and was at the front desk checking it out.

A conversation led to a lunch date at the local pub. Once the willowy Irish lass started talking, Danny Finn's bachelor days were numbered. Her brunette hair and infectious smile were captivating, but it was her intellect, not her beauty and sexuality, that impressed him most. She was brilliant and in no time taught him how to be a student of great books. As Kathleen had said over and again:

"No one, not even the scholars, can read classic literature without underlining key passages and writing notes in the margins. Since the library frowns on that behavior, create your own collection. All you need are paperbacks and a felt-tip pen."

Danny swallowed hard, then walked to the parson's table and picked up the wireless phone. He had a call to make, but first he glanced at the boss.

"As God is my witness, I enjoy your books. Many a late night I come up here and just read."

When Mr. Barbera nodded—his way of accepting the explanation—Danny began dialing. He knew the boss was anxious to reach his *consigliere*, Tom Kempner.

Danny turned away, counting ten unanswered rings. When he looked over his shoulder and locked eyes with the boss, Danny shook his head. Mr. Barbera showed no signs of anxiety, but the Irishman knew the boss was good at hiding his temper.

Admiral Eric Weiss, Deputy Director of the CIA, sat in his office in Langley, Virginia. He'd spent his military career in intelligence, not at sea, but he did admire one naval hero. An oil painting of John Paul Jones standing on the burning decks of his ship, *Bon Homme Richard*, hung on the wall across from his desk.

Usually that artwork inspired him, but today Eric was in a foul mood. His ill humor worsened when he dialed Tom Kempner's private number and got a busy signal.

"Son of a bitch!"

The deputy director clicked off the phone and stood up. He wanted to cuss again, but knew it wouldn't help. Since he needed to make contact, all he could do was keep trying.

Eric engaged the intercom. "Cissy... this is a direct order. No calls, no interruptions."

"Just got the coroner's report," Cissy Place replied, her voice echoing through the speaker. "Okay if I violate a direct order?"

"Don't be smug. What the hell are you waiting for?"

Ten seconds later, he nodded when his secretary handed him a manila folder.

"Glad we got things straight," Cissy said, standing at attention. "From here on in, I won't interrupt... unless it's an emergency."

"Sounds like a plan," he said. "You understand my priorities better than me."

Danny Finn hit the disconnect button, then put the wireless phone back in the charger.

"No answer, boss. Let it ring twenty times."

"Your instincts were right," Gary Barbera said, rising from his chair. "Tommy always picks up the private line. He must be furious with me."

"With the funeral and all, your boy has got to be tired. Even money says he's taking a nap."

Danny picked up a silver thermos, but as he poured mugs of coffee for the boss and himself, he saw the hardness in his Godfather's eyes. At that moment, Danny looked down at the Oriental rug and decided to stay where he was. Sometimes it was best to give the boss room to vent.

"Don't patronize me," Barbera snapped. "Tommy doesn't take naps."

When Danny lifted his head, the boss stopped rubbing one of his gold peregrine cufflinks and signaled for his coffee.

"I shouldn't have listened to the admiral. Damn, why didn't I keep Tommy posted?"

"You never had a choice," Danny said, putting both mugs on the lamp table between the two wing-back chairs. "Sailor-boy threatened us with all sorts of reprisals. If you ask me, he and his spy dickheads are a bunch of un-American thugs."

"Even a rogue cop wears a badge and uniform," Barbera added. "Admiral Weiss may be unprincipled, but he still represents the United States. We play ball with the enemy because crossing the CIA can be hazardous."

Danny knew that the boss's abhorrence was directed at Eric Weiss and not the CIA. The boss routinely engaged with many authoritarian agencies. He viewed it as a struggle between competing businesses. Even when events disappointed him, he operated under a strict code of conduct in which violence was only used to keep dishonorable men in line. The boss's son didn't share his father's views. Gary Thomas III (G.T.) was a disappointment and an ingrate.

"Slice it up, down, or sideways, I hate Sailor-boy's guts." Danny balled his hands into enormous fists. "Say the word. Just say the word."

"You sound like my son," Barbera replied, his voice even and his eyes calm. "Isn't that how G.T. feels about our journalist friend, Miss Patricia?"

"I'll take the fifth."

The Irishman knew G.T.'s missteps last spring had taken a toll. Events stemming from the punk's run-in with Miss Patricia Shaver were coming to a head. The attractive, rich, smart, and unfortunately, very nosy reporter had dug up a dossier on the boss's hidden payroll. The preliminary hearing to review the admissibility of evidence was on the docket for early next year. He knew the judicial wrangling meant difficult legal problems for Mr. Barbera and his son. Yet the boss considered Miss Shaver and her friend, Mrs. Eichler, to be honorable opponents. They hadn't hidden behind their skirts. Unlike Admiral Weiss, who mounted covert operations and used spies, the ladies had gone toe-to-toe with the Family. Some even had them winning round one.

"Wait and see, boss. Someday we'll get the goods on that fuckin' Weiss."

"If it ever happens, his pals at Langley will disavow him."

"That would be sweet," Danny said, "but right now, I got bad vibes."

"You're always worried about something," Barbera replied, staring at one of several Monets that hung in the library. "Be specific. I'm not good at guessing."

"What if Weiss and his moles knew your *consigliere*'s wife was a target all along?"

The boss turned and faced him. "Are you questioning the veracity of a revered agency?"

"What if Weiss has Dr. Gaylani in his hip pocket?" the Irishman asked, sitting down. "He might have called us just to see if we could penetrate his cover."

The boss eased back into the other wing-back and picked up his mug. "Hold off calling Tommy again. Before I do anything, we need a better handle on Dr. Gaylani and his wife."

Danny nodded. "On the other hand… Why would Weiss ask us to dig up dirt if the Gaylanis were working for him?"

"Elementary," Barbera said, his eyes hardening. "The admiral is a disgrace to his country. All traitors suspect turncoats in their own ranks."

Tom Kempner pushed away from the breakfast nook table, Bloody Mary in hand. The muted ring and flashing signal light on the wall-mounted phone had stopped, but he still needed to go back to his office. The Kempner/Weiss file was lying on his desk in plain view, and the answering machine hadn't been reactivated.

Last night, during one of his trips to the brandy cart, he'd taken a detour and turned the answering machine off. At the time, he was livid. But a while ago, when he'd called the doctor by his old nickname, he'd gotten the right reaction. If Dr. Tony Gaylani squirmed, why not make the CIA and Mafia uncomfortable too? Since men he'd trusted had treated him with disdain, why not stop answering the telephone and make them communicate with him via the message recorder? That would give him an opportunity to show his own lack of respect. That would also allow him to apply his own kind of pressure.

Tom stood. "Stay put, doc. Won't be gone long."

"Why the rush?" Tony asked. "The caller hung up."

"Maybe so, but I want to fix the message recorder."

"You're unbelievable," the doctor said, picking up his Bloody Mary. "The world is driven by technology and you can't keep an answering machine working."

"Watch me." He pointed as the light on the wall-mounted phone flashed and the muted ring sounded anew. "In a minute I'll have the recorder fixed."

"Better hurry, old man. Right now you're more popular than my wife."

Admiral Eric Weiss redialed Tom Kempner's private number. When it rang through, he sat at his desk and listened… And listened.

He clicked the disconnect button after fifteen rings. When he picked up the top secret report his secretary, Cissy, had brought in, he began fighting indigestion again. Instead of phoning in the results, the coroner had sent Katherine Kempner's medical examination through regular channels.

The admiral suspected she'd been murdered. The on-site autopsy notes confirmed a crushed larynx. That narrowed things down. There was a killer loose next door, and Tom Kempner had to be next on the list. Of course, he wasn't in the mood to protect a lawyer who defended Mafia scum, but more than ever, the Company needed Kempner's cooperation as badly as it had to have Barbera's.

He wasn't concerned about the old don's safety. His Irish bodyguard wouldn't let anybody get close. But Tom Kempner didn't have Danny Finn protecting his ass. The mob lawyer was an accessible target and, like all civilians, didn't follow orders.

Hadn't he made the rules crystal clear? Either pick up the phone or leave the recorder on. But that hadn't happened. Instead of obeying, Tom Kempner had apparently talked on his private line and then gone out.

Eric felt like smashing the wall. Instead, he walked over to his trophy case. He'd been the Naval Academy's middleweight champ four years in a row. Looking at those silver cups always perked him up. Maybe he wasn't the most handsome guy, but his chiseled physique, prominent cheekbones, cobalt-blue eyes, and short-cropped hair made him an imposing ring figure.

As he reevaluated the situation, he decided to overlook Kempner's transgression. With his wife dead, the guy probably wasn't feeling so hot. But Eric wouldn't wait forever. The mob lawyer needed to be told that now was not the time to leave his front door unlocked.

Tom Kempner stepped over the doggie gate. By the time he'd crossed the foyer and walked under the arched entry to his personal sanctuary, the private line had stopped ringing. But that didn't deter him. He had a plan to implement, and his neighbor, Tony Gaylani, was the target.

He could have started his gambit in Katherine's office, but that wouldn't have produced any new insights. Checking General Alan Cunningham's documents would just verify what he already knew. His wife hadn't lied. She'd read her grandfather's papers and reiterated what he'd written.

Tom chided himself for stonewalling Katherine's pleas. But even if he hadn't, it wouldn't have made a difference. The documents had been written in the forties. They referred to Tony's mother and father, not Tony. According to General Cunningham, Tony's father was an Iraqi nationalist who'd sent his son to grow up in America. But those avowals didn't prove that Tony was a spy. The courts would deem the general's documents as hearsay.

When Tom entered his office, another sobering thought crossed his mind. He was trying to nail the man who years before had saved his life. He was alive today because Dr. R.A. Gaylani was in a Vietnamese hospital when Tom needed him most.

A week before he'd joined the Army, Tom Kempner stood in Camp Randall Stadium and, along with five thousand other seniors, flipped the tassel on his mortarboard and became a graduate of the University of Wisconsin. Nineteen sixty-six was two years after the Tonkin Gulf Resolution and the sudden escalation of America's involvement in Vietnam. But for a bachelor without deferment, the choice was simple. Enlist or be drafted.

His soldiering had begun right away. He exchanged his civvies for an olive drab wardrobe, left his hair on the barber shop floor, and headed for the barracks. After eight weeks of basic training and a similar period in AIT (Advanced Infantry Training), he started OCS (Officer Candidate School).

Seven months later, a newly commissioned second lieutenant left Fort Bragg. Dressed in fatigues and combat boots, he began a two-stage forty-hour journey—an endless MAC airlift to Saigon, then a bumpy helicopter ride northward to Hue.

He'd celebrated his first anniversary in the military by pulling his duffel bag off an Army Huey. As he wondered if the cockiness of being an Airborne Ranger would help him survive in the jungles of Vietnam, he'd slung his pack and M-16 over his back and reported for duty. The horror of the Tet Offensive was still six months away. But for an unproven officer leading patrols in search of Viet Cong infiltrators, life in the rice paddies was daunting.

His squad had been ambushed during a reconnaissance mission just six days after he'd landed in Nam. Out of the eleven-soldier unit he led, only he survived. Seven were killed in the initial crossfire, and the other three died alongside him as a rescue chopper whirled its way back to a hospital outside Da Nang.

He'd been at death's door when fate and two stretcher bearers put his body on the operating table of a brash young doctor. He had no idea they'd ever meet again, but midway through the summer of 1967, Dr. R.A. Gaylani had plugged the bullet holes in his chest, then put his shattered right leg back together.

Tom sat at his desk and massaged his thigh. The physical pain was bearable, but his mental anguish was not. Somehow, some way, he had to avenge Katherine's death.

He took a deep breath and picked up the phone. He was certain Mr. Barbera had initiated the call. The ultra secret private line had been installed by the boss's techies and was dedicated to his private use.

Tom listened to the dial tone, then he closed his eyes and dropped the handset back in its cradle. No. Damn it to hell. He wouldn't be the loyal *consigliere* and call Mr. Barbera back. He'd play the game, but only on his own terms. He had to make Katherine proud. By nature, he wasn't a violent man, but this time the Airborne Ranger in him wouldn't back down. This time he'd do whatever it took to win.

* * *

Admiral Eric Weiss walked back to his desk. He picked up the speakerphone and speed-dialed James Fitzgerald, Director of the FBI.

"Mr. Fitzgerald, sir, on behalf of my boss and everyone associated with the Iraqi spy surveillance, I want to thank you for your willingness to accommodate my request."

Eric chose his words with care. All phone calls into the director's office were taped. And that wasn't the only reason. A new CIA directive made it clear that the Company and the FBI had to cooperate.

"We aim to please," Fitzgerald replied, "but we also have a mandate to put mobsters in jail."

Eric hated the patronizing tone, but chuckled anyway. Years ago, Police Commissioner James Fitzgerald had run a tight ship as the top cop in Chicago. The man knew how to fight street crime, but had never learned the nuances of doing battle with Mafia dons.

"Don't want to wear out my welcome, sir, but I need an undercover agent to watch over Tom Kempner."

"That's a tough one, Admiral. Normally, I'd assign someone to dress up like a gardener, but in the dead of winter that doesn't work."

"What about a maid?" Eric offered, wishing he could say, *No shit, Dick Tracy*. "Kempner doesn't have a live-in, but I know he has cleaning help at least three times a week."

"Might work," Fitzgerald said. "Fax me the name of the service he uses. We'll get them to tell Mr. Kempner his regular housekeeper is sick. After that, one of our female agents will show up as a replacement."

Eric smiled. "Like your idea, sir. You'll have the name and phone number in less than an hour."

CHAPTER TEN

Tom Kempner continued to sit in his office and eye the phone. He was happy he hadn't dialed Mr. Barbera back. The mobster could wait. Tom needed time to plan.

He pushed his leather chair away from his desk and scanned a space his wife had laughingly dubbed Forbidden Territory. Katherine and her entourage of architects, builders, and interior planners had designed, furnished, and decorated every part of their house except the ground floor of the west wing. In his private library, gym, and office, he'd laid out the rooms and chosen the décor.

He leaned back and stared at the ceiling, wondering what his parents would think if they could see him now. Regrettably, he'd never know. They'd died just weeks before he graduated from college. A drunk driver had broadsided their car as they'd driven back from Friday sundown services at the local Brooklyn synagogue.

Tom closed his eyes. The aftermath of their deaths had been difficult. For the most part, they'd been a close-knit family. But there had been a major unresolved issue.

That point of contention had nothing to do with scholastic or gang-related problems. Quite the contrary. He'd maintained a straight-A average, made friends easily, and stayed out of trouble. It was in matters of religion that he and his mother and father had parted company.

They were Orthodox and he wasn't. They believed in prayer and a simple life. He was a go-getter who thought wealth was the measure of a man's success. Saturday subway rides into Manhattan had opened his eyes. He saw limousines, gentile gals in short skirts, and a whole lot more. From then on, he'd not only craved to be known as a trendsetter, but also as a man who'd reached the pinnacle of his profession and looked down.

His mother, Nan, a striking woman who abhorred fashion designers, epitomized their differences: "Tommy, why must you talk about Brooks Brothers and co-op apartments? A proper Jewish boy doesn't concern himself with money or button-down shirts. He finds a nice Jewish girl and settles down."

Tom opened his eyes. Back then, he'd kowtowed to his mother, but once he started college, he'd cut the apron strings. How well he remembered their first and only showdown. It was Thanksgiving break of his freshman year. He'd come home looking very preppy. He'd taken a part-time job and used his paychecks to buy clothes.

Today he was defying another authoritarian force, one where the stakes were infinitely higher. But when he'd vowed not to acquiesce to Barbera and Weiss, he'd also taken the first step in going it alone. From now on, he had to keep the mob and the intelligence community off his back while he dealt with Dr. Tony Gaylani.

Since Vietnam, the doctor had added forty years and almost that many pounds. But while older and less fit, Dr. R.A. Gaylani was still someone to be reckoned with.

He'd used Tony's Vietnam nickname to knock the doctor off balance. Calling him R.A. had worked, but browbeating a hostile witness was just one part of the carrot and stick routine. The time had come to stroke his ego. Katherine's rush to judgment hadn't been a leap of faith. But in the eyes of the law, R. A. Gaylani's family background and desire to hide his Muslim heritage didn't make him guilty of a crime.

Tom walked to the windows and looked out at the panoramic view. Why hadn't he told Katherine about the doctor and the Da Nang hospital? Granted, until a few days ago, it hadn't mattered. Prior to taking Admiral Weiss's call, he'd viewed Tony as just a closet Iraqi who'd fallen for a beautiful Jewish girl.

He looked toward a distant corner of his property and eyed the barn near a stand of Douglas firs. All along, he'd figured Tony had done the smart thing. Upper-crust America rarely chose the healing hand of an Arab doctor. To save his career from culture-driven biases, a bright young surgeon had pretended to be an Italian-Catholic. As a Jew and Mafia lawyer, Tom knew all about profiling.

He turned on his heels, certain of only one thing. He should have broken his promise to the Family and the CIA when Katherine raised the subject of Tony's background. He and his wife had never kept secrets. But instead of leveling with her, he'd treated her charges with indifference.

He returned to his desk and took a sip of his Bloody Mary. Tom enjoyed a drink, but for many years, he had sworn off all mind-altering substances. Back in Nam, a different kind of drug had almost destroyed him. Dr. R. Anthony Gaylani might have pieced him together, but the side effects of the operation had left an invisible scar.

He took two swallows. Until last night, he'd blocked out that stint in Vietnam. Now the sounds of the firefight came back, and so did the images of his men being slaughtered.

When Viet Cong bullets had torn into his body, he hadn't felt a thing. His leg had buckled. And then a burning sensation in his chest. But other than that, everything had been a blank. Only after surgery had he felt real pain. Even in a drug-induced stupor, his body cried out. And that was just the beginning. Once the anesthesia wore off, the pain became intolerable. During every waking minute, he begged the nurses for stronger medication. Even blinking hurt.

Tom wiped a bead of sweat from his forehead. Army Captain R.A. Gaylani had been like two docs in one. He'd been his surgeon in the OR, and his internist once Tom was taken back to his hospital room. And guess what? The moment R.A. upped the dosages, the round-the-clock morphine injections worked. After a week of pain-free healing, he'd sat up, taken solid food, and asked questions.

The Army nurses said the doctor had used plates, screws, and pins to reconstruct his shattered femur. They gave Dr. Gaylani's performance a standing ovation. He wanted to join those applauding and also add a personal thank you. But the doctor never made rounds.

Tom stared at his Bloody Mary. Why was he sitting in his office, wasting time? He needed to tend to Katherine's murderer, not leave him stewing in the kitchen.

He got up, replaced the tape cassette in the answering machine, and clicked the cover in place. Drink in hand, Tom walked back to the breakfast nook, a small smile curving his mouth.

"Miss me?"

"Terribly," Tony said, looking up, "but lucky me, I had a beverage to while away the lonely minutes."

Tom took the doctor's empty glass. "Either kill me or accept my apology."

"Won't have to. Our stomachs will corrode if we keep pouring down this rot-gut." Tony stood. "Tell you what. You do the honors, I'll build a fire."

Tom watched the Roman Allah step over the doggie gate and head for the living room. The prospect of talking about Katherine's death suited him. But there were hurdles. He would have to be careful not to get emotional or imply that any of the emergency medical procedures had deviated from the standard of care.

Tom laced the doctor's Bloody Mary, disguising the potency with extra drops of Tabasco and Worcestershire. His plan set, he picked up the velvet hammer, but instead of seeking out Gaylani, he hesitated and remembered a time more than three decades ago when a devilish woman had pulled the same trick on him.

Harriet Cunningham O'Banyon had eventually bestowed her blessing on his marriage. But not before she'd pumped Bloody Marys into his system and then pumped him. Of course, the atmosphere had been friendlier. Katherine's surrogate mother had engaged in a spirited give and take, but when it was over, he'd had the pleasure of learning about a woman who had a history of intoxicating male egos.

During World War II, Harriet Cunningham had become a favorite with hundreds of men. The youthful volunteer nurse left her aristocratic title in Hyde Park and made daily journeys to the London hospitals that tended to the wounded.

Sean O'Banyon was a tough Irish teenager from an even tougher Chicago family. He'd been especially touched by Harriet's brand of medicine. Unlike thousands of other D-Day casualties who wanted to heal and be sent home, Sean prolonged his therapy. He'd fallen for the British nurse and needed time to win her over.

In the fall of 1944, over her mother's objections, Harriet eloped with the renegade Irishman. Following a honeymoon in Dublin, the newlyweds returned to England. General Cunningham had sympathized with his daughter's plight, but he allowed his wife's voice to rule. Attempts to make peace ended in frustration. Harriet would be an instant hit in Chicago, but as Lady Harry enjoyed a Thanksgiving drumstick, some members of her English family had voted her into the Cunningham Black Sheep Squadron.

"Damn it, Kempner," Tony complained, calling from the living room. "What's keeping you?"

Tom gathered the drinks and joined the doctor.

"It may not seem like it," he said, handing Tony the laced Bloody Mary, "but I appreciate everything you did for Katherine."

"Small comfort," the doctor replied. "Had there been symptoms, we might have saved her, but a brain aneurysm is almost always fatal."

"Did Katherine die right away?"

Tony nodded. "Never got a pulse."

"That's something," Tom said, rotating his glass slowly in his hands. "At least she didn't suffer."

"Even if death wasn't instantaneous, she felt no pain. Furthermore…"

As Gaylani began citing medical jargon, Tom tuned the doctor out. So far, he hadn't made any progress, and while that wasn't surprising, he had to figure out a way to either legally implicate the man drinking his liquor or dispose of him in a less constitutional fashion.

"What gives, old man?" Tony said, banging his glass down on the coffee table. "Didn't you fix that thing?"

"Sorry," Tom stammered, his thoughts vanishing. "You said something?"

"The phone," the doctor repeated. "The one that answers after the fourth ring."

"I must have pushed the wrong button," Tom said, standing up. "Hold on, I'll be right back."

Admiral Eric Weiss asked his secretary to find out who cleaned Kempner's house. He also asked her to fax the information to the director of the FBI.

When she left, the admiral picked up the phone and dialed. After ten rings, he hit the disconnect button.

"God damn you, Kempner," he said, banging his fist on his desk.

Tom Kempner entered his office, expecting to hear someone leaving a message. Instead, the phone just stopped ringing. Why had Mr. Barbera dialed back so soon? If the boss had been that anxious to have a conversation, he would have sent Danny Finn over to make sure it happened.

Tom sat at his desk, suddenly realizing Mr. Barbera's private line wasn't as private as before. Right after Admiral Weiss requested a meeting with his boss, Tom had given the admiral the number as a way to insure instant communications. Getting two calls back-to-back meant one thing. Powerful and impatient men were on his case.

He looked at the answering machine. When it was working properly, the red light either glowed or flashed. Since his did neither, he knew he hadn't engaged the on/off switch.

Tom chided himself for the mistake, but instead of pushing the switch down, he did nothing. When he'd vowed to deal with Dr. Tony Gaylani, he'd also pledged to stand up to his Mafia boss and the admiral. At the time, he wanted Barbera to call him back so he could set the record straight and give him a piece of his mind. Since Admiral Eric Weiss also had the number, he wondered if it made sense to turn the recorder back on.

Tom's body tensed. Since Katherine's death, one thought had dogged him: Was Gary Barbera working with Admiral Eric Weiss? He knew they were talking. He'd set that up before the end of the trial. But what if their conversations weren't restricted to assembling biographical materials on his neighbor, Dr. Tony Gaylani? And that wasn't his only concern. What if Tony Gaylani had gotten wind of the Mafia/CIA alliance? Could the doctor have been spooked into killing Katherine? Had the Chicago mob teamed up with the CIA and orchestrated his wife's death?

He stood up very slowly, thinking it through. He had the Kempner/Weiss file to hold over their heads. Somehow, he had to find out if Katherine's murder had been the byproduct of a clandestine collaboration between the Mafia and the CIA.

He reached for the wireless phone, his hand shaking. He wouldn't have to look up the numbers. He had each man on speed dial.

CHAPTER ELEVEN

Joanna Myerson Gaylani parked her Mercedes behind a large snow mound not far from Ellen Eichler's house. From an earlier drive-by, she knew that the Eichlers lived on a small farm on the outskirts of Barrington. During the same drive-by she had also noted that real estate developers had bought acres and acres of land around the Eichlers' property. Since the infrastructure had been built and the sales office was open, Joanna had all the cover she needed. On any given Saturday, prospective buyers parked off the road to check out lots for their dream houses.

She turned off the car engine. Even for a strong person, the last seventy-plus hours had been difficult. Events following Kitty Kempner's death had taken an enormous toll. But now was not the time to let down. Now was the time to show fortitude.

As she waited for the postman, her thoughts drifted back to that day in Palestine when a teenage Jewish girl had stood on the dirt floor of their two-room house and watched her parents die. Back then, like today, she'd felt enormous sadness and stress. But back then, unlike today, she hadn't been trained to make sure the people she loved hadn't died needlessly.

When the postal truck came by, Joanna looked up and watched the carrier stuff a rubber-banded packet of mail into the Eichlers' box. Shortly after he sounded his horn and drove away, Ellen ran out, picked up the letters, and went back inside.

Joanna waited, her face tense. As her fingers drummed on the steering wheel, she watched the seconds tick off the dashboard clock.

The mailman had done his job, but would Ellen Eichler do hers? Everything depended on her reaction.

The answer came sooner than Joanna had expected. Two minutes after retrieving her mail, Ellen rushed out the front door, clutching an envelope in her free hand. The woman was in such a hurry, she had forgotten to put on her coat. Instead, Ellen tossed her sheepskin into the front seat of her pickup. Then she got in, sped down the driveway, and turned right, the direction of Honey Lake and Patricia Shaver's cottage.

Joanna watched Ellen leave, but didn't start her car. She just stared through the windshield at the Eichlers' Victorian farmhouse.

Why had her mood darkened? Everything had gone according to schedule. The second Ellen Eichler had driven away, Joanna knew that the letter she'd taken from Kitty's mailbox on the afternoon of her death had finally been delivered, opened, and read.

Patricia Shaver was in her office. The converted stable that had once housed her grandfather's prized Arabians no longer smelled of horses. After she moved back onto the estate, her architects had not only freshened the air, but turned the space into a fabulous office, kitchenette, and storage facility.

When her phone rang, she turned away from the window and walked to her desk. Still immersed in her thoughts, she lifted the receiver, but before she could say hello, a very anxious voice screamed through the line.

"Patricia! We need to talk."

"What's wrong, Ellie?"

"Not over the phone. Got something to show you."

"Are you all right?"

Ellen didn't have to answer. Pat heard her rev the engine and downshift, an indication that a grandmother who always drove under the limit was speeding on snow-packed country roads.

But why? What could be so troubling that Ellen had decided to race over just hours before leaving on a trip to see her daughter and grandchildren?

"I'm not going anywhere," Pat said, "just say when and where."

"Don't move," Ellen ordered. "I can see your driveway just ahead."

Pat eyed the smoldering fire, then lifted her parka off the pegged rack. Her timing was perfect. She opened the door as a pickup truck backfired in her driveway.

"Where's the fire, Mrs. Eichler?"

Ellen stood grim-faced next to her pickup. She held her sheepskin coat in one hand and the envelope in the other.

"No fire," Ellen replied, nodding toward the envelope, "but you'll want to read this."

"Go inside the house and start the coffee. I'll join you after I collect the Frisbees."

Tom Kempner sat at his desk, a wireless phone clutched in his hand. A minute ago, he'd vowed to call Gary Barbera and Eric Weiss. Just now, he'd analyzed the repercussions of standing up to the deputy director of the CIA and the ruling don of the Chicago Mafia.

Tom hesitated, then put the phone back in the charger. As he weighed whether he was a coward or just being smart, he stared at the answering machine, depressed the lever, and watched the red light go on. Chickenhearted or not, it was important to have his recorder in good working order. He needed to know who was trying to reach him.

He rubbed his eyes. Maybe his hesitancy was an outgrowth of a sixth sense telling him to move slowly. If Katherine's death was part of a conspiracy, he had to do some preliminary legwork. Confronting Barbera or Weiss was a tall order. The task became suicidal if they were working together.

Tom looked at a framed snapshot on his desk. Katherine had

taken the photograph as he'd crossed the finish line, winning the sixty-and-older flight in the local bike race last September. That had been a happy time. Now it just rekindled painful thoughts.

He reached out and again picked up the wireless phone. Yesterday afternoon, during the reception at the house, he'd promised to call Harriet O'Banyon. He liked Katherine's aunt but knew he'd have to watch what he said. Her husband, Sean, had close ties to Barbera.

He dialed Harriet's number, feeling a little sheepish. He wanted to begin his investigation into Katherine's murder, but he'd never dreamed it would start with her adopted mother.

His worries were premature. On the fourth ring, Harriet's recorder picked up. He left a message, then leaned back in his chair and closed his eyes.

According to Katherine, Harriet and Sean O'Banyon enjoyed life to the fullest. Their marriage was a working partnership that brought profitability to the family's trucking business and spontaneity to their personal lives. They were lovers and pals, but in spite of their efforts, Harriet had never gotten pregnant.

About the time the O'Banyons had become reconciled to the void in their marriage, a couple on the other side of the Atlantic had thrown up their hands. Things in London had become so desperate that Katherine's narrow-minded father prevailed on his baby sister for advice.

Harriet hadn't hesitated. She wouldn't experience natural childbirth, but God had answered her prayers. Back in England, Katherine liked the idea too. A rebellious teenager had just joined Lady Harry to become the second member of the Cunningham Black Sheep Squadron. To Katherine, being banished to Chicago represented the best of all worlds.

"Pardon me, your holiness." Tony Gaylani extended his arm into the office and waved a Bloody Mary. "Okay to come in?"

Tom pointed to a chair, then quickly whisked the Kempner/Weiss file into the top drawer of his desk. "Sorry. Once I fixed the answering machine, I called Harriet."

"Did you?" the doctor said, putting his glasses in the breast pocket of his blazer. "How is she?"

"Wasn't home. Left a message on her recorder."

"Hers works?" Tony asked rhetorically, a smirk crossing his face. "Your wife always said Harriet was a dynamo. After yesterday, I understand where Kitty got her zest for life."

"Don't forget ambition," Tom added.

"Did Kitty's love of medicine get started with her Aunt Harriet?"

"Yes."

"Funny how things work out," Tony said. "She followed in her aunt's footsteps, then you two met each other at Hines."

"But not in the coffee shop. Her first job was to get me back on the straight and narrow. This soldier was a junkie."

Tom gazed out the window, recalling Katherine's first bedside visit. His new doctor had been professional and pleasant. He had acted like a self-centered brat.

As a man addicted to morphine, Tom hadn't cared that Katherine had graduated valedictorian from Northwestern's medical school. He hadn't known that she'd interned at Rush, then left one of Chicago's most prestigious medical facilities to join the staff at Hines, a bare-bones veteran's hospital that couldn't attract big-shot teaching doctors or afford state-of-the-art equipment. He also hadn't given a damn that she'd chosen an institution known principally for its slave wages and backbreaking schedules. But in the summer of 1967, Katherine had begun her residency in part to emulate Lady Harry's World War II example, and in part to voice a vote of support for those wounded in Vietnam.

Tom picked up his Bloody Mary, raising it in a mock toast to Tony. "When I laid eyes on Katherine, I saw double. Talk about a guy in trouble. Both images looked so good, I asked both of them out."

Tom had never told Katherine, but for him, it was love at first sight. He'd been captivated by the whole package—brains and beauty. Katherine hadn't shared his enthusiasm. She'd been more interested in getting him drug-free than getting involved.

"Well, well, counselor," Tony remarked, "I had no idea the man who makes his living keeping pushers on the streets once popped pills himself."

"Even a former dope fiend believes in due process," Tom replied. "For the record, doc, I got hooked when an Army MD gave out morphine shots faster than his nurses passed out aspirin. But, hell, you know all that. You're the genius who wrote the prescription."

"I was out of options," Tony said, arching his dark, bushy eyebrows. "Your wounds were severe, and like most Jewish soldiers, you couldn't handle the pain."

"Not so fast, doc. You never asked me a thing."

"Couldn't. You weren't doing much talking. But I figured, what the hell. I'll plug the grunt's holes, then make him a happy Hebe." Tony grinned. "Back then, you had no bitch. Putting you on cloud nine got Kitty to sign your dance card."

"My dependence certainly caught her attention," Tom replied, hoping his anger didn't show.

"Like I said, old man. I did all you Jews a service."

"Thanks for being so considerate," Tom responded. "Of course, I'm grateful a daughter of English royalty found time for a commoner like me, but I still wish God had given us another decade or two."

"Speaking of royalty," Tony said, "I didn't see any of Kitty's relatives at the funeral. Where were the bloomin' limeys?"

"Katherine's parents are dead. Several members of her family wired their condolences."

"You're too damn polite," the doctor sneered. "Someone should have showed up. Sending a telegram is tantamount to saying you don't care."

"You're being unfair."

Tony waved him off. "Maybe, but given her family's attitude, I'm surprised Kitty had an interest in keeping track of them."

"You can be fascinated by genealogy without caring about titles or bloodlines. The thought of getting her grandfather's papers sparked a bit of nostalgia."

"I suppose it's like looking at old picture albums," Tony agreed, leaning forward. "Ever find out why the boys in MI-6 held up the documents so long?"

Tom shrugged. "Maybe somebody marked the stuff classified."

"General Cunningham must have been privy to some heavy-duty secrets. If I remember correctly, he was the last British High Commissioner of Palestine."

"Very impressive," Tom replied. "Now for the sixty-four dollar question: Name the countries surrounding the general's home away from home?"

The doctor smiled. "Back in the forties it was Lebanon, Syria, Jordan, and Egypt."

"Right you are," Tom said, feeling a twinge in his stomach.

"It's important to understand the Middle East conflict," Tony continued, his voice firm. "I've made an effort to brush up. More often than not, once you understand the root causes, what appears to be lunatic behavior suddenly has a rationale."

"If you're talking about Israel, that's not a defensible theory," Tom answered, hoping to spark a debate. "Jews and Arabs have been arguing over Palestine since Moses and the Ten Commandments. If a consensus was possible, they'd have one by now."

"Hope you're not giving up," Tony said, taking out his tortoise-shell glasses and putting them on. "A fresh idea can be anywhere. Take the general's papers. He wrote about the region. Maybe there's a solution hidden in one of his journals."

"Anything's possible."

Tom was stunned by Tony's boldness. The doctor had looked over General Cunningham's documents last Wednesday morning, and right now, he wanted to look some more.

"Priceless paintings turn up in attics. Why not a diplomatic solution to the Middle East?"

"No argument here," Tony replied. "Let's wade through the files. If we find the answer, the world owes us a big favor."

"Not so fast," Tom cautioned. "They're Katherine's papers."

The doctor moved a step back toward the office door. "I'll let you in on a hot scoop. My sources think the wife of King George and General Cunningham were tight."

Tom stood up. The doctor was anxious to go up to Katherine's office and pore over the general's papers. He'd go along, fake disinterest, but watch his every move.

"Tell me, doc… Are you after kiss and tell?"

"Isn't everyone?" Tony asked, grinning wryly. "You must be a little curious too."

"Let's just leave it that I don't want to perpetuate an ugly rumor." Tom forced a smile. "I'll make a fresh pitcher, then we can go up and see if Katherine's grandfather was really a Casanova."

"Sounds good to me, old man. Sounds good to me."

Admiral Eric Weiss looked up when his secretary came in, flushed and breathless.

"You okay, Cissy?"

"Our fax machine just went down," she replied, gasping. "When a top secret message came into the director's office, they said pick it up ASAP."

Eric's boss was on the same floor, but a long way away on the far side of CIA Headquarters.

"Never hurts to stay in shape," he said. "Next time I go jogging, tag along."

Cissy, a workout freak, handed him the top secret communiqué, then left.

Eric ripped open the envelop and read James Fitzgerald's reply:

The subject has cancelled his cleaning help for the Christmas weekend. I can assist you on Monday morning. Advise. J.F., Director of the FBI.

Dr. R. Anthony Gaylani followed Tom into the kitchen. Once the mob attorney had made a pitcher of Bloody Marys, they walked toward the garage, stopping halfway down the hallway opposite the laundry room.

The elevator to Kitty's office opened into a dormered space built above the back side of the four-car garage. The large room had a feminine touch, and by the looks of the furniture, had also served as a place for Tom's wife to sew and do projects.

Tony moved toward a wooden crate with documents strewn about the base. He turned, eying Tom, trying to discern any kind of reaction. Tony felt relief when the mob attorney bypassed the papers and set the pitcher of Bloody Marys on a table.

Tony took a sip of his drink, then watched Tom grab a magazine and sit down. At that moment, Tony really gave thanks. Maybe this time he'd be able to thumb through General Alan Cunningham's memoirs without someone looking over his shoulder.

"You'd rather lounge than do research?" he asked, still trying to spot a telltale sign or some disharmony to contradict Tom's apparent disinterest.

"Reading old diaries seems like a snooze," Kempner replied, "but if you find anything worth talking about, let me know."

Tony went back to work, but after a minute of rummaging, the doctor began to worry. Why wasn't Tom paying closer attention? It seemed unlikely, but was it possible the mob attorney didn't know he'd stopped over on the morning General Cunningham's documents were delivered?

His wife, Joanna, knew. But she had no reason to tell Tom. For obvious reasons, he'd never broached the subject. That left his victim, Kitty Kempner.

Of course, Tony remembered every detail of the confrontational meeting with Tom's wife. On the morning before he'd choked her to death, Tony had also pilfered a memorandum. At first he'd thought he'd gotten away with it. But a few seconds after he shoved the memo in his sport coat, Kitty made up an excuse about having to get her nails done. Then she'd thrown him out.

Tony eyed Tom Kempner. The mob attorney appeared to be

engrossed, but why had he picked that magazine? Tom was into clothes and had an up-to-date wardrobe, but *In Style* covered ladies' fashions, not men's.

Tony did an instant reevaluation. Maybe Kitty hadn't complained about his aggressive behavior last Wednesday morning. Maybe Tom really was checking skirt lengths and had no intention of sorting through General Cunningham's papers. But so what? Tony still needed to lure the mob attorney away. As he scanned the diaries and documents, Tony realized the general's notations were more pointed than he'd recalled. While he'd taken the only memo he'd found that incriminated him, Tony had seen Kitty stick some papers into a manila folder. Until he could account for them, he'd be very cautious.

"Just remembered something," Tony said, walking toward the elevator. "Got an errand to run."

"You just started," Tom replied, glancing up from the *In Style* magazine. "Don't tell me the general's memoirs aren't racy enough?"

"Nothing like that. I need to pick up an item at Ace Hardware."

"Ace Hardware?" Tom questioned. "When did you become Mr. Fix-it?"

"Never had a choice in the matter," the doctor answered. "I can't be certain, but it looks like the cleaning help is drinking some of my wine."

"So you're going to lock it up?" Tom asked, smirking.

"Joanna thinks they do a great job. Since I can't fire them, the next best alternative is to padlock the temptation."

Tony pushed the call button for the elevator.

"Why not come along? You might learn something."

Tony didn't want Tom Kempner to see his purchase, but it was the lesser of two evils. Right now, his neighbor seemed uninterested, but he couldn't risk leaving him alone in the midst of General Cunningham's wartime memos. What if he got nosy?

* * *

Patricia Shaver didn't waste any time picking up the Frisbees in her driveway. She'd seen the concerned look on Ellen's face. It spoke volumes.

Once inside her house, Pat walked to the L-shaped counter that separated the cooking area from the rest of her country kitchen. While she dumped her parka on a chair near the maple table, Ellen hit the brew button on the coffee maker, then handed her a note-sized envelope.

"Read this."

Pat sat on a barstool and studied Mrs. Kempner's handwritten letter.

Wednesday afternoon
Ellie,

Grandfather's memos just arrived. Only had a chance to dig into a few, but what I've read really scares me.

Not trying to be an alarmist, but in one document, Grandfather said Rashid Ali el-Gaylani was a troublemaker who wanted to overthrow the pro-British government. He also said that R.A. Gaylani had big plans for his son.

Maybe I shouldn't point the finger at my neighbor, but I checked the dates on Grandfather's memos and they match up. A boy born before World War II would be about Tony Gaylani's age today.

I put some of Grandfather's memos into my horse purse for safekeeping. Maybe I'm nuts, but given the name correlation and Tony's behavior…

Next time we go riding, you can read them and decide for yourself.

Kitty

Pat finished the letter and looked up. Yesterday, after glancing at Mrs. Kempner's funeral service program, she'd had suspicions. Now she knew she'd been right. But rather than act like a reporter electrified over the fact that she'd discovered a diamond of a story, she decided to suppress her emotions until she could judge Ellen's true feelings.

For openers, Pat knew Ellen was concerned. She had proven that by showing her Mrs. Kempner's letter. But Ellen also had to be conflicted. Her friend hadn't mentioned their conversation after the funeral—especially the part where she'd outlined biographical data about Middle East personalities, including Rashid Ali el-Gaylani and his wife and young son. Ellen hadn't said anything because she realized that Kitty might have been the victim of foul play, but at present, wasn't ready to admit to it.

"Quite a note," Pat said, holding her voice neutral. "What's your take, Ellie?"

"Before I comment, I'd like you to read it again."

During a second run-through, Pat's gooseflesh welted up. She was as confident as ever that her theory was correct, and she was ready to pull out all the stops to see if Katherine Kempner's death could be tied in with General Cunningham's memos and the couple living next door. But again, Pat hesitated. Asking measured questions was the best way to bring Ellen onboard.

"I need some info," Pat said, glancing up. "Was the envelope sealed?"

Ellen nodded. "Isn't that the way the post office delivers them?"

"Yeah, but…" Pat bit her lip. "Forget I said anything."

The envelope was postmarked Thursday PM. The note itself had been written in ink, signed by Katherine Kempner, and dated *Wednesday afternoon*. Presumably the deceased had penned the text just hours before her death, then left it in the box for the postman to pick up when his route brought him back the following day.

But that scenario troubled her. Marooning the letter overnight might have made sense if it had been filled with inconsequential news. Under the circumstances, it seemed like an odd way to communicate an urgent message. Why write? If Katherine wanted to share her concerns with Ellen, why not pick up the phone?

"One thing bothers me," Pat said. "Why didn't Mrs. Kempner just—"

She didn't finish her question, remembering that on the fatal afternoon and evening, Ellen's husband was away on business and she and Ellen were Christmas shopping in the city. The Eichlers' answering machine was out of order, so if Katherine Kempner had felt danger, she had few choices but to entrust her message to the postal service.

But even that didn't make much sense. The envelope was postmarked Thursday. If she knew the carrier had already come by, why not jump in the car and mail it in town? Or better still, drive over and put it in Ellen's mailbox?

"Another small detail… In Mrs. Kempner's note—"

"Call her Kitty," Ellen said, using a raised hand to interrupt. "Had you ever met her, you would have been friends."

"Fair enough." Pat went on, "Kitty's note makes a strange reference. What's a horse purse?"

"One of our…" Ellen tensed. "It used to be one of our private jokes. We gave our equestrian equipment a feminine twist. Ergo, the saddlebags became horse purses."

Pat considered the inferences as her friend got two coffee mugs from a cabinet near the sink.

"Clever," Pat said. "Calling her saddlebags a horse purse was a good way to pinpoint the location of hidden documents."

Ellen's eyes widened. "Kitty used the word 'safekeeping.' You really think she meant to be devious?"

"From her note, it's obvious she was upset. Using language known only to you implies a strong desire to disguise the hiding place. I'm guessing Kitty saw danger and thought she needed to act."

Ellen filled one mug, then another, the rich aroma permeating the kitchen.

"Not exactly an urgent SOS. The thing arrived three days after she died. If the documents were so important, why didn't she go to the police or send the general's papers directly to the station house?"

"Don't know," Pat said, standing up and sipping her coffee. "The answer may be in the horse purse. We need to take a look ASAP."

"Tommy Kempner's a friend. Sneaking over would be an invasion of his privacy."

"I agree, but who said anything about sneaking?"

"How else will we get into his stable?"

"Does he ride?" Pat asked.

Ellen shook her head.

"Does he keep any of his personal stuff in there?"

Her friend shook her head again.

"So what's the problem?" Pat asked, putting her mug on the counter. "By my reckoning, we'll just be walking into Kitty's barn to retrieve a few papers out of Kitty's horse purse."

"Why not go to the authorities?" Ellen suggested. "We could tell the police about her note and ask them to gather up the documents."

"Get real. Your friend, Kitty, hid some papers in her saddlebags. She didn't sign an affidavit, and there's no hint she thought her life was threatened. The note just fingers Dr. Gaylani as a guy who seemed too interested."

"Are we reading the same note?" Ellen asked. "I think Kitty was more than concerned."

"Even if you're right, why stir up a hornet's nest? Let's find out why she took such careful measures. After that, if the material points toward some criminal activity…"

"Criminal activity," Ellen snapped. "One second you tell me not to sweat the small stuff, and the next you have me tracking down… My God. I can't even imagine what's running through your mind."

"Then don't try, and while you're at it, stop jumping to conclusions."

Pat checked her winter coat to be sure her fur-lined gloves were in the pocket. Several things had made her suspect something was amiss. Aside from the apprehension expressed in Katherine Kempner's note, there was the condition of the envelope, the woman's mysterious death, and three names—Katherine Balfour Cunningham Kempner and her neighbors, R. Anthony and Joanna Myerson Gaylani. Each had a last or maiden name that, when taken together, spelled out the ingredients for a Jewish-Arab conflict.

"One other small thing," Pat said, zipping up her parka. "In her note, Kitty intimated that you'd both read her grandfather's documents the next time you went riding."

"That sentence bothered me too," Ellen replied. "It makes no sense."

"Why not?" Pat asked.

"We rode Wednesday morning before you and I went downtown. We planned to do it again the next day. Kitty even suggested I leave everything at her place."

"Your stuff is still in Kitty's tack room?"

Ellen nodded.

"Does that include your horse?"

"He's in the stable too."

Pat was more convinced than ever that Katherine Kempner had safeguarded some of her grandfather's memos out of fear. Why else would she write a letter that couldn't have been delivered before she planned to see Ellen again? Kitty might have said she wasn't finger pointing, but her letter was proof that she wanted to be sure someone would look into Dr. R.A. Gaylani's background.

"Ellie, don't fight me on this. Since your horse is in Kitty's stable, we have a legitimate excuse to nose around."

Ellen buttoned her sheepskin, then pulled a knitted ski cap down over her ears. "Maybe so, but dropping in uninvited leaves me cold."

"Didn't he just take home one of your puppies?"

"Yep. Now he has two female dogs—the pup and an older stray Lab he just took in."

Pat whistled, a loud piercing sound that got Snowshoe and Shoe-Too's attention.

"I rest my case. Can you think of a better time to get his Labs acquainted with mine?"

CHAPTER TWELVE

Joanna Gaylani was in her Mercedes, her hands squeezing the steering wheel. She'd watched Ellen Eichler open her mail and speed away. Since then, she'd been on the move too, but instead of driving directly home, she'd opted for a circuitous route over snow-covered side roads.

Still some distance away, she gazed through the windshield and pushed back her blonde hair. Right now her mind was focused on images and memories—a dirt floor house in Palestine, her life in America as a Jewish orphan, the photo of her parents hidden in her jewelry box—all remembrances that could summon either happiness or violent hatred.

She came to another intersection. After looking both ways, she drove on, telling herself she'd made the right choice. She knew the letter she'd intercepted and rerouted to Ellen Eichler would start a chain reaction and have grave consequences for Tony. But why should she care? Joanna of all people knew her husband was a killer. Why carry a torch?

She braked her Mercedes, stopping behind the four-way stop sign. Kitty's murder had torn at her, but she'd kept her composure as was required. Like her husband, she too could plan a strategy with deadly precision, then put it into operation in a cold and professional way. Maybe she had deep feelings for Tony Gaylani, but they had to be suppressed. She had dedicated her life to nobler objectives.

Joanna—lovely, educated—sat comfortably in her car. As she

went over her own plans, she increased her speed and kept her eyes on the road. Ever since her marriage to Tony, she'd led two lives: In her public persona, as the wife of a successful orthopedic surgeon, she shopped at the right stores, had lunch at the right restaurants, and volunteered for the right charities. In her clandestine life as a political activist... Well, that facet of her existence was a well-kept secret.

Joanna was a senior officer in an organization called All Alone— a Zionist splinter group committed to keeping Israel strong and non-aligned with its Arab neighbors. All Alone believed that peace in the Middle East was possible, but only when Jews and Arabs recognized that their religious and cultural differences made living with open borders an impossibility.

The leader of All Alone was a man of vision. Lawrence Magel —her uncle and the man who had brought her to America after her parents died—preached non-violence, often closing his speeches with the phrase *oil and water don't mix*. That metaphor described his political ideology. He was an isolationist and thought good fences made for good neighbors.

All Alone had a budget of fifty million dollars—contributions collected annually from rich Jews worldwide. The organization had two offices and a hundred members, split evenly between New York and Chicago. The leader had purposely kept their numbers low. He'd also given their group an unusual name to underscore one theme: A small country like Israel survived in an arena dominated by super-powers when it adopted a foreign policy based on isolationism.

In a recent pep talk to the membership in Chicago, Lawrence Magel had summarized his philosophy:

"Global politics breeds strange alliances. Nations like the United States alter their domestic and world priorities after every presidential election. The rich and powerful have the muscle to send mixed messages and still impose their will. Countries with less economic and military might aren't so lucky. They protect themselves from their natural enemies and also look out for enemies that appear friendly. Take World War II, for example. Eight million Jews died while the leadership in Washington, London, and the Vatican turned a deaf ear."

Joanna swung onto Spring Creek Road, her blue eyes hardening at the thought of the Holocaust. Lawrence Magel had taught her well. Over the years, she'd learned that second-tier nations gained strength through self-sufficiency. They needed to fend for themselves.

The leader also knew that Israel's chance for survival was further complicated by politics. The Middle East oil producers had influence. Many in the Arab world wanted to finish the job Hitler had begun. To combat fanaticism, Israel had to manage its financial affairs and its image too.

On the money front, Israel needed to raise enough cash to field a strong standing army. Of course, defending its borders was only one of its military's missions. Along with local law enforcement and the Mossad (Israeli Secret Police), the army had to quell insurgents and insure homeland security. The Israeli government also had to fund research projects. Israel had nuclear weapons, but to deter belligerent neighbors, the government had to continually upgrade its delivery systems.

Polishing Israel's image was trickier. As Larry Magel often commented, "The court of world public opinion favors the underdog, unless they're Jews."

When Palestinian terrorists killed and raped Israeli women and children, the press printed the story on page three. But when the State of Israel struck back, newspapers from every corner of the Earth rose up in protest.

Joanna held onto the steering wheel with one hand and adjusted the thermostat with the other. As warmer air blew through the vents, she recalled how Republicans complained about the liberal press. Little did they know. The American media wasn't liberal, it was soft. TV anchormen and print journalists didn't understand the realities of existing in a hostile environment. They worried about human rights. They abhorred torture and profiling. But aggressive interrogation techniques and wiretaps were the keys to keeping tabs on a hidden enemy.

That belief, coupled with a desire to prove her mettle, had spurred Joanna to join a second Zionist organization. All Alone sought political solutions. The Ruling Council was action oriented. No matter the cost or method, its members were dedicated to preserving Israel's strength by plotting to expose Middle East Arab dictators for what they were—bigots interested in exterminating Jews.

The name "Ruling Council" was a misnomer. They didn't rule over anyone, and they were hardly a council. The group was a secret terrorist cell consisting of just three people—the leader of All Alone, the leader's son, and Joanna. Of the three, only the leader, Lawrence Magel, had a vote. But while he dictated policy and set the agenda, they were all committed to their single goal. Each would make the ultimate sacrifice to show the world that peace talks between Israel and its Arab neighbors were a sham—a fool's folly where liberal Jews who had no stomach for the truth pretended that moderate Muslims would eventually sway their governments so people of goodwill could live in harmony.

The leader had created All Alone and the Ruling Council to insure that atrocities committed against Jews were heard around the globe. While the two associations seemed at odds, both groups worked together, the nonviolent one wrapped around the other to protect it from detection.

All Alone's credo—good fences make good neighbors—was not the mainstream view, but the organization was small, preached non-violence, and rarely published a position paper. As a result, pundits in the West and Middle East considered them weak and ineffectual. That invisibility allowed All Alone to operate in the open and solicit funds from rich Jews.

The Ruling Council conducted business in the shadows. Only the three overlapping members even knew it existed. As a stealth operation, the Ruling Council siphoned off money raised by All Alone to finance worldwide events that kept tension high between Israel and its Arab neighbors.

In the past, the leader's son had carried out all their terrorist missions. Using the alias Charles Sweet, the crack marksman and demolitions expert had assassinated several low-level Arab leaders and also bombed many out-of-the-way mosques. While Chuck Sweet's deeds hadn't attracted a world audience, they had gotten wide local coverage and had served as a training ground as well.

In recent years the Ruling Council's ambitions had become more daring and their planning more sophisticated. The upcoming big event was a case in point.

Step one in their plan had come to life more than a decade and a half ago, a time shortly after Joanna had married Dr. Tony Gaylani and moved to Barrington. With the approval of the leader, Joanna had pretended to renounce her allegiance to All Alone. To highlight her change of heart, she'd joined the United Jewish Congress, a multi-thousand-member international society comprised of business executives, political leaders, and philanthropic Jews. The UJC was known for moderation, favoring open borders and the elimination of Israeli settlements in the West Bank and Gaza.

Step two of their plan had begun after Joanna established herself as a hard-working member of the UJC. Since joining, she'd served on many committees, using her charm and organization skills to rise through the ranks. Her tireless effort finally paid off. In the summer of 1999, she was elected to the UJC Board of Directors.

The aftermath of that election had been pivotal: As an acknowledgement of her long service and the superb job she'd done in coordinating the millennium convention in Jerusalem, Joanna had gotten the United Jewish Congress to name Chicago as the site of this year's conclave.

Having the upcoming convention in their back yard allowed the Ruling Council to refine their plans. With the location and date for their big event no longer in doubt, the other two members became proactive.

Late in the summer, several years ago, the leader's son—a.k.a. Chuck Sweet—had shut down his overseas terrorist operation and covertly entered the US. Lawrence Magel had also taken a more hands-on role in the big event. While he'd maintained his public persona as head man of All Alone, in private he'd advised Joanna so her star would keep rising in the UJC.

As he'd said to her just the other day, "I'll be a happy man if the world wakes up and allows Israel to reach its true destiny. But jealously and hatred are powerful forces. We're a strong, independent nuclear power, but we'll keep the Ruling Council operational until we can test and stockpile atomic weapons to suit our needs."

Joanna turned off Spring Creek and onto Oak Knoll Road. She drove a quarter mile, made another turn, and saw her colonial mansion.

As she hit the opener and watched the garage door retract, Joanna reflected on how far she'd come: Once a naïve teenager who'd cherished her Judaism, her family, and their simple life in Palestine; now a woman of prominence who would do anything and sacrifice everything to get her revenge for the atrocities she'd witnessed when Arab soldiers had entered her family's dirt-floored home many years ago.

Her face muscles taut, she pulled into the garage, noting that Tony's Mercedes SUV was gone. She suspected he was at Tom Kempner's house, but couldn't see over the plowed snow mounds that lined her driveway.

Joanna unfastened her seatbelt but didn't open the door. Instead, she stared through the windshield and recalled the extraordinary measures Lawrence Magel had taken to maintain the anonymity of the Ruling Council.

From its inception, the Ruling Council had relied on All Alone for field intelligence. Since any group with a political agenda had to protect itself against infiltrators, the leader had hired and trained a cadre of specialists who could spot people with phony aliases or forged identification. His moles either held sensitive positions or knew how to bribe the people who did. Of course, he never told anyone that the majority of the intelligence gathering was being done for the Ruling Council.

Joanna closed her eyes, remembering the first Ruling Council meeting almost twenty years ago. The leader had initiated the conference call from Chicago. She was patched in from her apartment in New York, and Lawrence Magel's son had dialed in from somewhere in the Middle East.

During that get-together, the leader had discussed world events in general and Dr. R. Anthony Gaylani in particular. The doctor, son of Rashid Ali el-Gaylani, had come on All Alone's radar screen following his marriage to Barbara Stein, one of their New York City members.

The elopement had caught All Alone by surprise and forced the intelligence branch of their organization to hurriedly piece together a detailed dossier. While Dr. Gaylani's ancestry raised a red flag, each time All Alone did further background checks, nothing ever surfaced. After many months had gone by, most thought Dr. Tony Gaylani was just a gifted surgeon who'd found his Iraqi heritage professionally detrimental and socially embarrassing.

Joanna leaned back against the headrest. While suspicion within All Alone had died down, it never disappeared. In the end, the cynics were vindicated when Tony's first wife died a little over a year after they'd married.

Barbara Stein Gaylani's sudden demise had been billed as a medical mystery, but the day after Tony bribed a mortician and had his spouse's body cremated, the Ruling Council met. Naturally, the leader had alerted All Alone of his concerns, but suggested they take no specific action. In the Ruling Council meeting (a conference call between Magel, Chuck Sweet, and Joanna), Uncle Larry had taken a different position. He had ordered Joanna to penetrate the Iraqi doctor's cover by any means possible.

Joanna remembered being nervous when she'd stopped by Tony's Manhattan co-op and introduced herself as one of Barbara's friends. After extending condolences, she invited him out for a cup of coffee. The rest was history. While he hardly seemed like a candidate to marry another Jewess, within weeks they'd become an item, and within months they were engaged. Shortly thereafter, when Tony accepted a position at a hospital near Barrington, Illinois, they'd exchanged marriage vows and moved to the Midwest.

Joanna squirmed in the car seat. The leader's plan had worked, but there'd been a catch. She'd agreed to the courtship, but nothing in his scheme had called for her to fall in love. Still, it had happened. From the moment she'd laid eyes on him, from their very first kiss, she'd known Tony Gaylani was the one for her. No matter how often she reminded herself that it was crazy, she couldn't change her feelings. Of course she told no one and continued to follow the leader's directives. He and his son, Chuck Sweet, would have gone ballistic had they known that she had let down her guard and believed in something other than the cause.

Joanna leaned forward and rested her head on the steering wheel. At first, Tony's behavior had been tender and passionate. Then he'd shown his true colors. In the late eighties, a year or so after their marriage and within months of moving into their house next to the Kempners, the bastard had made contact with an Arab operative.

She'd never realized her husband had reentered the world of espionage. But from day one, the leader, Lawrence Magel, had told the intelligence arm of All Alone to keep up the surveillance and watch Tony Gaylani's every move.

Joanna yanked the keys from the ignition and stuffed them into the pocket of her mink. The photographs of Tony passing papers to the other spy had ravaged her. To make matters worse, the leader had insisted she not let on. Uncle Larry thought the relationship might prove valuable. He'd even told her to keep up pretenses and playact the role of a loyal and doting wife.

It sickened her to perform for the enemy, but for years, she'd found imaginative ways to be an exuberant sexual partner. Each time Tony had taken her, she'd envisioned him as a hopelessly-in-love suitor, not a spy in the shadows. During bouts of foreplay, her mind projected pictures of a man plotting to seduce her. But make no mistake. She'd remained emotionally detached. Even when she'd moaned with pleasure as their sweaty bodies reached climax, she'd never allowed her broken heart a moment to cry.

Joanna and the leader had thought Tony's original rendezvous with another Iraqi operative would be the first of many. But it wasn't. To the best of their knowledge, the doctor had never again talked to, met with, sat beside, or looked at another foreign diplomat, politician, or spy.

As the years wore on, senior officials of All Alone began to waver. One after another they changed their minds and concluded that R. Anthony Gaylani's lone contact had been made for the sole purpose of resigning. They suggested that he really was a considerate husband and hard-working doctor. Lawrence Magel hadn't disputed their arguments. But for reasons only he, Chuck Sweet, and Joanna knew, Uncle Larry had also insisted that the intelligence arm of All Alone not relax their vigil.

That had been especially true during the most recent period. The invasion of Iraq had brought down Saddam Hussein and his regime, but the deposed despot's spy network had gone underground and continued to operate. She, Chuck Sweet, and Uncle Larry (the membership of the Ruling Council) weren't sure of Tony Gaylani's status as an Iraqi spy, but in order to pull off the big event and make the world aware of their Jewish struggle—and in order to prevent any breach in security—they'd quadrupled their efforts to make sure the doctor didn't upset their plans.

In that regard, Tony's interest in General Alan Cunningham's papers had raised the leader's eyebrows. Joanna had informed the two other Ruling Council members that both she and Tony knew Kitty Kempner had petitioned the British government for release of her grandfather's memoirs. Their next-door neighbor had told them quite offhandedly one night over cocktails. But during the ensuing days, when Tony pressed Kitty for the delivery date, a new red flag had been raised.

Joanna took two short breaths, recalling how last Wednesday morning had proven that point. Tony had told her he'd planned to use his day off to catch up on his reading. As he sat in the alcove of their second-story master suite, she noted that his rocker had been moved to capture vistas of the Kempners' property. Acting like a considerate wife, she'd brought up freshly-brewed coffee and asked if she could join him.

Tony's answer had been curt: "I can't have any distractions. This literature is too technical."

Rather than argue the point, she smiled and left. To be sure, she'd put her husband at ease, but her suspicions had never been higher.

She and Tony had dined with the Kempners the previous night. During a pointed conversation, Kitty had said her grandfather's papers were coming the following morning.

From Ruling Council meetings, Joanna knew Kitty's grandfather—General Alan Cunningham—was stationed in the Middle East at the time Tony's father was causing trouble in Iraq. When Joanna coupled the delivery date of the general's papers with Tony's incessant interest in Alan Cunningham's military service, she concluded the obvious: Tony worried that his true identity would be exposed after Kitty read her grandfather's memoirs.

To keep tabs on her husband, Joanna had dragged a chair from the breakfast nook table to the counter next to the twin kitchen sinks. Holding a wad of paper towels in one hand and a spray bottle of Windex in the other, she'd stepped from the seat of the chair to the granite counter.

When she stood on the floor and looked out, the snow mounds alongside the Kempners' driveway and turnaround blocked her view. But when she stood on the counter, the sightlines opened up.

At first, nothing happened. But a few minutes later, her skepticism was rewarded. After seeing a UPS truck pull into Kitty's driveway, Joanna watched the deliveryman struggle with a cumbersome wooden crate.

She'd reacted the moment she heard Tony bounding down the main staircase. By the time he'd come in and told her he had an appointment, she'd jumped to the floor and was leaning over the granite counter, wiping Windex off the lower portion of the sink window.

Joanna pulled off her driving gloves and smiled. Last Wednesday, after Tony left, she'd again stood on the counter and watched him park in the Kempners' turnaround. Two hours later, she'd heard a door slam. By then she was back upstairs, sitting in the bedroom reading alcove.

Since she only wanted to keep track of him, not gauge his mood, Joanna hadn't gone downstairs. If he stayed inside, she'd listen to his movements. If Tony ventured back next door, she'd observe him from his rocker.

Initially, her surveillance had only targeted her husband. Then a new development caught her eye. She might have let it pass had Kitty been dressed for the bitter cold. But when Joanna saw her friend run to the stable with a folder in her hand—when Kitty scampered through the snow protected by only a turtleneck, jeans, and a pair of loafers—Joanna had jumped to her feet.

She had no idea why Kitty wanted to brave the elements to drop off a folder of papers. But one thing was certain. It hadn't taken much time. Less than a minute after Kitty had gone into the stable, she'd left through the tack room door.

Joanna had continued to watch, expecting Kitty to go back inside her house. But that hadn't happened either. Instead, her friend had pulled an envelope from her pants pocket, then run down the driveway toward her mailbox.

In spite of the dangers, Joanna had let her inquisitiveness overrule her orders. She hurried downstairs and checked the den. To an indifferent shrug, she'd told Tony that she had to leave for an appointment at the beauty salon.

Her alibi in place, she'd cruised down her driveway, looking for signs of Kitty. Seeing none and presuming her neighbor had run back home, Joanna turned onto Oak Knoll Road. With no one around, she lowered her car window, pulled open the snap cover on the Kempners' mailbox, and grabbed an envelope addressed to Ellen Eichler.

Joanna remembered wondering what had motivated her friend to put her thoughts down on paper. Why hadn't Kitty hit the speed dialer? What had she written that couldn't be said in a phone call?

Joanna had driven away, fully aware of her other problem. If she ripped the letter open, it couldn't be resent. To get at the text undetected, she needed to be alone next to a steaming kettle.

She made a short side trip to one of her favorite boutiques to set up her excuse. Twenty minutes later, she pulled into the garage. As luck would have it, Tony was getting ready to leave. For a second he looked puzzled, but when she said the hairdresser had goofed on the dates, he launched into an explanation of his own planned activity.

While she'd been away, Tony had apparently reached Tom Kempner and discovered the mob attorney had once again found a legal loophole to beat the system. She knew Tony deplored judicial maneuvering. But in this instance he didn't put down their neighbor's victory. Fact was, Tony had wrangled an invitation for them to drink to it.

His departure to the liquor store to pick up a couple of special bottles of wine had given her a window of opportunity, But as he left, she'd wondered if the cocktail hour celebration might have been a smoke screen for a hidden agenda her husband had in mind.

Joanna banged the steering wheel with an open hand as her recollection nagged at her. Last Wednesday, she'd rushed into the kitchen, filled a kettle, and sat it on the gas burner. Once the water boiled and the steam loosened the bond, she pulled out the letter and began devouring Kitty's words.

The scripted message had churned her stomach. But it excited her too. She would put the letter back in the envelope and reseal it with Elmer's glue, but instead of going to the post office to resend it, she'd call Uncle Larry. She had formulated a new strategy and needed permission to implement it.

At the time, Joanna hadn't been sure her husband would target Kitty Kempner. When it had happened several hours later, she felt conflicted. Losing her close friend hurt, but the loss was tempered by a tactical advantage. The leader of the Ruling Council was always anxious to capitalize on Arab mistakes. Kitty's murder was a tragedy, but it had given their group a valuable option.

The big event was in the final planning stage. Every detail had been double checked, but neither she, the leader, nor the leader's son had been happy with the choice of a scapegoat. To create genuine outrage, a Jewish catastrophe had to be blamed on a specific person, not an unnamed Arab terrorist group.

Joanna knew the public would get worked up into a frenzy if the right villain was exposed. Her husband was a conniving doctor— a man who masqueraded as an American Catholic of Italian descent. Wouldn't he be a good candidate? Wouldn't the world be willing to hate an Iraqi spy who slaughtered innocent Jews? She thought so, and best of all, intercepting Kitty's letter had allowed her to incriminate Tony Gaylani.

Joanna felt chilled as she walked from the heated garage into her house. Uncle Larry and Chuck Sweet had been shocked when Tony murdered Kitty Kempner. Joanna hadn't been surprised by her husband's audacity. But she had been amazed by her sudden change in attitude. Kitty's death had triggered a craving for revenge. All at once, she was a hardened terrorist, stalking an enemy.

Last Wednesday, Joanna had had no idea how specific General Alan Cunningham's memoirs would be. Of course, she knew Kitty's grandfather and Tony's father were bitter enemies, and that Tony Gaylani was a vicious man who would protect his identity at all costs. But most of all, she knew her husband's history. His first wife, Barbara Stein, had died under equally suspicious circumstances.

While no one could accuse her of being an accessory to murder, Joanna had left her near-lifelong friend in harm's way. But what else could she do? With the Ruling Council in the final days of their countdown, she wanted to make sure nothing went wrong.

Joanna walked inside and tossed her mink coat on a kitchen counter. Ill at ease, she reached into her purse and pulled out a secure cellular phone. She needed to make a call to the leader.

Uncle Larry knew she'd redelivered Kitty's letter. He was a stickler for details and would expect a full briefing on Ellen Eichler's reaction.

Tom Kempner was in a quandary. Dr. Tony Gaylani had insisted on running an errand, but now, as they were driving back from Ace Hardware, Tom couldn't figure out why the doctor had been in such a hurry.

For openers, Tom doubted whether Tony's wine cellar had been raided, but even if some of his grape had disappeared, why make a special trip to buy a padlock? It was Christmas Eve. The cleaning help wouldn't be back for at least a couple of days.

The doctor slowed down, then parked his Mercedes SUV in the turnaround in front of the heated walkway.

Tom got out and started running. "Hurry up, doc, and don't leave my front door open."

As he waited in the kitchen for Tony to appear, Tom wondered about something else. The doctor had known exactly what he wanted, but after they got to Ace Hardware, Tony had made the padlock purchase in slow motion. Never had he seen one guy ask so many questions about a combination lock.

And there was more. Once Tony had expressed his brand preference and purchased a Master lock, the real Q & A had gotten underway. For the next twenty minutes, the doc asked the hardware store attendant to show him how to install the hinge and staple mounts. God Almighty, you'd have thought the SOB planned to padlock Fort Knox.

Tony strolled in, rubbing the palms of his hands. "It's cold out there. Guess we should have worn our parkas."

"Instead of stating the obvious, listen to my solution. How 'bout another Bloody Mary?"

"Some people sip hot toddies to get warm," Tony said, folding his arms across his chest. "You're the first to suggest an ice-cold drink."

"Hey, doc, it's a dual-purposed remedy. Installing padlocks is tough enough. You don't want to be all thumbs."

Tom decided to conduct a test. First he added ice and a little vodka to the Bloody Marys they'd left on the counter. Then he handed one to Tony.

"Here, old buddy, once you suck this down, you'll forget about wine pilferage."

"Thank you. Your concern is...?" Tony stared. "Now where the hell are you going?"

"Back upstairs. Don't you want to check out General Cunningham's love letters?"

"Actually, I'd rather relax by the fire."

"It's a free country," Tom said, "do whatever you want."

He turned and began walking toward the elevator. Above all else, he needed to gauge Tony's reaction. If the doctor followed him to Katherine's office, it might be significant. Since the Ace trip, Tony had been stalling. Alan Cunningham's papers wouldn't be relevant in a capital case against Tony Gaylani, but a charge of first-degree murder wasn't the only thing on the doctor's mind. Spies from Saddam's old regime wouldn't want to be extradited back to Iraq.

Tom pushed the up button, and like a shadow, Tony appeared at his side.

"Guess I'll tag along," the doctor said. "There's a pitcher of Bloody Marys up there. That's too much for one man to drink."

Joanna Gaylani stood in her kitchen with the secure cellular phone in hand. The call to Lawrence Magel had gone well. Uncle Larry had listened to her update without comment, then issued his one harangue and hung up. But his parting reminder to keep close tabs on Tony had her worried. His SUV wasn't there when she'd pulled into the garage.

She put the secure cell phone in her pocket. Joanna assumed

her husband had gone next door, but to be sure, she ran upstairs, stepping into the bedroom alcove just as Tony's Mercedes SUV stopped in the turnaround. She was relieved to locate him, but only until the men scampered inside without winter coats. That sight brought back a vision of events after Kitty Kempner had run to her mailbox.

Joanna slumped into Tony's rocker. Last Wednesday, after she'd reglued Kitty's unpostmarked letter and shoved it into her purse, Joanna knew there was no time to dally. Tony had been out running errands, but for how long? And there was the matter of the folder Kitty had left in the stable. The note addressed to Ellen Eichler had pinpointed the location of that folder. A broad-daylight invasion of the stable would be risky, but given what was at stake, it was a risk worth taking.

She'd bundled up in a heavy sheepskin coat, left via a side door, and trekked through the snow to the Kempners' stable. Her plan could have worked, but she'd run out of luck. Just as she neared the saddles, the tack room door had opened.

Joanna's face muscles tensed. How well she recalled telling Kitty that she'd been sewing all day and thought a riding break might give her weary eyes a rest. How well she recalled that Kitty had been too polite to say that her furry wide-toed boots were too big to fit in the stirrups. Talk about a defining moment. She'd looked into the eyes of her friend and made a decision. Not Katherine, not anything took precedence over safeguarding their plan to bomb the Jewish convention.

Joanna stood up and stared at the Kempners' turnaround. Tony's SUV brought back another memory. The morning after her friend had been murdered, Joanna had initiated a plan to place evidence in the hands of those who would unmask Tony's true identity. Step one had begun the moment her husband and Tom Kempner went to pick out a casket. Left alone, she'd slipped into the stable and read the papers in Kitty's horse purse.

Particularly damning were translated memos signed by Tony's

father, Rashid Ali el-Gaylani. The documents, as well as cover letters written by General Cunningham, had told a story of el-Gaylani's pre-World War II attempts to bring down the pro-British Iraqi government. The papers also made mention of a preexisting plan for Rashid's son (Tony) in case the Arab's revolution failed. As evidentiary material, the sixty-plus-year-old allegations proved nothing. But who gave a damn? She hadn't been looking to set her spouse up for murder. She needed a scapegoat, and in that regard, it was obvious that Tony's mother hadn't brought him to American just to attend medical school. No indeed. Joanna didn't know what Tony had been groomed to do, but she was sure killing Kitty Kempner hadn't been part of the original plan. Her best friend had been murdered because General Allan Cunningham's diaries and papers compromised Tony Gaylani's identity.

Joanna stayed by the window and looked down at Kempners' house. Last Thursday, after shoving the general's documents back into the saddlebags, she'd understood why Tony had killed Kitty in such a brazen way. Once unmasked, he would have no place to run. The CIA would brand him as a spy, and the new Iraqi government would disown him.

She looked past their neighbors' house toward the barn on the far corner of the property. That building would play a pivotal part in the Ruling Council's big event, but like all plans—even those that are well thought out—there were rough spots.

Take their big event, for instance. When Tony had murdered Kitty, Joanna saw an opportunity to turn the doctor into a fall guy. But to insure that the Ruling Council had someone who would take the blame, Joanna had to drop Kitty's letter at the post office. Naturally, she worried about the incongruity, but if someone noticed the note had been written and dated in life, but postmarked and delivered after death, so be it. Keeping attention away from herself had meant steering others to Tony Gaylani's true identity and giving them the wherewithal to make it stick.

Joanna turned away from the window and walked into the master bathroom. As she began brushing her hair, she recalled the final part of her gambit. At Friday's funeral, she'd told Ellen Eichler to expect an invitation to a Sunday morning get-together. She apologized for the late notice, saying that the gathering involved the planning of a charitable event to honor their friend, Kitty. The mailed summons had been a ruse, but she'd needed an excuse to make sure Ellen would be at home when the postman came by the following day.

Joanna hoped Kitty's note would be a catalyst. If Ellen felt danger, she would be shaken enough to seek the counsel of Patricia Shaver. Like the rest of the nation, Joanna had read the story of the Gary Barbera affair and the role the determined reporter had played. If Miss Shaver demonstrated the same dogged persistence, Joanna knew her plan to trap Tony would be in capable hands.

She sat at her dressing table and put on fresh lipstick. So far, everything was in place. Minutes after Joanna had seen the Eichlers' mail delivered, Ellen had driven away. A quarter hour later, as Joanna cruised by a Honey Lake address, she'd positively identified the pickup parked in front of the reporter's cottage. By now, she presumed that Pat Shaver had scrutinized Kitty's SOS. If correct, Ms. Shaver would track down Dr. Tony Gaylani to the ends of the Earth.

Joanna walked out of the bathroom and headed for the stairs. Steps one, two, and three had been implemented. Step four was to retrieve her husband.

She drove to the Kempners'. Without knocking, Joanna pushed open the unlocked front door, then searched out Tony and Tom in Kitty's upstairs office.

She gazed at the half-empty pitcher.

"When did our neighborhood get a new cocktail lounge?"

"Hello, honey," Tony said, holding a diary. "Glad you found us. Just been glancing at the general's letters. They're fascinating."

"Hardly the time, is it? We're due at the Sextons' in less than two hours. Remember, dear, Christmas Eve is your holiday." She eyed the two men. "Tommy, I know Connie hopes you'll come too."

"I'll take a rain check," Tom said. "I'm exhausted and, frankly, it doesn't feel much like a holiday."

CHAPTER THIRTEEN

Patricia Shaver stared out the passenger-side window, hardly noticing the rolling snow-covered landscape. Neither she nor Ellen had said a word since they'd left her house and loaded her Labs, Snowshoe and Shoe-Too, into the rear cab seat of Ellen's pickup. The reason was obvious. They each had read Katherine Kempner's note, and they each had interpreted it differently.

Ellen found it difficult to admit that Kitty might have met with foul play. She also had a strong sense of loyalty to Tom Kempner. Those two factors taken together, Ellen was a reluctant participant in a scheme to extract General Alan Cunningham's papers from the Kempners' stable.

"Nice day, huh, Ellie?"

Her friend nodded. "For those who like sunsets and sub-zero wind chills."

Pat leaned back. Why force a conversation? They'd hammered out a strategy to make Ellen's entry into the stable look routine. When they arrived at the Kempners', she'd let the general's papers speak for themselves.

Her mood brightened when Ellen turned onto Spring Creek Road and they passed the sign for Hill 'N Dale Farm. The white planked fences reminded her of Honeymead when it too had been a horse farm of some renown. It also reminded her of how she and Ellen had met.

They had first gotten acquainted in the late sixties. Twice a month, Ellen made trips to stock the stable at Honeymead. Back then, Pat hadn't cared about the delivery of hay and oats. She was a few months shy of her fifth birthday and just wanted to play with Ellen Eichler's dog. She knew that Bash—a champion yellow Labrador retriever—would be standing outside the stables with a clipboard in his mouth. Like any kid about to go off to kindergarten, she had been more interested in signing Bash's receipt than having a conversation with Bash's owner.

"The snow on the pines is beautiful," Pat observed, breaking from her reverie. "Winter or summer, I never tire of a drive on country roads."

"Me either," Ellen fired back, "especially when I'm alone."

After getting the same message a second time, Pat chose to reminisce, remembering that her carefree days around the stable had been short-lived. While away at boarding school, she occasionally saw Ellen in the summer. In the aftermath of the Honeymead fire, their contact had ended altogether. But fate had set the stage for a reunion after all the years she'd avoided Barrington to become a full-time academic.

Her grandfather had hoped future generations would live at Honeymead and perpetuate his legacy. That hadn't happened. Well before the fire, her father—R. D. Shaver—attacked the heart of Bill Zwilling's monument to himself.

As her father's marriage unraveled, he had reduced the horse stock. For him, each auction had been a symbolic stab at her mother's jet-setting ways. But Betty Shaver never heard the death knell. By then, Mumsy had stopped riding and was into fast men, fast cars, and fast planes.

Pat wiped away a tear. Maybe her mother and father hadn't had a great marriage, and maybe they hadn't been outstanding parents. But so what?

Her eyes welled up whenever she remembered the emergency call to her freshman dorm. The days following the fire had left her in shock. Rebuilding Honeymead had no appeal, but for nostalgic reasons, she couldn't let it go completely. To find some middle ground, she'd contacted Ray Cooper. When the former overseer of Honeymead agreed to help, she'd hired Coop to tend to what was left of Grandfather's horses.

During her college and graduate school years, she'd been an absentee owner. When she accepted a job with the *Chicago Tribune*, she decided to put the fire behind her and move into the caretaker's cottage. She'd never intended to give Grandfather's legacy a new lease, but once she'd set Ray Cooper up in an artist's studio in town, she'd driven out and unpacked her bags.

"Sorry about being rotten company," Ellen said, easing her grip on the steering wheel. "You're right. I owe it to Kitty's memory to get answers."

Pat nodded, but kept her eyes focused straight ahead.

"What's going on?" Ellen asked. "I'm ready to talk and you're looking out the window."

"Just mulling over old times. Remember what happened after I moved back into the caretaker's cottage?"

"How could I forget?" Ellen said, half-smiling. "By the time I got there, things had deteriorated."

Her friend was right. After dark on the third day of going it alone, all hell had broken loose. It had never occurred to Pat that horses weren't self-sufficient. But around 11:45 PM, she'd been jolted from her bed by a God-awful sound. While the root of their snorting remained unclear, their intent wasn't. The second the Arabian thoroughbreds began kicking the stable walls, Pat had tabled her investigation and dialed Ellen.

"Think about it, Ellie. Back then, I was in the same predicament Tom Kempner faces today."

"Not quite, my dear. When you arrived, Ray Cooper left. Tommy may not know one end of a horse from the other, but he's not alone. He's got Chuck Sweet."

"Chuck Sweet? Who's Chuck Sweet?"

"The young man who takes care of the Kempners' horses," Ellen answered. "And that's not the only difference. Chuck gets along with horses. Your stallions never considered you their favorite filly."

Pat just smiled, recalling how Ellen had rushed over and assessed the emergency. While her friend fed and watered the animals, Pat had stayed out of the way, wandering over to a stately pair of Labs. Ellen's male stud, Mailman, sat next to his pregnant mate, Snowcone. The dogs watched the hullabaloo from the cab of her friend's pickup.

"You were a blessing that night," Pat said, "and more important, you resolved the horse fiasco and freed me for a project I could handle."

"For the record, I didn't resolve your problem, I eliminated it."

"Either way, when you sold the Arabians, I said goodbye to the horses and hello to one of Snowcone's puppies."

"That's not the only thing you dumped," her friend added. "You also quit that horrible job."

Ellen had a point. Snowshoe's birth had coincided with the day she'd left the *Tribune*. But raising a puppy hadn't been the only reason she'd quit. During her short tenure, she discovered that it was easier to read a metropolitan newspaper than work for one. Of course, she adored her young boss, Ken Dale. But everything else connected with glamorous bylines and hard-nosed reporting had really sucked. The atmosphere in the city room overwhelmed her, and the pressure to increase circulation and sensationalize stories had turned her off too.

"Leaving the *Trib* was the right move," Pat acknowledged. "I got back my sanity… and had a ball hanging around the kennel."

"You can say that again," Ellen concurred, slowing down and turning onto Oak Knoll Road. "Once the puppy was born, you were there so much I figured you for part Labrador."

Pat nodded. She'd felt a loving bond during the daily visits before bringing Snowy home. But that wasn't the only connection being forged. Before long, Ellen Eichler became the mother she'd never had and the friend she'd always wanted.

Ellen turned again and drove down the Kempners' driveway. As they neared the house, Pat pointed at two Mercedes parked in the turnaround, a silver-gray E 55 sedan and navy-blue SUV.

"Looks like Mr. Kempner has company. Any chance Chuck Sweet is into German cars?"

Ellen shook her head. "The His and Hers plates belong to the Gaylanis. Chuck Sweet drives an old pickup. He's just a guy Joanna retains to keep Kitty's stable shipshape."

Ellen got out of the driver's side door, then coaxed Snowshoe and Shoe-Too out. Pat wanted to ask why Joanna Gaylani kept a stable boy on retainer for a barn owned by the Kempners, but it was too late. Ellen had the dogs heeling by her side and was walking toward the trio standing outside the entrance to the Kempners' Tudor mansion.

Pat hurried to catch up, watching Dr. Tony Gaylani pull up the collar of his winter coat.

"Is that the dragon slayer herself?"

Kempner nodded. "Miss Shaver is with her partner-in-crime, Ellen Eichler."

"Quiet, you two," Joanna said as she turned and waved. "Hello. Nice to see… Oh my. You're a foursome."

A round of canine and people introductions followed. But the moment the small talk resumed, Joanna tugged at Tony's coat.

"Time to leave."

"Whatever you say, dear." Dr. Gaylani acknowledged his wife, then turned to Tom Kempner. "Not too late to reconsider. Jewish or not, you're welcome too."

Joanna Gaylani pulled her husband's coat, this time harder.

"All right, all right," he replied. "Ladies, I'd love to stay and chat—"

"Tony! Now means now."

Pat watched Dr. Gaylani zip up his parka and tag along. To her, his dark features could have been Italian, but his coarse jet-black hair and mustache marked him as a Middle Easterner.

"Your neighbors make an interesting couple," Pat said, facing Tom Kempner. "Joanna is quite a beautiful woman."

"What about my pal, Dr. Gaylani?"

"Not my type," she replied. "Can't stand a doc with hard eyes. Kills his bedside manner."

Tom Kempner smiled. "If you'll permit me, I'd like to introduce a more amiable crowd."

Without further explanation, their host did an about-face and dashed inside.

"What do you think?" she asked, looking at Ellen. "Did he just give us the brush-off?"

Before her friend could answer, the outdoor floodlights came on and Tom Kempner reappeared with his two Labs.

Immediately, the dogs paired up. Snowshoe and Blizzard sat atop a snow bank. Below them, Shoe-Too and Snowflake chased each other on the cobblestone turnaround.

"Labs remind me of my grandchildren," Tom said, turning his back to the numbing north wind. "They have inexhaustible energy and never get cold."

Ellen adjusted her scarf. "You must be freezing."

He glanced down. "The dogs are having a ball, and I like the company... but if you don't mind, maybe I'll step inside for a warm-up."

Pat hand-signaled Ellen, then strolled to Tom's side. "Mr. Kempner, I'm with you. About now, I'd like to get the circulation back in my toes."

He started toward the house, then stopped. "Would you consider taking a blood-thinner? When it comes to hot toddies, my recipe is renowned."

"Why, Mr. Kempner, your offer sounds positively thermal."

"One small request, Miss Shaver. Tom or Tommy will do."

"Suits me as long as you reciprocate. Call me Pat... or if I've struck a nerve, Patricia."

At the front entrance Pat stopped and commented on the mahogany trim and hand-carved double doors. By prearrangement, she and Ellen had decided to wait until Tom gave them an opening. When it came, she'd occupy their host while Ellen checked the stable for documents.

"Go ahead," Ellen said, picking up Tom's puppy. "I'll join you in a few minutes. In my opinion, little Snowflake could use an obedience lesson."

"Ellie's a perfectionist," Pat said. "She'll have Snowflake saluting in no time."

"I'll be happy when she's housebroken." He turned toward Ellen. "Don't stay out too long."

"Thought I'd go to the tack room," Ellen replied. "I need a tether, and I know where Kitty stores the horse lines."

Ellen looked down, realizing she'd used the present tense. "Oh, Tommy. I'm so sorry."

"For what? Katherine is gone. Neither of us can get used to the idea, but neither of us can change the facts."

CHAPTER FOURTEEN

Dr. Tony Gaylani and his wife left the Kempners' and drove home in separate cars. As they walked from their garage into the kitchen, Joanna went on and on, glorifying Patricia Shaver and the article she'd written last spring. At first, he ignored his wife's comments. He didn't care to hear how the reporter had taken the Mafia to task. But then Joanna changed the topic.

"Talk about weird," his wife said. "Ellen Eichler told me she just received a letter from Kitty Kempner."

"Sounds like a waste of ink. Why write? Katherine and the Eichler woman used to see each other almost every day."

"Don't know, dear," Joanna answered, unbuttoning her mink coat. "But Ellen made one thing clear. The note had been written just hours before Kitty died."

Joanna's comments rocked him. Trying to keep his composure, Tony flipped down the hood of his parka and extended his arm.

"Can I hang your coat?"

She handed him the mink, then walked away, stopping at the base of the stairs. "Aren't you coming?"

"Be right up."

"Tony, dear. May I offer a suggestion?"

"Of course," he said, leaving his gloves on and his parka zipped.

"Take off your winter clothes before you get in the shower."

"Very funny, dear," he snapped, his brow moist with beads of sweat. "Let me worry about undressing. Right now I need to call the hospital."

"Can you dial wearing mittens?" she asked, smiling.

"Don't be overbearing. Trust me, I'll be shaved, showered, and dressed before you've finished drying your hair."

When his wife disappeared upstairs, Tony headed for the basement, retrieving the combination padlock and hinge assembly from his parka pocket. There wasn't time to put the wine cellar under lock and key, but he wanted to get the noisy part of the installation over.

He reached for his battery-powered drill the moment he heard water running through the drainpipe. After the necessary holes were bored, he breathed lightly, examining his work. He'd bolt the hinge and staple mount in place when they returned home from Larry and Connie Sexton's dinner party.

Quietly, Tony hurried upstairs and entered the His of the his-and-her master bathrooms. He turned on the shower and stripped down to his shorts. He let the water run while he shaved, then he turned it off and wrapped a towel around his waist. After he collected clothes from his walk-in closet, Tony tiptoed into the reading alcove and looked down toward the Kempners' turnaround.

As he watched the dogs play, his mind focused elsewhere. The arrival of the reporter and Ellen Eichler made him nervous, but it was Joanna's statements that really had him on edge. He couldn't recall when his wife and the dog breeder had been alone long enough to chat, but Ellen's disclosures sure put a new perspective on the visit next door. Spies smell trouble. Fifteen minutes ago, the stench threatening his survival had become overpowering.

He continued to dress and keep a wary eye on the Kempner house. The meddlesome women appeared harmless, but only until Tom and the Shaver woman took three of the dogs inside. Between fastening cufflinks and pulling on trousers, he watched, hoping Ellen Eichler would take the puppy and follow suit. But no such luck. Instead, Ellen scooped up the Lab puppy and walked around the back side of the garage.

For a few seconds, he lost sight of them. When Ellen and puppy reappeared, he watched the lights come on in the stable. He had

no idea what she was up to, but the combination of her strange behavior and Joanna's comments made him uneasy.

Tony tightened his tie. Why hadn't he grilled his wife on the contents of Katherine's note? At the time he'd thought it would look
suspicious, but now he wasn't sure. As a skilled Iraqi operative, he
understood the frightful implications. He knew what he'd seen when
he was in Katherine's office with her. And he knew what he hadn't
seen when he was in her office with Tom. A folder Katherine had
used to shelter some documents had disappeared.

From the Her bathroom, his wife turned off the blow dryer.
"What did you say?"

Fully dressed, Tony looked at her, his face calm. "Need to run
into town and get some cash."

He anticipated Joanna's disbelief and didn't wait for a reply.
Over his shoulder, Tony told her he'd be back before she was ready.

CHAPTER FIFTEEN

Patricia Shaver was pleased. Their plan had started flawlessly. Ellen had picked up Tom Kempner's puppy Snowflake and taken her to the stable. Pat knew her friend would teach the dog a few obedience lessons, but more importantly, she would find out what Kitty Kempner had hidden in her horse purse.

Pat accepted Tom's invitation and followed him into the house. Her role was straightforward. She planned to use her interrogative skills to pump their host.

"Wow. What a spot for a Christmas tree."

The huge Douglas fir dominated the entryway. More like a rotunda, the walls of the two-storied foyer were plastered above the wainscoting.

Tom unbuttoned his coat, looking at the lustrous ornaments. "Katherine loved Christmas trees."

"It shows. Hers is lovely."

Crystal, porcelain, and gold-filigreed decorations adorned the boughs. As the heir to her grandmother's collection, Pat knew a thing or two about antique Christmas ornaments. Katherine Kempner's tree belonged in a museum.

"Come closer," Tom said, walking to the tree. "The hanging pieces are either heirlooms or items my wife and I collected over the years."

Pat followed, touching a reindeer ornament. "They're all beautiful."

Tom took her parka and headed toward the closet. "Guess you'd call Katherine a Christmas freak."

"And the man of the house?"

He turned. "Jewish guys can only be closet Christmas freaks."

They both laughed as she looked around. Straight ahead was an enormous sunken living room. Unlike the foyer, which had large oil paintings and a couple of settees, the living room was filled with an eclectic array of furniture that bespoke more of comfort than origin.

To her right, carved mahogany newel posts secured the banisters for the curved staircase. Under the second floor landing, a pair of pocket doors opened into a paneled library. To the left of Tom's den, down an arched hallway, were more rooms. From her vantage point it was impossible to see the interiors, but she presumed it was his wing and off-limits.

Pat planned to saunter across the foyer and take a glimpse down the hallway, but when Tom said, "Ladies, how 'bout a cookie?" the dogs followed him and so did she.

His route took them along the perimeter of the living room and into the dining area, a space that had to have been furnished from an English country estate. Facing each other from opposite walls were the breakfront and the sideboard. Centered between the Edwardian antiques was the dining room table, a circular piece hewed from thick walnut planks and surrounded by sixteen chairs.

She stepped over the doggie gate and walked into the kitchen. "Whose castle did you loot? The stuff out there didn't come from a furniture mart."

Without looking up, he distributed dog biscuits, then began collecting the essentials for toddies. "Katherine's family is English. All the pieces came from her grandfather's hunting lodge. The general was quite a sportsman."

"The general?" she asked.

"Sir Alan Cunningham. He was Katherine's..." Tom eyed her, an apologetic smile creasing his face. "Sorry. With all the hoopla over his memoirs, I began to assume everyone had an interest in the man."

"Crazy as it sounds, count me among the legions."

"You're joking," Tom said, eying her. "In some circles Cunningham is famous, but isn't your brand of journalism more attuned to… How shall I say it?"

"Tough trial lawyers don't mince words," she replied, her tone a little too stern. "Go ahead, counselor, probe with impunity."

"Before I probe anything, let's clear the air." He faced her, his arms crossed. "Do I call you Patricia when you're being insufferable, or just when you're being nice?"

Nailed by his graceful candor, she lowered her gaze. "Sorry… as to my interest in the general, I'm researching an article and Sir Alan Cunningham's name came up."

"There's one for the books," he said, laughing out loud. "My firm knows about your fact-finding talents. But after reading your latest piece, I thought you made celebrities from the ranks of the living, not the dead."

"For the record, Mr. Kempner, General Cunningham figures into a much broader inquiry." She stared back and also crossed her arms. "I'm writing a treatise assessing the chances for peace in the Middle East. The conflict has root causes dating to Moses, but I chose to begin my inquiry with post-World War I events."

Tom didn't break eye contact. "Ramifications stemming from the Balfour Agreement?"

"When I began this project, the Balfour Agreement was the first thing I examined."

"Are you aware of my wife's full name?"

"Ellen showed me the program from her funeral service." Pat lightened her tone, recalling the elegant script: *Katherine Balfour Cunningham Kempner.*

"So there's no confusion," he said, searching her face. "Balfour was her mother's grandfather. General Alan Cunningham was her father's father."

"How interesting. Both sides of her family played important roles in Middle East affairs."

He began stirring spices into the pot of simmering toddies.

"That's certainly the opinion of my neighbor. Tony found the general's letters very engrossing."

She shrugged. "Some people like baby pictures. Others are intrigued by a peek into a bygone era."

"Maybe, but not when the snapshots are of another person's family."

The co-chair of the nationally prominent criminal defense firm Kempner & Bronner sniffed the aroma coming from the toddy pot. Tom's body language and benign comments cast him as anything but a courtroom titan, but Pat wondered whether their host's relaxed demeanor and seeming disinterest were part of a deadly serious game.

"Names are deceiving," she went on, clasping her hands behind her back. "Why, I've heard they can even confuse the identity of a nationality."

The pot bubbled, pungent and festive.

"What a striking observation," he said, facing her.

"It's a fact... maybe even a *striking* fact. Take a Pole named David Grun. More than a century after his birth, Jews idolize the man they know as David Ben-Gurion."

"Grun, huh? Wonder why he changed it?"

"There's another notable too," she went on, ignoring his question. "In Kiev, a baby was born twelve years after Ben-Gurion's birth. A couple of decades later, Golda Myerson, nee Mabovitch, taught school in Milwaukee. Three years after that—in 1921—she and her husband emigrated to Palestine. Today, Golda Meir gets a mixed report card, but virtually all historians recognize her as one of the forces who made the State of Israel a reality."

He spiked their toddy mugs with a shot of brandy, then added Kahlua.

"With Zionists changing their names and showing up all over the world, it almost makes you wonder if everyone has some Jewish blood."

Their eyes met and neither of them gave quarter.

"One thing's certain," she said. "Your case gets stronger if you count all the inter-religious marriages."

"More research, Miss Shaver… or a comment on my neighbors?"

"Joanna's Jewish. Her maiden name gives her away."

They walked to the breakfast nook table, hot toddies in hand.

"What about Dr. Gaylani?" he asked, sitting down. "Any surprises with him?"

"Depends. R.A. Gaylani may look the part, but I'm betting he *ain't* Italian."

"My goodness," Tom said, a look of surprise on his face. "If the Roman Allah isn't a Catholic choirboy, some of my theories are correct."

Pat's heart skipped a beat. She'd used Dr. Gaylani's initials to get a reaction. When Tom called his neighbor the Roman Allah, she figured their conversation was about to get focused.

"My research is clear on one point," she said, leaning forward, elbows on the table. "The Arabs hated your wife's great-grandfather. Arthur Balfour made lots of enemies when he legitimized the Zionists' claim on a large section of the Holy Land."

"But none of Balfour's recommendations ever happened," Tom replied, watching her over his toddy mug. "For a long time, Jerusalem stayed in Arab hands and, as a people, Jews continued to sit in the back of the bus."

"Yes, but only until Dr. Chaim Weizmann called in a debt."

"Who?" Tom asked.

"Weizmann was a chemist who devised a process to manufacture acetone. When he gave the formula to the Brits, their bombs exploded with much greater force."

"How interesting," he said. "Give the English military a bigger bang for their buck and they reciprocate. Back scratching has been popular since the dawn of man."

"Reminds me of the legal profession," she replied. "Nothing personal, but don't you barristers plea bargain more than you prosecute?"

As Kempner's grin faded, Pat looked over his shoulder. A phone was mounted on the wall behind him. Of the three incoming lines, the one on the right had a light to signal use, but not a connector button.

"Save the lawyer jokes for another time," he snapped. "Weren't we talking about Dr. Chaim Weizmann?"

Pat sipped her toddy and made note of the change in his inflection. "My knowledge is limited, but back in the twenties, the doctor wore two hats. His work with acetone brought him fame as a military chemist. His views as a political scientist didn't get the same accolades."

Tom glanced at her, eyes cold. "What were his views?"

"At the time, Dr. Weizmann was a British subject. Like Arthur Balfour, he believed that chopping up Palestine to make room for the Zionists would give the English an ally in the region. To him, the Middle East was the unstable part of the Empire."

"Ah, yes… the worldwide commonwealth." Tom set his mug on the table. "But by then, wasn't the sun setting on the British Empire?"

"To be sure, but like the Egyptians and Romans before them, the English enjoyed being a planet powerhouse. Tony Gaylani's homeland makes my case. Back in the early twenties, the British tried to shore up their Middle East influence by installing Faisal I as Iraq's king."

Tom studied her face. "Don't tell me. A Baghdad despot with a cockney accent."

"I can't comment on the accent, but he most certainly was a despot."

When Tom stood, Pat refocused on the wall behind him, wondering what made a kitchen phone line so private it lit up, but couldn't be answered.

"The twenties and thirties were turbulent times," he admitted, "but the Middle East was different. The English had figurehead rulers in place, and that kept the status quo in balance too."

"On the surface, yes. But behind all those puppet thrones, different factions vied for control."

"Unsuccessfully," he asked, "or did some of those *different factions* gain control?"

"For a very, very brief time, Arab rightists ruled in Iraq," Pat said, wondering if Tom had just made a reference to Tony's father. "In the late thirties, Rashid Ali el-Gaylani had secretly visited Nazi Germany and presented Hitler with a plot to undermine the British."

"Technically correct, but after the start of World War II, the British kicked the ultra-nationalists out of Iraq. It's possible they did the same thing in the Holy Land."

"I don't think so," she replied. "The Palestinians never fought British rule. It was a country without great natural resources. Nobody cared who ruled."

"If you're right, Katherine's grandfather was the British High Commissioner of a wasteland." Tom chuckled sardonically. "Why did King George send a general? Sounds like a lowly corporal could have handled the job."

"Not that simple," she said, rotating her toddy mug on the table. "During the war and after, Muslim nations pumped oil and didn't cause trouble. But years later, an area in the 'wasteland' got a catchy new name. Once the Jewish state of Israel came into being, lots of Arab leaders adopted the Palestinian cause."

"Funny how that works. A rock pile is only worthless until someone else wants it."

"Particularly in this case," she agreed. "Israel's creation stemmed more from the Holocaust than any ancient religious or territorial claims. To be frank, most politicians felt a need to make amends for looking the other way."

Tom leaned back in his chair and smiled wryly. "What a great world. It took Hitler and an Allied guilt trip to make the Zionist demands a reality. But guess what? I'm still not safe. Like a rabbi once told me, "When Jews stand back to back, murdering Arabs take note and steer clear."

* * *

Ellen Eichler flipped on the lights in Katherine Kempner's stable. She put Snowflake down, then searched for a training leash. When she heard restless hooves followed by whinnies, she sensed trouble. The puppy was prancing in and out of the stalls.

She tucked Snowflake under her arm and settled the horses. With order restored, she walked toward the wall where Kitty's western-style saddle was draped over a dowel rod.

Seeing her friend's riding gear caused her to pause and remember. In that second, when she relaxed her arm, Snowflake squirmed free and jumped to the floor. Once again, the search for the general's papers was delayed.

A minute or so later, Ellen tethered the puppy to a post. With the hide-and-seek contest over, she returned to the wall where the saddles were stored. Her primary job was to retrieve Kitty's hidden cache, but just as Ellen pulled the documents from the horse purse and started scanning the first page, Snowflake began yipping.

She heard the puppy and acted without thinking. Instead of shoving the papers inside her sheepskin coat, Ellen slipped them back into the saddlebag and turned around.

Dr. Tony Gaylani opened the tack room door and entered.

"Hello, Mrs. Eichler. Nice to see you again."

She stiffened, then moved away from Kitty's horse purse. "Are you here for a reason… or did you just get lost?"

"I live next door. You're the one on the wrong side of town."

Ellen saw two pictures. From the knees up, Tony looked like a gentleman ready for a night on the town. Below his gray chesterfield, he resembled an Iditarod musher ready to urge on his huskies.

"Quite an outfit. Are you and the missus traveling by dog sled?"

"Connie Sexton called and asked Joanna to bring over her new bridle."

"There's one for the books," Ellen replied, smirking, "show and tell at a cocktail party."

"Something like that."

Clearly not amused, Gaylani moved toward the saddle rack.

"My better half is running late. I'm only trying to save her some extra steps."

They stared at each other. His excuse was lame and he had to know it.

"If you need help," Ellen offered, "I can find Joanna's bridle."

"Wouldn't think of disturbing your...your..." Tony arched an eyebrow. "What exactly are you doing here?"

"Giving Snowflake some pointers," Ellen replied, "but we're almost done. When it comes to obedience, puppies are like men. Short attention spans."

"Not in my case," he said, taking another step toward Kitty's saddle. "When something interests me, I have the patience of a saint."

Ellen untied the puppy. "If you hang out here too long, you'll be late to Sexton's party."

The doctor leaned against Kitty's saddlebags. "Like I said before, Joanna is still blow drying her hair. Go ahead. Who knows, I might learn something."

Patricia Shaver didn't want to let Tom's "back to back" comment pass. It was a clear reference to a speech delivered by David Ben-Gurion. But before she could get him to elaborate, Pat felt a draft and saw the puppy scamper in.

"Hello, Snowflake, I see your drill sergeant is here too."

Wide-eyed, Ellen joined them at the breakfast nook table. "Tommy, you've got a fast learner."

"Was there ever a doubt?" He walked to the stove and began mixing a new batch of cinnamon-laced toddies. "We'll celebrate Mrs. Eichler's training triumph with another round."

Ellen leaned over and whispered to Pat. "Let's get out of here. We need to talk."

"No way. Tom Kempner should be a part of the dialogue."

"Ladies, I'd like to propose..." He looked at them, then set the toddy mugs down and stepped back. "Excuse me one second. You two probably want to be alone."

When Tom left, Ellen slid her chair even closer.

"Listen up. What I have to say, he can't hear."

"Hold on," Pat replied. "Tom and I just had a pointed discussion. He suspects something is very wrong."

"He's not alone. While you two played twenty questions, Dr. Tony came calling."

"What! Gaylani walked into the stable?"

"Yep," Ellen replied. "He was dressed to the nines except for his knee-high winter boots."

"Jesus. How did he know?"

"Have you forgotten who lives next door?" Ellen asked, her lips quivering. "For anyone looking, the stable is easy to see from the Gaylanis' bedroom window."

Pat knew the coincidences were too great. Her instincts hadn't lied. She and Ellen had somehow stumbled into the middle of a plot being played for the highest stakes imaginable.

"Listen to me," she said, grabbing Ellen's arm. "We've got to tell Tom."

"Everything?"

"Just about Kitty's letter. Until we get his reaction, we'll hold off on the part about your stable encounter."

Ellen pulled away. "You know that means we'll both be making phone calls."

She was correct. Once committed to stay the course, they both had to delay their Christmas plans.

Tom returned, stepping over the dog gate. "Okay to join you?"

Pat nodded, then faced Ellen. "Shall I start dialing, or do you want to go first?"

CHAPTER SIXTEEN

Joanna Gaylani stood in her dressing room, looking into a full-length mirror. Satisfied, she turned and stared at the jewelry box atop her chiffonier. For a moment, she hesitated. Then she raised the hinged top and lifted one of the trays.

A tear ran down her cheek as she looked inside. More moisture welled in her eyes as she retrieved a small black and white photograph she kept hidden under a coiled pearl necklace.

The picture of her parents standing in their dirt-floor home in Palestine always made her sad. In 1956, less than a year after the photo was taken, they were dead—Jewish civilians slaughtered in cold blood by Muslim soldiers.

The picture was her touchstone. It fueled an inner strength and also made her reevaluate. She'd dedicated her life to seeking revenge, but was her cause noble, or was her behavior no better than her enemies'?

Joanna dabbed at her eyes with a Kleenex, then glanced back at the mirror. Her outfit looked great and so did she. As for her plan to frame and murder her husband…? It continued to progress on schedule, and rightly so.

Just as she reassured herself that Tony deserved to die, her stomach knotted. Almost doubling over, Joanna took two quick breaths. She'd had bouts of remorse ever since she'd convinced Uncle Larry to use Tony as their scapegoat.

She straightened up. Not surprisingly, during prior instances she'd found relief by reasoning with her conscience. After all, her husband had killed her best friend. Kitty's murder had been premeditated. Tony was a heartless felon and spy who needed to be brought to justice.

Joanna replaced the black and white picture, then walked from her dressing room to the head of the main staircase. Okay... maybe her scheme was a roundabout way to ensure Tony got his due. But she wasn't a vigilante. The courts would never indict him. There was no evidence to bring him to trial.

She closed her eyes, thankful the ache in her abdomen had subsided. Framing the man she'd once loved was difficult, but it had to be done. That was why she'd given the Eichler and Shaver women an excuse to go to the stables. That was also the reason she'd taken an extended shower and fussed with her hair for an inordinate amount of time. For her overall plan to succeed, she needed to get Tony involved.

She'd seen her husband's jaw muscles tense the moment she'd told him that Ellen Eichler had received a letter written and sent by Kitty the afternoon before she died. Joanna had made up the story as they walked into the kitchen. She wanted Ellen to get to General Cunningham's papers first, but she also wanted her husband to watch it happen.

Her ploy had been a cunning move, adroit and subtle. Of course, there had been a chance that Tony wouldn't take the bait, but now as she began walking down the stairs to the foyer, she knew her fears had been unfounded. In testimony to his trespass, her fool husband stood in front of her, his boots dripping onto the marble foyer floor.

"You're a handsome man, dear," she said, stepping off the carpeted stairs and gazing into the eyes of a man she'd execute in less than seventy-two hours. "But what's with the boots?"

"Only a precaution," he replied. "If we have car trouble, I'd hate to walk for help in a pair of alligator loafers."

Joanna kissed his cheek, then asked him to get her coat. As he turned toward the closet, one part of her psyche thanked God for giving her the fortitude to live with the enemy. Another wondered why she couldn't hate him—why some remnant of her former love refused to die.

Less than twenty minutes ago, she'd stood by the window in the upstairs bedroom alcove. She'd held her breath until her husband stopped his car in the middle of their driveway, got out, and trudged through the snow toward the stable.

She hadn't seen Ellen Eichler go in, but figured Kitty's friend had had enough lead-time to get the job done. But a few minutes later, when Tony came out the tack room door right behind Ellen and the puppy, she wondered who had the papers. Her husband had begun walking toward their driveway, then lingered. He'd doubled back when the Eichler woman was out of sight.

As Tony approached with her full-length mink, Joanna stepped away from the staircase and did a slow about-face. From behind, she smelled his strong cologne. The photo of her parents conjured itself, and she had to hide a primal rage as his lips brushed her cheek.

"That was dreamy, dear," she said, faking a sigh. "Too bad we can't stay and cuddle."

Joanna began buttoning her coat, all the while replaying the last part of her surveillance.

Watching Tony go back into the stable had alarmed her. She'd counted on Ellen Eichler's getting hold of the general's papers, but after a moment's thought she realized it didn't matter. Even if Ellen hadn't retrieved them, she'd been alone long enough to get the gist of their meaning.

"Tony, dear. How's this for a delicious thought?"

She put her arms around his neck, brushed her lips against his, and began undulating in a way that produced friction and other signs of heat.

"Connie is famous for her hors d'oeuvres, but why don't we skip the cocktail hour."

"We can't," Tony said, leaning his head back, watching her. "The Sextons are expecting us. Besides, we're both dressed."

Joanna let her palms drift down the outside of her husband's sport jacket. When she felt something crinkle, she knew the general's papers were in his breast-coat pocket.

"Stand still, darling," she ordered. "After I undo your boots, we'll sneak upstairs."

He gently pushed her away.

"Control yourself, Joanna. It's bound to be an early evening. Once we're back, I'll be a slave to your wishes."

CHAPTER SEVENTEEN

Pat and Ellen got up from the breakfast nook table and excused themselves from Tom Kempner. With cell phones in hand, they retreated to the far end of the kitchen. She called Ken Dale and Ellen called her husband.

Pat knew her reporter's instincts hadn't lied. Something big was in the works. When she'd cautioned Ellen, "We've got to tell him," she'd conveyed one message. Tom Kempner knew much more than he was saying. To unravel the mystery of his wife's death, they had to show him Kitty's letter and pretend to be sympathetic to his plight. Anything less, and they'd never crack into his storehouse of information.

Pat slipped her cell phone into the front pocket of her jeans. With a game face, she joined Ellen and Tom at the breakfast nook table, very conscious of Tom's steadfast gaze.

"Tom, Ellie got a letter from your wife today."

"Oh?" he replied, his tone guarded.

"Yes," Pat went on. "The envelope was postmarked Thursday, but on the note itself, Mrs. Kempner had written *Wednesday afternoon*."

Tom Kempner let the incongruity between the postmark and the letter pass without a comment or a visible reaction, but when she outlined the contents, Pat noticed an abrupt change. He stiffened at the reference to Rashid Ali el-Gaylani. Then he became wide-eyed when she mentioned that Rashid's son would be about the same age as Dr. R. Anthony Gaylani.

"To think," Tom said, slumping in his chair, "Katherine wrote the letter, then died a few hours later. I'd like a look. Did you bring it along?"

Ellen shook her head. "No, but we had no right to keep it from you. Right now, I feel like a traitor."

"No way," he replied, "you and Katherine were close. Her note was frantic, the delivery was screwy, and she died suddenly. Why wouldn't your first obligation be with her?"

When Ellen didn't answer, he looked down at the tile floor, his shoulders bowed.

"Damn. If I hadn't dismissed her concerns, none of this would have happened."

Tom Kempner's body language sent a message of despair. But did their host feel like he'd been kicked in the stomach, or was he just acting like it? Shouldn't Tom have picked up on her statement that the doctor living next door was the same age as the son of Rashid Ali el-Gaylani? Why wasn't he making that connection?

"Tell me it's none of my business," Pat said, "but when did your wife become concerned?"

"*Concerned* is the wrong word. The process started last Tuesday evening, the night before her Grandfather Cunningham's papers were delivered." Tom rubbed his hand over his jaw. "We were having dinner with the Gaylanis. Katherine looked radiant, and as usual, Tony made a tactless comment, comparing Katherine's radiance with sexual afterglow."

Tom continued, saying the doctor had persisted until Katherine told him the real reason for her girlish blush.

"You're going to be disappointed, neighbor," his wife had explained. "I'm happy because I won the battle with MI-6. My grandfather's diaries and papers are being delivered tomorrow morning."

"Most people don't take on the British Secret Service," Pat said. "Why did your wife want to check out General Cunningham's documents?"

"It had nothing to do with espionage," he answered. "Katherine's reasons were personal."

For a moment, Tom looked irritated. Then he explained his wife's teenage deportation and unofficial adoption, saying that in spite of considering Aunt Harriet and Uncle Sean to be her parents, Katherine had been greatly affected when her real mother died thirteen months ago and her father passed away a short time later. As Tom saw it, the failure to reconcile had bothered her so much, she went to Aunt Harriet for advice.

"Did your wife's aunt suggest she contact the British government?" Pat asked.

"She insisted. Harriet has spunk and figured if Katherine read her grandfather's papers, she'd discover that at least one Cunningham male wasn't like her father and consumed with himself."

"Why MI-6?" Pat asked. "Harriet must have had some of her father's letters. Why not let your wife read them?"

"Wouldn't have worked. Katherine was a tough sell."

He went on, saying that his wife yearned for concrete proof that she wasn't to blame for putting a permanent wedge between herself and her parents. Harriet knew Katherine's grandfather had a bit of the devil in him and counted on the general's feisty personality to come through in his memoirs.

Tom concluded the anecdote, telling them that he'd been there the night Harriet banged her hand on their dining room table, looked his wife in the eye, and laid down the law:

"Listen to me, Katherine. My father, General Alan Cunningham, was a friend of Winston Churchill and served honorably during World War II. After the peace he spent his final days in the military as the High Commissioner of Palestine, trying to keep that part of the colonial empire from deteriorating into anarchy.

"But I'm not here to praise his accomplishments. I want you to read your grandfather's diaries and memoirs to prove one point: My father and your father may have shared the same genes, but they were as different as night and day. Your father had stern eyes—my dad's eyes sparkled. Your father spoke in low tones—the general's voice echoed vibrancy. And most important, your father waited for things to happen. My father—like you—made things happen."

Pat listened to the explanation. She acknowledged Harriet's ingenuity, but shuddered at the irony. All along, Kitty had scrutinized her grandfather's papers to free herself from guilt. Tony Gaylani had a far more sinister reason. He didn't want people pointing a guilty finger at him.

But now wasn't the time to initiate a character assassination. While Tom Kempner had used debasing terms to describe Dr. Gaylani's indiscretions, she knew their host was a master at hiding his true feelings. For some reason, Tom didn't want to admit that Dr. R Anthony Gaylani could have murdered Kitty.

"One question," Pat said. "What prompted the British authorities to release General Cunningham's memoirs?"

Tom pushed his toddy mug away. "The Brits have regulations similar to our Freedom of Information Act. There's lots of red tape, but if you ask nicely, have the right lineage, and send money for postage and copying, the folks in the archive department will forward the documents."

"Politicos amaze me," Ellen said, lifting Snowflake onto her lap. "They spend billions funding covert networks, then pass legislation making sensitive material just a Fed Ex away."

Pat smiled. "You've just defined a civilized society."

"Have I?" Ellen scoffed. "In that case, tell me why Dr. Tony Gaylani found General Alan Cunningham's observations so captivating?"

"You read Kitty's letter," Pat said. "Rashid Ali el-Gaylani tried to overthrow the pro-British government before the start of World War II. Tony and that guy share the same last name."

"Look, I know what Kitty wrote in her letter," Ellen replied, petting Tom's Lab puppy, "and I realize the initials and surname match up, but I still think the doctor is an Italian Catholic. My God! He's married to Joanna, and she's an active fundraiser with the United Jewish Congress."

Pat cocked her head. "You have Joanna pegged right, but you missed the boat on Tony. He found Sir Alan Cunningham's memos interesting because the general had contact with Jews and Muslims. I'm betting Tony and Joanna had relatives who knew Kitty's grandfather."

Tom nodded. "Good point. Your research confirms the logistics and timeframe. Joanna's grandmother and R.A.'s father may not have known each other, but they both had to have dealings with the general."

Ellen raised her arm like a traffic cop. "Hold on. Who's Joanna's grandmother?"

Pat stood, thankful Tom had finally admitted the obvious. Now she had to convince Ellen. Since Tom had heard the story before, she capsulized her response.

"Have I got this right?" Ellen asked, her eyes open wide. "You think Golda Meir's son was Joanna's father?"

"I'm not certain," Pat replied, slowly rotating the toddy mug in her hands. "But that's what I think. Keep in mind I began by researching historical figures. I never expected to see some of those names on Mrs. Kempner's funeral service program."

To a rapt audience of two, Pat outlined her case:

"By the late thirties, Rashid Ali el-Gaylani was married and had fathered a son. Aside from that, no reference had ever been made to his family, other than a rumor that his wife fled Iraq with her infant son and settled in America.

"The details of Golda Meir's offspring were equally sketchy. Her son and daughter-in-law had been listed as fatalities of the '56 Sinai Campaign. No mention had ever been made as to the whereabouts of their teenage daughter."

Pat glanced at Ellen, then Tom. "All this may seem like a stretch, but you must admit the names and dates of birth correspond to the couple next door. Is it just coincidence?"

"There are lots of Myersons in Chicago," Ellen countered, her face tense. "Who says Joanna's father and Golda Meir's son were one and the same?"

"Even if he isn't, Myerson is a Jewish name. Why would Joanna marry an Iraqi?"

Ellen rolled her eyes. "Do you expect me to believe that Dr. Tony Gaylani went from being an Italian to an Iraqi based on a nickname some Army nurses used?"

Pat looked at their host. "Tom is the one who said the nurses called him R.A. Why would they lie? What's to be gained?"

"I'm not accusing them," Ellen answered, her hands rising. "You're a journalist. Is this the kind of proof that passes muster with a tough editor?"

Tom tapped the table. "Go easy, you two. Concrete proof may be hard to come by, but I can add to the circumstantial evidence."

"Something better than Hot Lips and the RNs, I hope," Ellen said tartly.

Tom glared. "An admiral who works for the CIA once told me the chiefs run the Navy. I assure you, the nurses, not the doctors, run the military hospitals."

With that, Tom Kempner recounted how he'd been transferred to the recovery ward a few days after his surgery. One morning, as he sat up in bed, a nurse walked in, grabbed his chart, and mentioned that the Roman Allah had once again pulled off a miracle. Her remark might have passed, but when he laughed and asked if Jesus and not Allah had guided the scalpel, the RN got grim-faced and told him that Italian blood didn't run in Dr. R.A. Gaylani's veins.

"She knew," Tom assured them. "On a midnight shift, a few nurses had gone snooping in the record room. That was where they found his 201 file."

Ellen's eyebrow arched. "201 file? What's that? More rumor-monger material?"

"No, Mrs. Eichler, it's the military's answer to a J. Edgar Hoover dossier. Along with your name, rank, and serial number, it contains everything you've ever done as a member of the Armed Forces."

Ellen blinked. "If the nurses got it from the source, it must be on target."

"Now that that's settled," Pat said, "we have another confession. Ellie's trip to the stable wasn't to locate a horse line. She went to search the contents of a horse purse."

"A horse purse?" he asked. "What's a horse purse?"

After Ellen explained their code for saddlebags, she recapped her stable encounter.

"Gaylani showed up just after you got there?" Tom asked, his strained features telegraphing his surprise. "The man has a knack for barging in at the wrong moment."

"Or the right moment for him," Ellen said. "When did he do it to you?"

"Tony didn't exactly barge in," Tom corrected. "He tracked me down by phone."

Ellen leaned over the table. "And?"

"It occurred before the wine tasting," Tom said, his eyes afire. "Now will you get off my back?"

"Why so touchy?" Ellen asked. "You opened the door, I'm just asking questions."

"Then try another topic, Mrs. Eichler."

"Hold on," Pat said, "we're all on the same team. To get anywhere, we need to cooperate."

When Ellen and Tom sat back, a wobbly peace was reestablished.

"Let's bring some organization to our conversation," Pat suggested. "As with most things, it helps when you start at the beginning."

"Whatever it takes," Tom agreed. "The only woman I ever loved is gone. I can't change that, but when I think about the night she died, there are so many unanswered questions."

Pat listened to Tom's reply. His tone was fiery, but his statements lacked conviction. And there was that other oddity. At first Tom had avoided the connection between Rashid Ali el-Gaylani and Tony Gaylani, but later he embraced it.

All things taken together, Pat was sure Tom knew more than he was letting on. Like all experienced courtroom lawyers, he adopted a style and never let the opposition alter it. In this case, he agreed with her only when it became silly to hold out. Once again, Tom proved to be a master at managing the talk points.

"Before we try to answer some tough questions, I have a procedural suggestion." Pat smiled. "A wise man once said nobody works well on an empty stomach."

Tom stood, glancing at his watch. "Where did the time go? It's almost eight. The choice is yours, ladies. Anything in the fridge is fair game. Otherwise, DiPero's delivers great pizza."

Joanna Gaylani was standing amongst the other guests in the Sextons' living room. With her innermost thoughts focused on the planned bombing and Tony's execution, she snuggled up to her husband and put her arm around his waist.

"Honey," she said, whispering in his ear, "are you enjoying Connie's canapés?"

Tony flinched. "The jumbo shrimp are delicious."

Joanna bent down, plucked one by the tail, and gave it a shake.

"Icky," she said, happy her husband seemed uncomfortable. "Much too limp."

"Darling," he whispered, "you've made your point."

Tony was an aggressive sexual partner, but a prude in public. Of course, in a few days, he'd be neither. Soon he'd be their scapegoat—an Arab who'd falsified his identity and married a Jewess—an Iraqi doctor who had dedicated his life to terrorism. Yes, indeed. Soon the world would think Dr. R.A. Gaylani had detonated a bomb during the keynote speech at the upcoming convention of the United Jewish Congress.

Joanna felt her body tense, an involuntary reaction she'd begun to experience each day since Kitty Kempner's murder. Why, she wondered, had her friend's death triggered these pangs of conscience?

To be sure, Kitty's death had made her question the efficacy of her plan. But she, along with her Ruling Council colleagues, were engaged in a new type of war. And in this instance, the harsh realities were simple: They had to act. They had to do the unthinkable.

She, Chuck Sweet, and Lawrence Magel had discussed their decision *ad nauseam*. Of course, the murder of innocent Jews haunted them. But the greater good was at stake, and there were no other options. Someone had to turn public sentiment against the Arabs, the real evil force in the Middle East. Someone had to bomb the Jewish delegates at the UJC Convention.

Joanna bent down and skewered a crust-wrapped miniature frankfurter, desperately trying to get the images of mutilated Jewish delegates out of her mind.

"Look at this one," she said. "It's got the desired stiffness, but it's too small. I can hardly tell it's in my mouth."

"Joanna," Tony said, forcing a smile, "be a good girl and behave yourself."

Patricia Shaver set the DiPero's pizza box aside. While they ate, her cohorts had kept their conversation to a minimum. She hoped that meant each was anxious to get back to work.

Tom put three steaming mugs of Kona coffee on the kitchen table. "Cream or sugar?"

Pat shook her head, maintaining eye contact with their host. "To get this off on the right foot, someone has to frame our discussion. I'm the outsider… the only one who didn't know Kitty. Maybe it would be easier if I tried."

"With one proviso," Tom said, sitting down. "I expect tough questions."

"Of course," Pat replied, their eyes still locked. "Why not start by telling us what unnerved Kitty enough to write such a desperate letter?"

Tom jabbed a thumb at himself. "You're looking at him. I'm the root cause."

"How so?" Pat asked. "You're not mentioned in her note. She only wrote about Tony Gaylani and General Alan Cunningham's memoirs."

"The delivery of her grandfather's papers got things going, but my inaction forced her to write the letter." Tom looked away.

"Katherine called me at the office around 12:30. She was upset, but at the time, I was running late… tied up with an important trial. Frankly, I turned a deaf ear and blew her off."

"We've all let deadlines lead to ill-advised words," Pat said quietly. "I need specifics. Do you remember anything your wife said?"

"Not from our noontime conversation. But once I got home, Katherine unloaded on me in no uncertain terms."

Tom went on to say that after he and Barbera's three mob soldiers went to the courthouse and heard the judge dismiss the murder charges, they'd all gone out to celebrate.

"So you didn't call her back," Pat said. "You and Kitty didn't talk until you got home."

"Correct, but I did take one call. Tony phoned the office and bugged my secretary until she gave him my private cell number."

"What did he want?" Pat asked.

"It was weird," he continued. "Tony congratulated me on my courtroom performance and insisted we all get together to celebrate. A wine tasting, no less."

Pat shrugged. "You're neighbors. Why wouldn't he be happy for your success?"

"Like most folks, the doctor doesn't like my clients… something about extending judicial protection to bloodsucking pond scum."

"Ah," Pat said, smiling. "So you turned him down."

"At first, yes… but *no* isn't part of Tony's vocabulary."

Pat leaned back and looked out the window. When the conversation started, Tom had been contrite. His last few answers had seemed more assertive. Was he reassessing his culpability, or sending her a message?

"Given Kitty's earlier call, I mean, knowing how upset she was…"

"Don't sugarcoat your thoughts," he advised. "Maybe I should have checked in. Instead, I committed both of us to Tony's agenda."

"Tony's agenda?" Pat asked. "Did the doctor run the show that evening?"

"Tony thinks he's a wine connoisseur," Tom scoffed. "Claimed he'd discovered a couple of new chardonnays. The wine tasting was his venue to get our opinion."

Pat said nothing. Several things bothered her. Tom wasn't insensitive. Why refuse to return Kitty's call, then compound the problem by accepting Tony Gaylani's invitation? It made no sense unless other things had influenced his actions.

"Let's back up a second. You said your wife gave you an earful. Difficult or not, tell us what she said."

"I was half-lit when I agreed to Gaylani's wine tasting," Tom replied, his voice shaky. "Right after that, I got into Mr. Barbera's limo and headed for my house. I knew I had it coming, and I was right. Katherine went nuts when I walked through the front door."

Pat watched him lower his head. Without question, Tom talked and acted like a person whose indifference to his wife's concerns had led to a tragedy. But could that be true? And if so, was he a victim who hadn't had a choice in the matter?

"You asked how Katherine reacted," Tom said, his eyes open and alert. "She left nothing to the imagination. She told me, 'Go ahead and play footsie with the bastard. I've had a bellyful of that son of a bitch. You may think he's a Dago doctor. I'm betting he's a God damn Arab spy.'"

Pat listened, but she wasn't fooled. The language was too harsh. Even if Kitty Kempner had been irate, she would have chosen different words. Tom had made up the quote. But why?

"Were those her exact words?"

Tom nodded. "At the time I was ducking expletives and didn't think much about it. Now that I recall her outburst, it's obvious that Katherine had discovered something important."

"Hard to disagree with that," Pat replied. "What's your read on the doctor's arrival and departure times?"

Tom sipped his coffee, thinking it through. "Probably got to our house the moment the general's stuff came…say late-morning. As for leaving, Katherine called me during the tail end of the noon recess. Tony undoubtedly left shortly before that."

"No wonder the note came today," Ellen said, leaning across the table.

"What do you mean?" Pat asked.

"Kitty's mail delivery is between twelve and one," Ellen replied. "Even if she wrote the letter after she tossed Dr. Gaylani out, she must not have gotten it down to the box in time for Wednesday's pickup."

Pat let the comment pass. She was sure Ellen's reasoning was flawed, but rather than argue the point, she decided to shift the focus back to Tom and let him prove her friend wrong.

"Do you remember opening the mail before the Gaylanis came over?" Pat asked.

Tom shook his head. "Come to think of it, I can't recall opening any mail, either last Wednesday or any day since Katherine's death. For all I know, it's still in the box."

"That might be worth checking," Pat said, confident her deductions were correct. "For now, let's get back to Kitty. While she lectured you, did your wife indicate anything about the contents of the general's papers?"

"Never gave her a chance," Tom replied, his voice firm. "Once Katherine let loose, I went upstairs to shower and change. By the time I was dressed, the Gaylanis were ringing the doorbell. After that, the wine tasting began, and of course, the rest you know."

"But we don't," Pat said. "Ellie and I weren't there."

Yet another time, Tom Kempner had micro-managed the conversation. Like water trickling through a clogged pipe, the information he gave out was limited.

Pat wanted an accounting of Kitty Kempner's movements. That would allow her to check for contradictions in Tom's story and also observe his behavior. Many incongruities existed, but high on her list was Tom's claim of drunkenness.

According to him, on the fatal night, he'd come home inebriated. Fine. But if he'd been drunk then, how could he act sober now? He'd consumed several toddies over the last couple of hours. And what about the eye-openers? Just before he'd handed out dog bones and made his one-of-a-kind toddies, hadn't she seen a half-full pitcher of Bloody Marys on the counter? Didn't the two empty glasses reveal that he and Tony Gaylani had poured more than one drink? Yet, while showing no ill effects from today's bout of drinking, he'd gotten stiff during a similar time frame on the afternoon of his wife's death. Had he been inhaling drinks then and sipping them now… or had he used his liquor breath as an excuse to feign intoxication?

She concluded the obvious. When his wife had lambasted him, Tom Kempner hadn't headed for the shower to get sober. Similarly, when she'd asked pointed questions, he hadn't glossed over the details to spare Ellen and her from an uncomfortable description. No. In each instance, he'd tried to avoid a confrontation. But why? Even if he didn't want to debate the issues with Kitty, why purposely antagonize the woman he loved? Mother of God, her feelings mattered. They certainly took precedence over a wine tasting.

"Look," Tom said, hands on hips, "I haven't skipped over the facts. All that's left are the gory details. Is that what you're after?"

"Hardly," Pat answered, "but try this scenario: While going through the general's memoirs, Kitty spotted something she didn't want Tony to see. Calling Ellie was a dead end. We were Christmas shopping and her message recorder was on the blink. That left you, Tom. But guess who was either polishing a speech for the judge or polishing off drinks with…" She glared, purposely trying to goad him. "Sorry. Let's leave it that you made yourself unavailable."

"Guilty as charged," he replied, walking to the sink and pouring the pitcher of Bloody Marys down the drain. "I'd have done things differently had I known the consequences."

"Yeah, right," she sneered. "A hero like you would have brought home a bouquet of daisies."

He marched back and faced her. "No, Miss Shaver. I would have done much more."

Pat got up and made herself stand tall. "Okay, Superman, give me a for instance."

He leaned in. "For openers, I wouldn't have committed Katherine to an evening with the jerk who'd just made her day miserable."

Ellen rose and, like a referee separating tired boxers, stepped in front of Tom. "Hindsight's twenty/twenty. We're here to move forward, not to discuss what could have been."

Pat stared out one of the windows. Her attempts to provoke Tom had gone for naught. She'd pissed him off, but he'd stayed in control, a lawyer's discipline. Right now, he had no intention of telling them his innermost thoughts.

"Ellie's right. Let's move forward," Pat suggested. "The most productive thing we can do is take a look at General Cunningham's memoirs."

"My wife's office is upstairs," Tom said, walking toward a back hallway. "Once she told Dr. Gaylani to leave, she looked over the documents, then lugged them into the elevator."

Pat turned toward Ellen. "Would you mind getting the papers from Kitty's saddlebags? In the meantime, Tom and I will start going through the stuff in Kitty's office."

Dr. Tony Gaylani scanned the faces around the Sextons' dining room table. He hated mixed company gatherings. Either he had to endure humdrum jokes or listen to old fogies talk about their grandchildren and medical problems.

"Darling," he said, turning his head, "this party's a snooze."

"Don't blame me," Joanna replied, reaching her hand under the tablecloth and rubbing his inner thigh. "Refresh my memory, but don't we both know a gentleman who was worried about getting here on time?"

"I've met the aforementioned gentleman." He looked into his wife's eyes and saw light reflecting from the candles. "I assure you the man didn't mean a word he said."

"What a pity," she said, retracting her hand. "The aforementioned gentleman's wife isn't horny anymore."

Patricia Shaver thumbed through several documents, but saw nothing of interest. She was looking over one of General Cunningham's diaries when Ellen rushed into the attic office.

"They're gone. I put the papers back. Now they're gone."

"What?" Tom said. "How can that be?"

"There's a simple explanation," Pat replied, "if there's a window next to the tack room door."

"What diff—" Ellen grimaced. "Of course. While I pulled out the documents, he stood outside and watched."

"Possibly," Pat said, setting aside a batch of the general's letters. "Did you look over the stuff before Gaylani came in?"

"There were several sheets of paper," Ellen replied. "I only got a glimpse at the top one. It was a memo from General Cunningham to David Ben-Gurion. It listed radical Arabs known to be infiltrating Palestine. I can't be certain, but since you mentioned Rashid Ali el-Gaylani, I think his name was on the roster."

"No wonder the bastard had a sudden interest in the general's papers," Tom said. "Dr. Gaylani was covering his backside."

Pat closed a diary and looked up. "But why would a prominent surgeon go to such extremes? His father has been dead for years, and it's not like Kitty worked for *The Enquirer*. When Dr. Gaylani was just getting started… maybe. Today, he's established. He could easily weather… Unless…?"

Tom eyed her. "Unless what?"

"Maybe nothing," Pat replied. "On the other hand, how much does anyone really know about Dr. R. Anthony and Joanna Myerson Gaylani?"

Ellie's eyes widened. "Patricia. I hate it when you get that look."

"Don't get me wrong," Pat went on. "I'm not accusing anyone. But why don't we leave General Cunningham's papers for another day? Right now, I want to pool our knowledge. We need a profile of Tom's next-door neighbors."

They took the elevator downstairs. In the kitchen, they walked past the slumbering Labs, stepped over the dog gate, and continued into the living room.

Tom stood by the hearth. When he reached down and put a log on the fire, hot embers fell through the andiron.

"Why don't you begin," he said, nodding toward Ellen. "Katherine and I had no secrets, but I never asked her about Joanna's past."

Ellen took a deep breath.

"Well, let's see…"

CHAPTER EIGHTEEN

Patricia Shaver and Tom Kempner sat on the sofa. They both watched Ellen pace back and forth in front of the hearth. Each was anxious to hear the details of Joanna Myerson's life.

With the fire flickering behind her, Ellen eyed Tom. "According to your wife, Kitty and Joanna got acquainted by chance. Talk about the luck of the draw. In the mid-fifties, they happened to sit next to each other at a freshman assembly in the New Trier High School auditorium. Neither knew any of the other students. Each was an alien who'd recently come to live with relatives in the posh suburbs on Chicago's North Shore.

"Once the welcoming speech ended, the two looked at each other. Kitty wore a skirt and blouse, Joanna a denim shirt and jeans. They were at odds in dress, but the boring orientation had sparked a need to commiserate."

Ellen rested her arm on the mantel, telling them that Kitty's and Joanna's religious, social, and ideological backgrounds couldn't have been more different; but their accents—a feature which distinguished them as foreigners—was a uniting force that drew them together. They'd quickly established a dialogue. Once Kitty had shared her life story, Joanna began a narrative that proved fate had joined kindred spirits.

Ellen stared at the oil painting that hung above the mantel, then continued, saying that Joanna was born in a two-room house in Palestine. World War II was underway, but for Jewish families like the

Myersons, the conflict seemed distant. Even a few years after the peace, when Joanna's rocky playground became part of the Palestinian territory ceded to form the new State of Israel, the Myersons' detachment from war and politics remained intact.

That insulation ended abruptly in 1956. During the early days of the Sinai Campaign, Joanna's mother and father became civilian casualties in the first Arab-Israeli War.

"Joanna's uncle took charge after her parents were killed," Ellen said, sitting down on the sofa. "He was a wealthy industrialist living in suburban Chicago and a staunch supporter of Israel. He also believed in the Zionist cause, but thought a battlefield was no place for an orphaned teenager. After he buried Joanna's parents, the uncle brought his niece to America."

"All very fascinating," Pat replied, faking a yawn, "but can we move on? Why not tell us how Joanna met Dr. Tony Gaylani."

"Be patient, my dear," Ellen advised. "I'll get there after I set the stage."

"Don't take this the wrong way, but—"

"But nothing, Patricia. Just listen."

Pat stared straight ahead, admonished by Ellen's uncharacteristic outburst. Was her friend expressing frustration over Kitty Kempner's death, or something else?

"As I was saying," Ellen went on, clearing her throat, "whether a Yiddish twang or the King's English, Joanna and Kitty's accents turned out to be icebreakers. The two became very popular, but each greeted their notoriety from different ends of the study hall. Kitty dug into the books. Joanna didn't. Kitty got straight A's. Joanna made the Honor Roll, a remarkable feat considering she was out on a date almost every night."

Pat detected a change when Ellen got up. Her friend seemed tense, and her monotone was gone. Rather than continue to be a casual listener, Pat paid careful attention, tuning in mid-sentence to Ellen's more impassioned words.

"…considering Joanna's behavior, it's startling she didn't let down her guard. Throughout high school and the following decades, her facade never cracked. Not once did her face show signs of the hatred she felt. Nobody, not even Kitty, had any idea that Joanna's conduct was part of a long-range plan to build a network of political alliances."

Ellen let her words sink in. Then she focused on Tom. "Joanna was a masterpiece of deception. Take her teenage and college years. By playing the field and dating Jewish boys from influential families, she hoped to find a few young men who someday would be champions of democracy and captains of industry. These she would recruit as co-conspirators in her struggle to keep Israel strong, independent, and non-aligned with its Arab neighbors."

Pat listened and was dumbfounded. Had Joanna been a political activist back in her high school days? Had the fun-loving teenager from Hebron embraced the views of Israeli isolationists even before she was old enough to vote? Ellen had just said that the uncle who'd brought Joanna to America had sympathized with the Zionist cause. Had this man brainwashed an impressionable teenage girl?

Pat stared at the ceiling, trying to reconcile Ellen's words with Joanna's current position as a sixty-something-year-old member of the UJC (United Jewish Congress). But the two personas didn't match. Nobody could have changed that much.

She glanced at Tom, wondering whether he was confused. Their host sat ramrod straight on the sofa, his eyes alive with puzzlement. Apparently, he had some doubts too.

Ellen continued, seemingly oblivious to their distress, but when she skipped several decades in Joanna's life, Pat realized that Ellen had done it on purpose. Her friend's objective was simple. She was picking out specific anecdotes to serve notice that Joanna Myerson Gaylani wasn't to be taken lightly.

"Kitty, Joanna, and I got together several months ago." Ellen stood in front of the fireplace, her hands by her side. "After a few too many glasses of wine, Joanna asked if we knew why oil prices were so high. When we claimed ignorance, she filled us in, saying it was a surtax the Arabs had levied to fund a project to exterminate

Israeli Jews... especially the ones who favored a fence along the Palestinian border.

"Her words hit us like a sledgehammer," Ellen said. "Joanna hadn't changed. She was still the same high school and college student who'd joined a group of Zionists promoting isolationism. Joanna was on the board of the United Jewish Congress, but in name only."

"Stop peddling insanity," Tom said, shaking his head. "Jesus, Ellen. Who's kidding who? Joanna isn't a Zionist. She likes fast dancing and hard whiskey."

"You call her fun-loving; I say she's a gifted hustler," Ellen replied, her face impassive. "The UJC promotes moderation. The woman who makes a habit of massaging male egos hates Arabs. Joanna was once a teenager who watched her parents get slaughtered."

"Slaughtered?" Tom said, standing up. "They were casualties of war. But even if she had scars, they got buried years ago."

"Her wounds may look healed, but they still fester," Ellen argued. "She's like Hitler. Charismatic when it suits her... but calculating and cold-blooded to the core."

"Get realistic, woman," Tom bellowed. "We're talking about Gaylani's wife."

"Smart conspirators hide their agendas. Why couldn't she? Haven't you wondered why Joanna, Kitty, and I were the only Barrington Hunt Club ladies to ever ride western?"

"Ride western?" Tom asked, obviously startled. "What in God's name does horse gear have to do with anything?"

"Answer the question," Ellen persisted.

Tom's face reddened. "Bareback, English, or western, it never crossed my mind... but my guess is, they copied you. Before you introduced the total equestrian experience, Katherine and Joanna thought shoveling horse manure was a job for stable boys."

"Sarcasm doesn't become you, Mr. Kempner." Ellen gave Tom a long look. "We rode western as a way to Americanize the English fox hunting tradition."

Pat didn't say anything, but she knew the reason went deeper. The three women had sought to make a statement by separating themselves from the snootiest Hunt Club riders.

Ellen had told her that Kitty had instigated the change. Tom's wife believed that fox hunters should play down their elitist reputation. One way to make the sport more accessible was to encourage all types of riders to join in.

To be sure, all three donned their red blazers and felt hard hats. But on occasion, especially on nippy morning rides, they'd wear western-style leather vests under their blazers and pull on hand-tooled cowboy boots over their jodhpurs. And that wasn't all. Ellen had taken their single-mindedness a step further. To silently mock the prim and proper, she always wore Old Spice for Men whenever she hit the trails.

"I recall Katherine telling me some of the biddies made fun of your lassos and cowboy boots," Tom said, rolling his eyes. "But western or not, I still don't get the point."

"Then listen," Ellen ordered. "One day after a morning ride, some of the Hunt Club matrons joined our table for a long wet lunch. When they left, Joanna asked Kitty and me to wait. Without provocation, your neighbor let loose with some locker room words: 'Those gentile bitches are phonies, but that's not what really pisses me off. How can anyone contaminate a good English saddle by putting it on the back of a f...in' Arab horse?'"

Tom's mouth fell open.

"She wasn't joking?"

Ellen shook her head.

"I'm not defending Joanna," he said, "but after a few pops, she's been known to let her hair down."

"Not this time." Arms crossed, Ellen stared straight ahead. "The booze may have loosened her lips, but it didn't put the venom in the words."

"Any chance it was just an unfortunate slip?" Pat asked.

"Well put," Tom said. "There's no way Joanna's a bigot... or a militant promoting hatred."

"I'm not out to lynch Joanna Gaylani," Ellen answered, "but I know what I heard."

Ellen went on, saying that she and Kitty were stunned into silence. Neither spoke of the incident, but less than a month later, when Joanna blurted out the same message in a similar setting, they knew Joanna Myerson Gaylani was a zealot.

"Did I hear you correctly?" Pat asked. "Joanna made another unprovoked comment?"

Ellen nodded. "The entire incident might have been forgotten had we not been in Galena for the annual Midwest ladies fox hunt. The host club invited some breeders, among them a Saudi who was willing to let people test-ride a string of horses his stud farm was selling."

Ellen sat back down on the sofa, then looked up at the oil painting above the mantel—a portrait of Kitty Kempner. "The fireworks began after the first day. The group was well into the cocktail hour when Joanna got wind of the offer. As her face glowed red, she spoke in a loud voice. 'Arabs are like Indians—the only good ones are dead ones.'"

Pat and Tom looked at each other.

Ellen's face remained impassive. "When no apology came, everyone cleared out. With the place a ghost town, Joanna stared at Kitty and me and said, 'Sorry I made you two uncomfortable, but I meant every word.'"

"Tough talk," Pat said. "How did you respond?"

"Never got a chance," Ellen replied. "That was Joanna's opening volley. After that, she gulped down her drink and began the story of the real circumstances that brought her to America and her uncle's doorstep."

Dr. R. Anthony Gaylani stood in the reading alcove and looked down at his neighbor's house. Minutes ago, he and Joanna had arrived back home, but when he'd motored between the snow banks lining his driveway, Tony hadn't been able to see if Tom Kempner still had visitors. From a higher vantage point, he got two pieces of bad news. Ellen Eichler's pickup was parked in the turnaround, and the stable lights had been turned back on.

Joanna Gaylani sat under the covers and watched her husband. Suddenly her body began to quiver ever so slightly. The prelude to another bout with her conscience had started. First, involuntary muscle spasms; then a dull ache in the pit of her stomach.

"Tony, dear," Joanna purred, fighting to get hold of her thoughts. "Are you coming to bed?"

"In a minute, sweetie."

"Remember when I offered to unlace your mukluks?" she asked, forcing a giggle.

"You made that service available just before we went to the Sextons' party."

"The offer is still on the table," she said. "But before we do anything, I need your help."

"What's the problem?"

She held up the controls for the electric blanket. "It's on full-tilt."

"Are you uncomfortable?"

Joanna sat up. "I'm certainly overheating… and there's nobody here to take off my nightgown."

Her words were foolish and innocent, yet death—his death and the death of Jewish delegates—was only a few days away.

Patricia Shaver and her host, Tom Kempner, sat on the edge of the sofa. Ellen rose, walked to the hearth, and continued her story.

"All along, Kitty and I thought Joanna's parents had died during an Arab bombing raid. As we sat in the empty barroom, Joanna set the record straight."

Ellen recreated a grim picture, telling them that a budding teenager had watched in horror as Arab soldiers beat her father, then took turns raping her mother. Once the Muslim infantrymen had satisfied their lust, they stood over their fallen victims and used their rifle butts to smash her parents' kneecaps.

Moments later, an Arab major entered the house and sent his men outside. As Joanna's mother and father lay moaning in pain, the officer put his arm on Joanna's shoulder, restraining her when she tried to kneel down and give them comfort.

While she shook with fear and looked up teary eyed, he ripped open the top of her dress. Then he grinned, took out his pistol, and blew gaping holes in her parent's stomachs. The major wanted to be sure they convulsed in a slow agonizing death. He also wanted them to live long enough to witness the violation that would take their teenage daughter's virginity.

Ellen lowered her eyes. "Forgive my language. Those atrocities turned an innocent girl into a hardened revenge-seeker. A zealot."

Tom shook his head. "My God, to think Katherine knew and never breathed a word."

"Joanna pledged us to secrecy," Ellen said. "On that and her activities in America as well."

"There's more?" Tom asked.

Ellen nodded. "Once Joanna got started, she didn't hold back."

Ellen finished by describing how Joanna's life had become dual purposed. She put on a front in public to showcase her fun-loving passions. But hidden away was an angry activist. During her college years and thereafter, Joanna had quietly traveled around the country to solicit rich iconoclastic Jews. Her trips raised substantial sums and funded the campaigns for Knesset members who took a hard line with their Arab neighbors.

"So there's no misunderstanding," Pat said, brushing back a loose strand of hair, "you're saying Joanna was a Zionist fundraiser before she became a moderate?"

Ellen nodded, then began a mini-narrative, explaining that once

Joanna married Dr. Tony Gaylani and joined the UJC, she renounced her earlier philosophy. According to Ellen, Joanna swore them to secrecy, not to keep her prejudices under wraps, but rather to insure her past associations wouldn't hurt her status within the United Jewish Congress. While Joanna admitted she still couldn't look an Arab in the eye and not see someone who'd raped and plundered, her thinking had changed. She now saw herself as a stateswoman—a person who realized a peaceful settlement with the Arabs was in the best interest of all Israelis.

Pat eyed Ellen with a wary look. "The Red Sea parted and a voice told Joanna to marry the son of an Iraqi nationalist, join the UJC, and let bygones be bygones."

"Not funny," Ellen said, sitting down, "but for once we agree. Being intimate with an Arab man would be impossible."

Tom tilted his head. "Maybe not. This world breeds strange bedfellows. What if Joanna doesn't have a clue? What if she fell in love and actually bought into Tony's act?"

"I doubt it, counselor," Ellen said.

"Why not?" Tom asked. "Tony and I belong to the same golf club. The board welcomed me, but make no mistake: a token Jew is one thing, but Arabs are horses of a different color."

Ellen eyed Tom. "I get your point, but…"

"What's the problem, Mrs. Eichler? The whole town thinks he's Italian. Why couldn't he have duped his wife? Look at me. I knew Joanna had designer labels in her closet. Now I know she's got skeletons."

"Let's say I buy in," Ellen replied, straight-faced. "What's to be gained by misleading her?"

Pat stood. "As long we're talking about low probability events, I'll do you one better. What if the doctor's feelings are also genuine? Tony's father hated Jews, and Tony knew that a Jew-hating Arab isn't supposed to fall in love with an Arab-hating Jew. But what if it happened?"

Tom chuckled sarcastically. "Love conquers all. Instead of negotiating our differences, we'll root out worldwide prejudice with in-breeding."

Ellen glared. "Don't give up your day job. Your jokes stink."

"Sorry, Mrs. Eichler, did I offend your delicate sense of—"

"Cool it, Tommy," Ellen snapped. "Patricia, were you serious or, like Tom, yukking it up?"

Pat didn't answer. She was troubled by the way the conversation had gone. A reporter's instinct told her that Tony and Joanna Gaylani's marriage was no accident. They might have pretended otherwise, but each had known of the other's background. While she couldn't fathom what had inspired them to marry, it distressed her that Tom and Ellen didn't seem to have doubts.

Maybe the evidence wasn't ironclad, but weren't there enough smoking guns to make reasonable people suspicious of the Gaylanis? Didn't the doctor's actions prove he was bent on protecting himself from more than the embarrassment of a checkered past? Didn't the delayed transit of Kitty's note suggest that before landing in Ellen's mailbox, it had been looked over by another pair of eyes? Didn't Tony kill Tom's wife? Didn't Joanna suspect her husband, but not rat him out?

Pat kept her head down. While she had a good idea who was involved in Katherine Kempner's death, her scenario left questions unanswered.

What prize warranted murder? What motivated Tony and Joanna to operate with hidden agendas? What rationale drove people to such extremes? And another thing. Since Tom and Ellen didn't want to draw logical inferences from circumstantial evidence, how the devil was she going to find hard proof to convince them?

Pat looked at her friend. "We're all looking for answers. I wasn't being flip. Like you, I'm just trying to figure out why the Gaylanis ever got together."

"One thing's certain," Ellen conceded. "Theirs was no Romeo and Juliet romance."

"Meaning what?" Pat asked.

"Meaning, I hate it when things don't add up. I can understand a Roman Catholic doctor falling for a Jewish woman, but now with these new twists and the other thing."

Pat leaned forward. "What other thing, Ellie?"

"Tony and Joanna didn't bump into each other on a street corner. His first wife, Barbara Stein, introduced them."

"How convenient," Tom said. "Was Barbara Jewish too?"

Ellen didn't have to answer. She just stared at the fire, her face paling to ghost white.

"Well, well," Tom continued. "I knew there was another Mrs. Gaylani, but this... So much for the theory of Jew and Arab haters finding true love. Two in a row is a bit much."

Pat focused on Ellen. "Are you sure about your facts?"

"Everything I know came out of Kitty's mouth."

"Nobody knew Joanna better than Katherine," Tom said. "The floor is yours, Mrs. Eichler. Tell us what you know."

Ellen began by highlighting Joanna's academic achievements at Columbia—an undergraduate degree with honors, a Ph.D. in post-World War II political science, and a career as a tenured professor teaching courses in modern Middle Eastern history.

"Cut the background material," Pat suggested. "Tell us how Dr. Gaylani keeps meeting Jewish women."

Ellen eyed her two listeners, saying that Joanna had first run into Dr. Tony Gaylani when his wife, Barbara, brought him to a late-eighties Israeli rally. Joanna had expected to see her Jewish colleague, but had been surprised when Barbara's Italian and Roman Catholic husband tagged along. Most gentiles weren't interested or sympathetic to the views of Israeli hard-liners.

"Dr. Gaylani had another surprise for Joanna," Ellen went on. "A few weeks after his wife's unexpected death, he asked Joanna out on a date."

"Unexpected death?" Tom questioned. "What the devil does that mean?"

"You tell me," Ellen snapped. "According to Kitty, Barbara Stein was healthy one day and gone the next. Does that qualify as unexpected?"

"There I go again, doubting the wrong person." Tom looked up sheepishly. "Tony told me his first wife got sick. That's a far cry from keeling over."

"How'd she die?" Pat asked.

"It was a brain…" Ellen's face turned ashen. "Is a cerebral infarction and a brain clot the same thing?"

Tom nodded. "Why do you ask?"

"Kitty used that terminology to describe Barbara Stein's seizure. Back then, it didn't seem important."

Pat watched Ellen and Tom bow their heads.

"What am I missing? Why is it material now?"

"My wife died from a cerebral infarction," Tom answered.

"Oh," Pat said, closing her eyes. "I didn't know. I'm sorry."

"Don't be. Until now, it was just a medical term." He looked at the ceiling. "Am I crazy, or are these coincidences too coincidental?"

"You're not crazy," Pat replied. "Gaylani must have pursued Joanna because of her background, not in spite of it."

Ellen gasped. "That means Joanna might be in danger too."

Pat said nothing. She didn't believe Tony would hurt his wife, but the identical nature of Kitty Kempner and Barbara Stein-Gaylani's deaths made her skin crawl. It also reinforced a gut feel about Tony and Joanna Gaylani's involvements. But to prove the connection, she needed more data.

"Let's be smart," Pat said. "Before we go off halfcocked, why not hear the rest of the courtship story. I have a feeling we'll learn something important."

Ellen agreed, giving them an abbreviated rendition of Joanna's seduction, saying that following a ninety-day-plus whirlwind courtship, Joanna Myerson—dazzled, happy, and well over forty—said yes.

"Her first trip to the altar?" Pat asked.

Ellen nodded. "The service was held in Chicago at Temple Emanuel. Just before their marriage, Dr. Tony Gaylani had resigned as

Chief of Orthopedic Surgery at Columbia Medical Center to join the staff at Good Shepherd."

Pat frowned. "Doesn't that strike you as an odd career path?"

"Odd?" Tom questioned. "It's a comedown. I knew he'd left a good job, but I never realized he went from top orthopod to just another doctor on the staff of a community hospital."

"I'm bothered by something else," Pat said. "Why would a devout Catholic agree to a synagogue wedding?"

"Who said anything about devout?" Tom asked. "The bastard prayed on Sundays, but only that he'd hole some long putts."

"Point taken," Pat said. "That leaves us with a non-practicing Catholic-Arab who pulls up stakes, takes a less prestigious job, marries another Jewess, then moves... By the way, when did they move next door?"

"That was Katherine's doing," Tom answered. "She insisted we give the lovebirds a five-acre parcel as a wedding present. They wanted to build their dream house, and Joanna and Katherine were like sisters. I wasn't anxious to have a close neighbor, but I owed Tony my life. Back then, giving up some privacy seemed like a small price to pay."

"Makes sense," Pat said. "Did you and Kitty attend the wedding?"

"Attend?" he looked at her, laughing. "Hell, we were two thirds of the show. I was the audience, Joanna's uncle stood up for Tony, and Katherine was her maid of honor."

Pat stared at the flickering flames. Who was kidding whom? For such an important event, two noteworthy people could only field a cast of three? Shouldn't Tony and Joanna have lit up the Big Apple and got married amongst their friends?

"I'm puzzled. If Tony popped the question at the last minute, how'd they manage Temple Emanuel?"

"Joanna's uncle had influence," Tom answered.

"But Tony barely knew Joanna's uncle. Why'd he allow a stranger to stand up for him?"

"Logistics," Tom replied, his face flushed red. "Like I said, the wedding was in Chicago."

"So the doc spent years in New York, but never made any friends who would come to Chicago?"

"What do you want from me?" Tom asked, losing patience. "Her uncle was his best man, period. If that slant doesn't work, go next door and ask my buddy, Gaylani."

"No big deal," Pat said, "but there is one other thing. Was the reception as small as the wedding?"

"Smaller," Tom said. "The five of us had dinner at the Pump Room, but the uncle left before coffee."

Ellen yawned. "It's getting late. Maybe we should go too."

"Not yet," Tom said. "Pat wanted to frame some questions to better understand the Gaylanis' behavior. We've made some progress, but are at best, halfway home."

"How do you figure?" Pat asked, eying Tom. "We've exhausted that subject. Ellie told us what she knows about Joanna, and neither of us knows anything about Dr. Tony Gaylani. All that's left is the wine tasting… and again, Ellie and I weren't there the night your wife died."

"Very true," Tom said, his face determined, "but Katherine wrote a note out of genuine fear. If there's a bigger picture, I intend to explore it."

Pat pursed her lips. What a strange development. Suddenly, the lawyer who had trouble deciphering circumstantial evidence wanted to keep talking to the investigative reporter who kept shoving it in his face.

For a second, she thought about unloading the truth on him… but just for a second. Why tell a grieving husband that Kitty's death was only a small part of a bigger picture? Why say that the real question wasn't who killed her, but why the wife of the murderer sat back and watched it go down? While Tom and Ellen worried for Joanna's safety, she wondered why Joanna not only stayed with a man she had to hate, but stayed silent too.

Tom turned and caught her staring. When she looked into the sad eyes of a man who'd just buried his lover, friend, and spouse, she no longer saw a tough Mafia lawyer. Still, her suspicions persisted. Why did a man who'd either avoided full answers or completely dodged her probes want to give her another chance to ask more questions?

"You're the host," Pat said. "I can't speak for Ellie, but as long as you're agreeable, let's keep talking."

Joanna Gaylani's invitation hadn't worked. Instead of turning down the electric blanket, her husband walked back to the reading alcove, sat in the rocker, and picked up one of his medical journals.

Her curiosity aroused, she slipped out of bed and sneaked over. Before Tony could react, she faced him and straddled the rocker. As his eyes widened, she leaned forward and let the straps of her negligee slide off her shoulders. Joanna hated the man, but knew she had to keep him off balance and happy.

A half hour later, in bed, flushed and naked, she took a deep breath.

"My goodness, doctor," Joanna gasped, snuggling next to him. "Either my foreplay has improved, or that article on cardiac exercise got you going."

"My darling, you were wonderful."

"Then why are you leaving me?"

Joanna pouted, but was delighted when he tossed the covers aside and got up. Under normal circumstances, she would have tried to rouse him again, but at this moment, more important considerations preempted a repeat performance. If Tony had something on his mind, she would feign sleep, wait for him to leave the bedroom, then keep track of his next move.

"Patience," he advised, "be back in a little bit."

"But I need you now," she cried out, sounding distressed. "I promise to be good. In fact, if you bring your doctor books back to bed, I'll turn the pages."

When Tony kept walking through the open bedroom door, she sat up.

"Darling," Joanna cooed, "try not to stay up too late. And, dear, if you hear Santa, don't forget to put out some cookies and a glass of milk."

CHAPTER NINETEEN

Patricia and Ellen were alone in Tom Kempner's kitchen. Minutes ago, their host had pressed them to take a breather, then get together in the living room and resume their deliberation. Pat welcomed the break, but she held her enthusiasm in check. Tom had insisted that the hard questions be asked and answered, but she suspected he was motivated by other considerations.

Tom appeared, standing behind the doggie gate, peering into the kitchen.

"I'll toss a log on the fire, then we'll have at it."

The moment he left, Ellen hit the brew button on the coffee maker.

"This is nuts. Another round of *what ifs* won't solve anything."

"Maybe not," Pat countered, "but I want a parting shot at Mr. Kempner. The more he talks, the more I learn."

"You're beginning to sound like a prosecutor," Ellen replied, grabbing mugs from the cupboard. "You can't think he's involved?"

"Not directly, but he knows a lot more than he's letting on."

She left Ellen and went into the living room. Once seated on the curved sectional sofa, Pat watched Tom stoke the fire.

"Looks like you've got the knack."

He looked up. "Like trial work, practice makes perfect."

"Really?" she said, leaning back on a cushion. "I thought good litigators had a special gene."

Tom didn't comment, but when Ellen set three steaming mugs

on the coffee table, he stowed the poker and went to the liquor cart.

"Can I interest anyone in a brandy?"

"Why not?" Pat said. "Maybe it will sharpen my mind."

He reached for two crystal glasses, then poured generous drinks from a bottle of hundred-year-old Napoleon cognac.

"You be the judge," he said, handing her a snifter.

Ellen raised her coffee mug. "Shall we get on with it?"

"That's why we're here," Tom replied. "If it bothers you, Mrs. Eichler..."

"Not in the least, as long as we can move beyond cognac."

"Fine," Tom snapped, sitting near the corner of the curved sectional. "Let's get back to business."

For a long few seconds, no one moved or said a word. Pat waited too, but to get things moving, she stood up.

"Let's start by profiling Dr. Tony Gaylani," Pat said, looking at Tom. "Aside from his Iraqi heritage and the allegations your wife made, is there anything in his background that strikes you as suspicious?"

Tom shook his head. "Fact is, when it comes to Gaylani, my knowledge is sketchy at best."

"He's your son's godfather," Ellen said, leaning forward. "Aren't guardians and parents well acquainted?"

"Trevor was a teenager when Joanna and Tony signed the papers. Trust me, it was a symbolic gesture." Snifter in hand, he got up and moved to the hearth. "Joanna's gynecologist delivered the bad news. A routine checkup revealed some problems. After the hysterectomy, Joanna got depressed and asked Katherine if she could be Trevor's second mother. When my wife said yes, I went along too."

Pat picked up her brandy. "You and Tony played golf on weekends. Some of your conversations must have touched on subjects other than sports."

"The doc is a closed-mouthed guy," Tom answered. "We're neighbors, but when it comes to his life, I'm out of the loop. Most of what I know came from the Army nurses."

Pat wasn't shocked to discover that Tony had a face, but no history. A good spy blended in. Unless Dr. Gaylani made a mistake, they'd never amass anything beyond a superficial biography.

"I'm curious about one thing. From Vietnam till their wedding, had your paths ever crossed?"

Tom put his snifter on the mantel and shook his head. "No."

"Then yours was an interesting reunion. He had to be surprised to see you again."

"Meaning what?"

"Meaning, he patched you up," Pat replied, staring at him. "He did remember, didn't he?"

"Hell, no," Tom answered, his voice rising. "Army surgeons dealt with bodies, not faces."

"But once you broke the news… You did tell the man?"

He gave her a misbehaved smile. "At the reception, I incorporated it into my toast."

"And?"

Tom chuckled. "As we clicked glasses, Dr. Gaylani's face looked like molded steel. Later, during a private moment, he made it clear that Nam was a closed chapter in his life."

"Is that a fact," Pat said. "I'm a little surprised."

"Don't be," Ellen injected. "We've got friends who served in Vietnam. To a man, no one wants to talk about the experience."

"Maybe for combat troops, but Tony was a doctor." She glanced at Ellen, then focused on Tom. "Wouldn't most medical men be proud of their accomplishments?"

"Most were," he answered, "but I gave the doc a reason to chill me out. During my toast, I dusted off his old nickname."

"No way," Pat said, arching an eyebrow. "You actually called him the Roman Allah?"

"More like a back-door compliment," Tom replied, sipping his brandy. "First, I praised his skill, then I said he even made wounded Jewish soldiers believe in Allah."

She couldn't believe her ears. Tom's story was becoming less probable by the second. But why was he using a fabricated tale to dispense critical information?

"Your reference to Allah must have gotten a rise."

Tom grinned. "If looks could kill... but I didn't care. From day one, the only thing I admired about the man was his doctoring. When he showed up with a Jewish fiancée on his arm, I decided to see if the old Nam prejudices were still alive."

"Wait a sec," Pat said. "Before all this wedding stuff, we were talking about a man trying to disguise his ethnicity. Now you're saying you suspected him of being a Jew-hater?"

"In Nam," Tom explained, "the Army nurses nicknamed everyone. Branding their superiors was as normal as eating. Most times it wasn't malicious, and had I not heard Tony curse the Star of David, his nickname wouldn't have aroused my curiosity."

Pat tensed. "The doc made inflammatory remarks in your presence?"

"Indirectly," Tom replied. "I was on crutches. As part of my therapy, I dragged my body down the hospital corridors. During one walk, I overheard him talking to another surgeon."

"And?"

Tom stared off, his eyes open, but not focused. "The two doctors roared after Gaylani suggested a change in Army regulations."

"What kind of change?" Pat asked.

"It was a sick joke," Tom answered, his face muscles hardening. "Dr. Gaylani wanted to make it mandatory for all Yids to open the top buttons on their fatigues."

Pat held up her hands. "What am I missing?"

"Many Jewish soldiers wore the Star of David around their necks. Like Gaylani said, it gave the Gooks something shiny to shoot at. From then on, I knew the nurse's scuttlebutt was true. The guy who saved my life was an Arab bigot."

"My God," Pat said, biting her lip, "what a horrible thing to discover."

"Hey. War is hell. Besides, I never expected him to be a neighbor. Anyway, back then, I remember being grateful I didn't wear any bull's-eyes."

Pat searched Tom's face. "I don't understand."

"Tony never knew I was Jewish. In fact, until Katherine's family boycotted our wedding, I didn't know I was Jewish."

Ellen stood up. "That's off base, Tommy. Your wife was the most tolerant—"

"Hold on, Mrs. Eichler. I pointed the finger at Katherine's family, not Katherine. She made me focus on my heritage and insisted I be proud of it."

Pat waited to see if Ellen had anything further to say. When her friend stayed mum, Pat leaned forward and eyed their host.

"Can we get back to Dr. Gaylani and his knowledge of your background?"

"There's not much to tell," he replied. "Introductions in a M.A.S.H. tent are one-sided. Until Tony got me stabilized, about all he could see was bloody tissue and smashed bones."

"What about afterward?" Pat asked. "Weren't you comatose for several days?"

"Sure didn't feel like chatting," he agreed. "I never saw Gaylani stop by, but my chart spoke volumes. Everything about me was on a clipboard hooked to my bedpost."

"How convenient," she said. "Back then, like now, you were an open book."

"Are we sparring, Miss Shaver?"

"If we are, it's because I'm surprised you never told your wife any of this."

"Katherine and Joanna were best friends," he said, staring at the carpet. "I thought he was a bigot, not a killer. Given my line of work, who was I to cast stones?"

"We're all human," she said. "Once they moved next door, it must have galled you."

"In the real world, prejudice makes unwanted house calls," Tom replied. "Don't forget, it was Katherine and Joanna who were inseparable. Tony and I played some golf, and as couples, we got together, but that only happened once or twice a month."

Pat was both frustrated and heartened by his detached attitude. On the one hand, she couldn't push him to get straight answers, but on the other, Tom didn't try to avoid her questions.

"Guess your motto is live and let live."

Tom nodded. "I've never trusted Dr. Gaylani, but over the years, we built a superficial but cordial relationship. Why throw the first stone? I defended Italians and he looked like one."

"Men like the doc have good memories," Pat said. "When you tweaked him at his wedding, you might have thrown the first stone."

Tom looked at her for a long second, his face showing fear. "My God, you might be right. Dr. Gaylani had to assume that General Alan Cunningham's papers would mention Rashid Ali el-Gaylani. If the bastard thought I'd told Katherine about the Nam nurses and my experiences with the Roman Allah… It's possible my comment all those years ago put him on guard."

Tom balled his hand into a fist, but Pat wasn't buying his guilt trip. She was more convinced than ever that his storytelling was a way to alter his strategy. As the discourse inched along, Tom Kempner kept steering the dialogue. Plain and simple, he was still being very careful. If she ever hoped to get inside his head, she'd have to craft questions that tested him and, at the same time, signaled her loyalty.

"Let me get things straight," Pat said. "You made reference to his nickname at their wedding, but until today, never called him the Roman Allah to his face?"

Tom nodded, then stared at the oil hanging over the mantel, a large painting of Katherine sitting on a western saddle aboard her favorite horse, Ascot. His wife wore a Stetson, her red hunting blazer, and cowboy boots

"Something about Katherine's death didn't sit well," he said. "Even before you mentioned the note, I had concerns."

"Can you elaborate?" Pat asked.

"Hard to put my finger on it," he replied, still staring at the oil painting. "That's why I'm so frustrated."

"Going over the last hours might help," Pat suggested. "Start with Tony's interest in your courtroom victory."

"My clients don't wear white hats," Tom said. "Most of our friends don't talk about the people I defend. Gaylani was different. He referred to me as the champion of those who dwell in the sewer."

"Did the doctor's comments bother you?"

Tom shook his head. "I'm thick-skinned. People either accept what I do or they don't."

"But you must have been surprised by Tony's apparent change of heart."

He nodded. "I'd won plenty of court cases before, but this was the first time he wanted to celebrate the occasion."

"So you went along?" Pat asked.

He glanced at his snifter. "I'd had a few drinks and, frankly, it felt good to be congratulated."

She looked at Ellen. Her friend hadn't said much, but her intent expression indicated she wasn't bored.

"What about your wife?" Pat asked, turning back to Tom. "You had to suspect she wouldn't want to drink wine with Dr. Gaylani."

"I figured she'd take it philosophically," he answered. "Remember, she knew Joanna would be there."

"Right," Pat agreed. "When did Tony start the tasting?"

"Immediately."

"Did everyone enjoy the wine?" Pat asked.

"It got a mixed review," Tom said. "Joanna and I thought it was too sweet. Gaylani sided with Katherine. They said, if anything, it had a slightly bitter aftertaste."

"Did Tony say it first or just agree with your wife?" Pat asked.

"He agreed with Katherine."

"Time out," Ellen said. "Exactly what are you suggesting?"

"Give me a second," Pat replied, waving off her friend and zeroing in on Tom. "Who watched him pour the wine?"

"No one. Dr. Gaylani was alone in the kitchen." Tom stood and glared at the fire. "I've heard lots of expert witnesses. They all say barbiturates leave a bitter taste."

"Stop pretending I'm not here," Ellen complained. "Did Dr. Gaylani give Kitty a lethal overdose?"

"Not lethal," Pat corrected, "just enough to knock her out."

She hoped her short answer would satisfy Ellen and keep her quiet. Right now, she wanted to grill Tom.

"When did your wife's condition really scare you?"

"Right after I went to Tony's car and got his bag. Once back inside, I noticed Katherine's chest wasn't moving and her lips were blue."

"Was that the case after she slid off the couch and passed out?"

"I can't be certain," he answered, "but just before Katherine collapsed, her eyes got glassy. If she hadn't been breathing, I'd have realized that too."

"When did Tony come on the scene?"

His face reddened. "In a flash. Joanna screamed and he was there."

"Is that when Tony started issuing orders?"

Tom nodded. "Yes. He sent Joanna to the kitchen to call 911."

"Why the kitchen?" Pat pointed at an antique phone on a nearby end table. "911 operators want you to describe the scene. Joanna should have stayed close to the patient."

"Maybe," Tom agreed, "but things were chaotic."

"Did you go after Tony's bag the moment Joanna went to the kitchen?" Pat asked.

"Yes."

"How long were you gone?"

"A minute, two at the most."

"Was Joanna in the living room when you came back inside?"

"No," he said, "she was still on the phone with the 911 operator."

"What happened next?"

"I dropped Gaylani's bag, then went to check in with Joanna."

"Whose idea was that?"

"Gaylani's," Tom answered. "The doc wanted to know when the paramedics were due."

"How long did you stay in the kitchen?"

"Less than sixty seconds."

"When did you first realize your wife wasn't breathing?"

"When I came back from the kitchen."

"Think hard," Pat said. "Is three minutes a reasonable estimate of the time it took you to get the medical bag, drop it off, go to the kitchen, and report back to Tony?"

Tom's face turned scarlet. "Is there something significant about three minutes?"

"I just want you to be specific," Pat demanded. "When you returned to Tony's side a second time, what was he doing?"

"Administering mouth to mouth resuscitation."

"Where were his hands?"

"One pinched Katherine's nostrils. I can't remember seeing the other one."

"How about your wife's neck?" Pat asked. "Was it visible?"

"I don't think so, but I can't be sure."

"Not a good answer, Mr. Kempner. Either it was or it wasn't."

His jaw tensed. "About that time, I heard the sirens and ran for the front door."

"What about Joanna?" Pat asked. "Was she still in the kitchen?"

He nodded. "Jesus, haven't you ever heard a 911 call? The operators talk slow and never let you off the phone."

"That's their job. Tell me what you did when the emergency vehicle arrived."

"I screamed into the kitchen," he replied. "I wanted to let Joanna know the paramedics had come. Then I went out to direct them."

"So they were still outside," Pat concluded. "How long before they got into the house?"

"Hell, I don't know," Tom said, balling his fists. "Long enough for Gaylani to finish the job, if that's what you mean."

"We're talking about motive and opportunity, Mr. Kempner."

"Okay, Ms. Shaver. The bastard had the opportunity. But motive? Why do something so… so insane? Tony isn't stupid. The doc wouldn't kill just to protect his reputation."

Pat looked for signs of rage, but saw none. He'd raised his voice plenty of times, but genuine anger had never materialized.

"What if this isn't about salvaging his good name? What if he's more than just a doctor of Arab descent? What if marrying Jewish women in die-hard Israeli coalitions is part of a well-thought-out plan? What if Tony is here because of his father's grand dream?"

Ellen sat up straight, incredulous. "You're saying he murdered Kitty? That he's a spy who killed to protect his identity? That he's engaged in some form of espionage?"

Pat watched Tom slump. She'd pushed him to the brink. It was time to tone down the rhetoric. Why inflict pain on someone who didn't fight back?

Tom Kempner was a man who had passionately loved his wife … a man who realized his neighbor had strangled the life from her body… a man who should have been raging for justice. But instead, he was a man who sat on his sofa, blankly looking at the living room carpet.

But why so passive? Why would a man who'd butted heads with the toughest legal minds… a man who could have picked up the phone and asked one of the Family to even the score… why would this man sit still and not seek revenge?

Pat was sure Tom hadn't taken part in his wife's murder. True, he'd failed to return Kitty's call and had accepted Tony's invitation. But those acts were lapses in good judgment, not unpardonable sins. Why, then, did Tom behave like his missteps had caused the tragedy?

She was short on answers, but was heartened nonetheless. Tom Kempner hadn't stopped her inquiry. That meant one of two things. Either he was a man with a guilty conscience, or one whose sense of guilt drove him to get others to probe where he was forbidden to tread.

"If Tony is a murderer," Ellen said, "we should call the police."

"Won't do any good," Pat replied. "Without hard evidence to prove he's the guy, we're stuck."

"Oh, he's the guy, all right," Tom said. "My only goal is to get him. If it's the last thing I do. Somehow. Some way. I'm going to bring Gaylani down."

Pat picked up her brandy snifter. "If things break right, that may be possible."

"Name it," he said. "Right now, I'll do anything."

"Earlier this evening, you talked about an admiral in the CIA who said the chiefs ran the Navy. How well do you know him?"

"Eric Weiss and I grew up together," Tom replied. "After high school we went our separate ways. He graduated from the Naval Academy, then served in Nam as an intelligence officer. When the Nguyen Cao Ky regime fell, he resumed his career as a CIA military advisor. Currently, he's deputy director."

"How interesting," Pat said, bringing the snifter to her lips. "The deputy director of the CIA must be privy to top secret material."

"I've never seen a published job description," Tom replied, "but rest assured, Eric Weiss knows what's going on. Take the other day, for instance. The admiral came to me on the QT. I think a senior official at the State Department sent him, but of course, they would never admit it. At Foggy Bottom, everyone wears white gloves. Messy situations are handled by nonexistent emissaries."

Pat put down her snifter, trying to remain calm. By her reckoning, Tom Kempner had just opened the door and was about to divulge something important.

"Let's say I agree that the stuffed shirts at State use nonexistent emissaries." She eyed their host. "Why enlist Eric Weiss? No offense, Tom, but he's the deputy director of the CIA. Hobnobbing with you could wreck the man's career."

"You've described our relationship all wrong," Tom said, eyeing her right back. "The admiral and I have history, but when we meet, we don't hobnob."

"Okay… then tell me what he said."

"His message was brief: 'Set up an untraceable call. I want to talk to Barbera.'"

Well, well, well… Tom Kempner had just become loose-lipped. But where was he going? The State Department and the CIA might be interested in rooting out spies, but what message could they possibly want to convey to the don of the Chicago Mafia?

"A mob/CIA collaboration brings one idea to mind," she said, staring at Tom. "Sounds like our goodwill ambassadors were predisposed to take another shot at Castro."

"Like I said, Miss Shaver, I wouldn't know. Men like Admiral Weiss don't justify their requests. It's like dealing with the IRS. You're told and you comply."

"Did he and Gary Barbera ever talk?" Pat asked.

"I have no idea. I just made the phone introduction."

"Is that a fact? Could you alter the procedure and try your hand at arranging a face-to-face with me?"

"I don't think so," Tom said, chuckling. "Given you're on opposing sides in the upcoming trial, it's probably not a good idea to put you and Mr. Barbera in the same room."

"Not him," she said. "I don't want to meet your boss."

"Then who?"

"The Navy guy," she replied. "Of course, calling the admiral would be delicate too. You'd have to handle him with kid gloves."

The scene was almost surreal. She was the star witness against Gary Barbera in a hearing scheduled for early next year. In all probability, Tom Kempner would be cross-examining her.

Yet, just now, he'd chosen to bring the crime boss squarely into the picture. But why betray the attorney/client privilege? Why imply that Gary Barbera's name belonged on a list of people involved in Katherine Kempner's murder? Jesus, Mary and Joseph, where was this going?

"Your smug look puzzles me. Is it easier to put together a meeting with Admiral Weiss than with your boss?"

"I'd rather steer clear of both men."

"Why? After your last courtroom performance, I'd say Gary has to be singing your praise. As his *consigliere*, you must be on a first-name basis."

Tom shook his head. "Miss Shaver, you're one of the few people in the world that ever dared to address Mr. Barbera by his first name."

"It wasn't my doing. As I recall, he insisted I call him Gary."

Pat let a faint smile crease her face. As the conversation continued to get more bizarre, she played along. To be sure, she and Mr. Gary Barbera were on a first-name basis, but it had nothing to do with their being close.

Last spring, after six stressful days, she'd confronted Gary Barbera and his stooge—a long-time family friend, Senator Scott Sheppard. She'd inadvertently discovered a file her father had prepared before his death. When she held the lists of payoff names over Barbera's head, she'd kept the initiative at their first get-together. But that had only been round one in a legal battle due to resume any day.

"If it's not too late, let's get your friend Admiral Weiss on the phone."

Tom's face turned steel hard. "Just so there's no confusion, the admiral and I are not friends."

"I stand corrected. What about phoning? Is it too late?"

"Eric Weiss is on duty 24/7. People engaged in espionage never sleep, and neither do the ones in charge of homeland security."

"Does that mean you'll dial him right now?"

Tom didn't answer. Instead he got up and started walking out of the living room. When he got to the foyer, he stopped. "What exactly do you want to know?"

"Why not make it a conference call?" Pat suggested. "I'm sure Ellie would like to listen."

"My office is private," he replied. "Depending on the nature of your demands, it might be better if I talk to him alone."

"Have it your way. As for specifics, I'm on a fishing expedition. At this point, I'd welcome anything on Dr. Tony Gaylani, his wife, and maybe even a short bio on Joanna's uncle."

Without agreeing to her request, Tom left them and headed to his office.

"Patricia," Ellen said, "did Tommy just implicate his boss?"

"I think so."

"If that's true, why did you encourage him to call Admiral Weiss? The CIA doesn't like guys who share their secrets. If the admiral finds out we're involved, Tommy will be in big trouble."

Pat shrugged her shoulders. Without question, Admiral Weiss would be upset if he found out about tonight's conversation. But Tom Kempner was smart enough to couch his questions without mentioning names.

Right now, she needed information on the Gaylanis. To make her case, she had to prove that Joanna might be as dangerous as her husband.

"Looks like we'll be hanging around. How about making another pot of coffee?"

Ellen started toward the kitchen. "You're not coming?"

"Not this minute. You grind the beans, I'll take the dogs for a walk."

She had hoped to accompany Tom into his private quarters, but if she couldn't be part of the conversation with Admiral Eric Weiss, she'd confirm one of her conjectures. Once she rounded up the four Labs, she'd go down to the end of Tom's driveway and look in his mailbox.

Dr. Tony Gaylani stood in his downstairs den and looked through the windows. His anxiety ratcheted up a notch when he saw the nosy reporter open Tom Kempner's front door. He suspected Shaver just meant to let the dogs out, but changed his mind when she came out of the house and started running down the driveway.

"Son of a bitch," he cursed, "now where the hell are you going?"

He worried that Joanna might still be awake, but decided to take the risk. Tony pulled on his boots, grabbed a coat, and headed for the side door. The bitch reporter had to be on a mission. Only a fool ventured out without a coat on a night of sub-zero wind chills.

Danny Finn made another pass in front of Tom Kempner's mansion. After driving out of sight, he slowed and hit the speed dial on the hands-free car phone. His boss, Mr. Barbera, answered on the first ring.

"A new development," Danny said. "Miss Shaver never went to the airport. She's with a bunch of dogs near the end of the driveway."

"Did she see you?" the boss asked.

"Couldn't miss the car, but there's no way she made the plates."

"I don't like it. Tommy's not loose-lipped, and he sure as hell isn't plea bargaining. What can they be talking about?"

Several hours ago, Mr. Barbera had sent him to Barrington. The precautionary measure had produced results, but not the ones the boss wanted. Now, as Danny Finn listened, he tried to gauge the gentleman don's frame of mind. The Irishman understood first hand that when Mr. Barbera's suspicions grew, his mood became menacing and cold.

"Whatever they're discussing, it's long-winded," Danny advised, reducing the limo's speed to a crawl. "Mrs. Eichler's pickup hasn't moved. Been by the house every thirty minutes for the past four hours. If you think it makes sense, I can stay in the area."

"Too risky," the boss replied. "If she's walking the dogs, they're in no hurry to leave."

Danny Finn took the next right and headed east. He knew Mr. Barbera was livid. He also knew the boss would want to put a contingency plan together.

Patricia Shaver slammed the front door. To warm up, she began doing abbreviated jumping jacks. She'd risked being frostbitten, but the trip to the mailbox had confirmed her hunch.

Ellen walked into the foyer. "Back so soon?"

"It's cold," Pat said. "Where's Tom?"

"Right here."

Pat turned as Tom walked across the foyer and joined them. "Any luck reaching the admiral?"

"Left a message," Tom replied. "Guys like me only have priority two status. When you're a no-account, you go through the Company's switchboard."

"Think he'll call right back?"

"Can't be sure," Tom admitted, "but I'm hopeful."

"Your optimism is shortsighted," Ellen said. "There's no way. It's Christmas Eve."

Pat checked her watch. "Time's flying, Ellie. It's already Christmas Day."

"All the more reason to leave." Ellen gave her the *let's go* look. "It'll only take a minute to wash up the brandy glasses and turn off the coffee pot."

"Leave everything," Tom said. "It'll give me something to do while I'm waiting for Weiss's call."

Pat turned to their host, eyes pleading. "If you think the admiral might call, I'd like to hang around."

"We've overstayed our welcome," Ellen said. "The admiral is probably in bed, and I'm sure Tommy would like to go to sleep too."

"Mrs. Eichler is right," he agreed. "It may be awhile before Admiral Weiss's staff gets up the nerve to wake him. In the meantime, I've got some important papers in my desk drawer to file away. That will keep me busy for quite some time."

"Okay," Pat said, both confused and startled by his latest disclosure, "but no matter what the hour… no matter how benign his message… call me. I'll go, but only if I have your promise."

CHAPTER TWENTY

Patricia Shaver felt trapped. She didn't want to leave Tom Kempner alone, but when Ellen whistled and Snowshoe and Shoe-Too raced to the front door, she knew her friend was determined to get moving.

"Here's a thought," Pat said, facing Tom. "I'll stick around and wait for the admiral's call. Once Weiss checks in, I'll borrow one of your cars and drive home."

Ellen kissed Tom's cheek, then turned to Pat. "Why are you so intent on keeping everyone up? It's late. I need some sleep and so does Tommy."

"Am I the only one who's got a second wind?" Pat asked, looking at Tom for encouragement. "Are the rest of you pooped?"

When he responded with an indifferent shrug, Pat zipped up her parka and wished him a Merry Christmas. No one else shared her apprehensions.

Neither she nor Ellen spoke during the short drive to her house. She desperately wanted to express her concerns, but her friend needed to see solid evidence, and at this point, the case against each of the Gaylanis was loaded with more conjecture than proof.

Ellen parked near the steps to the open-air porch. After Pat coaxed her Labs out of the pickup, she leaned through the driver's side window and kissed her surrogate mother's forehead.

"What a way to start Christmas."

Ellen half-smiled. "Let's say good night and talk when the sun comes up."

Pat scaled the three icy stairs, then turned back. "Damn it, Ellie. I'm worried."

"Why?" her friend asked, her breath condensing against the cold night air. "Tommy's a big boy."

"Think he'll call?"

Ellen stopped the window halfway up. "You gave him your phone number three times. If he hears anything, you'll be the first to know."

Pat checked her watch—12:45 AM. As the pickup's taillights disappeared down her driveway, she saw Snowshoe and Shoe-Too standing on the porch, ready for her to open the front door.

The house seemed peaceful, but her anxiety was stronger than ever. The moment she began climbing the stairs, she had a feeling Ellen's optimism was shortsighted.

Once in her bedroom, Pat stared at the quilted Hawaiian bedspread her dad had given her many years ago. For a second she thought about the happy times they'd spent together at the Mauna Kea Beach Hotel. She'd loved their annual trips to the Big Island. Each day, they'd played golf in the morning, had lunch on the beach, then paddled out to go surfing. Being away from her mother was always a pleasant reprieve. Betty Shaver's alcoholism had made Honeymead a living hell.

She yanked off the bedspread, remembering. A moment later, Snowshoe and Shoe-Too leapt to their nightly resting spot at the foot of the mattress.

"Pleasant dreams, girls."

As the dogs settled in, she strolled into her walk-in closet, left her jeans and sweater on the floor, then slipped into her favorite nightgown—an extra large Chicago Bulls t-shirt commemorating Michael Jordan and their first NBA title. Still out of sorts, she walked toward the wall-sized window at the end of her bedroom. For her, sleep wasn't in the cards. Tom's startling revelations had her reporter's instincts strung tight.

The outside floodlights mounted under the eaves illuminated

the perimeter of her house and gave her a sense of protection. Tom Kempner probably had a sophisticated home security system, but right now he had to feel vulnerable. His actions said it all. First he'd compromised the attorney-client privilege, and then he'd called Admiral Weiss.

Tom hadn't told her why the CIA had contacted the Mafia, or admitted that a meeting between Eric Weiss and Gary Barbera had even taken place. But it was obvious he feared both organizations and thought each might have played a role in his wife's death.

Patricia kept the temperature of her home at seventy, but when her body began to shiver, she hurried back to her bed and slid between the sheets. As the weight of the comforter warmed her, she turned off the bedside lamp, but not the outside floodlights. On most nights, seeing the winter landscape had a calming effect. Tonight she hardly noticed the deep snow that had drifted and formed sloping dunes. Instead, she wondered if leaving Tom's place had been a mistake.

She reviewed the evidence, playing back her visit to the Kempner mailbox. Once she'd counted the four rubber-banded bundles of envelopes—a packet for each day, including the day Katherine Kempner had died—she'd confirmed another one of her suspicions. Why, then, hadn't she told Tom that his wife had put her letter in the mailbox before the postman came by?

Pat stared at her sleeping dogs. Had she kept her mouth shut because she didn't want to tell him what else she'd seen? The limousine had gone by before she caught the license plate. But that hadn't mattered. When the black Cadillac was framed between the snow banks at the end of Tom's driveway, she'd focused on a recognizable object. From last May's face-to-face confrontation, she knew Gary Barbera had a gold falcon embossed under the rear door handle.

She closed her eyes. The gentleman don was watching his lawyer's house. Did he also have a tap on Tom Kempner's phones? If she wanted to stay in the loop, why hadn't she dragged Tom back into his office and told him his wife's letter had been intercepted?

Pat picked up the phone, but didn't dial. Broaching the subject would be tough. How could she say, *Gee, Tom, I'm sitting here in the middle of the night wondering two things. Why does your boss have a limo cruising by your house… and when is your pal the admiral going to let you in on the Company's grand strategy?*

She set the phone back in its cradle. No mob attorney would dare confront a Mafia don or the deputy director of the CIA.

She got out of bed and walked into her closet. It wasn't hundred-year-old Napoleon cognac, but the fifth of brandy she pulled from the shelf would have to do.

She carried the bottle into the bathroom and poured two fingers into a water glass on the vanity counter. For a moment, she did nothing. Then she dumped the cognac into the sink, rinsed the glass, and returned the bottle to the shelf in her closet.

Tom Kempner answered his front door. He was surprised to see his visitor, but not shocked. Tom had accomplished most of his goals earlier in the evening, but not all of them. His early morning visitor would allow him to take care of unfinished business.

"Come in," he said. "I had a feeling I'd see you again."

"Guess our brain waves must be on the same frequency. I wasn't tired, so I decided to pop back over."

"Can I take your parka?" he asked. "I was just about to pour myself another brandy. You'll join me, of course."

Dr. Tony Gaylani walked in and smiled. "Of course."

Patricia Shaver spent a fitful night. Once up, she showered, dressed, and bounded downstairs. As the sun added light to the frozen landscape and officially welcomed Christmas Day, she fed her two Labs. Only then did she make a phone call.

After several rings, Tom Kempner's answering machine clicked on. She hesitated, then hung up. A part of her was concerned; another part said he'd turned off the bedroom phone and was sound asleep. Either way, she needed to know. Her heart racing, she grabbed car keys and a parka.

As her Mercedes sped over the snow-packed roads, Pat gripped the steering wheel and yelled into the hands-free phone.

"Ellie, I've called several times. There's no answer."

"Why would there be?" Ellen groaned, obviously roused from a sound sleep. "It's six-thirty. Now, if there's nothing else..."

Before she could respond, Pat heard Ellen's husband ask a groggy-voiced question.

"Yes, dear. It is Patricia. I'll be sure to send along your holiday cheer."

Pat listened, wincing. "Tell him I'm sorry."

"Won't help," Ellen replied.

Pat eased off the accelerator and turned onto another snow-packed road.

"How do I do it? Your husband's pissed and Tom won't pick up."

"Maybe he went to church," Ellen suggested.

"He's Jewish. He doesn't go to church."

"Why me, Lord?" Ellen sighed. "Give me a second. I'll buzz you back from the kitchen."

"No need. Just put on the coffee. I'm almost there."

Joanna Gaylani was awakened by Tony's tender touch. It never failed. When she wanted to sleep in, the horny bastard insisted on making love.

Joanna felt his naked body slide alongside her. She couldn't say no. Zero hour was at hand. To minimize him as a threat, she needed her husband to be happy and content.

She pulled her nightgown above her waist to encourage his advances. Then she turned on her side and used her foot to rub the inside of his leg.

"Oh, my," she said, feeling more than just his hands, "first a Christmas goose, now another gift. But shame on you, Tony. Your present isn't wrapped."

He kissed her cheek. "Italian men deliver their gifts without frills. It's traditional."

"Is that a fact?" she said, rolling on top of an aroused partner and wiggling seductively until they interlocked. "What about bows?"

"That's the other part of the tradition. No ribbons."

Patricia Shaver flipped down the visor as the sun rose above the horizon. She was conscious of Ellen sitting beside her in the Mercedes. Old Spice for Men wafted in the car. Ellen used the cologne whenever she got mad and wanted to make a statement.

"You should have listened to me," Ellen said, grimacing as the roadster skidded. "My Explorer holds the road better than this bucket of bolts."

Pat glanced at her, then turned the steering wheel hard right. When the Mercedes went into an ice-abetted power slide, she turned the wheel back and fishtailed into Tom's driveway.

"Hang on."

"Slow down," Ellen cautioned. "This isn't Le Mans."

Under normal circumstances, Pat would have taken her friend's advice. She wasn't a reckless driver. But every time she thought about Tom Kempner, she got more anxious.

Halfway down his cobblestone driveway, she hit a patch of ice and lost control. Ellen locked her arms and braced her hands on the dashboard. "For God's sake. Pay attention."

"Give me a break," Pat replied. "I'm not doing this on purpose."

Something caught her eye near the end of the driveway. It looked like a dog, but she couldn't be sure. Yellow Labs are buff white and from a distance blend in with the snow.

Pat eased off the gas and continued to turn the steering wheel in the direction of each skid. When the car stopped fishtailing, she pumped the brakes.

"Look to the left of the walkway," Pat said, "then check out the snow bank."

"I already saw her," Ellen snapped. "Now will you listen and cut your speed?"

As the Mercedes slowed and they neared Tom's house, she realized her eyes hadn't deceived her. Blizzard was in trouble. The dog hadn't reacted to the sound of the car coming down the driveway. Instead she lay motionless on her side, her head and legs encrusted under the base of a snow bank near the point where the heated walkway intersected the cobblestone turnaround.

Once parked, she and Ellen got out, slammed the car doors, and started running.

Joanna Gaylani sat up as her husband bolted from the bed. She'd chosen to ignore the outside noise, preferring to watch Tony's reaction. Mindful she'd lost her nightgown during their last bout of lovemaking, she held the blankets over her chest.

"Darling, if you must go, hurry back. I want to cuddle."

"All in good time," Tony said, running toward the reading alcove. "I swear I heard car doors slam."

Patricia Shaver had experienced her share of anxiety, but her heart had never beaten faster.

"Are they alive?" she asked.

"The puppy is." Ellen was on her knees, pulling the dogs out from under a cave-like opening at the base of a snow bank. "Can't tell about Blizzard. The old girl's survival instincts were good, but she took the brunt of the weather."

Ellen was correct. Blizzard had acted with great foresight. First the Lab had lain on her side and clawed out the opening. Next she'd coaxed Snowflake to lie under the icy ledge. Finally, Blizzard had squeezed in after the puppy, using her body to seal the opening. With an assist from the heated walkway, the maneuver had protected the dogs from the wintry wind.

"My God," Pat said, "why would Tom leave them out all night?"

Ellen handed her Snowflake. "Who knows? Try the doorbell. I'll bring Blizzard."

The front door was ajar. She hip-shoved it open, set Snowflake down, then turned back to Ellen.

She helped her carry Blizzard into the kitchen. Once they set the Lab on the tile floor, Pat looked around until she spotted the puppy.

"The little one's no worse for wear," she said. "How's Blizzard doing?"

"To early to tell," Ellen replied. "We need to make her a warm nest."

Pat began to improvise, sliding Snowflake's sleeping cushion in Ellen's direction.

"What about blankets?" she asked.

Ellen moved Blizzard onto the dog bed, then pointed. "There's a storage closet in the laundry room. Look in there."

As they cocooned the older dog in a mound of down-filled comforters, the puppy pranced up and licked Blizzard's face. The reciprocal act of kindness was touching, but when Snowflake dog-kissed Blizzard again, Pat's stomach muscles tensed. When they'd entered the kitchen, neither she nor Ellen had stepped over the doggie gate.

Her disquiet intensified. If she shared her dread, Ellen would immediately begin a search of Tom's house and garage. Assuming her worst fears were correct and their hunt produced his body, Ellen would insist on calling the police. That was what she couldn't risk. Call it callous, call it immoral, call it anything, but if Tom Kempner had met with foul play, she didn't want to compound an earlier mistake. Right now she needed free rein to investigate before Chief Carlton Cherrigan and his Barrington deputies cordoned the place off.

"Thank God," Ellen said, kneeling down, "Blizzard's coming around."

While the dogs drowsed, Pat motioned her friend toward the foyer.

"Tom is probably sleeping it off. You guys are pals. Maybe it's best if you try the bedroom."

When Ellen began climbing the stairs, Pat walked into the living room. Her pulse quickened when she focused on the coffee table. Along with the mugs, a third brandy snifter was next to the ones she and Tom had left. The inference was clear. Tom had entertained someone after they'd left.

"Where are you, Patricia?"

Pat scanned the coffee table one more time, then walked back into the foyer and looked up at the second-story landing.

"Any luck?"

Ellen shook her head. "Nobody's slept in his bed."

"What about the other rooms?"

"Nothing."

Pat couldn't be sure, but she figured Tom was dead. That meant her next move had to be decisive. More than ever, she needed to gain access to Tom Kempner's office.

She pointed toward the arch-shaped hallway. "Bet he's snoozing in the no-female zone."

"Forget it," Ellen replied. "Even Kitty didn't go in there unannounced."

"Don't worry," Pat said, walking across the foyer. "I'll knock before entering."

"Why do I bother?" Ellen scoffed. "To you, off-limits means a green light."

"Hardly," Pat replied. "But what if he suffered a heart attack or something?"

"Spare me the what-ifs." Ellen started down the stairs. "Check out his office. I'll see if Tommy's car is in the garage."

Dr. Tony Gaylani hadn't bothered to put on his robe. He stood bare-assed, watching the canine rescue mission unfold. At first, Shaver and Eichler's early morning visit had upset him, but once the women took the mutts inside Tom Kempner's house, Tony had calmed down. While he sensed they were up to no good, he needed someone to find Kempner's body and call the cops. He wanted to be on the scene, but only after the Barrington police arrived.

Tony shuddered as goosebumps welted up all over his body. For sleeping comfort, he and Joanna kept their bedroom at sixty degrees. Since the daytime thermostat didn't kick in until eight AM, the chill he felt was real.

"Welcome back," Joanna said, flipping the covers aside and drawing him in. "I liked the other view, but having you close is better."

Tony played along when his wife pulled the electric blanket over their bodies. As he and Joanna snuggled, Tony waited, knowing the siren on Police Chief Cherrigan's squad car would alert him.

"Just once," he said, kissing Joanna's nose, "I'd like you to cry uncle first."

"Quit jabbering," she replied. "I'm starting to cool off."

He smiled and got down to business. Tony hated to admit it, but he did enjoy the work. Of course, he'd liked banging his former wife, Barbara. She was just as voluptuous, and when it came to lovemaking, every bit as hard to satisfy.

Tony ran his hand along the nape of Joanna's neck. His top priority as an Iraqi spy was to monitor Jewish organizations that took a hard line against Arab nations. Since he didn't look like a Jew, he couldn't infiltrate into one of their groups. But that didn't stop him from gathering useful intelligence.

First he'd pretended to be sympathetic to the Zionist cause, then he'd seduced and married one of their members. That was all it took. A contented woman in love had a hard time keeping secrets.

As his hands stimulated Joanna's sensitive parts, he remembered his first wife, Barbara. One night after sex, she'd told him that she wanted to resign from All Alone and start a family. Not good news, but information he had to deal with. The next morning he'd strangled her.

Tony breathed in deeply. When he kissed the underside of Joanna's neck, her breath became labored too.

* * *

Pat watched Ellen head toward the garage. Before going into Tom Kempner's very private office, she detoured into the library.

Light streamed through monastery-like windows. Recessed bookshelves were spaced along the walnut-paneled walls and crammed with leather-bound editions. The room felt like a scholar's haven, but not all the appointments reeked of cobwebs and academia. A Gainsborough landscape hanging over the fireplace added a modicum of cheeriness and reminded her that everything, from the pricey masterpieces to the oriental rugs, reflected a discerning taste.

Pat left the library. Ten steps down the corridor, she stood in the doorway of the gym. Based on Tom's trim waistline, she knew the array of Nautilus equipment had been put to use.

The last door in the wing opened into a replica of the Oval Office. The rug didn't have the Presidential Seal, the square latticed windows weren't made of bulletproof glass, and the dimensions didn't measure up to the real thing. But there was no mistaking the intent.

"Patricia!"

She looked back at the doorway. "Right here, Ellie."

"Where the hell are you?"

Pat took a deep breath. "Are you deaf?"

She accepted the inevitable. Before Ellen came striding through the door, Pat knew her friend had found Tom's body. The reason was elementary. Ellen never used even mild profanity.

Joanna Gaylani stood in her bathroom next to her husband. When Tony patted her derriere, she used a flirtatious wink to disguise her murderous intent.

"Tony, dear, got anything special on your agenda?"

"Probably just relax and recover my strength." Tony kissed the top of her head. "There are a couple of important games on the tube. Maybe I'll watch football over at Tom's."

"Sounds like a dreadful way to spend Christmas. Besides, won't he be going to his son's house?"

"Took a pass," Tony said, finger-combing his hair. "Told Trevor it would kill him to be there when the grandkids opened all the presents Kitty had wrapped."

She nodded. "Christmas will never be the same."

Since being awakened at dawn, Joanna had made passionate love to Tony, wallowed in his arms, and then soaped him down during a steamy shower. But as they lolled in her bathroom clad only in terry-cloth robes, she sensed he wanted to leave.

To test the strength of his football-junkie mentality, she undid the sash of her bathrobe, put both arms around his neck, and pressed close.

"My sweet," she cooed, "I'm glad we put on clean sheets. Now that we're spic and span, why don't we go muss up the linens?"

"Out of gas, Snookums."

"That's funny," she replied. "I swear the end of your pump just moved."

She dropped her hand and found an opening in his robe. God, how she loved playing the game.

Earlier, she too had heard the two car doors slam. Of course, she'd acted disinterested, but later, while Tony readied the shower, she'd looked at their neighbor's driveway.

The Mercedes with SNOWSHOE plates was parked in the center of Tom Kempner's turnaround. Ellen and that Shaver woman had come by again. It never failed. She'd purposely put them on Tony's trail because she'd never dreamed it would interfere with her plans. But now she wasn't so sure. During crucial times, busybodies with a nose for trouble always got in the way.

Patricia Shaver stood in the laundry room doorway and looked out. The garage door was open, but she could still smell the fumes.

"I meant what I said, Ellie. We're both staying, and neither of us is calling the cops."

Pat moved toward Katherine Kempner's car. As she took a closer look, her friend fidgeted, focusing on everything but the dead mob attorney. Ellen had reason to be unnerved. A minute ago, she'd found Tom Kempner slumped over the wheel of Kitty's Mercedes.

Pat circled the car, hands at her side. "Have you touched anything?"

Ellen shook her head.

"The engine," she asked, "was it running?"

Ellen shook her head again. "My God, he committed suicide. We have to notify the authorities."

"Plenty of time to get the cops involved. For now, we wait."

Pat walked past the rear of the car, knelt down, and checked the undercarriage. She assumed Tony Gaylani was monitoring their activities from afar. She also figured he would hold off making a move.

Ellen backed away. "We can't leave Tommy like this."

Pat nodded. "That much I figured out for myself."

Using her handkerchief to cover the handle, she opened the passenger-side door. One thing was paramount. She wanted to inspect his head without smudging any prints he or Tony might have left on the driver's side.

She'd known Tom Kempner less than twenty-four hours. In that span, her opinion had changed. He'd become more than just another lawyer hired to keep a Mafia don out of trouble. Tom had a realistic perspective on himself, a sense of humor, and a deep devotion to his wife. In her book, that meant he deserved better than this.

Pat took short breaths to control her emotions. For a moment, she thought about taking matters into her own hands. Of course, she was hardly in a position to dispense vigilante justice. But she could make a call to someone who would. While a frank talk with Gary Barbera conjured up images of justifiable revenge, she closed her eyes and let the idea drop. She wanted Tony Gaylani to get a killer's due, but she also needed to nail the killer's wife. To accomplish both, she'd get the Chicago Mafia and local cops involved on her timetable.

She had first-hand knowledge that Carlton Cherrigan, the Barrington Police Chief, was on the mob's payroll. Since Tom had disregarded the attorney/client privilege and in so doing brought Gary Barbera to the periphery of Katherine Kempner's murder, she figured any investigation the chief conducted would whitewash all hints of complicity and proclaim the suicide the act of a lovesick widower.

"This is crazy," Ellen said, her voice quivering. "We have to do something."

"Do me a favor and don't state the obvious." Pat glared, then bent down and knelt on the front passenger seat. "Make yourself useful and see if he left a note."

"Why?" Ellen shot back. "I've already been in all the upstairs bedrooms."

"Then check the bathrooms. If there's nothing there, scout around in the dining room."

"Five minutes, lady!" Ellen shouted, stomping away. "In five minutes, I'm dialing 911."

With the clock ticking, Pat began examining Tom's body, taking special note of his posture. She knew that carbon monoxide induced sleep. That meant a suicidal victim would pass out and either fall sideways on the seat or recline back on the headrest.

Tom had done neither. He was seated with his upper torso pitched forward, his shoulders square and parallel to the dashboard, his arms hanging free, and his head aligned on the steering column. As she viewed his profile, it appeared the bridge of his nose was wedged against the curved inside rim of the steering wheel.

An emotionally distraught man might go to extremes and inhale gas fumes, but would he pass out, then rock forward and come to rest in balanced symmetry? Wouldn't the impact have caused his head to turn to one side?

To get a better view, she crouched down. To gain stability, she curled the fingers of her left hand around the top of the passenger seat. Then she looked up and peered between the circular part of the steering wheel and the rectangular housing that held the air bag.

She'd expected Tom's skin to look bluish and pasty, but she wasn't prepared for the eyes. Instead of being shut as in sleep, they were wide open, offering an opaque emptiness.

Cold sweat moistened her brow. She stared, frozen, then closed her mouth and breathed through her nose. Tom's pallor disturbed her, but for a long second she gawked and he seemed to gawk back. Then bubbly foam dribbled from his mouth.

Pat gagged and jerked backwards. Her head cleared the underside of the steering wheel, but as she let go of the top of the seat, her left hand banged the back of Tom's skull.

Heart pounding, she watched as he toppled sideways and fell slow-motion onto the center console. She knew screaming wouldn't help, but did it anyway. Then she took a deep breath.

Pat put her hands under Tom's head and shoulder and lifted him back into a sitting position. Returning Tom to his original spot confirmed her worst thoughts. The golf-ball-sized knot on the back of his head had to be the result of a sharp, deliberate blow.

"Are you okay?" Ellen asked, rushing into the garage.

Quaking, Pat ignored her and backed out. "How can homicide cops do this day after day?"

"For openers," Ellen replied, "they don't disturb the evidence."

"No kidding," Pat said, her jaw tensing. "I made a mistake."

Using her knee, she slammed the Mercedes door. After taking another deep breath, she brought Ellen up to speed.

Her friend's eyes widened. "You think Tommy was murdered?"

"He's got a goose egg on the back of his skull, and there's no mark by his nose or forehead. Even if he didn't bruise his head as he fell forward, you'd expect an indentation."

Ellen stepped closer and looked into the interior of the Mercedes. "Are you saying he was knocked out, stuffed in the car, and then positioned that way?"

"He wasn't leaning against the steering wheel," Pat replied, "he was balanced on it."

Her friend stared at the body. "Why is this happening?"

"Stop whining," Pat said. "We both hate it, but we both have work to do."

"Like what?"

"Did you find a note?"

"Why would I?" Ellen snapped, her lip quivering. "You just suggested that someone had done Tommy in. Which is it? Murder or suicide?"

"Jeez, Ellie, give me a break."

"No way. I've had enough of this madness. I'm calling the police."

"Not yet!" Pat grabbed her friend's shoulder. "Our next stop is his office."

"Forget it," Ellen said, breaking free. "Rummaging through his personal effects isn't the answer. This matter should be handled by the authorities."

"For God's sake. Have you forgotten who represents the law in this town?"

They walked through the laundry room, then past the slumbering dogs. But once in the dining room, Pat stepped in front of Ellen and stopped.

"Think what you want, but I'm not playing some silly game. I believe Tom's a victim, but to be certain, check under the beds and anywhere else that comes to mind. Once we're sure there's no suicide note, we'll call Chief Cherrigan."

Ellen paused as if debating the issues. Then, without saying a word, she strode into the foyer and headed toward the stairs.

To take advantage of the short reprieve, Pat hurried back through the laundry room, reached her hand into the garage, and pressed the automatic door button. She had lots of details to attend to, but none took precedence over making Tony Gaylani nervous. If the killer spy was watching, he'd expect them to call the cops, not seal Kempner's body in a makeshift morgue.

Pat entered Tom's office and focused on the built-in file cabinets. Ellen didn't think they should snoop, but her friend's instincts were wrong. Ellen believed in people and couldn't comprehend that public servants like Chief Cherrigan perverted justice for money. But Pat knew. She'd seen him in action firsthand.

Last spring, when she'd confronted Gary Barbera over her father's secret file, she learned about the back scratching that existed between the Chicago mob and the Barrington police chief. The public saw Carlton "Cherry" Cherrigan as a congenial, conscientious country cop. To them he maintained the status quo and, when not showing his face around the village, used his radar gun to nab an occasional out-of-town speeder.

Pat knew otherwise. On the night Honeymead had burned to the ground, Cherry hadn't been the head man. More than two decades ago, Sergeant Cherrigan took orders from another chief. But a few months later, when Chief Paul Cassasa's bullet-riddled body had turned up in a Chicago alley, Carlton was promoted.

He hadn't taken this new job for granted. Carlton Cherrigan lorded over his constabulary force, but treated his benefactor with kid gloves. The mayor of Barrington signed his paycheck, but the gentleman don supplemented Cherry's income with cash.

Along with following orders, Chief Cherrigan had other attributes. Take the Honeymead fire, for instance. In all likelihood, Cherry had suspected that Gary Barbera had struck the match. How could he have thought otherwise? Sgt. Cherrigan had watched it burn, then walked through the ashy rubble.

It hadn't mattered that none of the evidence supported the claim that a cigarette dropped by her drunken mother started the blaze. A sergeant who had an eye on promotion knew what to do. And once Cherrigan had written the police report, the case was closed.

Pat sat in Tom Kempner's office, her mouth dry. Why had she chosen this moment to dig up unpleasant recollections from her past? What relevance could…? Unless…?

The parallel struck her. Chief Carlton Cherrigan's investigation had been inept because in his world, a savvy policeman never put two and two together. Tom Kempner had also used the same tactic. When Kitty had confronted her husband, the mob attorney had played dumb and feigned no knowledge of Dr. Tony Gaylani's Iraqi background.

She scanned the items on Tom Kempner's desk. Her mind should have been ferreting out clues to his death, but instead she kept thinking about the past. Had other people she'd known also acted like Tom Kempner?

Pat sat back in his chair and closed her eyes. It was a bit of a stretch, but she could see the correlation. Of course, the circumstances that had influenced their behaviors were very different, but Tom Kempner and her father, R.D. Shaver, had reacted the same way.

To friends and business associates, her dad appeared to be a rich and successful banker. That perception was wrong. R.D. Shaver was a white-collar crook who lived off bribes paid into a numbered Swiss bank account. Of course, her dad wasn't all bad. Before he died, R.D. had created a file of Gary Barbera's secret payroll and threatened to take it to the authorities.

She squirmed in the tufted leather chair and looked around the office. Hadn't her dad's packet of names and Swiss bank account numbers been assembled to soothe a contrite conscience? Similarly, hadn't Tom Kempner become guilt-ridden and given her sensitive data as a way to insure that his wife's death wouldn't go unpunished?

She stood and looked at the ceiling. Was it possible Tom Kempner had created his own file and then entrusted it to her? Had he realized his life was in danger and purposely implicated everyone who might have wanted to kill him?

If so, her plan of action had a short fuse. A very short fuse.

CHAPTER TWENTY-ONE

Dr. Tony Gaylani, clad in his bathrobe, stood in the bedroom alcove. As he stared at his neighbor's house, Tony realized his mistake. While he'd done Joanna a second time, one of the snoops—either Shaver or Eichler—had closed Tom Kempner's garage door. His dallying had been fun, but it had cost him valuable time. He needed to make an onsite visit and see what was going on next door.

He dressed hurriedly, went downstairs, and grabbed his car keys. He drove to the Kempner house, but instead of parking behind Pat Shaver's Mercedes, he pulled up next to the service entry.

Tony smelled traces of car exhaust fumes when he opened the door on the far side of the garage. His instincts to bypass the front entrance had been right.

Events hadn't transpired as planned. He'd counted on the women discovering the body and maybe even airing the place out, but under no circumstances had he figured they'd close it up. Wouldn't a sane person scream bloody murder and call the cops?

But not those two. No. They had another agenda. They had closed the garage door, hoping their trespass would go unnoticed. For reasons that made him nervous, they wanted to buy time to be alone in the mob attorney's house.

Patricia Shaver sat at Tom Kempner's desk, looking out the lattice-style windows. Just as she decided on a course of action, Ellen walked in.

"No note, Patricia. Another thing. Cherrigan may be on the mob's payroll, but we have to tell someone."

"In due time," Pat said, keeping her head down. "Right now there are more pressing needs."

"What could be more pressing than notifying Tommy's son? Trevor has a right to know."

"Agreed… but for now, leaving Tom in the garage can't be helped." She stopped leafing through Tom's desk drawers and looked up. "If all this makes you uncomfortable, go check on the pooches."

"They're doing fine, sleeping like babies."

"And the general's files?" she asked, scanning Tom's desk. "Someone needs to go up in the elevator and make sure they're still intact."

Pat assumed Gaylani had taken General Alan Cunningham's papers, but she sent her friend to Kitty's office anyway. Ellen's sense of propriety was getting in the way of her investigation. Right this moment, she needed more time to rummage alone.

When Ellen left, Pat used her handkerchief to pull out another desk drawer. She planned a thorough search, but when the blinking red light again caught her eye, she hit the replay button instead. The answering machine clicked, then the tape played.

Admiral Eric Weiss's voice immobilized her. As goose flesh welted up on her arms, Pat hit the re-play button again to be certain of what she'd heard.

"Sorry about your loss, buddy-boy. Wish I could have attended the funeral, but we both know that would never fly. And another thing… be a sport and don't use the private number. Wouldn't want the taxpayers to get the wrong idea."

There was a pause in the taped recording; then the admiral cleared his throat and continued:

"Remember one thing above all else. Life goes on. We're survivors, buddy-boy. And you know why? The rabbi in the old neighborhood taught us well. We're Jews, and we stand back-to-back."

She kept staring at the answering machine, her jaw muscles tight. Admiral Weiss hadn't admitted to a CIA/Mafia collaboration, but his tone suggested that he expected Tom Kempner to be cooperative. The part about the old neighborhood and the rabbi's words was a clever code saying that they'd face their common enemy together. Yesterday evening, when she and Tom Kempner had sat alone in his breakfast nook, he'd recited the same quote—borrowed words from a David Ben-Gurion speech.

Pat released the tape, put it in her pocket, then wiped her prints off the answering machine. Hearing the admiral's words had motivated her. Handkerchief in hand, she opened the bottom cabinet drawer and was surprised to see a manila envelope resting atop the hanging file folders.

"My, oh my," she murmured, pulling out a set of documents entitled "Kempner/Weiss file."

She read the cover letter and was astounded. Then she flipped it over and began thumbing through a small stack of dossiers on men with Hispanic names.

"Patricia! You won't believe this," Ellen said, rushing in. "The general's papers are gone."

Pat kept her eyes riveted on the Kempner/Weiss file—a dozen or so single-spaced biographical sheets with information that, if leaked to the press, would make Barbera and Weiss sweat bullets.

"Did you hear me?" Ellen asked, her voice fever-pitched. "They're gone."

Pat turned the chair to block Ellen's view, then stuffed the folder under her sweater. One thing was certain. If she didn't make these papers vanish, Police Chief Cherrigan would.

"Glad you're here," she said, swinging Tom's chair around. "Start with the file cabinets. See if anything pops out."

"You're not surprised, are you?" Ellen's face hardened as she moved in front of the desk. "You had it figured all along… but you still sent me to Kitty's office."

Pat looked up, knowing her friend hadn't seen her sleight of hand. "I figured the papers were gone, but didn't know for sure."

Ellen leaned over the desk. "When you figured out the general's stuff got snatched, did you also figure it was okay to rifle through Tommy's desk?"

"No, Mrs. Eichler. I figure we're investigating a murder and that gives us the right."

Their views stated, they stared at each other. A moment later, without uttering another word, they signaled a truce. As Ellen walked toward Kempner's file cabinets, Pat bent down, but only pretended to go through his desk drawers. She knew she'd found the prize. Tom Kempner, like her father, had been murdered. And Tom Kempner, like her father, hadn't died in vain. Each had left a file that incriminated people who had broken the law.

Ellen sighed. "Huh... Huh..."

Pat swiveled around, watching as her friend pulled a file from one of the cabinets. "What have you got?"

"A ranch file full of invoices. Machinery repairs, fertilizer, that sort of thing."

"No criticism intended," she said, "but we're not here to audit Tom's horse ranch."

"I'm not auditing anything," Ellen replied, shuffling through the folder. "There's something here that doesn't make any sense."

"Okay, what's so—Jesus!"

They both turned toward the noise. From somewhere inside the house, a man had screamed. Then he'd slammed a door.

"It's got to be Dr. Gaylani," Pat said. "Shove everything back, but don't push the ranch file all the way down. Leave it visible."

Dr. Tony Gaylani knew he'd made another mistake. He wanted to announce his presence, but he'd slammed the front door too soon. First he should have checked out the living room.

He waited several seconds. When the two women didn't come out to investigate, he made a beeline toward the coffee table.

Tony smiled. The snoops—Shaver and Eichler—hadn't been thorough. Seeing that nothing had been disturbed, he picked up the three snifters by their stems and headed for Tom's office.

"Well, look who's here," he said, walking in. "You ladies must have taken a wrong turn."

The blonde reporter looked up. "Did we?"

"Got that right, Shaver." He kept his hands behind his back, then stepped in front of the desk. "Visitors aren't allowed in this wing."

"Really?" she replied. "Seems sorta sexist, don't you think?"

"A word of advice, lady." He was annoyed by her composure, but grinned anyway. "Look elsewhere. If Tom finds you in here, there'll be hell to pay."

"Maybe," the reporter said quietly, "but I'll take my chances."

He watched her lean back and clasp her hands behind her head. While blondie kept smiling, Eichler looked petrified.

"People in journalism are notorious for treating private property as their own. By now, I assume you've micro-filmed all Mr. Kempner's documents?"

"You're confused, doc," she replied. "Cub reporters write. Only spies use miniature cameras."

Tony squinted at her, wishing he was back in Iraq, a country where insolence cost a woman her tongue. "Are you quite comfortable, Shaver?"

"Very," she answered. "Oh. I keep forgetting. You don't think I belong. But tell me, doc. If off limits is off limits, how do Italian Catholics rate?"

"Tom invited me," he snapped, "asked me over to watch the football games."

Shaver leaned sideways, trying to see what he held behind his back. Tony eyed her scrubbed face and hastily combed ponytail, wondering why American males allowed their women to be seen in public wearing bulky sweaters and jeans.

"Guess you're into the NFL," she said, still straining to see what he held. "Da Bears didn't make it this year. What team do you like?"

"New England is my favorite. No glory hogs, just a group of men committed to teamwork."

"It figures," she scoffed, "an outstanding American like you would have to root for the New England Patriots."

Tony decided to reclaim the initiative when Shaver added sarcasm to her blank stare. Slowly, he brought his hands forward and lined up the three brandy snifters on Tom Kempner's desk.

For a long few seconds, he waited for her to react. When she ignored his display and kept talking about pro football, he began at one end of the row and, in sequence, wrapped his hands around the bubble part of each snifter.

"I never thought to call and ask you over because I didn't know you followed pro football. But no harm done. Barging in uninvited seems to be one of your strong suits."

"You got me wrong, doc," Shaver said, her eyes focused on the snifters. "Ellie and I called Tom's home phone, but nobody answered. You must be the only one with the magic number."

"Actually, we agreed on a time yesterday. But to someone who's observant, there's a perfectly logical reason why Mr. Kempner didn't answer."

"Like what?" she asked.

Tony pointed to the open compartment at the top of the answering machine. "When the tape is missing, it zeros out the phone."

He was lying, and he suspected she knew he was lying. But it didn't matter. He no longer wanted to spar with her. The two women had been meddling in Tom Kempner's house for a long time, and aside from the pilfered tape, he wanted to find out what else they'd taken.

"Ellie's the only expert I trust," Shaver said, looking at her friend. "What do you think… is the doc right?"

Like a wooden soldier, the Eichler woman stepped forward and pushed the tape compartment closed. When the green light went on, the nosy reporter turned toward him, smiling.

"Told you Ellie does good work. Except for the missing cartridge, it's working fine."

Tony folded his arms. "I wonder who took it?"

"Who knows? Probably the guy who used the third brandy glass."

"Talk straight, Shaver. I'm not following you."

"Then listen carefully," she replied. "Last night, Tom and I were the only ones drinking. Ellie abstained. The third glass must belong to the thief. Got any ideas?"

"Sorry, sweetheart, don't have a clue."

"Too bad. If you hadn't smudged the glasses, we could have called the cops and had them dusted."

Tony's stiffened. Without knowing it, the reporter had warned him. He'd been careless after he'd killed Kempner and dragged him into the garage. He'd stuffed the mob attorney into his wife's Mercedes, but Tony had forgotten to wipe his prints off the car key and door handle.

He kept his arms folded and tried to look disinterested, but he needed to rectify his mistake. His next task was to get back into the garage.

"Well, ladies. We're making no progress in here. Shall we spread out and look for Tom?"

The reporter nodded and stood up. Before he could react, she leaned across the desk and extended her arms, curling her fingers and thumbs to hook the inside lips of the brandy snifters.

She flashed a smile and lifted them off Tom's desk. As the glasses swayed like three fish dangling from the end of a stringer, she began walking toward the door.

"I'll wash these up in the kitchen. As long as I'm there, I might as well check out that end of the house. As for the rest… why don't you and Ellie divide it up?"

Patricia Shaver knew Dr. Tony Gaylani was upset. His face had steeled when she took off for the kitchen. They all knew Tom Kempner was dead and sitting in Kitty's Mercedes. She didn't care who made the official discovery, but maybe Tony felt differently.

Pat sensed the doctor had no intention of giving her free rein. To make use of her limited time, she checked on Blizzard and Snowflake, then went into the laundry room and hid the brandy snifters in the pantry. That done, she stepped past the slumbering dogs. Once in the breakfast nook, she phoned the Barrington Police Department. Her anonymous call complete, she hung up on Chief Carlton Cherrigan's 911 operator just as Tony entered the kitchen.

"Heard voices, blondie," he said, looking at her. "You talking to anyone?"

"Buzz off, doc. You didn't hear a thing."

"Don't fuck with me, sister," he snarled, his dark eyes cold. "I said I heard voices."

"Oh, yes, now I remember." She stepped out of the breakfast nook and back into the kitchen. "I had a chat with the dogs. What a tale they told."

When Dr. Gaylani took another step into the kitchen, Blizzard sprang to her feet, her back hairs up.

"What's with the mutt?"

"She's temperamental," Pat said, walking between him and the dogs. "Be careful. I might be wrong, but I don't think she likes you."

Ellen came in and knelt by Blizzard's side. "What's the matter, girl?"

Tony kept edging back. "Like most broads, she's either finicky or looking for a handout."

"If that's the case, be a sport and give her a treat." Pat pointed toward the dog biscuit jar. "If you keep backpedaling, you'll trip over the doggie—"

She turned toward the door to the dining room and pretended to be surprised.

"Well, I'll be, some fool took the doggie gate down."

"A doggie gate?" he asked. "Why would anyone care?"

She didn't respond, but noted that Tony's dirty look and menacing tone still had Blizzard's attention. The Lab growled even louder, then took a step forward, teeth bared.

He retreated behind one of the dining room chairs. "Keep that damn mutt away."

Again, she didn't respond. Instead, Pat walked through the laundry room, opened the door to the garage, and pushed the opener. "Hey, girls, let's go out."

Blizzard and Snowflake wagged their tails, but before they could follow her, Pat screamed.

"In here! Oh, my God! Tom's in here."

Tony rushed past her, stopping near the driver's side of Kitty Kempner's car. "I was afraid of this."

Pat turned toward the open door. "Ellie, call 911. Tell them to send the paramedics."

Pat prayed that the emergency equipment she'd already requisitioned wouldn't arrive while Ellen was on the phone. For her own reasons, Pat wanted Dr. Gaylani to assume he had a few minutes before Chief Cherrigan and the bluecoats arrived.

"You're not surprised?" she asked, walking toward him. "You really saw this coming?"

The doctor moved closer to the Mercedes. "After Kitty's funeral, I expected him to be more resilient. But it never happened. Tom didn't set his jaw and become determined. His old spirit never materialized."

She noticed Dr. Gaylani reach into his pants pocket. When he pulled out a handkerchief, she again walked in his direction.

"You idiot," she snapped, "for God's sake, don't touch a thing."

"Go easy," he said, the handkerchief covering his hand. "I need to check Tom's pulse."

"Why? The man's deader than a doornail."

Dr. Tony Gaylani didn't hesitate. Using his handkerchief, he grabbed the handle and pulled the car door open. To complete the eradication of his prints, he reached under the steering wheel and removed the keys from the ignition.

"Don't worry," he said, all smug. "I'll put them back."

Pat's shoulders dropped, choreographing defeat. When she heard the sirens, she turned and watched a squad car speed down the driveway, lights flashing.

"How's that for a quick response?" Ellen said, coming into the garage. "Just got off the phone."

As Chief Carlton Cherrigan got out of his patrol car, the paramedics arrived in their emergency vehicle.

"Hello, Cherry," Pat said. "We found Mr. Kempner in his wife's car. It's supposed to look like a suicide, but I think somebody murdered him."

Chief Cherrigan didn't move. Puffing out his chest, he used his imposing physique to advantage. "No offense, ma'am, but if it's all the same to you, I'll conduct the inquiry."

"Be my guest," Pat replied, "but if I were in your shoes, I'd be mighty thorough. Tom Kempner's firm represents a man near and dear to our hearts. From what I hear, Mr. Barbera doesn't take kindly to people bumping off his friends."

The chief checked to see if they were alone. "Lady, not only is your mouth big, now you're talking out your ass."

"Why, Cherry. You certainly know how to sweet-talk a girl."

"Get lost, Miss Shaver."

"Just trying to be helpful," she replied. "If you don't want to dust the door handle and ignition key for prints… fine. But don't come bellyaching to me if someday Mr. Barbera thinks you and your deputies did a shoddy job."

"As long as your mouth keeps flapping, I can't get to work."

"Then I'll make it simple," she said, stepping closer. "Answer one question. How does a suicidal man climb into a car without leaving any prints?"

Cherrigan's eyes widened, visual confirmation her spoon-feeding operation had succeeded. Buoyed by the knowledge that the chief's sense of self-preservation would spur him to action, she did an about-face and headed toward her other target.

"Man, it's cold," Pat said, stopping in front of Dr. Gaylani. "I'm freezing, how 'bout you?"

"Cold weather doesn't bother me."

They stood in the garage, staring at each other. When the doctor turned to leave, Pat grabbed his parka. "Before I give Cherrigan my theory on the murder, there's one thing about this case I wouldn't mind discussing."

"Theorize all you want," he replied. "We've got nothing to talk about."

She let go and took a step toward the laundry room door. "Suit yourself. Just figured I'd give you a chance to explain."

"Explain what?" he asked, following her.

She ignored him and continued to walk with Ellen into the laundry room.

"All right, blondie," the doctor said, hustling to catch up. "What's on your mind?"

"Not much," she replied, "except for what happened last night."

"What's that supposed to mean?"

"Tom was a real chatterbox," she answered. "One minute Vietnam, the next your wedding."

"Sounds pretty dull."

"Maybe to you," she said, "but learning why those catty nurses called you the Roman Allah was worth the price of admission."

"I'm… ah… I'm afraid you're way ahead of me."

Pat poked him playfully. "Oh, come on, R.A. Loosen up. We won't tell any of your sandbox buddies that you're kind of partial to kosher delis."

For a moment it looked like he might overlook her comments. But then his face got red and he called her a bitch.

Ellen stepped between them. "For the love of God, you two! Be civil."

"Not easy, but I'm trying," Pat replied, still eying the doctor. "Tony… or should I call you Rashid? Why don't you get on your camel and ride out of town."

She watched him stomp back into the garage. Once Tony got past the police and paramedics, she lost sight of him, but seconds later she heard his Mercedes SUV start up and roar away.

"I thought that went very well. What did you think?"

Ellen didn't answer. Instead, she went into the kitchen and picked up Blizzard. Pat followed, wrapping Snowflake in her arms.

They left through the garage and headed toward her Mercedes. Pat knew Ellen was upset, but it couldn't be helped. She was on a mission, and nothing was going to change her plans.

"Be right back. Just need to talk to the chief."

Before beginning the short journey to Honey Lake and her house, she sought out Cherry and added to his storehouse of information. Dr. Gaylani was a murderer, and now he was angry at her. She wasn't afraid to stand up to the Iraqi spy, but that didn't mean she was inclined to take unnecessary risks.

CHAPTER TWENTY-TWO

Patricia Shaver drove toward her home on Honey Lake. While Blizzard and Snowflake slept in the back seat of her Mercedes, Ellen sat crossed-armed in the front, fuming in silence. The situation was bad, but salvageable. As Ellen stared out the windshield, Pat talked, recapping what they knew about Kitty and Tom Kempner's murders and how that aligned with her revised plan to bring Tony and Joanna Gaylani to justice.

"What do you think?" Pat asked. "Am I on track?"

"Before I endorse anything, I want answers," Ellen replied. "Why did you let Dr. Gaylani wipe his prints off the door handle and ignition keys?"

"Let him?" she replied. "I begged him."

"Either way, the result is the same. When Chief Cherrigan dusts the car, he'll just find smudge marks."

"Exactly," Pat said, keeping her eyes on the road. "But sometimes smudge marks are more telling than a fresh set of prints."

"Talk sense," Ellen demanded. "Why didn't you want the chief to find Dr. Gaylani's fingerprints on the door?"

"Because it wouldn't help convict him," Pat said, her exasperation showing. "Think about it. The doc has a perfect alibi."

She went on, expanding on the story Dr. Tony Gaylani could spin to the police: As a medical man, he would try to help. The smell of gas fumes and the sight of Tom Kempner would prompt him to rush over, open the car door, and check to see if his neighbor was alive.

She glanced at Ellen, then explained that a lack of prints meant

Tom Kempner didn't get into the car by himself. A suicidal man wouldn't slide in, start the engine, and then wipe his fingerprints off the door handle and ignition keys.

"Sound reasoning," Ellen agreed. "Tony goofed big time. Toweling away his calling card was a huge mistake."

Pat nodded, but her triumph was short-lived. Ellen leaned forward, her face showing doubt.

"Hold on one second. We believe he wiped off his fingerprints, but we can't prove it. A lack of prints tells a prosecutor that Tommy was murdered, but it doesn't point the finger at the killer."

"Get real. We both know Tony Gaylani is guilty."

"Do we?"

"Okay," Pat conceded, "maybe we're short on admissible evidence, but damn it… if the doc isn't punished it will be a travesty of justice."

"More like the way we do business," Ellen replied. "In America it's innocent until proven guilty."

Pat pumped the brakes and turned right onto another snow-packed road. "It's tough to convict a killer who destroys evidence, but who knows? Maybe he'll have an accident and save the taxpayers the cost of a trial."

"What!" Ellen barked. "When did vigilantism become part of our legal system?"

Pat avoided her friend's eyes. "Must justice only be handed out in courtrooms?"

"I won't dignify that question with a response." Ellen leaned forward, straining against her seatbelt. "But I'm curious about two things: What's your plan, and more importantly, why aren't you leveling with me?"

Pat's grip tightened on the steering wheel. "What could I possibly be holding back?"

"You're big on scenarios. What if Chief Cherrigan gathers the evidence, but doesn't put two and two together? Will you step in and make the call to the one person who doesn't care about courtroom procedures? Are you prepared to rub elbows with Mr. Barbera?"

"It's not what you think, Ellie."

"Isn't it? Why did you remind the chief that Mr. Barbera doesn't like it when his people get killed?"

"I'm not joining forces with Gary Barbera. I only goaded Cherry into doing his job." Pat glanced quickly at her friend. "My strategy is to create mad money. We know the dough is in our wallet, we just hope it never has to be spent."

"Was insulting Tony Gaylani another way to put money in our hip pocket?" Ellen asked, banging a gloved hand on the dashboard. "First you sparred over brandy glasses, then a few minutes later you forced the laundry room scene. My God, you barely stopped short of accusing him of murder."

"That man killed the Kempners. Why can't you accept that?"

"What I accept and what you can prove are two different things. You're not Roy Bean and this isn't the Wild West."

"I'm trying to get proof. Why do you think I hammered the doc with embarrassing facts? Maybe Tony will forget they're not relevant and conclude we know more than we do."

"And the brandy glasses?" her friend asked. "How does a mad money strategy fit in with the brandy glasses?"

Pat saw an icy patch in the road and steered carefully.

"We left Tom Kempner alone after midnight. The answering machine logged Admiral Weiss's call in at 2:02 AM. By then, Tom was breathing exhaust fumes and the killer was gone."

Ellen nodded. "Tommy answers the phone if he's alive. But if Tommy is dead and the murderer is there, he does what you did. He listens to the tape and lifts it. That still doesn't tie in the brandy glasses."

"Tom and I left our brandy snifters on the table. When Dr. Gaylani surprised us this morning, he brought three snifters into the office. The inference is overwhelming. After we left, Tom sipped brandy with a visitor he thought he could trust."

Ellen looked out, tensing as the road unwound before them.

"Even if I agree, once Tony Gaylani covered each one of the brandy glasses with his prints, he made the glasses less, not more important."

"Not by my reckoning," Pat countered, shaking her head. "The doc made another mistake."

"Really?" Ellen said, her eyebrow arching.

Pat laid out her case, explaining that by cradling balloon-style snifters in their fingers and palm, connoisseurs allow body heat to warm the brandy.

"Fine," Ellen agreed, "it releases the bouquet. What's the point?"

Pat went on, theorizing that in spite of Tony Gaylani's actions, each glass still had an untouched set of prints. The doctor had smudged the sides, but hadn't disturbed the saucer-shaped bottom.

"Assuming all that's true," Ellen said, "how do you plan to time-stamp Dr. Gaylani's glass? Have you forgotten that he removed all the snifters from the living room before Chief Cherrigan arrived on the scene? We're the only ones who saw the third glass on the coffee table. Besides, even if we swore it was sitting there, you took it into…"

Ellen turned and glared.

"Wait a minute. Did you wash those glasses or put them somewhere else?"

Pat shrugged, keeping her eyes on the road.

"Well, well, Patricia. This is a new low."

"What do you mean?"

"Where did you hide them?" Ellen asked.

"Behind some #10 cans labeled Whole Grapes."

"Wonderful," Ellen scoffed. "How'd you plan to have the glasses turn up? An anonymous tip to Chief Cherrigan or a direct phone call to Mr. Barbera?"

"These matters aren't always straightforward."

"Maybe not to a judge," Ellen said, her voice rising. "But in Mr. Barbera's hands, the glasses would be the linchpin that proved Tony Gaylani was the last person to see Tommy alive."

Pat didn't dare look. She already knew her friend's face had gotten beet red.

"Jeez, Ellie, don't get mad. Everything I've done is just insurance in case—"

"In case what?" Ellen demanded, her tone unwavering. "It's one thing to make sure the authorities don't overlook lawful evidence. It's quite another to create damning suggestions in the eyes of a man who's capable of taking the law into his own hands."

Pat didn't offer a rebuttal. How could she? Ellen's argument was irrefutable. But in spite of having no moral, philosophical, or legal ground to stand on, she was committed to keeping all her options open.

She turned the Mercedes into her driveway, realizing she had phone calls to make and a dangerous strategy to implement.

Dr. Tony Gaylani knew he'd been conned. The Shaver woman had gotten him so mad, he'd left without thinking. It pained him to think how he'd stormed past Chief Cherrigan's deputies without bothering to notice why they were still examining Kitty Kempner's Mercedes. Worse still, until he entered his house, he'd forgotten he hadn't tracked down the brandy snifters.

Tony sought out Joanna, telling her about Tom's suicide. When she expressed concern, he suggested they go back to the Kempners. He could find out what Chief Cherrigan's men had come up with and also see if the brandy snifters had been washed and put away.

Tony drove over and parked in Tom Kempner's turnaround. While Joanna greeted the chief, he walked through the garage and into the kitchen. Even before he opened the dishwasher and looked in, he knew the answer.

Several seconds later, he felt a tap on his shoulder.

"Dear," Joanna asked, "why are you looking in Tom's dishwasher?"

"Not now, sweetie. I'm busy."

Tony wanted to scream. First the cassette. Now the brandy snifters. Joanna tapped his shoulder again.

"Chief Cherrigan and his crew are getting ready to take Tom to the morgue. Maybe you should go along?"

He looked up from the dishwasher. "Did you say the morgue?"

"Cherry didn't elaborate, but I got the feeling he's conducting a full-scale investigation."

"Why? Everyone knows Tom committed suicide."

"Apparently not everyone, dear."

Patricia Shaver sat on one of her kitchen stools. As Tom Kempner's dogs reacquainted themselves with Snowshoe and Shoe-Too, Ellen pushed steaming mugs across the counter.

"Thanks," Pat said, taking a sip. "You make good coffee."

"Cut the small talk. Let's get on with it."

"Pick a starting point," Pat said, holding her mug. "There are so many crosscurrents, I hardly know where to begin."

Ellen came around the L-shaped divider and sat on a stool. "Go with the cassette."

Pat flipped open the cover on her answering machine, replaced the cassette with the one from Tom Kempner's office, and hit the replay button. She'd given Ellen a paraphrased version, but Admiral Weiss's exact words still had an impact.

"His voice gives me the creeps," Ellen said. "That last part… the way Jews stand. What does it mean?"

"A clever warning Ben-Gurion coined during the first Arab-Israeli War."

"Talk straight," her friend said. "Why suggest that Jews stand back to back?"

"So they can always be face to face with the enemy."

"Oh," Ellen replied. "Looks like Admiral Weiss thought Tommy's life was in danger too."

"Why guess?" Pat asked, grabbing the phone. "One call answers that question."

"Don't waste time phoning the admiral," Ellen said. "It's Christmas."

"Last night, Tom said spies never sleep. Maybe that means they also work holidays."

Pat dialed directory assistance, accepted the additional charge for ringing the call through, then heard the CIA receptionist.

"Seasons Greetings to you too. Admiral Eric Weiss, please."

The phone rang several times, then the admiral's recorder boomed out instructions. After it beeped, she responded:

"Hello, Admiral. You don't know me. We have... Check that. We had a friend in common. I was there last night when Tom Kempner called you. Unfortunately, between the time we left him and you called back, someone entered his house, killed him, and faked his suicide. At your convenience, I'd like to discuss the matter."

Pat caught Ellen's eye, then finished with her name, phone number, and a postscript:

"My cohort and I wrote the *Inquirer* article last spring. You remember. The one that let everyone know about Gary Barbera and his super-secret payroll."

Ellen winced. "As usual, you overdid it... but I'm guessing it won't matter. Odds are the admiral will plead amnesia."

"Maybe, but no matter what he says, we win."

"How do you figure?"

"Easy. If Eric Weiss denies everything, that's proof Barbera and the CIA are working together."

"I don't think so," Ellen replied. "At best, it proves they might be talking. But even if I buy into your story, it doesn't mean Dr. Gaylani is their target."

Pat didn't answer. To fully understand why Tom and Kitty Kempner had been murdered, she needed to figure out a few other things. Of course, she wanted Ellen's help, but not if her friend questioned every aspect of her plan. While she thought Ellen believed that Dr. Tony Gaylani was the killer, Pat was sure her friend didn't think Joanna was involved. Until she knew how all the players interfaced, she'd keep her innermost conjectures to herself.

Pat slid off the stool and stretched her arms over her head. Keeping Ellen on the sidelines wouldn't be easy. Her friend expected to hear a sensible explanation. Anything less and she might take what they knew to the police.

"To preserve anonymity," Pat said, "a high-ranking operative in the CIA would be reluctant to use an intermediary to contact a Mafia don. If Weiss wanted to make contact with Barbera, he would have placed the call himself."

When Ellen nodded, Pat went on, saying that the current situation was a special case. Tom Kempner lived next to the Gaylanis. He was also the *consigliere* to Gary Barbera and had grown up in the same neighborhood with Eric Weiss. Taken together, those facts made him a desirable go-between and a person who could bring hard evidence to the table. The admiral may have wanted to enlist Barbera first, but once he got him on board, the admiral planned to brief Tom Kempner on his role.

Ellen eyed her, then stared at the ceiling. "You're saying Tommy deliberately lied to Kitty... that all along he knew the CIA had contacted the mob as a way to get information on Dr. Gaylani."

"That's what I'm saying."

"Strong stuff," her friend said, gazing out the window. "If true, it means that while Kitty ranted and raved, Tommy knew her allegations were correct."

"Not quite that cut and dried," Pat cautioned, raising a finger.

"Didn't you just say that Tommy knew why Admiral Weiss came calling?"

"Yes, but with one caveat. Tom Kempner knew that Tony Gaylani was the subject under discussion, but until General Cunningham's papers arrived and he got a first-hand account of the doc's reaction, Tom didn't know his wife had uncovered an Iraqi spy."

Ellen rubbed her chin. "Are you suggesting that Tommy miscalculated... that when he found out, he either didn't react quick enough or didn't think Kitty was in any immediate danger?"

"I don't believe he did anything to intentionally put his wife in harm's way."

"Patricia!" her friend snapped. "Don't patronize me."

"Fine," Pat said, "then read between the lines."

"You do it for me."

Pat stopped pacing and eyed her friend. "Tom was a smart lawyer who made a terrible error in judgment. First he let his loyalty to the mob blind him, and then he compounded matters by thinking his old neighborhood pal, the admiral, would keep him informed. When neither happened, he got hung out to dry."

"You're saying Tommy's commitment to Mr. Barbera and Admiral Weiss cost Kitty her life?"

"Well… yes and no."

"Yes and no," Ellen grumbled. "How do I read between those lines?"

"By listening to me," Pat replied. "Admiral Weiss made contact before the general's papers arrived. At that stage in the negotiation, Tom Kempner's role was still being defined. Since no one had seen General Alan Cunningham's documents, Tom couldn't know that his wife would become a target. He just acted like a *consigliere* was supposed to act. He treated sensitive matters sensitively."

Ellen folded her arms across her chest. "Bottom line… Tommy made a pledge to Mr. Barbera and Admiral Weiss. But once he agreed to keep his mouth shut, neither the mob nor the CIA made any attempt to protect Kitty."

"It's likely Barbera was less culpable," Pat said quietly. "There's no reason to believe he knew General Cunningham's papers were in transit or carried a powerful message."

"I get it," Ellen muttered, her tone angry. "Your buddy Gary is a great big hero?"

"I'm just giving you the facts, not defending him."

"Powerful men treated Tommy and Kitty like pawns on a chessboard." Ellen bowed her head. "That kind of behavior makes me want to call the editor of the *Tribune* and tell him everything we know. Maybe an op-ed piece would send Admiral Weiss a message."

"We're both frustrated," Pat cautioned. "Before we take any action, we need to think things through."

Tears streaked Ellen's cheeks. "In some ways, I'm madder at Tommy. Barbera and Weiss create havoc for a living. He should have known better."

"It's not too hard to see how he got caught in their web," Pat replied. "Fact is, Tom Kempner was a good man with a good heart."

"Did Tommy's good heart tell him not to have an autopsy performed on Kitty?"

"I beg your pardon?"

Pat swallowed hard. Ellen had just broached a subject she didn't want to discuss.

"You heard me," Ellen said. "Kitty was a doctor who got annual checkups. As far as I know, she had no illnesses. Wouldn't a caring husband want an autopsy to identify the cause of death?"

"Guess that's a personal matter. Some people would, some wouldn't."

"No question it was personal," Ellen said, her voice reverberating. "Kitty made it personal. On the day she died, she accused Dr. Gaylani of being a spy."

"Let it go," Pat pleaded. "We've been through all this before."

"Except for one very important thing. An autopsy would have told Tommy exactly how his wife died."

Pat tried to mask her worry. First her friend had threatened to go to the papers; now she'd brought up the idea of an autopsy. Of course, Tom Kempner had suspected his wife had been murdered. But the man was also a pragmatist, seasoned in mob ways. He didn't dare ask for an autopsy. When the Mafia and CIA did business, no one got in their way.

"It's hard to be clinical," Pat said at last, "but consider this scenario: The CIA has reason to believe Dr. Gaylani is a spy. In an effort to collect evidence, Admiral Weiss contacts the mob through his old friend, Tom. Once Barbera agrees to help, the admiral calls Tom Kempner back and asks him to get chummy with his neighbor."

"Even if I accept your premise," Ellen said, daubing her eyes with a handkerchief, "why didn't Tommy ask questions? When a guy at Langley tells you to moonlight, it should raise a red flag."

"Maybe it did," Pat admitted, "but Tom was dealing with the deputy director of the CIA and the Godfather of the Chicago Mafia.

These men issue orders. They don't discuss strategy with subordinates."

"Are you suggesting that the admiral told Tommy to eavesdrop on his neighbor, but conveniently forgot to tell him why?"

"That's how I think the plan evolved," Pat said, her shoulders slumping, "but we'll never know for sure. Before Admiral Weiss could gather enough evidence to indict Dr. Gaylani, Kitty got murdered."

"No wonder Tommy blamed himself." Ellen stared at the handkerchief bunched in her hand. "A moment ago, you said he had a good heart. I disagree. When Tommy was between a rock and a hard place, he left his wife to fend for herself. He lacked courage when Kitty needed him most."

Pat lowered her eyes. "Taking orders from Admiral Weiss and Gary Barbera couldn't have been pleasant. Who knows… maybe that's why Tom finally turned a deaf ear on them and started confiding in us."

"Slow down, Patricia. You just spent five minutes telling me why Tommy had no recourse but to follow their commands. Now you want me to believe that he suddenly found his backbone and said good-bye to Langley and the mob?"

"I don't know why he opened up to us," Pat said, "but why debate his thought processes? Let the time lines tell us his reasons."

"What time lines?"

"The ones that defined Tom's actions. Before the delivery of General Cunningham's papers, he played the part of the loyal *consigliere*. Tom took Admiral Weiss's call, then set up a meeting between the admiral and his boss, Gary Barbera."

"Why repeat things I already know?"

"To highlight the differences," Pat replied. "When we went to his house after his wife's death, he kept us at arm's length, but once we told him about Kitty's letter, Tom's attitude changed. You heard him. He became more talkative and without any prompting, violated the attorney/client privilege and also brought up Admiral Weiss's name."

"That's right," Ellen said, "Tommy told us about the Mafia/CIA meeting and even placed a call to the admiral."

Pat didn't comment. Rather, she watched Ellen take a sip of coffee, then slide off the kitchen stool and begin pacing back and forth.

"Why," Ellen murmured to herself, "why did he confide in us?"

"Who else could he trust?"

"Maybe no one," Ellen agreed, turning and facing her, "but that's no reason to bare your soul. Guys like the admiral don't like it when their recruits discuss Company projects."

"No argument," Pat said, "but don't forget the time lines. Maybe it was our disclosure of Kitty's letter, or maybe it was for some other reason, but by then, Tom was treating us as allies."

"Fine," Ellen said, looking impatient. "I had a long friendship with Kitty, and you're a forthright journalist. Tommy had every right to be mad and feel betrayed, but he was also a professional. Why tell us about the Barbera/Weiss liaison? Why blow the whistle on the CIA? Why disregard the attorney/client privilege? Like you said earlier, he had to understand there would be consequences."

"I'm sure he did, but by then it didn't matter," Pat answered. "By then, he feared for his life."

"Am I nuts? If he feared for his life, why give us information about two men who don't fool around? The mob and the CIA play for keeps."

"Yes, but after Kitty's death, Tom probably figured he'd be someone's target no matter what he did."

A remembrance flashed into Pat's brain. Earlier, the discovery of the Kempner/Weiss file had excited her. The cover letters and Hispanic-American trucker biographies had outlined how the Chicago Mafia and the CIA had engaged in covert and illegal activities for more than two decades.

At the time, she'd thought Tom Kempner had created the file to incriminate people he no longer trusted. While that was still a reasonable explanation, now she wondered why Tom had left it in an unlocked desk drawer. The mob attorney wasn't stupid. He had to know that in the event of his death, Gary Barbera would send in Chief Carlton Cherrigan to purge all the files in his office.

"Just so there's no confusion," Ellen said, her voice firm, "you're saying that Tommy was a marked man… that he joined forces with us to make sure everyone who had a hand in his wife's murder paid for it?"

Pat nodded, still troubled that Tom had left the Kempner/Weiss file unprotected. Unless…? Suddenly, she remembered what he'd said just before she and Ellen had left last night: "It may be awhile before Admiral Weiss's staff gets up the nerve to wake him. In the meantime, I've got some important papers in my desk drawer to file away. That will keep me busy for quite some time."

Last night, she'd thought his answer was strange. But right now she wasn't so sure. Had Tom left the Kempner/Weiss file there on purpose?

A safety deposit box would have been more secure, but not necessarily a better place. Upon his death, officialdom would have opened it and confiscated the file as evidence in the government's continuing legal battle against organized crime. Under that scenario, the CIA and FBI would have made sure the Kempner/Weiss file never saw the light of day.

"It's scary to think about," Ellen said, "but if all your suppositions are true, Kitty was a victim of circumstance. She asked for her grandfather's memoirs, not knowing what was in them. But once the Brits tipped off the CIA, other wheels were set in motion."

"Yes. The operation went into high gear the second Admiral Weiss figured out that General Alan Cunningham's papers could help him nail Dr. Tony Gaylani."

Ellen sat back on the stool, her face pale. "You think our government is working with the British to set Tony up?"

Rather than answer, Pat reached over the L-shaped counter and poured herself more coffee. She hoped the people at MI-6 and the CIA had worked in concert, but she couldn't be sure how much either agency had studied the general's documents. In a world of espionage and computers, it was possible the top-secret memoirs had been improperly reclassified, and like a book in the library, sat in the archives waiting until Kitty Kempner checked them out.

"I believe our spies and theirs were working together," she finally said. "At least we know the time lines fit."

Pat held her breath. Throughout their give-and-take, she'd purposely kept one of her well-thought-out conjectures from Ellen. While she hated being less than forthcoming, until she verified her suspicion she saw no advantage to correcting one of her friend's blind spots.

All the circumstantial evidence indicated that Tony Gaylani had killed the Kempners without any help from his wife. But if that was true, wouldn't it follow that Joanna had intercepted, opened, and re-sent Kitty's letter? Lord knows, the doctor wouldn't steal and then mail a self-incriminating note. And Joanna wouldn't frame her husband if they were working together. But if they each had their own agendas…

Ellen stood up. "Everything you say makes sense. Tommy opened up after we gave him reason to suspect Admiral Weiss and Mr. Barbera."

Pat nodded. "Tom had plenty of misgivings, but once we paraphrased the contents of Kitty's note, he knew we were on his side."

Ellen sipped from her coffee mug. "Tommy was a sharp guy, but in this case, he got manhandled. His old neighborhood buddy Weiss sent him to the front lines with a gun loaded with blanks."

"That's when he decided who could be trusted and who couldn't," Pat said.

"One of your predictions turned out to be accurate. In their own way, they each sent out an SOS. I got Kitty's letter, and last night Tommy told us about his conversations with the admiral."

"As with many things," Pat remarked, "after the fact, everything is as plain as day."

She tacitly agreed, but she knew Ellen was wrong. Tom's conversations with the admiral were just a prelude of things to come.

He'd sent out his SOS when he left the Kempner/Weiss file in his office drawer. But as with other components in this investigation, Pat decided it was better to keep Ellen in the dark.

"You're right, Ellie. When Tom joked about getting second class treatment, he really meant there was a big picture, but he wasn't privy to it."

Ellen stirred her coffee. "Now they're both dead… and we failed them."

"Not in my book," Pat said, grabbing her friend's shoulders. "No one could have predicted this. But if we ignore the clues and let the matter drop, we'll have failed their trust."

"Is that why you called the admiral?"

"You're damn right. So help me God, if our government screwed up… If somehow the Kempners became expendable because Admiral Weiss didn't think through all the ramifications of going after Tony Gaylani… Well, if that's what happened, it's our duty to bring it to light."

Pat's phone rang and they both jumped. Why did it seem louder than normal? Was it because she knew who was calling?

She told herself to calm down. Even if the CIA and Mafia were working together—even if she and Ellen were in the way—she'd figure out a way to be a formidable opponent.

As the phone rang again, Pat felt her heart rate slow. Last spring she'd faced off with Gary Barbera and survived. This time there would be an additional player. She didn't know how Admiral Weiss operated, but at least one thing was certain. Spies—even admiral-type spies—worked on holidays.

CHAPTER TWENTY-THREE

Gary Barbera stood in front of a credenza. It was late morning and he was in his downtown Chicago office on the 102nd floor of the Sears Tower. Christmas Day was normally his favorite holiday, but at the moment, he didn't feel in the Christmas spirit.

Gary glanced across the office at a picture that hung in a place of honor behind his desk. The framed photograph—taken in the late 1890's—showed his father, then a seven-year-old boy, standing with his parents in front of their store in Palermo, Sicily.

Gary had never gotten to see much of his grandparents, but he'd loved them just the same. During his formative years, he'd often asked his father to tell him stories of the old country. At the time, he didn't realize that his father's association with the Mafia had driven a wedge between him and his Palermo relatives. Of course, no one ever acknowledged the estrangement. Birthday greetings and Christmas cards were exchanged. To an outsider, they looked like a happy family. But as he grew older, Gary understood all was not well. He also felt the same alienation his father had endured.

In a way it was ironic. The values his grandfather and grandmother had instilled in his father had been learned and passed down to him. His own cherished code of honor had been built around those teachings. But sadly, he would never go back to Sicily and thank them. The law-abiding Barbera shopkeepers had had a profound influence on his life and his father's life, but they would have been embarrassed to hear about it.

He motioned to Danny Finn, then walked to his desk. As the Irishman moved away from a panoramic view of the Chicago sky-line, Gary wondered if Finn also harbored a burning urge to avenge the Kempners' murders.

Over the years, Gary had watched people die. Some he'd mourned; most he had not. Fatalities stemming from conflicts among compet-ing crime bosses or street battles with the FBI and local police were part of his business. But Tommy and Katherine Kempners' deaths were different. They'd been executed by a different kind of enemy. They'd been victims of a terrorist plot.

"Hear any news from Chief Cherrigan?" Gary asked, watching Finn sit in the chair across from him.

"Our favorite flatfoot phoned in some preliminary results."

"Really?" Gary said, picking up a gold pen. "Did he come up with anything of interest?"

"More than I expected," Finn answered. "Without being told, Cherry conducted a full-bore investigation."

"That is surprising," Gary said, moving some papers closer for his signature. "I wonder what possessed him?"

"Don't know, but as you predicted, your *consigliere* didn't com-mit suicide."

Gary stopped signing the documents. "Did the killer attempt to get Tommy's prints in the right places?"

Finn shook his head "The door handle and ignition key were wiped clean."

"What about Tommy's body? Any word from the morgue?"

"Our contact in the coroner's office said your boy Kempner had a mound on the back of his skull big enough to tee up a golf ball."

"Will that be included in his report?"

"No," Finn replied. "The coroner will list the cause of death as suicide."

"Good. How about Weiss and his team at Langley? Anything new there?"

"You called that one too," the Irishman answered. "I don't know who filled them in, but those bastards got wind of Kempner's murder almost as fast as Chief Cherrigan."

"I'm surprised the admiral sent in his men," Gary said. "The CIA charter prohibits them from investigating domestic homicides."

"Sailor-boy used his FBI contacts. Cherrigan overheard one of their agents say his orders came straight from Washington. The top dog in the Bureau was doing the Company a favor."

"Sounds like the admiral's handiwork. As a rule the CIA are inept, but unfortunately, Eric Weiss is clever. He knew Dr. Gaylani was dangerous, but he kept it from me. By the time I realized the threat, my friend and his wife were dead."

Gary's fingers squeezed the gold pen. Like an old-school Sicilian don, he craved revenge. But, as always, he controlled his emotions. Long ago, Gary had learned that lashing out to exact retribution often created more problems than it solved. To insure the survival of his Family, a modern-day don never ordered a hit until he considered the full consequences of his actions.

In this case, the CIA had an interest in Dr. Tony Gaylani. Gary wanted to punish the man, but he would do nothing until Admiral Weiss gave him the nod.

"Sailor-boy may be an inventive prick," Finn said, "but I got another problem. It's my job to plug the leaks. Right now, I don't have a clue who's feeding Weiss information."

Gary looked up, his thought interrupted. "Were all our calls placed from secure phones?"

The Irishman nodded. "No one violates your standing instructions."

"Then simple logic tells me the loose lips aren't ours."

Finn leaned forward in his chair. "You think it's the chief or one of his people?"

"Unlikely," Gary said, pushing his paperwork aside. "Years ago, Cherrigan collected the remains of his predecessor and zipped up the body bag. Our friend may be slow to comprehend certain things, but that was sufficient warning, I think."

"I'm sure you're right, boss."

"No need to worry. Sooner or later, our network will find their source."

The Irishman set his jaw. "Let's make it sooner. Later doesn't sit well with me."

"If that's the way you feel, up the ante. I'm a big believer in paying top dollar for quality information."

Gary rose, touching one, then the other of his gold peregrine cufflinks. As his fingers felt how decades of rubbing had worn the embossed peregrines smooth, he stared at a miniature model airplane he kept on his desk.

His father had designed and made the balsawood model two years before the end of World War I. The single-engine fighter with a sweptback wing had the look of an F-16. But Hermann Goering— then an ace in the German air force—had dismissed the design as unstable. Had Adolph Hitler's future air minister been smart and put the warplane into production, it might have changed the outcome of WWI, or, at the very least, given Germany a big advantage in the next world war. But after the armistice, when his father moved his family to America, he also took the balsa model and blueprints.

"Coffee?" Gary asked, walking toward the credenza.

"Thanks, boss. Black would be great."

He poured a special blend of Etruscan coffee from a Lorenzo de' Medici server. All the silver pieces were from a tea set crafted from a da Vinci design celebrating falconry. The antiques had been a gift to his father from Al Capone.

Gary returned to his desk, remembering how his father had put guests and subordinates at ease by serving them coffee whenever they visited him in his office. That courtesy, like so many other things he'd learned, had come from a man who'd begun his business career with Samuel Insull, then used modern management skills to change the face of racketeering. Yet, for all his achievements, his father had always found time to measure out and brew the coffee and espresso served in his office. Gary Barbera, Sr., had been an important man, and he proved it by his willingness to recognize the people who helped him prosper.

After handing the Irishman a cup of coffee, Gary sat down behind his desk. His father had taught him well. Leaders build allegiances by example and fair play. Violence couldn't be eliminated, but it had to be used judiciously to defend the Family or to punish blatant infractions of his code of conduct.

"My father drummed one thought into my head: 'When you don't have a code to guide you, discipline vanishes.'"

"No argument, boss. Your code gives the Family purpose and allows all of us to set priorities."

"That's our strategic advantage," Gary said. "Langley doesn't have a code. They do some things right, but when one of their operations goes bad, they withdraw and try to place the blame on others."

Coffee cup in hand, Finn rose and walked behind his chair. "That's the problem. No matter how they do business, we still have to deal with them."

"Which reminds me," Gary replied. "Did Chief Cherrigan and the coroner take my advice?"

"Yes. They're being cooperative and are telling the authorities the same story." Finn stared at the hearth. "Shit, Boss, their performance has been so good, you'd swear the fuckers were taking acting lessons."

Gary noted that the Irishman's voice sounded jovial, but his face looked solemn. "You seem conflicted. Is there another problem?"

"I hate when the lackeys on the admiral's payroll get pushy," Finn replied. "Those bastards instructed the Feds to snatch Kempner's body out of the morgue. When we stalled them, they had the Bureau cordon off your lawyer's house and post agents inside."

"Haven't they locked an empty barn?" Gary's lips turned up— a wry smile he'd copied from his father. "As I recall, our people cleaned up the loose ends the second Chief Cherrigan and his crew left."

The Irishman nodded. "Another instance where I took your advice."

Gary listened as Finn described how he'd gotten hold of Cherrigan at the crime scene and told him that the mob's Sanitation Team needed to borrow two police uniforms. Finn went on to say that his men had masqueraded as cops and arrived moments after the chief's investigation ended. Ten minutes later, Tom Kempner's office had been emptied of all sensitive files.

Gary rolled his pen between manicured fingertips, then laid it on the desk pad. "You did say the coroner followed instructions?"

"As ordered, he dragged his heels," Finn replied. "Gave the Feds some bullshit about notifying the next of kin. With your approval, I'll instruct him to go ahead and release Kempner's body."

"Tell him he did a fine job," Gary said. "I like a man who can't be bullied."

"I'll make sure he gets a special holiday bonus," Finn replied, grinning. "Anything else?"

"No. Except the more I think about it, the more I want to know Admiral Weiss's source."

Gary again touched one of his gold peregrine cufflinks. He had important issues to deal with, but each time he tried to plan his next move, he started thinking about his father.

Any remembrance of family was welcome, but right this moment, he was annoyed that his concentration had drifted off point. Certainly, there were few parallels between the Kempners' murders and his father's untimely death. Or were there?

His jaw muscles tightened.

Well before Sunday morning, December 7, 1941, his father had sized up the combatants and concluded that Japan would eventually join Hitler and fight for world dominance. Gary, Sr., was born in Sicily and had strong ties to Italy, but he'd had no interest in supporting the Axis powers. He and his beloved wife had come to America to raise a son and start a new career. America had treated him justly, and he'd planned to return the favor.

Gary got slowly to his feet. It had just occurred to him why his memories kept coming back. His father, like his friends the Kempners, had been taken in a violent act initiated by a hostile foreign power. Now it was his turn to be a patriot. Just like his father, he would use Family assets to see that America triumphed.

He motioned to Finn.

"I want to find out who's providing information to Admiral Weiss. Once we get the source, we'll understand why the CIA is so interested in Dr. Gaylani and his Jewish wife."

"Read you five-by-five, boss."

"Give this matter top priority," Gary said, keeping his voice level. "We've got a score to settle. I'm confident we know who murdered Tommy and his wife, but since I've been forced to work with the admiral, I need to be sure."

The Irishman nodded. "That fuckin' Iraqi doctor did it, but before I have his arms and legs ripped off, I'll get confirmation."

Gary stared out at Lake Michigan. "He's my first choice, but Eric Weiss seems interested in Mrs. Gaylani's activities too. Men like the admiral are trained to send out false signals. His protocols are often sophisticated, and that makes it difficult to know who's really under his microscope."

"Don't worry, boss. We control enough military moles to outflank Sailor-boy. If he's interested in one or both of the Gaylanis, the brass on our payroll will report back in a matter of hours."

"Good. When it comes to taking care of our own, we must be decisive. Before I dispose of Tony Gaylani, I want to be sure his wife, Joanna, won't turn out to be a bigger thorn in my side."

CHAPTER TWENTY–FOUR

Patricia Shaver looked at Ellen Eichler. They were in Pat's country kitchen, seated on stools near the bend of the L-shaped granite counter. The phone was close by, but neither moved as it rang once, then again, and a third time. Finally, before the fourth ring, Pat grabbed the receiver. The caller I.D. window flashed PRIVATE, but they both knew who was on the line.

"Hello, Admiral. Thanks for calling back."

For the next minute, Pat listened while Eric Weiss feigned amnesia on all points except that he and Tom Kempner had grown up together.

"I'm sure you're right," she said. "Just a big misunderstanding."

When Admiral Weiss clicked off, she dropped the phone on the granite counter, seemingly oblivious that the impact damaged the end piece, allowing the battery to fall out.

Ellen picked up the receiver, shoved the battery back in, and snapped the broken plastic cover in place. "Careful, these things have limited warranties."

"Sorry, it's just…" She breathed in. "That jerk must think I'm an idiot."

"If you're still upset, buzz him back."

"Why?" Pat asked. "He'll just tell me the same thing."

"Then fill me in."

"The man talked in circles. For openers, he said he was shocked to hear from Tom after all these years. After that, he claimed the sum total of their business relationship was nothing more than a donation he promised to make to the University of Wisconsin Alumni Association."

Ellen smiled. "Who says our government is heartless?"

Pat slid off the stool and walked to a lakeside window. "Langley will come up with any alibi to save their butts."

"You're the card-carrying cynic. Why so surprised?" Ellen reached for the coffee pot and topped off her mug. "Forget the CIA. We need to get cracking."

"Let me start with a recap," Pat said, coming back and leaning against the counter. "We know Kitty Kempner kicked Dr. Tony Gaylani out, then wrote a letter and left it for the postman. We also know that before the afternoon pickup, someone took the letter from her mailbox, steamed it open, read it, glued it shut, and a day later, sent it to you."

Ellen rummaged in her handbag, pulled out the letter, then took a close look at the envelope.

"The date on the letter doesn't jibe with the postmark, but the business about steaming and gluing sounds like pure conjecture."

"Look closely at the letters and numbers," Pat said, using her index finger to point at the scripted address. "See how the ink ran just a smidge?"

"Big deal," Ellen replied. "The postman probably had snow on his gloves. It rubbed off and melted when he put the envelope in his truck."

"That would have created blotches. These ink runs are uniform... almost as though all the writing got the same treatment."

Pat leaned over the granite divider and held the letter above one of the gas burners.

"Assume there's a boiling pot of water below my hand."

"Fine," Ellen replied, "but even if your theory is plausible, it would be hard to prove."

Instead of answering, Pat turned the envelope face down and lifted the flap. "Run your finger along the glue line. Notice any irregularities?"

Ellen nodded. "The bumpy stuff sure wasn't put there by the manufacturer."

"I'm guessing a police lab would identify it as ordinary household glue."

"Suppose I buy your story," Ellen replied. "Aren't you forgetting one thing? Kitty was upset when she wrote the letter. Why would she leave it if the postman had already been by?"

"She wouldn't," Pat countered. "Kitty dropped it off before he came."

Ellen jumped off her stool. "How can you be so sure?"

"I counted the packets."

"You counted... Damn it, Patricia! What does that prove?"

"Do you remember when Tom said he didn't recall seeing the mail the night Kitty died?"

Ellen nodded. "He told us he hadn't seen it then, or picked it up any time since."

"I rest my case," Pat said, lifting her coffee mug. "We both know the Barrington postmen put rubber bands around each day's mail. Last night, when I walked the dogs, I also looked in Tom's mailbox. There were four packets. One for Wednesday, Thursday, Friday, and Saturday. That means two things: When Kitty dropped off the letter, the box was empty. When the postman came by sometime later, Kitty's letter had been taken."

Ellen pursed her lips, tacitly agreeing. "Someone had to be watching. We know Tony was home. Tommy told us Kitty got rid of him sometime around noon. But it makes no sense. That letter incriminates him."

"It wasn't Tony," she said. "Another person played postwoman."

"Post...? Not Joanna! You can't mean Joanna?" Her friend turned ashen. "My God! I just thought of something. At the church, a few minutes before Kitty's funeral, Joanna asked about my Saturday mail delivery. Said she'd sent an invitation for a Sunday morning get-together, but hadn't dropped it at the post office until late Thursday. She expressed concern that it might not get to me if I was on the morning route."

"Morning route?" Pat questioned. "What difference would that make?"

"None, but I was preoccupied with Kitty's service and didn't give it a second thought."

"That's not the only oddball thing." Pat placed her mug on the counter. "Why schedule a deli brunch for Christmas?"

Ellen nodded. "The idea of creating a foundation in Kitty's memory was appealing. Frankly, I never paid attention to the date."

Pat picked up Kitty's ill-fated letter and tapped it on the counter.

"This was the brunch invitation, and I'll bet that after Joanna Gaylani rerouted Kitty's letter, she hid and watched your reaction."

"There's more," Ellen said, fidgeting with her hands. "Remember when I tried to tell you about the file I saw in Tommy's office?"

"Those horse expenses?"

"Yes. Based on the invoices, it appears Tommy has been double-ordering ammonium nitrate for the last three years."

Pat kept her emotions under control. She knew Ellen was watching for a reaction. She also knew NH4NO3 was extensively used by farmers. In granular form, the chemical was added to certain fertilizers to bolster their performance. As a powder, it was dissolved in water and sprayed directly on plants and grasses. Of course, after the Oklahoma City bombing, she'd become aware it could be converted into something more deadly.

"Have I got this right? You're saying Tom Kempner double ordered ammonium nitrate?"

"Hold on," Ellen replied. "I said it *appears* he doubled ordered. But it's entirely possible he didn't know it."

"Come on," Pat muttered, "either he did or he didn't."

"There's no question he did it. His ranch file contained summer-month receipts for a product I was already supplying."

"But if you and another guy were delivering this stuff, how can you say he didn't know?"

"It's slightly complicated," Ellen said, taking a deep breath. "Joanna Gaylani has always shared stable space and grazed her horses in Kitty's pasture. About three years ago, as a thank you, she asked me to bill her for all the horse fodder and fertilizer. When I told her I supplied everything but the ammonium nitrate, she asked me to get it anyway. Claimed the extra cost was easier than dealing with another delivery person. Her payment methods were odd, but overall it seemed like a nice gesture."

"Forget about nice gestures. I'm interested in the odd payment methods."

"Joanna settled everything in cash," Ellen replied. "But that's not all. When my delivery guy finished and came to her front door, she took the bill, but refused to sign the receipt."

"That is weird," Pat agreed.

"What can I say? Joanna told me that she never wanted the Kempners to know the monetary amount of her generosity."

"But they already knew," Pat protested. "Until Joanna started picking up the tab, they were paying your bill."

"I said the same thing," Ellen replied, shrugging. "I also mentioned that the government didn't cotton to nameless accounting."

"And...?"

Ellen balled her hand, her knuckles whitening. "First she gave me a look that would kill. Then she demanded I keep it on the books as account X."

Pat's mind whirled. To effect a double order, Joanna Gaylani needed two suppliers. To accomplish that objective, Joanna must have told Tom that she'd take care of the hay, oats, and organic fertilizer, but he'd have to continue to use his supplier of ammonium nitrate.

"Over the three years, how much ammonium nitrate did you bring in?"

Eyes closed, Ellen pondered the question. "Give or take... two or three hundred pounds."

"And the organic fertilizer?" Pat asked. "How much of that?"

"About five tons."

Pat frowned. "I've seen the Kempners' stable. There's no way it's big enough."

"Right, that's why everything got dropped off just outside the barn doors. From there, Chuck Sweet took over."

Pat wanted to ask two questions, but decided the location of the barn could wait. "Is Chuck Sweet the same guy you mentioned when we made our first trip to Tom Kempner's?"

Ellen nodded. "He's the stableman Joanna hired three years ago."

"The man must be a glutton for punishment. Why deliver the hay and oats to some remote barn? The horses are in the stable near the house."

Ellen said she'd asked the same question. "To us, it didn't matter whether we split the shipment or unloaded it inside the barn or out. But Chuck was adamant. He wanted it done his way."

Pat picked up her coffee mug and slowly rotated it in her hands. "Where is this barn? I don't ever remember seeing it."

"You wouldn't," Ellen answered. "It's painted off-white and hidden in the far corner of the Kempners' property behind a stand of Douglas firs. With all the snow on the roof, it's almost invisible."

"So no one uses it in the winter?"

"Correct," Ellen said. "It's accessed by a dirt road that runs along the property line. To push through the drifts, you'd need a pick-up truck with a plow."

"What am I missing?" Pat asked. "If the barn isn't available year-round, where did you dump the turf *builder* in the winter? On the turnaround in front of the Kempners' mansion?"

Ellen grinned. "Nobody fertilizes after a killing frost. During the cold months that shipment stops. As for the hay and oats… we deliver to the stable near Tommy's house."

Pat pushed aside her half-empty coffee mug. "Don't tell me. In the wintertime, Chuck lets you stack the horse delicacies inside the stable."

Ellen smiled. "How'd you guess?"

"About this barn… have you ever been inside?"

"I've ridden by it, but that's all. I'm not pitching hay bales anymore, but our deliverymen tell me it's always padlocked."

"Doesn't that strike you as odd?" Pat asked. "Why would the Kempners let Joanna's man have the keys to their barn?"

"Why not? It's full of machinery and supplies. Neither one had any reason to go out there."

Pat slid off her stool and stood. "What do you know about this Chuck Sweet fellow?"

"Joanna found him. He supposedly lives in the area and seems knowledgeable about horses. Beyond that, nothing."

"Does he work for any other Barrington horse owners?"

"Don't think so," Ellen replied. "Why do you ask?"

She glanced at her watch, then handed Ellen her parka. "We're going to be late."

"Late. Late for what?"

"Didn't Joanna invite you to a Sunday morning get-together?"

Ellen nodded. "That's what she said, but—"

"But what?" Pat countered, moving toward the staircase. "Give me a sec to freshen up. If we leave in a minute or two, we'll get there before noon."

Instead of powdering her nose, she went up to her bedroom and hid the stuff she'd stolen from Tom Kempner's office. Until needed, the Kempner/Weiss file and the answering machine tape would stay under her mattress.

Moments later, jingling her keys, she bounded downstairs. "Don't give me that look, Ellie. I'm driving."

As her friend moved with a slow resignation, Pat envisioned her plan of attack. Their next move was to catch Tony Gaylani off balance. She assumed that after killing Tom, the doctor had taken the general's papers. She also believed that given the cumbersome nature of the memoirs and the late hour when they'd been snatched, he had to have hidden them close by. In view of their earlier confrontation, she hoped a surprise visit would encourage Tony to leave. At the very least, she expected her presence to send him sulking off to his den. Under that scenario, Ellen would occupy the lady of the house while Pat did some snooping.

* * *

Admiral Eric Weiss grabbed his sheepskin coat from the hall closet in his Georgetown house. He wasn't happy. Jerald Cash, Director of the CIA, had just beeped him. Instead of using Christmas Day for R & R, he was getting ready to leave for a meeting at Company headquarters.

"Don't worry, dear," Eric said, eyeing his wife. "I'll be home before the kids and grandkids get here for dinner."

Eric headed for the garage, happy he'd had the foresight to ask James Fitzgerald, the director of the FBI, to send agents to Tom Kempner's house. Several minutes earlier, he'd called Miss Patricia Shaver from his upstairs office. The conversation had been tense, but he'd answered her questions without giving up any information. Still… some of her claims had made him nervous. If the reporter was right, there were loose ends to connect.

Patricia Shaver cradled Tom Kempner's puppy in her arms. Ellen Eichler stood by her side and rang the Gaylanis' front doorbell. During the short drive, Ellen had expressed reservations, but agreed to participate in Pat's scheme.

Joanna Gaylani answered the door, staring wide-eyed. "Hello, you two. What a surprise."

Ellen smiled. "Hi, Joanna. We're here for the get-together."

"The get-together," Joanna asked. "What get-together?"

"Who is it, Joanna?" Tony joined his wife at the door. "Oh, it's you two again."

"Gee," Pat said, forcing a grin, "twice in one day. Like a dream come true."

After she and the doctor glared at each other, Pat turned toward Joanna.

"Hope you don't mind. When Ellie mentioned the brunch, I asked to tag along."

"I'm confused," Joanna said, rubbing her eyes. "About the get-together. Could you help me out?"

"That wife of yours is really something," Pat replied, winking at the doctor. "She's gorgeous to a fault, and now she's pretending this wasn't even her idea."

"Hush, Patricia." Ellen acted mad, then turned and faced Joanna. "I never got anything official, but we came anyway. You remember? We talked just before Kitty's funeral. You said the invitation was mailed late Thursday. You were worried it might not get delivered on time."

"Goodness me," Joanna replied, "didn't I tell you I'd rescheduled?"

When Ellen shook her head, Joanna raised her hands to her cheeks.

"First I plan a brunch for Christmas, then I forget to cancel. Forgive me, but now, with the terrible news about Tom's passing... Well, I'll keep you posted."

While Pat listened to Joanna make amends, Tony stood close by. She felt the doctor's dead stare, but ignored him, petting Snow-flake, then turning her attention to the Kempners' house. Several agents with yellow FBI letters blazoned on their overcoats had just strung crime scene tape around the perimeter.

"I'm heartened to see the Feds are involved," Pat said. "It's scary to think there's a killer on the prowl."

"Killer, Miss Shaver?" Tony asked, his voice rising. "Didn't Tom commit suicide?"

"Chief Cherrigan doesn't think so," she continued, careful not to make eye contact. "Why do you think he called in J. Edgar?"

"I'd ask him myself, but with an informed authority at our doorstep, it hardly seems worth the effort. Please. Fill us in."

Pat looked down at Snowflake. "I've probably said too much. We journalists have to protect our sources."

"Of course you do." Tony moved forward and got in her face. "It's too bad, but since you ladies are under a gag order, there's noth-ing left to say. Feel free to barge in next Christmas."

"Tony! What's come over you?" Joanna motioned them in and closed the front door. "I asked Ellen and Pat over."

"Then you watch 'em, sweetie-pie. I promised Trevor we'd finalize the arrangements."

As he walked by, Pat noted that Tony made a special effort to bump her shoulder.

"Choose your words carefully," he said. "Journalists have selective hearing. To them, 'off the record' sounds like 'feel free to print every word I just said.'"

Tony never looked back. Instead he kept going down the hallway toward the garage.

"Sorry," Joanna said, her face softening. "The Kempners' murders have us both unglued."

Pat took note that while Tony was around, Joanna had made reference to Tom's passing. Once the doctor had left, his wife had characterized the Kempners' deaths as murders.

"I understand why Tony feels unglued," Pat said. "The doc was the last one to see each of them alive."

Joanna cocked her head. "Weren't you and Ellen with Tom last night?"

"Yes," Pat replied, "but according to Chief Cherrigan, Tony stopped by for a brandy after we left."

"Patricia, please." On cue, Ellen disciplined her again. "The chief pledged us to secrecy."

"Me and my big mouth," Pat said, rolling her eyes. "Don't tell anyone. I wouldn't want your hubby to think I'm a gossip."

"Tony has nothing to hide," Joanna replied. "If he went over for a nightcap after I went to bed, so be it. As for his whereabouts when Kitty died... I was there and he was in the kitchen."

"You misunderstood me," Pat said. "When I said time alone, I meant all those hours they spent together that day. Weren't they going over the general's papers when you came over with the wine?"

"Heavens no," Joanna replied. "My husband came back well before one PM. Later he picked up the chardonnay and ran some other errands."

Wasn't that interesting? On the day Mrs. Kempner was murdered, Joanna had had an opportunity to steal Kitty's note. But that left an unanswered question. After she'd steamed it open, why had Joanna waited a full day before sending it along?

"Joanna, I love your house." As Pat stood in the foyer rocking Snowflake in her arms, she did a slow three-sixty. "Who's the decorator? The furniture and appointments are magnificent."

"She's too humble to say anything," Ellen replied.

Ellen continued her praise, going on about Joanna's ability to coordinate wall coverings with different furniture styles and fabrics. As Pat agreed with her friend's assessment, she also kept thinking about Katherine Kempner's letter.

A minute ago, she'd wondered why Joanna Gaylani had held the letter back. Now she'd figured it out. Until Tony had committed a crime, mailing the letter had served no purpose. But once he'd killed, the doctor might become a useful fall guy.

Snowflake's cold nose found her cheek. Well, well, well. Joanna might act like just another pretty face, but the lady from Hebron knew how to put Tony's head on a chopping block. First she'd set him up, then she'd made sure the trail of clues couldn't be traced back to her. My, oh, my. They weren't dealing with a rookie.

"I'm overwhelmed." Pat did another spin, this one near the arched entryway to the living and dining rooms. "From what I can see, your place is *Architectural Digest* material. Any chance for a complete tour?"

For the next half hour, Joanna guided them through the house. In each room, their hostess pointed out the Mastercraft sofas, Henridon breakfronts, and Lalique vases. Pat nodded as big-ticket items were name-dropped, but at each stop, her eyes took in more than the furnishings.

Upstairs in the master suite, she edged into the reading alcove and studied the views of the Kempners' house and stable. Downstairs in Tony's den, she commented on the curtain fabric as a way to check out the sight lines to the mailbox.

But vistas weren't her only interest. When Joanna instructed them on the nuances of capturing glare-free natural light, Pat checked the window frames for alarm circuits. When their hostess pointed out the custom-made door hardware, Pat looked near the jamb for pressure sensors. When Joanna bragged about the waxed plaster finish, Pat scanned the upper walls for motion detectors.

Once finished with a tour of the upstairs and downstairs, they stopped near an oversized door close to the kitchen.

"Joanna, you're a woman after my own heart," Pat said, nodding approvingly. "Finally, a storage area with access. Don't tell me. This opens to the basement."

"There are drawbacks," Joanna acknowledged. "Tony and I are savers. Nothing ever gets trashed."

"Amen to that," Pat said, smiling. "I'm a pack rat too."

Ellen stepped forward. "The basement isn't all cedar closets and mothballs. Isn't your gym down there too?"

"Yes, along with the steam room, sauna, and my husband's precious wine cellar."

"I'm thinking of upgrading my grape dispensary," Pat said, twisting the doorknob and opening the basement door a crack. "Any chance I can take a peek at his?"

"He keeps it locked, I'm afraid," Joanna replied, her face tensing ever so slightly. "You know how men are. Tony's got a notion the cleaning help are into Chateau La Fayette."

Pat wrinkled her nose. "Speaking of palates, if that coffee tastes as good as it smells, bring it on. What's that delicious aroma?"

"A Starbucks special," Joanna answered, waving them into the kitchen. "Ethiopian coffee. How 'bout a cup?"

"If it's no imposition," Pat said. "Are you game, Ellie?"

When Joanna turned and reached into a cabinet above the twin stainless steel sinks, Pat slipped down the hall and shooed Snowflake through the cracked basement door.

"Snowflake, you little devil." Pat's voice rose. "Don't you dare go—"

Just as Joanna finished pouring the coffee, Pat eased back into the kitchen and looked at their hostess with helpless eyes.

"Back in a jiffy. That puppy just scampered down the basement stairs."

During the house tour, Pat had noted that the ADT security system, like hers, had sensor plates on each door, but none on the windows. That style of protection was the most popular because it was the least invasive on the homeowner's freedoms. It worked well if an intruder came through an outside door and broke the electric circuit. And it also worked when an unwelcome visitor got in through a window, then used an interior door to access other rooms. When any entryway was opened, the resultant breach activated the alarm.

But the system had one drawback. If an intruder jimmied a window and climbed inside, nothing happened. As long as the person didn't open a door or try to go from room to room, he didn't trigger the alarm. Since the room she planned to invade was the Gaylanis' basement, the flaw served her purposes.

Her excuse in place, Pat flipped on the lights, ran down the stairs, and scooped up Snowflake.

She cradled the puppy in one hand, then checked out the padlock on the wine cellar door. Once she noted it hung with the dial facing in, Pat made her way toward the southeastern wall.

Her plan was simple. First she'd locate a window that had the most protection from blowing snow, then she'd release the inside metal handle.

When the window fell open, she reached into her pocket. She was in search of paper, but all she found was a couple of hundred dollar bills.

Quickly she folded them over and wedged the bills between the casement and the frame. When she closed the window again, the fit was much tighter. It wasn't a perfect solution, but on short notice, it was the best she could do.

Pat raced up the stairs with the puppy. As she entered the kitchen, she tried not to appear winded. "This tigress was training for a marathon. I found her on the treadmill."

"So young and already an athlete," Joanna replied, acting matter-of-fact. "Cream or sugar?"

"No thanks. Black is fine." Pat accepted the mug, then took a sip. "Great flavor, huh?"

"Very tasty," Ellen agreed, looking at Joanna. "Have any of the arrangements been made?"

"The wake is tomorrow night, and the funeral is scheduled for Tuesday morning," Joanna replied. "You heard Tony. He went over to finalize things with Trevor."

"If there's anything I can do…"

Joanna had no children, but she stared at Ellen with a mother's grief-stricken eyes. "It's a godparent's nightmare. Twice in one week."

"My heart is in pieces too," Ellen sighed. "Patricia, drink up. Joanna doesn't need us milling about. It's time we got going."

CHAPTER TWENTY-FIVE

Dr. Tony Gaylani was in a mild state of panic. Several minutes ago, he'd left Shaver and Eichler standing in his doorway. At the time, he'd thought their visit brazen and annoying. Now he felt threatened, wondering if the reporter and her pal were up to no good. Of course, he'd wanted to stay and make them feel unwelcome, but that wasn't possible. He had a meeting to attend that couldn't be postponed.

As Tony drove through Barrington, he checked the rearview mirror. No one was following him, but he would continue to check and take evasive action. His mission wasn't to stop by his godson's house. Instead of working out the funeral arrangements in person, he wheeled into an empty grade school lot and called Trevor Kempner from his cell phone. Once they'd finalized the details for the viewing and burial, he turned to the real reason for his trip.

Tony had spent his adult life as doctor and spy. In both professions, he'd never had a partner. To be sure, he needed some assistance in the operating room, but when it came to espionage, he'd been groomed for a special task and had always acted alone.

He liked working solo. In fact, with the exception of a single meeting initiated by Baghdad about a year after his marriage to Joanna, he hadn't met with anyone who could compromise his identity. He hadn't needed to. Long ago, his mother had coached him.

Tony wasn't supposed to steal America's nuclear secrets or get his hands on the Pentagon's Star Wars plans. His role was passive.

He was part of a cell that monitored some of the more radical Zionist groups.

Iraq and the other Middle East nations shared a common goal. They wanted to weaken the Israeli lobby in the United States. To that end, men like Tony were given new identities. They were encouraged to marry or get romantically attached to Jewish women who belonged to Zionist organizations.

Finding candidates wasn't difficult. The American constitution guaranteed freedom of speech. Even the most radical of groups could organize and broadcast their views. Take Tony's first wife. He'd found Barbara Stein after he'd attended a few All Alone rallies in New York. Unfortunately, she'd gotten the maternal urge and had to be eliminated. But lucky him. His next recruit had come along shortly after he'd had Barbara's body cremated.

Events had gone smoothly for many years, but a couple weeks ago, at the Kempners' tree-trim party, Tony Gaylani had gotten a real jolt. As a student of post-World War II Middle East history, Tony knew all about General Alan Cunningham. When Kitty mentioned that the British government had released the general's papers, the doctor realized his life in the shadows would never be the same.

Fearing his identity would be compromised the moment the general's papers were delivered and read, he'd made up an excuse, telling his hosts he'd been beeped for an emergency. But instead of going to the hospital, he'd driven around, and after calming himself, had dialed Andy Douglas. His handler was an American citizen who had been recruited by Baghdad many years ago to be Iraq's liaison to its US spies.

The following day he'd met Andy on the fifth-floor corridor of the hospital. The man hid his face behind a surgical mask and wore scrubs. Stressing each word, Andy Douglas delivered a crystal clear message:

"Protect your identity, no matter the risk. Kill those who can expose you. There's no place to run. The Iraqi embassy is not a safe haven. The new regime has disavowed all Saddam's agents. But keep one thing in mind. Under no circumstances are you to initiate an action against any member of the Zionist organization All Alone."

Tony had listened carefully, then designed a cunning scheme to carry out his orders. But in the end, what had it gotten him? Sure, he'd eliminated the Kempners, and yes, Shaver couldn't make the murders stick. But like flies on shit, Miss Moneybags kept dogging his trail.

A distasteful remembrance complete, Tony looked through the windshield of his SUV and scanned the parking lot. Seeing no cars, he phoned Andy, had a brief conversation, and hung up. Just now, like a fortnight ago, he'd broken silence and risked CIA detection. Just now, like a fortnight ago, he'd heard Andy Douglas reaffirm the same instructions.

In the silence of his car, Tony cursed Allah. Since Saddam's fall, Ba'ath Party loyalists had run their intelligence operation from an underground headquarters. Unfortunately, their ability to gather useful information had gone underground too. The Iraqi agents were less informed than he was.

Joanna and her group underscored that point. For years, he'd bided his time, passing intelligence on to Baghdad, but mostly waiting for the right circumstances to assassinate All Alone's leaders.

All well and good until a few moments ago. The time was right, but when he'd gotten specific and suggested a plan to dispatch Joanna and her uncle, Andy had become very angry.

Tony remembered Andy Douglas's admonishment after Katherine's tree-trim party. He knew that members of All Alone were off limits. Even so, he'd still been shocked by his handler's reaction.

According to Douglas, their superiors in Baghdad had not only halted all terrorist activity against All Alone, but they'd halted all terrorist activity against all their enemies in America. As Andy had said, "Something big is on the horizon, but right now, Iraqi intelligence doesn't have a clue how big or which horizon."

Tony banged the steering wheel with the palms of his hands. He needed to know if Osama bin Laden and his Al-Qaeda operatives were planning another major attack. Of course, he'd be delighted if an American city was hit again. But the ensuing hysteria would not be good for him. Given his family background, he'd eventually be rounded up.

Tony stared out the windshield at an empty parking lot. His plan of action was clear. If Baghdad couldn't figure out the big picture, he'd review what was going on in his backyard and develop a scheme to protect himself.

He assumed Kitty Kempner had tipped off her pals, Shaver and Eichler. Hadn't Joanna told him that Mrs. Eichler had received a letter written by Kitty shortly before her death?

At the time, he'd been rattled by the news. But as it turned out, Joanna's bombshell had saved him. Had he not been diligent and followed the Eichler woman into the stable, she would have retrieved some very damaging material. Even so, she must have gotten a look at the general's papers. Judging from Shaver's remarks, someone had put holes in his cover.

He scanned the empty parking lot, wondering if Tom Kempner had talked too much. Last night Tony had stopped by his neighbor's house after the two snoops had left. Once inside, he certainly noticed that Kempner's attitude had changed.

Over brandy, the Jew had acted standoffish. Tony wasn't sure Kempner's behavior was directed at him, but then again, he wasn't sure that it wasn't. To be safe, he'd made the percentage play. Wasting the mob's *consigliere* had allowed him to remove the general's papers, the evidence that had forced the Kempner killings.

Tony pressed his temples, massaging them with his fingers. Talk about a long shot. He'd almost been unmasked by unclassified letters written by a British general more than sixty years ago. Thank God computers hadn't been processing information in the forties. Instead of cross-referencing the documents, governments merely warehoused sensitive reports in archives so big they dwarfed even the largest library.

Tony shook his head. First a Jew Army officer got wounded in Vietnam and landed on his operating table. Next the Jew recovered and married the granddaughter of a World War II British general who'd served in Palestine. Finally, the Jew's wife requested a single box of manuscripts, one carton amongst the tens of thousands. As isolated events, each could have happened. But taken together, the probability was extremely small.

He took two deep breaths. For years, his undercover operation had gone unnoticed. But recently his luck had gone bad. While he vowed that neither a meddlesome reporter nor a box of old documents would be his downfall, he also scolded himself for allowing his temper to flare.

Remembering his father's words, "Unbridled anger only creates futility," he leaned back against the car seat and allowed a quiet to engulf him. Right now, he wished his father were here. Right now, he needed advice from a brilliant man.

The late thirties had been a turbulent time for all Arab nationalists. Since the end of The Great War and the Treaty of Versailles, the British had watched much of their worldwide empire dwindle. The inhospitable lands of the Middle East seemed an unlikely place to make a stand, but oil had become an important commodity and a bargaining chip of increasing value in the international economic picture.

In 1939, his father, Rashid Ali el-Gaylani, was a militant leader in the small but growing faction of Iraqi right-wingers. Rashid realized that unsettled conditions had put his ambitious plans for himself and even bigger dreams for his son in peril. Because his father understood that it would be tough to kick the English and their puppet monarch out of Baghdad, Rashid asked his wife to take their only son and be part of a contingency plan.

Years later, Tony's mother had explained why her husband had sent them on a circuitous route through Europe and on to America. To solidify the masterful scheme, his father wanted the diplomatic corps in England and the United States to think his wife had taken their son and fled Iraq rather than stay and be part of an insane attempt to start a civil war.

Had the revolution succeeded, Rashid would have brought them back for a triumphant reunion. But in the end, the Nazis had lost, the British ruler had prevailed, and Rashid had spent his remaining years in prison. There, a bitter father took heart that his wife had detailed instructions to carry out his contingency plan. His son would be groomed into an Iraqi agent.

As his mother had told him when he was old enough to appreciate his father's cunning, the campaign to make Tony into a spy had begun the moment she stepped onto American soil. To mask her neighborhood identity, she'd told his schoolmates that she was a widowed Roman Catholic. For officialdom, the story was markedly different. On immigration department records, she'd listed his father by name and nationality, making it easy for investigators to know her son had been sired by a revolutionary zealot. The tactic worked perfectly. The State Department, CIA, and FBI knew his identity and assumed the amateurish cover-up stemmed from an understandable embarrassment. After all, what self-respecting person wanted to be branded as the son of an Iraqi insurgent who had allied himself with Hitler?

Once free of scrutiny by the authorities, his mother had taught Tony the rudiments of espionage. She'd also instilled in him a hatred for the Zionist movement and all Jews. Her effort was rewarded. Before she died, Tony's mother knew she'd raised a skilled surgeon and a man capable of killing without remorse to further the cause he'd been bred to embrace.

Tony's eyes popped open. He put the car in gear and eased out of the grade school lot. For the last several minutes, he'd forgotten about the snoops, Shaver and Eichler.

Tony was in a hurry, but he didn't speed. When he neared his house, he saw Shaver's car. Slowly he pulled into his driveway and parked. As he watched the nosy reporter and her pal come out, he gripped the steering wheel, feeling a growing impulse to kill again.

Smiling, he got out and slammed his car door. "Leaving so soon? What a shame."

"No reason to stay," Shaver said, matching his smile. "Your missus just served coffee. I was hoping you'd gone out to buy a couple bottles of chardonnay."

"It's Christmas. Some of us keep the holidays sacred." He glared, watching Shaver cuddle the puppy. "Like mother, like daughter. She never needed an excuse to drink. Why would your genes be any different?"

"Speaking of genes," the reporter said, "what do you hear from your cousins back in Iraq? Guess they feel like your old man. Once you've ridden a losing horse, a guy thinks twice before climbing back on."

Tony wanted to smash her filthy mouth.

"For your information, Shaver, my father was a patriot."

"Come, come, R.A.," the reporter replied, "get with the program. What would George Washington say if he heard you call Papa a flag-waver?"

The Eichler woman pulled on Shaver's coat sleeve. "We ought to leave."

"One second." She turned toward him. "Rashid, old buddy, thanks for the friendly welcome… but I got this thing about rubbing elbows with a murderer."

He took a step toward her, then another. "A nosy bitch like you should watch those slanderous remarks. Someone might sue you for libel."

She smirked. "If illegal aliens can file lawsuits, sue my ass. Nothing would please me more than to meet you in front of a judge."

"Don't hold your…" He reached out and patted the puppy. "On second thought, sweetheart, be my guest. In fact, if you should ever want any breath-stopping assistance, give me a holler."

Tony eyed her, waiting to see if she dared to reply. When none came, he took heart. The reporter had talked tough, but blinked when he'd made reference to strangulation.

* * *

Joanna Gaylani looked through the kitchen window and watched her fool husband trade verbal blows with Pat Shaver. She couldn't hear what was being said, but based on Tony's pained expressions, she judged he was getting the worst of it.

Joanna smiled, happy for his discomfort and pleased with the state of affairs. With zero hour and the fruition of three years of meticulous planning at hand, she couldn't think of any unattended details. But best to go over everything one more time.

She focused on a far stand of Douglas firs. As she stared at the pine trees surrounding the Kempners' barn, Joanna began reviewing the plan she'd conceived, then brought to Larry Magel—her uncle and the leader of All Alone and the Ruling Council.

Years ago, after she'd married Tony and moved to Barrington, Joanna had conceived a cunning idea. Wouldn't her value to All Alone be greatly enhanced if she devised a way to lead a double life? Instead of openly soliciting wealthy Zionists sympathetic to their cause, why not conduct fundraising efforts on the sly? Her comrades would know her as the same militant, Arab-hating isolationist. The rest of the world would see a new Joanna Gaylani. How perfect. She'd be a chameleon and pretend to publicly renounce her allegiance to All Alone. Then she'd approach the moderate members of the United Jewish Congress and ask for their forgiveness. Wouldn't all the peace-loving Itzak Rabin do-gooders be supportive? Wouldn't she be accepted by the mainstream Jewish community?

Joanna smiled. For more than a decade, she'd followed that game plan, serving on numerous UJC committees and even chairing a few. The effort had finally paid off. Several years ago, during the annual congress, the convention delegates had elected her to the United Jewish Congress Board of Directors.

As she stood by the window and watched Tony and Pat Shaver argue, Joanna thought about a far less confrontational debate. Early in 1999, her first year on the board, she'd made her presence felt. Instead of delivering an acceptance speech filled with platitudes, Joanna proposed, in a formal motion, to change the date of their next convention from mid-November to the days preceding the New Year.

The gathered assemblage had given her a standing ovation when she expounded that for Jews worldwide, the significance of holding the millennium convention in Jerusalem would be far greater if the dates coincided with the ushering in of the new century. In fact, in their enthusiasm, the delegates had said yes to her other suggestion. In appreciation, they'd not only slated the week after Christmas for future conventions, but had agreed to hold this year's meeting in Chicago.

Joanna kept staring at the pine trees, then refocused on her husband. Watching Tony brought to mind an all-important principle: Even when a good plan is in place, it never hurts to keep going over the details.

Great schemes can be simple. In that regard, hers stood out. Only she, Uncle Larry, and Chuck Sweet had any idea what had been planned. From the beginning, they'd agreed never to discuss any aspect with others. She and Chuck Sweet would implement the plan by themselves. If anything went wrong, the blame would fall on a rogue Jewess and a stableman she had hired.

Joanna looked at the Kempners' house and felt a tinge of remorse. Their deaths, especially Kitty's, had been regrettable. But what could she have done differently? Friendships were subordinate to All Alone's goals. Besides, she hadn't killed them. She'd only been opportunistic. She'd just used their murders to enlist Tony as her scapegoat.

Joanna breathed in and reviewed their strict timetable. In a few hours, Chuck Sweet, her co-conspirator, would begin to doctor up his appearance. To change into a Tony look-alike, he'd dye his hair black, wear tortoiseshell glasses, and glue on a mustache and fake eyebrows.

Tomorrow, Chuck would take a taxi to a U-Haul agency. There he would rent a large panel truck with a plow. For identification,

Chuck would use a driver's license she'd taken from Tony's wallet. Months ago, she'd stolen the ID, then reminded her husband to apply for a replacement.

Later tomorrow night, while she and Tony greeted mourners at Tom Kempner's wake, Chuck would drive into Barrington and plow a path to the Kempners' barn. After opening up their cache of stored ammonium nitrate and organic fertilizer, he'd load the truck, travel back to Uncle Larry Magel's horse farm and complete the bomb preparations.

The following morning, Joanna and her husband would sit in church with Trevor Kempner and his family. While they attended the funeral service, Chuck would disengage the plow and drive the panel truck to her house. He'd gain access using the garage door opener she'd put in the mailbox. Once parked in the garage, he'd disarm the security system and go inside.

Her role was well defined too. When the Tuesday morning service ended, she would—

The front door slammed, instantly ending her recollections. She waited... then smiled as Tony came into the kitchen.

"Oh, hi dear," she said. "Why the sad face?"

"That reporter is a royal pain in the ass," he replied. "Why, for two cents..."

"Now, now. Don't be so hasty."

Scavenging through a drawer, Joanna thought about the root cause of her husband's annoyance. Why had Pat Shaver and Ellen Eichler come over? She'd sent Ellen the note Kitty had written, not an invitation. Another thing. Hadn't the basement door been closed, and if so, how had that puppy gotten down the stairs? For that matter, why had Miss Shaver brought the damn dog over in the first place? Was the mutt a decoy? Maybe Tony was right. Maybe the rich gentile reporter and her church-going buddy had served out their usefulness.

"Dear, did you say a penny for your thoughts?" She tossed a pair of copper coins on the counter. "Or was it two cents to get into your knickers? Either way, consider yourself paid in full."

CHAPTER TWENTY-SIX

Patricia Shaver was shaken. The doctor's blatant reference to strangulation had upset her. She didn't want to give the Iraqi murderer the last word, but she chose not to speak. She feared her voice would give away her fright.

She and Ellen left quickly. They got into her Mercedes and drove toward Honey Lake. On the way, they discussed their horrific morning. Unfortunately, that turned into a frustrating experience too. She disagreed with her friend, claiming that any discussion with the likes of Chief Carlton Cherrigan or Admiral Eric Weiss was a waste of time.

"The solution to our problem is simple," Pat said, turning the Mercedes into her driveway and stopping alongside the Sunday paper. "Someone needs to put Tony's lights out."

"We're both upset," Ellen replied, "but that kind of ranting is pointless. Still, it's strange. I realize he's a killer, but it's Joanna's role that disturbs me most."

"The lady swiped Kitty's note," Pat said, her voice ringing with annoyance. "Doesn't that say it all?"

Ellen nodded, then unfastened her seatbelt. "But after Joanna read it, why mail it to me?"

"Maybe Joanna wants us to blow the whistle on Tony."

"For what?" Ellen asked, her eyes hardening. "We may think he murdered Kitty, but we can't prove it."

"Good point. You only set someone up if you want him to take a fall. Kitty Kempner's note isn't flattering, but it's not sending Dr. Gaylani to jail either."

"We've gone full circle again. We know Joanna took the note, read it, and sent it to me. But we still don't know why."

"There is one possibility," Pat suggested. "Sweet Joanna might be praying we'd buy into the circumstantial evidence."

"What would that accomplish?"

"Depends on your point of view," Pat replied. "Joanna has put the gun in our hands. Maybe she's hoping we'll pull the trigger."

"For the love of God, Patricia! Get serious."

"Would you cry if someone put a bullet between Tony's eyes?"

Ellen lowered her head. "Bad as it sounds, maybe not."

"That's progress, but first things first. Right now we have to find out why Joanna made a special effort to let us know she's married to an evil man."

"Agreed," Ellen said. "If she stole the note, odds are Joanna also went into the stable and read the material Kitty stashed in her horse purse. Let's face it, that stuff had to be an eye-opener. If she didn't suspect her husband before, once Kitty died, Joanna had to know."

"That may be relevant, but for now, I want to focus on Joanna and her motives. Last time I checked, a director of the United Jewish Congress isn't supposed to be an avowed Arab hater who double-orders ammonium nitrate."

"You think you know a person," Ellen said, closing her eyes, "and then this happens."

"She's a clever woman, but why make a special effort to get us involved? What gets a person—"

Her thoughts were derailed the moment she looked at Ellen and her stupid grin.

"Okay, Ellie. What's so funny?"

"Why are we sitting at the end of your driveway? Your car is comfortable, but isn't there a better place to talk?"

"Yes, but first open the door and reach down."

She'd run over her Sunday paper on each of her several trips in and out of the driveway. This time Pat had decided to park where *The Tribune* could be retrieved.

Ellie picked up the paper. "Mission accomplished. Unless you expect me to get out and push, let's get a move on."

Admiral Eric Weiss was having a bad day. He'd driven to CIA Headquarters in Langley, Virginia, to be sure the investigation into Tom Kempner's death was on track. Earlier he'd asked James Fitzgerald, director of the FBI, to send in agents. Eric wanted to make sure the local police didn't miss anything. At the time, he wasn't worried, but after he picked up the phone and talked to an FBI man on the scene, he felt a gush of heartburn.

"You're not making any sense," Eric said, his voice rising.

Ted Sinclair, the agent quarterbacking the FBI team, couldn't supply crucial answers. Irritated, Eric rose from his desk and leaned toward the speakerphone.

"If the Barrington Police Chief doesn't have the cassette, who took it out of Tom Kempner's answering machine?"

"Sorry, sir," Agent Sinclair said, his voice less than robust. "I don't have a good answer."

"Then find one!"

Red-faced and feeling uneasy, Eric hit the disconnect button, then stared across his office at the oil painting of John Paul Jones' ship, *Bon Homme Richard*. Aside from the missing cassette, he wondered about Tom Kempner's office cabinets. When the Feds had examined the mob attorney's business papers, they'd found some folders empty and some jammed full. Very strange, especially after he'd listened to a pair of conflicting voice mails.

The county coroner had left word that Tom Kempner had breathed in a lethal dose of gas fumes. But Patricia Shaver made a far different claim. According to her, Barbera's *consigliere* hadn't committed suicide. Shit! If the reporter had it right, it meant Tom Kempner had been murdered. Maybe his queasy stomach was a precursor of more surprises to come.

The admiral picked up the phone and instructed a subordi-

nate to book him on a morning flight to Chicago. He needed feedback, but interviewing people on Christmas Day wouldn't be productive. Besides, he had a more pressing problem. In ten minutes,
America's top spy, the director of the CIA, wanted an official update on a very unofficial operation.

Until Tom Kempner died, Eric had thought he had things under
control. Sure, the feedback from Barbera had been slow in coming.
But that was to be expected. Whenever the CIA and the Chicago
Mafia did business, the old don acted like he was running the show.

Normally, Eric would have told Barbera to get the information
flowing or else, but in this instance, an ultimatum might have backfired. Cutting the mobster down to size would have soothed his ego,
but jeopardized the quality of the information.

In most cases, CIA intelligence was excellent, but when he
looked at the reports on Dr. R. Anthony and Joanna Myerson Gaylani, he saw lots of holes. The bio on the doctor's spy activities was
sketchy at best, and the file on Joanna's involvement with All Alone
and the United Jewish Congress was equally thin. In short, until
Katherine Kempner had requested the release of her grandfather's
wartime papers, he'd had no excuse to dig deeper.

Eric rose, ran his hand across his trophy case, then began pacing around the office. The British Secret Service had dragged their
feet, only informing him of Katherine Kempner's request months
after it had been made. Of course, the moment he'd been briefed
that General Alan Cunningham's papers had been cleared for delivery, he saw an opportunity to pressure Dr. Tony Gaylani.

When the admiral had approved MI-6's shipment of the general's documents, he wasn't sure how Dr. Gaylani would react or even
if he would find out. All he could count on was Katherine Kempner's sense of propriety. Because she was a respected physician, Eric
hoped Mrs. Kempner would read the explosive material and pass it
along to the local authorities.

As things turned out, Dr. Gaylani had proven to be a very resourceful man. Somehow he'd gotten wind that the papers were in transit.

Eric had had no idea Dr. Gaylani would pay Mrs. Kempner a visit on the morning the general's documents were delivered. A part of him was sorry he'd inadvertently put her in harm's way, but another part wasn't. He needed proof, and when the doctor had killed to protect his identity, Eric knew something big had to be in progress.

He looked down at the carpet and continued pacing. After Mrs. Kempner was murdered, Eric had thought about warning her husband. But approaching Tom Kempner would have been tricky. How could he come out and say that the general's papers contained damning material and might have been the catalyst for killing the man's wife? No. To keep his operation alive and clandestine, he had to sit back and see what Dr. Tony Gaylani did next.

Grim-faced, the admiral stopped in front of his trophy case. The doctor hadn't kept him waiting very long. Tom Kempner had met his maker a couple of days after burying his wife.

Eric had decided to get the FBI involved once the Barrington Police Department began investigating the crime scene. He figured Dr. Gaylani would be watching the activity next door, but Eric hadn't thought the doctor would be spooked by the presence of Bureau agents. Tom Kempner was a mob attorney, and the FBI routinely looked into all matters pertaining to organized crime.

He opened the glass door and pulled out one of the silver cups. He made a point of polishing each of his trophies because he was proud of his boxing achievements. The same couldn't be said for the operation he was currently running.

The admiral hadn't been shocked when Tom Kempner got killed. He also hadn't been surprised when the Bureau agents couldn't find any of the general's papers. Dr. Gaylani might have had multiple reasons to murder the Kempners, but protecting his identity had to be high on his list. How could the man commit two homicides and leave circumstantial evidence behind?

Eric returned the silver cup to the trophy case, then walked to his desk. Once seated, he knew why his stomach was still churning.

Not long ago, he'd returned a call placed earlier by Patricia

Shaver. In the message she'd left on his voice mail, Miss Shaver had said that she and Ellen Eichler had spent part of last night with Tom Kempner. Her recorded message also made other claims, but at the moment, only one thing concerned him: Why would Tom Kempner have given either woman the time of day? What could they have said or done that would make a smart mob lawyer jeopardize the attorney/client privilege? Miss Shaver and Mrs. Eichler were about to be the star witnesses in a court hearing against his boss, Gary Barbera. Tom Kempner knew the rules. He knew there would be repercussions. Yet he'd blatantly disregarded them.

While Eric agonized over the mob attorney's insubordination, he realized there were other loose ends. Within minutes of each other, there had been two 911 calls to report Tom Kempner's death. Both were placed from Kempner's house, both were female, but only Mrs. Eichler had identified herself. The other—the anonymous caller—had disguised her voice.

Ted Sinclair, an FBI agent, had briefed Bob Stanojev, one of his men in Chicago. Neither knew why two calls had been made. But even if they found out, Eric wondered what had possessed Miss Shaver and Mrs. Eichler to come over in the first place. Christ Almighty, two women who shouldn't have been around had gone to Tom Kempner's house early Christmas morning and, without permission, nosed into things that didn't concern them.

Eric shook his head slowly. No matter how he spun it, the events didn't fit into an airtight package. But that wasn't his only concern. When he rocked his chair forward and saw the manila folders on his desk, Eric understood that he had two other problems.

He picked up the thin folder, the one that contained information on Joanna Gaylani. It was small because evaluating Joanna was difficult. Eric knew she'd dedicated her life to making Israel an independent nation, non-aligned with its Arab neighbors. She had advocated isolationism, and as an outspoken member of All Alone, raised millions to further that cause.

Then she'd reinvented herself. Years before, after she'd married

Dr. Gaylani, Joanna had found a new kind of religion. She'd renounced All Alone and joined the United Jewish Congress.

Her new colleagues had embraced her, and she'd risen in the ranks to become one of their managing directors. True, she hadn't ceased all formal communication with All Alone. From time to time, Joanna made contact with the leader, Lawrence Magel. But Magel was also the rich old Chicago Jew who'd brought her to America. That made the uncle her only real family. That gave them a reason to talk.

Eric balled his hand into a boxer's fist. He wasn't convinced. Even if Joanna's rebirth had been genuine and even if she no longer shared the same political ideology, Eric remembered how he always cautioned young CIA operatives, "A leopard doesn't change its spots."

If Joanna's loyalties had been hard to pinpoint, Dr. R. Anthony Gaylani's hadn't. The US Army had drafted Tony, commissioned him as a captain, then sent him to Vietnam for a thirteen-month surgical tour. While his performance had been brilliant, a troubling byproduct of his patients' post-op recovery had ultimately caught the attention of high-ranking non-medical officials.

As Henry Kissinger conducted peace talks in Paris, the Surgeon General commissioned a study to investigate the incidence of drug addiction among Vietnam vets. Once the records of VA hospital patients had been compared with their battlefield medical files, the correlation showed that one doctor had operated on an abnormally high number of users. With great regularity, Jewish soldiers coming from a Da Nang hospital had become addicted to morphine.

The entire episode could easily have gone undetected. But when the analytical probe went further and screened for religious anomalies among the attending physicians, the program revealed that only Jewish soldiers under Dr. R.A. Gaylani's care had a high incidence. Since the doctor's 201 file was already red-tagged by the State Department, the results had been forwarded to the CIA.

The admiral leaned back and recalled the day Dr. Gaylani's records had first hit his desk. They'd gotten acquainted in July 1972. Eric had finished his last Nam tour, joined the CIA, and been promoted to lieutenant commander. Back then he'd had no desire to create waves. As a junior agent, he'd only written a memo that highlighted the doctor's background.

Eric squirmed to get comfortable. More than thirty years and several promotions had passed, but then, two weeks ago, he'd taken another look at Dr. Gaylani's file. The dossier had collected more dust than entries, but this time he'd given it greater scrutiny.

The admiral regularly came in on Sunday. Routine paperwork was easier when his phone wasn't ringing. Of course, on the Sunday in question, he hadn't known that a man would panic and break his silence for the first time in many years. But sure enough, fourteen days ago, Dr. Gaylani had dialed his Iraqi handler, Andrew Douglas. Of course, the doctor hadn't known it, but he'd also lit up the switchboard in Langley, Virginia.

Eric remembered how the agent monitoring the wiretap had rushed into his office without knocking. Seeing the glint in the man's eye had brought back his own memories. But the thrill of eavesdropping notwithstanding, he'd sat the young agent down and asked for a profile on the spy Dr. Gaylani had just contacted. The young man had his facts in order and gave him a comprehensive biography.

Andrew Douglas had a regular white-collar job, a house in suburbia, a wife, and a couple of kids. In his spare time Andy liked to play golf, eat junk food, and drink Classic Coke. To his neighbors, he seemed like an ordinary guy, but looks can be deceiving.

On the QT, Andy Douglas loved to gamble. He got an adrenaline rush each time he placed a big bet, but unfortunately, his narcotic highs were usually followed by a hangover. Pure and simple, Andy made bad wagers. In fact, during one stretch years ago, he'd hit a prolonged losing streak. Unnerved by the size of his markers and the people who held them, Andy had considered a back-door exit out of town.

Eric smiled, recalling how Lady Luck had befallen Andy Douglas and, indirectly, the Company too. As events played out, Andy had never bought a bus ticket. He had gotten a proposal that paid off his debts and put him on easy street as well.

The Iraqi Secret Police was a spy network desperately short on born-and-raised American operatives. To them, addicted gamblers made excellent candidates. When they'd discovered Andy was a non-descript, middle-management computer specialist to boot, Baghdad thought they'd hit the jackpot.

Eric twisted in his chair. The recollection of the Douglas briefing also reminded him of his contempt for the underworld scum who controlled illegal wagering. Regrettably, it also called attention to the means he and his associates used to identify people like Andy Douglas.

From time to time, the Company found it convenient to trade favors. In accordance with an unwritten proviso, whenever the Mafia sold bad debts to foreign agents, they also passed along the names to the admiral's staff. For that mandated courtesy, the CIA showed its appreciation by getting the FBI to give the mob advance warning on their next scheduled raid.

Eric couldn't remember what they'd traded for Andy Douglas's name, but he recalled what he'd done once Dr. Gaylani made his call a fortnight ago.

After listening to the tape a second time, he had devised a plan. A female agent wearing a nurse's uniform had been wired with monitoring gear and stood close by. But when Dr. Gaylani and Andy Douglas met in the hospital corridor the following day, nothing intelligible had been recorded.

Eric leaned back in his chair and stared at the ceiling. He couldn't be sure what had prompted Dr. Gaylani's sudden re-entry into the espionage arena, but the timing fit. Two days before the doctor broke silence, MI-6 had called, saying they'd notified Katherine Kempner that her grandfather's papers were being released. How well he'd remembered the way the English stuffed shirts had also covered their asses. The official memo out of London read: *General Alan Cunningham's memoirs are no longer Top Secret. As declassified documents, they can be forwarded without checking their contents.*

MI-6 might have disavowed any knowledge of their contents,

but apparently Dr. Gaylani had done his homework. The admiral remembered being impressed that even before the doctor had seen the documents, he'd realized that Mrs. Kempner's grandfather had been stationed in Palestine at the same time Dr. Gaylani's father was causing trouble in Iraq.

Eric's face tensed as he recalled his next move. In the past, when he'd needed to avail himself of Gary Barbera's unique talents, the admiral had used his boyhood friend, Tom Kempner. This occasion had been perfect for enlisting him once more.

Eric knew Kempner had a difficult trial in the works. He also knew Barbera's *consigliere* was smart enough to never ask for favors. With that backdrop, Eric called Kempner and told him to arrange a meeting between himself and the crime boss.

The admiral recalled that Tom Kempner hadn't wasted any time. Within an hour, Barbera's *consigliere* had set up a conference call. Kempner had hung up before any words were exchanged, but Eric felt the mob attorney knew what he planned to offer Barbera and also what he hoped to get in return.

Eric stood, easing the tightness in his back and shoulders. From the beginning, he'd never planned on warning Tom Kempner that General Alan Cunningham's papers might contain explosive material. As an agent watching over the people of the United States, he had to look at the big picture. Of course, he'd been surprised by Dr. Gaylani's fast reaction, but after the Kempners had been murdered in two rapid-fire events, he knew his decision was correct. If a terrorist plot was in the offing and Dr. Anthony Gaylani had killed to protect more than just his identity, Eric would be ready. He had never forgotten the pictures of 9/11. Not on his watch.

Eric rubbed the small of his back. What he'd done next, like all aspects of the operation, had been off the record. The Company's charter didn't authorize him to investigate domestic homicides, but to confirm Katherine Kempner had been murdered, he'd dispatched agents dressed as gravediggers to examine her body. Dr. Gaylani had managed to get her released to the mortuary faster than Eric had anticipated, and the funeral parlor had drained her blood before his people could do tests. But another group—his team of forensic specialists—had had no trouble going to the cemetery and diagnosing a crushed windpipe.

The intercom buzzed, but he let his secretary, Cissy, pick it up. Before facing the director of the CIA, he wanted to go over the details of the latest Gaylani-Douglas contact.

Less than two hours ago, Dr. Gaylani had left his house and driven to a vacant parking lot. The agent tailing the doctor hadn't gotten close enough to read his lips, but the CIA man did report that Dr. Gaylani talked on a cell phone. Unfortunately, when Langley people double-checked the Douglas wiretap, they could only verify that the doctor had called. Andy Douglas had installed a scrambler a day after the Kempners' tree trim party.

Their mumbo jumbo hadn't stayed mumbo jumbo for long. The phone conversation had become meaningful when another Company agent saw Andy Douglas leave his home with a can of Classic Coke in one hand and his car keys in the other. The two spies had set up a meeting, and once Douglas and Gaylani arrived in separate cars, they were able to walk up and down the Walgreens aisles without anyone monitoring their conversation.

The admiral left his office and went down a very long hall. He paused outside the CIA director's door. God-damn-it-to-hell, he hated this kind of situation. His well-prepared plan had gone into the toilet. Instead of finally understanding what R. Anthony and Joanna Gaylani were up to, he was back to square one.

Without knocking, Eric walked into Jerald "Jerry" Cash's office. Once told to sit, he'd tell the director that Dr. R. Anthony Gaylani was an Iraqi spy who'd killed twice, most probably in anticipation of initiating some covert act during the upcoming United Jewish Congress Convention. He'd go on to say that because Joanna Gaylani was the keynote speaker at the opening luncheon, it would be difficult, but not impossible, to deny her husband access to the Grand Ballroom. Naturally, the admiral wouldn't compromise the director's position by detailing how unfortunate accidents happened, but as he discussed alternative approaches, Eric would be on the lookout for a sympathetic nod. When he got it, he'd get up and leave.

Eric fidgeted as he stood in front of the director's desk. He had reason to be nervous. Just now, he'd had a disturbing thought. Was it possible that Katherine Kempner had told Dr. R. Anthony Gaylani about her grandfather's papers?

The doctor had made his call on a Sunday afternoon. As part of his investigation, Eric had sent out feelers to the Chicago CIA agents. One agent, Rick Eichman, had been especially creative. He'd asked around and determined that Dr. Gaylani's neighbors, the Kempners, had held their Christmas tree trimming party that Sunday afternoon.

The admiral waited patiently for CIA Director Jerald Cash to make eye contact. When that happened, he'd express himself with confidence. He still had lots of questions, but Director Cash didn't want to hear hedged statements. Like everyone else in the profession, Jerry Cash knew espionage work drew specific inferences from limited facts.

But this operation was different. Eric had a warehouse of limited facts and no specific inferences. To be sure, he'd express himself confidently, but in truth, he didn't have a clue.

CHAPTER TWENTY–SEVEN

Patricia Shaver parked the Mercedes in her detached garage. She and Ellen got out, Pat hitting the button to close the garage door, her friend grabbing the Sunday paper. They both left through the side door, puffing out frosted air as they raced toward the icy three-step riser and the covered porch.

"Nice work, Grandma," Pat said. "My front door is open. Give it a shove."

The two were happy to feel the heat of a warm house. Ellen tossed the *Tribune* on the L-shaped counter, then dispensed dog bones to a quartet of wagging tails. Meanwhile, Pat dropped her coat on one of the kitchen stools and checked the answering machine.

"Great headline." Ellen pointed at the *Trib*. "But all's not lost. My husband flew out today. At least one of us will be with Lauren and the grandkids."

Pat glanced at the block-lettered **MERRY CHRISTMAS TO ALL**. Her friend had reason to be sarcastic. Ellen was hurting. Who wouldn't be? She'd lost another friend and had postponed her travel plans.

In past years, Ellen's daughter, Lauren, had brought her two children to Barrington. Celebrating Santa's arrival with the grand-parents had become a tradition. But last summer Lauren had gotten divorced and, as part of her changed lifestyle, had decided to stay home for Christmas.

"Your family is all that matters," Pat said. "If you want to take off and be with them…"

"I belong right here," Ellen snapped. "There's Tommy's wake and funeral to contend with."

"It's your call, but if you change your mind, it's fine with me." Pat walked behind the L-shaped counter, watching Ellen stare at the paper. "What's so important?"

"Guess who made the front page of the *Trib?*"

"No clue," Pat said.

Ellen spun the paper around and pointed. "That's Joanna, isn't it?"

Pat nodded, then read the caption under the photograph: *Joanna Myerson Gaylani, a Director of the United Jewish Congress, welcomes delegates to the annual convention being held at the Conrad Hilton Hotel.*

She slid the paper back in Ellen's direction and began grinding beans for the coffee maker. Her mind raced, but again, she didn't want to show any emotion.

"Still checking out the UJC story, or maybe something else has caught your fancy?"

Ellen held up her index finger, then gestured toward the article under the picture. "We knew Joanna was a big wheel, but I wasn't aware she'd be delivering a keynote speech."

"At what?"

"The United Jewish Congress shindig. According to this, over a thousand people will be at their national convention."

Pat pushed the start button. "When does it begin?"

"Tuesday." Ellen flipped to the next page. "They're kicking it off with a luncheon in the Grand Ballroom of the Conrad Hilton."

Pat thought she was prepared, but when her friend quoted the text, "They're kicking it off with a luncheon in the Grand Ballroom of the Conrad Hilton," the words floored her.

"Why have a big convention between Christmas and New Year's? Seems sort of weird, doesn't it?"

"Not if you're Jewish," Ellen replied. "According to the article, it's a holy time for them too. In fact, it quotes Joanna on that very subject."

Pat listened as her friend paraphrased the article, saying that several years ago, Joanna had suggested they begin their convention after the last day of Chanukah and conclude on the first day of the millennium. Since the 2000 meeting had been so well received, Joanna Gaylani had used her influence as a UJC director and asked for a similar time for all succeeding conventions.

"What a unique idea," Pat said. "It'll be dark in a few hours, won't it?"

Ellen looked up. "So what?"

"Let's go horseback riding. It might be fun."

"Get real, Patricia! It's Christmas and it's cold." Her friend's gaze steadied. "Wait a minute. I know that look. What's going on?"

"Nothing much. But we do need to sneak over to the barn."

"The barn?" Ellen asked. "Whose barn?"

"Tom Kempner's, of course."

She kept the explanation short. When her friend gave her a grudging nod, they grabbed their parkas and said good-bye to the Labs.

Pat continued to map out a strategy as she drove to Ellen's. At first her friend sat in stunned silence, but after reflecting, Ellen agreed to provide the horses and help with the break-in. The Eichlers' trucks were fitted for plowing, but for this operation they needed secrecy. Until they knew whether Joanna had bomb-making material, it made no sense to get anyone else involved.

They went inside and raided Ellen's closets. When they left for the Eichlers' stable, each had donned heavy long underwear, fur-lined foul-weather gear, and boots.

"No chance I'll be cold," Pat predicted, putting a bridle on her horse. "I'm already sweating."

Ellen cinched her saddle and stayed deadpan. "Have you heard the weather report?"

"Those jokers are never right. I'm betting the blizzard misses us."

"And if you're wrong?" Ellen asked, pulling her stocking cap down over her ears. "For a couple of hours, a young lady is going to find out if her frozen backside is also saddle tough. And that's just the trip over. It's two hours coming back."

"Jeez," Pat moaned, "don't you know some shortcuts?"

"That is the shortcut. The direct route would take at least three."

"Then let's get a move-on." Pat grabbed the saddle horn and hoisted herself up. "By the way, is the crowbar in your saddlebag?"

Ellen nodded. "Along with the flashlights, hammer, and rope."

Admiral Eric Weiss stood in the foyer outside the dining room of his two-story red brick house. His meeting with CIA Director Jerald Cash had gone well. But since arriving home, his luck had changed. The minute he'd sat down to dinner, things began running afoul.

"They're doing what?" he roared, holding the phone in a death grip. "You interrupted my dinner to say they went horseback riding?"

Like many Jews married to Christians, Eric had invited his kids' families over for a holiday feast. He was annoyed, but didn't slam down the phone. As the Chicago FBI agent, Bob Stanojev, mustered an apology, Eric re-evaluated. Miss Shaver and Mrs. Eichler weren't fools. If they'd chosen to go riding on a frigid night, there had to be a good reason.

"Follow them. I want to know where they go."

He listened, then clenched his teeth. Eric felt as helpless as the agent who'd just told him that they'd taken off through the woods and were already out of sight.

Patricia Shaver hadn't been on horseback for some time. She knew she'd be sore, but for the moment the cold weather had numbed her body.

During their ride, she laid out her case against Joanna Gaylani. Unfortunately, she never got past square one. Time and again, Ellen asked how a woman who'd changed her political ideology could suddenly become militant. Since her friend didn't accept violence as a solution to anything, Pat gave up, responding that she wouldn't prejudge Joanna Gaylani. She'd let the contents in Tom Kempner's barn speak for themselves.

Holding one subject in abeyance didn't halt conversation. While Pat felt uncomfortable getting into the specifics of her relationship with Ken Dale, discussing some aspects of her romantic life did have a therapeutic benefit. As Ellen grilled her, the tension between them evaporated.

Pat stood up in her stirrups and did a three-sixty. "Are we getting close?"

"Don't change the subject," Ellen grumbled. "What did Ken say?"

"Yesterday he sounded like a jilted lover. Today he understood."

Early last evening, Pat had called Rome from Tom Kempner's kitchen. Ken was still working in his office at CNN Headquarters-SW Europe Bureau. When she told him she needed to delay her trip, he hadn't been happy. Today, when she'd outlined the circumstances of Tom Kempner's death and the faked suicide, he acted like a newsman, telling her to stay on the story and keep him posted.

Pat sat back down in her saddle, then ducked to avoid evergreen branches as her horse zigzagged through a stand of gigantic firs.

"Ken knows we have a job to do," she said, noting that Ellen's horse stayed clear of the low-hanging boughs, "but once we figure things out and notify the authorities, we can both leave."

"Amen to that," Ellen replied, turning back and facing her. "How long will you stay?"

"Don't know. I left the return part of the ticket open."

"Sounds like the right thing to do. Think he'll pop the question?"

"Rest assured, you'll be the first to know."

When Ellen turned and faced forward, Pat knew the interrogation was over. That was when she mused about the only man who'd ever captured her fancy and also her heart.

To compress a long story, she'd grown up last spring and salvaged what she should never have lost. In the late eighties, when she'd begun working for the *Tribune*, Ken Dale had been a senior editor and her boss. After a dozen or so weeks on the job, she'd left the paper, but hadn't stopped dating Ken.

While their romance had lasted longer than her stint as a cub reporter, it had flopped too, mostly due to her inability to commit. But after going their separate ways, they'd kept in touch. From time to time they'd call each other, and occasionally they'd visit. She thought she was building a relationship with a male friend. That was true, but something else had happened too.

She'd called Ken Dale this past spring at the height of the Gary Barbera investigation. When Ken dropped everything and offered his help, she'd realized two things: Ken meant the world to her, and absence and time really had made her heart grow fonder.

Since then, they'd been much closer. Ken worked overseas, but they'd managed to be together for at least one long weekend each month. Either he'd come to Chicago on the pretext of following up some international story, or she'd fly abroad on absolutely no pretext at all.

"The barn is dead ahead." Ellen broke the silence. "Once we get clear of these trees, you'll see lights in the distance. They're coming from the Gaylanis' house. I shouldn't have to say it, but from now on, be careful."

Pat heard Ellen's warning, but her mind was on Ken and their rendezvous on the French Riviera. As she wondered how long her trip would be postponed, she reached into her saddlebag, pulled out a flashlight, and turned it on.

"For the love of God," Ellen yelled, "turn that thing off."

At first the barn had blocked Pat's view, but when they rode past the last of the Douglas firs, she saw the far-off lights.

* * *

Joanna Gaylani was doing something unusual. Most evenings she and Tony went out, but tonight she was in her kitchen, adding the final touches to her Christmas dinner. While the thought of a condemned man eating a hearty meal made her smile, a flash of light coming from a spot near the barn caught her attention. As she squinted, trying to make sense of what she'd seen, her husband sneaked in, grabbed her affectionately, and spun her around.

"Whatever you're cooking, it smells great."

"Tony, please."

She broke loose and turned back to the darkness. Seeing nothing, she relaxed. Stress must have played tricks with her eyes. According to her timetable, the road to the barn wouldn't be plowed for another twenty-four hours. Besides, who in his right mind would be out on a night like this? Still, she'd mention it to Chuck Sweet. If there were tracks near the door or signs the tractor had been moved, she'd abort the operation.

Her husband's hands started making advances.

"Tony, stop that. Can't you see I'm cooking?"

"The hell with the food. You're the one that looks good enough to eat."

Patricia was embarrassed. After turning off her flashlight, she and Ellen rode to a blind spot near the back of the barn. As the wind swirled and snowflakes blew against her face, they dismounted. When Ellen gave her a nodding okay, Pat pulled another flashlight from her saddlebags and turned them on.

"What's the deal? When it's this cold, it's not supposed to snow."

"Don't tell me," Ellen replied. "Talk to the jokers at the weather bureau."

She ignored her friend's sarcasm and instead focused the lights as Ellen wedged the crowbar under an eighteen-inch-wide plank of barn siding.

"A little closer," Ellen said, "but be careful where you point those flashlights."

Her friend applied pressure and pried a board loose. Then she tied a loop in one end of the rope, flipped it around the top part of the siding, and tied the other to the saddle horn. The horse did the rest. Ellen yanked on the reins, the horse stepped forward, and the plank fell on the crusted snow.

"After you, Mrs. Eichler."

They squeezed through the opening. Once inside, they let the flashlight beams crisscross the walls. To Pat's dismay, nothing incriminating popped out. A Deere tractor, complete with all the attachments, was parked in the middle of the barn. As she continued to play the light, this time toward her feet, there was no sign of the ammonium nitrate.

"Do these things come with basements?" Pat asked.

She sensed a difference in the uneven floor and used her boot to scrape away a thin layer of straw. Most of the barn had a dirt floor, but under the tractor it was wood.

"Try enunciating," Ellen replied, joining her. "What are you mumbling about?"

"Not mumbling, just wondering." Pat continued to look down and use her boot as a scraper. "Why would the tractor be sitting on a wooden floor?"

"Why would...?" Ellen looked down. "Well, I'll be."

Without any explanation, her friend climbed aboard the tractor. Once in the driver's seat, Ellen began feeling the control panel with her hands. "Rats, no keys."

"Put it in neutral," Pat suggested. "The floor is pitched. If we give this beauty a shove, I'll bet it moves."

Ellen took the tractor out of gear and hopped down. That was all it took. Once they walked to the front and pushed gently on the engine cover, it began to roll backward. In fact, before they knew it, the damn thing was free-wheeling.

"Jesus," Pat screamed, "how do we stop this sucker?"

With masterful agility, Ellen jumped back onto the driver's seat and hit the brake. Had she not acted, the Deere tractor would have made short work of the padlocked barn door.

"Nice work," Pat said. "That was a close call."

Instead of answering, Ellen jumped down and grabbed one end of a heavy plank. Working as a team, they lifted the boards and moved them to the side. Once the cache was opened, Pat shined her flashlight into a crudely-dug underground storage bin.

"I'll be a son of a bitch. Joanna Gaylani gives hate a whole new meaning."

Pat had anticipated the discovery, but seeing a couple of hundred, fifty-pound sacks of organic fertilizer and a far lesser number of smaller bags of ammonium nitrate still had a profound effect. She'd had a similar reaction more than two decades before, when she'd walked around in the ashy rubble that had once been her home. Then, like now, her heart had pounded and her stomach muscles had tensed. But back then, she'd only witnessed the destruction. Right now, she was visualizing the magnitude of the potential disaster.

Ellen stepped into the shallow pit for a closer look. "It's hard to believe."

"Yes it is." Pat banged her heavy gloves together. "Joanna is a very sick woman."

"And clever." Ellen turned toward one corner of the underground storage area and flashed the light on the bags of ammonium nitrate. "Joanna has been stockpiling this for some time."

"How can you tell?"

"This is the only brand I ever bought." Ellen pointed the beam at one of the labels. "Been using this company for three years."

"What about the fertilizer? Are those bags yours or someone else's?"

"Can't be sure," her friend replied. "I use that brand, but so do a lot of other landscape outlets. This kind of organic fertilizer is easy to come by."

"I'll say. Along with the ammonium nitrate, there must be several tons here." Pat eyed her friend. "Enough to pack a big punch."

"For sure," Ellen agreed. "Right now, I'm scared, I'm mad, and I don't know what to do."

"Not me," Pat replied, her confidence echoing off the walls. "I know exactly what to do."

Ellen stepped out of the pit. "Any chance it involves something intelligent, like getting our fannies out of here and calling the cops?"

"Trust me," Pat said. "That won't help. You and I need to do something else."

"Like what?"

"For starters, the floor needs to go back in place. After that, you have to figure out how to get the tractor back over it."

"We're in over our heads," Ellen warned. "We should call the authorities."

"Damn it," Pat said, "I don't want to hear that kind of garbage. The cops can't get involved. We've got nothing to show them."

"But…?"

Pat stepped toward her friend. "But nothing. I barely knew Tom and Kitty Kempner, and I'm livid. Let's do something to set this straight."

"Two wrongs don't make a right."

"Give me a break. I'm looking for justice, not revenge." Pat took a deep breath. "First we need to do some housecleaning. After that we'll talk about the big picture."

Once they got the flooring in place, Ellen slipped out the back. A few seconds later, she reappeared, holding one end of a heavy rope. Pat got into the driver's seat as Ellen tied the line to the front end of the tractor. The rest was easy. Ellen went back outside and climbed into the saddle. When the horse pulled, Pat steered, and the tractor rolled quietly back into its original spot.

They checked to be sure the interior looked like they'd found it, then they squeezed through the opening. As they stood outside, Pat held the board and Ellen nailed it back in place.

"Well done," Pat said, patting her friend on the back. "Covering the hammer with the handkerchief was a nice touch too."

"Noise travels," Ellen replied. "It's a carpenter trick to muffle sound."

Their work complete, they got back on their horses.

"Never thought I'd pray for snow," Pat said, watching the large flakes begin to cover their tracks. "If this blizzard continues, nobody will ever know we've been here."

For several minutes, they rode in silence. Then Ellen reined in her horse.

"Been thinking, Patricia. We should call Ethel."

"Even if I wanted to, we can't. Neither one of us brought a cell phone."

Ellen used her heel like a spur. When her horse moved, they both started riding again. Hoping the silence would last, Pat thought about Ethel Iverson, the woman she and Ellen had met last spring.

Pat's publisher had introduced them. Ethel was the Deputy Superintendent of the Chicago Police Department and had come into their lives during a crucial time in her face-off with Gary Barbera. Once on the scene, Ethel Iverson had pulled strings. First she'd managed to cross jurisdictional lines, then she'd thwarted Chief Cherrigan's efforts to suppress evidence.

"I'm dead serious," Ellen said. "The authorities should be involved."

"I'd phone Ethel in a second, but we don't have any proof."

"My God, woman! If what we know isn't proof, what do you call it?" Ellen's voice rose. "We know Tony Gaylani killed the Kempners. We also know the CIA and Mr. Barbera are in the thick of it. Now we've got proof Joanna Gaylani has bomb material stashed and is going to blow up God knows what."

"That's not a secret anymore. I've figured out her target."

"Is that a fact?" Ellen's face showed surprise, then anger. "When were you planning to let me in on the secret?"

"Don't be mad. Everything you said is true."

"I hate being patronized, Patricia. Just tell me the target."

"First, listen to my explanation," Pat said, brushing snow off her face. "We both know Joanna used her position as a director of the United Jewish Congress to persuade her colleagues to hold their convention in Chicago."

"And?"

Pat squirmed in the saddle, her eyes focused away from her friend. "Joanna plans to assemble a bomb and use it to kill the Jewish delegates at the UJC Convention. She is a chameleon, lethal and two-faced."

Pat waited for a reaction. When Ellen stayed quiet, Pat grabbed the saddle horn, leaned back, and glanced at the heavy low sky. "My guess is the CIA would concur with our allegations. We're both sure something is going down. But neither of us can prove it."

They nudged their horses forward, Ellen looking straight ahead.

"A while ago you got angry at me," Pat went on. "Back then, I wanted to pass sentence before the trial started. Now you understand my frustration. We still have the same problem. Until Tony and Joanna Gaylani make a mistake or do something illegal, there's not a shred of evidence to arrest them or a court in the land to keep them in jail."

Ellen's shoulders slumped. "Do you *really* think she'll try to blow up the convention?"

"I can't be sure," Pat admitted, "but it's an educated guess you can bank on."

"Isn't that all the more reason to call Ethel?"

"You still don't get it," Pat said, an edge of impatience in her voice. "Storing ammonium nitrate and organic fertilizer isn't a crime. Right now, we've got a king-size quandary… and only one option. Like it or not, we have to ask Gary Barbera for help."

"Barbera!" Ellen's voice rose anew. "Are you nuts?"

Pat continued to stare straight ahead. "Look. I know this must come as a surprise."

"What's surprising?" Ellen answered, her laugh brittle with fear. "Doesn't everyone link arms with the Mafia?"

Pat was cold, and now she'd begun to ache. She refocused on her friend, knowing she hadn't been honest. All along, she'd thought it would take outside help to nail the Gaylanis. The gentleman don, Gary Barbera, could handle the situation, but did she have enough leverage to enlist him?

"This job is too big for us. To move forward, we need someone to keep an eye on the Gaylanis and to do some checking too. Gary Barbera has the manpower to do both."

"Whoa, Patricia." Ellen used a gloved hand to wipe snow off her horse's mane. "Even if we weren't star witnesses against Mr. Barbera and his son, why use the Mafia? Maybe the Barrington cops aren't the answer, but it sounds like the authorities could get things done."

Pat winced. Once again, Ellen wanted the FBI or CIA to handle a situation that needed to be done on the sly. Gary Barbera was better equipped to nose around without making either Tony or Joanna Gaylani suspicious.

"The authorities are good at some things," Pat agreed, "but Barbera is in touch with the right people to get the information we need. Face facts. Before the fertilizer and ammonium nitrate can be moved, somebody has to bring in a good-sized panel truck with a plow."

"Okay, but why call Mr. Barbera?" Ellen asked. "Kitty's aunt is married to a guy in the trucking business. Sean O'Banyon could find out who rented that kind of vehicle."

"Right, but if I've done my homework, Barbera is in a better position to get those details."

"No way," Ellen argued. "Once Sean O'Banyon knows why we're asking, he'll move heaven and earth to help."

"We need it done quietly," Pat said. "As I see it, Gary Barbera is the only one who can keep O'Banyon's temper under control."

Their horses stood abreast of each other, heads high. Ellen's posture looked far less confident. Her eyes were closed and her shoulders were slumped down.

"Are you telling me that Lady Harry's husband works for the mob?"

Pat faced her friend. "You really want to know?"

"I guess not."

They rode on in silence. Moments later, Ellen straightened her back and reined in her horse. "One of us is losing it," she said. "We're talking about asking Mr. Barbera for help. He's a crime boss, a hardened criminal."

Pat looked Ellen in the eye. "I've never said this to anyone, and I don't expect you to fully understand, but last spring, when he and I negotiated, I got a sense for this man. It sounds crazy, but much of his behavior is dictated by a private code of honor. Sure, he runs a horrible business for a despicable organization. But the man is a standup guy."

"What an interesting take," Ellen said. "I didn't know a standup guy could run a horrible business for a despicable organization."

They rode on for a bit, then Pat slowed her horse again.

"We can deal with Gary Barbera one-on-one," Pat said. "Trust me, Ellie. We'll strike a bargain that's mutually acceptable."

"Then do me a favor," Ellen said. "When you're hammering out the particulars, ask him how he plans to pull off the surveillance. Having his thugs parked in a limo, spitting distance from the scene of two murders, might look strange."

Ellen trotted ahead. Pat waited a moment, then slapped the flank of her horse. Once she caught up, she held out her arms and let snowflakes fall on her gloves.

"Have you forgotten what's piling up all around you?" she asked. "There's no room to park anything on the side of these roads."

Ellen smiled. "Only trying to make a point."

Pat nodded in acknowledgment and also noted that her friend seemed to be opening up to the idea. "In this instance, I'm thinking of a moving surveillance. Gary Barbera can have Chief Cherrigan send a squad car by every couple of hours. By my estimation, it would take that long for Joanna and her associates to plow the road, load up their truck, and get out."

"May the Lord forgive me," Ellen said, looking heavenward. "For once, I'm glad we know a cop on the take."

* * *

Admiral Eric Weiss picked up the bedroom phone. His grip tightened as Bob Stanojev, the agent assigned to watch the Eichlers' house, gave him an update.

"What," he said, "you're telling me they just got back?"

Eric had eaten a Christmas dinner and opened presents. His married kids and their families had gone home. Five hours after the initial call, he was hearing that Dale Evans and Annie Oakley were just climbing off their mounts. If ever a message awakened him to a continuing nightmare, this was it. Something had gone down, and he hadn't been a part of it.

"Those dames were gone long enough to ride into Chicago. Where the hell…"

He stopped himself. No need to ask the obvious question. None of the Chicago FBI agents knew where Miss Shaver and Mrs. Eichler had gone.

"Pay attention, damn it. At first light, I want someone to follow their tracks."

Admiral Weiss's smile disappeared.

"You can't be serious," he said. "A blizzard? I'll be a son of a bitch."

CHAPTER TWENTY–EIGHT

Pat and Ellen unsaddled and fed their horses. They'd said very little since getting back to the Eichlers' barn. That silence held as the two made the short walk to Ellen's Victorian farmhouse.

While Ellen went to the kitchen, Pat stayed in the foyer. In spite of a throbbing backside, she managed to pull off her boots, shed her parka and pants, and change into dry jeans.

She limped into the living room and headed toward the fireplace. When the kindling in the hearth caught, she closed the steel curtain and let the gathering blaze thaw out her body.

Minutes later, Ellen came in with two steaming mugs. Pat skirted around the coffee table and settled as her friend sat down on a needlepointed divan.

For a long moment, neither moved, then Ellen gestured toward the phone and speaker box. Pat hated herself for sinking to such depths, but calling Gary Barbera seemed like their only option.

She hit the hands-free button on the speakerphone and began dialing the gentleman don at his Lake Forest mansion. Last May, she and Barbera had met eye-to-eye. The negotiations had concluded with a firm handshake and a personal guarantee that all aspects of the bargain would be followed to the letter. As a symbolic gesture, he'd given her an eleven-digit number. This special code—a numerical access to a very private cellular phone—could be used in the event his son ever threatened her again. While she'd never anticipated dialing it, she also hadn't tossed it in the trash.

"My dear," the crime boss said, "did you call to wish me a Merry Christmas?"

"It's that time of year, Mr. Barbera." The fire had warmed Ellen's living room, but hearing him gave her chills. "I hope you had a nice holiday."

"It was wonderful," he said, his voice carrying an air of amusement and curiosity. "Danny joined me and my wife, Maria. But without one of your favorites at our table, it hardly seemed like a family gathering."

"I'm sure G.T. found a unique way to celebrate." Pat's fingers gripped the coffee mug, and her vocal cords tightened. "He's the inventive sort. A guy who pushes every boundary."

"My dear, you do my son a grave injustice."

"I admit to some prejudices," Pat said, glancing at Ellen. "But in the final analysis, what I think doesn't matter. The courts will settle our constitutional issues."

Pat knew Gary Barbera enjoyed sparring, but when the subject centered on G.T., she also realized the mobster's playful manner could change without warning. She'd come away from their springtime encounter with a gut feeling that he knew his son was an egotistical sex fiend with an uncontrollable mean streak. But even if Gary Barbera had pegged G.T. for what he was, the mobster hadn't disowned him. Embarrassment or not, blood was indeed thicker than water.

"As usual, you bring the gentleness of a woman's perspective to bear," he said. "You're right, this is a day for reflection and gift giving. But I fear you've caught me empty-handed."

"The stores may be closed," Pat replied, "but we may find something worth exchanging."

"The suspense is overwhelming. As God is my witness, I do love the way you bring me to the bargaining table."

Ellen continued to glare, tacitly signaling that the gentleman don's flamboyance was getting a mixed review.

"In the interests of full disclosure," Pat said, "be advised, you're on the speaker phone."

"How generous of you to inform me. Might I ask if you're alone … or does the audience include a group of my fans?"

"I'm at Ellie's. We're by ourselves, and I assume we're the only ones using this phone line."

"To be sure things stay that way, I'd like to dial you back." His tone turned businesslike. "If I patch our conversation through my office, people I trust will make sure our privileged call stays privileged."

"Fine with—"

Before she could agree, Pat heard a dial tone.

"Don't think he hung up to be rude. I bet he calls right back."

"Then what?" Ellen asked, staring angrily.

"Then we'll deal with him."

Pat stood, still sore from the horse ride. As she looked around a Victorian living room full of Victorian artifacts, her gaze settled on the mantel and an ornately framed picture of Queen Victoria seated in front of her faithful Scottish servant, John Brown.

Pat knew that several years ago, Ellen had bought the small reproduction when she and her husband had visited the Tower of London. Decades before their trip, during a college lecture on English history, Ellen had become enamored with Queen Victoria and her tireless defense of her relationship with John Brown.

Pat stretched her arms, wondering if the parallel she saw between Victoria and herself was just a figment of an overactive imagination. From her own research, she knew that Queen Victoria had detested the behind-the-back comments referring to her as Mrs. Brown. Right now, her phone call to Gary Barbera could be viewed as a similar betrayal to William Pavin, the federal district attorney in Chicago, and Admiral Eric Weiss, deputy director of the CIA. While she was prepared to seek help from any source, she wasn't sure if Ellen realized that from here on, the Mafia might turn into their new best friend.

* * *

Admiral Eric Weiss was in bed under the covers, looking at the first page of a novel he'd received from one of his grandchildren. When the bedside phone rang, he answered.

For a moment, he said nothing. Eric was a master at hiding his emotions. But after being briefed by Rick Eichman, one of the Chicago agents, the admiral felt his heart race.

"Did I hear you right?" he asked, his voice rising. "First, Miss Shaver called Barbera from Mrs. Eichler's house. Then after exchanging pleasantries, he hung up so the call could be rerouted through his office. What the hell does that mean?"

Over the years, the admiral's wife had grown accustomed to all-hours phone calls. She also knew how to deal with them. When his words reverberated off the bedroom walls, a head full of roller curlers came to life. She didn't say anything. She didn't have to. He sensed her look.

"Give me that again," Eric said, whispering. "Barbera dialed the reporter back, but the moment Miss Shaver answered the phone, all you picked up was static?"

"Not exactly static, sir," Rick answered. "Initially they scrambled the line; now I'm hearing Christmas carols."

"Christmas carols!"

Eric was infuriated, but when his wife sat up, he got quiet. He'd learned to live with face cream and roller curlers, but her fiendish smile and the squint in her eye… that unnerved him.

"Listen carefully," the admiral said, turning away and hushing his voice. "I want to hear what Miss Shaver and Barbera said. Patch their conversation through to my phone."

"The call she made?" Rick asked. "The one that ended when Barbera dialed-toned her?"

"That's the one."

"On it, sir. Give me a few seconds to set everything up."

Eric waited, the receiver held close to his ear. To soothe his wife, he glanced over and told her that his business would end in a matter of minutes.

The moment she pulled the bed covers over her curlers, Eric also began to calm down. Why worry? No hood would dare cross the CIA. When Barbera had hung up to reroute the call, he had to be exercising caution. Tomorrow night, they'd meet and—

"Jingle Bells" blared into his ear.

"God damn it! Get that sleigh ride shit off the air." Eric swung his legs over the side of the bed. "Don't patch what you're hearing. I want to listen to what you heard."

"Sorry, sir," Rick said, his words quavering, "got my wires crossed."

Eric said nothing. Instead he took short breaths and closed his eyes. Why was this happening? Hadn't he taken the proper precautions? Sure, he had some qualms about unlawful bugging. But didn't he have to put an emergency tap on Miss Shaver's and Mrs. Eichler's phones? Once he'd discovered the two women had found Kempner's body and roamed around the house before the authorities arrived, he figured it was his right to know what they knew.

"It's working, sir," Rick said. "You should be getting—"

"Yeah, yeah," Eric replied, "it's coming in loud and clear. Now shut up and let me listen."

As his wife headed for the guest bedroom, he made no effort to make amends. To understand the nuances of the recorded conversation, he concentrated on every word.

"Shall I play it again, sir?"

"Once is enough," he said, his voice expressing relief. "Heard it just fine."

Eric had known he had nothing to fear after Miss Shaver told Barbera they were on a speakerphone. The mobster's excuse to switch to a scrambled line was in accordance with the CIA's standing instructions. All phone conversations concerning the Kempner/Gaylani matter were to be taped. He'd judged Barbera correctly after all. The old bastard would have a transcript ready for their meeting tomorrow.

"Good work, Rick. Make a copy and get a dupe sent to my office." His grip on the phone eased. "See you and the boys tomorrow. Unless it's earthshaking, no more calls."

Patricia Shaver sat beside Ellen on her friend's Victorian couch. Since Gary Barbera had hung up, neither had said much.

Seconds later, when the phone rang, Pat hit the speaker box button. She listened as Barbera apologized for the delay, then inquired about the clarity of the connection.

"There is one other thing, my dear," he said, sounding all business. "I'm taping our conversation. Do you want a copy?"

Pat thanked him, but declined. His willingness to record their conversation surprised her, but once she thought it through, she understood why. If Barbera offered a transcript to Admiral Weiss, the mobster would protect himself from CIA reprisals.

Pat picked up her coffee mug. "Once I start speaking, you'll realize why my safekeeping rests with whoever doesn't hear the tape, not who has a copy."

"My dear, I'm more intrigued than ever. But before we get started, may I digress?" The gentleman don's businesslike tone softened. "Mrs. Eichler, I'd like to offer an apology for my son's behavior. I was appalled at his conduct during the divorce proceedings. As before, you, Lauren, and her children have my assurance that none of you will ever be troubled by G.T. again."

While Ellen thanked him, Pat shook her head and sat back. Who'd have thought a crime boss of Gary Barbera's stature would atone for his son's sins? But then again, who'd have suspected the son of a crime boss of Barbera's stature would wind up married to Ellen's daughter? Nevertheless, it had happened.

Lauren Eichler was an expert horse jumper and Olympic silver medalist. More than fifteen years ago, she'd followed up on a tip from her riding coach and sent her resume to a PO box. After two exhausting interviews, Lauren became the assistant manager of Falconcrest, a Kentucky horse farm owned by the chairman of Holly

Corporation. Of course, neither she nor her family knew that the man with a fascination for Arabian thoroughbreds was Gary Thomas Barbera, Jr., the Chicago crime boss and the chairman of Holly Corporation. For that matter, they didn't know he also had a handsome son. But a few weeks after Lauren was hired, Gary Thomas III (G.T.) came down to spend a weekend.

With his father away on business, G.T. had free run of the place. In no time, he'd worked his charms. When Ellen and her husband found out, they urged caution. But it was too late. A few months later, G.T. completed Lauren's seduction by eloping with the Eichler's eighteen-year-old daughter.

"Let me say one more thing." Gary Barbera's voice broke the unpleasant silence. "With Lauren's permission, I'd consider it a privilege if I might drop by and say hello. While I'm sure it pains you to hear me say it, they're my grandchildren too."

"It doesn't pain me," Ellen said, "but I do have one question."

Her friend lifted her hand, letting it settle near her sternum. Pat had seen the same reflexive gesture many times. Under Ellen's turtleneck sweater was a medallion on a chain. After the '84 Games, she'd begun wearing the smaller-sized replica of Lauren's Olympic silver medal. Ellen never took it off, but since her daughter's recent divorce, she had covered it with a layer of clothing.

"Clarify one thing," Ellen said, facing the speakerphone. "Are our grandchildren bargaining chips in this negotiation?"

"Never," he snapped. "I'm a businessman, Mrs. Eichler. I will evaluate Miss Shaver's proposal on its merits."

"My quarrel is with your son," Ellen replied. "If you control him, I'd be grateful. As for visiting your grandchildren... If Lauren stays on to manage your horse farm, I suspect you'll want to go down and oversee your investment."

Pat's mouth fell open. Her friend's graciousness meant only one thing. Grandparents do share common bonds.

"Thank you for your kindness, Mrs. Eichler." The gentleman don cleared his voice. "Now to business. I believe you called me, Miss Shaver."

"I'll get right to the point," Pat said, leaning toward the speaker box. "On the day Mrs. Kempner died, she received a shipment from the British government. The documents were written by her grandfather during his World War II assignment in Palestine. Unbeknownst to her, they also contained disclosures that compromised Dr. Tony Gaylani's cover. Once the doctor made that connection, he acted to protect his status as an Iraqi spy. That's when we believe he murdered Katherine Kempner."

"Hold on, my dear," Barbera replied, his voice rising through the speakerphone. "You're going too fast for an old man. Maybe if you substantiated some of these... these allegations."

"Where shall I start, Mr. Barbera?"

"Start by slowing down. After that, I'd appreciate it if you'd call me Gary."

Pat smiled. She took his request to be addressed by his first name as a sign of trust.

"Gary, let me begin with some facts." She glanced over at her friend. "Kitty Kempner wrote Ellen a note and mailed it just hours before she died. Ellen received the note a day after Kitty's funeral and immediately showed it to me. Once I looked it over, I suggested we visit your lawyer, Mr. Thomas Kempner. After he read his wife's note, we began a brainstorming session that ended with a midnight call to Admiral Eric Weiss. As you know, the deputy director of the CIA had been in contact with you regarding a request transmitted by your—"

"My dear," the gentleman don said, "if you'll pardon me for interrupting, your so-called facts sound more like a soap opera than real life."

"Do they?" she questioned. "What if I can prove that Dr. Tony Gaylani visited Tom Kempner during the early hours this morning? That the doctor lulled his neighbor into complacency over a brandy or two? That Gaylani knocked Tom unconscious, dragged his body to the car, and faked his suicide?"

"My dear. You're doing it again."

"We discovered Mr. Kempner's body," she said. "We had first access to the crime scene. Believe me, Gary, I know what I saw."

She and Ellen stared at the speakerphone… and waited. Pat concluded his sudden quiet meant he suspected much of what she'd said was true. But she also knew that before the gentleman don aligned himself with them and subjected his Family to repercussions from the CIA, he'd need two things: Positive proof of Dr. Tony Gaylani's complicity, and a scapegoat to protect him from Admiral Eric Weiss's wrath.

If Barbera sent a tape of their conversation to the admiral, he'd certainly make her the fall guy. As to providing solid proof and enlisting the mobster in their cause… She had things he would like to possess, but convincing Gary would be more delicate.

Two items she'd lifted from Tom's office—the cassette of Eric Weiss's call-back and the Kempner/Weiss file—did not prove criminal wrongdoing. But things not admissible in a court of law often served a higher purpose.

Take the admiral's taped message left on Tom Kempner's answering machine: *Sorry about your loss, buddy-boy. Wish I could have attended the funeral, but we both know that would never fly. And another thing… be a sport and don't use the private number. Wouldn't want the taxpayers to get the wrong message.*

Admiral Weiss might not have admitted to CIA/Mafia collaborations, but the inference was clear and damaging. The admiral would have to resign his post if a public disclosure of his relationship with the mob was ever leaked to the press.

The other item she possessed—the Kempner/Weiss file—also had great value. Both the admiral and the Chicago crime boss would want it destroyed or put away in a very safe spot.

The Mafia had unwritten rules when a don from one of the Families provided assistance to the CIA. Each of the other Families expected a full accounting of the activities and a commensurate share of the benefits. But in this case, the gentleman don wouldn't want his Mafia brethren to know he'd supplied the Company with bios on

Hispanic-American trucking executives. Anything that reduced the flow of cocaine reduced the mob's bottom line.

Gary Barbera would covet both items, but if Admiral Eric Weiss had a tap on Ellen's line, Pat couldn't dangle her carrots over the phone. Gary Barbera had gone on record as electronically recording the entire conversation. Sure, the mobster's people were scrambling the audio right now. But that would just make the admiral more anxious to get a transcript of the entire tape.

To protect herself, she'd have to find a forum to present the cassette and the Kempner/ Weiss file. As she saw it, that meant baiting Gary into accepting an invitation to a meeting tomorrow night. Ideally, he'd agree to get together with her in the funeral parlor parking lot before Tom Kempner's wake.

Pat glanced at Ellen, then leaned toward the speakerphone.

"Trust me, Gary. Much of what I'm saying may seem farfetched, but I'm telling the whole truth."

"That's my dilemma," he replied. "You've mixed your beliefs and facts in such a way that it all sounds like unsubstantiated declarations. I hardly know which one to challenge first."

Pat knew Ellen was watching for a reaction. She didn't dare smile, but so far, she was pleased. Barbera's feigned indecision was masterful. As a sly tactician, the gentleman don realized he couldn't be charged with complicity or obstruction of justice if all he did was listen.

"Let's try a new approach," she offered. "I'll kick things off, starting with Kitty's note."

"One second, my dear. I'm an old man and logical deductions often escape me, but by my reckoning, you might be holding a fraud."

"Is that a question, Gary?"

"An observation," he replied. "Of course, if you'd like me to elaborate, I'm happy to oblige."

"Ellie and I are all ears."

Barbera cleared his throat. "Tommy Kempner's wife died on Wednesday. If she mailed a note hours before her death, why wasn't it delivered to Mrs. Eichler on Thursday or Friday?"

"Why, Gary… you have been paying attention." Pat bent down toward the speakerphone and rubbed her sore legs. "Ellen and I think the delay was probably nothing but a bureaucratic snafu. The Post Office does a great job, but occasionally a letter gets misplaced."

"Why are we playing cat and mouse?" he asked. "Had you not noticed the irregularity, I doubt you'd have pointed it out to me."

She kept still, trying to come up with a reasonable response.

"Are you there, my dear?"

"Yes," she replied sheepishly. "Mind if I offer a theory that's pure conjecture?"

"By all means."

"Your position is well-founded," Pat said, sitting down and eying Ellen. "We believe the note was taken from Kitty Kempner's mailbox before the postman could pick it up. Sometime late Thursday, after it had been steamed open, read, and reglued, the letter was mailed again."

"Someone tampered with it?"

They'd reached a critical point. To keep her scheme on track, Pat had to lie. But that wasn't all. She also had to pray Gary Barbera's knowledge didn't include background information on Joanna Gaylani. As she took a steadying breath, Pat needed the gentleman don to believe that Tony was the only felon.

"All the arrows point in one man's direction. When Dr. Gaylani discovered Kitty was in receipt of General Alan Cunningham's papers, he insisted on coming over. While they were together, we believe Kitty Kempner read something that blew Tony's cover. Her discovery was so upsetting that she tossed the doctor out, then sat down and wrote Ellen."

"All well and good," he said, "but if Mrs. Kempner saw such powerful evidence, why didn't she call?"

"Ellie and I were downtown shopping. To compound matters, her answering machine wasn't working."

"I see," Gary said, dropping his voice. "Who has the papers that prove Dr. Gaylani is a spy?"

"Can't be sure," Pat replied, "but I'm guessing Mr. Kempner was murdered so the doctor could steal them."

"If true," he added, "Dr. Gaylani is quite a nasty fellow. Mail tampering, murder, and burglary are police matters. You should notify them."

"Our proof is circumstantial," she admitted. "To make it stick, we need your help."

"I'm not sure I could help even if I wanted to," Gary said. "Of course, the deaths of Tommy and his wife are distressing. If you outline your evidence, maybe I can offer a suggestion as to how you might proceed."

Pat glanced at the ceiling and savored the moment. At last, a mini breakthrough. But Gary's overture was conditional. He'd protected himself.

In a courtroom, he could argue he hadn't given advice, he'd only sought to steer them to the proper authorities. But one thing pointed toward his eagerness to hear more. Throughout the conversation, she'd referred to his lawyer as Mr. Kempner. Yet repeatedly, Gary chose to call him Tommy. To her, the use of a nickname meant they were more than client and attorney. Unless she missed her guess, the gentleman don considered Tom Kempner a part of his Family.

"You asked me to list our physical proof," Pat said, recapping Barbera's request. "Unfortunately Ellie and I only control Katherine Kempner's note."

"That's all?"

"Yes." After telling one boldfaced lie, she explained. "We believe the bulk of her grandfather's wartime documents were taken from the house. We also think a smaller cache of papers was removed from the stable. Mrs. Kempner made reference to both sets of documents, but we never found them."

Pat waited for a response, but when none came, she continued. "Before we go on, I'd like to make one observation and phrase it in the form of a question: How does a man with a golf-ball-sized knot on the back of his head walk to his wife's car, get in, turn on the ignition, and in the process, not leave a single print?"

"My goodness, my dear," Barbera replied, his voice sounding whimsical. "I realize you've been busy, but when did you find time to dust Mrs. Kempner's Mercedes?"

"I didn't, but Barrington has a fine police chief. I'm positive he's informed the coroner of the lump on Mr. Kempner's head and also included fingerprint analysis in the official report."

"Then there's nothing to worry about," he added. "The chief sounds like a lawman who won't rest until the perpetrator of this horrible crime is brought to justice."

"There's one problem," she said. "A blow to the head and a lack of prints may dispel the notion of suicide, but it does nothing to identify the killer."

"Is it possible the chief overlooked some evidence?"

"Who can be sure?" Pat said. "But I'll bet if someone looked in the pantry behind some #10 cans and found three brandy snifters, that person could take the glassware to a criminologist for analysis."

"Brandy snifters?" he asked. "A criminologist?"

"They fit together," she said. "What if I told you that on the night Tom Kempner was murdered, he and I had a glass of brandy? But the next morning, after we found him, I noticed three snifters on the coffee table?"

"If there were three," Gary replied, "I'd conclude someone came by after you left."

"What if I went on to say that the rounded underside of each snifter had a different set of prints? One with mine. One with Mr. Kempner's. One with Dr. Gaylani's."

"Elementary," he said. "If, as you say, the doctor's prints are found on the bottom of the third glass, the police might be persuaded to believe that Tommy's visitor was Dr. Tony Gaylani."

Pat eyed Ellen, then spoke into the speaker box. "Persuaded enough to look into some other things?"

"That depends on the legality," he answered. "The Constitution won't permit one crime to be committed in order to solve— Hold on a second."

Unexpectedly, Gary interrupted his own train of thought. A moment later, as she and Ellen exchanged quizzical looks, his voice came through the speaker box.

"Sorry," he said, his tone harried. "My office just called. There's going to be a short delay. The tape is about to run out. Once they get another one, we'll resume."

When the speakerphone went silent again, she and Ellen exchanged more quizzical looks. Then, as before, Gary broke in.

"Are you still there, my dear?" he asked.

"We're both here," Pat answered.

"Good." His voice deepened. "While my staff is locating a fresh cassette, why don't you tell me what information you need to convict Tommy's killer?"

Pat was caught off guard by his change in tone. Then it hit her. Gary had just agreed to help. Nixon should have taken lessons from this savvy old fox. Instead of trying to erase sensitive material after the fact, he pretended to be out of tape. That ploy allowed him to cooperate with her at the same time he appeared to be honoring his pact with the admiral.

She didn't waste any time outlining a wish list, including a request to keep the barn under police surveillance.

Admiral Eric Weiss was restless. He'd hung up with the Chicago agent more than fifteen minutes ago. At the time, he'd felt a controlled sense of optimism. But once he'd turned off the reading lamp and put his head on the pillow, lots of unanswered questions kept him awake.

Would Barbera figure out where Miss Shaver and Mrs. Eichler had gone? Would the bastard also get the goods on Dr. Tony Gaylani and finally put an end to the rumor that the doctor's wife, Joanna, was still politically involved with her uncle, Lawrence Magel?

Eric rolled over on his back. The room was pitch-dark, but he stared at the ceiling anyway. As a career naval and intelligence officer, his job was to preserve democracy and the American way of life. That meant he routinely made decisions that kept the vast majority of law-abiding citizens safe. Regrettably, that also meant he had to walk a fine line balancing right and wrong with the need to formulate the difficult policies insuring the greater good.

He blinked into the darkness. At present, he was in the midst of a delicate operation. While certain his decisions were correct, he also realized that asking the Mafia to help had to be kept secret. If his investigation of Dr. Tony Gaylani and his wife, Joanna, ever got out and was debated in the newspapers, the rightness of his position would be lost.

He blinked again. Congress had insured that the CIA could initiate certain inquiries without getting subpoenas or seeking indictments. In their wisdom, they'd authorized the Company to use covert operations to defend the vital interests of the United States. Of course, his authority got a little hazy when he and his agents became involved in domestic homicides. But he wasn't worried. Only a mob lawyer and his wife had gotten killed. No one was going to organize a congressional hearing over them.

He closed his eyes. He hated feeling unappreciated, but most of all, he detested having to assure himself that he was an honorable man in an honorable profession. When he wore his Navy whites, people treated him with respect. Civilians viewed him as a seafaring man who defended his country's shores. When he left his uniform in the closet, the adoration disappeared. Why did his image change when he took command of the ship fighting espionage? What made intelligence an ugly battleground? Christ Almighty, the military killed people and no one said anything to them. Wasn't his job the same? He and the Company were embroiled in a deadly ideological war. So what if opposing governments didn't identify their armies? Like all great conflicts, it was shoot to kill, even if innocent people occasionally had to be sacrificed.

He sat up, opening his eyes and staring at the darkness. Okay. Maybe, in this instance, he'd skated over some thin ice. Certainly,

Mrs. Kempner's death had been regrettable. But he hadn't deliber-ately left her or Tom Kempner in the crosshairs. The doctor had been bold and caught him off guard.

He blinked several times, trying to clear his vision. With Joanna Gaylani the situation was different. Sometimes, to gain the initiative, a commander had to suffer casualties. Wasn't she a case in point? Wouldn't she be the next victim in her husband's rampage?

Of course, he couldn't warn her. She'd freak if she knew her husband was an Iraqi spy. And what about the doctor's other nasty habit? If Joanna ever learned her bedside Romeo was a murderer, she might cancel her keynote address. That would ruin everything.

None of this was his fault. Until the Jewish convention got under way, he had to give the doctor free rein. He needed concrete proof. If he locked Dr. Gaylani up, the liberal courts would just put him right back on the streets. That left him no other choice. To protect the greater good, he had to go outside the law. To save America from its enemies, he had to hope the doctor would try to kill again.

Eric tried to relax. When he got to Chicago, maybe things would become clearer. Maybe Barbera would put a new spin on all this. Maybe he'd be able to sort things out before anyone else got killed. He'd keep his fingers crossed, but wouldn't bet on that kind of good fortune.

He yawned, a reminder of something else. In his business, need-less worry didn't pay dividends. Why ruin a good night's sleep over stuff you couldn't control?

CHAPTER TWENTY–NINE

Gary Barbera stared straight ahead. As the fire in the hearth warmed him, he turned and disconnected the speakerphone. He and Danny Finn were in the library. They sat in claw-footed wingback chairs juxtaposed between antique lamp tables.

Gary mulled over his conversation with Patricia Shaver and the one he'd just had with Tommy's law partner, Bill Bronner. Then he lifted a demitasse cup of espresso. Before taking a sip, he smelled the aroma. Instantly he was reminded of his father and the story of how Lavazza coffee had become a staple in the Barbera household.

Almost ninety-seven years ago, after completing his freshman year in college, his father had spent the summer touring Italy. While in the northern city of Turino, he'd stopped at an outdoor café. Luigi Lavazza, the owner of a local grocery store who roasted coffee beans on the side, was hawking his wares to the chef and maitre d'. Being a coffee lover, his father had listened. When Luigi's pitch was over, he asked if he could join the tasting.

That was all it took. Following the sales call, he'd accompanied Luigi back to his store. After more coffee and some lively political discussions, his father canceled his reservation at a mountain villa, stayed in town, and bought Luigi dinner at a nearby bistro.

Before leaving the next morning to continue his trip, his father knew two things: He'd made a new friend, and he'd never serve anything but Lavazza coffee.

"Great stuff, boss," the Irishman said, hoisting a near-priceless antique—a Royal Crown Derby oversized teacup. "Lavazza beans are the real deal."

"Glad you're enjoying the flavor," Gary replied, "but why not take it in smaller doses? You've got a week's worth of caffeine in that cup."

"No offense, boss, but those demitasse mugs don't hold squat. A guy like me drinks espresso 'cause he wants to feel the full effect. That means getting a jolt."

Gary smiled. The espresso was outstanding, and the Irishman's frankness had improved his spirits. Of course, the session with Miss Patricia Shaver had lightened his mood too. But that phone conversation had a downside. It had reminded him of a shortcoming in his genetic family.

Since his first contact with Patricia last May, Gary had known that his son didn't have the smarts or pizzazz of the stylish journalist. But now was not the time to speculate on how an intelligent and beautiful young woman would run a Family business. His energies had to be concentrated elsewhere. Mistakes could bring the CIA down on him. It would take all his skill to protect his organization and still make sure that the Kempners' killer felt the sting of justice.

"I like Miss Patricia," he said. "A pretty good journalist and a nice girl, don't you think?"

Finn nodded. "It's the holiday season and I'm in a charitable mood, but I haven't forgotten about the payoff file and our run-in last spring."

Gary stood, tossed a hickory log on the fire, then grabbed the poker and stoked the white-hot embers. "I'm not adding her to my Christmas card list, but in this instance, we may be able to do each other a favor."

"She's already answered one question," Finn said, draining his espresso. "Miss Shaver must have batted her baby blues at Cherrigan. He didn't turn into a smart cop by himself."

"That's true, but I'm more interested in her undercover role." Gary unbuttoned his Irish knit, a Christmas gift from Danny Finn many years ago. "She was there when Tommy phoned the admiral. She and Mrs. Eichler were also first on the scene. That means she took the answering machine tape. Didn't Chief Cherrigan say the lid was up, but nothing was inside?"

"That's not the only things she's up to," Finn predicted. "I'm also betting we don't have a leak. Weiss got the FBI in there fast 'cause she tipped him off."

"That's worrisome," Gary admitted. "Every journalist knows the rules. Langley invented *no comment*. Telling Admiral Weiss she knows the CIA contacted Tommy won't get him to disclose anything. Unless…"

Gary watched the flames build, wondering whether subtle hints could also be part of Miss Patricia's charm. "When the Sanitation Crew went through Tommy's drawers and cabinets, how many empty folders did they find?"

"Just the one marked Kempner/Weiss file."

"Ah, yes. The Kempner/Weiss file." Gary frowned, absently rubbing one of his peregrine cufflinks. "Almost forgot about that one."

"What is it, boss? Don't think you ever mentioned it to me."

"Just some ideas Tommy and I kicked around a long time ago."

He winced, hoping the Irishman didn't notice his tension. Of course, he remembered all about the Kempner/Weiss file.

Of late, it had been inactive. His *consigliere* hadn't added any dossiers since the mid-nineties. But from the early eighties till then, Admiral Weiss had requested information on persons of interest at a rate of more than one per year.

While he didn't believe his Mafia family could be connected to the disappearances of the Hispanic trucking executives, he was surprised by the report the Sanitation Crew had submitted after they'd cleaned out Tommy's office. Years ago, Tommy had given him the location and combination. But when the Sanitation Crew pulled up the rug, opened the trap door, and scrolled in the numbers, they discovered an empty safe. The only evidence of the Kempner/Weiss file was an empty folder lying on some hanging files in the bottom drawer of Tommy's desk

If his *consigliere* had removed the Kempner/Weiss file from the safe and destroyed it, all well and good. But, if Tommy had gotten careless… That was something else.

Gary didn't want the contents of that file to ever become public. Such a breach would foster embarrassing and troublesome questions from all the crime Families. And something else. Eric Weiss and his CIA superiors would come under the scrutiny of congressional committees.

"Not trying to be nosy," Finn said, "but is there any sensitive shit in that file?"

"Nothing at all," he said, booming out his attestation. "Just wondered why someone would take the contents of a file and then leave a titled folder behind?"

"Only one reason, boss. That nice girl, Miss Shaver, wants you to know she's got that too."

Gary nodded his head slowly. "It makes me wonder what else she's commandeered."

"We traded with her before. Why not do it again?"

"Have you forgotten about Eric Weiss?" Gary asked. "The admiral must be monitoring their phones. When he flies out tomorrow, he'll want the tape."

"Fine," Finn said, "tell Sailor-boy you're meeting the journalist at the wake. Make it sound like you expect to get something big. Once you see what she has to horse-trade, you'll know whether she's worth protecting."

"But what if she's got something we want?" Gary asked rhetorically. "One thing is guaranteed. If we think it has value, the admiral will think so too."

"Who cares?" the Irishman said, shrugging his beefy shoulders. "If our new girlfriend comes across with the right kind of insurance, you can tell Weiss to fuck off."

"One thing never changes," he said, trying to sound blasé. "Your Irish logic is flawless."

"Got it from my mother," Finn quipped. "Oh, about Miss Shaver's request. Shall I call Cherrigan?"

Gary nodded. "Tell him to send a cruiser by Tommy's property every two hours, around the clock."

"What about those snifters in the pantry?"

"They're untouchable at the moment," Gary replied. "Eric Weiss got his pals at the FBI to cordon off Tommy's house."

Finn shook his head. "Too bad."

"You're not listening," Gary snapped. "I said they're untouchable *at the moment*. If Bill Bronner's new approach works out, that may change."

Tommy Kempner had been his *consigliere* for many years, but during that time, Gary had always been very impressed with his law partner, Bill Bronner.

"What's his angle?" Finn asked.

"I won't bore you with the legalese, but if we prevail, the Feds will be forced to leave. Unfortunately, nothing can happen until the courts open tomorrow."

"Bronner is a creative guy," the Irishman said, sitting back in his chair. "If anyone can figure out a way to boot out the FBI, it's him. But what about Chuck Sweet? The journalist thinks he's important… and frankly, I agree. If you don't mind, now might be a good time to tell you why he's a key player."

"But I do mind."

Gary glared, tacitly reminding his most trust lieutenant that he had just broken a cardinal rule. Subordinates, even Danny Finn, were never supposed to offer unsolicited advice.

"Sorry, boss, it's just…" Like an animal signaling submission, the Irishman dropped his shoulders and looked down. "Normally, I wouldn't say anything, but…"

"But, what?"

"Damn it, boss!" The Irishman sat up straight and stared him in the eye. "Chuck Sweet is involved with Joanna Gaylani and that uncle of hers, Lawrence Magel. Chew my head off if you must, but it's important you know how this bird fits in."

"Haven't I made myself clear? Fishing expeditions aren't on today's agenda."

Gary chided himself. He knew his anger stemmed more from his concern over the missing Kempner/Weiss file than a challenge to his tyrannical power. In truth, Finn's initiative had pleased him. To run his Family business, he needed men who packaged backbone and intelligence with respect for authority.

"All right. By all means, table everything. Why is this *bird* so important?"

Finn's eyes became animated. "Remember when Weiss told us to check out Joanna Gaylani's uncle?"

Gary put down his cup. "I recall him asking if we could get a line on the old buzzard."

"Right, Boss," Finn said. "That's what I meant. Once you agreed to honor Sailor-boy's request, Chuck Sweet's name popped into the picture."

"I'm confused," Gary replied. "Our journalist friend, Miss Patricia, thinks Joanna Gaylani hired Chuck Sweet to do chores for the Kempners."

"No way," Finn said. "Joanna didn't hire anyone. Sweet's services are free."

Gary looked up. "Explain."

"It started when we ran intelligence on the uncle's employees."

"His employees?"

"Lawrence Magel lives on an estate overlooking Lake Michigan," Finn said, "but along with his Winnetka joint, the uncle owns a horse farm just west of Barrington in Wayne. Magel rarely goes out there, but Chuck Sweet and several other men live and work on the grounds."

"Why should I care if Sweet and several co-workers reside in the bunk house on Lawrence Magel's horse farm? What am I missing?"

"Two technicalities," Finn replied. "Sweet dresses and acts like a stablehand, but talks like a professor. And he doesn't live with the others. Sweet bunks down in the uncle's ranch house."

"If opposites attract, you've described your alter ego." Gary noted that Finn's conservative GQ togs contrasted sharply with his

blue-collar mouth. "Tell me, did this academic charlatan get his credentials from Harvard or Yale?"

"No one knows," the Irishman said, getting up and walking to
the hearth. "Our people can't get a line on him. As far as we can tell,
there's not even an official record of Chuck Sweet's birth."

"How unusual. A man with a name but not an identity. Reminds
me... hmmm." Gary dismissed the unpleasant memory. "But back
to basics. Let's say this Chuck Sweet lives in a ranch house owned by
Joanna's uncle. What makes him of interest to us?"

"It's a little complicated, but fully explained in the unofficial bio
our people pieced together."

"Don't toy with me," Gary snapped. "Get to the point."

"Sorry, boss. It begins years ago, when Sweet's mother cooked
for Joanna's uncle."

"Great." Gary tapped his fingers on the antique lamp table. "A
story about a mother and her well-fed lad."

"Well-fed, but not from her kitchen. Before Chucky took his
first bite, Mama started singing with the angels. She died during childbirth."

"How tragic."

"Yeah. Quite a tear-jerker, especially since she was young and a
real looker too."

"When did she die?"

"In the mid-seventies," the Irishman answered. "That puts
Chucky in his late twenties, maybe thirty. He's strong as an ox and
also handsome."

Gary leaned in. "Would you say he inherited his looks from his
mother?"

"No proof either way," Finn said. "The Warehouse snoops never
dug up any old pictures of Larry Magel. Today, he could stand to drop
twenty pounds, but I gotta admit, the old fart ain't bad looking."

"So the uncle rescues his niece and feels compelled to raise his
cook's son?"

"I said no one can prove it, but take it from me, Chucky is Magel's son." The Irishman rested his forearm on the mantel. "Word has it, Larry banged Sweet's mother morning, noon, and night."

"Is this soap opera going anywhere?"

Finn nodded. "Sweet's name surfaced again when I started investigating Joanna Gaylani. At the time, I was trying to figure out whether she and her uncle had more than a social relationship."

"An illegitimate son is living in the main house on his father's horse farm," Gary said, sitting back in his chair. "How does that affect Joanna's relationship with either one of them?"

"Chucky was only born there. Before he was a week old, Magel sent him abroad to be raised in Switzerland. About three years ago, he brought Chucky back to Barrington."

"What?" Gary squinted. "You're telling me there's no way to check where he's been from birth until three odd years ago?"

Finn smiled. "Haven't you made people vanish?"

"A determined man can hide almost anything… but that's another story." Gary got to his feet and took a deep breath. "At the moment, I'd like to understand how Chuck Sweet fits between an old-guard isolationist and the bleeding-heart UJC liberal."

"Chucky is the connecting rod," Finn answered firmly. "About three years ago, that bleeding-heart liberal hired iron-man Sweet to do part-time work in the Kempners' stable."

"The prodigal son returns so he can be hired out by the uncle's niece." Gary glanced up at the ceiling. "Will the coincidences never cease?"

"That's why I wanted you to hear the story."

Gary tugged at his cuffs, touching the gold peregrine links. "Have we passed any of this along?"

The Irishman shook his head. "If you like, I can include it in the materials being prepared for your meeting tomorrow with the admiral."

"No. Let Admiral Weiss figure that out for himself."

Stone-faced, Finn nodded. "What about the panel truck? Are we still going to locate it?"

"Why not?" Gary shrugged. "Sean O'Banyon owes me a favor."

"You won't tell him why we're looking… will you?"

"What's the harm?"

"Don't get sore, boss… but you do recall that O'Banyon's wife and Katherine Kempner's adopted mother are one and the same." Finn turned and walked from the hearth to a fireside window. "When that crazy Mick finds out why he's tracking down a truck… Shit, boss, he'll go berserk."

"Really?"

Finn cocked his head. "Remember, I'm a crazy Mick too."

Gary acknowledged the warning, but his mind was focused elsewhere. All at once, things began to make sense.

He'd understood who'd intercepted Katherine Kempner's note the moment Danny Finn made him aware of Joanna Gaylani's involvement. He'd kept still when the journalist rambled on, making it seem like the doctor had taken it. Naturally, he'd had his suspicions. He knew from experience that not all of Miss Patricia's charms were befitting of her societal standing.

Bluffing, innuendo, and deception were also part of her repertoire. But she wasn't the only one who played by those rules. Of course, when he realized what she was doing, he chose not to challenge her allegations. When talking over the phone, one never knew who else might be listening.

CHAPTER THIRTY

Admiral Eric Weiss arrived at O'Hare International Airport on Monday morning. He was driven to a rundown building on the outskirts of Chicago's downtown business district. Once settled into one of the Spartan rooms the Company leased, he met with the local agents to outline his strategy. After each man had been given his assignment, the admiral excused himself, went into a conference room, and phoned the old don, Gary Barbera.

The gamesmanship began immediately. When pressed on certain facts, Barbera balked. Aside from trying to cut their discussion short, the crime boss would only say that he'd hand over the taped conversation with Patricia Shaver and be armed with new insights.

The response made the admiral uneasy. He'd dealt with Barbera before and knew the bastard was unprincipled. But right now, he needed his help. Right now, he had to limit his anger to glaring at the speakerphone

"Stay focused, Barbera. I deal in facts, not insights."

"We both want answers," the crime boss replied agreeably. "If you must criticize my effort, at least wait and see what I produce. I'm getting together with Miss Shaver at 8 PM. Since we both plan to attend Tommy Kempner's wake, I suggested a meeting in the parking lot."

"How chummy," Eric said, forcing a laugh. "After a chitchat in your limo, you and the society dame can stroll into the funeral parlor hand in hand."

"We're getting together in the parking lot," Barbera repeated. "Once our business is done, she'll go in by herself. From then on, I'll be at your disposal."

"Got that right." Eric banged his fist on the metal conference table and watched the speakerphone bounce. "I'll be watching your every move."

Patricia Shaver checked her watch. 7:48 PM. She looked out her living room window, then reached into the cookie jar and passed out dog bones. Ellen was due any moment. While the Labs munched on unexpected treats, she rechecked the time.

Twenty-four hours ago, she'd thought the authorities would figure things out. The horseback ride to Tom Kempner's barn and the discovery of the ammonium nitrate had changed her mind. Storing fertilizer wasn't a crime, but now a bomb threat had been added to the double murders.

She closed her eyes, feeling the stress. It was a nightmare. She knew Joanna Gaylani wanted to create mayhem. She knew Tony Gaylani had killed the Kempners. But that knowledge was useless. Tony had covered up his crimes, and so far Joanna hadn't done anything illegal. Both were untouchable. To her, that meant one thing. She and Ellen had to solicit Gary Barbera's assistance.

She looked through her window and remembered their call last night. They'd just come back from their horseback ride. She and Ellen had listened to Barbera, but after agreeing to a strategy and hanging up, Ellen had had misgivings. Instead of allowing Gary Barbera to get involved, Ellen wanted to call Ethel Iverson, Deputy Superintendent of the Chicago Police Department.

To be sure, Ethel was an honest cop with plenty of resources. But Pat had also argued that officialdom couldn't act until someone collected evidence proving the Gaylanis' complicity. She'd gone on to say that Eric Weiss and the CIA were better equipped to handle espionage and foreign nationals.

She and Ellen had sat in Ellen's Victorian living room and talked until dawn. To reach a compromise, she'd promised to confide in Ethel, but only after involving the CIA. Ellen had also made concessions. She'd okayed a meeting with Gary Barbera to be held during Tom Kempner's wake. Pat's marching orders were simple. With the mobster's assistance, she would try to get hold of General Alan Cunningham's papers.

Her thoughts were interrupted when headlight beams flashed in her driveway. She ran to the front entry, put on her parka, and picked up a large duffel bag. As Ellen came around the Explorer and opened the rear passenger door, Pat walked down the porch stairs, tossed her stuff in the back seat, then climbed in the front.

"Hi, Ellie. How's everyone doing in Lexington?"

"Santa was good to the grandkids, and Lauren seems to be managing," Ellen said, half-smiling. "They all loved the presents you sent."

Pat snapped on her seatbelt. "Tell me the truth. Are you okay?"

"Be fine once I get to Kentucky," Ellen answered. "For now, I'm just trying to get used to the idea of being in bed with the Mafia."

Bad as it sounded, her friend had it right. From now until things got resolved, they'd be aligned with Gary Barbera and his Family. Desperate conditions required desperate solutions. Tony and Joanna Gaylani needed to be stopped. Given the stakes, the ends justified the means.

"You know I'd never do this if there was any other way," Pat said.

Ellen slowed the Explorer and turned onto Main Street.

"Stow it. Nobody put a gun to my head. Somehow, I let you talk me into this fool idea. But now that we're ready to go, I've got very mixed emotions."

"Even if justice is served?"

"Yes, Patricia. In some ways, it will scare me more if our methods produce a just result."

Ellen pulled the Explorer into the far corner of the funeral parlor lot and parked next to a black limousine with a gold falcon embossed under the door handle.

* * *

Admiral Eric Weiss sat next to Rick Eichman, one of the three Chicago agents under his command. They were in a four-wheel-drive, unmarked CIA vehicle. The Company car was parked parallel to Barbera's limousine, but in the opposite corner of the funeral parlor lot.

As the admiral glanced down at his watch, he also noted that two-thirds of the spaces were full. Why, he wondered, did a Mafia lawyer rate such a big turnout? The overnight blizzard had left a foot of new snow, yet despite the storm, it seemed like the whole town had bundled up to mourn the loss.

"Is that Mrs. Eichler's Explorer?"

Rick lowered his binoculars and nodded.

"I'll say one thing. When Barbera sets something up, it happens." Eric leaned forward and looked toward the mobster's limo. "The Eichler woman looks properly dressed, but what's with the reporter? Her get-up hardly fits the occasion. Am I missing something?"

"Well, sir," Rick said, fidgeting with his gloves. "Dollars to doughnuts, Miss Shaver doesn't plan to go in. Rumor has it, she and Kempner weren't friends."

"Big goddamn deal," Eric barked. "Barbera isn't exactly keeper of the Holy Grail, yet Shaver has no problem dealing with him. She's too involved not to pay her respects. Son of a bitch! If that debutante saddles up again, I'll personally shoot her horse."

Eric focused on Miss Shaver and her sidekick. While Goldie Locks tossed a duffel bag inside Barbera's limo, Mrs. Eichler walked toward the funeral parlor entrance.

"Hey," he said, elbowing Rick, "I want you and what's-his-face to double up."

"You mean Donald Haider, sir?"

"Yeah. Go sit with Haider." He pointed toward another beat-up Chevy Blazer. "When Barbera finishes with the reporter, follow her."

"But, sir… What if Miss Shaver goes inside?"

"Dressed like an upscale derelict?"

Eric stared at the limo, then motioned the field operative out of the car. He hadn't counted on the two broads separating, but sure as hell knew that the reporter wouldn't have dressed like his teenage granddaughter if she planned on attending Kempner's wake. Shaver had something else scheduled, but unfortunately, he had only one vehicle available to follow her.

He watched Rick Eichman get out and walk toward Donald Haider's car. Aware that both men seemed totally intimidated by his presence, he picked up the hand-held radio transmitter and called D. Maynard, the last of the three men under his command.

"It's quiet here," Maynard said, his voice flat. "The Gaylanis left a while ago. You should see them shortly. As for Kempner's place, the house is pitch-dark. Been that way all evening. Aside from the craziest snowplow you ever saw, nobody's come by since the Feds left."

"Tell me about the snowplow," Eric said, his jaw muscles tense.

"Ever hear of a front-end loader?" Maynard asked. "Construction crews use them for excavating."

Eric's grip on the radio receiver tightened. "For Christ's sake, I know what a god-dammed front-end loader is. Since when are they used for plowing?"

"A Midwest trick," Maynard said. "With this much snow and no place to push it, the only way to clear a driveway is to scoop it up and pile the stuff in big mounds."

The explanation seemed logical, but something about the timing made Eric pause. "Do me a favor. Before getting your butt back over here, cruise by the target houses one more time."

Eric continued to stare at Barbera's limo. He felt uneasy about pulling the surveillance off the Kempner and Gaylani properties, but he had no choice. When Shaver showed up wearing jeans, knee-high snow boots, and a parka, Eric had realized he'd eventually be short of manpower. Since the females had separated, he needed Maynard to keep surveillance on the Eichler woman. His other men would watch Miss Shaver, and he'd spend time with Barbera.

* * *

Gary Barbera pushed open the rear passenger door of his Cadillac limousine.

"Good evening, my dear. You certainly came dressed for the weather. Of course, when it comes to braving the elements, tonight is just cold. But Christmas… that was a *horse* of a different color."

"It certainly was," Pat said, tossing her cumbersome duffel bag onto the forward of the facing back seats. "Sorry I'm late."

"A minute or two is hardly a cause for alarm." He watched her slide in and pull the door shut, noting she looked radiant even with her blonde hair tucked under a knitted ski hat.

Eying her, so inappropriately dressed for a wake, he wondered what had become of their original plan. Since she'd obviously scrapped the idea of accompanying Mrs. Eichler, he was curious if Miss Patricia would try to alter anything else on their agenda.

"I should have consulted with you," she said, unzipping her parka. "Bottom line… I decided a short appearance might create more suspicion than none at all. Ellie will alibi for me."

"What's in the duffel bag?" he asked. "You're dressed for the outdoors. Did you bring snowshoes for Danny and me?"

He purposely mentioned snowshoes, an item he knew she'd purchased. He'd gotten curious when Chief Cherrigan reported that Mrs. Eichler had phoned in the second 911 call on the morning Tommy Kempner's body was discovered. Since then, he'd had Miss Patricia and Mrs. Eichler watched.

"I pack for every contingency," she said, her eyes studying him. "A girl can't be too careful."

"We all have to exercise caution."

"So I see," she agreed, nodding toward the Irishman.

He noted her pointed reference to Danny Finn. The moment the journalist sat down in the back seat, the Irishman had lowered the driver's partition. With his 9mm automatic out but concealed under his enormous hands, Danny had turned his body so he had an unobstructed view of the proceedings.

"Forgive me," he said, smiling. "Sometimes my manners are abominable. I keep forgetting, you've never met my good friend and associate, Danny Finn."

"Mr. Finn, my pleasure," she said, patting his hands. "You're working. We'll shake later."

Ellen Eichler walked into the funeral parlor. She greeted several people, then headed toward the coatroom. When she came out, Joanna Gaylani was waiting.

"Where's your friend?" Joanna asked. "I'm surprised you and Pat didn't come together."

Ellen extended her hand, noting Joanna's husband was moving toward them. "Pat got tied up with some last minute things. I expect she'll be along in the next half hour or so."

"Should I send out a search party?" Dr. Tony Gaylani inquired, muscling between them. "It makes me nervous when I can't keep my eye on the likes of her."

"Behave yourself, Tony," Joanna said. "This is not the place for a scene."

"Just expressing the sentiments of our godson," the doctor replied. "Trevor is anxious to talk to Miss Shaver. Something about asking a muckraker to let him bury his family in peace."

"I'm warning you," Joanna said, her lip curled. "When Pat gets here I expect you to be civil."

"Not to worry, my sweet. Unlike Miss Shaver, I know what's in good taste."

Chief Carlton "Cherry" Cherrigan parked his squad car in a makeshift spot just past the entrance to the funeral parlor lot. Once in place, Cherry put his hand around the radio receiver and depressed the transmitter button.

"Okay, boys and girls. It's showtime. Pay attention… and no mistakes."

The chief had the entire Barrington Police Department on the same wavelength. While the dispatcher, Marge Schwartz, listened in from the station house, his patrolmen monitored the call from squad cars in different parts of town.

"Tonight is special," Cherry said, his voice strident. "All my directives must be followed to the letter. Hughes, do you copy me?"

"Yes, Chief," Patrolman Matt Hughes replied.

"Cruise Main Street, nothing else. When I call and ask if you've seen a stretch limo with FALCON 1 plates, I want you to say that you saw it heading south on 59 toward the toll road."

"Got it, Chief. No problem."

Cherry loved being chief. He only had two deputies and his command post was a police cruiser, but controlling the operation fed his ego.

"Iverson. Speak up. Anything happening at Kempner's house?"

"After the FBI pulled their people, a front-end loader came in. Other than that, it's been quiet." Sergeant Dick Iverson—Ethel Iverson's son—cleared his throat. "By the way, Chief, no one has plowed the road to the barn."

"Sergeant, I didn't ask about the status of the road. I want to know if anything is happening at the Kempners'."

"Sorry, Chief. I see no signs of life at the house or barn."

"In that case, Sergeant, I want you to leave the area and join me at the entrance to the funeral parlor."

"Five-by-five, Chief. On my way."

Cherry clicked off his radio transmitter when his special cell phone rang. Mr. Barbera's calls always got his undivided attention.

Patricia Shaver sat in the old don's limo, delighted Gary Barbera had accepted her revised plan. She was also impressed. A second after he'd hung up his cell phone, Chief Cherrigan responded. Even from across the parking lot, the red and blue flashers beamed light into the interior of the mobster's limousine.

"Cherry does have a flair for the dramatic," she said. "Should I be grateful he didn't blast his siren?"

Gary Barbera offered her a tired smile. "My dear, that arrangement is also just a phone call away."

She unzipped the duffel bag and handed him two pieces of evidence—the Kempner/Weiss file and the cassette featuring the admiral's voice.

"Here's a little insurance," she said. "In a couple of hours, I hope to increase our coverage."

"These pages don't look like Xerox copies," he mused, examining several pages of the Kempner/Weiss file. "Is this the original?"

"Yes," she answered, "anything wrong?"

He shook his head, then held up the cassette. "Same deal here? The original."

She nodded. "I thought you'd want the originals. Got a duplicate of the cassette and a copy of the file in my duffel. We'll give those to the admiral."

"What about your records?" he asked. "Did you make copies for yourself?"

"No," she lied, "I didn't think it was necessary."

"It's not," he said, his voice strong. "We have a deal, and I'll live up to my side of the bargain."

As she wondered whether the gentleman don believed her, she noted that Mr. Finn seemed puzzled by their exchange.

"I'd like to show my gratitude," Gary went on, holding up a CD. "Here's a copy of last night's conversation."

"Don't need it," she replied. "I just hope your voice scrambler is as good as you claim. We'll both be in trouble if Admiral Weiss ever gets wind of the part after you said, 'the tape just ran out.' "

"I'm far from an electronics whiz," he said, "but my staff is the best money can buy. While we talked, our Langley friends heard nothing but Christmas carols."

"Your legal team must be as good as your techies," she replied, fiddling with the duffel. "Today, they earned their keep. Getting the FBI booted off Kempner's property was quite a feat. What did J. Edgar's guys do? Violate somebody's constitutional guarantees?"

"Bill Bronner went into federal court and got an injunction," Gary answered. "He claimed undue harassment of Tommy's heirs. Said the Feds went overboard the moment they occupied his house."

Pat looked up. "What's the logic on that one?"

"Elementary, my dear," Barbera replied. "Bronner argued that suicide isn't a felony. Therefore, the FBI had no reason to treat the area as a crime scene. Obviously that put them in a bind. To stay put, they had to charge Tony Gaylani with murder."

"Even the government knows they can't make that stick."

Barbera nodded. "Admiral Weiss also realizes Joanna Gaylani could panic if her husband is indicted."

Pat flinched, amazed at how quickly the gentleman don had pieced together the puzzle that put Joanna Gaylani in the center of things. Even before she'd gotten around to telling him about the barn and the ammonium nitrate, he'd figured out that Joanna and her uncle were still politically tight. And that wasn't all. The mobster had some amazing insights about Chuck Sweet too.

"Very thorough," she said. "Good thing Eric Weiss doesn't have access to your research staff. With it, he could eliminate the guesswork."

"Never underestimate the admiral," Gary cautioned. "He's a repulsive human being, but he's no fool. Right now he may be guessing, but take it from me, Eric Weiss is a good guesser."

"Then I suggest we preoccupy him with something other than speculations." Pat looked across the parking lot at the admiral's Chevy. "Why don't Danny and I take a ride?"

Barbera flipped up his overcoat collar. "Had you warned me of the rescheduling, I'd have dressed differently."

"Don't worry," she said. "You're wearing gloves. That's the most important item in all our wardrobes."

"Quite right, my dear." He rubbed a miniature gold falcon embossed in the leather on top of the door handle. "Be careful, you two, and good hunting."

CHAPTER THIRTY-ONE

Admiral Eric Weiss sat alone in the dinged-up Chevy Blazer. He stared across the funeral parlor parking lot at Gary Barbera's limousine. A short time after Patricia Shaver had stepped into the Mafia don's Caddy, Eric had sent his agent Rick Eichman to go sit with Donald Haider. Since then, a few cars had come and gone, but things had stayed quiet.

Eric rested his big-knuckled hands on the steering wheel and closed his eyes. Why couldn't he get front-end loaders out of his mind? Why did he think there was something amiss?

"Admiral! Barbera's taking off."

His head shot up as Haider's voice blared through the radio speaker. He hadn't seen the black Caddy move, but once his agent's warning got him to focus, he watched the limousine fishtail around parked cars and start to accelerate.

"Jesus Christ," Eric screamed, depressing the transmitter button. "What the hell are you waiting for? Follow that car!"

He saw Haider's CIA Blazer move, but by then Barbera's limo had sped the wrong way through the entrance to the funeral parlor. Eric's annoyance increased as he realized the escape maneuver must have been planned.

"Son of a bitch," he cursed, his fists banging the steering wheel.

He watched, helpless. The second Barbera's limousine cleared the lot, Chief Cherrigan turned on the blue and red flashers and pulled across the single lane. With the avenue of pursuit blocked, Eric saw

Haider's Blazer skid in front of Cherrigan's squad car, narrowly avoiding a broadside crash. By the time he drove up, a bad situation had deteriorated. His men and the chief were yelling at each other.

"Chief," Eric said, sloshing through salted snow, "my men are on official business. Let them through."

"Official business?" the chief replied, opening the driver's side door. "Mister, you don't look the type to be on official business."

The admiral knew all about small town cops and their big city egos. To jumpstart the process, Eric reached into his breast coat pocket. He'd hoped to avoid an ugly confrontation, but when the taillights of Barbera's limousine disappeared around the corner, he pulled out a Company ID.

"Chief, we're in pursuit of that limo."

The chief squinted at his laminated identification. "Come on, Admiral, quit joshing. You Company dudes can't be after our governor?"

"Governor!" Eric protested. "The governor isn't in that car."

Cherrigan rubbed his chin. "That's funny. His office said he'd be attending. When I saw that stretch Caddy exit against the one-way sign, I assumed it was a politico."

"For Christ's sake, Chief. Did you happen to see the damn license plate?"

Cherrigan nodded. "FALCON 1 is kinda catchy, don't you think?"

"For a mobster," Eric responded, "but not for the governor of Illinois."

As the chief's face turned red with embarrassment, Eric watched Barbera approach.

"Good evening, Admiral. Are you and Chief Cherrigan having a problem?"

Eric glared. "Where the hell did you come from?"

"My car, of course," the crime boss replied. "I thought we were getting together, but when you started racing around the parking lot, I wasn't sure what was happening."

The admiral banged his open hand on the hood of Cherrigan's squad car. "Are you fuckin' nuts? Your limo just blew out of here."

Barbera smiled. "Our journalist friend, Miss Patricia, is thinking about buying one. Once we concluded our business, I told my chauffeur to show her what the car can do. He's Irish and impulsive. She's single and beautiful. The lad may have driven a bit recklessly, but boys will be boys."

"So help me God," Eric said, his voice low and cold. "If I find out this is another one of your cons…"

"My goodness, man, no need to get upset. If it makes you feel better, I'll give you their route." The old don adjusted his cashmere scarf. "Let's see. Danny's taking the big loop. First, south on Route 59 to the tollway. Then southeast toward—"

"Cut the loop bullshit," Eric said, raising his hand.

"Hold on, Admiral." Chief Cherrigan butted in. "I got a man with a radar gun checking speeders near 59 and the tollway. If FALCON 1 is cruising in the vicinity, Hughes will know."

Eric stared at Cherrigan. "Back up your squad car. Once my men start making this loop of yours, we'll tell Hughes to be on the lookout."

Danny Finn zoomed out of the funeral parlor parking lot. He made a right turn, but didn't ease off the accelerator. Even as he traveled on the snow-packed streets outside the tiny business district, he kept up his speed. Patricia Shaver didn't seem to mind. The journalist was kneeling on the forward back seat of the boss's limo with her head and arms sticking through the partition.

"Impressive," she said. "This buggy handles like Ellie's Explorer."

"I'm cheating, Miss. With chains, it's hard to get stuck."

He continued to zigzag, this time through the residential part of town. Once confident they weren't being followed, the Irishman turned onto a country road that would take them to Tom Kempner's house.

"Mind if I ask you a question?" she asked.

"The boss told me to be polite. Fire away."

"How did Mr. Barbera know Ellie and I went horseback riding?"

Danny grinned. "Sailor-boy isn't the only one that's good at guessing."

"Sailor-boy?" she asked. "Sounds like you don't care for the admiral."

"We have conflicting business interests."

"You and I aren't exactly batting on the same team, yet we talk civilly."

"Right again, Miss," he replied, swerving around another S-shaped curve. "Let's just say Weiss isn't my type."

"Funny you should say that. He's not my type either."

Conscious of being beguiled by her charms, Danny Finn doused the headlights and turned into Tom Kempner's driveway.

Gary Barbera sat on the front passenger seat of the admiral's poorly-heated, unmarked CIA Blazer. Everything had gone well. Danny Finn and Miss Patricia had left unhindered. Chief Cherrigan had followed orders to the letter. Now was his chance. But before he made the admiral's life miserable, Gary looked out over the funeral parlor lot and listened to Weiss bark instructions over the radio.

"Okay, Rick. Follow Route 59 and step on it." Weiss clicked off the radio transmitter. "My men should make visual contact with your limo in a few minutes."

"Fine," Gary replied, "but if they don't, be patient. Danny will be back in no time. How else would I get home?"

"Don't look at me," the admiral snapped. "Hell will freeze before I'll drive you anywhere."

Gary detested the man sitting next to him, but enjoyed watching Weiss strut. When the CIA pulled rank, it meant the Company thought they had the upper hand. To keep the admiral's superiority complex intact, he handed him a CD, then lowered his eyes.

"This ought to get me back in your good graces," he said softly. "As promised, the tape of last night's conversation."

"That's all you got?" Weiss questioned.

"The CD speaks for itself. Why not listen to it?"

Weiss loaded it into the CD slot, but didn't push the play button. "What's your read on Joanna Gaylani? Is she politically in bed with her uncle?"

"My instincts tell me she's not a United Jewish Congress do-gooder, but according to my people, there's not a shred of evidence to prove it."

The admiral leaned forward. "Not helpful, Barbera."

"I'm doing my best," Gary responded, staring at the plowed banks of snow, "but without hard proof I can only draw inferences."

"What about Shaver and Eichler?" the admiral asked. "Were the fuckin' Bobbsey twins training for the Kentucky Derby last night?"

Gary looked straight ahead. He was a master at using his eyes to diminish opponents, but he knew Weiss had similar aptitudes.

"Do us both a favor, Admiral. Play the tape. Once you've heard it, my answers will make more sense."

"How so?" Weiss asked. "At the time it was made, you didn't know they were out gallivanting."

"That's true, but the cassette conveys a sense of their paranoia."

"What does paranoia have to do with a horseback ride?" Weiss questioned, his voice icy. "If you're fucking with me, you'll be one Dago who never sees the light of day."

Gary didn't answer. He just stared at the funeral parlor and the shoveled banks of snow flanking the entrance.

Patricia Shaver steadied herself as the Irishman wheeled the gentleman don's limo down Tom Kempner's driveway. The moment he stopped near the side of Kempner's garage, she got out. From there, she used hand signals and directed Danny Finn as he backed the limousine into a man-made open-air carport near the service en-trance.

When she'd planned her strategy, Pat realized she and Danny needed to enter the house from a point other than the front door. On Christmas morning, Dr. Tony Gaylani had left his car in the perfect location. But the service door entrance had one drawback. She wanted to keep the limo hidden from anyone looking out from the Gaylanis' bedroom alcove.

Ellen had solved the problem. A few hours before the wake, she'd contacted a man with a front-end loader. After Sam Durso brought his loader over, he called Ellen back. Together they traded ideas until a three-sided carport had been constructed.

The structure was simple to design. Sam used his front-end loader to erect two snow walls. The embankments were ten feet apart, eight feet tall, and fifteen feet long. Each was built perpendicular to and on either side of the service entrance to the garage.

Pat unzipped the duffel bag and handed Danny a pair of snowshoes.

"What do you think?"

"Well, Miss," he said, smiling, "a Mick like me will try anything. But this will be a first."

"If they don't work, we'll sink together."

Pat knelt down. While Danny Finn lifted one foot and then the other, she strapped on what looked like a pair of tennis racquets. When he was fitted out, she put her snowshoes on, then grabbed a backpack. With the tools they needed slung around her shoulder, she and Danny spent the next several minutes trudging across fluffy new snow.

They moved around the back of Tom Kempner's house. Once past the corral and stable, they shuffled across the Gaylanis' property, heading toward the basement window she'd left open.

Both breathing hard, they unbuckled their snowshoes. While she held a flashlight, Danny pried off the grate and lowered himself into the basement window well.

"Now what, Miss?"

"Say a prayer. If you see the ends of some folded hundred dollar bills, we're home free."

"Beg your pardon, Miss?"

She saw the puzzled look on his face. Rather than explain, she trained her flashlight on the corner of the casement. When she saw the folded money sticking out between the window frame and the metal housing, she knew her makeshift wedge had worked.

"Crouch down," she said, "and get eye-level with the window."

As the Irishman bent down, she dropped to her knees.

"Push the window open and lift it off the swivel hinge. Once it's free, you can turn the window sideways and pass it up to me."

After Danny handed her the casement, he sat in the window well, dangled his feet inside, and slithered through the opening. Once on the Gaylanis' basement floor, the Irishman picked up her money, signaling success with a thumbs-up.

"Next comes the light load," she said, lowering him the backpack and casement. "After that, we'll see how strong you are."

She sat in the window well, leaned back, and let her body slide forward. They were both dressed for sub-zero weather, but when she dropped into his arms she felt the hardness of his muscles.

"Good catch. Let's clean things up, then we'll we go to the wine cellar."

"Is that where Dr. Gaylani stashed the general's papers?"

"I hope so… but like everyone else in town, I'm guessing."

Pat spread a terrycloth bath towel under the window well and mopped up some melted snow. As she waved Danny over, she stood on the towel to dry the soles of her boots.

"It's best if we don't leave tracks."

"Agreed," the Irishman said, handing her the C-notes. "Lead on, Miss."

Using the flashlight to guide them, Pat led the way to Gaylani's wine cellar. She knew few things for certain, but she did realize that on the night Tony had killed Tom Kempner and stolen the general's memoirs, he'd had few options. The cumbersome load of memos and diaries had to be stashed quickly. Taking them to a dumping ground was out of the question. Raising the garage door and motoring down the driveway might have awakened Joanna. But even if his wife had slept through it, Tony couldn't run the risk of being seen by a passing motorist. During the time of Tom's murder, the doctor had to have an airtight alibi.

Pat opened her backpack and took out another powerful flashlight and a heavy-duty bolt cutter. As Danny watched, she shined the beam on the padlock securing the wine cellar door.

"Your turn to do the honors," she said.

"Top of the line tool," Danny replied, grabbing the bolt cutter. "Where did you get it?"

"Ace is the place."

With one motion he cut through the lock. After she tossed the bolt cutter and combination lock into her knapsack, Danny opened the door.

"Nicely done, Miss. The papers are in here."

Flashlight in hand, she peered into Tony Gaylani's wine cellar. The cedar-paneled space was lined with floor-to-ceiling wine racks. But her eyes were drawn to the general's documents stacked on the tasting table.

"Wow, the doc likes pricey grapes." Danny checked the label on a bottle of champagne he lifted off a wine rack. "I know all about *le grande marque*—Piper Heidsieck. It's in Rheims, just down the street from the Boyer, one of the boss's favorite eateries."

Pat nodded, more than surprised by his knowledge. Last spring, when she and Ken were in Paris, they'd made the short drive to Rheims to have dinner at the Boyer. The place was not only a romantic inn, but it housed one of the world's finest restaurants. And that wasn't all. As they dined, the sommelier had poured champagne, saying, "This is a product of the House of Piper Heidsieck—one of *les grande marques* of France since the sixteenth century."

"We'll treat our palates later," she said. "First let's sample his collection of papers."

They worked quickly. As she readied a small microfilm camera, Danny pulled the general's memoirs from the wine cellar and began laying out sheet after sheet on the basement floor. The Irishman held the two high-intensity flashlights while she photographed the documents. For five minutes nonstop, they labored. Each time they completed the process, she collected and stacked the evidence, then waited while he got more pages.

"That's enough, Danny. A couple rolls of microfilm should convince Weiss." She pointed to the bottle of Piper Heidsieck. "Pack up. By the time we finish our next objective, that will be cold enough to drink."

Admiral Eric Weiss sat in his car and listened. Ten minutes later, he eyed the Chicago hood, Barbera, then pulled the CD from the deck and put it in his overcoat pocket.

Eric had doubts. The CD contained some information, but neither Shaver nor Barbera had said a single incriminating thing. Instead, the reporter and the mobster had orchestrated a scenario that pointed the finger at Dr. Tony Gaylani.

"Interesting," Eric said. "Your friend Miss Shaver sure believes Tony *is* a real bad boy."

Barbera nodded. "You have access to the coroner's report and the results of the FBI investigation. If they confirm her analysis, she's probably on to something."

Eric had been trained to read facial expressions. Tonight his expertise was wasted. The well-dressed crime boss didn't give any telltale signs.

"Did Miss Shaver take the cassette from Kempner's answering machine?"

"Don't question me," Barbera answered. "I wasn't at the crime scene."

"And the brandy glasses?" Eric asked, letting his voice grate. "If she had time to hide them, she had ample opportunity to rifle Kempner's office."

The admiral knew the FBI had cordoned off the house and done a thorough search of the mob attorney's office. Unfortunately, the Feds' quest for evidence had stopped there. They hadn't bothered to look in any other rooms, including the pantry.

"You keep asking the wrong person," Barbera said, his face hard as stone. "My chauffeur and our friend Miss Patricia ought to be back any time. Why not interrogate her?"

"Speaking of joy rides," Eric snarled, "tell me why Shaver and Eichler went on horseback last night."

He eyed Barbera, but the son of a bitch kept staring out the windshield. "For the last time, where did they go, and why the fuck did it take five hours?"

"No offense, Admiral, but your bedside manner needs an update."

"You're here to answer questions, not criticize me or my manners," Eric growled. "Just tell me why they used horses?"

"How else could they approach the doctor's house without being seen?" Barbera adjusted his scarf, made eye contact, then quickly turned away. "The FBI was staked out at Tommy Kempner's. With all the snow, there was no place to park on the road."

Eric's stomach got queasy. Something in Barbera's statement made him pause. But why did he think the bastard was playing with his mind? Who cared if there was no place to park on the road?

"Using horses was an ingenious way to get there," Eric admitted, "but why that address? What did those misfit broads want from Gaylani's house?"

"Evidence, Admiral. They wanted to find something that would pin the Kempners' murders on the doctor."

"What kind of evidence?"

"Remember the documents Mrs. Katherine Kempner received the day she died? That kind of evidence."

Eric hated Barbera's condescension, but until he could put his finger on the inconsistency, he had no choice but to go along. "Ah, yes. General Alan Cunningham's papers—the memoirs from my asshole colleagues at MI-6. Just another piece of the puzzle we've never found."

"Neither did they," Barbera answered, his gloved hand examining the crease in his trousers. "On Christmas, when they discovered the body, all the papers had already disappeared from Mrs. Kempner's office."

"Have I got this right?" Eric asked. "You expect me to believe that Shaver and Eichler went out last night in search of those documents?"

"Believe what you want," Barbera replied, talking in a monotone. "That's what she told me."

"Did Goldie Locks also tell you how she planned to get into the doctor's house?"

Barbera nodded. "Quite clever, really. Miss Patricia intends to go through a basement window well. She believes the documents might be hidden in Gaylani's wine cellar."

"Is that a fact?" Eric said, shaking his head. "This gets more preposterous by the second."

But he knew it wasn't preposterous at all. Court order notwithstanding, Eric realized his mistake. Instead of having his forces chase a looping limousine, he should have had them positioned around the scene of the murders—Tom Kempner's house.

Eric needed more manpower but knew he couldn't get hold of D. Maynard, the man he'd called off the Kempner-Gaylani surveillance. His third agent was down the hall. While he and Barbera listened to the CD, Maynard had knocked on the Blazer window and asked permission to drive to a nearby gas station.

Eric grabbed the radio transmitter, his anger boiling. "Check in, dammit. That means everybody."

"Admiral, it's Rick Eichman. Haider can't talk. He's got both hands on the wheel."

Road sounds mixed with static came through the speaker.

"Where are you?" Eric asked, his tone ugly. "And where is that fuckin' limo?"

"Haven't seen it, sir," Rick replied, his voice barely audible. "Unless the chauffeur is flying, we should have caught him."

Eric banged the steering wheel with his open hand. "God damn it to hell!"

"Did you say something, sir?"

"Yeah," he snapped. "Get your asses back here ASAP."

Eric's worst fears had materialized. Barbera had played him. There was no cop sitting off the road with a radar gun. The damn hood had said it himself. With all the snow, there wasn't any room to park. And speaking of snow, the front-end loader story had to be a sham too.

Christ, how stupid could he be? The blizzard had hit last night. The court order to vacate Kempner's place was issued at noon today. Since the FBI had left shortly thereafter, someone had to have come over much earlier to plow them out. Whoever had brought in excavation equipment late this afternoon had done it after the Feds were long gone, and for an entirely different reason.

Eric wanted to react, but couldn't. He was a stranger in this Godforsaken town. He knew what had to be done, but he had no idea how to get to where he needed to go.

"Pay attention," Eric said, grabbing Barbera's shoulder and pulling him around. "You and I are going to take a little trip."

"You're calling the shots," Barbera replied, his face expressionless.

Eric was fuming. Why hadn't he picked up on it right away? When the hood had said "she plans to go through the basement window," he'd used the present tense. What could be plainer? Hadn't he signaled that Shaver's caper was happening as they spoke? That was where the SOB's limo had gone. The reporter and the chauffeur planned to rifle the doctor's wine cellar.

"Stow the innocent look," he snapped. "I'll drive. You call out the directions to Kempner's."

"Sorry, Admiral. I'd like to help, but I'm just a man who rides in the back seat."

Eric glared, his face congested with anger. "You lying no-good bastard!"

"Now, now, Admiral. These outbursts must stop."

He saw the change in Barbera, and it scared him. Like the sun reappearing after a total eclipse, the Mafia don's expression seemed to shine with new defiance.

"Last chance," Eric said, boring in. "I want directions."

"I'll bet you do, but this isn't Langley. Chicago is my town. I suggest you get used to it."

Eric wanted to empty his revolver into the two-bit wop. Instead, he kept his anger in and let a ghoulish smile crease his face. "This is far from over."

"You're wrong, Admiral. There's nothing left for us to discuss."

Barbera opened the Blazer door, but paused before getting out. "Here's some free advice. You don't need directions to Tommy Kempner's, you need a roadmap back to Langley."

Patricia Shaver shined the flashlight all around the Gaylanis' basement. Danny also made a visual check, then began stuffing General Alan Cunningham's papers into a duffel bag. While the Irishman completed the cleanup, she put a new padlock on the wine cellar door.

She realized she was taking a chance. The Master combination lock wouldn't open if Tony scrolled in his numbers. But that was all she could do. She had to pray the doctor would be satisfied with it being affixed face in, the odd way he'd left it.

Danny grabbed onto the lower part of the basement window frame, bent his knees, and sprang up. Using his arms and elbows as levers, he squirmed into the window well.

"Ready, Miss?"

When she nodded, the Irishman stayed on his knees and extended his arm into the basement. The second she grabbed on with both hands, he lifted her out.

Once on the snow-packed ground outside the window well, Pat prepared for the hike back to the limo. While she made sure some of the general's papers were zipped up in one duffel, the Irishman fitted the casement onto the swivel hinge.

"In a bit of a pickle," he said, looking up. "The locking handle is on the other side. There's no way to pull the window closed."

"No problem," she replied, holding up a roll of duct tape. "This should do the trick."

She hopped into the window well and ripped off two foot-long lengths of three-inch-wide duct tape. While the Irishman stood aside and held one, she pressed the sticky side of the other onto the center part of the glass casement. Using the tape as a pull cord, she raised the window into its metal frame.

"So far, so good," she concluded, knowing the job was only half done.

To keep the window in place, she told the Irishman to gently press the other piece of duct tape along the line where the top of the casement window butted into the frame. That accomplished, she released the tension on the first strip of duct tape, then pulled it off the glass pane and used it in a similar manner to also hold the window in its frame.

"Like the way you improvise," Danny said. "Good work, Miss."

Their jury-rigged lock in place, they stepped out of the window well and dropped the metal grill back down.

"Only one thing left to do," she said. "Buckle on your snow-shoes and we're out of here."

They each flipped a duffel over their shoulders and began the trek back to the man-made carport.

"We're right on schedule," she said, checking her watch. "Time to switch to more comfortable footwear."

They left their snowshoes on the floor of Barbera's limo and began the second and last phase of their operation—breaking into Tom Kempner's Tudor manor.

Pat held the flashlight while Danny picked the lock on the service door. They crossed the garage, then teamed up again and worked on the laundry room entrance.

They doused the flashlights before making their way through the house to Kempner's office. Moonlight was sufficient. When the Christmas blizzard had blown out of town, it had taken the clouds too.

"Do you see it?" she asked, looking through the bay windows that shaped the rear portion of Tom Kempner's oval office. "Am I imagining things, or is there a light flashing every now and then?"

"Where, Miss?" the Irishman asked.

She pointed. "The Kempners' barn. It's out by that stand of pine trees."

"If the dark shadow is the pines, I see that," Danny said, standing behind her. "But I'm sorry, Miss. I don't see anything blinking."

As the full moon bathed the outdoors with lunar twilight, she left Danny and walked over to Tom Kempner's desk. While the Irishman pulled opera-size binoculars from his coat pocket and looked toward the barn, she reached into her parka and pulled out a copy of the fertilizer, ammonium nitrate, and horse food invoices Ellen had billed to Joanna Gaylani. When Pat had given Gary Barbera his copy of the cassette and the Kempner/Weiss file, she'd held those items back.

"Miss, you were right. Something is moving out there."

"Didn't I tell you?"

She turned her head. As he continued to check out the activity near the barn, she slipped Ellen's invoices into the Kempner/Weiss file. Then she stepped away from Tom Kempner's desk and faced the Irishman.

"What's going on?"

"It's kinda weird," Danny said, lowering his binoculars. "First, a guy parked a panel truck with a plow outside the Kempners' barn. Then he unlocked the doors, walked in, and several seconds later, drove a John Deere tractor out."

"That is weird," she agreed.

"There's more. After the guy jumped off the tractor, he got into the panel truck and backed it into the barn. I can't see inside, but I'm guessing he put the truck in position to load it up."

"Sounds plausible, but why do ranch work at night?"

She kept her eyes on Danny. As he lifted the small but powerful binoculars and focused out past the stand of Douglas firs, she waited for a reaction or comment. When none came, she breathed easier, then let her thoughts go back to her negotiation with Gary Barbera.

She'd done the best she could, but her effort had still come up short. Earlier, in their meeting in the funeral parlor parking lot, she'd asked the gentleman don for copies of the ranch bills Tom Kempner had paid. She knew Barbera had taken those invoices from Tom's office. She also knew that together, the two sets of documents would enable Admiral Weiss to figure out how Joanna Gaylani had double ordered the ammonium nitrate.

She stepped away from Tom Kempner's desk and watched the Irishman adjust his binoculars. Sadly, she'd only been able to leave one set of bills. Gary Barbera had assured her that Admiral Weiss would get the other set of invoices, but they would be delivered on the gentleman don's time schedule, not hers.

Pat walked to Danny's side, satisfied, but not entirely happy. She knew the display was incomplete, but she also knew there was no quick remedy.

"Mind if I take a look?"

The Irishman handed her his theater-sized binoculars.

"Talk about top-drawer," she said, gripping them in the pale light. "With this telescope my opera seats would seem like orchestra pit."

"Bought them with that in mind," he agreed. "While the boss watches the stage, I keep tabs on the audience."

Pat held the high-magnification opera glasses to her eyes. Once focused on the front of Kempner's barn, she watched someone slide the door closed, get back in a truck, and without turning on the headlights, motor slowly down the plowed road.

The bomb-making material was being transported, and that frightened her. But it was important for the Irishman to see the fertilizer being removed. She handed him the glasses and pointed, praying Danny Finn hadn't detected her fear.

"Your glasses have a great field of vision," she said, watching him follow the bomb truck until it turned on Oak Knoll Road and drove away. "Let me know where you bought them."

"Go you one better, Miss," he replied. "Next time the boss decides not to use his opera tickets, I'll ask you to join me in his box."

"A deal I can't refuse," she said, smiling around her nervousness. "But I'm curious about one thing. When did your boss get interested in opera?"

"Owes that to his old man. Gary Barbera, Sr., loved all forms of classical music. And get this, Miss. In the fall of 1929, when the Civic Opera House opened its doors for the first time, the boss's father was in the audience."

"I know a little Chicago opera history," she said. "*Aida* played that night, and the lead was sung by—"

They answered in unison. "Rosa Ponselle."

"Very good, Miss. You are a buff."

"I wouldn't call you a slouch," she said. "It takes a real effort to appreciate opera."

"And good seats," he said, lowering his eyes. "You won't need the glasses where we sit."

Pat felt her cheeks redden. Like the Irishman, she was blushing. But why had Danny's gesture touched her?

Before she could figure it out, her cell phone rang.

CHAPTER THIRTY-TWO

Admiral Eric Weiss sat alone in the Chevy Blazer. A crime boss had just insulted him. He was shocked, irate, and humiliated. No one snubbed the deputy director of the CIA.

He watched Barbera walk into the funeral parlor. For a moment, he indulged his fantasy. But putting the Blazer in gear and running down the wop bastard would be counterproductive. Barbera had gone to great pains to choreograph a show for his benefit. Of course, he dreaded what he would see, but he knew he had to go out to Tom Kempner's for a look.

Eric revved the Chevy and drove off. He hated to admit it, but Barbera had been right. He needed directions to get to the mob attorney's house.

His luck changed at a nearby gas station. First he spotted D. Maynard's Company car, then he spotted Maynard.

He waved the agent over. "You big guys sure take your sweet-ass time."

"Sorry, sir. Had I known you needed me…"

Eric pushed open the passenger-side door. "Get in. We're running late."

He didn't wait for Maynard to buckle up. Eric accelerated, and as the rear wheels spun and the dashboard tachometer shot to the red line, the car began to fishtail. Safety wasn't an issue, only speed.

"Stop cringing, Maynard, and get with the program. I need to know which way to turn."

The agent pointed to the next intersection, then started calling out directions.

"Get hold of Haider and Eichman," Eric snarled. "Tell them to pick up your car, then get their asses back to the funeral parlor and keep an eye on Barbera."

Many years ago, the admiral had raced stock cars as a hobby. Tonight it wasn't for fun. He threw the Blazer into the sweeping S-shaped turns. For a while, it worked. Then the Chevy hit an ice patch and began to skid sideways. Maynard yelled and hitched up his seatbelt. Eric paid him no mind, but he did use both sides of the road to regain control.

"How much farther?"

Maynard gulped. "At this rate, sir, we'll be there in no time."

Ellen Eichler stood next to Mr. Gary Barbera in a funeral parlor anteroom. By design, they were far away from Tommy Kempner's open casket.

Ellen listened as the mobster described his confrontation with Admiral Weiss. When she realized an irate naval intelligence officer was headed in Pat's direction, Ellen hit the speed-dial on her cell phone.

"Listen up," she whispered as Dr. Tony Gaylani approached. "The admiral is on his way to Tommy's house."

"This is a solemn occasion," Tony said, glaring at her. "Cell phones aren't appropriate."

Mr. Barbera stepped in front of Dr. Gaylani.

"Excuse me," he said, "have we met?"

The doctor looked at him, his dark eyes calm. "I know who you are and what you represent."

"Tell me," the mobster replied, touching one of his peregrine cufflinks. "Who am I and what do I represent?"

"Cut the act," Dr. Gaylani answered smugly. "Your kind doesn't scare me."

He turned his back to the doctor. "Does this man belong, Mrs. Eichler?"

"He's Tommy's neighbor," Ellen replied. "As for belonging, that depends on who you ask."

He rotated back and faced Dr. Gaylani. "Sir, you're beginning to annoy me."

The doctor retreated a step. "Is that a threat?"

"I don't make threats, but I do keep promises." After glaring, he refocused his attention. "Mrs. Eichler, once I've had a word with Tommy's son, could I prevail on you for a ride?"

She nodded. But as soon as he walked away, she felt both guilt and fear. Why was she so taken by a man she wasn't supposed to like?

"Scumbag," Dr. Gaylani said, his voice sounding unsettled. "Barbera has some nerve being here."

"Funny," Ellen replied, "I was thinking the same thing about you."

"What's that supposed to mean?"

"You're a bright boy," she answered, "figure it out."

"I can figure out lots of things. Like maybe that no-show buddy of yours is up to no good."

Ellen smiled. "I'll be sure to tell Patricia how much you missed her."

The doctor raised a clenched fist, waist-high. "Eichler, I said it before. If you value your health, stay clear of me."

Admiral Eric Weiss saw headlights illuminate the embankment on the other side of the road. He edged over and took his foot off the gas. A car passed quickly in the opposite direction.

"Who the hell went by?" he asked. "Answer me, Maynard. Was that a limo?"

"Missed it, sir. I'm watching for Kempner's driveway."

Eric stared ahead, holding the steering wheel in a death grip. The encounter had come too fast. Even a quick glance in the rearview mirror hadn't helped. The driver of the other car had turned off his lights.

He thought about turning around, then recalled something else he'd overlooked. When Barbera's limo entered the parking lot, Eric had noted it had chains strapped around the rear tires. At the time, he'd dismissed it as an overly cautious bodyguard worried that the old man in the back seat wanted a skid-free ride. Now he knew differently. Now he understood that Barbera had prepared his car for a fast getaway. Now he realized he'd missed another glaring indication the mobster and the reporter were working together.

"Please slow down, sir," Maynard cautioned. "The driveway is dead ahead."

"Don't wet your pants, buddy-boy."

Danny Finn kept his eyes on the road. With the headlights off, he reduced his speed.

"Did you see the driver, Miss? Was it Admiral Weiss?"

Pat nodded. "With reinforcements."

"Surprised he got here so fast."

She unfastened her seatbelt and settled back facing Danny. "Maybe the admiral had chains wrapped around his rear wheels too."

"No way," Danny replied. "When we parked at the wake, I checked his car."

"Good," she said, "looks like we're home free."

Danny turned the headlights back on. "I know this isn't your kind of work, Miss, but you handled yourself like a pro."

She touched her gloved hand to her cheek. "Thank you, Danny. That's sweet."

Eric Weiss drove into the Kempners' driveway and got a first-hand look at what a front-end loader could do. Two, three-foot-wide ridges of snow flanked the service entrance to the garage. The snow walls ran parallel to one another and were long and wide enough to shield a large automobile from the next-door neighbors.

He parked within the confines and got out. The open-air car-port had been designed to insure more than just anonymity. When he directed his flashlight against the garage wall, Eric saw he had ready access to Tom Kempner's house.

D. Maynard walked alongside the Chevy Blazer. "Seems like a lot of unnecessary work. Why would anyone want to build two mounds of snow?"

Eric shined the light on the doorknob. "Let's go in and see. I'm betting it's open."

Ellen Eichler motored toward Honey Lake, chatting with a man she'd never thought would be a passenger in her car. Their conversation was friendly, but her stomach was in a knot. Mr. Barbera was speaking warmly about the prospect of seeing his grandchildren, but she had a horrible feeling that Pat and his bodyguard were involved in activities testing the limits of the law.

"Sorry you're not comfortable with this," he said, softening his tone.

"Playing God doesn't work," Ellen replied, slowing the Explorer and turning onto Signal Hill Road. "When people rise above the law, tyranny is the result."

"Including people of good will?"

Ellen let the comment pass as she accelerated to the top of a wooded bluff, flipped on the turn signal, and made a left into Pat's driveway.

"Why are we quibbling?" she asked. "As an educated man and a student of political science, the answer has to be obvious."

"In the real world, truth is a voice that frequently gets shouted down. How can I assure you that I have no intention of being a party to anything illegal?"

"You just did," she replied. "But unfortunately, you can only speak for yourself."

* * *

Admiral Eric Weiss stood in Tom Kempner's oval office and balled his fists.

"Son of a fuckin' bitch! Assholes. You fuckin' assholes!"

As Maynard retreated to a corner, the admiral marched up to the display. He glared, fully understanding why it had been created. Like dinnerware sitting prominently on *Fuck You, Weiss* place mats, everything they'd gathered had been left on Kempner's desk.

"Buddy-boy! Go get the evidence bags."

When Maynard left the room, Eric closed the top of the answering machine and depressed the message-repeat button. As he heard his recorded voice connect him with Tom Kempner, Eric began to take a closer look at the other items.

During the parking lot meeting, Barbera had told him about the brandy glasses and theories on fingerprint identification. As he stood alongside Kempner's desk, Eric stared at three snifters and a whole lot more.

With detective-like efficiency, he inspected each item. The mound of documents with a spool of microfilm on top had to be General Alan Cunningham's papers. Next to the archive material was something that gave him heartburn. After thumbing through a number of single-spaced reports, he began to appreciate why not everything belonged in evidence bags. Tom Kempner had violated his standing order. Instead of destroying the detailed dossiers on the Hispanic trucking executives, he'd kept them and put the bios, along with a cover letter, in a manila envelope labeled as the Kempner/Weiss file.

He stuffed the brown envelope inside his breast coat pocket. He was curious about a group of receipts that had been attached by a paper clip to the cover letter. The copies of invoices Mrs. Eichler had billed to Joanna Gaylani were obviously not a part of the file.

Oat, hay, and fertilizer bills didn't interest him, but the appearance of ammonium nitrate on any list always made CIA operatives nervous.

He assumed the fertilizer had been used to keep Tom Kempner's pastures lush and green. But the admiral was a cautious man. He'd not only check and see how much fertilizer a fifty-acre horse farm used, but he'd ask a CIA agronomist if ammonium nitrate was used on grasses where horses grazed.

The admiral moved a half-step and picked up the final document on the desk. He read Katherine Kempner's letter through once, then again. Initially he found the message surprising, but once he compared the postmark on the envelope with the scripted date Kempner's wife had written on the note, events began to fall into place. During the taped phone conversation he'd listened to earlier this evening, Patricia Shaver had made it seem like Tony Gaylani had intercepted it. But after reading the contents, he knew the doctor would never have put the letter back in the mail.

Son of a bitch. As allies, Barbera and Shaver made a clever team. The two had figured things out, copied the pertinent documents to insure against government reprisals, then like good citizens, they'd returned the originals to the crime scene.

Maynard reentered Kempner's office loaded with an armful of boxes and bags.

"Got everything you asked for, sir."

"Good. Once we pack this stuff up, I want to have another chat with Barbera."

Dr. Tony Gaylani's dark angry eyes watched Barbera and the Eichler woman leave the funeral parlor. He hadn't been suspicious at first, but Tony decided to play it safe. The reporter was a no-show, and the egotistical hood was acting chummy with a grandma who was a prosecution witness against his son.

He located his wife and her mink coat. After getting Joanna into his Mercedes jeep, they drove home and went upstairs to the reading alcove of their second-story bedroom.

"Somebody is in the Kempners' house," Tony said. "I see lights coming from several rooms."

"Don't be silly," Joanna scoffed. "The FBI left them on."

"No way. I checked before we went to the wake. The house was dark when the front-end loader was in the driveway."

Tony moved to get a better viewing angle of the snow mounds someone had constructed near the Kempners' garage.

"There's no car in the driveway," Joanna said. "If there's somebody inside, they must have parachuted in."

Tony was more convinced than ever that the reporter, Shaver, had gone snooping. He didn't know if she was next door, but the thought of nailing her in the act was too tempting to resist.

"Whatever the explanation, I'm calling 911."

Danny Finn turned into Miss Shaver's driveway, then parked next to Mrs. Eichler's Explorer. He walked around the front of his boss's limo and opened the front passenger door.

"Miss, would you like your equipment brought into the house?"

"Thanks, Danny. Just toss it inside the door."

He smiled and she smiled back. He'd chauffeured a lot of people, but no one compared to her. Why would a rich, gorgeous lady take enormous risks to help solve the murders of people she barely knew? But then again, look at the boss and himself. In a matter of weeks, she'd be a star witness against Barbera's son. Yet in their own way, each was attracted to her and neither wanted to sever relations.

For him, she represented what might have been—a grown-up version of his murdered daughter. The boss talked a tougher game, but Danny sensed that was just chatter. Judging by his tone of voice, Gary Barbera thought she had the brains and pizzazz to take over a Family business.

Barrington Police Chief Carlton "Cherry" Cherrigan sat in his squad car in the funeral parlor lot. The moment he got beeped by the stationhouse dispatcher, the chief picked up his radio receiver.

After listening to Marge Schwartz's message, Cherry asked her to patch in Dr. Tony Gaylani's 911 call. Then the chief put his squad car in gear and jammed the accelerator to the floor.

As he sped out of the lot, the chief grabbed the radio handset. But before he could say anything, Dr. Gaylani started talking, a rambling tirade about unauthorized people roaming the neighborhood at will.

A mile from the Kempners' Tudor mansion, Cherry broke in, reassured Dr. Gaylani, then said good-bye. He'd cut the call short to satisfy a more important priority. The chief had to make an important call.

Dr. Tony Gaylani glared at the phone. He was happy he'd called, but found it difficult to talk civilly with the self-righteous police chief.

When he rejoined his wife at the window, Joanna didn't say anything and he kept quiet too. Tony guessed she was interested in what was happening at the Kempners', but like him, wasn't inclined to share her innermost thoughts.

Just as their silence got awkward, a man opened their neighbor's front door. They watched him struggle with some plastic bags and cardboard boxes. Thinking a robbery was in progress, Tony wondered why the man had come out in full view, then lugged his heist behind the snow mounds. Wouldn't a housebreaker go through the garage and out the service door?

Neither he nor Joanna commented, but when they saw a light go on behind the snow mounds and a few moments later, heard the muffled sound of a hatchback being slammed, he understood why they hadn't seen the getaway vehicle.

"What do you think?" he asked, eying Joanna. "Is this clown the same guy who brought in the front-end loader?"

"Who knows, but if that's the case, he's the dumbest burglar alive."

Tony nodded in agreement, watching the man walk out from behind the snow mounds and back inside.

* * *

Chief Carlton Cherrigan kept his eyes on the road. As he navigated the icy turns, he had Marge Schwartz put him through to a Honey Lake number. Miss Shaver picked up, and after a short but cool exchange, she put Mr. Barbera on the phone. The timing was perfect. His secret employer finished giving him guarded instructions just as he wheeled his squad car into Tom Kempner's driveway.

Dr. Tony Gaylani peered out the second-floor bedroom alcove. He pointed when he saw headlights flash at the end of Kempner's driveway.

Both he and Joanna pressed closer to the window as a Barrington squad car stopped in the turnaround. Again, neither spoke. They watched Chief Cherrigan get out of his patrol car and stride to the entrance. The chief paused at the front door as if to unlock it, then slipped into Tom Kempner's house.

"Cherry didn't waste any time getting here," Joanna said. "But how did he get in? The chief of police isn't supposed to have access to locked private property."

"Don't get your nose out of joint," Tony replied. "The FBI had the place cordoned off. Maybe they gave the chief a set of keys."

Chief Cherrigan entered Tom Kempner's house and felt a rush of excitement. The foyer was dark, but when he turned toward the sound of muted voices, he realized that someone had turned on the lights in the arched hallway under the sweeping staircase.

Silently, the chief followed the sound, stopping in the doorway of the mob attorney's office.

"Talk sense, Maynard!" the admiral snarled, all the while keeping his eyes focused on Kempner's desk. "What do you mean, we got company?"

"The boy seems tongue-tied," Cherry said, unzipping his parka and flipping down the hood. "Course, he's probably a little nervous. Breaking and entering might be routine in Washington, but here in Barrington, we respect private property."

"Well, well. If it isn't Radar Gun himself." Weiss looked up. "Go back and check out the funeral parlor. I hear there's a traffic jam in the parking lot."

Cherry stomped his feet, leaving chunks of snow on the berber carpet. "No can do, Admiral. When you came into Mr. Kempner's house, you trespassed. The way I see it, you're just another lawbreaking city slicker."

Weiss scoffed. "Speaking of lawbreakers, have you flagged anyone down?"

"You're joshing me, right?" the chief said, chuckling. "Any fool knows it's silly to set speed traps when the roads are treacherous."

When under orders to behave, Cherry knew how to be polite, but when given the opportunity, he also knew how to rub it in. Earlier, at the funeral parlor, Mr. Barbera had cautioned him to mind his manners. Minutes ago, his Mafia benefactor had taken off the shackles.

Cherry recalled every word of Mr. B.'s message: "Chief, you're representing the village of Barrington. As our Ambassador of Goodwill, I want you to engage our friend the admiral, and in the process, feel free to show him our brand of country hospitality."

Cherry had no idea what had changed, but he looked forward to cross-examining a highfalutin' CIA officer.

"Did you and your boy walk from the funeral parlor?" the chief asked. "Didn't see that spanking-new Chevy parked outside."

"Parked near the service entrance," Weiss snapped. "With so many speeders on the road, I wanted to be out of the way."

His arms crossed, the chief stepped forward and faced the admiral from the other side of Tom Kempner's desk. "Did you say speeders?"

The admiral squinted. "Maynard and I saw a limo with chains that was moving at a fast clip."

The chief glanced at the ceiling. "Don't recall seeing a limo."

"You don't remember FALCON 1," the admiral asked, "the car you mistook for the governor's?"

"Can't say that I do," Cherry replied, leaning forward and putting his fists on Kempner's desk. "Except for some gate crashers, all the townsfolk I saw stayed within the limit."

"You made your point, Cherrigan." The admiral glared back, then put his fists on the other side of Kempner's desk. "Now get out of my face."

Cherry held his ground, but when he looked into the admiral's steely blue eyes, he got uncomfortable.

"Sailor," he said, a bit of moisture forming on his brow, "in spite of your bad attitude, the Barrington Police Department extended you professional courtesies. But no longer. Right now my patience is wearing thin."

"Disappear, Cherrigan. I eat country bumpkins like you for breakfast."

"That tone of voice doesn't sit very well." Cherry unsnapped the leather holster strap that secured a .357 Magnum. "Around these parts I was elected to enforce the law."

"Back off. You're in over your head."

"I only see one person drowning," Cherry replied, cocking his pistol and pointing it at Weiss. "Gentlemen, turn around and head for the front door."

"Cherrigan," the admiral growled, "you'll live to regret this."

"Read your charter," Cherry said, waving his service pistol to get Weiss and his agent to move. "The CIA isn't authorized to stick its nose into domestic affairs. By my reckoning, unless you become real cooperative, a high-ranking Company admiral might find himself in front of the House Intelligence Committee. You know the group. All those liberal congressmen who love hearing about un-sanctioned covert operations."

Weiss glared. "I've survived congressional committees before, and I'll do it again."

"I suppose you have," Cherry said, "but one thing is puzzling. What do you say when those left-wing Democrats look at your budget and question you about the entries marked 'Joint Operations with the Mob'?"

Dr. Tony Gaylani was running out of small talk. While he and Joanna watched Tom Kempner's house, Tony became more and more alarmed at the amount of time Chief Cherrigan had spent inside. Why hadn't backup patrol cars been dispatched? Why hadn't Cherry cuffed the man and taken him into custody?

Joanna gasped. "Now there are two of them!"

Tony nodded, watching the chief, gun drawn, follow the two men out the Kempners' front door. As the scene unfolded, he bent down, trying to get a look at their faces. But to no avail. Both men walked with parka hoods up and faces down.

"Wonder who they are?" he asked.

"Must be burglars," Joanna replied. "The chief has them in custody."

"Maybe… but maybe not."

Tony exchanged a quizzical look with his wife, then stood in silence as Cherrigan made a move that dumbfounded him. After ushering the two men across the plowed cobblestone turnaround to the snow mounds near the far side of the garage, Cherry holstered his pistol and walked back toward his squad car.

A moment later an old Blazer backed out and came into view. When the Chevy turned at the end of the driveway, the chief started up his patrol car and followed.

Gary Barbera sat in Patricia's living room. When the telephone rang he watched her walk toward the L-shaped counter. The second she answered, he checked his watch, then took in the surroundings.

He wasn't surprised by the décor. Like his home and office, her place was refined and tasteful. But one thing troubled him. It felt curiously detached, even cold. Aside from a framed photo of her with Mrs. Eichler and a yellow Lab puppy, there were no mementos.

In his library and office, the works of great artists dominated the walls. But every mantel, coffee table, and desktop was loaded with photos and remembrances of his heritage. He even had a demitasse cup with "Lavazza" embossed on the side that dated back to his father's 1911 trip to Tuscany and Turino.

"For you again," she said, holding up the phone. "Chief Cherrigan can't seem to get enough of your wise counsel."

"I have no secrets," Gary said, standing. "If no one minds, I'll take it here."

He listened, his face calm. In truth, he was very pleased. Chief Cherrigan completed his recap, making a point to say that Admiral Weiss and his CIA agent had confiscated all the items arrayed on Tom Kempner's desk.

"Fine job, Chief. Once again, you've done the citizenry proud."

Gary hung up, noting Miss Patricia was watching him, her reporter's eye probing.

"Did I do something wrong?" he asked. "If it's about the call, I'm happy to discuss it."

"I don't much care what Cherry said. But I would like to know how it feels to have a police chief in your hip pocket."

"I'm a property owner in Barrington," he protested with a hint of a smile. "Aren't I entitled to the same services as you?"

"Of course you are. No more, no less."

Mrs. Eichler stood. "Stop picking on Mr. Barbera. He's assured me he doesn't wish to be a party to any illegal activity. I assume that also means he'll cooperate with the authorities. If so, I for one would like to know how he plans to be helpful."

Dr. Tony Gaylani pulled at his mustache, confounded by events. First he'd observed a man load a vehicle with items taken from his neighbor's house. Next, the local police chief arrived and got the situation under control. But then, instead of arresting the two men, Cherrigan had sent them packing without even a perfunctory look at the items they'd loaded into their car.

The chief's behavior was odd, but whom would Tony confide in? Joanna was the only one around, and he had no intention of sharing his thoughts with her.

Tony sensed something was wrong, and without giving his wife a reason, he excused himself and headed for the basement. He couldn't pinpoint the trouble, but his survival instincts had never failed him.

Who wouldn't be nervous? The reporter, Shaver, was unaccounted for, and the police chief had just escorted two men out of his neighbor's house. Sure, Tony had been relieved when they'd come back from the wake and he'd disarmed the alarm. But even though his security system had worked perfectly, to be safe, he'd double-check everything.

"Dear?" Joanna stopped midway down the basement stairs. "Oh, there you are."

He let go of the Master combination lock. He'd dialed all but the last number, but with his wife gawking, he didn't dare open it up.

"Yes, sweetie? What's so all-fired important?"

"Chief Cherrigan is on the phone. Says he'd like to explain what went on next door."

"Did he now?" Tony said. "Be right there."

The moment his wife disappeared, he got back to his task. But just as he flipped up the lock he'd specifically mounted face-in and began redialing the combination, Tony heard footsteps coming back down the basement stairs.

"Make up your mind," Joanna demanded. "Either talk to the chief or I'm hanging up."

Tony wanted to hear Cherrigan's explanation, but first he needed to check the wine cellar. Unfortunately, Joanna was making that difficult. With the general's papers sitting inside on the tasting table, he couldn't risk opening the wine cellar in her presence.

"Tell the chief to hold on. Just take me a second to get us a bottle of your favorite port."

"Darling," Joanna said, "I don't need any port, and I certainly don't need to chitchat with Chief Cherrigan. If you want something from your precious wine cellar, give me the combination and I'll get it."

"Naw… if you're not interested, neither am I."

Joanna grinned. "Dearest, I said I wasn't interested in port. I certainly didn't say I wasn't interested."

Tony eyed his wife. It was useless to keep stalling. He took a last look at the surrounding area and headed toward the stairs. Joanna was hinting at sex, and the chief waited for him on the phone. Not an opportune time to check his wine cellar.

But why worry? Everything in the basement looked normal. The Master combination lock was attached face in, and the floor, as always, was spotlessly clean.

"Darling," Joanna nagged, "I'm about to turn off the lights."

"I'm coming, I'm coming."

Tony ran upstairs, remembering one bothersome item. The air downstairs had felt a tad chilly. He'd make a note to call the heating contractor.

"Give me a second," he said, taking the portable kitchen phone from his wife. "After I talk to the chief, I'll meet you in the bedroom."

Instead of taking Cherrigan off hold, he watched Joanna leave, then leaned up against a granite countertop. All at once, checking the wine cellar and the general's papers faded in importance. A review of recent events combined with a sudden awareness of a startling omission made him break out in a cold sweat.

Of course, he'd talk to the chief. He wanted to know about the men who'd looted Tom Kempner's house. He'd also take care of his wife's carnal lust. But once he'd sent Joanna to dreamland, he would sneak out of the bedroom and take a huge but necessary risk.

Breaking silence carried a big price tag. Spies only interfaced with their handlers over crisis-level matters. The risks of detection were too high. Their code had worked in the past, but phoning Andy

Douglas because of a gut feeling would get his Iraqi superiors agitated.

But he didn't care. Right now his survival instincts were scraping his nerves raw. Within the space of a little over an hour, he'd seen Ellen Eichler cozy up to a Mafia kingpin and Chief Cherrigan brandish his gun. Those things alone would spook any spy, but when coupled with his wife's apparent indifference toward tomorrow's UJC Convention, the situation became frightening.

Tony stared at the phone. A bead of perspiration rolled down his forehead. Joanna had been instrumental in bringing the damn convention to Chicago. She was scheduled to give the keynote address. Granted, she had to be one of the horniest broads on the face of the planet, but with the opening proceeding a little over twelve hours away, shouldn't she be practicing her speech? But no. Nada. Not a word. Not a script. Nothing.

CHAPTER THIRTY-THREE

Patricia Shaver had been on guard from the moment Danny Finn tossed her gear through the front door. With an eye toward privacy, she'd suggested her house as a staging point. She knew Danny Finn and Gary Barbera needed an out-of-the-way place to reunite. She also figured some items in the duffel bag were best unpacked when she was alone. But mostly, she thought her cozy bungalow would be a great spot for Barbera to tell Ellen that he planned to sit on the sidelines and let the authorities handle Tony and Joanna Gaylani.

Pat sat in her living room, looking across the coffee table at the gentleman don. By her calculations, she'd covered all the contingencies. Unless... could she have missed something?

She began to worry when he picked up his mug. His hand was steady and his face exuded confidence, but ever since Chief Cherrigan's second call, Gary Barbera had acted way too smug.

Nervous, she walked to the kitchen counter and reached for the coffee pot. "Be a sport, Gary. Tell Ellen you want the CIA to arrest the Gaylanis."

He said nothing as she topped off everyone's coffee. But once she'd settled in next to Ellen on one of her sofas, Barbera slowly got to his feet.

His opening comments were complimentary of law enforcement, but made no mention of the CIA. That got her attention. Seconds later, as he continued, Pat noted a change in his inflection. Instead of saying he didn't expect to be involved, Barbera implied that his presence might be required.

"Mrs. Eichler," he said, "any tampering was done with only the best of intentions."

"Of course," Ellen acknowledged. "I never doubted your sincerity."

"You should also know I didn't ask to be involved." He eyed Ellen, then sat down. "A few days before Katherine Kempner's unfortunate death, Tommy called and told me I had to meet with the admiral or face the full prowess of the CIA."

"Really?" Ellen's smile disappeared. "I'm surprised the CIA would seek your help."

"Please understand. It wasn't a formal invitation."

"Oh," Ellen said, "the CIA's message was clear, just not in writing."

"Congress has passed legislation outlining the scope of the Company's authority." Barbera looked toward the hearth, where Danny Finn stood. "As with most things, there are gray areas. It's not my place to tell the CIA how gray the gray areas are. I'm only a practical businessman trying to survive in a hostile environment."

"I'm a little confused," Ellen said, "but are you saying that as a businessman, you felt obliged to respond even though the CIA's request fell in the gray area?"

Barbera's expression was pained. "In a competitive world, everyone tries to cooperate with the authorities, but everyone wants a return on his investment too."

Ellen touched a finger to her lips. "Were you paid for being cooperative?"

The gentleman don eased himself forward to the edge of the couch. "In exchange for information on the Gaylanis, Admiral Weiss offered me a degree of immunity. But the man is a little slow. Had we not teamed up to set the record straight, I fear he might have overlooked the real culprit and jeopardized the lives of many innocent conventioneers."

"Your concern for the innocent is heartening, Mr. Barbera, but are the conventioneers really out of danger?"

He cupped his hand around his mug, drawing warmth into his

fingers. "We've given Admiral Weiss all the evidence he needs to figure things out. In a way, we did the public a service. By standing up
to his roughshod tactics, we've encouraged the admiral to do his job.
Of course, we hold duplicate copies of the items he received. That's
our protection. Eric Weiss can't afford to go after any of us without
putting himself and the CIA in a tenuous position."

"Goodness," Ellen said, a little tartly, "sounds more like black-
mail than encouragement."

Barbera glared, his eyes fixed on Ellen. "The admiral is a spy working for an egotistical agency. No one tells them what to do... but
sometimes they need prodding."

"Doesn't the CIA conduct operations in secret?" Ellen asked,
her tone more congenial. "How would you know where or when to
prod?"

He squirmed, then his thumb found his cufflink, smoothing it.
"They keep things quiet, but above all else, the CIA is a political animal. In front of congressional committees, they seem to be guided
by noble patriotic principles. But that's a facade. In truth, they'll grovel
behind closed doors with anyone who can further their agenda."

Pat listened to them spar, troubled by the drift of his conversation.

"I'm not trying to put you in a box," she said, eying the gentleman don. "But most everyone... and that certainly includes me...
agrees that U.S. intelligence gathering leaves something to be desired.
But just because the FBI and CIA aren't perfect, it doesn't mean they
shouldn't be trusted to handle sensitive operations."

Barbera appeared troubled by her assessment, but didn't respond. When Danny Finn's cell phone rang, Pat, Ellen, and Barbera
turned and listened.

"Okay," Finn said, staring at the floor.

"Right," he went on, taking in the caller's message. "I'll pass it
along. Thanks for the update."

Without looking up, Danny Finn disconnected his cell phone,
then walked toward a hall tree in the entryway. Once he put his parka
on, he grabbed Gary Barbera's coat.

"According to Cherrigan," the Irishman said, "the admiral drove back to the funeral parlor, had a brief meeting with his three agents, then sent them on their way."

"Anything else?" Barbera asked, his face impassive.

"Cherrigan assigned some copper named Hughes to follow the admiral's boys out of town."

"And Admiral Weiss?" the gentleman don asked. "Is Cherrigan on him?"

"Affirmative," Finn replied, helping the boss with his overcoat. "The chief thinks Sailor-boy may be headed this way."

"Not surprising," Barbera said, adjusting his coat, "but not something I'd counted on either."

Ellen raised an eyebrow. "What an odd thing to say, Mr. Barbera. If you've washed your hands of this affair, why would you want to track the admiral's movements?"

Pat noted the Mafia don's tension. She'd never thought he would turn his back on Dr. Tony Gaylani or let the admiral bring him to justice. But when it came to stopping Joanna, her read wasn't as certain. Pat knew the Mafia credo called for Barbera to avenge lost comrades to his very death. When it came to protecting innocent civilians, she wasn't sure his course of action would be as clear.

"Mrs. Eichler," Barbera said, "thoroughness is the hallmark of any well-run business. While I have no intention of stepping in and doing the admiral's job, I have a stake in seeing that justice is done. Monitoring his progress is one way to be certain the man does the right thing."

"Is the admiral doing the right thing by coming here?" Ellen asked.

"Yes and no," Barbera said, ignoring Danny's impatience to leave. "He's to be congratulated for swallowing his pride. But that isn't the whole story. When a person of his rank is reduced to begging, it indicates his analytic powers are on the decline."

"In what way?" Ellen asked.

"Isn't it obvious? The man hasn't figured out what Joanna Gaylani aims to do."

"How could he?" Ellen demanded, her voice sounding vexed.

"You didn't give him the necessary information to make that connection."

Pat's heart tripped a beat. Jesus, Mary, and Joseph! Ellen had done it again. Drawing inferences from God knows where, her friend had figured out that Barbera had turned the tables and stayed in control.

But how had she done it? How had Ellen identified the one part of their plan that had come up short? How could her friend have known that the evidence she and Danny Finn had stacked on Tom Kempner's desk was incomplete?

The ranch expenses Ellen had billed to Joanna Gaylani were included. Earlier, Pat had told her that she planned to put them on Tom Kempner's desk. At that time, they had thought Gary Barbera would give them copies of the horse ranch expenses he controlled—the bills Tom Kempner had paid over the years. When laid out side-by-side, the two sets of documents would have told Admiral Weiss that Joanna Gaylani had double ordered enough ammonium nitrate to make a bomb.

Finn stepped forward. "Boss, excuse me for interrupting, but do you want to be here when Sailor-boy arrives?"

Barbera moved toward the door, then stopped and faced Ellen.

"Mrs. Eichler, I'm sorry to leave without giving you a satisfactory answer. I believe if you speak with Miss Patricia, she'll be able to explain my position. Before undertaking any of this, I briefed her on my intentions."

Without a hint of malice, he looked Pat in the eye. For a second they each gave no quarter, then, with a glint that said he'd won, Gary Barbera turned back to Ellen and smiled.

"On a personal note, thanks for being so considerate. Asking Lauren to allow me to see my grandchildren will make this grandpa very happy."

Joanna Gaylani waited patiently. She was perched atop the covers and clad in her sexiest negligee. She knew Tony's phone call with Chief

Cherrigan was over, but she made no move to find him. Staying composed was part of her plan.

When Tony finally came through the door, she beckoned him to their bed. As always, he pretended not to be interested. And as always, she pursued until he relented. Of course, this time it was extra special. This time she made passionate love with the man she planned to execute in twelve hours.

Joanna lay back on the pillows, breathing heavily.

"Tony, darling, you're the antsiest guy I ever met. Now where are you going?"

"Got a taste for brandy. If you'd like, I'll bring a glass up for you."

"You and your brandy," she said, faking a pout. "Go if you must, but remember, you're not the only one with an unquenchable thirst. Promise me you'll be back."

"I will… but in the meantime, why not work on your speech?"

"My speech? I don't—" She caught herself. But had Tony noticed the questioning inflection in her voice? "You know I never rehearse my speeches. I jotted down a few key points the other day. That's all I need."

When her husband shrugged, Joanna smiled. Then she watched the bare-assed fool grab his bathrobe off a chair. Undoubtedly, he was headed for the wine cellar to make sure the general's papers were still safe and sound. She didn't have to look. She already knew they were locked up. She'd unraveled that mystery on Christmas Eve, shortly after she and Tony had left Tom Kempner's to come home and get ready for Connie Sexton's party.

Her husband thought she'd gone up to take a shower. Instead, she'd turned on the water, sneaked downstairs, and stood at the basement door. When she heard the sound of the drill, she had all the information she needed.

The next morning, about the time Tony and the nosy women had found Tom Kempner's body, she went downstairs for a closer look. It hadn't taken a genius to locate the keys to his handiwork.

Neatnik Tony had left the combination tag in the Ace bag when he'd tossed it in the garbage.

Joanna sat up in bed and stretched her arms over her head. For fifteen years, Tony had left hundreds of bottles of vintage wines and cognacs unlocked. Of course, in this instance, he'd had no choice but to padlock the cellar. When Tony had stolen and warehoused General Alan Cunningham's memoirs, he'd also placed himself at the scene of Tom Kempner's murder.

As a single tear ran down her cheek, Joanna slipped her nightgown back on. Why couldn't she dismiss her feelings? She had lots of reasons to hate the man. Making love to him was just part of her job.

Okay. Maybe messing with Tony did get her heart rate up and was more fun than pedaling a stationary bike. But the pleasure was physical. Time and again, she told herself that she was not emotionally connected.

Joanna pulled the covers to her chin and snuggled with the pillow. None of the lamps were on, but light from the full moon beamed in, making the boudoir glow like dusk after a setting sun. It also made her skin turn to goose flesh.

She wanted to regain her focus and not think about Tony. She wanted to fall asleep without any feelings of guilt. Her husband deserved to die. Why dwell on what could have been?

Soon a bomb would explode and all her years of work and sacrifice would be vindicated. Soon an Iraqi spy would be the Ruling Council's scapegoat. Soon her Tony would be blamed for an act that would become a Zionist rallying point for a strong, independent Israel. Soon Jews everywhere would believe that even when a rogue state is defeated and its leader deposed, Arab terrorists would continue to traumatize the world.

Patricia Shaver watched Gary Barbera nod to the Irishman, then say good-bye to Ellen. When they departed, she felt totally isolated. She knew her friend wouldn't waste any time. Ellen had grilled the gentleman don and, based on her accusatory eyes, Pat realized she was next.

"Excuse me a second."

She made a beeline for the powder room. Once inside, she lowered the wooden lid over the commode and began retracing earlier events.

Around noon, she'd called Barbera. She needed to confirm the time of the limo meeting in the funeral parlor lot. She also wanted to give him a sketchy outline of a plan she'd conceived and Ellen had reluctantly approved.

She and Ellen knew it was important to provide Admiral Weiss with the proof he needed to have Dr. Tony Gaylani arrested for the Kempners' murders. But that wasn't all. They also wanted the admiral to receive the two sets of invoices that proved Joanna Gaylani possessed the raw materials for making a bomb.

Gary Barbera had bought into her scheme. As a shrewd businessman, it made sense to cooperate. He needed the pieces of evidence she and Ellen controlled. Kitty Kempner's note, the cassette featuring the admiral's voice, and the Kempner/Weiss file could be held over the admiral's head like a paid-in-full insurance policy against future CIA reprisals. As for them, she and Ellen wanted to be certain the display on Tom's desk included the one item Barbera possessed—the paid invoices for ammonium nitrate in Tom Kempner's horse ranch file.

Of course, she hadn't been totally forthcoming. During her noontime call to Barbera, she hadn't told him about the fertilizer invoices Ellen had billed out to Joanna Gaylani. But instead of suggesting they combine the two sets, she'd just asked Barbera if he would make Kempner's invoices available. When he'd agreed to include them, she thought she'd scored a mini coup. But later, when they'd sat in the back seat of his limousine, Gary Barbera had claimed that by including the invoices, he'd meant getting them directly into Admiral Weiss's hands.

Maybe she should have pinned Barbera down by asking him to give her Tom Kempner's horse ranch file. But tactical mistake notwithstanding, even now, as she sat in the powder room, she couldn't fathom why he'd chosen to make such a fine distinction.

Pat took a deep breath and looked up. She cherished the small oil painting that hung on the wall opposite the commode. The framed portrait of Snowshoe's head usually gave her a lift. But not right this second. When she remembered who was waiting in her living room, her thoughts returned to the meeting in the funeral parlor lot.

She'd expressed some unhappiness, but stayed calm when Barbera stated that the ammonium nitrate invoices billed to Tom Kempner would not be part of the display placed on Tom's desk. After all, he hadn't refused to give them up. He'd just chosen to be directly involved in their delivery. As Barbera had said: "If I thought the CIA, the FBI, and the courts would do their job, I'd give the admiral the receipts promptly. But I don't trust them. Keeping temporary possession is my way to make sure they do the right thing."

She'd accepted Barbera's statement without interrupting, but didn't waste any time seeking a clarification. First she'd demanded a firm time of delivery, then she'd asked him to define how he would keep an eye on things and still stay within the law.

As expected, he'd given her blanket assurances: "My dear, don't concern yourself with frivolous details. You have my word. The invoices will be in the admiral's hands in a timely manner. As for any illegal tampering, I'll let you be the judge. If at any point you sense I'm being an obstructionist, feel free to contact the admiral and tell him everything you know."

Maybe she should have bored in for guarantees. But in truth, his reticence had merit. Above all else, she'd wanted the Gaylanis to pay for their crimes. Unlike Ellen, who had faith in the system, Pat sided with Barbera.

Why wouldn't she be mistrustful? Senator Scott Sheppard had buried the truth during the investigation into her parents' deaths. That experience had taught her a tough lesson: When the Feds got involved, their self-interest always dwarfed everyone else's search for justice.

And of course, practicality had to be considered too. Being adversarial with the crime boss made no sense. To get justice, she needed Gary Barbera's and Danny Finn's help. Without their assistance, she wouldn't have been able to decoy Weiss and his three agents. Without their involvement, she wouldn't have gotten into the Gaylanis' basement or put an array of evidence on Tom Kempner's desk.

Pat cracked the powder room door and looked out. Ellen was sitting on one of the sofas, skimming through a magazine. She wasn't sure it was safe to face her friend, but she walked into the living room anyway.

"Don't be mad. On my word of honor, I haven't been holding out on you."

"Of course you haven't," Ellen replied, tossing the *Vanity Fair* on the coffee table. "But either way, what's the big deal? Don't all good friends look each other in the eye, then lie through their teeth?"

Ellen's words carried a sting, but her friend's delivery was almost jovial. Had Ellen just taken a page out of Barbera's playbook? Was she toying with her?

"Keep one thing in mind," Pat said. "Technically, I never lied."

"How so? Didn't we agree to have Tommy's invoices included with everything else?"

"We agreed," Pat admitted, "but Barbera didn't."

She was about to beg for Ellen's forgiveness when it hit her.

"Wait a minute. Speaking of people holding back, you're as bad as I am. How did you know Barbera didn't give me Tom Kempner's stable invoices? You weren't in the limo when I asked. You were inside the funeral parlor."

"I didn't know for sure. But I also didn't forget your instructions the day we searched Tommy's office." Stone-faced, Ellen leaned forward. "Come, come, Patricia, don't you remember telling me to pull up the ranch file folder before I closed the cabinet drawer?"

"Suppose I do," she conceded. "What's your point?"

"Simple," Ellen said. "You wanted to take a closer look, but knew I'd never let you steal it. The next best thing to controlling it yourself was making it obvious to someone who would."

"And?"

"You suspected Mr. Barbera would send Chief Cherrigan in to purge Tommy's files. I just took that piece of information and coupled it with a trick Ken Dale taught you."

As Ellen sat back, looking confident, Pat leaned over the coffee table. "You coupled what?"

"The adjuratory authority routine," Ellen said. "Surely you recall that one?"

Nodding, Pat remembered last spring. During a strategy session, her fiancé, Ken Dale, had told her how to get a tightlipped person to speak up and validate sensitive information.

"Adjuratory authority only worked for Ken. When I gave it a whirl, it flopped."

"Guess you needed a more gullible person," Ellen replied. "You fell for it hook, line, and sinker."

"So… just now… you didn't know for sure? You just guessed and watched my reaction?"

She recalled Ken's lesson on adjuratory authority. According to her fiancé, only two things mattered: Be self-assured, then state your conjectures as though they were fact.

"I made an educated guess," Ellen replied, "but my instincts guided me too. Since historians starting keeping records, men like Mr. Barbera have always wanted to be in control."

"I tried to fight him," Pat said. "We needed his help, but before I said yes, I got Gary to make a major concession."

"Well, well, how chummy. First it's Gary to his face. Now it's Gary when he's not around." Ellen walked to the lakeside window. "Tell me, Patricia, what concession did Mr. Barbera make?"

"He gave us complete latitude. You and I are free to tell the admiral everything we know about Joanna Gaylani and her plans to bomb the UJC Convention."

Ellen continued to look out at the lake. "Barbera insisted on that?"

"He's understandably gun-shy of the authorities. But I swear, Gary isn't looking for Mafia justice. Just like you, he wants the Gaylanis arrested by law enforcement."

Ellen turned and faced her. "Fine, but what if Admiral Weiss doesn't believe us?"

"The admiral has no reason to think we'd lie," Pat argued. "But if Weiss won't heed our warning, as a last resort, Gary will step in."

"I knew there had to be a catch."

"Jeez, Ellie. We can't sit on our hands and let Joanna slaughter innocent people." Pat pleaded, her eyes hopeful. "If the authorities won't listen to reason, we have to stop her."

As she defended the gentleman don's case, Pat's stomach knotted around a horrible thought. Could he be using them to set up the admiral? Had Barbera devised his own scheme and purposely left her and Ellen out? Had he hoped all along that Eric Weiss would fail to put things together? Would the crime boss knowingly allow a bomb to be detonated just to make the admiral and the CIA look incompetent? Could Barbera stoop to such depths just to get even?

She took a deep breath, careful not to make eye contact with Ellen. What if the gentleman don had set her up? It made a certain amount of sense. It explained why Barbera hadn't handed over Tom Kempner's invoices. If he really wanted the admiral to know that Joanna Gaylani had double-ordered ammonium nitrate, why not let Danny and her put the file on the desk with the rest of the evidence? What could be the risk? Admiral Weiss had no way of knowing who'd rifled Tom's office. Yet, as things stood, she only had Barbera's word that Weiss would ever see the invoices.

Mary, mother of Jesus! Had she abetted a man who'd schemed to find a way for one radical Jew to exterminate her brethren? Had the gentleman don remembered their springtime encounter and set his sights on her? Without her knowing it, had Gary Barbera placed her finger on the detonator?

"I'm disappointed," Ellen said, breaking an uncomfortable silence. "By not insisting that Tommy's invoices be included, you in effect winked at Mr. Barbera's proposal. That tacit approval makes us his co-conspirators. If things get out of hand, we'll be as guilty as him."

"Ellie, please. Before you get completely bent out of shape, why not wait and see how the admiral reacts to our story?"

CHAPTER THIRTY-FOUR

Admiral Eric Weiss checked his rearview mirror. The police cruiser behind him kept a two-car interval. Annoyed, he pressed down on the accelerator. For a second, he pulled away. But when he checked again, the gap in the two-car interval had closed.

Eric thought about slamming on the brakes. In the end, he decided not to test Cherrigan's ability to react. Why screw around with a police chief who was just following orders? Cherrigan's blatant contempt for him and the CIA had to be Barbera's idea.

The moment he put on his turn signal and made a snail-like swerve into Patricia Shaver's driveway, the sheriff stopped tailgating. As if to end their game, Cherrigan flashed the flashers, hit the siren, and sped off, a flamboyance that brought a small curl to Weiss's mouth.

The admiral followed the plowed driveway until he saw the two buildings. He'd been informed that the reporter, Shaver, lived in the dormered cottage to the right. The sight of it made his jaw muscles tense. He was anxious to debrief both Shaver and Eichler, but he also dreaded what he might hear.

He pulled up, but didn't park in the empty space to the right of the Ford Explorer. Instead of taking the spot closest to the reporter's home, he stopped on the left side of Mrs. Eichler's car.

He got out, circled around the back of his vehicle, then walked just past the rear of the Explorer. When he bent down and rubbed his hand over an embedded tread, he knew Barbera had come and gone. Chiseled into the snow pack were the imprints left by an automobile equipped with chains.

His examination finished, he walked up the steps, crossed the porch, and rang the bell.

"Good evening, Miss Shaver. I'm Eric Weiss."

He extended his hand to a young woman he'd only met through photographs.

"Sorry it's so late," he said. "Whenever you and I try to get acquainted, we end up passing like ships in the night."

"Don't give it a second thought," she replied. "Lately, Ellie and I have been staying up way past our bedtimes."

Gary Barbera relaxed in the back seat of his limo. As Danny Finn drove toward Lake Forest, Gary unbuttoned his cashmere overcoat and adjusted the climate control.

"Is everything set for tomorrow?"

"Yes, boss. Several carloads of our people will be in place. No matter which direction Chuck Sweet takes the truck, we'll have men watching him."

"Will Sean O'Banyon be going with us?"

The Irishman nodded, then eased the limo around a wide-sweeping curve. "The funeral is at nine-thirty. Sean will come by the house at eight AM sharp."

"Good. Is the service being held at his wife's church?"

Finn nodded again. "Like Mrs. Kempner, their son was raised Episcopalian. Trevor made the decision to have an Anglican burial for his father."

"Tommy won't mind. In matters of religion, he didn't quibble over orthodoxy."

Gary smiled. Things had fallen into place. He hadn't anticipated Mrs. Eichler's insightful probing, but in the end, it had worked to his advantage. To be sure, he didn't relish Miss Patricia's dilemma. About now, she was probably reeling from Mrs. Eichler's questions.

"Has Chief Cherrigan checked in?"

"Not yet, boss."

"Call him." Gary pulled off his leather gloves and placed them on the seat. "I want to be kept posted on Weiss's whereabouts. And one other thing. Has Cherrigan been fully briefed?"

"The chief knows the score," Finn replied. "When it comes to pranks, he's a master. Before it's over, Sailor-boy will be frustrated enough to eat nails."

The car phone rang and the Irishman answered it.

"Chief," Finn said, "the boss was just asking about you."

Admiral Eric Weiss walked into Miss Shaver's bungalow with his head high. While the reporter closed and locked her front door, he slipped off his parka and looked around.

She lived in a quaint house full of junky antiques. It didn't suit his taste, but he wasn't a society honcho with millions to spend on stuff you couldn't sit on.

"May I take your coat, Admiral?"

He ignored her, first dropping his hooded parka on a wooden bench, then kneeling down.

"This looks familiar. Any chance the duffel bag got tossed into old man Barbera's limousine?"

"Could be," Pat replied. "With so much going on, who can be sure?"

Eric unzipped it. "Good quality stuff… but an unusual mix."

He decided to conduct a test. If an illegal invasion of the reporter's private property didn't cause a stir, it might indicate she planned to cooperate. As he fingered through the paraphernalia, he held up the microfilm camera.

"Does this Brownie come with a flash attachment and a tele-photo lens?"

The reporter didn't smile. "Is owning a camera a crime?"

"Take it easy, missy. I'm not accusing you of anything."

He noted the tame objection and continued the probe, this time hoisting what remained of a Master combination lock.

"Isn't this ingenious? For an Alzheimer's patient, a bolt cutter eliminates the need to memorize numbers."

"It's late, Admiral. I'm tired and you're here of your own volition. In good faith, I invited you in." The reporter walked over and squatted down. "If Ellie and I can be helpful, we'd be happy to answer your questions. If this is an exercise in one-upmanship, I'm going to bed."

"I know Barbera was here," Eric said. "Did he put you up to this?"

"Mr. Barbera doesn't tell either of us what to do." She rose and strolled into her living room. "When you finish rummaging, come join us."

Called to task, he followed, nodding to Mrs. Eichler as he sat on a cushioned sofa opposite them.

"I heard the recording of your call to Barbera," he said, eying Pat. "In the interest of time, let's skip right to Katherine Kempner's note. On the tape, you imply Dr. Tony Gaylani stole it, but given the content, it seems unlikely he'd have put it back in the mail."

"Ellie and I think Joanna took it."

"Joanna Gaylani? Why would she resend it?"

"Mrs. Gaylani is very innovative," the reporter replied, giving him a hard stare. "She needed a fall guy, and her husband fit the bill."

"A fall guy?"

She put her coffee mug down. "Admiral, do you know anything about this woman?"

"With all due respect, ma'am, I'll run the interrogation."

To save face, he talked tough. In truth, he felt like a man in command of a rudderless ship. He hated swallowing his pride, but he needed information, and the Shaver and Eichler women were the only ones who could provide it.

Mrs. Eichler leaned forward. "I'm not sure which is worse. Your bull or Patricia's arrogance. In either case, shall we stop dancing and get down to business?"

"No can do," he said, shaking his head. "As deputy director of the CIA, it's not my habit to discuss national security issues with civilians."

Mrs. Eichler jumped to her feet, waving her index finger. "For the love of God, Admiral! I don't give a hoot about you or the CIA. While you're sitting on your high horse, Joanna Gaylani is getting ready to set off a bomb. Are you interested in protecting the delegates at the UJC Convention, or are you concerned about red tape and security clearances?"

He looked straight ahead, hoping his face muscles hadn't telegraphed his surprise. Unlike the bomb Eichler claimed would go off, one had just exploded in his head.

"Think what you're saying, woman. Why would Joanna Gaylani bomb her own people?"

Mrs. Eichler sat down. "Like Patricia said. How much do you know about Mrs. Gaylani?"

He was stunned. Could it be possible? Had the two misfits gathered information the CIA had failed to uncover?

Embarrassment hardly described his feeling. But now was not the time to defend his ego. Along with everything else that had gone wrong, the last thing he needed was to have a renegade Zionist blow up the UJC Convention right under his Jewish nose.

"To answer your question, Mrs. Eichler, we monitor her uncle, Lawrence Magel, and his group. We know Joanna came to live with him after her parents were killed. We also know she joined and later renounced his organization. If she still harbors radical views and is sympathetic to her uncle's group, I assure you, it's news to the UJC."

"Begging your pardon, Admiral," the reporter said quietly. "Ellie and I don't care what the UJC knows. Our concern is you... and right now we're wondering if Joanna Gaylani and Chuck Sweet's involvement is news to you and the CIA."

It felt like his heart had stopped beating. Who the hell was Chuck Sweet? He'd never heard the name. "Can't seem to place him. Why is Chuck Sweet important?"

"I'll let you decide." The reporter's mouth molded into a sly smile. "For openers, the young man is a ranch hand who doesn't have a past. Joanna Gaylani hired him three years ago to do chores around the Kempners' stable and barn. And guess what? When he's not at the Kempners', he lives and works at Lawrence Magel's horse farm over in Wayne."

"That is a coincidence," he replied, afraid of what might come next. "We keep an eye on Mr. Magel, but he rarely goes to his horse farm. It's not surprising I'm not familiar with the names of his ranch hands."

"In this instance, only one 'ranch hand' is important, but unfortunately, our knowledge is also incomplete." She looked at him, her face unreadable, a reporter's skill. "We know Chuck Sweet is involved in the scheme to stockpile and hide the fertilizer. Beyond that, we're speculating. We think he's a co-conspirator with Joanna Gaylani and Larry Magel. We're also guessing he's the guy who will drive the bomb truck into Chicago."

"That's the problem, Miss Shaver. You think this and you're guessing that." He chuckled, trying to make light of another potential hole in his investigation. "Not much to go on."

"My God, Admiral," Mrs. Eichler scolded, "you've pushed my patience to the limit."

"And you mine," Eric snapped, jumping up. "How many times must I say it? The CIA doesn't discuss national security matters with civilians."

He stared at the duffel bag, just visible from the living room. Then he took a deep breath and exhaled.

"I will admit one thing," he said, sitting down. "You both seem like forthright women. For that reason, I'll make an exception. If you two want to report an incident and expand on your allegations, as a representative of your government, I'd be happy to listen."

"In that case," the reporter said, "you might want to pay real close attention. Ellie and I think Joanna is very cunning. We believe she knows her husband is an Iraqi spy. We also believe she re-sent

Katherine Kempner's note as a way to get our suspicions up. Think about it, Admiral. If Joanna can implicate her husband in the Kempners' murders, she can also set the stage to blame him for the bomb."

"I'm not questioning your sincerity, Miss Shaver, but let's be honest. Your scenario sounds a bit farfetched."

To hide his mortification, he wiped his hand across his mouth. Jesus fuckin' Christ. It was difficult to understand how he'd missed it, but now that the two women had steered him to a new point of view, many of the oddities in Joanna Gaylani's behavior didn't seem so perplexing. Suddenly, a woman he'd thought was either stupid or paralyzed with fear had become a manipulative conspirator.

As he balled his hands into white-knuckled fists, the admiral thanked God he'd come alone. If the solution had to come from this pair, at least he'd suffer the indignation without being the laughing stock of the Company.

Slowly he got to his feet. He couldn't sit and let them barrage him with proof that would mark the doctor's wife and her stable boy companion as international terrorists. Instead, he began to piece together his own synopsis.

The Company knew Dr. Tony Gaylani was one of Saddam's spies. Since he didn't have the new Iraqi government's support, the doctor was undoubtedly operating under the auspices of the underground old régime.

Why couldn't Joanna Gaylani be a similar animal? The reporter had said the doctor's wife was clever, cunning in fact. Why couldn't she have publicly renounced her affiliation with Lawrence Magel's organization, All Alone, then privately cooked up a scheme to polarize Jews against an Arab bomber she'd frame? If Joanna Gaylani had kept her plan between herself, her uncle, and this guy Chuck Sweet, it was possible even the CIA might not have caught on.

But there was one gaping hole.

If Joanna Gaylani expected to bomb a gathering the size of the UJC Convention, she'd have to detonate a very powerful device. While Company agents had their faults, they also had a worldwide network of eyes and ears open to anyone who tried to purchase the ingredients necessary to assemble an explosive. Until he had proof the doctor's wife had bomb-making materials, he couldn't act.

Miss Shaver walked to his side. "Admiral, time is short. Are you aware of a barn on the far corner of the Kempners' property?"

"The one behind a bunch of pine trees?" he asked.

The reporter nodded. "By chance, did you notice that as of this evening, a barn once surrounded by snow is now accessible?"

Eric had seen the end of the plowed road as he and Maynard had driven back to the funeral parlor. "Tell me, ma'am. Why is it a big deal when someone plows a path to a barn door?"

"Not just any barn door, Admiral." The reporter grabbed his arm. "If you want proof the doctor's wife isn't a well-meaning board member of the UJC, why don't we go over and take a look?"

CHAPTER THIRTY-FIVE

Gary Barbera stood in the library of his Lake Forest mansion. He looked toward the arched entryway, waiting for Danny Finn to join him. When the Irishman didn't appear, Gary turned and stared across the room at his lone holiday decoration—a ten-foot balsam that had been flown in from the low mountains around Tuscany.

His choice of Christmas trees—like so many things in his life—was influenced by his father. Gary Barbera, Sr., had steered him in many positive directions, but none of his dictates had been clearer or repeated more often:

"Touring northern Italy in 1911 taught me two things. No man's house is complete without Lavazza roasted coffee beans and a backyard full of Tuscan balsams."

Gary smiled. He'd taken his father's landscaping message to heart. Not only did towering balsams grow within his walled estate, but each year he put strands of white Italian lights on his perfectly shaped Christmas tree.

He moved toward the corner windows. After touching some of the short-needled boughs, he looked up at the mantel. A framed photo changed his mood. Some remembrances were pleasant, others were bittersweet.

As if doing penance, he kept staring at the picture. The photograph had been taken an hour or so after his wedding in 1939. He and Maria stood with his mother and father. Surrounding them on the church steps were his grandparents and the rest of the Barbera relatives.

He and his bride had just been married in the most lavish Mafia church service and reception Florence had ever seen. The entire Barbera family had come over from Palermo. But in spite of the embraces, kisses, and well-wishes, it was obvious his relatives had been uncomfortable.

Gary bowed his head and closed his eyes. He kept the photograph in a prominent place because it marked his father's final trip to Italy. Regrettably, it also marked one of his last visits.

He'd confirmed his suspicions when he and Maria had gone back to Europe after the War. In Florence, things were fine, but not so in Palermo. It was in their eyes. His father was the first Barbera to be in the Mafia, and he was the second. To staunch law-abiding Catholics, that had been an unpardonable sin.

Gary looked off as Danny Finn walked into the library. The Irishman nodded dutifully, but before they had a chance to talk, Finn's specially-programmed cell phone rang. When the Irishman answered and signaled that all was well, Gary slipped on his cardigan and took a seat in one of the wingback chairs facing the hearth.

He stared at the dying flames. His heart was heavy with the recollection, but not burdened by it. He'd accepted his role as a crime boss and would make no apologies to anyone.

Gary listened as Finn finished his conversation. He also watched the Irishman go to the bar cart, pour Napoleon cognac into two brandy snifters, and place the drinks on the lamp table between their chairs.

"Cherrigan just checked in," Finn said. "The first part of your assignment is complete."

"Good. That means the chief had time to leave Tommy's ranch file in the barn and still vacate the area."

Finn nodded. "After he followed the admiral to Miss Shaver's house, he drove to the barn and dropped off the file. From there, Cherry said the timing was tight, but he did manage to double back. Just before the ladies and Admiral Weiss came out and got in separate cars, he positioned himself in the cul-de-sac close to the journalist's bungalow."

"Cherrigan watched all three of them leave?"

"Yes," Finn replied. "Weiss got in his car, then followed the ladies in Mrs. Eichler's Explorer."

"What about the second part to the surveillance?" Gary asked.

"Cherry will follow your instructions. He'll hold his position another minute or two, then drive just past the road to the barn and hide in a driveway off Oak Knoll Road."

"Very good," Gary said, watching the reflection of the hearth embers dance across the brandy snifter. "Will the chief call us after he makes a final check?"

Again, Danny nodded. "Once the ladies and the admiral leave the barn, he'll go out and make sure the ranch file is gone."

Gary smiled approvingly as the Irishman sat down. He sensed Finn wanted to pick up his snifter, but knew his confidant would wait. In Lake Forest, the host took the first sip.

"Well, Danny, if my calculations are correct, we have a half hour to enjoy our brandy."

Patricia Shaver sat in the passenger seat of Ellen Eichler's Explorer. As they sped past Tom Kempner's Tudor mansion, Pat verified that Admiral Weiss's car was behind them.

"Slow down," Pat cautioned, "we're getting close."

As she pointed toward a stand of Douglas firs, Ellen turned the Ford SUV onto the recently plowed road. In no time, they reached the barn. Soon after they got out and stood on either side of the Explorer, Admiral Weiss pulled up and flipped on the Blazer's brights.

Pat saw that the padlock on the barn door had been snipped off and knew Barbera had upstaged her again. She closed her eyes. It couldn't be coincidental. First he'd out-negotiated her. Now the gentleman don was about to prove he was a man of his word. His shrewdness knew no bounds. Like it or not, she would have to take full credit for the papers she, Ellen, and the admiral would find inside.

Pat stepped forward. As long as it was a *fait accompli*, she decided not to act surprised.

"Before we go in, take note of two things. The barn isn't padlocked, and there are lots of footprints around the door. Whoever plowed the road had more on his mind than clearing a pathway."

Weiss walked to the wooden door and eyed the metal latch.

"Cleverly done, Miss Shaver. I commend you on your thoroughness. But what would you have done if I hadn't gone through your duffel bag?"

"I'm thankful you're a curious man," Pat replied. "Why don't we go in and see what awaits us?"

She knew Ellen and the admiral assumed she and Danny had used the bolt cutter to snip off the lock. Just as she couldn't admit the combination lock in her duffel bag had come off Dr. Tony Gaylani's wine cellar door, she also couldn't speak up when they turned on flashlights and found Tom Kempner's ranch file.

Barbera had planted the invoices, but she was powerless to insist she hadn't taken part. Still, what was the harm? She didn't understand the gentleman don's motives, but one thing was clear. When Admiral Weiss saw the stack of bills and asked Ellen about the fertilizer she'd delivered for Joanna Gaylani, he understood that an extra five tons of explosives had been accumulated without the CIA's knowledge.

"Very enlightening, ladies," he said, using a flashlight to scan the invoices. "If you don't mind, I'll log these items in as official evidence."

Pat knew their mission was over the moment Admiral Weiss stuffed the fertilizer receipts in his breast coat pocket and turned toward the barn door. Once outside, she and Ellen said good-bye, then watched him leave, his taillights fading as he drove off.

Gary Barbera looked at his watch. He'd enjoyed sipping cognac with Danny, but thirty-one minutes had passed, and he wanted a report.

"By my reckoning…"

He smiled when the Irishman's cell phone rang.

"A little late, but within tolerable limits."

Finn answered, listened, then pressed the disconnect button. "Cherry says the deal is done. The ladies and Sailor-boy went to the barn."

Gary stared at the remnants of hickory logs smoldering in the fieldstone fireplace. "And they found Tommy's ranch file?"

"According to Cherry, they stayed less than ten minutes. The chief drove out and checked once the ladies and the admiral left. The file was gone."

"Glad that's over," Gary said. "Now I've satisfied my end of the bargain."

He took a sip of cognac and looked at Danny Finn. Gary knew the Irishman was too respectful to ask why they hadn't just handed the file to the admiral. Of course, he hadn't ordered the direct transfer because he hadn't wanted to lie or tip his hand.

Gary had begun developing his own plan on Christmas night. After he'd stopped taping the call and went off the record, Miss Patricia had presented a large wish list. At first, he wondered why most of her queries seemed to concentrate on Joanna Gaylani and not Tommy Kempner's murderer. Later, after Finn had told him about the young man who dressed like a stablehand but talked like a professor, he'd realized Miss Patricia's questions pointed in a disturbing direction.

"Think back, Danny. Do you remember who asked us if Chuck Sweet had rented an oversized panel truck with a plow?"

"Sure, boss. Miss Shaver couldn't have been more emphatic."

The snifter warmed in Gary's palm. "Do you also recall how we got the answer?"

"You called Sean O'Banyon," the Irishman replied. "Told him to work with the warehouse bean counters and computer nerds until they got a line on it. Sean's the man when you're looking for a vehicle with stiff shocks and more than four wheels."

Gary swirled his brandy and smelled the bouquet. "When O'Ban-yon sent us a copy of the U-Haul lease agreement, did that confirm what Miss Patricia must have suspected?"

"No question," Finn answered. "It gave us proof someone using Doc Gaylani's driver's license rented the truck."

"Yes," he agreed, "but the truck was never driven to the doc-tor's address."

"Right again," Finn said. "That's when our long-range surveil-lance team made an important discovery. Not only had Chuck Sweet parked the truck in a garage on Lawrence Magel's horse farm, but he'd gotten a beauty makeover too. Christ, Boss, with his new hair-cut and dye-job, he could pass for that sawbones Gaylani."

Gary took another sip of brandy. "My suspicions were aroused the moment you told me the son of a fanatical Zionist had forgone the good life to work three years as a stablehand."

"I may have supplied the info," Finn replied, "but you spotted the red flag."

"And that flag got redder when you indicated the same bright young man rented a panel truck on the eve of a national UJC Con-vention. From then on, everything pointed in one direction. Nowa-days, a bomb is the terrorist's weapon of choice."

Finn nodded. "That old Jew, Magel, may be rich and well-dressed, but he's still fighting the first Arab-Israeli War. Shit, it's no wonder some of his ideas rubbed off on his niece and son. Still, not everyone who uses an alias and rents a truck plans to blow up a con-vention of Jews."

"In that regard, we owe Mrs. Eichler an assist," Gary said, nod-ding toward the hickory logs stacked in an open compartment on one side of the hearth

"Really?" Finn replied, adding wood to the fire. "How'd she help?"

"Mrs. Eichler signaled us," Gary answered, watching sparks burst up the chimney. "Once the sanitation crew brought Tommy's office papers to the warehouse, didn't our analyst make note of two file folders?"

"Yep. The Kempner/ Weiss folder was empty. Totally gutted. The other one… The folder full of Kempner's ranch bills was slightly pulled up and slanted, as though shoved back in a hurry."

Gary swirled his cognac. "When I checked a schematic of what was found where, something else caught my attention. The Kempner/Weiss folder came from Tommy's desk drawer. The ranch invoices were stashed in a free-standing cabinet located some distance away. Since Miss Patricia grabbed the message machine cassette, I assumed she went through the desk."

"Fine," Finn agreed, "while she rifled Kempner's drawers, Grandma was elsewhere. What's the big deal?"

"Isn't it obvious?" Gary asked. "The ever-alert Mrs. Eichler must have noticed Tommy was buying a like amount of ammonium nitrate from another supplier at the same time she was delivering the identical product via her deal with Joanna Gaylani."

"Jesus," Finn said, "how'd you come to that conclusion?"

"Since Mrs. Eichler found Tommy's ranch invoices interesting, I got interested too."

"You've always been a curious man, but in this case I don't see the relevance."

"Really quite elementary," he replied. "When our people analyzed the invoices, they noted a conspicuous lack of horse fodder. Tommy paid all sorts of bills, including the ones for the ammonium nitrate, but never any for hay and oats."

"Why do I feel like the straight man?" Finn asked. "Horses eat hay and oats. If your lawyer forgot to feed them, they'd be anorexic."

"But they didn't starve, because three years ago Joanna Gaylani adopted the good neighbor policy. As a thank-you, she began buying ranch supplies from Mrs. Eichler."

"So that's how the ammonium nitrate got doubled up?"

"Yes," he answered, "a simple, but ingenious plan."

"No offense, boss, but how'd you unravel that riddle?"

"I called Mrs. Eichler's delivery man," Gary replied, setting his snifter on the lamp table. "When I identified myself as a potential customer referred by Joanna Gaylani, the man told me everything I wanted to know."

"Speaking of tell-alls," Finn said. "How come you didn't clue in the journalist about Chuck Sweet and the rented truck?"

"For the same reason our friend Miss Patricia conveniently forgot to inform us about Joanna Gaylani's plan to stockpile ammonium nitrate."

Gary recalled their phone conversation. During that negotiation, Miss Patricia asked if Chief Cherrigan had confiscated Tommy's office files and, if so, could the ranch invoices be included amongst the items displayed for the admiral.

"Think about it," he said. "Before anyone could prove a planned conspiracy, we needed a way to tie Chuck Sweet to a truck rental and into Lawrence Magel's organization as well."

"You amaze me, boss. At the time, I wondered why you placed so much importance on Miss Shaver and Mrs. Eichler's Christmas night horseback ride. Now I get it. You and the journalist were approaching the same problem from different angles. Even if she didn't realize that Larry Magel and Chuck Sweet were father and son, sure as shit, she knew Joanna Gaylani and Chuckie-boy were stockpiling bomb-making fertilizer."

For a second, Finn smiled, self-satisfied. The he suddenly sat up ramrod straight.

"Jesus fucking Christ! Now something else makes sense."

"I'm not following you, Danny."

"This evening, while we were arranging the display on Kempner's desk, the journalist called my attention to some activity at your lawyer's barn."

"What kind of activity?"

"A guy driving a panel truck with a plow backed his vehicle into the barn. Shit, boss, I even commented that it looked like he was getting ready to load it up."

Gary nodded. "A very insightful observation. It seems our friend Miss Patricia wanted to make sure we didn't miss a thing."

The Irishman lowered his eyes. "With all due respect, boss, if you already knew that Joanna Gaylani was stashing fertilizer and ammonium nitrate in your lawyer's barn, why didn't we give her copies of Kempner's ranch invoices? If you combine the ranch file with Mrs. Eichler's bills, even a moron like Sailor-boy would put two and two together."

He decided to hold off answering. When the Irishman's body stiffened a few seconds later, Gary knew his test had worked. Finn had just figured out that Miss Patricia was not only beautiful and clever, but devious too.

"Stop the damn music," the Irishman barked. "Did our friend the journalist ever show us the invoices Mrs. Eichler billed to Joanna Gaylani?"

Gary shook his head. "Miss Patricia probably forgot to give me a copy, but I'm guessing she left one on Tommy's desk."

"Don't think so, boss," Finn replied. "I watched her arrange the stuff. Those invoices weren't there."

"Remember the manila envelope entitled Kempner/Weiss?"

"Sure," Finn answered. "She had it in the duffel bag when we met her in the funeral parlor parking lot. The original was for you and the copy was for Kempner's desk."

"By any chance, did you thumb through it after she put it on Tommy's desk?"

When the Irishman got beet red, Gary held his snifter up to the light to check for clarity.

"Don't worry. Things worked out just as I'd hoped. I wanted the admiral to figure things out on my timetable. If both sets of ranch invoices had been put together, it would have made my life more complicated."

"Boss, you're losing me."

"It's straightforward, Danny. Before I played fairy godmother and delivered the ranch invoices, I had to be sure Miss Patricia had been neutralized."

"Neutralized?" Finn asked. "Didn't you give her permission to clarify things for the admiral?"

"I did."

"Then what am I missing?" Finn sat back and stared at the ceiling. "When you held back Tom Kempner's ranch file, you also left Miss Shaver with only one option. To convince Sailor-boy of Joanna Gaylani's involvement, the journalist would have to show him where the fertilizer was hidden."

"Right again."

"But, boss. It wasn't there! She and I saw a truck leave the barn. She had to reckon Chuck Sweet had moved the stuff out."

"Correct," Gary said. "You're very perceptive."

"Then why do I feel so stupid?"

"Think about it, Danny. At that point, I'd neutralized her."

"But not for long. Once they got to the barn and found the invoices, Miss Shaver was off the hook."

"With the admiral and Mrs. Eichler," Gary replied, "but not with me."

"You're doing this on purpose… right, boss?"

"Doing what?"

"If you're on the level, I need to switch gears." The Irishman's face grew puzzled. "Once I give you my Dick and Jane version, you'll understand why I'm so confused."

He nodded and Finn continued.

"You knew Cherrigan had been out to the barn and, per your instructions, left copies of the invoices. You knew that the second Sailor-boy saw Tom Kempner's ranch file, he'd buy into the bomb theory. You also knew that about now, Miss Shaver would wise up and realize you'd figured out the double-order business."

Gary silently agreed and again motioned for Finn to continue.

"Jesus, boss. What am I missing? Why hold the ranch invoices in abeyance, then a few hours later, have Cherrigan set them out in plain view? To me, that's a crazy way to neutralize somebody."

"You might be correct," he said, shrugging, "but I'm not in the habit of telling boldfaced lies. I told Miss Patricia I'd make Tommy's invoices available, and so I did."

"Fine, boss. But if you planned to make it available all along, why not give it to her when you met in the limo?"

"Call it a horse trade," he said. "She knew I wanted to monitor Admiral Weiss's activities. Temporarily holding back the invoices forced her to cut me some slack. Remember, she had Mrs. Eichler to consider. Her friend believes in law and order."

"Boss, we believe in law and order too." Finn grinned. "Once you lay down the law, everyone follows your orders."

"Now, Danny," he cautioned, "let's not be hasty. In a perfect world, Mrs. Eichler's position on crime is correct."

"Who wrote *Utopia*?" Finn asked. "Milton or Dante?"

"Sir Thomas More authored *Utopia*," Gary answered, thinking it unlikely the Irishman had picked those writers at random. "But that's an unnecessary detail. Now that Tommy's file has been discovered, my conscience is clear."

"What if Miss Shaver blows the whistle?" Finn asked. "She has to know you're responsible for getting that file out to the barn."

"There's a risk she won't take credit for planting it, but it's one I'm willing to take."

Gary held his snifter toward the hearth and stared through the curved crystal globe. He'd stretched his code of conduct to the limit, but he'd still played within the rules. Once Miss Patricia had accepted the stipulation that he'd deliver the ranch bills to the admiral… once she hadn't demanded the invoices be part of the stash placed on Tommy Kempner's desk… she'd left herself with no bargaining chips and had been neutralized.

As firelight lit up his cognac and made it shimmer, Gary recalled being surprised that Miss Patricia hadn't made an issue of his demand to stay involved and keep tabs on the admiral. He knew she required his help, but she had cards to play too. She had to realize that he not only wanted the cassette, but desperately needed to get his hands on the Kempner/Weiss file.

Whatever her motive, he was certain his skill as a negotiator wasn't the only reason she hadn't pressed her advantage. No. She'd let him off easy. Too easy. Unless…?

Gary chuckled. Was it possible they shared similar philosophies? Could she have given him extra latitude to insure that the Gaylanis didn't escape through a legal loophole?

"Hear me out, boss," Finn said, leaning forward. "Even if Miss Shaver has reason to take the bows, my gut says she won't."

"Forget your gut," Gary warned. "We have logistics working in our favor."

All at once, Gary sensed he had a lot more than logistics abetting his cause. That bright young lady, Miss Patricia, was a pragmatist. She knew the doctor and his wife were guilty and was ready to let the ends justify the means.

He looked at Danny Finn and held back a smile. Why hadn't Maria conceived a bright, beautiful baby girl? Instead of grooming his son, G.T., he could have taught her the Family business.

"As I said, Miss Patricia will take the credit for putting Tommy Kempner's ranch file in the barn. Don't forget that the admiral knows you and she were in the vicinity earlier this evening. That puts her in a slight bind. When the discovery occurs, both Admiral Weiss and Mrs. Eichler will conclude that you two put it there."

"But boss," the Irishman said, "how does that neutralize her?"

"Simple," Gary answered. "If she reneges and says we're responsible, Mrs. Eichler might think our interest in law and order is greater than Miss Patricia's."

"Sailor-boy would have a cow too," the Irishman agreed, laughing. "Wouldn't that be a pisser? After the deputy director and Mrs. Eichler screamed at Miss Shaver for holding out, they'd stand back and give us high marks for saving the day."

"I'd like to be the white knight," Gary said, "but for all concerned, it's better if Admiral Weiss thinks we've been forthright in helping solve the case. A quid pro quo, if you will."

"Won't he be mad that you forgot to say something earlier?"

"On the contrary," Gary said, "by not laying the solution out in a humiliating face-to-face session, I've made it clear that all I want is to live and let live."

"But that's not all you want."

"Why, Danny, I was right. You are perceptive." Gary eyed the Irishman and noticed he was frowning. "Something else bothering you?"

"Yes," Finn said. "What if the journalist tells the admiral you're not backing off? That you plan to pursue Family justice?"

"Accusing me of mischief might backfire," Gary cautioned. "Since I've been an honest broker, there's no reason to suspect I have ulterior motives. Besides, Miss Patricia has her friend to consider. It would be dangerous to talk vigilantism in Mrs. Eichler's presence."

Finn stood and picked up the poker. "From your standpoint, the key was making sure they took the admiral to the barn?"

"Getting them there was a calculated risk," he said, "but one where the odds were in my favor."

Gary joined the Irishman on the other side of the hearth.

"Put yourself in their place," he said. "To convince Admiral Weiss that Joanna Gaylani is the mad bomber, they had to offer proof. Mrs. Eichler could produce her records to confirm the purchases Joanna made from her, but when it came to the double order, she could only allege to have seen the duplicate invoices in Tommy's file."

"Right, boss," Finn said. "They were in a bind with few options … but that brings me back to an earlier point. Wouldn't Miss Shaver have to admit seeing a truck leave the barn while she and I put all the stuff on Tom Kempner's desk?"

"I doubt the question ever comes up," Gary replied. "But if it did, Miss Patricia can claim she planted it there on purpose."

"Boss, I'm not good at riddles."

Gary smiled. "She'll say she assumed the admiral saw that the road had been recently plowed… that he would have been curious and investigated it for himself. According to your account, he had to go by the access road on his way to and from the Kempners'."

Gary hesitated a moment, then reached for his snifter.

"Another thing," he said. "I solidified her position by instructing the chief to leave the barn wide open. When I saw the bolt cutter in her duffel bag, I specifically told Cherrigan to snip off any lock that might be on the door. That potentially gave her additional ammo. Admiral Weiss is clever. Earlier this evening at the funeral parlor, he would have watched Miss Patricia toss the duffel bag into the back seat of my limo. When he arrived at her home, his curiosity had to be piqued. If he got into her duffel and saw bolt cutters, the admiral would assume they were used to unlock Tommy Kempner's barn."

Gary took a sip. Since the Irishman seemed absorbed in his explanation, he went on.

"All along, I wanted to create an atmosphere where the admiral could judge for himself whether he thought Miss Patricia and Mrs. Eichler were being forthright and honest."

"I'm impressed," Finn said. "Once you got involved, the Gaylanis didn't stand a chance. Now it looks like the admiral and our female buddies are dancing to your tune too."

"I didn't do anything special. Most anyone could have put my plan in motion."

Gary walked toward the bathroom.

"Give me a moment to freshen up. There's another matter we need to discuss."

CHAPTER THIRTY–SIX

Patricia Shaver's mind was whirling. She and Ellen said good-bye to Admiral Weiss, then started driving back toward Honey Lake. Pat tried to figure out the ramifications of Gary Barbera's ploy, but as she listened to Ellen go on and on about the way events had played out, she found it difficult to concentrate.

Yes, she was happy the admiral was up to speed. But she couldn't shake a growing anxiety. Why would the gentleman don go to such extremes? He'd promised to get the file to Admiral Weiss, but after Barbera had bested her in the negotiation, why not give the ranch bills to Danny Finn and ask him to leave them on Tom Kempner's desk?

Ellen parked near the front porch and got out. Pat opened the passenger-side door but stayed seated. She kept thinking about the book *Men Are from Mars, Women Are from Venus*.

Maybe that was the way to describe how she and Gary Barbera interacted. As members of the opposite sex, they behaved differently and thought differently. Given those parameters, how could they take the same set of facts and arrive at the same conclusion?

She closed her eyes, heartened by one thing. So far her plan was still on track. She knew Ellie abhorred the idea, but in this case, the ends did justify the means.

"End of the road, Patricia." Her friend walked to the front of her Ford SUV and leaned against the warm hood. "The choice is yours. Either spend the night in my car, or go inside and get warm."

Pat glanced through the windshield, then slid out without commenting. Once through the front door, she and Ellen greeted the dogs.

"Talk about a roller coaster ride," Pat said, her mind still in space. "Maybe after tomorrow, this thing will be over."

"I hope so,"her friend agreed. "But if it isn't, the CIA will have no one to blame but themselves."

Ellen draped her sheepskin over one of the chairs by the maple table, then sat down on a stool at the L-shaped counter. "On a personal note, I owe you an apology."

"Don't be silly." Pat replied. "We're a team."

"Maybe so, but this time you carried the load." Ellen reached for the coffee pot and filled a couple of mugs. "Leaving the duffel bag out in plain view was smart. Letting the admiral find the bolt cutter and lock was masterful. But getting Barbera to let you leave the invoices in the barn… that, Patricia, was off the charts. Frankly, I'm ashamed for doubting your sincerity."

Pat wrapped her hands around the warm coffee mug, continuing to worry about Gary Barbera's motives. Had he delayed the delivery of the ranch invoices just to buy a little time, or did he have a more sinister reason? "I hope you weren't too embarrassed."

Ellen shook her head. "Not telling us about the empty fertilizer bin was a stroke of genius too. Admiral Weiss saw my mouth drop. He knew I was shocked, but he also realized everything else was exactly as I'd described. If he had any doubts, they disappeared."

Pat's stomach tightened. Had she just figured out the gentleman don's intention? Granted, she'd held out on Barbera, but look what he'd done to her. By letting her leave Tom's file, he'd made it impossible for her to blow the whistle or speculate on his future plans. Her leverage was gone. Going forward, she'd be in the dark.

Ellen took a sip of coffee, looked at her watch, then headed for the front door.

"Got to go. Pick you up tomorrow… say a half hour before Tommy's service?"

Pat wanted to stop the charade and tell Ellen the truth, but when she opened her mouth, a new wave of heartburn singed her throat. As things stood, the admiral finally had all the pieces to the puzzle. But was that enough?

Admiral Eric Weiss drove toward Chicago, a cell phone held to his ear.

"Maynard… call Eichman and Haider. I want the three of you to meet me at the Conrad Hilton."

Eric felt great. Finally he realized how Joanna Gaylani had collected enough ammonium nitrate to make a powerful bomb. Finally he understood why Joanna had renounced her allegiance to Lawrence Magel and his organization, All Alone. Finally, he'd figured out Joanna's motive. The renegade Zionist and terrorist had joined the United Jewish Congress so she could bring their convention to Chicago and bomb their delegates.

Of course, he wouldn't let it happen. His strategy would be straightforward and foolproof. He'd commandeer a cadre of plainclothes cops from the Chicago Police Department. They would spend the rest of the night going through the Conrad Hilton with bomb-sniffing dogs. If Joanna's explosive was already on the premises, he'd find it and defuse it. At the same time, he'd have another group of administrative police call every trucking firm in the area. One way or another, he'd locate whoever had rented an oversized panel truck with a plow.

He suspected the hotel sweep would come up empty. If true, tomorrow morning he'd dress a legion of cops as parking attendants, baggage handlers, receptionists, waiters, and barmen. Nobody but authorized personnel and registered guests would be allowed in the hotel. Every vehicle, especially trucks, would be checked. Nothing would enter the parking facilities or stop in the turnarounds and side streets.

Eric tried to concentrate on the road, but his thoughts kept zeroing in on the glory of apprehending Joanna and her tight-knit group of conspirators. He drove on, the Sears Tower guiding him like a lighthouse.

There were moments when he'd doubted the efficacy of his tactics. But now he'd been vindicated. The Kempners hadn't died in vain. They were victims in his battle to rid the world of terrorists.

The admiral pushed the accelerator to the floor, fantasizing himself a vigilante rushing down the highway to save mankind. The speedometer kept moving. Seventy-five… eighty… and higher. Nothing was beyond his grasp.

Then his cell phone rang.

"For Christ's sake, Maynard. Why are you calling? Weren't my orders clear?"

He listened, his speed dropping as his agent spoke of Dr. Tony Gaylani's latest indiscretion.

"Cut the bullshit, buddy-boy, and play the tape. Let the doctor and Andy Douglas hang themselves."

Danny Finn stood in the library facing the fireplace. As he waited for the boss to return, he looked up at the mantel, cluttered with photos and keepsakes from Sicily and Tuscany.

There was irony here, the kind he read about in his classic books. His wife and daughter had died in a mob hit, but he was welcome in the old Irish neighborhood and often dined with his in-laws. Why, he wondered, was the boss—the don of the Chicago Mafia—snubbed by his friends and relatives?

Were the people back in Palermo jealous of the financial success the boss and his father had enjoyed? Or maybe it was about marriage and family. He and the boss were each devoted to his spouse and child. But there was a difference. He'd loved his daughter and wife more than life itself. The boss felt differently. The gentleman don could distance himself from that emotion.

As the Irishman saw it, Gary Barbera protected his son, nothing more. As for his wife… Well, the boss made all the right moves. He remembered her birthday and their anniversary, but always without passion. That was the key word. Gary Barbera didn't blame Maria for their loveless union, and he was always very discreet.

Hawaii was a case in point. Whenever they traveled to the Big Island, the boss asked him to book the appointments. Gary Barbera was always very specific. He allotted time for business and time for Jane. Danny knew because when everything was settled, he called the boss's longtime lover and gave her Gary Barbera's schedule.

Danny heard footsteps in the hallway. He turned away from the mantel and greeted the boss as he walked back in the room.

"I'm ready, Danny. Let's get started."

Gary Barbera sat in his wingback chair, quiet and seemingly at ease. During times of stress and crisis, his demeanor never changed. The Irishman knew the drill. Their exchange would be short, and to an outsider, violent and ugly. From experience, he knew that once the justifications had been aired, Gary Barbera would issue his commands.

"About tomorrow," the boss said, picking up his snifter and joining him at the hearth. "If at all possible, I want you and Sean O'Banyon to inflict the utmost pain on our enemy. But when you send my personal regards, always remember that we're members of the community and want to protect our good name."

Danny's orders were cold and clear. The boss wished to leave a bloody imprint, but as a businessman, he understood how to operate in the public domain. Mobsters could slaughter each other as long as no private citizen was harmed.

As always, Danny would minimize the risk of publicity by shielding the innocent. Only the Gaylanis and Sweet would receive Family justice.

He made eye contact with his Godfather. "Count on me. We'll be very careful."

"Of course you will, but in case Chuck Sweet does the unexpected, have you picked a site to revoke his driver's license?"

Danny nodded. Under no circumstances could the bomb-laden truck get anywhere near a populated area. If Chuck Sweet turned and started heading away from the Gaylanis' home, his truck would be surrounded and Sweet would be shot.

"I've visited several stretches of uninhabited road along his probable route. There will be opportunities to stop him."

The boss nodded approval. "That covers everything except the call to Admiral Weiss. If you don't mind, I'll ask you to give him my wish list. All this excitement has made me sleepy."

Danny said good night, then watched Gary Barbera leave the library. For a moment he stood still, marveling at the gentleman don's style. Yet again, Gary Barbera had stayed true to his code of conduct. But that was only part of his ingenious plan. Once the boss made sure he'd kept his word to all concerned, the man went forward with a lethal strategy that allowed him to bend the CIA to his will.

"Oh, Danny?" The boss stopped midway up the staircase. "After you speak with the admiral, don't stay up too late. I want you fresh for tomorrow morning."

He waved from the library entrance. "Got my word, boss."

Finally alone, the Irishman walked back to a table near the fireplace and picked up the phone. In preparation for the morning mobilization, he called five of his most trusted lieutenants. To each he issued a twofold command: *Meet me at the warehouse within the hour. By then I want each one of you to have called your best soldiers. The boss wants ten armed carloads of men available at 8 AM tomorrow morning.*

Danny knew that the Warehouse—a suburban structure located inside a twenty-acre fenced-in site—was the correct staging point for tonight's meeting and tomorrow's mobilization. The Warehouse was more than an office building and storage facility for trucks, bulldozers, graders and other heavy equipment necessary to run Holly Corporation, the boss's giant construction company. Below the area where architects drew plans was Gary Barbera's underground computer center—a hidden complex of conference rooms and offices where a few skilled analysts kept track of the Family's business interests and monitored intelligence information from informants.

Danny Finn arrived at the Warehouse around one AM. After being waved through the gates, he drove behind a heavy-equipment garage. Once inside, he took an elevator to the lowest of the underground floors.

The five lieutenants arrived shortly thereafter. The men were dressed like suburban commuters, their faces quiet and benign. They had been roused on a post-holiday night, but none complained. They sat around a table, awaiting instructions.

Danny didn't stand on ceremony. He placed an enlarged road map on an easel, then outlined Gary Barbera's basic plan. Using a pointer, he indicated how the cars would be positioned on all of the several streets Chuck Sweet might use as a route.

As Danny demonstrated how they would follow the fertilizer truck once it began to move, he prayed Chuck Sweet would drive toward the Gaylanis'. The boss had assumed Joanna Gaylani would want Sweet to come by her house after she and Tony left for the funeral. In that scenario, Sweet would park the truck in the Gaylanis' garage and wait for Joanna's return with her husband. According to the boss's theory, any woman as dedicated as Joanna Gaylani couldn't pass up being a part of the final act.

Danny thought Gary Barbera had it figured to a tee. But he also knew that nobody had perfect foresight. And that wasn't the only danger. Danny knew that the best of plans didn't always play out as they appeared on the drawing board.

To cover the unexpected, he continued his briefing with a contingency agenda. If, for some reason, Chuck Sweet veered away from the Gaylanis' house and turned his truck toward Chicago, Danny told the lieutenants to fake a fender bender on an isolated stretch of the road and then summarily execute the young terrorist as he slowed to get around the blocked lane. The Irishman knew that machine-gunning Chuck Sweet in broad daylight wasn't the cleanest hit, but the boss had been emphatic: *If you can't do Joanna and her stableman together, do them separately.*

CHAPTER THIRTY-SEVEN

Admiral Eric Weiss spent a long night conferring with high-ranking members of the FBI and the Chicago Police Department. With their plan in place, he called a second meeting.

The morning sun slanted into the living room of his suite at the Conrad Hilton as he briefed his agents with last minute details. Donald Haider, Rick Eichman, and D. Maynard would facilitate communications between himself and the other law enforcement agencies under his command.

Eric dismissed his men, confident he had anticipated every contingency. If all went well, he—and only he—would stand in front of the media and tell the country how the CIA had thwarted a dangerous terrorist plot.

Alone in his suite, Eric strutted into the bathroom. After showering and shaving, he donned his Navy blues. Feeling like a man in control of his destiny, he went into the closet and pulled out his large roller-type suitcase. For a moment he hesitated. Then he reached inside and grabbed a small leather tab. When the false bottom opened, he took out his old Navy .45 and a couple of extra clips of ammo.

He set out for Barrington and Tom Kempner's funeral at 8 AM. Less than an hour later, he drove into the village and followed Main Street to the top of the highest hill in the township. Then he turned right and drove past a larger-than-life statue of Jesus—the unofficial marker of the grounds surrounding St. Mark's Episcopal Church.

The parking lot was U-shaped, the spaces running along the

sides and back of the church. Since Eric wanted to be seen, he avoided the lot and pulled up in the sweeping circular turnaround in front of St. Mark's.

The attendant checked his clipboard, but before the man could wave him off, Eric flashed his credentials. The uniformed attendant seemed unimpressed, but did walk down to the end of the reserved spaces and move a couple of orange cones.

Irritated he'd been relegated to a spot more than a hundred feet from the church entrance, Eric decided to make himself conspicuous. Rather than park alongside the curb, he backed the dinged-up Chevy Blazer perpendicular to it.

Feeling chilled, he pushed the temperature lever to maximum and turned the blower on high. Seconds later, as tepid air filled the inside of the Blazer, a hearse drove up. To get a better look, Eric wiped condensation from the inside of the passenger side window.

Off to the right, three members of the funeral parlor staff struggled with Tom Kempner's casket. As they carried the dead mob attorney up the wide steps leading to the Episcopal church, Eric balled one of his gloved hands into a fist. *Keep it together, damn it, this is your big moment.*

When the casket disappeared behind the elegant doors with the stained-glass inlays, he closed his eyes. Eric hadn't slept, but he wasn't tired. Adrenaline invigorated him. And why not? His meticulous plans to protect the UJC conventioneers had been carried out to the letter. A sizable force of plainclothes cops had probed the building, parking lots, and streets surrounding the hotel with a diligence the likes of which no Windy City innkeeper had ever witnessed.

During last night's operation he'd sat in the Conrad Hilton's finest penthouse suite—dubbed Command Headquarters—and directed the FBI to intensify their hunt for Chuck Sweet and the panel truck with a plow. He wanted that truck. But he'd also been relieved when the all-night search came up empty. High on his list of priorities was to nail Joanna Gaylani in the act. Not finding the bomb truck had reinforced his belief that she would personally launch her attack to coincide with the opening of the United Jewish Congress Convention.

Eric adjusted his aviation-style sunglasses as the mourners began entering the church. With the hint of a smile creasing his face, he marveled at the audacity of Joanna Gaylani's scheme.

To point the blame at her husband and his Arab comrades, she had to accomplish two things: link Dr. Gaylani to the bomb truck, and establish an alibi for herself. Both could be done if two other things happened: First, Chuck Sweet had to drive over and park the bomb truck in the Gaylanis' garage. Second, Joanna had to fake an illness just before the procession carrying Tom Kempner's casket left the church and headed for the cemetery.

As Eric saw it, Joanna Gaylani would act faint and ask her husband to take her home. Once Dr. Gaylani obliged and they went inside, Chuck Sweet would not only kill him, but make sure the doctor carried lots of ID's—a wallet containing his driver's license and other credit cards.

While Chuck carried Gaylani's body to the truck, sliding it behind the seats in the cab, Joanna would call the UJC president, saying she'd been delayed. Then after parking her husband's SUV in their garage, she'd get into her Mercedes and prepare to leave.

By then, Sweet would be ready to drive downtown too. Having given Joanna a slight head start, he'd follow her to the Conrad Hilton Hotel.

Eric shifted his weight and leaned one arm against the steering wheel. Still engrossed in his analysis, he visualized how the rest of her machination would play out.

When the bomb exploded, Joanna Gaylani would want it to look like her husband had met Allah all by himself. She'd want to stand outside the hotel talking to reporters while Chuck Sweet drove around back into the area reserved for food deliveries. As the television cameras rolled, she'd want to talk about Arab-Israeli peace prospects, waiting for Chuck to park in a bay under the Grand Ballroom. Then after a few more minutes of Q & A—enough time for

Chuck to leave the area and detonate the bomb by remote control—she, along with the other press and media personnel, would react to the muffled sound of a powerful explosion.

That was what Joanna Gaylani wanted, but Admiral Eric Weiss wasn't going to let it happen. No, indeed! Joanna had to be counting on surprise. Homeland Security's color-coded terror alert was at its lowest level. Chicago residents were suffering from arctic blasts, but a bomb threat wasn't on their radar screen.

Given those circumstances, Joanna probably thought a panel truck could drive behind the Hilton without being checked. But even if she painted the side panels with a logo advertising a food company that made daily deliveries to the hotel, surprise would not be Joanna's ally. He'd devised a superb anti-terrorist operation. On this occasion, only she would be surprised.

When the admiral saw Dr. and Mrs. Gaylani walk briskly toward the church and disappear behind the twin doors, he took off his sunglasses and laid them on the dashboard. For a moment, he sat still, gearing up for what lay ahead, but the second he got out and locked the dinged-up Chevy, his stomach tightened. He was a man with an acute sense for political survival, but he worried that an eleventh-hour change in his plan would come back and bite him. Still, what could he do? When Danny Finn had called last night, Eric was out of options. How well he remembered the smug Irishman's bravado.

"Good evening, Admiral. Hope all is well with you."

"Get to the point, Finn. I'm a busy man."

"Precisely why I'm calling. The boss has an idea that may lessen your workload."

"What kind of idea?"

"Pay close attention, Admiral. You won't want to miss a single detail."

Last night, Eric had listened. Then he'd done his best to hammer out a deal that protected him and the Company too. But he wasn't dealing from strength. Gary Barbera still possessed duplicate copies of the damning evidence that had been displayed on Tom Kempner's desk. And that wasn't all. According to Finn, the mobster had more pieces of evidence in his arsenal. If Eric played ball, two documents—both authenticated—would be identified and delivered before the funeral today.

With that kind of firepower pointed at his head, he'd had little choice but to agree with the mobster's pre-sunrise wish list—concessions that Eric thought made a certain amount of sense, and more importantly, only caused a minor logistical headache to his plan to shut down Joanna Gaylani. Still, he'd dealt with Barbera before and realized the old don could be devious.

Eric stayed next to the Chevy Blazer and glanced up at the narrow wooden bell tower. He hated giving up any control, and he knew firsthand that the local jurisdiction took orders from Barbera. But Danny Finn had insisted that as long as Joanna Gaylani stayed in Barrington, only Chief Cherrigan and his deputies could monitor her movements. The Irishman had demanded that the army of law enforcement personnel under CIA command had to stay outside the Barrington village limits.

Finn's arguments had been persuasive. He said his boss wanted Tom Kempner's church service and burial to be a solemn occasion, but more to the issue at hand, Barbera thought Joanna Gaylani would be spooked by any noticeable increase in security. She was a smart woman who lived in an affluent community. Plainclothes cops tried hard, but were given no-frills Ford and Chevy sedans to drive. Another thing. None had any style. The guys looked and acted like they shopped at Wal-Mart. That alone would be a red flag to a person on high alert.

Eric walked along the shoveled walkway. With no clouds to block the sun, he thought about going back and getting his sunglasses, but as his anxiety increased, he realized that protecting his eyes was the least of his concerns. Finn had been direct and persuasive, but Eric couldn't shake the feeling that he'd been duped. Yet each time he went over his plan, he couldn't find a way for Barbera to best him.

Didn't he have state police covering every road out of the Godforsaken town? So what if his men couldn't cross the border? Let Joanna Gaylani ride around and do her thing. The second she and Chuck Sweet set foot out of Barrington, he'd arrest their asses.

He looked up and was amazed by the number of people weaving their way through the parking lot. As Barrington's social elite streamed up the stairs and into the white, wood-sided church, the admiral continued to wonder if Gary Barbera had a secret agenda.

Naturally, the old don wanted revenge; but Eric couldn't imagine Barbera being stupid enough to sneak thugs in to gun down the doctor and his wife. Still, to guarantee that no one got trigger happy, he'd added his own proviso to their negotiated settlement.

He insisted that he be allowed to attend the funeral. His reasoning was straightforward. If he had free run of Barrington, he could keep Dr. and Mrs. Gaylani under surveillance. Should conditions be right, he might even have a chance to introduce himself at the church. It would be a special kick to view his pigeons up close and personal.

When a car door slammed close by, he turned and watched Danny Finn move quickly around the limousine toward the rear curbside door. As he thought about how to maintain contact with the Gaylanis, he also wondered why the Irishman was dressed so casually. Even if Gary Barbera had decided to go into the church without his bodyguard, the old don's fetish for propriety would have demanded that Finn respect the occasion and dress in black.

Eric approached the church doors, his hands balled into tight fists. He was certain Joanna Gaylani's amateurish operation had no chance of succeeding. He'd also been assured by Gary Barbera that the mob wouldn't interfere. But he still couldn't dismiss the final part of the conversation last night with Danny Finn:

"Like the boss said, nobody can stop Chuck Sweet from loading sacks of organic fertilizer and ammonium nitrate into a panel truck. Transporting that kind of stuff isn't a crime."

"I don't recall saying it was," Eric had said. "So do me a favor, Finn. Say something I don't know or say good-bye."

"Just emphasizing why the boss wants to keep law enforcement out of Barrington."

"You're boring me, Finn. Get on with it."

"The boss realizes the CIA has demolitions experts, but he thought it would be useful to point out that until the nitro-methane—racing fuel—is added to the mixture and the detonator is put in place, a panel truck loaded with fertilizer is just a panel truck loaded with fertilizer."

"When did I ask for a chemistry lesson, buddy-boy?"

"Just thinking out loud, Admiral."

"Then talk about something relevant."

"Fine. The boss would like you to listen to the following hypothetical: Why would a prominent Barrington woman want a bomb truck parked in her garage?"

"You disappoint me, buddy-boy. I thought you and your esteemed boss were bright."

"Humor us, Admiral. It's a simple question."

"Then here's a simple answer," he had said. "A prominent Barrington woman wouldn't want a truck parked in her garage unless she intends to frame her husband. Get with the program, Finn. How else will she get Dr. Gaylani's body into the cab?"

"Have I got this right, Admiral? You think Sweet will already be on the premises?"

"Why not?" he had asked. "Chuck Sweet works around the stables, so his presence won't raise any suspicion."

"You're saying Sweet is going to drive the panel truck over before Joanna and her husband arrive home?"

"Jesus Christ, Finn, you Irish are all alike. Even when I connect the dots, you can't see the picture."

"Sorry, Admiral. I'm doing my best… but I need your help."

"Then try this hypothetical: Sweet parks in their garage and waits inside until the Gaylanis arrive. When they come in, he overpowers the doc, drags his dead ass back to the bomb truck, then stuffs him behind the seats."

"Interesting wrinkle, Admiral. The boss thought Sweet would keep the bomb truck hidden until the last minute, but your scenario makes more sense."

"Glad we're on the same page," he'd crowed.

"We are, but please don't tell the boss I sided with you."

"Your secret is safe, buddy-boy. Now, if there's nothing else…"

"Just one footnote. You, the boss, and I do share one wish. Wouldn't it be great if Superman flew into town and saved the citizens of Barrington the cost of a trial?"

With Danny Finn's odd statement fresh in his mind, the admiral stiffened as the old don stepped from his limo. When Gary Barbera stood next to Finn, Eric realized that powerful people surrounded themselves with a small cadre of trusted lieutenants. In that regard, Joanna Gaylani was like the old don. Her group of conspirators had maintained their operational effectiveness by keeping their numbers few. Of course, he was the undisputed champ. When it came to inner-councils, Eric relied on himself.

He wanted to go inside, but knew he had to face Gary Barbera one more time. Last night's agreement had called for the transfer of two documents. While he was certain it was a mere formality, Danny Finn had been insistent: "The boss wants to give you the lease and affidavit. Then he wants to stand outside the church doors and shake your hand."

All well and good, but he still had a big problem. He couldn't get the Superman remark out of his mind.

Gary Barbera stood on the curb next to his limousine. The Irishman was on the other side of the Cadillac, his forearms and elbows leaning on the roof.

"Good luck, boss. Hope Weiss goes for your deal."

"Why wouldn't he?" Gary asked. "If you handled last night's phone call as well as I think, the admiral won't have a choice."

"Followed your instructions to the letter," Finn replied. "Sailor-boy is tough to read, but I know he enjoyed treating me like an imbecile."

"It's humbling," Gary said, "but the best way to dupe a person is to present yourself as the fool. In our business, the end, not the means, is the only thing that matters."

Finn nodded. "Speaking of business, Sean and I need to get our asses in gear."

He watched Finn slide into the driver's seat and close the door. When the black-tinted passenger-side window came down a half inch, Gary bent down.

"Last chance. If either of you two have questions, now's the time to ask."

Dressed in a black suit and overcoat, he rested a gloved hand on the car roof. When no questions were asked, he rapped the hardtop and then rubbed his fingers over a miniature gold-plated replica of a falcon riveted below the door handle.

"Good luck, gentlemen. After the service, I'll hitch a ride to Miss Patricia's."

Eric Weiss stood near the three broad stairs leading to the entrance to St. Mark's. As he watched the old don approach, his stomach got queasy. He wasn't intimidated by Barbera, and he knew how to handle stressful situations, but he still felt on edge.

"Good morning, Admiral. I think this is the first time I've seen you in uniform."

"Cut the small talk, Barbera. What have you got that's so vital to my interests?"

"An insight and two documents," the mobster said.

"An insight?" Eric asked, chuckling. "If it's about Superman, save your breath. That Irishman of yours may be good at some things, but his powers of reason are piss poor."

"I'm surprised," Barbera said. "The man is an avid reader of the classics. He always struck me as quick-witted."

"Dim-witted fits him better," Eric replied, leaning in and squinting. "But he's your hired gun, not your mouthpiece. Go ahead, Barbera. Impress me with one of your insights."

"Actually, it's more of a question. I'm wondering how you plan to nail Mrs. Joanna Gaylani."

Eric was taken aback. "What do you mean?"

"Sorry," Barbera said, "I thought I was being straightforward."

"Then why ask a stupid question?" He glared into the old don's quiet eyes. "I'll *nail* her like I *nail* any other criminal. First I'll assemble a ton of supporting evidence. Then I'll catch Mrs. Gaylani in the act. This case will be a slam-dunk."

"I know you can detain Mrs. Gaylani, but to keep her in custody your evidence needs to be ironclad and admissible."

"Either you've been reading classics with your boy Finn, or this is one of your sick jokes." He snarled, but Barbera didn't blink. "The woman's a terrorist. Remember the receipts? They show how she double ordered ammonium nitrate. Those invoices prove she's going to bomb the UJC Convention."

"Those receipts only prove one thing: Tommy Kempner ordered ammonium nitrate and so did Joanna Gaylani." Barbera continued to look at him, deadpan. "You know she engineered the double order. And I know it. But without some proof she did it with purpose, I doubt if a judge will agree."

Eric's fists curled. For yet another time, the mobster was attempting to toy with him. While not in the mood for games, he didn't like the snide look on Barbera's face and decided to play along.

"You want proof, Barbera? How about the panel truck?"

"Ah, yes, the bomb truck," Barbera said, adjusting his scarf. "The one loaded with organic fertilizer, ammonium nitrate, and nitromethane."

"That's the one. Tell me that doesn't qualify."

"It certainly is incriminating, but as before, it doesn't incriminate Joanna Gaylani."

Rather than scream anew, Eric controlled himself, treading carefully. "How do you figure? By my logic, it implicates her co-conspirator, Chuck Sweet."

"I'm not disagreeing with your logic, Admiral. You and I know

Chuck Sweet rented it. But the hard evidence points the finger at their scapegoat, Dr. Gaylani." Barbera looked away, watching the churchgoers. "Last night, Danny told you I had two additional documents for your file—a lease agreement signed by Dr. Gaylani, and an affidavit signed by the U-Haul employee attesting that a man fitting the description of Dr. Gaylani presented his driver's license and rented the truck in question. These documents prove that neither Joanna Gaylani nor Chuck Sweet rented the panel truck. But don't throw them away. I think you'll find they will be useful."

"I don't give a shit who rented it," Eric snapped. "Only one thing matters. Chuck Sweet will be in the driver's seat when my men pull him over."

"A valid point, Admiral, and when you arrest him, Sweet will be in a bind. But just Sweet. At that moment, Joanna won't be with him. She'll be driving her Mercedes toward the Conrad Hilton Hotel." Barbera grinned ever so slightly. "Tell me, Admiral. Do you plan to surround her car with police cruisers, then drag her out of the front seat and cuff her? How do you justify Rodney King treatment on a woman who's heading downtown to make a speech?"

"Aren't you forgetting one thing?" he asked. "She'll have to explain the disappearance of her husband. When we stop the bomb truck, we'll find Dr. Gaylani's body."

"What's to explain?" Barbera replied, shrugging. "Joanna will just say they left the funeral to go home so her husband could pick up another car and drive to the cemetery. Once she dropped the doctor off at the front door, she headed downtown. It would be news to her if Sweet was waiting inside to murder him."

Eric laughed out loud. "You're saying Chuck Sweet will be a stand-up guy and take the fall? That he'll claim credit for the plot to bomb the UJC Convention?"

"Seems reasonable to me," Barbera said. "Joanna ordered the fertilizer and ammonium nitrate, but Sweet was the one who took delivery and dug the underground cache in the Kempners' barn. He's been living at Lawrence Magel's horse farm in Wayne. Over the last three years, he could have *borrowed* enough bags of organic fertilizer to keep Tommy Kempner's pastures green."

"Your story is preposterous."

"Is it?" Barbera tilted his head. "Lawrence Magel is a Zionist. His organization isn't mainstream. Why couldn't he have thought up this plot and hired Chuck Sweet to carry it out?"

The admiral leered, but in spite of his contemptuous façade, he felt like a man who'd been gutted with a jagged knife. No wonder Barbera had insisted that no law enforcement personnel be in Barrington. Joanna's trip back to her house would be the only time she and Chuck Sweet would be together.

The mobster had set him up. All at once, Danny Finn's Superman remark made sense. Barbera wanted to become the man with the big S on his chest. The Mafia don craved to be the Superman who would save Barrington the cost of a trial.

"Okay, Barbera, you made your point. Where do we go from here?"

"First, take these two documents." The old don handed him an envelope. "Before this is over you'll need them."

"Anything else?"

Barbera nodded. "We should have a little chat."

Eric let his shoulders slump, feigning a man who'd just suffered a catastrophic loss. But he was far from beaten. Barbera might have pointed out a major flaw in his strategy, but there was still time to make a mid-course correction.

The solution came to him after he remembered one of Barbera's statements: *"A valid point, Admiral. When you arrest him, Sweet will be in a bind. But just Sweet. At that point, Joanna won't be with him. She'll be driving her Mercedes toward the Conrad Hilton Hotel."* Then the punk hood had continued: *"Tell me, Admiral. How do you justify Rodney King treatment on a woman who's heading downtown to make a speech?"*

Barbera was right. He couldn't justify Rodney King treatment. Joanna was the ringleader, but she'd covered her tracks. Worse still, once she and Sweet separated, his opportunity to get her vanished.

But what about before they separated? The window was small, but it existed. After the funeral, when Joanna and her husband went back to their house, Sweet would be there too. At that moment, his three pigeons would be together. And they would be vulnerable.

It was too late to call in his law enforcement personnel. Not only was there no place for them to hide, but they'd be in the way. Sure, they could arrest her, but they couldn't make it stick. Under those circumstances, what was the point?

He chuckled to himself. But what if he acted as a lone assassin? Then he didn't have to make it stick. He knew she was guilty. And that wasn't all. He brought a unique quality to the action. He was an experienced attacker. His training as a Navy SEAL made him lethal. And he had something else on his side. He belonged. He wouldn't spook the Gaylanis. He was Tom's old neighborhood buddy. And he was also a part of the funeral congregation.

Eric crafted his plan. He would introduce himself to Joanna and Tony Gaylani. After the service, he'd be sympathetic, but not overly maudlin. He'd probe too. Asking questions and prolonging the conversation would give him a chance to gauge their anxiety. But he wouldn't press too hard. The second they expressed a desire to get on their way, he'd politely say good-bye and head for the Chevy Blazer.

His Navy .45 was hidden under the driver's-side seat. While he waited for the Gaylanis to come out of the church, he'd put the pistol in his overcoat pocket and get the extra clips from the glove compartment.

He knew he could follow them without raising suspicion. He also knew it was unlikely that he'd be able to catch any of them in the middle of a felonious act. But if he couldn't get Joanna by the book, he'd break into her house and disrupt her rendezvous with Chuck Sweet. Maybe he wouldn't have probable cause, but once the shooting began, he'd make sure all the terrorists were taken down.

* * *

Patricia Shaver looked straight ahead. Ellen nodded to the man with the clipboard, then pulled her Explorer inside the reserved area —a spot a couple of cars closer to the church than Admiral Weiss's irregularly parked unmarked Chevy.

As they got out and began walking, Pat was bothered by three things: Gary Barbera and Eric Weiss were standing together near the doors to St. Mark's; Danny Finn was nowhere to be seen; and the gentleman don's limo, FALCON 1, wasn't parked in the reserved area.

"Look at them," Pat said, knowing that something was wrong. "The admiral and the Mafia don acting like they're good friends."

She and Ellen were bundled up and dressed in black. The occasion was solemn, but Pat's thoughts were not on the impending funeral service.

"I wonder what changed?" Ellen asked. "Last night, Mr. Barbera said the admiral would rather be dead than caught publicly in his company."

That's right," Pat replied, "and he meant it too."

She felt a twinge in her stomach. Something crucial had to have happened. The moment she and Ellen approached, Barbera and Weiss had stopped talking. Then, without acknowledging their presence, the admiral tucked an envelope into the breast coat pocket of his Navy overcoat and walked away, his gold braid gleaming in the sun.

Pat wanted to bait him with a snide comment, but she was too late. As he departed, an elegantly-attired woman walked up.

"Ellen, dear," the lady said. "How are you?"

"Oh, hello, Harriet," Ellen greeted Harriet "Lady Harry" O'Banyon, Katherine Kempner's aunt and adopted mother. "It's always nice to see you. I only wish the circumstances were different."

"It's been an unbelievable week, hasn't it?"

Pat watched. A woman she'd never met addressed Ellen, then looked in her direction.

"You must be the young lady Ellen took under her wing. Hello, I'm Harriet O'Banyon."

Pat extended her hand. "Nice to meet you, Mrs. O'Banyon."

"Please, skip the formality. It's Harriet, or better still, Lady Harry."

Gary Barbera sidestepped into the group and bowed slightly.

"Good morning, Mrs. O'Banyon. Your ladyship is looking rather fit."

"Hello, Gar… Hello, Mr. Barbera."

Pat knew Sean O'Banyon and Gary Barbera had business dealings, but was surprised when the gentleman don and Lady Harry responded so warmly to each other. Her surprise continued when Gary Barbera took Harriet O'Banyon's gloved hand and brushed it against his lips.

"Where's that Irish husband of yours? He can't be driving eighteen-wheelers today."

"No," Harriet replied. "Sean was called away unexpectedly."

Dr. Tony Gaylani stood next to his wife Joanna in the foyer of St. Mark's Episcopal Church. As Trevor Kempner's godparents, they acted as greeters, often speaking briefly to the mourners before directing them toward the ushers.

"Holding up okay?" Tony asked, leaning over and whispering to his ashen-faced wife. "You look a little shaky."

"I'll be fine, darling. Just a bit nauseous." Joanna glanced at him, then stared at a man who'd just entered the church. "Who's the man with the gold braid?"

Tony took a very long look. Could the Navy admiral be one of the guys Chief Cherrigan had escorted from Tom Kempner's house?

"Don't have a clue. Never seen him before."

"Maybe it's someone from Tom's Vietnam days?"

"Not likely," Tony answered. "See the stripes and a star? A flag officer wouldn't be an infantryman's cup of tea."

He gave the man a closer look. His build was the same as one of the intruder's, but from his vantage point in the bedroom alcove Tony had only seen the lower part of their faces. Both home invaders had been wearing hooded parkas when Chief Cherrigan marched them out at gunpoint. Still, as his survival instincts kicked in, Tony wondered why a Navy admiral had made a conspicuous appearance. For that matter, he also wondered about his wife. Her pasty color bespoke more of a person about to vomit than one in grief.

"Joanna. Are you sure you're feeling all right?"

"Maybe a little light-headed," she replied, squeezing his hand. "First Kitty, now Tom. Coming so close to our convention, it's unnerved me."

CHAPTER THIRTY–EIGHT

Chief Carlton Cherrigan had been briefed and knew his role. In accordance with Danny Finn's instructions, the chief wheeled his Barrington squad car into St Mark's parking lot, timing his arrival to coincide with the halfway point in Tom Kempner's funeral service.

He pulled up just past the front of Admiral Eric Weiss's dinged-up Chevy. After unfastening his seatbelt, he picked up the radio transmitter with one hand and grabbed a Dunkin Donuts doughnut with the other.

"Iverson! Hughes!" he barked. "Ask questions now. Once the show begins, I won't tolerate any mistakes."

"In position, Chief," Officer Matt Hughes answered. "If that panel truck comes by, there's no way I'll miss it."

"What about you, Iverson?"

"Ditto, Chief," Sergeant Dick Iverson responded. "I'm in a sheltered spot off the road not far from the Gaylanis' residence. Nobody can see me, but I have a great view of the garage."

"Well done, boys," Cherry said, dunking a doughnut in his coffee mug. "Sit tight, and remember... when a black limo comes by and parks at Kempner's, pay it no mind. The men inside are part of a security detail I sent to protect the house during the funeral service and burial."

Danny Finn turned the boss's limo onto Oak Knoll Road. He and Sean O'Banyon rode in silence. The trip from St. Mark's to Tom

Kempner's house was short. Had this been any other occasion, the two friends would have had a spirited conversation. But this was not any other occasion.

"We're here," Danny said, stopping the limo in the open-air carport. "Let's go."

Sean O'Banyon got out and stretched. He was ruggedly handsome, with freckles and silver-gray hair. He was also taller, older, and heavier than Danny Finn.

"Quite an operation. First we pack snowshoes, now we park in an igloo. What gives?"

"O'Banyon, try something unusual. Be patient." Danny opened a rear passenger door and tossed out two sets of snowshoes. "Here. Put these on."

"Are you kidding?" Sean replied. "I'll fall flat on my face."

"You're an old dog. Learn a new trick." Danny bent down and buckled on one of his snowshoes. "Watch me and do the same."

"Who taught you the ropes… Nanook of the North?"

Danny looked up. "I learned snowshoeing from a lady."

He waited for one of O'Banyon's wisecracks. When none came, Danny reached into the duffel, grabbed two cell phones, and shoved them into his parka pockets. With his primary and back-up instruments in hand, he checked over the UZI-SMG's. Satisfied the two automatic weapons were fully loaded and had the safeties engaged, Danny put them in a knapsack along with a magnetized rectangular box equipped with a timer dial.

"How you doing, Sean?"

O'Banyon took a few steps, then almost fell down.

"This is hard work," he said, regaining his balance, "and not something a lady would do."

"How would you know?" Danny asked, motioning him with his arm.

"I get around, and I've seen plenty of ladies… but none have ever worn snowshoes."

Danny looked over his shoulder, noting that O'Banyon followed, his forehead sweaty. "Take it from me, the lady who taught me how to walk on snow is all woman."

"You going soft on me?" O'Banyon asked, pulling even with Danny. "Sounds like you got a case of the touchy-feelies."

Danny felt his face flush, but before he could react, one of his cell phones rang. He answered, listened without talking, and hung up.

"Let's go. Chuck Sweet has left Lawrence Magel's horse farm and is moving in our direction. If he's headed for the Gaylanis', we need to get there before he does."

Danny guided O'Banyon over a snow-packed trail he'd helped forge some twelve hours before. As he strode ahead, Danny wondered whether the duct tape he'd used to seal the Gaylanis' basement window had held.

"Hey, Danny. Did they say whether Sweet was headed toward us?"

Danny looked back. "Yeah, but there's time for him to change course. He's still a few miles away."

"Here's hoping the son of a bitch comes calling." Condensed air came from O'Banyon's mouth. "Remember the boss's promise. Alone or with others, I get to do the honors."

"No problem. I'll soften them up, you put them away."

Joanna Gaylani listened to the Episcopal priest's closing prayer. Tom Kempner's church service was over. Her act was about to commence.

As the recessional began, Joanna clung to Tony's arm. She hoped the pill she'd taken would keep her facial pallor white and make her look sick.

"I feel awful," she said, leaning against her husband.

"You've been under enormous pressure," Tony replied. "The funerals, now a speech. It's a wonder you're functioning at all."

"Oh, my God, the speech!" She squeezed his upper arm with both her hands. "I forgot my notes. I left them at home."

"No problem, dear," he said. "I planned to drive you to the hotel. We'll just make a short detour and pick them up along the way."

Danny Finn arrived at the back side of the Gaylanis' house. He'd undone his snowshoes and stepped into the window well by the time a red-faced and panting Sean O'Banyon clumped across the snow.

"Glad you finally got here," Danny said. "The next part should be easier. In fact, think of it as follow the leader."

He pulled the duct tape off the metal frame, then pushed the casement open and lifted it off the swivel hinge. Using his left hand and arm to hold the window over the front of his body, Danny twisted through the opening to the basement floor.

O'Banyon tried to follow. He sat down near the edge of the window well and caught his breath. Then he handed Danny their snowshoes and other gear. But when he leaned back and pushed off, he was tilted too far to the left. Sensing his predicament, he tried to compensate. It didn't work. Instead of hitting the basement floor with both feet, he landed off balance. Then he fell on his ass.

"Nice landing," Danny said, grinning. "A man with your agility should take up gymnastics."

O'Banyon got to his feet, rubbing his backside. "My entrance may have been clumsy, but your lady friend is to be congratulated. Figuring this out took lots of smarts."

Danny ignored the comment and continued to check out the area. Daylight coming through the basement window wells allowed them to move around. But to be safe, he pulled two flashlights from his knapsack and handed one to O'Banyon.

"Never thought I'd say it," Sean said, "but we could use someone with her brains."

Danny nodded agreement. "After this is over, let's write a memo and ask the boss to adopt her and demote his son."

"Great idea," Sean replied, laughing. "We'll call it Operation Snowshoe."

"That suits me," Danny said. "When we type it up for the boss, we'll stress one point. Without Miss Patricia Shaver's insights—"

"Did you say Patricia Shaver?" O'Banyon questioned, his face turning to steel. "The same broad who wrote the article last spring?"

"That's her."

"How is it possible?" Sean asked. "The old man can't be working with her."

"It's a long story and we're in a hurry."

Danny pulled away and began moving toward their entry point, the stairs on the other side of the basement.

"I'm patient," O'Banyon said. "After we're done here, I'll buy the beers. For this explanation, I want to hear every detail."

When O'Banyon started climbing the stairs, Danny restrained him. "Not so fast. Miss Shaver also figured out the Gaylanis' security system. There are sensors on all the outside and interior doors. Until someone with the code gets here and deactivates the system, we have to stay put."

"Jesus, Danny. She got the skinny on the security system too?"

"Told you it was a long story."

Admiral Eric Weiss sat in the last pew at the rear of the church. When the funeral service ended, he left first. After positioning himself near the church entrance, Eric smiled the moment he saw them coming.

"Dr. and Mrs. Gaylani, I'm Eric Weiss."

"How do you do." Joanna nodded, but used both hands to hold onto her husband's arm. "My military knowledge isn't very good. Is it Captain Weiss?"

"It's Admiral… but I'm not a guy stuck on formality." He slowly brought his feet together and, after standing at attention, returned her visual once-over with a clubby smirk. "Please call me Eric."

Joanna, like her husband, seemed more interested in examining his face than making eye contact. He obliged, first giving them a straight-on shot, then turning for a profile.

He was more amused than worried. Last night, when pistol-happy Chief Cherrigan had escorted him and Maynard out the front door, he'd flipped up the hood of his parka and kept his face down. The precautionary move was automatic. The second he'd noticed lights burning on both floors of the Gaylanis' mansion, he realized someone had come home.

"Nice seeing you." Dr. Gaylani extended his hand. "You look familiar. Have we ever met?"

He shook his head. "Doubt it. Tom and I grew up in the same neighborhood, but once we went off to college, we lost touch."

The doctor kept staring, his dark eyes penetrating. "That's probably why Tom never mentioned you."

"Career officers have just one duty," Eric replied. "Our life belongs to the Company."

Dr. Gaylani tensed. "The Company?"

"Sorry," Eric answered. "Chalk it off to a senior moment. I meant to say the country."

He loved playing mind games. In this case, the Iraqi spy had flunked. A skilled agent wouldn't stiffen, telegraphing his tension.

"I'm feeling light-headed," Joanna said, tightening her grip. "We should say good-bye to Trevor and his family."

"Excuse us, Admiral," the doctor said, eyeing him again. "My wife's not feeling very well, and we're on a tight schedule."

"Perfectly understandable," Eric replied, clasping his hands behind his back. "Losing your neighbors in rapid-fire incidents has to be terrible."

"Incidents?" Dr. Gaylani questioned. "I'd characterize Kitty's stroke and Tom's suicide as something other than incidents."

"Sorry, again," he said, bowing his head. "Sometimes I forget everyone isn't in the military."

Gary Barbera stood in the reception area of St Mark's Episcopal Church. When Miss Patricia and Mrs. Eichler approached to express their condolences to Trevor Kempner and his family, he acknowledged the women with a courtly nod. Then he excused himself, and along with most of the mourners, went outside.

The air was clear and crisp, but Gary wasn't cold. He spotted Chief Cherrigan and wasted no time walking over to have a word.

"Any news, Chief?"

"Just got off the horn with Hughes," Cherrigan replied. "Your limo went by his position about twenty-five minutes ago."

"What about the panel truck?"

"Came by later," the chief answered. "When it passed a few minutes ago, Hughes radioed Sergeant Iverson and alerted him."

"Are two officers enough to handle the job?" Gary asked, slipping on black leather gloves.

Cherrigan nodded. "They have both ways in and out of the Gaylanis' under surveillance. Now that the truck's on the scene, they're under strict orders to keep their distance and watch the house through binoculars."

After taking a step closer, Gary put the fingers of his gloved hand inside his overcoat sleeve and rubbed the gold peregrine cufflinks.

"I need more details, Chief. Tell me exactly what your boys saw."

"Well, sir," Cherrigan replied, "when the truck stopped at the Gaylanis' mailbox, the driver retrieved a small package. After proceeding up the driveway and opening the garage door, he pulled the vehicle in and closed things up tighter than a drum."

"Interesting. So far, I've guessed right."

"Yes, sir. You sure knew where to stick my deputies. They've had a bird's-eye view."

Gary watched Miss Patricia and Mrs. Eichler come out of the church. With one more private item to discuss, he put his arm over Cherrigan's shoulder and guided him toward the nearby squad car.

"Order your deputies back to the stationhouse," he said.

"But, Mr. B," the chief replied, "don't you want them to keep up the surveillance?"

"Didn't I make myself clear?" Gary asked, keeping his arm on

Cherrigan's shoulder. "Your men are no longer needed. Get them out of there."

"Yes sir, Mr. B. Anything you say."

"By the way, Danny told me about your secret weapon. The pipe idea is very clever."

Chief Cherrigan had a bounce in his step as he walked back to his patrol car.

Danny Finn listened, waiting. As the Gaylanis' garage door opened with a groaning wail, he nodded. In unison, he and his partner, Sean O'Banyon, cocked their UZI-SMG's.

"It's showtime."

Danny put two fingers across his mouth, signaling silence. When he picked up the sound of the garage door being closed, then heard footsteps walking on the floor above them, Danny knew that Chuck Sweet had disarmed the alarm.

He glanced to Sean, using more hand signals to coordinate their moves. When his partner nodded, they crept up the stairs.

Danny opened the oversized basement door, and the two burst out. By listening to the footsteps on the floor above, Danny had gauged Chuck Sweet's location. That wasn't the only safeguard he'd taken. Just to be sure the terrorist had no escape, he and O'Banyon attacked from both flanks.

Their precise timing hadn't been necessary. Danny came through the door and was on Sweet before the man had a chance to draw a weapon. Backing him against the wall, Danny shoved the barrel of his UZI into the startled young man's chest. When Sean joined them seconds later, Chuck Sweet was disarmed and handcuffed.

"Chuckie-boy, my name is Danny Finn."

He slashed the UZI barrel across Sweet's face. The blow—a surprise to the wide-eyed young man—came with such force that it split his nose wide open and knocked him to the kitchen floor.

"I'd like to introduce Sean O'Banyon," Danny said, looking

down at the bleeding terrorist. "I consider myself lucky to call him a friend. Unfortunately, you'll never share my good fortune."

Danny knelt down and grabbed Sweet's hair. Slowly he pulled his head up until he could see the man's eyes.

"As I was saying… my buddy, Sean, runs a trucking business. In fact, he controls every fat-tire diesel rig in this part of Illinois."

To be sure he had Sweet's undivided attention, Danny used his boot to mule-kick the young man's rib cage.

"Sean tells me you've been very, very careless. In spite of his warnings, you haven't paid attention to the rules."

Chuck Sweet buckled into the fetal position and moaned.

"I asked Sean to give you a second chance, but patience isn't one of my friend's strong suits. Your latest parking violation was the straw that broke the camel's back."

He used the UZI barrel to lift Sweet's chin.

"Any idea how we punish people who are guilty of parking violations?"

When Sweet didn't answer, Danny took a step back. For a second, he saw a look of disbelief on the terrorist's face. But for only a second. After he motioned for Sweet to stand, Danny aimed and fired twice.

Sweet's face contorted. The nerve endings in what remained of his shattered knees had sent violent impulses of pain.

Danny watched as Chuck Sweet collapsed, caving in on one leg, then the other. In that moment, the muscular terrorist became hysterical. Of course, no one could hear his agonizing pleas for mercy. The whole town was in church.

CHAPTER THIRTY-NINE

Patricia Shaver stood by a window near the entrance to St. Mark's. The church was located on a high hill, and from inside and out, parishioners enjoyed panoramic vistas of the rolling, snow-covered countryside.

After Ellen hugged Trevor Kempner and said good-bye to his family, Pat pushed open one of the double doors with the stained-glass inlays. It was bright outside, but when Ellen put on sunglasses, Pat knew her friend was shielding more than just the glare. Ellen had also reached into her purse and taken out a handkerchief.

As they walked down the steps, Pat wondered why Chief Cherrigan was off to the side talking with Gary Barbera. The parking lot was beginning to empty out, but with many cars funneling toward a single exit lane, traffic was at a crawl. The chief hadn't attended the funeral service. Shouldn't he have positioned himself to alleviate the congestion?

Pat nudged Ellen and they started walking toward Cherrigan and Barbera. "I can't be certain, Ellie, but it looks like Cherry has a new set of priorities."

"Our work is done," Ellen replied. "Let's go home."

"In a minute. It would be impolite not to say goodbye."

Nothing else seemed out of the ordinary, but the moment they got close, the chief moved away. As Cherry walked toward his police cruiser, Pat stared into the gentleman don's eyes and prayed all was as quiet as it appeared.

"Do I have a problem? Every time I get within earshot, people start taking a hike. If it continues, I may get a complex."

"Don't be hasty, my dear. The chief and I were just discussing a community works project."

"Knowing you, it works," Pat said, taking a step closer. "The bigger question is whether it works for the community?"

She glanced over Ellen's shoulder. She saw the admiral's Blazer parked perpendicular to Cherry's squad car, but didn't see Gary Barbera's limo, FALCON 1.

"Where's your chauffeur and limousine?"

"It appears Danny has abandoned me," he answered, his face waxing puzzlement. "Ever since your night of gallivanting, he's acted a little confused."

"Mr. Finn kept the snowshoes," she said. "Are you suggesting he's practicing?"

She purposely joked, but she wasn't joking. Under normal circumstances, Gary Barbera wouldn't have allowed his trusted lieutenant to drop him off and then disappear. And Danny Finn wasn't the only absentee. Lady Harry had come to the service by herself. That meant Sean O'Banyon—magnate of Illinois truckers—was also unaccounted for.

Pat bit her lip. When two mobsters don't show up as expected, expect them to show up where they're unwanted. The conclusion was obvious. Gary Barbera's people had used Sean O'Banyon's connections to find the panel truck with the plow.

"I'm afraid I left my pager in the car," he said, facing her. "Can you give me a ride?"

"Ellen and I would be happy to oblige," Pat replied. "Unless you'd rather go with your buddy, Chief Cherrigan."

He looked toward the chief, then shook his head. "Cherry has other matters to attend to."

"Of course," Pat said, "the public works project."

As she watched the chief tip his hat to the last mourners, her eyes were drawn to a three-inch black pipe that extended straight out the rear of Cherrigan's squad car trunk. Whatever its purpose, one thing was certain. The chief hadn't volunteered to do pro bono plumbing.

Danny Finn felt no remorse for Chuck Sweet. The young terrorist could talk, but Danny didn't want to hear what the man had to say. From the moment the bullets had shattered his knees, Sweet had thrown up, then yelped like a newborn puppy. Blood and vomit pooled around him, but it was his cries for mercy that annoyed Danny most. To cut down on the noise and make sure Sweet stayed conscious, Danny stuffed a handkerchief in the man's mouth and tied tourniquets above each of his knees.

Danny remembered the boss's orders. Since Mr. Barbera wanted Chuck Sweet to suffer, Danny dragged the young terrorist out of the kitchen and into the garage. While Sean O'Banyon held the UZIs and watched, Danny eyed Sweet, then muscled the young terrorist into the cab of the panel truck.

After chaining and handcuffing Sweet to the steering wheel, Danny stood outside the open cab door and watched him struggle, his chest heaving in and out with each short breath. Finn was the man often entrusted with administering Family justice. As such, the Irishman was accustomed to seeing signs of runaway fear. In all his reading of the classics, that was what intrigued him the most. The Crusades, the Inquisition—down through history, the manifestation of fear in the human condition.

Danny left Sweet in the cab and walked to the rear of the truck. Once he opened the hinged doors, he motioned O'Banyon over. The two surveyed the young terrorist's handiwork. He was adept at constructing a bomb.

"We're on the verge of a farming breakthrough," Danny said, eyeing O'Banyon. "Talk about exciting. With our detonator and Chuck's ingredients, we can make our young agronomist the farmer of the week."

"Is that a fact?" O'Banyon asked.

"It's a certainty," Danny said, speaking loud enough for the young terrorist to hear. "Once his bomb goes bang, young Chuck will be credited with spreading enough nitrates to fertilize the county."

Finn attached the magnetized rectangular box with the timer dial to the side of the truck. He synchronized the clock to his watch, then spliced wires to the detonation mechanism, making sure the trip switch hadn't engaged.

"Damn," he said, giving O'Banyon a playful shove. "We may have a problem."

His friend grinned and shoved him back. "How so, Farmer Finn?"

"It has to do with young Chuck's ingredients."

"Like what? Does Chuck have the mixture wrong?"

"That's a tough call," Danny answered. "He's got enough nitromethane... that much I can smell."

"Isn't that a good sign?" O'Banyon said, solemnly. "My father was a gardener. He always said a little racing fuel gets the plants off to a flying start."

"Normally I'd agree. But I'm troubled by something else."

O'Banyon squinted. "Like maybe his formula-one concoction is low on octane?"

Danny pointed to a torn piece of a fertilizer bag. "No, it's the chemical additives. See for yourself. It reads 22-10-8."

"That is distressing. Twenty-two percent nitrogen is wonderful, but without more phosphorus and potash, the flowers won't bloom."

During their conversation, he and O'Banyon had moved back near the cab. To make sure Sweet heard it all, Danny leaned in and smiled.

"There still may be a way to save the day. The human body, when properly dissected and left to decompose, releases many plant pick-me-ups."

"Right," O'Banyon agreed, "but do we have enough? Chuckie-boy has lots of muscles, but he can't weigh more than two hundred pounds. For this much fertilizer, that seems like a drop in the bucket."

"It's a start," Danny replied. "Besides, we've always been two lucky Micks. If we say our prayers, maybe God will send us some more volunteers."

Patricia Shaver watched Chief Cherrigan nod to the last mourner and then walk back to Gary Barbera's side. Mindful that she and Ellen were standing nearby, the chief whispered.

"Wonderful, Chief," the gentleman don said, "glad you've handled everything."

Moving closer, Pat decided to emulate Ellen and take a page out of Ken Dale's book. Her fiancé called it "strutting with adjuratory authority." She'd be happy if the ploy just produced some answers.

"How could Cherry have things handled?" she asked, glaring at Barbera. "Your public-works specialist hasn't used the pipe. See for yourself, Gary. It's sticking out his ass-end."

"Get a load of the mouth that roared," Cherrigan whispered, stepping closer. "Careful, missy. The next one of these church socials might be for you."

"Speak up, Cherry," she said, trying to look menacing. "We wouldn't want your boss to miss any of your solicitous words."

"Like I said, Miss Shaver, it's a solemn occasion." Cherrigan's face turned crimson. "Why not show some respect for the dearly departed?"

Pat was frustrated. She'd pushed the chief and gotten him mad, but he still hadn't given out answers. And that wasn't all. She was battling a nervous stomach over other matters.

Danny Finn was missing, but it was Sean O'Banyon's absence that really troubled her. They'd given Admiral Weiss enough information to thwart Joanna Gaylani's bomb plot, but there was no way to put him onto Sean O'Banyon. She had unimpeachable sources linking the trucking magnate to the mob, but just like her grandfather and father, Lady Harry's husband had avoided brushes with the law.

She looked past Cherry. Tony and Joanna Gaylani were coming

down the church steps and heading to their car. Seeing them intensified her anxiety. Again, she thought about the two Irishman and considered what conditions were necessary to warrant their being absent.

Even if Sean O'Banyon had located the panel truck, why send
him and Danny Finn to disarm it? Gary Barbera hated Eric Weiss and
wanted his own brand of revenge. But the gentleman don wasn't
stupid enough to pull a stunt right under the admiral's nose. My God,
without Weiss's nod, that kind of…

She froze. Like being shocked by a hot wire, jolting impulses
paralyzed her body. Holy Mother of Mercy, could it be possible? She
wanted to run and hide, but her brain kept summoning nightmare
images that rooted her in place.

Before the funeral, two men who hated each other had stood
outside the church and conversed. Neither Barbera nor Weiss looked
happy, but they'd only stopped talking when she approached. That
was also the point when the admiral had put an envelope in his breast
coat pocket.

Had the unthinkable happened? Had they struck a bargain? Had
Barbera convinced the admiral to back off?

"Hey, missy, don't run away." Cherrigan reached out and put his
hand on her shoulder. "Had I known you were so sensitive, I'd have
minded my manners."

She turned and glared. "If you really want to mind your manners, do me a favor. Take your sensitivity and your pipe and shove it."

Cherrigan didn't flinch. "I would, missy, but it's a replacement
part. During the Christmas blizzard, the main water line to my bathroom froze."

Silence crackled in the cold. Then Admiral Weiss walked around
Gary Barbera and stepped between them. She was grateful for the
reprieve, but realized the intervention wasn't chivalrous. The admiral looked preoccupied, and she understood why. Dr. Gaylani had
just helped Joanna into his Mercedes SUV.

"Damn it, Chief," Admiral Weiss said, grabbing Cherrigan's
shoulder and spinning him around. "I'm in a hurry and you're blocking my car. Find someplace else to park."

"Sorry, Admiral, I'll move it right away." Cherrigan lumbered away. "Who'd have guessed a man of your stature would still be driving a beat-up Chevy Blazer?"

"I haven't got all day," Weiss called after him.

"Doing the best I can, but there're patches of ice everywhere, and it makes walking treacherous." Cherrigan pointed as he continued to move toward his police car. "Well, looky here. Mr. Deputy Director went and got himself a set of chains. What a great idea for improving traction."

The mini-drama had begun. The admiral got in and started his vehicle. The chief jumped in the squad car and revved up his engine. Weiss honked, showing impatience. Cherrigan nodded, signaling his intention to move. But the chief didn't pull forward to create a lane. Instead, he put the patrol car in reverse, turned the steering wheel hard right, and floored it.

For a split second—before the airbag covered his face—no one looked more surprised than Eric Weiss. When the back of Cherrigan's police cruiser rammed the front of the admiral's Chevy, the black pipe punctured the radiator.

Pat stood with Ellen and Barbera less than twenty feet away. The sound and sudden impact made them jump. The deliberate collision reminded her of an Army recruit bayoneting a dummy. But that impression changed when the chief shifted from reverse to drive, inched his squad car forward, and withdrew the pipe with great deliberation.

"Cherry must be a precursor of bad luck," Barbera said. "Everywhere the chief goes, pipes are bursting."

They all watched as the admiral squeezed out from behind the air bag and got out of his car. Pat's mind was awash with conflicting thoughts, but she bit her cheeks when he walked forward and slipped on the coolant pouring from the radiator.

Weiss's eyes were murderous as he regained his balance. "This was no accident."

"But it was," the chief replied. "Somehow the car slipped into reverse."

Pat watched the two exchange barbs, wondering if an arrangement existed between the CIA and the Mafia. What was going on out here? Was Weiss angry or playing his role? Had the admiral left his forces in Chicago on purpose? Had he come alone only to witness the proceedings, not to arrest the participants? Had Barbera promised to spare the government the expense of several difficult trials as long as the Mafia don staged his vendetta in a remote location where there was no chance of civilian casualties?

As she asked the key questions, frightening in their portent, she became fearful. All the answers had a common denominator. Gary Barbera and Eric Weiss had to be working together. They'd played risky games against each other, but both knew it made more sense to forgive, forget, and cooperate than go it alone.

That explanation made everything fit, including the admiral's presence. As befitting an egomaniac, Eric Weiss had undoubtedly agreed to be a lone observer. But just as probably, he hadn't agreed to be inconspicuous. In all likelihood, the admiral had put his uniform on display to counteract Barbera's effort to administer vigilante justice.

Weiss wanted the CIA to have the glory of apprehending the Gaylanis and Chuck Sweet. By strutting around with his medals gleaming in the sun, the admiral was undoubtedly trying to spook one of the conspirators. Why wouldn't he hope Tony or Joanna would get nervous and make a run for it? Why wouldn't Eric Weiss have men positioned on the perimeter to take them into custody?

Pat's stomach churned. She'd figured things out on Gary Barbera's timetable, not her own. Of course, she wasn't the only one he'd duped. But it was small comfort to know that the gentleman don had upstaged the admiral too. Chief Cherrigan's antics hadn't been an accident. And Eric Weiss's shocked expression hadn't been faked.

If she guessed right, Barbera had taken out another insurance policy. By immobilizing the Chevy, he guaranteed himself a battlefield free of CIA interference.

She wanted to grab Barbera by the lapels and shout obscenities in his face. But that would have to wait. Act II of the mini drama looked like it was about to begin. Cherrigan had just inspected the rear of his squad car.

"My vehicle is operational," the chief said, directing his comments to the admiral. "If you're in such an all-fired hurry, I could provide the wheels."

Dear God.

Pat looked at Gary Barbera, but instead of questioning him, she watched him gently tug at one of his French cuffs, then rub his gold peregrine cufflink.

CHAPTER FORTY

Joanna Gaylani sat in the passenger seat of her husband's Mercedes SUV. She and Tony had left St. Mark's Episcopal Church to pick up her speech notes. During the short trip back to their home, she continued to feign nausea and say very little. Why talk? By now Chuck Sweet had parked the panel truck in their garage. By now her co-conspirator was at the front door, ready to incapacitate Tony. Soon, she and her husband would never speak to each other again. Soon, she'd watch him die.

Joanna glanced at Tony, then looked back out the windshield. Suddenly, she felt her facial muscles tense, an instant reminder of the one flaw in her plan.

If everything was on schedule—if Chuck was lying in wait at the front door—she would be exposed too. In order to transport Tony's body to the hotel, she'd had to trick her husband into going back to their house. That meant bringing the fully armed bomb truck into her garage. Likewise, that also meant she and Chuck would be surrounded by incriminating evidence and vulnerable to detection.

Joanna's head jerked forward as Tony stopped his Mercedes SUV next to the shoveled walk not far from the front entrance. To playact her role, she kept her eyes closed and tilted her head back against the headrest. She wanted to keep up pretenses, but she hadn't expected to show emotion.

When a tear ran from the corner of her eye down her cheek, Joanna rubbed it away and tried to regain her focus. Tony was her enemy. Why couldn't she hate him? Why couldn't she be happy that her effort was coming to a glorious conclusion?

"Don't know what's the matter," she said, pushing the car door open. "All at once I'm light-headed."

Joanna made a feeble effort to get out, then gasped, faked dizziness, and slumped back into the front seat.

"Stay right there," Tony ordered. "Looks like you need some help."

"Oh, darling. Would you mind terribly?"

Admiral Eric Weiss stood in front of St. Mark's Episcopal Church next to his dinged-up Chevy Blazer. As he watched warm antifreeze drip out of the radiator and melt a small circle in the snow pack covering the cobblestone turnaround, he reached into his overcoat pocket and felt the extra clip and his Navy .45. Right now he should have been sneaking into the Gaylanis' house, ready to gun down Joanna, her husband, and Chuck Sweet.

The admiral turned and eyed Patricia Shaver, Ellen Eichler, and Gary Barbera. They were standing on the sidewalk some thirty feet away and, as it turned out, were the only witnesses to the disabling of his Chevy Blazer. Everyone else had left for the cemetery.

"If you're in such an all-fired hurry," Chief Cherrigan had said, "I could provide the wheels."

The chief's offer got Eric to thinking. As originally conceived, his plan would have succeeded only if he alone killed Joanna Gaylani, her husband, and Chuck Sweet. But what if he deputized Cherrigan as a US marshal and ordered him to drive to the Gaylanis'? While he went inside to surprise the terrorists, the chief could be posted outside to capture anyone who tried to escape. Under that scenario, Cherrigan would hear the shots, but couldn't testify who had opened fire first.

Eric grimaced at Barbera and the two women, then hustled to the police cruiser, pulled open the door, and got in.

"No more bullshit. From now on you're a deputized US marshal. I'll give the orders and you'll follow them. Am I making myself clear?"

"Whatever you say, Admiral."

Eric told the hick flatfoot to step on it, but when Cherrigan pressed the accelerator to the floor, the squad car went into a series of skids. At first the admiral thought things were under control. The chief corrected each fishtail by turning in the direction of the slide. But as the patrol car neared the single-lane exit, Cherrigan turned away from the skid and sent the car into an ice-induced three-sixty.

"For Christ's sake!" Eric screamed. "Watch where you're going."

"I'm trying, Admiral! I'm trying."

Eric watched, helpless, as they stopped spinning and began skidding off the road. He could only cower when the front of the squad car plowed through a snow bank and slid down an embankment. They were moving in slow motion, but a crash was inevitable. Dead ahead was the larger-than-life statue of Jesus that stood at the entrance to St. Mark's.

He didn't try to protect himself. He just stared through the windshield. But when the gap closed and the police car made contact, he ducked and closed his eyes.

Miraculously, neither of them was hurt. The same couldn't be said for the statue of Jesus. When the front bumper of the squad car banged into the lower part of the wooden pedestal, the colorful replica of the Son of God began to wobble.

Eric hadn't seen the dislodged figure. Since the police cruiser was facing nose-down, his view of the Father's only begotten Son was blocked by the roof. In fact, right after the vehicle stopped, he looked out and wondered if they'd missed the pedestal altogether.

The answer came quickly. A moment or two later, the statue toppled onto the hood. That started a chain reaction, and for the second time in less than five minutes, Eric Weiss found himself face deep in an airbag.

He sat quite still, angry enough to kill. His opportunity to assassinate the Gaylanis and Chuck Sweet had been lost. Once again, he'd been bested.

"Cussing won't help," the chief said, trying to free himself from behind his seat. "You're the man with the experience. How do you deflate this thing?"

Danny Finn stood in the foyer of the Gaylanis' colonial mansion. The Irishman looked through a peephole as the couple walked up. Just as Dr. Gaylani reached into his pocket and pulled out his keys, Danny yanked the front door open.

"Good morning," he said. "Won't you come in?"

The instant Danny brought up his hand, Joanna's eyes widened. The 9mm semi-automatic, equipped with an ugly-looking silencer, also got her husband's attention. Dr. Tony Gaylani took a step back and sideways, positioning himself behind his wife.

"What's going on?" Joanna asked, looking over her shoulder. "Do you know this man?"

Her husband didn't move, stunned.

"Answer me," Joanna said, her voice rising. "What's he doing in my house?"

"Take it easy," Danny said, keeping his weapon aimed waist high. "Come in and get warm. There's someone I want you to meet."

Once inside, he had them remove their coats. As they complied, he closed and locked the front door. Then he wagged the silencer snout and pointed them toward the kitchen.

"My name's Danny Finn. My friend and I stopped by to lodge a complaint."

Tony Gaylani stepped out from behind his wife. "Take your fuckin' complaint and shove it up your ass."

The doctor's boldness surprised him. But when Danny eyed the Iraqi and took in the nervous blinks, he dismissed it as bravado. "R. Anthony, my man… The original grievance didn't include insubordination. If you insist, I can amend the citation."

"You Micks are all alike—large mouths and stupid jokes. Cut the crap and tell me what you want."

Danny's face froze. "First, I'd like you to show some respect."

"Respect?" the doctor questioned, holding up his hands. "Look around, snapper. See anything worth respecting?"

Danny lowered his 9mm semi-automatic and fired a single shot. For a millisecond Tony didn't blink. The silencer had reduced the bang to a pop, but once the shell splintered the bones in his instep, Dr. R. Anthony Gaylani cried out and fell onto the floor.

"Let me ask again," Danny said, stepping closer. "See anything worth respecting?"

Joanna knelt next to her fallen husband and checked his wound with a mix of detachment and fear.

"Why are you doing this?" she asked, looking up.

Sean O'Banyon stepped out from the shadows of the hallway. "Hello, Joanna. Remember me? Lady Harry's husband, at your service."

Chief Carlton Cherrigan deflated his airbag. Once out of his police cruiser, he walked to the front and checked out the dented hood.

"Admiral, I should have been smart like you," the chief said, surveying the damage. "Only a fool tries to get by without chains. Still, it's a miracle… Almost like a sign from the Almighty Himself. Take a look. Not even a crack. The ceramic likeness of Our Savior is totally intact."

The admiral stood next to the chief and ran his finger over a small area where the paint on the eight-foot figurine was chipped away.

"Jesus Christ, Cherrigan. Open your eyes. It's nothing but painted metal."

Danny Finn stood near the open passenger-side door of the bomb truck. He watched as Sean O'Banyon followed the Gaylanis into the garage. The doctor, his arm over his handcuffed wife's shoulder, limped on his shattered foot. A smell of blood trailed behind.

Danny poked his head inside the cab. "Hey, Chuckie, you've got company."

When the young terrorist looked up, Danny glanced in the other direction to follow the Gaylanis' progress.

"Hurry up, you two. I'm anxious to see if we have enough chemical nutrients to balance the fertilizer."

With Joanna acting as a crutch, the doctor and his wife stepped onto the cement floor. As they moved slowly in his direction, Danny noted that like Chuck Sweet's, Tony's eyes continued to flicker with fear.

"Mr. Finn," the doctor pleaded, "I don't want to die."

"What's the big deal? No matter whose God you pray to, we all have to go sometime."

"None of this is my doing," Tony persisted. "My wife's the one you want. She's the member of the Zionist organization. I'm just a doctor."

"Shut up," Joanna cried, her face tense. "For once in your life, act like a man."

Saliva ran from the doctor's mouth. His foot was sodden with blood.

"Didn't I tell you? She's talking crazy. You want her, not me."

"Got a point, doc. My beef is with your bride and Chuckie." Danny winked at Sean. "What do you think, should we let him go?"

"Why not?" Sean answered. "Aside from associating with an unsavory element, the good doctor hasn't done anything wrong. Go ahead. Get out of here."

"You mean it?" Gaylani said, his eyes brightening. "Thanks. You'll never regret this."

Danny watched Tony turn and begin hobbling toward the laundry room door. A new lease on life seemed to strengthen the Iraqi's resolve. Christ, the doc even nodded as he approached Sean. But then another pop sounded and everything changed.

In disbelief, Tony Gaylani gazed back at Sean O'Banyon. For a moment, Danny wondered if the paralytic effect resulted from the shot or the curl of smoke that drifted from the silencer of Sean's pistol.

The doctor seemed in denial. But his fantasy was short-lived. Once Tony Gaylani shifted his weight onto the newly wounded leg, it buckled and the Iraqi crumpled onto the garage floor.

"Before you go," Sean said, "there's one little matter I need to clear up."

Danny watched, noting that when the doctor tried to use his hands to compress his shattered knee, he did it alone. Joanna Gaylani stood apart, but she did not relish his pain.

"Tony, old man," Sean said, stepping closer. "Do you think Katherine suffered before she died?"

"What do you mean?" the doctor asked.

"It's a simple question," Sean said, his voice hardening. "Why must I repeat it?"

Danny continued to observe the scene, impassionate. When Sean O'Banyon squeezed the trigger again, his aim was perfect. Dr. Tony Gaylani let out a primal screech as the bullet fragmented his other knee.

"You're making this more difficult than need be," Sean said, seeing blood spurt through Gaylani's protective fingers. "Now, doctor, for the last time…"

" I… I swear," Gaylani cried out. "I didn't kill her."

"You must be hard of hearing," Sean said. "We all know you choked her to death. I'm asking if Katherine suffered."

Dark stains radiated from the kneecaps of Tony Gaylani's pants. Danny glanced at Joanna, satisfied the boss's wishes were being carried out. She was teary-eyed, and as he shifted his focus back to Sean, he pitied her.

"Let's get it over with. The doc's looking a little weary."

Sean nodded and pulled the trigger. He re-aimed. Then he pulled it again.

"My hands!" Tony screamed, looking at his wrists. "I'm a surgeon. I need my hands."

The hollow-point bullets had done their job. Tony Gaylani's

physical agony was over. The doctor's brain had blocked his sense of pain. The Iraqi could talk, but his body had gone into shock.

"Arabs are slow learners," Danny reiterated. "As God is my witness, he's not receiving your message."

Sean fired twice more, this time into Gaylani's ankles.

"Must be doing something wrong. Before this son of a bitch talks, I'll be out of bullets."

Danny shrugged. "It's a moot point. We're out of time."

Like a worm skewered to a fishing hook, Gaylani writhed. Fractured hand and foot bones were attached to his body by skin only. As blood spread on the garage floor, the doctor grew glassy-eyed and ashen. Then he looked in Joanna's direction, moved his mouth, but made no sound. Seconds later, Gaylani's head rolled to one side and his breathing stopped.

"Looks like it's too late to call 911," Sean said, turning his attention to Joanna. "You're next, toots."

"Go ahead," she said, her face tear-stained, but her voice firm. "Shoot me as many times as you like."

"Not a chance, lady. You wrote the script, now you'll be treated to a front row seat." Sean pointed toward the cab of the panel truck. "Joanna belongs next to her young stud. Kinda like the shit-shoveler gets cheek to cheek with the horse whisperer."

Danny helped Sean lift Joanna Gaylani into the cab. As her eyes opened wide at the sight of Chuck Sweet, Danny chained her to the steering wheel.

"Say good-bye, Joanna."

Like a cobra itching to sink its fangs into an enemy, she recoiled. "I'm not afraid to die."

"Good," Danny said. "In a few minutes you'll have a chance to prove it."

CHAPTER FORTY-ONE

Patricia Shaver stood on the sidewalk near the steps of St. Mark's Episcopal Church. She was flanked by Ellen and Gary Barbera. As they watched Chief Cherrigan and Admiral Weiss jaw at each other from opposite sides of the chief's squad car, Pat realized that something was radically wrong.

Why was the admiral still standing by the fallen statue of Jesus? Why hadn't he run back and commandeered Ellen's Explorer?

Pat stared at the shoveled walkway. The answer was obvious. Her assumption had been right. Eric Weiss had been the sole Barrington watchdog. The deal he'd negotiated with Gary Barbera allowed him to keep tabs on Tony and Joanna Gaylani, but only him. Once the doctor and his wife left the church and escaped to places unknown, the admiral had to wait until they drove out of the village limits before he could engage his men.

As if to confirm her thinking, Admiral Weiss made no effort to seek help. Instead, he walked back and forth near Cherrigan's squad car. Even when the chief got into his cruiser and picked up the radio transmitter, the admiral folded his arms across his chest and glared at the Barrington sky. Minutes later, after a wrecker arrived and began hoisting the chief's car, Weiss still hadn't called for backup. He just stared in their direction, then turned away and strode down to the opposite side of the large turnaround.

Shortly thereafter, Sergeant Dick Iverson, one of Cherrigan's officers, drove in and parked close to the admiral. At first, Weiss ignored the Barrington policeman and continued kicking clumps of snow. A few moments later, he leaned down, exchanged a few words, and nodded. Then he pointed a menacing gloved finger in Barbera's direction, got in the back seat of the sergeant's car, and was chauffeured away.

Pat wondered if the admiral was headed back to Langley. As she mulled things over in the cold, she noted something else. Ellen had gotten into her Explorer and started the engine.

Events had taken an ugly turn. While her friend sat behind the wheel, unhappy, but reconciled that nothing could be changed, she stood next to Barbera, coming to grips with the same dilemma. The problem was simple. Tony and Joanna Gaylani had already been sentenced. Sure, they were guilty of crimes punishable by death, but neither had been charged or convicted.

Her stomach was queasy and her brain struggled with contradictory images. But rather than give up, she faced Barbera—not only the judge, jury, and executioner, but the man who was directing all the players and every scene.

"Tell me, Gary… are we waiting for Danny Finn or just enjoying the sub-zero temperatures?"

He didn't answer. Instead the crime boss pushed at his overcoat sleeve to expose his watch.

"Why don't you level with me?" she said. "You've gone after them, haven't you?"

"Gone after whom?"

"Don't play games."

Pat wanted to tell him that she was a good guesser too. She wanted to impress him with her intuitive powers. She wanted him to admit he'd schemed and hadn't played fair. But mostly, she wanted to stop feeling like she was an unwitting part of a machination that had started with a noble cause.

"I know you and the admiral worked out some sort of deal."

He looked at her, eyes focused and alert. "Who told you that, my dear? I never said anything, and I don't recall hearing you talk to the admiral on the subject."

"Why else would he come by himself?" she asked. "When the CIA goes after a group of terrorists, they don't send an unarmed admiral dressed in his Navy blues."

"Admiral Weiss is a potent force, my dear. Some would even say he's an army unto himself."

She stood in the cold, staring in disbelief at this man. "You're not going to tell me, are you?"

"Do you really want to know?"

"I suppose not. Hearing the details would just make me feel dirtier."

"Hold on one minute," he said, his gloved hand touching her shoulder. "That kind of talk pains me. You've done nothing to be ashamed of."

"Look in that car, Mr. Barbera." She turned and stared at Ellen. "Even if I rationalized my own behavior, I've let Ellie down. Knowing I made her part of something ugly doesn't sit very well."

The gentleman don's eyes radiated compassion, but if she sought words of redemption for the role she'd played, she got none.

CHAPTER FORTY-TWO

Joanna Gaylani felt like crying. For one of the few times in her life, she didn't have a plan. She'd just been chained to the steering wheel next to Chuck Sweet. As she watched Danny Finn back out of the cab and disappear toward the rear of the panel truck, she tried not to lose all hope. Instead, she twisted her head and let her ears be her eyes.

Almost immediately she heard a short clicking sound, the noise a kitchen timer makes when it's being set. Earlier, when she and Tony had been led into the garage, she'd noticed a metal box attached to the side panel of the truck. She wasn't a demolitions expert, but she assumed Danny Finn had just set an automatic fuse. Seconds later, after listening to the garage door open, her suspicions were confirmed. Cold air chilled the sweat on her forehead. Then Joanna overheard Finn ask O'Banyon if he'd finished his tasks. She also heard the Irishman tell Sean O'Banyon to move out, that once he'd made a final check, he would strap on his snowshoes and catch up.

Joanna assumed that the duffel bag she'd noticed on the garage floor contained snowshoes and other gear. She and Tony hadn't seen a getaway car, so their captors would use snowshoes to get back to the Kempners' and then make their escape.

Sensing her fate had been sealed, Joanna turned and looked through the open cab door. Her husband lay sprawled in blood, his chest no longer heaving with labored breaths. Tony's struggle was over, and for just a moment, she envied him. So far she hadn't been hurt, but her situation was even bleaker. She and Chuck Sweet were handcuffed and chained to the steering wheel. Their lives had been reduced to a nerve-shredding wait until they were blown to bits.

Again, Joanna heard the sound of something shuffling over snow. She knew O'Banyon had already taken off. That meant Danny Finn had just left too.

Silence was broken only by the sound of the ticking timer. In desperation, she turned toward Chuck Sweet. He leaned in her direction, his chin held high. Joanna got the message. She bit down on the handkerchief and pulled his gag free.

"Sorry," she moaned, "never thought it would end like this."

"Save the tears. We've got work to do."

"Work?" she asked. "What kind of work?"

"There's a bolt cutter under the seat," he replied, using his head like a pointer. "Get it… and be quick about it."

Along with his obvious pain, Joanna saw hope. Sparked by Chuck's renewed confidence, she took a deep breath, then slid away from him, stretching the chains to the limit. With all the slack taken out, she leaned forward and reached down. There, as Chuck had said, she touched the wooden handle of the bolt cutter he'd purchased before picking up the fertilizer and ammonium nitrate. Chuck Sweet had brought the heavy-duty metal snips on the slim chance the Christmas blizzard might have frozen or rusted the combination lock on Kempner's barn.

"I can feel it," she said, "but I can't get my fingers around the damn thing!"

"No excuses, Joanna. Try harder!"

Danny Finn kept striding atop the snow. A few minutes ago, he'd strapped on his snowshoes, stepped over the plowed snow bank paralleling the Gaylanis' driveway, and begun backtracking along the trail that led to the igloo-style carport on the far side of Tom Kempner's garage.

At the halfway point, he caught up to Sean O'Banyon.

"Keep moving," he said, "the timer's set to go off in about eight minutes."

Beet red with effort, Sean arm-waved him around. "Go ahead. I'll follow you."

Danny started to shuffle by, but when O'Banyon's face tensed, he stopped.

"What's wrong?" he asked.

"I forgot to take the keys."

"Keys?" Danny questioned. "What keys?"

"The keys to Sweet's panel truck."

"Damn it, O'Banyon! The last thing—"

"I know," Sean said. "I meant to pull them out of the ignition."

Sean O'Banyon began turning around.

"Forget it," Danny snarled. "There's no time."

"The old man gave us strict orders," Sean replied. "Innocent people can't be put in jeopardy. Joanna and Chuckie-boy may not be able to wiggle loose, but if they get the damn truck started, there's still time to drive into a populated area."

"Jesus, you're right," Danny said, "but you're not going alone. We'll go together."

"It's my mistake. I'll take care of it."

"Don't be a fool. I can move faster."

Sean O'Banyon's eyes hardened. "It's not up for discussion. I'm going back alone."

Joanna Gaylani was beset by hope and despair. She stared at Chuck Sweet and saw a man who looked more dead than alive. But notwithstanding the cracked ribs, the smashed nose, and other injuries, he had managed to slide flush against the driver's side door. The vice-like tourniquets wrapped around each of his thighs had cut off circulation to his lower legs, but his maneuver had given her room to pull the bolt cutter from under the seat.

"No excuses, Joanna."

"Damn it," she complained. "I'm not strong enough."

Prior attempts had failed. She'd opened the mouth of the bolt cutter and guided it around the chain, but she was unable to exert enough leverage to cut though the links.

"The bolt cutter is in position," Chuck said, his eyes aglow with desperation. "You can do it. We didn't come this far to die like a couple of animals."

His voice was weak and hoarse, but his words resonated in her ear.

Danny Finn glided into the open-air carport and unstrapped his snowshoes. He looked up, knowing it was too early to see any signs of Sean O'Banyon.

He tossed the backpack and snowshoes in the rear seat of the boss's limousine. Then he looked at his watch. Four minutes before the timer hit zero.

He walked outside the carport and stared at the sunlit, compacted-snow trail leading to the Gaylanis' house. Why worry? He'd given Sean a set of simple instructions to reprogram the detonator. O'Banyon was a veteran. He'd get the job done. Assuming the man was on schedule, it was still too soon to expect him back.

Danny stepped back inside the snow-sided, open-air garage. How could anything go wrong? Even if Joanna Gaylani and Chuck Sweet saw the ignition keys and managed to get the truck started, there was little chance they could drive it. Chuck was sitting on the driver's side, and his legs were useless. To make sure the young terrorist hung around for the finale, he and Sean had tied tight tourniquets around his lower thighs.

And that wasn't the only thing working in their favor. Since Chuck Sweet's position made it near impossible for Joanna to depress the clutch, shifting the gears became a low probability event. But even if they somehow got the truck in gear, Joanna was chained to Sweet in a way that would make it difficult to turn the steering wheel more than a few degrees.

Danny told himself there was no danger. The panel truck would never move, and the bomb wouldn't do significant damage. He'd purposely left the rear of the truck open and the garage door up. He knew that by not encasing the device, much of the bomb's destructive power would be dissipated out into the open air. The blast would level the house, but probably not destroy the area beyond the Gaylanis' property line.

He breathed in, then exhaled. Why wouldn't the gnawing feeling in his stomach go away? O'Banyon was a big boy. He could take care of himself.

Danny knew his sheltered position behind the Kempners' garage gave him total protection. But his sixth sense didn't share that optimism. When he looked at his watch a second time and saw that the original ten minutes were almost up, Danny Finn knelt down beside Barbera's limousine.

Joanna Gaylani summoned all her strength. When the bolt cutter hacked through one of the links, she felt exhilarated. She was still handcuffed, but she was free of the chain holding her to the steering wheel.

"Good job," Chuck said. "Now do your stuff."

Sweet had given her specific instructions: "Reset the timer for thirty minutes, then come back and cut me free. Once I'm out of the way, you can drive. We'll make our statement locally. It won't be as spectacular as bombing the UJC Convention, but it's noontime and downtown Barrington will be loaded with people."

She scrambled out of the cab and moved to the side of the truck. In her haste, she hadn't seen him. But once she put her hands on the timer, she knew she wasn't alone.

"Going somewhere?" he asked.

Joanna turned her head. Sean O'Banyon was red-faced, panting, and sweaty. But he was also ready. His 9mm automatic was out and the safety was off.

"Why, Mr. O'Banyon, what are you doing here?"

She stared at him, keeping her hands on the timer.

"Be a good girl," he said, "and step away from the truck."

She followed half of his instructions. She let her hands drop to her side.

"If you came back to keep me company, take your snowshoes off and stay a while."

"You can make this easy or hard," he said. "Move away from the truck."

"Is your first name Sean?"

Snowshoes on, he stepped closer. "My name isn't important. Now…"

She held up her hand like a traffic cop. "Don't bore me with macho chatter. Your leverage is gone, so shut up and listen."

Joanna eyed him, then gave a quick look at the timer.

"In a few seconds, there's going to be a big bang," she said. "It's your choice. Leave your gun where you stand, turn around, and go find your pal. Or stay here and become part of the fertilizer."

"Sweetheart, I don't like it when broads fuck with me."

Sean O'Banyon started trudging awkwardly across the garage floor. Joanna looked back at the timer, then faced him. She smiled, staring straight into his eyes. A second later, she fell to her knees as if in prayer.

Danny Finn knelt by the front wheel of the gentleman don's limousine and watched the second hand of his watch. From his position inside the manmade carport, he only heard and felt the deafening blast. But that was enough. He didn't have to see the devastation to know he'd underestimated the bomb's power.

His ears rang from the explosion and his body trembled from the shock waves that shook the frozen earth under his feet. He didn't move. He continued to kneel, eyes squeezed closed. He'd been spared, but once he heard pieces of the Gaylanis' house start coming back to earth, he knew that Sean O'Banyon was dead.

Danny didn't waste time offering a prayer. He had to leave. Within minutes, emergency vehicles would come rushing to the scene. He couldn't let them find him or the boss's car.

He jumped in the limo, started the engine, and began backing up. He expected to see significant destruction, but as he pulled out of the snow garage and moved forward onto the Kempners' driveway, even he was shocked. The Gaylanis' two-story colonial mansion was gone. An earthen crater, twice the depth of their basement and half again the circumference of their house, had consumed the standing structure. Considering the precautions he'd taken to defuse the bomb's potency, the magnitude of the force flabbergasted him. Trees no longer ringed the Gaylanis' house. Fifty-foot oaks and pines had been uprooted and flung in all directions.

The doctor's mansion had been obliterated. Several hundred feet away, the exposed part of the Kempners' Tudor manor had sustained enormous damage. All the windows were blown in and many of the slate shingles peeled away. Sections of the roof and exterior had also been sheared off.

Flying debris was everywhere. Like a mammoth shotgun blast, fragments of cement and painted brick had created large pockmarks and gaping holes in the stucco. Much smaller particles had whitewashed the dark planking with dust.

Danny was on a tight schedule, but he stopped the car and got out. Over the years, he'd fought in his share of street battles, but he'd never seen anything like this. First, his body convulsed. Then he began to shiver.

The devastation reminded him that terrorists could stalk and strike any time, any place. Fighting them was like going after an enemy you couldn't see.

A siren calling the all-volunteer Barrington Fire Department to the stationhouse pierced the winter air. He hated to leave his friend behind, but he had no choice. Sean O'Banyon, like himself, had been a soldier. They'd known and accepted the risks.

CHAPTER FORTY-THREE

Patricia Shaver had asked Gary Barbera for an explanation. She got one without the gentleman don saying a word. As she stood near the entrance to St. Mark's Episcopal Church and looked into his eyes, she saw, then heard the fruition of his plans.

In the distance, a flash brightened the already sunlit sky. A second later, a thunderous boom sent sonic shock waves though the air.

She pointed and Gary Barbera turned. Billowing skyward, a dust-colored cloud mushroomed out of the snow-covered landscape. Quivering, she stepped back. Overcome with an eerie sense of *deja vu*, she was a college freshman again, standing near the ashy rubble that hours before had been a home where her parents had perished.

Ellen rushed from the car.

"Did you hear that?"

Pat nodded. "Who could have missed it?"

They watched a grayish blot rise above the tree line and begin to dissipate. None of them spoke. Finally, Ellen stepped in front of the gentleman don.

"Is this part of your handiwork, Mr. Barbera?"

"Think what you will of me and my methods, but I assure you, nothing happened today that in any way jeopardized the safety of innocent people." He faced Ellen, his eyes quiet, wet with cold. "The very law enforcement personnel you demanded be part of this operation had the situation completely under control."

Ellen moved in closer, standing toe to toe. "Did the authorities detonate the bomb, Mr. Barbera... or did the Gaylanis get careless with a truckload of fertilizer?"

"I wasn't there, so I can't say."

"What would you say if I asked you to speculate?"

"In my business, it's dangerous to speculate." He glanced away, watching the dirty cloud flatten and spread against the bright blue sky. "I deal in facts... and these are the facts: The people in the government charged with enforcement wanted to press for the full measure of the law. But some—the admiral included—were concerned about the ramifications of an open trial."

"Does that mean a sentence without a judge and jury, Mr. Barbera?"

"You've put your finger on Admiral Weiss's dilemma. We live in the post 9/11 world. People are polarized. In that environment, the admiral is powerless to negotiate a plea bargain."

"I'm surprised the admiral chose to reveal his strategy."

"This morning, we had occasion to talk." Barbera reached inside his overcoat sleeve and touched a gold cufflink. "Last night, one of my lawyers informed me of a truck leasing contract our people had run across. Naturally, when I learned who'd signed it, I thought it might be significant. But I knew Dr. Gaylani was a prominent man. Before saying anything, I wanted to be sure the document wasn't a fake."

"A fake?" Ellen asked.

"It happens... and in this case, the authentication process took some time." Barbera fidgeted, looking back at her. "All the t's weren't crossed until early this morning. I was about to leave for Tommy's service when my legal team showed up at the house. Once they indicated the procedures used to establish the validity of the documents, I called the admiral."

"Hold on one damn minute," Pat said, interjecting. "Your lawyers found conclusive proof that Dr. Tony Gaylani leased the panel truck with the plow?"

His shoulders shrugged under his winter coat. "Let's just say, a truck similar in every way to the one you and Danny saw last night was leased to a man who identified himself as Dr. R. Anthony Gaylani."

"Don't play word games," Pat said. "You expect me to believe that Tony Gaylani leased the bomb truck?"

"Believe what you want," he replied, a tired smile lining his mouth. "I'm only saying that this morning my lawyers handed me an envelope containing two documents: the truck rental contract and a signed affidavit. In the sworn statement, taken in the presence of Chief Cherrigan and a court stenographer, the leasing agent attested that the man who signed the truck rental contract paid cash, and established his identity with a valid driver's license. The U-Haul employee also stated that the man who handed her the picture ID looked like the man in the photograph Cherrigan presented during the deposition. Based on that eyewitness identification, the chief concluded that Dr. R. Anthony Gaylani had rented the truck."

"What about the signature on the leasing agreement?" Pat persisted. "Was it verified?"

"It appears to be Tony Gaylani's, but unfortunately, the doctor used a fountain pen. During transit to me, the contract got wet and the ink ran." Barbera looked away, watching the debris cloud dissipate on eddies of air. "One thing is certain. In the affidavit, the leasing agent states that at the time of the transaction, she compared the signature against Dr. Gaylani's license."

"Your legal team should be congratulated," Pat said. "They've seen to every detail."

Time and again, she'd painted Gary Barbera into a corner. Time and again, the man with rich colors on his palette had deftly applied his brush, eluding her.

He'd bested her at every turn… and now it was too late to do anything. At this stage, she only knew one thing.

At long last, she finally understood the ins and outs of his plan. And what a plan. He had every contingency covered. Gary Barbera, the Mafia maestro, had gotten it done his way, and in the process he'd covered his butt, her butt, and the admiral's butt too.

Whatever had made her think she and Ellie were any match for this man? Whatever—

"Mr. Barbera," Ellen said, her voice ringing out. "You've said your piece, and you've made sure we saw your display. If the show is over, I suggest we leave. I'll drop you anywhere you say."

His gloved hand reached out, but Ellen turned away, walking toward her Explorer.

"Please don't think ill of me, Mrs. Eichler," he called out. "As God is my witness, I did what I thought was right."

Ellen stopped and faced him. "Each of us makes peace with his own conscience. If you're satisfied, far be it from me to be your accuser."

Pat sighed. Ellen detested Barbera's tactics, but refused to condemn the man. Her best friend was truly a Christian woman. A person who had an unshakable faith in God and His teachings.

Pat thought about what had transpired as the first foul smell from the explosion reached her and tainted the air. She was a Christian woman too. She also had a high opinion of the human spirit and its ability to regulate ethical behavior. But her tolerance to forgive was limited.

Pat studied the gentleman don. In spite of his precious code of honor, she felt sure that at least part of his behavior had been motivated to insure his Family's survival. But who was she to question the roots of his morality? Her own conduct had fallen woefully short.

She stared into the crime boss's eyes and he stared back. Were the two of them more similar than different? Did she have a conscience of convenience? Had Barbera outplayed her, or had she just refused to ask the hard questions? Either way, who wouldn't marvel at how nice and tidy all the pieces fit?

To avenge Tom and Kitty Kempner's deaths and avoid criminal prosecution, Gary Barbera had to have assurances he could operate with impunity. But he wasn't the only one who had specific needs. In order to shield the CIA from unfavorable publicity and, at the same time, give the Chicago crime boss a free hand to execute Tony and Joanna Gaylani, Admiral Weiss required credible fall guys.

She and Ellen had gathered many pieces of evidence, but none of their documents had the appeal of the truck rental agreement and the witness affidavit. When Barbera offered his most alluring carrots, Admiral Weiss accepted. This morning, on the steps of St. Mark's, an envelope had changed hands. With that exchange, the conditions both men demanded were met and a mutually beneficial trade was consummated.

Gary Barbera knew that all the evidence he'd supplied, including copies of Tom Kempner's ranch invoices, hadn't been enough. The truck rental agreement and the witness affidavit were the missing items. Handing Admiral Weiss authenticated proof that the blurred signature on the U-Haul contract matched the one on Dr. Tony Gaylani's license completed the necessary paper trail. Armed with those linchpins, the admiral could link the fertilizer truck to the doctor and his militant Jewish wife. He could also claim the explosion had occurred as the husband-wife terrorist team inadvertently detonated a bomb they'd built to derail the Arab-Israeli peace talks.

That was undoubtedly how it had been orchestrated. Barbera and Weiss had forged a deal last night and sealed it this morning. From their standpoints, cooperating behind the scenes made sense. Once the admiral had his scapegoats, what did he care if the gentleman don took care of business and administered Family justice? As things stood, Admiral Weiss and the CIA were breathing a collective sigh of relief.

Pat looked away, watching the dirty cloud thin into wisps. Without question, the CIA had bumbled. Instead of coordinating with their British counterparts, they'd allowed General Alan Cunningham's papers to become the catalyst that had led to Katherine Kempner's murder.

With Tom Kempner, their record had been equally unimpressive. Instead of protecting him, they'd left the mob attorney vulnerable. As circumstances stood, the Company could claim their fast action had prevented a disaster at the United Jewish Congress Convention. But in truth, it had been Gary Barbera's involvement that had saved them from criticism.

No wonder the CIA was happy to see Tony and Joanna Gaylani eliminated. It would have been a disaster if the doctor and his wife had been put on trial. But with both of them dead, the CIA could claim that the Gaylanis had acted together: Joanna, an All Alone terrorist who was hardened by her parents' brutal murders; and Tony, an Iraqi Muslim who'd converted to Catholicism, married Jewish women, and become sympathetic to their cries for a strong Israel, non-aligned and isolated from its Arab neighbors.

Pat's journalistic eye visualized a courtroom with the Gaylanis on trial. What a scene that would have been. Tony and Joanna could have told a story of how they'd each operated undetected for decades as independent terrorists, one representing Jihad Arabs, the other Zionists.

Their testimony would have created a sea of red faces and cries for change. The CIA, FBI, and Homeland Security would have come under a new wave of Congressional scrutiny. The only winner in that debacle would have been the press.

She looked out at the mounds of plowed snow in the church lot. The surface was pure white. But underneath—where salt kept the parking spaces and access lanes free from ice—the slush was dirty.

As she stared, Pat realized that the gentleman don had not gone unscathed. Barbera might have killed a trio of no-goods and evened an overdue score, but when he'd gotten in bed with the CIA, he'd also turned his back on Tom Kempner, his trusted *consigliere*. Under the tenets of any moral code, that had to be an unpardonable sin.

Distant sounds of sirens brought her back. She looked at the man who ran the Chicago Mafia. His profile showed no signs of anxiety, yet she wondered how he felt inside.

What drove men like Barbera and Weiss? Did the male psyche secrete a hormone that permitted them to ignore other people's rights when they engaged in their lethal games?

Take the admiral, for instance. Even after making a deal with Gary Barbera, Admiral Weiss couldn't resist going for glory. Why else had he gotten decked out in his dress blues, come to the funeral, and strutted like a peacock? When he'd tried unsuccessfully to follow the Gaylanis, he must have had something on his mind. And given his ego, it had to be an attempt to get in the gentleman don's way. She couldn't be sure, but she suspected that all their extracurricular activities served one purpose: Each wanted to one-up the other.

Pat looked out over the rolling hills, trying to remember exactly where the dust cloud had been. From her perspective, the snow-covered landscape seemed unchanged. But then again, to the unknowing eye, she seemed unchanged too.

CHAPTER FORTY–FOUR

Patricia Shaver walked back to the Explorer, opened the rear passenger door, and climbed in. There was nothing left to be said, observed, or processed. She'd looked at things with a reporter's eye. Now she felt empty.

Gary Barbera held the door for Ellen. When he moved around the front of the car and got in, no one spoke. But halfway into the drive from St. Mark's to her home, Barbera broke the silence and tried to convince Ellen to accept his generous offer.

"I beg you to reconsider, Mrs. Eichler. My plane is going to Kentucky whether you hitch a ride or not."

Pat knew he parked his G-5 at a private airstrip nearby. But was his jet really loaded with saddles and other gear destined for his Lexington horse farm? In all probability, he was making a nice gesture.

"Thank you," Ellen replied, "but it's not right. I'll fly commercial."

"Don't be silly," Pat said, leaning between the front passenger seats. "Hop on Mr. Barbera's plane and cut hours off your travel time."

"She's right, Mrs. Eichler."

Ellen glanced at him, then looked back at the road.

"I feel funny accepting, Mr. Barbera."

"Nonsense. You gave up part of the Christmas holiday to help Tommy. He'd want you to say yes. I feel it's the least I can do."

"Patricia…?"

"Go for it, Ellie."

Pat was heartened when her friend nodded, but her happiness was short lived. Seconds later, when Ellen turned the Explorer into her driveway, Pat saw the stretch limousine parked near her home.

"Your ride is here," she said, her stomach muscles tightening. "As always, Mr. Finn is attentive."

"Indeed he is." The gentleman don smiled, then turned toward Ellen. "Thanks for the lift, Mrs. Eichler."

When Ellen parked next to the Cadillac limousine, Gary Barbera handed her a folded piece of paper.

"Directions to my airstrip, Mrs. Eichler. The plane will take off when you arrive." He extended his hand, and this time Ellen shook it. "I'll say my goodbyes to Miss Patricia after you leave. Right now, you both should have a private moment."

Gary Barbera lifted the door handle and got out. As he walked toward his limo, Ellen turned toward the back seat.

"His jet would accommodate you, Patricia. Grab your bags and come along."

"I appreciate the thought, but tonight I take off to see Ken." She forced a smile, but with a teary glint. "Christmas is a family time. You should be with your husband, daughter, and grandkids."

"You're family," Ellen said. "Right now it's not a good idea for you to be alone."

"I'll be fine," Pat replied, dabbing an eye and water-staining her black leather glove. "Wish everyone a belated Merry Christmas."

With her thoughts choked out, she leaned over and hugged the only woman who'd ever loved her like a daughter and spoken to her like a friend. Ellen hugged back, but only for a second. Pat knew it was time to cut their good-byes short as they pulled apart and her friend began to take quick breaths.

She got out and closed the rear passenger door, staring ahead. But when Ellen lowered the driver's-side window, Pat leaned in and kissed her on the forehead. A moment later, she watched the Explorer motor down her driveway.

"Mrs. Eichler is a fine woman," Barbera said.

Pat nodded. "God broke the mold after he made her."

"And that's not all," he added. "She lives in a Victorian house and has Victorian values. But she also mixes compassion with an uncanny sense of right and wrong."

"Just like you, Mr. Bar—" She looked down and put her hand over her mouth.

"Don't trouble yourself," he said. "I'm comfortable with my morals. Whether Mrs. Eichler would say they meet her high standards… Well, that's a different question."

When she looked up, he stared at her, his eyes fixed, but not hostile.

"As for compassion," he went on, "why don't we just leave that one alone."

"I'm so sorry, Gary. I was way out of line."

"It's been a long stressful day," he replied, taking a step toward his limo. "It's time for me to go. You've got an overseas flight this evening and undoubtedly have some last-minute packing."

"Yes," she said, "but if you and Danny want to come in, I'd be happy to brew a fresh pot of coffee."

Pat stared at the stretch Cadillac and the heavily tinted windows, wondering why Danny Finn hadn't joined them. Initially she'd thought his behavior odd, but then remembered that Harriet O'Banyon had come to the funeral by herself.

"Is Danny being shy," she asked, "or is he sitting next to someone I'm not supposed to see?"

"Of course not. Even when I try to hide things, you decode all my secrets." Barbera rapped his gloved hand on the limousine roof. "All right, you two. Come out and say hello."

They waited for an interminable five seconds. When he rapped again, Danny loomed from behind the darkened glass. His eyes dull, the Irishman glanced at her, unsmiling. Then he closed the driver's side door and walked to the front of the car.

"Hello, Miss. Pleased to see you again."

She was confused. Why was Danny Finn slump-shouldered? He created mayhem for a living. Eliminating Tony and Joanna Gaylani and leveling their house couldn't weigh heavily on a pro.

As her stomach churned, she felt a little faint. She had asked to meet Danny Finn and Sean O'Banyon, hoping they'd make up a fairy tale and tell her that they hadn't executed the Gaylanis. She wanted to hear that the bomb had gone off accidentally before either Irishman had had a chance to administer Family justice.

She eyed Danny. "You look a little shaken. Are you okay?"

"Yes, Miss, I'll be fine."

"We missed you at the funeral today," she went on, searching for words that would make her look strong.

"Yes... Well... ah..." He looked down. "Another matter came up unexpectedly."

Danny didn't want to talk. But what about her? Should she keep rambling as a way of punishing herself? Should she press until Barbera's enforcer admitted that he'd learned from the master? That without seeing it done, he'd never have used the snowshoes to sneak over and bomb Tony and Joanna Gaylani's house?

"Your engagement must have been important," she said, pushing hair from her face. "Lots of people were concerned about your whereabouts."

"Quite right, my dear," the gentleman don added. "I, for one, was worried."

He waited, but when Danny Finn didn't speak and kept his eyes focused on the ground, Gary Barbera's face tensed. "Come, come. Explain your behavior."

Finn looked up. "Boss, can I talk to you in private?"

"I just told Miss Patricia, we have no secrets." Barbera's eyes darkened. "I'm a man of my word. You hem and haw, and your buddy... By the way, where is Sean?"

"Boss. I really think it's important..."

"Who's in charge?" Barbera asked, raising both arms in the air. "For the love of God! You're tongue-tied and the other Mick has stage fright."

"I'm not trying to be difficult, boss." The Irishman kept staring at the snow-covered ground. "As you know, we went snowshoeing."

Danny Finn probably didn't mean to make her feel guilty, but the second he mentioned *snowshoeing,* a phobic vise tightened on her gut.

"You and Mr. O'Banyon…" Pat edged closer, finding it difficult to breathe. "You two were involved, weren't you?"

Barbera stepped between her and Danny. "Let's remember that we're friends and this conversation is off the record."

She nodded. "I'm not after a story, I just want to understand—"

"What's to understand?" the gentleman don asked. "Of course they were involved, but don't be so bashful. You deserve a lot of the credit. After all, using the snowshoes was your idea."

When Barbera formally acknowledged that the snowshoes were her brainchild, she felt paralyzed by fear and anxiety. She finally understood. She was as guilty as the person who had detonated the bomb.

"Tell her," Barbera insisted, "tell the pretty lady how much you enjoyed yourself."

"Actually, Miss," Danny said, stepping back, "this time I didn't."

She stepped away from Barbera too, but when she looked up at Danny Finn, she wondered why his emerald eyes weren't sparkling. His boss had led her to the slaughterhouse. Why not admit she'd devised one part of the scheme and shared in their criminal triumph?

"Did I hear you correctly?" Barbera asked. "Why didn't you enjoy yourself?"

"If you wouldn't mind, boss, I'd rather not say."

The gentleman don's eyes hardened. "But I do, damn it! Now, please go on."

Each time he pressed his trusted lieutenant, Pat felt more nauseous. While Danny seemed reluctant to elaborate, she knew he'd eventually agree that introducing the snowshoes had made her a central figure in their despicable operation.

As she waited, she looked out over ice-covered Honey Lake. Her charade was over. She might not have set the timer, but she'd had a hand in soiling the Barrington sky. Nobody else had seen it, but when the gray cloud of dust rose above the horizon, it had spelled out her name.

"We're waiting, Danny," the gentleman don said.

"We suffered a casualty." The Irishman looked his boss in the eye. "Sean didn't make it."

Pat's body began shaking. She turned and stared at Barbera. He had closed his eyes, taking the blow.

"My dear," Barbera said, reaching his gloved hand inside his overcoat sleeve, "don't concern yourself with any of this. I was wrong to force the issue."

He moved to her side, his voice breaking ever so slightly.

"You had no part in the last act. I and I alone directed the players. Rest assured, I never contemplated letting you be privy to my plans."

"Maybe so, but like it or not, I'm involved. I took part."

Trembling, she finally understood Ellen's position. All along Pat had told herself that her motives were unselfish and simon-pure. Yet, all along, she wasn't a reporter on the trail of truth. Her actions had only paved the way for vigilantism and revenge. She was uncertain how she could have played it differently, but once again she felt less than human.

"Mr. Barbera, is this how it feels when you win dirty?"

"You're not to blame, my dear. I'm an old warhorse and have witnessed many tough campaigns. This one was as difficult as any. Now it's over. You acted with honorable intent and showed great character. You tried to help my friend at a time when I should have been at his side. For that, I'm forever grateful." Gary Barbera touched her hands. "You're a fine young woman. I regret our differences, but most of all I regret putting you in a position where your sense of fair play compromised your faith. Over the years I've become immune to watching men bend the rules. While I find myself technically innocent of misleading you, I do feel guilty for making sure the game was played on my field. For that, I apologize and beg your forgiveness."

"You held my hand, Mr. Barbera, but I chose the path. Just me."

"Good-bye, my dear. As God is my witness, I pray you enjoy your trip to Rome." He reached for the passenger door. "I also hope the next time we meet, it won't be in a courtroom sitting at opposite tables."

"So do I, Mr. Barbera, so do I."

As she watched the taillights of his limousine disappear down the driveway, her mind whirled. Barbera was a conniver and killer who'd manipulated the deputy director of the CIA and run roughshod over her. Yet, though she knew she'd been had, she also knew how she felt.

How could it be possible? How, after all that had happened, could she be touched by a gentleman who expressed his emotions with empathy and yet enforced his code of honor with violence?

EPILOGUE

Admiral Eric Weiss never went out to view the crime scene. Instead, he flew to Washington, took a limo to CIA headquarters, and began composing a memorandum.

A package, anonymously delivered and placed on his desk, interrupted the admiral's dictation. His secretary, Cissy Place, watched him open the plain wrapped box. Cissy also noted that after seeing the contents, her boss called for a maintenance man, then continued to draft a short memo he coded OPERATION SNOWSHOE.

Several minutes later, when she handed the typed memorandum back to him, Cissy concluded the file name must have been influenced by the unsigned gift. While waiting for him to initial the original, she watched a man on a ladder hang the latest addition to the admiral's office memorabilia. A lone antique snowshoe with an engraved gold plate was mounted horizontally on the wall behind his desk.

Cissy didn't comment at the time, but after he left early that day, she took a closer look.

The engraved inscription simply read: *A Memory from Barrington and the Christmas Blizzard.*

Weiss's secretary remembered typing the town name, Barrington, in her boss's memo. That coincidence prompted her to pull the file and reread the admiral's short communiqué.

To: Jerrold Cash, Director, CIA
From: Eric Weiss, Deputy Director, CIA
Subject: Detonation, Barrington, IL

Dr. R. Anthony Gaylani and his wife, Joanna, long suspected to harbor terrorist views, inadvertently detonated a fertilizer bomb in their garage today.

The blast was so powerful that all traces of the conspirators as well as remnants of the bomb and delivery mechanism were destroyed.

Our investigation has uncovered conclusive proof (see attached truck rental agreement and eyewitness affidavit) that the couple planned to transport and detonate this bomb during the United Jewish Congress National Convention being held in Chicago.

The Company has monitored the movements of both suspects for many years. Throughout this long investigation, there has never been any indication either R. Anthony or Joanna Gaylani was associated with a foreign power or subversive group. It is my belief the two terrorists acted alone.

Case closed.

E.P. Weiss

END

Case Approach
to Counseling
and Psychotherapy

Case Approach to Counseling and Psychotherapy

Gerald Corey

California State University, Fullerton

Diplomate in Counseling Psychology

American Board of Professional Psychology

BROOKS/COLE
CENGAGE Learning™

Australia • Brazil • Japan • Korea • Mexico • Singapore • Spain • United Kingdom • United States

BROOKS/COLE
CENGAGE Learning™

Case Approach to Counseling and Psychotheraphy, Seventh Edition

Gerald Corey

Senior Acquisitions Editor:
Marquita Flemming

Assistant Editor:
Christina Ganim

Editorial Assistant:
Ashley Cronin

Technology Project Manager:
Andrew Keay

Marketing Manager:
Karin Sandberg

Marketing Communications
Manager: Shemika Britt

Project Manager, Editorial
Production: Rita Jaramillo

Creative Director: Rob Hugel

Art Director: Vernon Boes

Print Buyer: Judy Inouye

Permissions Editor:
Deanna Ettinger

Production Service:
International Typesetting
and Composition

Text Designer: Lisa Henry

Copy Editor: Kay Mikel

Cover Designer: Lisa Henry

Cover Image: Jack Dykinga/
Getty Images

Compositor: International
Typesetting and
Composition

For product information and technology assistance, contact us at **Cengage Learning Customer & Sales Support, 1-800-354-9706.**

For permission to use material from this text or product, submit all requests online at **www.cengage.com/permissions.** Further permissions questions can be emailed to **permissionrequest@cengage.com.**

Library of Congress Control Number: 2007904192

Student Edition:
ISBN-13: 978-0-495-55334-2
ISBN-10: 0-495-55334-4

Brooks/Cole
10 Davis Drive
Belmont, CA 94002-3098
USA

Cengage Learning is a leading provider of customized learning solutions with office locations around the globe, including Singapore, the United Kingdom, Australia, Mexico, Brazil, and Japan. Locate your local office at: **www.cengage.com/global.**

Cengage Learning products are represented in Canada by Nelson Education, Ltd.

To learn more about Brooks/Cole, visit **www.cengage.com/brookscole.**

Purchase any of our products at your local college store or at our preferred online store **www.ichapters.com.**

Printed in the United States of America
3 4 5 6 7 8 9 12 11 10

To Kyla and Keegan, my beloved grandchildren, who by their very presence have enlivened my life and given new meaning to playing in the sand.

ABOUT THE AUTHOR

GERALD COREY is a Professor Emeritus of Human Services at California State University at Fullerton. He received his doctorate in counseling from the University of Southern California. He is a licensed psychologist; a Diplomate in Counseling Psychology, American Board of Professional Psychology; a National Certified Counselor; a Fellow of the American Counseling Association; a Fellow of the American Psychological Association (Counseling Psychology); and a Fellow of the Association for Specialists in Group Work.

Jerry received the Outstanding Professor of the Year Award from California State University at Fullerton in 1991. He teaches both undergraduate and graduate courses in group counseling and graduate courses in ethics in counseling at various universities. He is the author or co-author of 15 textbooks in counseling currently in print, 3 student videos with workbooks, and more than 60 articles in professional publications. *Theory and Practice of Counseling and Psychotherapy* has been translated into the Arabic, Indonesian, Turkish, Portuguese, Korean, and Chinese languages. *Theory and Practice of Group Counseling* has been translated into Chinese, Spanish, and Korean.

Along with his wife, Marianne Schneider Corey, Jerry often presents workshops in group counseling. In the past 30 years the Coreys have conducted group counseling training workshops for mental health professionals at many universities in the United States as well as in Canada, Mexico, China, Hong Kong, Korea, Germany, Belgium, Scotland, England, and Ireland. In his leisure time, Jerry likes to travel, hike in the mountains, bike ride, and drive his 1931 Model A Ford.

Recent publications by Jerry Corey, all with Brooks/Cole Publishing Company, include:

- *Theory and Practice of Counseling and Psychotherapy* (and *Manual,* Eighth Ed., 2009)
- *The Art of Integrative Counseling,* Second Edition (2009)
- *Theory and Practice of Group Counseling* (and *Manual,* Seventh Ed., 2008)
- *Issues and Ethics in the Helping Professions,* Seventh Edition (2007, with Marianne Schneider Corey and Patrick Callanan)
- *Becoming a Helper,* Fifth Edition (2007, with Marianne Schneider Corey)
- *Groups: Process and Practice,* Seventh Edition (2006, with Marianne Schneider Corey)
- *I Never Knew I Had a Choice,* Eighth Edition (2006, with Marianne Schneider Corey)
- *Group Techniques,* Third Edition (2004, with Marianne Schneider Corey, Patrick Callanan, and J. Michael Russell)
- *Clinical Supervision in the Helping Professions: A Practical Guide* (2003, with Robert Haynes and Patrice Moulton).

Jerry is co-author, with his daughters Cindy Corey and Heidi Jo Corey, of an orientation-to-college book entitled *Living and Learning* (1997), published by Wadsworth. He is also co-author (with Barbara Herlihy) of *Boundary Issues in Counseling: Multiple Roles and Responsibilities,* 2nd Edition (2006), and *ACA Ethical Standards Casebook,* Sixth Edition (2006), both published by the American Counseling Association.

He has also made four CD-ROM (or DVD) programs on various aspects of counseling practice: (1) *CD-ROM for Integrative Counseling* (2005, with Robert Haynes); (2) *Groups in Action: Evolution and Challenges—DVD and Workbook* (2006, with Marianne Schneider Corey and Robert Haynes); (3) *Ethics in Action: CD-ROM* (2003, with Marianne Schneider Corey and Robert Haynes); and (4) DVD/Online Program, *Theory in Practice: The Case of Stan* (2009). All of these CD-ROM or DVD programs are available through Brooks/Cole.

ALVIN N. ALVAREZ, PhD, is Associate Professor and Coordinator of the College Counseling Program at San Francisco State University. His professional interests and scholarship focus is on Asian Americans, racial identity, and the psychological impact of racism. Dr. Alvarez is the current President of the Asian American Psychological Association (AAPA) and recently received the Early Career Award from AAPA.

JENNIFER ANDREWS, PhD, is a faculty member in the Department of Counseling and Family Sciences at Loma Linda University. A licensed marriage and family therapist, Dr. Andrews teaches classes that emphasize postmodern ideas and has co-authored a number of journal articles on postmodern perspectives.

JAMES ROBERT BITTER, EdD, is Professor of Counseling in the Department of Human Development and Learning at East Tennessee State University. He is a consultant in the areas of individual and group therapy and in the application of Adlerian principles to the counseling of children and families. Dr. Bitter has written many journal articles on family mapping and family constellation, created memories versus early recollections, and family reconstruction, and a textbook entitled, *Theory and Practice of Family Therapy and Counseling* (Brooks/Cole, 2009).

WILLIAM BLAU, PhD, has a private practice and teaches as an adjunct instructor at Copper Mountain College in Joshua Tree, California. Although his theoretical orientation is psychoanalytic, he often uses techniques from other approaches. His specialty areas include clinical biofeedback and the psychotherapy of psychotic people. Dr. Blau and his wife, Cathey Graham Blau, LCSW, BCD, work together in providing biofeedback training and couples therapy.

DAVID J. CAIN, PhD, ABPP, CGP, is the editor of *Humanistic Psychotherapies: Handbook of Research and Practice* and of *Classics in the Person-Centered Approach*. He received his doctorate in clinical and community psychology from the University of Wyoming. He teaches at the California School of Professional Psychology, San Diego (Alliant International University) and the psychology department at Chapman University. Dr. Cain is the founder of the Association for the Development of the Person-Centered Approach. He maintains a private practice in Oceanside and San Marcos, California.

GRACE A. CHEN, PhD, is a licensed psychologist at Counseling and Psychological Services at California State University, East Bay in Hayward, California. Her professional interests include Asian Americans, identity development, multicultural counseling, and college student development. She earned her PhD in Counseling Psychology at the University of Texas at Austin. Currently Dr. Chen serves on the directorate body of the Commission for Counseling and Psychological Services, a division of ACPA–College Student Educators International.

ROBERT C. CHOPE, PhD, is Professor of Counseling at San Francisco State University, and the founder of the career specialization. He is the author of four books and over 40 articles and chapters in books. Dr. Chope is a Fellow of the National Career Development Association (NCDA) and the 2004 winner of the NCDA Outstanding Career Practitioner Award. His daughter Luisa serves as an economic policy analyst for the National Council of La Raza in Washington, D.C.

DAVID J. CLARK, PhD, is a psychotherapist for Kaiser-Permanente Southern California, Psychiatry Department, where he is participating in a pilot project that is offering solution-oriented group therapy for brief treatment of depressed people. Dr. Clark has had a specialty in the area of addictions for more than 20 years. He is a licensed MFT and a clinical member and approved supervisor of the American Association for Marriage and Family Therapy (AAMFT).

ANDRÉS J. CONSOLI, PhD, is Associate Professor of Counseling at San Francisco State University, and former coordinator of the marriage and family specialization. He has written articles on client–therapist matching, psychotherapy integration, stress and anxiety, and Latino/a mental health. Dr. Consoli's research interests are in multicultural supervision, access and utilization of mental health services by Latinos/as, and the social representation of psychotherapy. He is the proud father of two boys, Julián and Benjamín.

BARBARA BROWNELL D'ANGELO, PhD, is a California-licensed psychologist with a behavioral orientation. Dr. D'Angelo had a private practice in psychotherapy in Santa Ana, California.

FRANK M. DATTILIO, PhD, ABPP, is on the faculty of psychiatry at both Harvard Medical School and the University of Pennsylvania School of Medicine, has been a visiting lecturer at many universities internationally, and is a clinical psychologist in private practice. Dr. Dattilio is the foremost authority on cognitive-behavior therapy with couples and families and has authored or co-authored 13 books and more than 200 professional publications worldwide. His works have been translated into 24 languages.

ALBERT ELLIS, PhD, ABPP, is considered to be the father of rational emotive behavior therapy and the grandfather of cognitive behavioral therapy. Dr. Ellis remained professionally active until his death at age 93 in 2007. He published more than 75 books and more than 800 articles, mostly on the theory and application of REBT. He gave workshops throughout the world and saw individuals in his counseling practice.

KATHY M. EVANS, PhD, is Associate Professor of Counselor Education at the University of South Carolina and is both a licensed professional counselor and a licensed psychologist. She has taught courses in multicultural counseling and counseling theory for the past 15 years. Her research, publications, and practice focus on issues important to women and ethnic minority men. Recently, Dr. Evans has devoted much of her time to studying the racial, gender, and feminist identities of African American women.

JON FREW, PhD, ABPP, is a Professor at Pacific University's School of Professional Psychology and is in private practice in Vancouver, Washington. He has published extensively in the field of Gestalt therapy and is on the editorial board of the *Gestalt Review*. Dr. Frew co-authored the book, *Contemporary Psychotherapies for a Diverse World*. He is co-director of the Gestalt Therapy Training Center Northwest and has conducted training workshops in the United States, Canada, and Australia.

WILLIAM GLASSER, MD, is Founder and President of The William Glasser Institute in Chatsworth, California, and is the founder of reality therapy. Dr. Glasser presents many workshops each year, both in this country and abroad. His practical approach continues to be popular among a variety of practitioners and teachers. He has written a number of books on reality therapy and choice theory.

ELIZABETH A. KINCADE, PhD, is Associate Professor and Coordinator of Outreach and Consultation in the Center for Counseling and Psychological Services at Indiana University of Pennsylvania. She is a licensed psychologist, counselor, supervisor, and teacher. Dr. Kincade's research and training interests are in the areas of feminist theory and therapy, multicultural issues in counseling, and supervision of emerging mental health practitioners.

KELLIE N. KIRKSEY, PhD, is Assistant Professor of Counselor Education at Malone College, as well as a clinician in private practice. She is a licensed clinical counselor, supervisor, and a rehabilitation counselor who blends traditional modalities with spirituality and creative expression for healing and wellness. Dr. Kirksey infuses diversity and multiculturalism into all of her courses. She is married to Cesar Augustin and has three children, Kelsie, Dominic, and Gabrielle.

ARNOLD A. LAZARUS, PhD, ABPP, is Distinguished Professor Emeritus in the Graduate School of Applied and Professional Psychology at Rutgers University and the executive director of the Lazarus Institute in Skillman, New Jersey. He is a Diplomate in Clinical Psychology of the American Board of Professional Psychology. Dr. Lazarus developed the multimodal approach, a broad-based, systematic, and comprehensive approach to behavior therapy, for which he has received numerous awards. He is considered a pioneer in the field of clinical behavior therapy.

MARY MOLINE, PhD, Dr.PH, is Professor and Chair of the Department of Counseling and Family Sciences at Loma Linda University. She is a licensed marriage and family therapist in California. She received her PhD in marriage and family therapy from Brigham Young University and her doctorate in public health from Loma Linda University. Dr. Moline is a clinical member and an approved supervisor of the American Association for Marriage and Family Therapy.

GERALD MONK, PhD, is a Professor at San Diego State University and teaches a range of conflict resolution and counseling courses. He has played a significant role in the development and international expansion of the narrative metaphor in therapy and mediation over the last 15 years. Dr. Monk has published numerous articles in the areas of narrative therapy, social constructionism, and mediation, and has co-authored three books. He has conducted workshops on narrative therapy and mediation in Canada, the United Kingdom, Iceland, Ireland, Cyprus, Mexico, Austria, New Zealand, Australia, and the United States.

WILLIAM G. NICOLL, PhD, is Professor and Chair of the Department of Counselor Education at Florida Atlantic University in Boca Raton, Florida. Dr. Nicoll provides training in Adlerian-based interventions across the United States as well as in Europe, Asia, Latin America, and Africa. His writings focus on the applications of Adlerian brief counseling with individuals and families and with the school-related problems of children and adolescents.

JOHN C. NORCROSS, PhD, ABPP, is Professor of Psychology and Distinguished University Fellow at the University of Scranton and a clinical psychologist in part-time practice. A long-time advocate of psychotherapy integration, his 16 books include *Psychotherapy Relationships That Work; Evidence-Based Practices in Mental Health; The Psychotherapist's Own Therapy; Leaving It at the Office;* and the *Handbook of Psychotherapy Integration.* Dr. Norcross has conducted training and workshops in 24 countries.

J. MICHAEL RUSSELL, PhD, PsyD, is Professor Emeritus in both the departments of Philosophy and of Human Services at California State University, Fullerton. He is a Research Psychoanalytic and Training and Supervising Analyst for the Newport Psychoanalytic Institute. His academic and research interests include existential psychoanalysis, philosophical assumptions of psychotherapy, existential group, and philosophical counseling. Dr. Russell has received numerous awards for excellence in teaching from California State University, Fullerton.

SUSAN R. SEEM, PhD, is a faculty member in the Department of Counselor Education at the State University of New York College at Brockport. Her past work experience includes both college and community counseling. Dr. Seem's publications include articles on gender bias in counselor training and in clinical judgments, counseling gay and lesbian adolescents, feminist therapy, the consideration of gender in college counseling center practice, and the development of a safe school environment.

MIA SEVIER, PhD, is Assistant Professor in the Human Services Department at California State University, Fullerton. She regularly teaches a variety of human services courses, including a survey of contemporary theories and techniques of counseling. Dr. Sevier received her doctorate in clinical psychology from the University of California, Los Angeles, and specializes in couple therapy.

ROBERT E. WUBBOLDING, EdD, is Professor Emeritus of Counseling at Xavier University. He is the director of the Center for Reality Therapy in Cincinnati and also the director of training for the William Glasser Institute in Los Angeles. He has taught reality therapy cross-culturally throughout Asia, Europe, and the Middle East, and frequently gives workshops in the United States. Dr. Wubbolding has written numerous journal articles, book chapters, and has published 10 books on reality therapy, including *Reality Therapy for the 21st Century*.

CONTENTS

4   Case Approach to Existential Therapy   72

5   Case Approach to Person-Centered Therapy   87

6   Case Approach to Gestalt Therapy   107

7   Case Approach to Behavior Therapy   122

8   Case Approach to Cognitive Behavior Therapy   144

PREFACE

 Case Approach to Counseling and Psychotherapy reflects my increasing emphasis on the use of demonstrations and the case approach method to bridge the gap between the theory and practice of counseling. Students in the courses I teach have found that a demonstration in class often clears up their misconceptions about how a therapy actually works. This book is an attempt to stimulate some of the unique learning that can occur through seeing a therapeutic approach in action. It also gives students a chance to work with a case from the vantage point of 11 counseling approaches: psychoanalytic, Adlerian, existential, person-centered, Gestalt, behavior, cognitive behavior, reality, feminist, postmodern, and couples and family systems therapies. This book also provides students with the opportunity to consider a single case from multicultural and integrative perspectives.

The format of this book provides an opportunity to see how each of the various therapeutic approaches is applied to a single client, Ruth Walton, who is followed throughout the book. A feature of the text is an assessment of Ruth's case by one or more consultants in each of the 11 theoretical perspectives. New to this edition are six consultants who address counseling Ruth from multicultural and integrative approaches. Highly competent practitioners assess and treat Ruth from their particular theoretical orientation or their integration of several approaches; they also provide sample dialogues to illustrate their style of working with Ruth.

The various theory chapters use a common format, allowing for comparisons among approaches. This format includes a general overview of the theory, the guest commentary or commentaries, followed by my way of working with Ruth from that particular perspective. I discuss the theory's basic assumptions, an initial assessment of Ruth, the goals of therapy, and the therapeutic procedures to be used. The therapeutic process is concretely illustrated by client–therapist dialogues, which are augmented by process commentaries explaining the rationale for my interventions. Questions for Reflection at the end of each chapter help readers apply the material to their personal lives and offer guidelines for continuing to work with Ruth within each of the theoretical orientations.

New to this seventh edition is Chapter 13, "Counseling Ruth from Multicultural and Integrative Perspectives." Guidelines are provided for working with Ruth as a member of various cultural groups. In this new chapter various contributors show how their approach with Ruth would incorporate cultural themes if Ruth were African American, Latina, or Asian American. In addition, one consultant demonstrates the value of an integrative counseling approach with Ruth. All of the contributors in this chapter combine concepts and techniques from both multicultural and integrative perspectives in their work with Ruth.

Chapter 14 brings all of the approaches discussed in the book together and helps students develop their own therapeutic style. I demonstrate how I would counsel Ruth in an integrative fashion by drawing on most of the therapeutic approaches discussed in this book.

Supplementary Resources

Ideally, *Case Approach to Counseling and Psychotherapy* will be used as part of an integrated learning series I have developed for courses in counseling theory and practice. In a separate book, *The Art of Integrative Counseling,* I describe how to develop your own integrative approach to counseling and provide guidelines for acquiring a personal style of counseling practice. Ruth's case is used to illustrate this integrative perspective. *Case Approach to Counseling and Psychotherapy* can supplement the core textbook to enhance students' learning of theory by letting them see counseling in action. In the textbook, *Theory and Practice of Counseling and Psychotherapy,* 8th edition, students are given an overview of the key concepts and techniques of the models of contemporary therapy. The accompanying *Student Manual for Theory and Practice of Counseling and Psychotherapy* contains many experiential activities and exercises designed to help students apply the theories to themselves and to connect theory with practice.

A self-study *CD-ROM for Integrative Counseling* illustrates my own integrative perspective in working with Ruth. References to the CD-ROM are given throughout this book by using an icon to help students coordinate the counseling sessions in the CD-ROM program with the topics in this book. The CD-ROM program brings together several of the therapies discussed in this book and provides concrete illustrations of my ways of working with Ruth.

New to this edition is an online and DVD program, *Theory in Practice: The Case of Stan,* in which I counsel a client named "Stan" from 11 different theoretical orientations. This interactive program builds on the sections for each of the theory chapters in *Theory and Practice of Counseling and Psychotherapy.* The aim of each of the sessions is to demonstrate selected techniques applied to the case of Stan. This online and DVD program can be tied in well to the discussion of all of the theory chapters in *Case Approach to Counseling and Psychotherapy.*

Acknowledgments

I appreciate both the support and the challenge given by those teachers of counseling courses and clinicians who read the revised manuscript for this seventh edition and provided specific and helpful comments for improving the effectiveness of the case presentations. These people are:

- Mary Jo Blazek, University of Maine at Augusta
- Patrick Callanan, California State University, Fullerton
- Monit Cheung, University of Houston
- Grafton Eliason, California University of Pennsylvania
- Erica Gannon, Clayton College and State University
- Mike Nystul, New Mexico State University
- Robert Peterson, Metropolitan State University

Special thanks are extended to Marianne Schneider Corey, my wife and colleague, for her contributions to this revision. Based on her clinical experiences as a marriage and family therapist, she went over the case of Ruth and reviewed the guest contributors' pieces as well.

I am particularly indebted to those individuals who reviewed a chapter in their area of expertise and who also contributed by writing about their way of working with Ruth from their particular therapeutic perspective. Most of the original contributors updated and expanded their selections in this edition, and there are eight new contributors. A complete list of these contributors appears in the About the Contributors section.

This book is the result of a team effort, which includes the combined talents of several people at Brooks/Cole. It continues to be a positive experience to work with a dedicated staff of professionals who go out of their way to give their best. These people include Marquita Flemming, senior editor of counseling; Meaghan Banks and Ashley Cronin, editorial assistants, who monitored the review process; Karin Sandberg, senior marketing manager; and Rita Jaramillo, content project manager. We thank Ben Kolstad of International Typesetting and Composition, who coordinated the production of this book. Special appreciation goes to Kay Mikel, the manuscript editor, whose sensitivity and editorial skills contributed in important ways to the readability and interest of this text.

— GERALD COREY

CHAPTER ONE

Introduction and Overview

Structure of the Book

In teaching theory courses I have found that even after reading about a theory of therapy and discussing it in class, students are sometimes still unclear about how to apply it. I began experimenting with asking my students to volunteer for a class demonstration in which they served as "clients." Seeing concepts in action gave them a clearer picture of how therapists use various approaches in their work. This book illustrates 11 therapies in action and shows how to selectively borrow concepts and techniques from these therapeutic approaches. In addition, I encourage you to integrate techniques that are appropriate to your client population in a style that is an expression of who you are as a person. Effective counseling combines your personality with the technical skills that you employ. To apply techniques appropriately, it is essential to consider your personal style and theoretical orientation in relation to each client's unique life situation.

Before this large task of developing a personalized approach can be accomplished, however, you will need to know the basics of each of the theories and acquire some experience with these therapies. This book aims to provide a balance between describing the way therapists with a particular orientation might proceed with a client and challenging you to try your hand at showing how you would proceed with the same client.

This initial chapter deals with methods of conceptualizing a case, and it provides background material on the central figure in this book, Ruth Walton, who is also the "client" in the accompanying program, *CD-ROM for Integrative Counseling*. Refer to Ruth's intake form and autobiography frequently as you work with her in the 11 theory chapters. Ruth is not an actual client, but is one that I have created by combining many of the common themes I have observed in my work with clients. However, I believe the characteristics ascribed to Ruth are representative of clients you may meet in your practice.

Ruth appears in each of the chapters on individual theories (Chapters 2–13), and in Chapter 14, which describes my own integrative approach. Chapters 2 through 13 begin with commentaries by one or more "outside consultants" on Ruth's case. There are 26 guest contributors (consultants) who demonstrate their approach in assessing and treating Ruth. Each consultant was given Ruth's background information and also read my perspective on her for the theory under discussion. Then this representative wrote a section describing the following:

- The core concepts and goals of his or her therapeutic approach
- The themes in Ruth's life that might serve as a focus for therapy
- An assessment of Ruth's dynamics, with emphasis on her current life situation
- The techniques and procedures that would probably be used in counseling Ruth
- Illustrations of the therapy in action through dialogue between Ruth and the therapist

After the guest contributors' discussion of their perspective on Ruth in each chapter, I look at the basic assumptions of the approaches, make an initial assessment of Ruth, and examine the theory's therapeutic goals and procedures. The therapeutic process is made concrete with sample dialogue I have with Ruth, along with my process commentaries to provide an explanation of the direction therapy is taking. In addition, I provide my own version of the theory as I draw from key concepts and selected techniques in my way of counseling Ruth.

You will notice that there are two invited consultants for Chapter 7 (behavior therapy), Chapter 8 (cognitive behavior therapy), and Chapter 9 (reality therapy). For Chapter 10 (feminist therapy) three consultants work as a unified team with Ruth. For Chapter 11 (postmodern approaches) there are three invited consultants, one for each of the major postmodern approaches: social constructionism, solution-focused brief therapy, and narrative therapy. Thus, in Chapters 7 to 11 you have the advantage of reading two or more different styles of working with Ruth from practitioners with the same general theoretical orientation. Chapter 13 ("Counseling Ruth from Multicultural and Integrative Perspectives") is new to this edition; it focuses on how to work with Ruth if she were from various racial/cultural backgrounds and by applying integrative perspectives in counseling her. Five different contributors show how they would counsel Ruth if she were a Latina, an Asian American, or an African American. Another contributor describes his integrative perspective in counseling Ruth.

With the contributors' and my work with Ruth, you are exposed to 27 different therapeutic styles in helping Ruth challenge her self-imposed or external limitations and shape her new identity. In a sense, all counseling is aimed at helping clients transcend their limitations and tap their inner resources for change. In our various ways, we are attempting to assist Ruth in reaching to the sky to tap the limitless possibilities in making choices to become the person that she never dreamed she could become.

You are encouraged to become an active learner by evaluating the manner in which the consultants and I work with Ruth from the various theoretical perspectives. You are asked to show how you would work with her as your client, using the particular approach being considered in the chapter. To guide you in thinking of ways to work with Ruth, each chapter ends with "Questions for Reflection." In addition to thinking about these questions by yourself, I suggest that you arrange to work with fellow students in small discussion groups to explore various approaches.

You can further enhance your learning by participating in a variety of role-playing exercises in which you "become" Ruth and also by participating in discussions in small groups based on various ways of working with her. Rather than merely reading about her case, you can use various perspectives to stimulate reflection on ways in which you have felt like Ruth. In experiential practice sessions, you can also draw on your own concerns in becoming the counselor. Think of as many ways as possible to use this case to stimulate introspection and lively class discussion.

In Chapter 14 you are encouraged to consider the advantages of eventually developing your own integrative approach and counseling style. Such an integrative perspective of counseling entails selecting concepts and methods from various sources and theories. An integrative approach does not necessarily refer to developing a new theory; rather, it emphasizes a systematic integration of underlying principles and techniques of the various therapy systems. I encourage you to strive to build a unified system that fits you and is appropriate for the particular setting in which you practice. It is also essential that you be willing to challenge your basic assumptions, test your hypotheses as you practice, and revise your theory as you confirm or disconfirm your clinical hunches.

I demonstrate my integrative approach to counseling in the *CD-ROM for Integrative Counseling,* which shows segments of individual counseling sessions in which Ruth explores key themes in her life.[1] Throughout this book I will refer you to specific sessions in the CD-ROM program that demonstrate the application of these diverse theoretical perspectives from the initial to ending phase of therapy with Ruth. The CD-ROM and this book are ideal companions. In addition, *The Art of Integrative Counseling* also uses the case of Ruth as the central example in illustrating an integrative approach to counseling practice.[2] This book expands on material presented in Chapter 14 here, which is devoted to bringing the approaches together and illustrating how you can develop your own therapeutic style.

As I mentioned in the Preface, there is a new online and DVD program titled, *Theory in Practice: The Case of Stan,* in which I counsel a client named "Stan" from 11 different theoretical orientations. The aim of each of the 13 simulated counseling sessions is to demonstrate selected techniques applied to the case of Stan. This program can be used to enhance your understanding of each of the chapters in this book.

Overview of the Therapeutic Perspectives

In the chapters to follow, the case of Ruth will be analyzed and discussed from various therapeutic perspectives. For each of these perspectives we will consider its basic assumptions, its view of how to assess clients, its goals for therapy, and its therapeutic procedures. This section presents the essence of the various approaches. As a way of laying the foundation for developing an integrative approach, we will look for common denominators and differences among the 11 perspectives.[3] For further study, I highly recommend the following books on psychotherapy integration: *Handbook of Psychotherapy Integration* (Norcross & Goldfried, 2005) and *A Casebook of Psychotherapy Integration* (Stricker & Gold, 2006).[4]

Basic Assumptions

When therapists make initial contact with clients, their theoretical perspective determines what they look for and what they see. This largely determines the focus and course of therapy and influences their choice of therapeutic strategies and procedures. As you develop your counseling stance, pay attention to your own basic assumptions. Developing a counseling perspective is more involved than merely accepting the tenets of a particular theory or combination of theories. Your theoretical approach is an expression of your unique life experiences.

How do theoretical assumptions influence practice? Your view about the assessment of clients, the goals you think are important in therapy, the strategies and techniques you employ to reach these goals, the way you divide responsibility in the client–therapist relationship, and your view of your function and role as a counselor are largely determined by your theoretical orientation. Attempting to practice counseling without at least a general theoretical perspective is somewhat like flying a plane without a map and without instruments. But a counseling theory is not a rigid structure that prescribes the specific steps of what to do in therapeutic work. Instead, a theoretical orientation is a set of general guidelines you can use to make sense of what you are doing.

One way to approach the basic assumptions underlying the major theoretical orientations is to consider six categories under which most contemporary systems fall. These are (1) the *psychodynamic approaches,* which stress insight in therapy (psychoanalytic and Adlerian therapy); (2) the *experiential* and *relationship-oriented approaches,* which stress feelings and subjective experiencing (existential, person-centered, and Gestalt therapy); (3) the *cognitive* and *behavioral approaches,* which stress the role of thinking and doing and tend to be action-oriented (behavior therapy, rational emotive behavior therapy, cognitive therapy, and reality therapy); (4) *feminist therapy,* which stresses egalitarian relationships and social and political activism to combat oppression; (5) *postmodern approaches,* which include social constructionism, solution-focused brief therapy, and narrative therapy; and (6) *family therapy,* which stresses understanding the individual within the entire system of which he or she is a part.

Although I have separated the theories into six general groups, this categorization is somewhat arbitrary. Overlapping concepts and themes make it difficult to neatly compartmentalize these theoretical orientations. What follows is a thumbnail sketch of the basic assumptions underlying each of these 11 therapeutic systems.

Psychoanalytic Therapy The psychoanalytic approach views people as being significantly influenced by unconscious motivation, conflicts between impulses and prohibitions, defense mechanisms, and early childhood experiences.

Because the dynamics of behavior are buried in the unconscious, treatment consists of a lengthy process of analyzing inner conflicts that are rooted in the past. Therapy is largely a process of restructuring the personality; therefore, clients must be willing to commit themselves to an intensive, long-term process.

🕮 **Adlerian Therapy**   According to the Adlerian approach, people are primarily social beings, influenced and motivated by societal forces. Human nature is viewed as creative, active, and decisional. The approach focuses on the unity of the person and on understanding the individual's subjective perspective. Adler holds that inherent feelings of inferiority, or feeling less than one should or needs to be, initiates a natural striving toward achieving a higher, or greater, level of mastery and competence in life. Like all living organisms, humans strive throughout life to grow, evolve, and become more fully developed and capable. The subjective decisions each person makes regarding the specific direction of this striving form the basis of the individual's lifestyle (or personality style). The style of life consists of our views about others, the world, and ourselves; these views lead to distinctive behaviors that we adopt in pursuit of our life goals. We can shape our own future by actively and courageously taking risks and making decisions in the face of unknown consequences. Clients are not viewed as being "sick" or suffering from some disability or disorder needing to be "cured." Rather, they are seen as being discouraged and functioning on the basis of self-defeating and self-limiting assumptions, which generate problem-maintaining, ego-protective behaviors. Thus, clients are seen as being in need of encouragement to correct mistaken perceptions of self and others and to learn to initiate new behavioral interaction patterns. Counseling is not simply a matter of an expert therapist making prescriptions for change. It is a collaborative effort, with client and therapist actively working on mutually accepted goals and the facilitation of change at both the cognitive and behavioral levels.

🕮 **Existential Therapy**   The existential perspective holds that we define ourselves by our choices. Although outside factors restrict the range of our choices, we are ultimately the authors of our lives. We are thrust into a meaningless world, yet we are challenged to accept our aloneness and create a meaningful existence. Because we have the capacity for awareness, we are basically free. Along with our freedom, however, comes responsibility for the choices we make. Existential practitioners contend that clients often lead a "restricted existence," seeing few if any alternatives for dealing with life situations and tending to feel trapped or helpless. The therapist's job is to confront these clients with the restricted life they have chosen and to help them become aware of their own part in creating this condition. As an outgrowth of the therapeutic venture, clients are able to recognize outmoded patterns of living, and they begin to accept responsibility for changing their future.

🕮 **Person-Centered Therapy**   The person-centered approach rests on the assumption that we have the capacity to understand our problems and that we have the resources within us to resolve them. Seeing people in this light means that therapists focus on the constructive side of human nature and on what is right with people. This approach places emphasis on feelings about the self. Clients can move forward toward growth and wholeness by looking within rather than focusing on outside influences. They are able to change without a high degree of structure and direction from the therapist. What clients need from the therapist is understanding, genuineness, support, acceptance, caring, and positive regard.

🕮 **Gestalt Therapy**   The Gestalt approach is based on the assumption that individuals and their behavior must be understood in the context of their present environment. The therapist's task is to support clients as they explore their present experience. The fundamental method to assist in this exploration is awareness of the internal (intrapersonal) world and the external environment. Clients carry on their own therapy as much as possible by doing experiments designed to heighten awareness and to engage in contact. Change occurs naturally as awareness of "what is" increases. Interruptions in the process by which clients develop awareness and move toward contact with the environment are monitored. Heightened awareness can also lead to a more thorough integration of parts of the client that were fragmented or unknown.

🕮 **Behavior Therapy**   Behavior therapy assumes that people are basically shaped by learning and sociocultural conditioning. This approach focuses on the client's ability to learn how to eliminate maladaptive behavior and acquire constructive behavior. Behavior therapy is a systematic approach that begins with a comprehensive assessment of the individual to determine the present level of functioning as a prelude to setting therapeutic goals. After the client establishes clear and specific behavioral goals, the therapist typically suggests strategies that are most appropriate for meeting these stated goals. It is assumed that clients will make progress to the extent that they are willing to practice new behaviors in real-life situations. Continual evaluation is used to determine how well the procedures and techniques are working.

🕮 **Cognitive Behavioral Approaches**   From the perspective of rational emotive behavior therapy (REBT), our problems are caused by our perceptions of life situations and our thoughts, not by the situations themselves, not by others, and not by past events. Thus, it is our responsibility to recognize and change self-defeating thinking that leads to emotional and behavioral disorders. REBT also holds that people tend to incorporate these dysfunctional beliefs from external sources and then continue to indoctrinate themselves with this faulty thinking. To overcome irrational thinking, therapists use active and directive therapy procedures, including teaching, suggestion, and giving homework. REBT emphasizes education, with the therapist functioning as a teacher and the client as a learner. Although REBT is didactic and directive, its goal is to get people to think, feel, and act for themselves. Therapists consistently encourage and challenge clients to do what is necessary to make long-lasting and substantive change.

Other cognitive behavioral therapies share some of the assumptions of REBT. Many of these approaches assume that people are prone to learning erroneous, self-defeating thoughts but that they are capable of unlearning them. People perpetuate their difficulties through their self-talk. By pinpointing these cognitive errors and correcting them, clients can create a more fulfilling life. Cognitive restructuring plays a central role in these therapies. People are assumed to be able to make changes by listening to their self-talk, by learning a new internal dialogue, and by learning coping skills needed for behavioral changes.

Reality Therapy   Reality therapy operates from the premise that all relationship problems are in the present and must be solved in the present. Problematic symptoms are the result of clients trying to deal with a present unsatisfying relationship. Once a significant relationship is improved, the troubling symptom will disappear. Reality therapists challenge clients to consider whether their current behavior is getting them what they want. Clients are encouraged to explore their perceptions, share their wants, and make a commitment to counseling. Because clients can directly control their acting and thinking functions more than they can control what they are feeling, their actions become the focus of therapy. Clients explore the direction in which their behavior is taking them and evaluate what they are doing. They then create a plan of action to make the changes they want.

Feminist Therapy   A basic assumption of feminist therapy is that power inequalities and gender-role expectations influence individuals from a very early age. There are detrimental effects of gender socialization for both women and men, for all individuals are capable of possessing a range of characteristics and behaviors that go beyond rigid and restrictive cultural stereotypes. Therapy is conducted in a gender-sensitive manner. This includes having a positive attitude toward women and being willing to challenge patriarchal systems, empowering both women and men by helping them transcend gender socialization, and assisting women in finding their voices and discovering meaning in their lives. The therapist's role is to sensitize clients to the impact of gender, class, race, ethnicity, and other aspects in their lives. Feminist therapists are aware of the potentially destructive power dynamics in the client–therapist relationship and build mutuality into the therapeutic process. Therapy is viewed as a cooperative and collaborative relationship.

Postmodern Approaches   The postmodern approaches challenge many of the assumptions of traditional therapies. Postmodernism is marked by acceptance of plurality and the notion that individuals create their own reality. Some of the main assumptions are that people are competent and healthy, have the capacity to find their own solutions to difficulties they face, and are the experts on their own lives. The postmodern approaches have in common the basic assumption that we generate stories to make sense of ourselves and our world. People are empowered by learning how to separate themselves from their problems. Clients learn that the person is not the problem—the problem is the problem. Therapists help clients to free themselves from problem-saturated stories and open space to co-create alternative stories. In essence, clients reauthor their stories about themselves and their relationships. Therapy is a collaborative venture aimed at helping clients construct meaningful goals that will lead to a better future.

⬯ **Family Systems Therapy**   Family systems therapy is grounded on the assumption that the individual cannot be fully understood apart from the family system. A basic principle is that a change in one part of the system will result in a change in other parts of the system. If the family unit changes in significant ways, these changes will have an impact on the individual. Likewise, if the individual makes changes, the entire family unit will be affected. Thus, therapy involves assessing and treating an individual's concerns within the context of the interaction among family members. From a systemic perspective, being a healthy person involves both a sense of belonging to the family system and a sense of separateness and individuality. Some of the assumptions of family therapy include the notion that a client's behavior (1) may serve a function or a purpose for the family, (2) may be the result of the system's inability to function effectively, and (3) may result from dysfunctional patterns that are passed on from generation to generation. The family therapist intervenes with individual clients in ways that will enable them to deal more effectively with significant people in their lives, whether or not these other people are physically present in the therapy session.

Multicultural Perspectives Underlying Practice

The contemporary theories of therapeutic practice are grounded on assumptions that are part of Western culture. Many of these assumptions may not be appropriate when working with clients from non-Western cultures. The basic assumptions of many of the theoretical orientations described in this book reflect values such as choice, the uniqueness of the individual, self-assertion, personal development, and strengthening the ego. Therapeutic outcomes that these models stress include improving assertive coping skills by changing the environment, changing one's coping behavior, and learning to manage stress. In contrast, non-Western orientations focus on interdependence, play down individuality, and emphasize losing oneself in the totality of the cosmos.

Western therapeutic approaches are oriented toward individual change. Non-Western approaches focus more on the social framework than on development of the individual. The techniques associated with some of the contemporary counseling models may need to be modified when they are applied to other ethnic and cultural groups. In Chapter 13, different contributors demonstrate how they would work with Ruth from various multicultural perspectives. Themes that might be addressed from a cultural perspective are illustrated in three different pieces: Ruth as a Latina client, Ruth as an African American client, and Ruth as an Asian American client. In each of these cases in which Ruth assumes a different cultural identity, the counselors demonstrate how they adapt their own integrative approach to various multicultural themes.

Seeking professional help is not customary for many client populations, and individuals typically first may turn to informal systems (family, friends, and community). In an increasingly pluralistic society, there is an ethical imperative to avoid forcing all clients to fit a mold that may not be appropriate for their cultural background. As counselors, we need to be aware of how our assumptions and underlying theoretical orientation influence practice.

Using Techniques From All Approaches

Whatever techniques you employ, it is essential to keep the needs of your client in mind. Some clients relate best to cognitive techniques, others to techniques designed to change behavior, and others to techniques aimed at eliciting emotional material. The same client, depending on the stage of his or her therapy, can profit from participating in all of these different techniques.

As a therapist, you would do well to think of ways to take techniques from all of the approaches so that you are able to work with a client on *all levels* of development. For example, when working with Ruth (whom you will become very familiar with in this book), your initial interventions may be directed toward getting her to identify and express *feelings* that she has kept bottled up for much of her life. If you listen to her and provide a place where she can experience what she is feeling, she is likely to be able to give more expression to emotions that she has distorted and denied.

As her therapy progresses, you may well direct interventions toward getting her to think about critical choices she made that still have an influence in her life. At this time in her therapy you are likely to shift the focus from exploration of feelings to exploration of her attitudes, her *thinking processes,* her values, and her basic beliefs. Still later your focus may be more on helping her develop *action programs* in which she can experiment with new ways of *behaving,* both during the sessions and outside of them.

In addition to working with Ruth as an individual, there may be significant therapeutic value in bringing in members of her family of origin, her current family, and significant others. It could also be useful to work with Ruth as someone who has been oppressed by gender-role stereotyping. Seeing Ruth as part of a system will provide another dimension that can deepen therapy. An important part of Ruth's therapy could involve encouraging social action on her part, geared to changing certain aspects of the *environment* that are contributing to her problems. It is not a matter of working with one aspect of Ruth's experiencing while forgetting about the other facets of her being; rather, it is a case of selecting a focus for a particular phase of her therapy. The challenge you will face as you encounter Ruth is how to utilize an *integrative approach* as you draw on a variety of techniques to help Ruth work through her struggles.

In working within a *multicultural framework,* it is especially important for you to use techniques flexibly. Clients should not be forced into a strict mold. Rather, techniques are most effective when they are tailored to what the individual client needs, which means you will have to modify your strategies. Some clients will resist getting involved in techniques aimed at bringing up and expressing intense emotions. Highly confrontational techniques may close down some clients. In such cases it may be best to focus more on cognitive or behavioral techniques or to modify emotive techniques that are appropriate for the client. Other clients may need to be confronted if they are to move. Confrontation at its best is an act of caring. It is designed to challenge clients to examine what they are thinking, feeling, and doing. Relying strictly on supportive techniques with certain clients will not provide the impetus they need to take the steps necessary to change. Techniques work best when they are designed to help clients explore thoughts, feelings, and actions that are within their cultural environment. Again, the value of bringing the client into the counseling process as an informed partner and a collaborator with you as a therapist cannot be overemphasized.

Perspectives on Assessment

Some approaches stress the importance of conducting a comprehensive assessment of the client as the initial step in the therapeutic process. The rationale is that specific counseling goals cannot be formulated and appropriate strategies cannot be designed until a thorough picture of the client's past and present functioning is formed. In this section I describe various views of the role of assessment in therapy. I also present some ways of conceptualizing an individual case, emphasizing what information to gather during the initial stages of therapy.

Psychoanalytic Therapy   Psychoanalysts assume that normal personality development is based on dealing effectively with successive psychosexual and psychosocial stages of development. Faulty personality development is the result of inadequately resolving a specific developmental conflict. Therapists are interested in the client's early history as a way to understand how past situations contribute to a dysfunction. This approach emphasizes the importance of comprehensive assessment techniques as a basis for understanding personality dynamics and the origin of emotional disorders. However, some analysts shy away from gathering information, preferring to let it unfold during the process of analytic therapy.

Adlerian Therapy   Some Adlerians prefer to engage in a more structured assessment process utilizing a detailed lifestyle questionnaire to gather information regarding the client's family of origin, parental relationships, sibling relationships, and family values so as to begin to see the client's perceptions of life and the context in which his or her unique style of life developed, which includes one's view of self, others, and life. Others prefer to use a more informal process, incorporating aspects of the formal lifestyle assessment (for example, family-of-origin information, birth order) as well as any of a variety of other assessment techniques that help to reveal the underlying cognitive framework of the client's personality. Early childhood recollections, family genograms, favorite childhood stories, family-of-origin stories, art therapy activities, and other such projective techniques can all be utilized in the assessment process by Adlerian therapists.

Existential Therapy   Existentially oriented counselors maintain that the way to understand the client is by grasping the essence of the person's subjective world. The primary purpose of existential clinical assessment is to understand the assumptions clients use in structuring their existence. This approach is different from the traditional diagnostic framework, for it focuses not on understanding the individual from an external perspective but, instead, on grasping the essence of the client's inner world. Existential therapists prefer understanding and exploration of the client's subjective reality, as opposed to formulation of a diagnosis.

Person-Centered Therapy

In much the same spirit as existential counselors, person-centered therapists maintain that traditional assessment and diagnosis are detrimental because they are external ways of understanding the client. They believe (1) the best vantage point for understanding another person is through his or her subjective world; (2) the practitioner can become preoccupied with the client's history and neglect present attitudes and behavior; and (3) therapists can develop a judgmental attitude, shifting too much in the direction of telling clients what they ought to do. Focusing on gathering information about a client can lead to an intellectualized conception about the person. The client is assumed to be the one who knows the dynamics of his or her behavior. For change to occur, the person must experience a perceptual change, not simply receive data. Thus, therapists listen actively, attempt to be present, and allow clients to identify the themes they choose to explore.

Gestalt Therapy

Gestalt therapists are interested in the "backgrounds" out of which the "figures" that guide their work emerge. Many Gestalt therapists gather certain types of information about their clients to supplement the assessment and diagnostic work done in the present moment. Gestalt therapists attend to interruptions in the client's contacting functions, and the result is a "functional diagnosis" of how individuals experience satisfaction or blocks in their relationship with the environment.

Behavior Therapy

The behavioral approach begins with a comprehensive assessment of the client's present functioning, with questions directed to past learning that is related to current behavior patterns. It includes an objective appraisal of specific behaviors and the stimuli that are maintaining them. Some of the reasons for conducting a thorough assessment at the outset of therapy are these: (1) to identify behavioral deficiencies as well as assets, (2) to provide an objective means of appraising both a client's specific symptoms and the factors that have led up to the client's malfunctioning, (3) to facilitate selection of the most suitable therapeutic techniques, (4) to specify a new learning and shaping schedule, (5) to predict the course and the outcome of a particular clinical disorder, and (6) to provide a framework for research into the effectiveness of the procedures employed.

Cognitive Behavioral Approaches

The assessment used in cognitive behavioral therapy is based on getting a sense of the client's patterns of thinking. Attention is paid to various beliefs the client has developed in relation to certain events. Therapists are not merely concerned with gathering data about past events but are also alert to evidence of faulty thinking and cognitive distortions the client has incorporated. Once self-defeating thought patterns and beliefs have been identified, the therapeutic process consists of actively challenging these beliefs and substituting constructive ones.

🐚 **Reality Therapy**   Assessment of clients is typically not a formal process; psychological testing and diagnosis are not generally a part of this approach. Through the use of skillful questioning, reality therapists help clients make an assessment of their present behavior. They have little interest in learning the causes of clients' current problems or in gathering information about clients' past experiences. Instead, the focus is on getting clients to take a critical look at what they are doing now and then determine the degree to which their present behavior is effective. This informal assessment directs clients to pay attention to their pattern of wants, needs, perceptions, successes, and personal assets to evaluate whether their lives are moving in the direction they want.

🐚 **Feminist Therapy**   This approach is less than enthusiastic when it comes to traditional diagnosis. Feminist therapists criticize the current classification system for being biased because it was developed by White, male psychiatrists. Also, the classification system tends to focus on the individual's symptoms and not on the social factors that cause dysfunctional behavior. The assessment process emphasizes the cultural context of clients' problems, especially the degree to which clients possess power or are oppressed. Some assessment and treatment approaches include gender-role analysis, power analysis, assertion training, and demystification of therapy.

🐚 **Postmodern Approaches**   Like feminist therapy, the postmodern therapies do not emphasize assessment, diagnosis, or categorization of individuals. Postmodern therapists do not want to assume the role of judging clients or thinking and talking about them in terms of pathological categories. These therapists do not get caught up in totalizing descriptions of an individual's identity, especially if these descriptions are anchored in terms of a problem. Instead, the emphasis is placed on an individual's competencies and establishing relationships with clients whereby they become senior partners in the counseling venture. Rather than looking at what is wrong with people, this approach focuses on the client's strengths and resources.

🐚 **Family Systems Therapy**   In most systemic approaches both therapist and client are involved in the assessment process. Some systemic practitioners assist clients in tracing the highlights of their family history and in identifying issues in their family of origin. The premise underlying the significance of understanding and assessing one's family of origin is that the patterns of interpersonal behavior learned there will be repeated in other interactions outside the family. Individuals may be asked to identify what they learned from interacting with their parents, from observing their parents' interactions with each other, and from observing how each parent interacted with each sibling. Clients may also identify the rules governing interactions in their family. These family precepts include unspoken rules, messages given by parents to children, myths, and secrets. Family rules may be functional or dysfunctional.

THE PLACE OF ASSESSMENT AND DIAGNOSIS IN COUNSELING AND CASE MANAGEMENT Assessment consists of evaluating the relevant factors in a client's life to identify themes for further exploration in therapy. Diagnosis, which is sometimes part of the assessment process, consists of identifying a specific category of psychological problem based on a pattern of symptoms. There are several types of diagnosis. *Medical diagnosis* is the process of examining physical symptoms, inferring causes of physical disorders or diseases, providing a category that fits the pattern of a disease, and prescribing an appropriate treatment. *Psychological diagnosis* entails identifying an emotional or behavioral problem and making a statement about the current status of a client. It includes stipulating the possible causes of the individual's emotional, psychological, and behavioral difficulties. It also entails suggesting the appropriate therapeutic techniques to deal with the identified problem and estimating the chances for a successful resolution. *Differential diagnosis* consists of distinguishing one form of psychiatric disorder from another by determining which of two (or more) diseases or disorders with similar symptoms the person is suffering from. The 2000 fourth edition, text revision, of the American Psychiatric Association's *Diagnostic and Statistical Manual of Mental Disorders* (*DSM-IV-TR*) is the standard reference for the nomenclature of psychopathology.[5]

A practitioner's view of diagnosis will depend on his or her theoretical orientation, as we have seen. For instance, psychoanalytically oriented therapists tend to favor diagnosis as one way of understanding how past situations contribute to an individual's current dysfunction. Practitioners with a behavioral orientation also favor diagnosis because they emphasize observation and other objective means of appraising both a client's specific symptoms and the factors that have led to the person's malfunctioning. Such an assessment process allows them to employ techniques that are appropriate for a particular disorder and to evaluate the effectiveness of a treatment program. On the other side of the issue are person-centered practitioners, who maintain that diagnosis is not essential for counseling because it tends to pull therapists away from a subjective way of understanding their clients and fosters an external conception about them.

Regardless of your theoretical orientation, it is likely that you will be expected to work within the framework of the *DSM-IV-TR* if you are counseling in a community agency. Even if you are in private practice, you will have to provide a diagnosis on the client's claim form if you accept insurance payments for mental health services. Because you will need to think within the framework of assessing and diagnosing clients, it is essential that you become familiar with the diagnostic categories and the structure of the *DSM-IV-TR*.

MY PERSPECTIVE ON ASSESSMENT Assessment, broadly construed, is a legitimate part of therapy. The assessment process does not necessarily have to be completed during the intake interview, however, nor does it have to be a fixed judgment that the therapist makes about the client. Assessment is a continuing process that focuses on understanding the person. Ideally, assessment is a collaborative effort that is part of the interaction between client and therapist. Both should be involved in discovering the nature of the client's presenting problem, a process that begins with the initial session and continues until therapy ends. Here are some questions that are helpful for a therapist to consider during the early assessment phase:

- What are my immediate and overall reactions to the client?
- What is going on in this person's life at this time?
- What are the client's main assets and liabilities?
- What are his or her resources for change?
- To what degree does this client possess the power to change his or her situation?
- Is this a crisis situation, or is it a long-standing problem?
- What does the client primarily want from therapy, and how can it best be achieved?
- What should be the focus of the sessions?
- What major internal and external factors are contributing to the client's current problems, and what can be done to alleviate them?
- What are the cultural and systemic influences of current behavior?
- In what ways can an understanding of the client's cultural background shed light on developing a plan to deal with the person's problems?
- What are the client's beliefs and experiences pertaining to spirituality? How might these beliefs and experiences be resources that can be drawn upon in dealing with a problem?
- What significant past events appear to be related to the client's present level of functioning?
- What specific family dynamics might be relevant to the client's present struggles and interpersonal relationships?
- On what support systems can the client rely in making changes? Who are the significant people in the client's life?
- What are the prospects for meaningful change, and how will we know when that change has occurred?

As a result of questions such as these, therapists will develop tentative hypotheses, which they can share with their clients as therapy proceeds.

This process of assessment does not have to result in classifying the client under some clinical category. Instead, counselors can describe behavior as they observe it and encourage clients to think about its meaning. In this way assessment becomes a process of thinking about issues *with* the client rather than a mechanical procedure conducted by an expert therapist. From this perspective, assessment and diagnostic thinking are vital to the therapeutic procedures that are selected, and they help practitioners conceptualize a case.

Even if mental health practitioners are required to diagnose clients for administrative or insurance reasons, they are not bound rigidly to that view of their clients. The diagnostic category is merely a framework for viewing and understanding a pattern of symptoms and for making treatment plans. It is not necessary to restrict clients to a label or to treat them in stereotypical ways. It is essential that practitioners be aware of the dangers of labeling and adopt a tentative stance toward diagnosis. As therapy progresses, additional data are bound to emerge that may call for modification of the original diagnosis.

GENERAL GUIDELINES FOR ASSESSMENT The intake interview typically centers on making an assessment and prescribing an appropriate course of treatment. As you have seen, this assessment may take various forms depending on the practitioner's orientation. For example, Adlerians look for ways in which the family structure has affected the client's development, whereas a psychoanalytic practitioner is interested in intrapsychic conflicts. I have pulled together some guidelines that might be helpful in thinking about how to get significant information and where to proceed with a client after making an initial assessment. Ten areas that are a basic part of conceptualizing an individual case are discussed here.

1. *Identifying data.* Get details such as name, age, sex, appearance, ethnic background, socioeconomic status, marital status, religious identification, and referral source (who referred the client, and for what purpose).

2. *Presenting problem(s).* What is the chief complaint? This area includes a brief description, in the client's own words, of the immediate problems for which he or she is seeking therapy. The presenting situation includes a description of the problems, how long they have existed, and what has been done to cope with them.

3. *Current living circumstances.* Information to collect here includes marital status and history, family data, recent moves, financial status, legal problems, basic lifestyle conflicts, support systems, and problems in personal relationships.

4. *Psychological analysis and assessment.* What is the client's general psychological state? For example, how does the person view his or her situation, needs, and problems? What is the client's level of maturity? Is there evidence of detrimental influences in the client's life? What are the person's dominant emotions? Is the client excited, anxious, ashamed, or angry? This phase of assessment entails describing the client's ego functioning, including self-concept, self-esteem, memory, orientation, fantasies, ability to tolerate frustration, insight, and motivation to change. The focus is on the client's view of self, including perceived strengths and weaknesses, the person's ideal self, and how the client believes others view him or her. What is the client's level of security? What ability does the person have to see and cope with reality, make decisions, assert self-control and self-direction, and deal with life changes and transitions? Standardized psychological tests of intelligence, personality, aptitudes, and interests may be used.

Another assessment procedure is the *mental-status examination,* which is a structured interview leading to information about the client's psychological level of functioning. This examination focuses on areas such as appearance, behavior, feeling, perception, and thinking. Under the behavior category, for example, the counselor making the assessment will note specific dimensions of behavior, including posture, facial expressions, general body movements, and quality of speech in the interview situation. Under the thinking category it is important to assess factors such as the client's intellectual functioning, orientation, insight, judgment, memory, thought processes, and any disturbances in thinking. The mental-status examination is also used to screen for psychosis.

5. *Psychosocial developmental history.* The focus here is on the developmental and etiological factors relating to the client's present difficulties. Five types can be considered: (1) precipitating factors—for example, maturational or situational stress, school entry, divorce, or death of a parent; (2) predisposing factors—for example, parent–child relationships and other family patterns, personality structure, and hereditary or constitutional factors; (3) contributory factors—for example, a current or past illness or the problems of family members; (4) perpetuating factors—for example, secondary gains such as the sympathy that a sufferer from migraine headaches elicits; and (5) sociocultural factors—that is, customs, traditions, family patterns, and cultural values.

From a developmental perspective these questions could be asked: How well has the client mastered earlier developmental tasks? What are some evidences of conflicts and problems originating in childhood? What were some critical turning points in the individual's life? What were some major crises, and how were they handled? What key choices did the client make, and how are these past decisions related to present functioning? How did the client's relationships within the family influence development? What was it like for the client to be in the family? What are family relationships like now? How are the client's cultural experiences related to his or her personality? This section might conclude with a summary of developmental history, which could include birth and early development, toilet training, patterns of discipline, developmental delays, educational experiences, sexual development, social development, and the influence of religious, cultural, and ethical orientations.

6. *Health and medical history.* What is the client's medical history? What was the date of the client's last consultation with a physician, and what were the results? Is there any noticeable evidence of recent physical trauma or neglect (for example, battering, welt marks, bruises, needle marks, sloppy clothing, sallow complexion)? What is the client's overall state of health? This section should include an assessment of the client's mental health. Has the client been in treatment previously for the present problem? Has there been a prior hospitalization? Has the client been taking medications? What were the outcomes of previous treatments? Is there any history of emotional illness in the family? It is important to be alert to signs that may indicate an organic basis for a client's problem (such as headaches, sudden changes in personal habits or in personality, and other physical symptoms). Regardless of the therapist's orientation, it is essential to rule out organic causes of physical symptoms before proceeding with psychotherapy.

7. *Adjustment to work.* What work does the client do or expect to do? How satisfied is the client with work? What is the meaning of employment to the person? Does he or she have future plans? What are the benefits and drawbacks of work? What is the client's work history? Has the person had long-term employment or a history of work problems? What is the balance between work and leisure? What is the quality of the client's leisure time? "Work" is used in the broad sense, whether or not the person receives pay for it. For instance, it would be important to inquire about a woman's satisfaction with her work as a homemaker and mother, even if she is not employed outside the home.

8. *Lethality.* Is the client a danger to self or others? Is he or she thinking about suicide or about hurting someone or something? Does the client have a specific plan either for committing suicide or for harming another person? Does the client have the means available to kill him- or herself? Have there been prior attempts at self-destruction or violent behavior toward others? Is the client willing to make a no-suicide contract as a condition of beginning therapy?

9. *Present human relationships.* This area includes a survey of information pertaining to spouse, siblings, parents, children, friends, colleagues, and other social ties. Included are the person's level of sexual functioning, family beliefs and values, and satisfaction derived from relationships. What are the client's main problems and conflicts with others? How does he or she deal with conflict? What support does the client get from others?

10. *Summary and case formulation.* Provide a summary of the client's major defenses, core beliefs, and self-definition of current problems, strengths, and liabilities, and make an assessment. What are the major recommendations? What is the suggested focus for therapeutic intervention? This formulation might specify the frequency and duration of treatment, the preferred therapeutic orientation, and the mode of treatment. The client might be included in the assessment process as a collaborator, which tends to set the stage for a shared therapeutic venture.

After the initial assessment of the client is completed, a decision is made whether to refer the person for alternative or additional treatment. Again, it is important to include the client in this decision-making process. If the client is accepted by the therapist, the two can discuss the assessment results. This information can be used in exploring the client's difficulties in thinking, feeling, and behaving and in setting treatment goals. Assessment can be linked directly to the therapeutic process, forming a basis for developing methods of evaluating how well the counselor's procedures are working to achieve the client's goals. Because most work settings require an intake interview, familiarity with these assessment procedures is essential.

Therapeutic Goals

After the initial comprehensive assessment of a client, therapeutic goals need to be established. These goals will vary, depending in part on the practitioner's theoretical orientation. For example, psychoanalytic therapy is primarily an insight approach that aims at regressing clients to very early levels of psychological development so that they can acquire the self-understanding necessary for major character restructuring. It deals extensively with the past, with unconscious dynamics, with transference, and with techniques aimed at changing attitudes and feelings. At the other extreme is reality therapy, which focuses on evaluating current behavior so that the client can develop a realistic plan leading to more effective ways of behaving. Reality therapy is not concerned with exploring the past, with unconscious motivation, with the transference that clients might develop, or with attitudes and feelings. It asks the key question, "What is the client doing now, and what does the client want to be doing differently?" It assumes that the best way to change is by focusing on what one is doing and thinking. If these dimensions change, it is likely that the client's feelings and physiological reactions will also change.

Therapeutic goals are diverse and a few include restructuring personality, finding meaning in life, substituting effective behaviors for maladaptive ones, correcting mistaken beliefs and assumptions, finding exceptions to their problems, and facilitating individual differentiation from the family system. Given this wide range, it is obvious that the perspectives of the client and the therapist on goals will surely have an impact on the course of therapy and on the therapeutic interventions chosen.

Despite this diversity of goals, all therapies share some common denominators. To some degree they have the goal of identifying what the client wants and then modifying the person's thoughts, feelings, and behaviors. Although there is common ground, each theoretical orientation focuses on a particular dimension of human experience as a route to changing other facets of personality.[6]

I attempt to integrate goals from most of the major theories by paying attention to changes clients want to make. My early interventions are aimed at helping clients identify specific ways in which they want to be different. Once they have formulated concrete goals, it is possible to utilize a variety of techniques that foster modification of thinking processes, feelings, and ways of behaving.

When counseling culturally diverse client populations, it is important to consider the degree to which the general goals and methods employed are congruent with the cultural background and values of clients. It is essential that both therapist and client recognize their differences in goal orientation. For example, it can be a therapeutic mistake to encourage some clients to be assertive with their parents and tell them exactly what they are thinking and feeling. A client from a Middle Eastern culture might believe it is rude and disrespectful to confront one's parents and that it is inappropriate to bring out conflicts. The therapist who would push such a client to be independent and to deal with conflicts within the family would probably alienate this person.

Therapists must listen to their clients and enter their perceptual world. The process of therapy is best guided by the particular goals and values of each client, not by what the therapist thinks is best. Questions therapists frequently ask of their clients are "Why are you seeking counseling from me?" "What is it that you would like to explore?" and "What is it about yourself or your life situation that you most want to change?" By staying focused on what their clients want, therapists can greatly reduce the danger of imposing their own goals on clients.

Having considered the basic assumptions, views of assessment, and goals of therapy, let us now consider a specific case. As you study Ruth's case, look for ways to apply what you have just read to gain a fuller understanding of her.

The Case of Ruth

The themes in Ruth's life are characteristic of those of many clients with whom I have worked. As mentioned earlier, I took typical struggles from a number of clients and compiled a clinical picture of a client I call "Ruth." Ruth's intake form and autobiography, reproduced here, will provide you with much of the information you need to understand and work with her. Each of the theory chapters will provide additional information. As you read the next 13 chapters, refer to this information about Ruth to refresh your memory on some of the details and themes in her life.

In addition to what is presented here, Ruth is also the subject of an interactive self-study program titled *CD-ROM for Integrative Counseling.* See Session 1 ("Beginning of Counseling") in particular for more information about Ruth.

Ruth's Autobiography

As a part of the intake process, the counselor asked Ruth to bring the autobiography she had written for her counseling class. Although most therapists do not make it a practice to ask their clients to write an autobiography, doing so can be beneficial. It provides clients with a way of reviewing significant life experiences and gives therapists insight into their clients' self-perception. Here is what Ruth wrote:

> Something I've become aware of recently is that I've pretty much lived for others. I've been the one who gives and gives until there is little left to give. I give to my husband, John. I've been the "good wife" and the "good mother" that he expects me to be. I realize that I need John, and I'm afraid he might leave me if I change too much. I've given my all to see that my kids grow up decently, but even though I'm trying my best, I often worry that I haven't done enough. When I look at my life now, I don't like what I see. I don't like who I am, and I certainly don't feel very proud of my body. I'm very overweight, and despite my good intentions to lose weight I just can't seem to succeed. I enjoy eating and often eat too much. My family nagged me as a child, but the more they wanted me to stop, the more I seemed to eat, sometimes to the point of making myself sick. I make resolutions to start an exercise program and stick to a diet, but I've yet to find a way to be successful.
>
> One of the things I do look forward to is becoming a teacher in an elementary school. I think this would make my life more meaningful. I worry a lot about what will become of me when my kids leave and there is just John and me in that house. I know I should at least get out and get the job as a substitute teacher in a private school that I've wanted (and have an offer for), yet I drag my feet on that one too.
>
> One thing that troubles me is the feeling of panic I get more often. I never remember feeling that bad. Often during the day, when I'm at school, I feel dizzy, almost like fainting, and have difficulty breathing. Sometimes in class I get hot flashes, and then sweat profusely. At times my hands tremble, and I'm afraid that others will notice this. There are times when I wake up at night with my heart beating very fast, in a cold sweat. I feel a sense of doom, but I don't know what over. I get scared over these feelings, which just seem to creep up on me. It makes me think that I might go crazy.
>
> I worry about death—about my dying—a lot. As a kid I was motivated by fear. Nine years ago I finally broke away from my strong fundamentalist church because I could see that it was not me. A philosophy class in the community college years ago got me to thinking about the values I was taught. When I was 30, I made the break from the fundamentalist religion that I had so closely lived by.

TABLE 3.1

CLIENT'S INTAKE FORM

AGE	SEX	RACE	MARITAL STATUS	SOCIOECONOMIC STATUS
39	Female	Caucasion	Married	Middle Class

APPEARANCE

Dresses meticulously, is overweight, fidgets constantly with her clothes, avoids eye contact, and speaks rapidly.

LIVING SITUATION

Recently graduated from college as an elementary education major, lives with husband (John, 45) and her children (Rob, 19; Jennifer, 18; Susan, 17; and Adam, 16).

PRESENTING PROBLEM

Client reports pervasive dissatisfaction. She says her life is rather uneventful and predictable, and she feels some panic over reaching the age of 39, wondering where the years have gone. For 2 years she has been troubled with a range of psychosomatic complaints, including sleep disturbances, anxiety, dizziness, heart palpitations, and headaches. At times she has to push herself to leave the house. Client complains that she cries easily over simple matters, often feels depressed, and has a weight problem.

HISTORY OF PRESENTING PROBLEM

Client made her major career as a housewife and mother until her children became adolescents. She then entered college part time and obtained a bachelor's degree. She has recently begun work toward a credential in elementary education. Through her contacts with others at the university she became aware of how she has limited herself, how she has fostered her family's dependence on her, and how frightened she is of branching out from her roles as mother and wife.

Ruth completed a course in introduction to counseling that encouraged her to look at the direction of her own life. As part of the course, Ruth participated in self-awareness groups, had a few individual counseling sessions, and wrote several papers dealing with the turning points in her own life. One of the requirements was to write an extensive autobiography that was based on an application of the principles of the counseling course to her own personal development. This course and her experiences with fellow students in it acted as a catalyst in getting her to take an honest look at her life. Ruth is not clear at this point who she is, apart from being a mother, wife, and student. She realizes that she does not have a good sense of what she wants for herself and that she typically lived up to what others in her life wanted for her. She has decided to seek individual therapy for the following reasons:

- A physician whom she consulted could find no organic or medical basis for her physical symptoms and recommended personal therapy. In her words, her major symptoms are these: "I sometimes feel very panicky, especially at night when I'm trying to sleep. Sometimes I'll wake up and find it difficult to breathe and my heart will be pounding. I toss and turn trying to relax, and instead I feel tense and worry a lot. It's hard for me to turn off my thoughts. Then during the day I'm so tired I can hardly function, and I find that lately I cry very easily when minor things go wrong."

- She is aware that she has lived a very structured and disciplined life, that she has functioned largely by taking care of the home and the needs of her four children and her husband, and that to some degree she is no longer content with this. Yet she reports that she doesn't know what "more than this" is. Although she would like to get more involved professionally, the thought of doing so frightens her. She worries about her right to think and act in her own best interests, she fears not succeeding in the professional world, and she most of all worries about how all this might threaten her family.

- Her children range in age from 16 to 19, and all are now finding more of their satisfactions outside of the family and the home and spending increasing time with their friends. Ruth sees these changes and is concerned about "losing" them. She is having particular problems with her daughter Jennifer, and is at a loss about how to deal with her. In general, Ruth feels very much unappreciated by her children.

- In thinking about her future, Ruth is not sure who or what she wants to become. She would like to develop a sense of herself apart from the expectations of others. She finds herself wondering what she "should" want and what she "should" be doing. Ruth does not find her relationship with her husband, John, satisfactory. He appears to resist her attempts to make changes and prefers that she remain as she was. She is anxious over the prospects of challenging this relationship, fearing that if she does, she might end up alone.

- Lately, Ruth is experiencing more concern over aging.

All of these factors combined have provided the motivation for her to take the necessary steps to initiate individual therapy. The greatest catalyst for her to come for therapy was the increase of her physical symptoms and her anxiety.

PSYCHOSOCIAL HISTORY

Ruth is the oldest of four children. Her father is a fundamentalist minister, and her mother is a housewife. She describes her father as distant, authoritarian, and rigid; her relationship with him was one of unquestioning, fearful adherence to his rules and standards. She remembers her mother as being critical, and she thought she could never do enough to please her. At other times her mother was supportive. The family demonstrated little affection. In many ways Ruth took on the role of caring for her younger brother and sisters, largely in the hope of winning the approval of her parents. When she attempted to have any kind of fun, she encountered her father's disapproval and outright scorn. To a large extent this pattern of taking care of others has extended throughout her entire life.

One critical incident took place when Ruth was 6 years old. She reported: "My father caught me 'playing doctor' with an 8-year-old boy. He lectured me and refused to speak to me for weeks. I felt extremely guilty and ashamed." It appears Ruth carried feelings of guilt into her adolescence and thus repressed her own emerging sexuality.

In her social relationships Ruth had difficulty making and keeping friends. She felt socially isolated from her peers because they viewed her as "weird." Although she wanted the approval of others, she was not willing to compromise her morals for fear of the consequences.

Ruth was not allowed to date until she completed high school; at the age of 19 she married the first person that she dated. She used her mother as a role model by becoming a homemaker.

I'm now attending a less dogmatic church, yet I still feel pangs of guilt that I am not living by the religion my parents brought me up with. My parents haven't formally disowned me, but in many ways I think they have. I'll never win their approval as long as I stay away from the religion that's so dear to them. But I find it more and more difficult to live by something I don't believe in. The big problem for me is that I so often feel lost and confused, wanting some kind of anchor in my life. I know what I don't believe, but I still have little to replace those values with that I once lived by. I sometimes wonder if I really did discard those values.

As part of my college program I took a course that was an introduction to counseling, and that opened my eyes to a lot of things. One of our guest speakers was a licensed clinical psychologist, who talked about the value of counseling for people even though they are not seriously disturbed. I began to consider that maybe I could benefit from getting some counseling. Up until that time I had always thought you had to be mentally ill before going to a psychotherapist. I see that I could work on a lot of things that I've neatly tucked away in my life. Yet even though I think I've almost made the decision to seek therapy, there is still this nagging fear within me. What if I find out things about myself that I don't like? What will I do if I discover an emptiness inside of me? What if I lose John while I'm getting myself together? I so much want magical answers. All my life I've had clear answers to every question. Then 9 years ago, when I became a questioner to some extent, I lost those answers.

What I most want from therapy is that the therapist will help me discover the things I need to do in order to change. My fear is that I could settle for a comfortable life that I have now, even though a great part of it drives me nuts. Sure, it's boring and stale, but it's predictable. Then again it's uncomfortable to be where I am. I'm scared to make the wrong decisions and that in doing so I'll ruin not only my life but John's life and the future of my kids. I feel I owe it to them to stay in this marriage. I guess I'm trapped and don't see a way out. Sometimes I wonder if I should turn my life over to God and let Him take over. I so much wish He would take over! I don't know what lies ahead. I'm afraid and excited at the same time.

Diagnostic Impressions of Ruth

While I was revising an earlier edition of this book, I had a telephone call from Michael Nystul, a professor of counseling at New Mexico State University, who told me that he was using *Case Approach to Counseling and Psychotherapy* for one of his summer courses.

"Dr. Corey," he asked, "what diagnosis would you give Ruth? My students are discussing her case, and they are interested in getting your opinion about her diagnostic category."

"Well," I replied, "I generally don't think in diagnostic terms, so I would be hard pressed to give Ruth a diagnosis."

"But if you *had* to give her a diagnosis," Dr. Nystul insisted, "what would it be?"

We exchanged our views on a possible diagnosis for Ruth. Because several possible diagnoses seemed to fit in her case, I began thinking about the process a practitioner goes through in attempting to identify the most appropriate diagnostic category for a client. I then asked several of my colleagues at the university who were familiar with Ruth's case to suggest a diagnosis. Interestingly, I got a variety of interpretations, each with a good supporting rationale. I also asked some of those who were reviewing this manuscript to give me their impressions of the most appropriate diagnostic category for Ruth. As you might suspect, there were a variety of diagnostic impressions.

At this point you are just beginning to familiarize yourself with Ruth. What would be your provisional diagnosis for Ruth? Justify the diagnosis you select on the basis of the information presented in this chapter. In learning about the various approaches to counseling Ruth, you may find new evidence or emerging patterns of behavior that warrant modifying your original diagnosis. This section deals with diagnostic impressions of Ruth, but this topic is revisited in each of the following theory chapters. I've asked the guest contributors to give their diagnostic impressions of Ruth and to discuss how their views of diagnosis and assessment influence their practice.

Rather than identifying one specific major disorder, I will describe a number of possible provisional diagnoses that *may* be appropriate for Ruth's case. As you review the different theories, consider these diagnostic classifications from the *DSM-IV-TR* to see which category you think best fits the case of Ruth.

Adjustment Disorder   The key feature of adjustment disorder is the development of clinically significant emotional or behavioral symptoms in response to psychosocial stresses. Some stressors may accompany specific developmental events, such as beginning school, becoming a parent, having children leave home, or failing to attain educational or career goals. There is some basis for giving Ruth a diagnosis of adjustment disorder, possibly with anxiety. She is experiencing some key developmental crises. A number of stressors are resulting in symptoms such as nervousness, worry, and fear of separation from major figures in her life. She could also be classified as adjustment disorder, unspecified, which reflects symptoms such as physical complaints, social withdrawal, or work or academic inhibition.

Panic Disorder   Individuals who have unexpected panic attacks typically describe their fear as intense and report that they feel as if they are going to die, lose control, or have a heart attack. In general, Ruth presents evidence of an anxiety disorder; specifically, her pattern of symptoms meets the diagnostic criteria for panic attack: palpitations of the heart, sweating, shortness of breath, dizziness, trembling, hot flashes and cold sweats, fear of dying, and fear of losing control or going crazy.

Dysthymic Disorder   The essential feature of a dysthymic disorder is chronic depression, which occurs for most of the day on more days than not for at least 2 years. Individuals with such a disorder often describe their condition as feeling "down in the dumps." When people experience a depressed mood, they often manifest some of the following symptoms: overeating, insomnia, low energy or fatigue, low self-esteem, difficulty making decisions, and feelings of hopelessness. At times, individuals are self-critical and view themselves as uninteresting or incapable. Ruth appears to fit this picture. She exhibits a long-term depressed mood that is part of her character but not severe enough to be considered major depression. She also manifests dependent personality traits in that she consistently puts the needs of others ahead of herself and has low self-esteem. She exhibits a number of physical complaints but does not indicate any serious physical disease necessitating surgery or other severe medical intervention.

✇ **Identity Problem**   Ruth's patterns fit the syndrome of identity problem. The main features of this classification include uncertainty about long-term goals, career choice, friendship patterns, sexual orientation and behavior, moral and religious values, and group loyalties. Affected clients respond to their uncertainty with anxiety and depression and are preoccupied about their lack of a sense of self. These people doubt themselves in everyday situations. One of the most common questions asked by the person with an identity disorder is "Who am I?"

I asked two of the reviewers of *Case Approach to Counseling and Psychotherapy* to provide their diagnostic perspectives on Ruth's case. They are Dr. Michael Nystul, who was introduced earlier, and Dr. Beverly Palmer, professor of psychology at California State University at Dominguez Hills.

DR. NYSTUL'S *DSM-IV-TR* DIAGNOSIS   The three key factors I use to facilitate the process of a differential diagnosis are onset, severity, and duration. Normally, I would explore these three issues within the context of a clinical interview, which would include a mental-status exam. In this instance, I must base my diagnostic impressions on Ruth's autobiography.

The *DSM-IV-TR* provides guidelines for a comprehensive assessment leading to a diagnosis. There are five categories, called axes, in the *DSM-IV-TR* that can be used by clinicians in formulating a treatment plan:

- *Axis I.* Clinical disorders; other conditions that may be a focus of clinical attention
- *Axis II.* Personality disorders; mental retardation
- *Axis III.* General medical conditions
- *Axis IV.* Psychosocial and environmental problems
- *Axis V.* Global assessment of functioning

As I read Ruth's autobiography, the major symptoms that stood out for me were anxiety and depression (Axis I disorders). The primary considerations for a differential diagnosis in this case appear to be an adjustment disorder with mixed anxiety and depressed mood, a panic disorder without agoraphobia, or a dysthymic disorder. For example, Ruth's diagnosis could be an adjustment disorder if (1) her symptoms (anxiety and depression) occurred within 3 months of the stressor and were resolved within 6 months of the termination of the stressor, and (2) her symptoms did not fulfill the criteria for one or more Axis I disorders such as a panic disorder or a dysthymic disorder. If her symptoms fulfilled the criteria for one or more Axis I disorders such as a panic disorder and dysthymic disorder, then those disorders would be recorded on Axis I and adjustment disorder would not be recorded.

Axis I also includes other conditions that are not mental disorders but may be a focus of clinical attention. Some of the "other conditions" that may be appropriate for Ruth include parent–child relational problem, partner relational problem, occupational problem, identity problem, and phase of life problem. I would use the clinical interview to determine if one or more of these "other conditions" would be included in Ruth's *DSM-IV-TR* diagnosis on Axis I.

In terms of Axis II, I would want to rule out a dependent personality disorder. The history suggests "she has fostered her family's dependence on her" and has "pretty much lived for others." If she did not meet the full criteria for a dependent personality disorder, I would record "dependent personality traits" on Axis II if I believed Ruth had prominent maladaptive personality features relating to dependency.

I would record "none" on Axis III (general medical conditions) because the history notes that a physician did not find anything medically wrong with Ruth.

Axis IV requires a listing of the psychosocial and environmental problems Ruth has experienced within the last year (or longer if she had experienced a posttraumatic stress disorder). A stressor that would be included for Ruth is discord with child. (The history suggested Ruth was having significant problems with Jennifer.) If my clinical interview suggested marital discord, that would also be included on Axis IV.

Axis V allows for the determination of Ruth's Global Assessment of Functioning (GAF). Based on *DSM-IV-TR* guidelines, I would estimate her current GAF to be 60, which would indicate that she has moderate symptoms or moderate difficulty in her overall psychological functioning.

DR. PALMER'S *DSM-IV-TR* DIAGNOSIS   Ruth's case is difficult to diagnose because she is a person on paper rather than a person in front of me of whom I can ask questions and notice her nonverbal behavior. Yet the *DSM-IV-TR* category of panic disorder without agoraphobia (300.01) is the one most supported by the evidence presented. She experiences unexpected panic attacks and is worried about having additional attacks. The symptoms of a panic attack she experiences are dizziness, heart palpitations, shortness of breath, trembling, sweating, and a fear of going crazy. All of these symptoms occur within a 10-minute period and occur both at school and during the evening when she is trying to sleep. Presently, there is no evidence that she has agoraphobia (anxiety about being in a place from which escape might be difficult, which often causes the person to not want to leave her house). However, I would want to monitor her for agoraphobia because recurrent panic attacks can develop into panic disorder with agoraphobia. Ruth's binge eating puts her in another *DSM-IV-TR* disorder: eating disorder not otherwise specified (307.50)—specifically, binge eating disorder. She reports eating more than she should when she is depressed and being very overweight. She also ate to the point of making herself sick when she was a child, and she has tried exercise and dieting but is unable to stick to either. Thus, it appears that in a discrete period of time Ruth eats an amount of food that is larger than most people would eat and that she experiences a lack of control over eating during these episodes.

Ruth has two other *DSM-IV-TR* conditions: a phase of life problem (V62.89) and an identity problem (313.82). She is concerned about what her life will be like after her children leave home or if she begins a professional job, and these concerns are characterized by the existential therapist as components of a midlife crisis. She is struggling with the identity issues of finding the values she does believe in and who she is apart from the expectations of others. Ruth is also having conflicts with her teenage daughter and with her husband, but it is difficult to determine whether these relational problems are causing clinically significant symptoms or significant impairment in family functioning. Thus, two other *DSM-IV-TR* conditions, a partner relational problem (V61.10) and a parent–child relational problem (V61.20), are probably not warranted from the evidence given.

As important as ruling *in* a particular diagnosis is ruling *out* other possible diagnoses. Ruth mentions several times that she feels "depressed" and that she eats more when she is depressed, yet there are not enough symptoms of depression to diagnose a mood disorder such as dysthymic disorder according to the *DSM-IV-TR*. Ruth does have low self-confidence and she does overeat, but her depressed mood and crying are not present for most of the day almost everyday for at least 2 years. Her tiredness during the day may be due to the panic attacks that make it difficult for her to sleep some nights. If she had "depression," she would feel tired even though she had had a good night's sleep, and her insomnia (typically early-morning awakening) would not be due to worrying or panic attacks. Many people use "depression" as a catch-all term to describe their present condition, but dysthymia does not fit this case as well as does an anxiety-based disorder such as panic disorder. The difference between self-diagnosis and a therapist's diagnosis is often in the degree of understanding of the psychological, social, and biological theories that are the foundation of the *DSM-IV-TR* categories. Of course, sometimes beneath the panic attacks and anxiety is a depression that can pop up once the panic attacks are alleviated. Another factor that must be eliminated when making the diagnosis of panic attacks is that there is no substance use or general medical condition (such as hyperthyroidism) that might cause the symptoms Ruth reports. She did have a recent checkup by a physician, which is always a wise recommendation for every therapist to make during the initial assessment.

The *DSM-IV-TR* is a multiaxial system of diagnosis, and so far I have given only Axis I diagnoses. Axis II is used to diagnose personality disorders or personality features that might also be the focus of treatment. Sometimes a person can have only an Axis I or only an Axis II diagnosis, but usually a person has diagnoses on both axes, and the two axes influence each other in treatment. In the case of Ruth there is no Axis II diagnosis, although she does show a few dependent personality features. As the behavior therapist says, Ruth has trouble stating her viewpoints clearly, and she often accepts projects in which she does not want to get involved. She admits dragging her feet in getting the substitute schoolteacher job she wants, which may be an indication of the dependent personality trait of having difficulty initiating projects or doing things on her own. Ruth shows only three dependent personality traits, so she does not have the full-blown picture of dependent personality disorder. The therapist also has to be careful that those traits typical of the socialization of a woman Ruth's age are not pathologized into dependent personality disorder.

Axis III is the place to indicate the results of her recent medical consultation and her problem with being overweight. Her physical condition and physical problems interact with her psychological problems reported on Axes I and II, so it is important to record them in this multiaxial system of diagnosis. For example, her being overweight affects her self-esteem, and her self-esteem affects her weight. Also, her panic attacks might be treated by medication as well as by psychological means, so health professionals from all fields need to communicate with one another. This multiaxial system is an ideal way to start this communication.

Axis IV is the place to record any social or environmental factors in Ruth's life. She reports relational problems with her daughter and with her husband, so it is on this axis that these social issues are recorded as problems with her primary support group.

The final axis, Axis V, is used to report Ruth's overall level of functioning. The usual way of recording this is by using the GAF scale. Ruth has some moderate symptoms, such as occasional panic attacks, which cause her to have some difficulty in her functioning at home, so she receives a GAF score of between 51 and 60.

One important axis is missing from the *DSM-IV-TR,* and that is one that records Ruth's strengths. Ruth has many strengths: she has recently pursued higher education successfully, and she has good insight into her present condition as well as a thirst for exploring her future directions. Ruth's strengths will be used in treatment just as much as will her difficulties, so it is important to have a record of them along with the *DSM-IV-TR* system of diagnosis.

In looking over the provisional diagnoses described here, what patterns do you see in these assessments taken as a group? Which ones do you tend to agree with the most? Why? If you do not agree with a particular diagnostic formulation, give your reasons. What are your legal and ethical responsibilities when diagnosing Ruth? Under what circumstances, if any, would you be likely to share your diagnostic impressions with her?

This section on diagnostic procedures with Ruth is necessarily brief. I encourage you to consult the *DSM-IV-TR* as a reference tool because it will introduce you to the categories and the labeling system that are part of the assessment and diagnostic process.

Notes

See the DVD/Online Program entitled Theory in Practice: The Case of Stan (Session 1: Intake and Assessment) for ways that assessment is applied to working with Stan.

1. Corey, G., & Haynes, R. (2005). *CD-ROM for Integrative Counseling.* Belmont, CA: Brooks/Cole.

2. Corey, G. (2009). *The Art of Integrative Counseling* (2nd ed.). Belmont, CA: Brooks/Cole.

3. This book and G. Corey (2009), *Theory and Practice of Counseling and Psychotherapy* (8th ed., Belmont, CA: Brooks/Cole) have parallel coverage of each of the theories you will be studying. As a basis for understanding the guest contributors' presentations on working with Ruth in the chapters that follow, refer to my theory book for background information on the basic assumptions, key concepts, elements of the therapeutic process, and application and techniques for each of the theories.

4. Two excellent books on the subject of psychotherapy integration are J. Norcross and M. Goldfried, eds. (2005), *Handbook of Psychotherapy Integration* (2nd ed., New York: Oxford University Press); and G. Stricker and J. Gold, eds. (2006), *A Casebook of Psychotherapy Integration* (Washington, DC: American Psychological Association).

5. The official guide to a system of classifying psychological disorders is the *Diagnostic and Statistical Manual of Mental Disorders* (4th ed., compiled in 1994, with a Text Revision in 2000), by the American Psychiatric Association. The *DSM-IV-TR* gives specific criteria for classifying emotional and behavioral disturbances and shows the differences among the various disorders. In addition to describing neurotic, psychotic, and personality disorders, this revised edition also deals with a variety of other disorders pertaining to developmental stages, substance abuse, moods, sexual and gender identity, eating, sleep, impulse control, and adjustment.

6. In Session 3 ("Establishing Therapeutic Goals") of the *CD-ROM for Integrative Counseling,* I demonstrate my way of assisting Ruth in formulating her goals, which will provide a direction for her counseling.

CHAPTER TWO

Case Approach to Psychoanalytic Therapy

Introduction

In this chapter and most of the chapters to follow, first you will read one or more sections written by experts in each of the theoretical orientations that illustrate their way of working with Ruth. These sections introduce each therapeutic approach. A brief biography of each of these guest consultants is provided in the "About the Contributors" section in the front of this book. Then I will assume the identity of a therapist from the particular orientation being considered, and, staying within the spirit of each specific approach as much as possible, I will show you my interpretation and my own style of working with Ruth. In each chapter I give an overview of the particular theory by describing (1) the basic assumptions underlying practice, (2) my initial assessment of Ruth, (3) the goals that will guide our work, and (4) the therapeutic procedures and techniques that are likely to be employed in attaining our goals. A section on the therapeutic process shows samples of our work together. It is illustrated with dialogue between Ruth and me, along with an ongoing process commentary that explains my rationale for the interventions I make and the general direction of her therapy.

There are many differences in therapeutic style among practitioners who share the same theoretical orientation, and there is no "one right way" of practicing psychoanalytic therapy or any of the other systems. I encourage you to do your best in assuming each of the separate theoretical perspectives as you follow the case of Ruth. Doing this will help you decide which concepts and techniques you want to incorporate in your own therapeutic style.

It is a good practice for counselors to consult with other practitioners at times, for doing so provides them with ideas of other ways to proceed with a client. In working with Ruth, I am using this model of consultation. Background data on Ruth's case were sent to well-known representatives of each approach, and they were asked to answer these questions: "How would you assess Ruth's case?" "On what themes would you probably focus?" "What procedures would you likely use?" and "How would you expect the therapeutic process to unfold?" You can gain much from examining these working models.

General Overview of Psychoanalytic Therapy

The main goal of psychoanalytic therapy is to resolve intrapsychic conflicts, toward the end of reconstructing one's basic personality. Analytic therapy is not limited to problem solving and learning new behaviors; there is a deeper probing into the past to develop one's level of self-understanding.

From the psychoanalytic perspective, all techniques are designed to help the client gain insight and bring repressed material to the surface so that it can be dealt with consciously. Major techniques include gathering life-history data, dream analysis, free association, and interpretation and analysis of resistance and transference. Such procedures are aimed at increasing awareness, gaining intellectual and emotional insight, and beginning a working-through process that will lead to the reorganization of personality.

Psychoanalytic clients are ready to terminate their sessions when they and the therapist agree that they have clarified and accepted their emotional problems, have understood the historical roots of their difficulties, and can integrate their awareness of past problems with present relationships. Outcomes of therapy are subjectively evaluated, primarily by the therapist and to some extent by the client. The main criteria used to assess outcomes are the client's degree of emotional and cognitive insight and the degree to which he or she has worked through the transference relationship.

A Psychoanalytic Therapist's Perspective on Ruth

by William Blau, PhD

Assessment of Ruth

🔖 **Psychoanalytic Perspective and Overview of Case Material**   As a psychoanalytically oriented therapist, I suspect that Ruth's background descriptions of her parents, her siblings, and herself are less than objective. Moreover, I predict that the areas of inaccuracy will turn out to be clues to the core of her personality problems. I anticipate finding that her symptoms (anxiety attacks, overeating, fear of accomplishment, panic over being 39, fear of abandonment, and so forth) can be interpreted as outward manifestations of unconscious conflicts that have their origins in childhood experiences and defensive reactions to these experiences that were necessary to her as a child. I suspect, given her intelligence and motivation, that her current exacerbation of symptoms is related to her recognition of discrepancies between what makes sense to her logically and what seems to drive her emotions and behavior. I hypothesize that Ruth is experiencing a split (a struggle between opposing dimensions of herself). This conflict is between the part of her that wants to change and the other part of her that clings to old patterns that were once necessary and have helped her maintain mental stability all her life. Although some of her defenses seem maladaptive from my perspective, I believe I cannot give her the most effective help unless I can fully understand why her patterns of defense seem necessary to her now and why, once, they were necessary to her psychological survival.

In contrast to some therapeutic practitioners, I am very interested in why Ruth thinks, feels, and behaves as she does. I have no interest in excusing her behavior or condemning others, but I believe her problems can be most fully helped by answering the "why" as well as the "what" questions regarding her life. This fundamental interest in the "whys" of an individual client's experience and behavior is a critical distinction between analytic therapy and other approaches.

Unraveling the dynamics of her history and filling in the story of her life with newly emerging memories will be an ongoing part of Ruth's treatment; hence, this aspect of assessment is never complete although it becomes less important in the final phases of treatment.

Assessing Ruth's Suitability for Analytic Therapy   Before establishing a contract to do analytic therapy with Ruth, I need to ascertain whether she is a good candidate for the treatment and whether she has the perseverance and resources to make this approach the treatment of choice. Assessment of her need for analytic therapy would include determining whether she wants and needs to understand the unconscious roots of her neurosis. If simply teaching her about the irrationality of some of her beliefs would lead to significant change, she would probably not need analytic therapy. Didactic, cognitive approaches would suffice. I suspect, however, that Ruth does not consciously know why she reacts in symptomatic ways and that she is repeatedly frustrated when she has been given good advice by others (or by herself) but still finds the old patterns persisting.

Ruth's case history does include a number of factors suggesting that she could be a good candidate for analytic treatment. Her autobiography shows her to be a woman for whom understanding the meaning of her life is important and for whom achieving individuation is a meaningful goal. Her autobiography also shows that she has the ability to look at herself from a somewhat objective perspective. Her need for symptom alleviation is sufficient to provide strong motivation for change, yet her symptoms are not currently incapacitating.

Ruth may expect that her therapist will tell her what to do with her life and take the place of her father and the God of her childhood religion. In contracting with her for treatment, I would let her know that fulfillment of such expectations is not provided by analytic psychotherapy; however, this would by no means end the issue. Despite the formal contract, I anticipate that Ruth will continue to demand that the therapist take charge of her life. This aspect of transference may be of ongoing significance in treatment. On the whole, Ruth is the sort of client for whom analytically oriented psychotherapy might be indicated.

Diagnosis   Analytic therapy is more clearly indicated for some disorders than for others, and some disorders require extensive modification of technique. But traditional, symptom-based diagnosis is limited in that an individual's ability to form a therapeutic alliance, which is the key issue in assessment for analytic treatment, is largely independent of diagnosis. Moreover, *DSM-IV-TR*[1] diagnoses typically fail to convey the essence of the client or of the client's suffering. From a diagnostic standpoint, the most important issues (once it has been demonstrated that Ruth is not suicidal or homicidal) would be to determine the role of organic factors in her symptomatology and to determine whether she should be referred for medication.

Ruth's reported unhappiness with her life could be her way of expressing symptoms of depression that might be helped by medication in addition to psychotherapy. Although she does not appear to meet the criteria for a major depressive disorder, a *DSM-IV-TR* diagnosis of dysthymic disorder should be considered if she is depressed "for most of the day, for more days than not" for a period of at least 2 years. Her panic attacks could be related to a cardiac condition, and her other psychophysiological symptoms could have organic as well as psychodynamic origins. In *DSM-IV-TR* terms, Ruth meets the following diagnostic criteria:

300.01: panic disorder without agoraphobia

313.82: identity problem

Neither of these diagnostic categories, in my opinion, conveys a feeling for Ruth as she is described in her autobiography and intake form. *DSM-IV-TR* diagnoses tend to reify symptom clusters rather than promote understanding of the client as a person.

Panic attacks are the essential elements of the *panic disorder* diagnosis, and I would consider treating these attacks initially with the cost-effective techniques of psychophysiological counseling and biofeedback rather than psychoanalytic psychotherapy. *DSM-IV-TR* diagnoses of panic disorder are coded as either with or without agoraphobia. I specified "without agoraphobia" because Ruth doesn't describe herself as being unduly afraid to travel or to be in crowds or similar social or confining situations.

The *DSM-IV-TR* category of *identity problem* is descriptive of the contents of Ruth's concerns. However, it is not a "clinical disorder" in *DSM-IV-TR* terms, and it minimizes the intensity of her very real suffering. The real, human Ruth presents a blending of neurotic symptoms and existential concerns.

Ruth's symptoms seem to be at a critical stage and could flower into an eating disorder, a counterphobic impulsive behavior, a generalized anxiety disorder, or a psychosomatic conversion disorder, as well as agoraphobia or a dysthymic disorder as previously discussed. Ruth's difficulties in establishing a sense of self suggest that her individuation is an important goal of treatment. I do not anticipate overtly psychotic symptoms, and her basic reality testing appears sufficiently stable that she can be expected to undergo some degree of regression in the course of treatment without danger of precipitating a psychotic break.

Key Issues and Themes in Working With Ruth

🕮 **Intrapsychic Conflicts and Repression of Childhood Experiences**   As a psychoanalytically oriented psychotherapist, I accept the role of detective in ferreting out the secrets of the past that are locked away in Ruth's unconscious. Although I am guided by theory to suspicious content areas, her psyche and the secrets therein are uniquely hers, and it is ultimately she who will know the truth of her life through her own courage and perceptions.

I suspect that the psychosexual aspects of Ruth's relationships with her parents (and possibly her siblings) remain key conflict areas for her, even now. In the classical Freudian model of healthy development, she would have experienced early libidinal attraction to her father, which she would eventually have replaced with normal heterosexual interests in male peers; likewise, her feelings of rivalry with her mother for her father's affection would have been replaced with identification with her mother. In the ideal model, moreover, she would have experienced rebellion against parental constraints, particularly during the developmental period associated with toilet training and also in adolescence.

In reality Ruth appears to have superficially avoided normal rebellion and to have suppressed her sexuality except for adopting a wifely role with the first man she dated. Although she followed the format of using her mother as role model and having children by an acceptable husband, she apparently abdicated in the struggles of sexuality, rebellion, and identification, leaving these conflicts unresolved. Her conscious recollections of her parents are of a rigid, fundamentalist father and a "critical" mother. I would be interested in knowing what these parents were really like, as perceived by Ruth in childhood. How did her father handle his feelings for his children? Did his aloofness mask strongly suppressed incestuous feelings that she intuitively sensed? Were these ever acted out?

A Freudian view of her father's harsh reactions to Ruth's "playing doctor" would emphasize the Oedipus/Electra aspects of this father–daughter encounter. Her father's refusal to speak to her for weeks after this incident suggests jealousy rather than simply moral rejection of childhood sexual activity. This suspicion is supported by the parentally imposed isolation of the children that delayed dating until after high school. Ruth's attempts to win her father's approval by supplanting the role of her mother (in caring for her younger siblings) is also consistent with these Oedipus/Electra dynamics. Ruth internalized her father's overtly negative attitude to sexuality.

If these hypotheses are correct, a theme in therapy will be Ruth's reexperiencing of the sensual aspects of her attachment to her father and his response to her. As she is able to fully remember, accept, and "own" these repressed feelings and fantasies, she will begin to loosen her unconscious attachment to them. She can become open to an adult relationship in which her sexuality is appreciated rather than scorned or distorted.

Although there is no direct evidence of sexual abuse in the case material, the family dynamics are such that there is the possibility of actual incestual acts by the father, the memories of which have been repressed by Ruth. Even more likely is the pattern wherein the father's incestuous feelings were not overtly acted out but were so intense that he developed defenses of reaction formation and projection, labeling her sexuality (rather than his) as reprehensible. The jealous response of Ruth's mother is consistent with either of the above patterns of paternal behavior, but the mother's response is more pathological (and more pathogenic) if actual abuse occurred.

Oedipus/Electra feelings by both parent and child are considered part of normal development. However, intense conflicts and guilt regarding these feelings or experiences are very common in clients seeking counseling or psychotherapy, and all too often actual molestation is eventually determined to have occurred.

Regardless of the details of the actual memories and buried feelings unearthed in therapy, the analytic therapist is alert for indications of psychological traumas in the client's early life, psychic wounds that may be associated with a family *secret* that the client has needed to protect from exposure through suppression, denial, and repression. The probability of a secret being at the heart of Ruth's neurosis is increased by the indication in the case material that she was socially isolated and that her lack of relationships outside the family was enforced by her parents, at least in terms of dating. The entire family may have lived with their unspoken secrets in relative isolation. Although incestuous themes in one form or another are the most common secrets unearthed, other "unthinkable" secrets may be at the center of the repression—namely, the hidden mental illness, homosexuality, or alcoholism of a family member.

To what extent is Ruth bringing themes from her family of origin to her present family? She defines her husband only by what he is not (her father) and by his potential to reject her (as her father had rejected her). Does she know the man she married at all, or is he merely a stand-in for the real man in her life? Is her husband's apparent rejection of her attempts at personal growth a facet of his personality, or is he being set up? Her reaction to her daughter Jennifer may very likely be related to her own failure to rebel. Acceptance and nurturance by Ruth of the suppressed child-rebel aspect of herself may well improve her relationship with her daughter.

Symptoms and Psychodynamics

A psychoanalytic approach views psychological symptoms as active processes that give clues to the client's underlying psychodynamics. Some acute symptoms are valuable in that they alert the client that something is wrong. Other symptoms, particularly when chronic, may be extremely resistant to intervention and may be disabling or even, as in the case of anorexia, threaten the life of the client.

Ruth's symptoms suggest compatibility with psychoanalytically oriented therapy. I would use analytic theory to help Ruth understand the role of anxiety in her life and the methods she uses to control her anxiety. I view Ruth's current existential anxiety as related to these issues: Her early training by her parents clearly made individuation (in the object-relations sense) a very scary proposition for her; hence, any attempt toward individuation is anxiety provoking. She is, therefore, terrified not only of acting impulsively but also of acting independently. She hopes to make her own choices in life but also hopes that her therapist will make her decisions for her.

Ruth's symptom of overeating probably gratifies her need for affection, but a psychoanalytic approach to this symptom would also explore its developmental origin. Oral gratification is the primary focus of libidinal energy in the earliest stage of development. Symptoms associated with this stage can appear if the client suffered deprivation during this period. If this is the case, the adult tends to be fixated on getting the satisfaction never adequately obtained during the childhood stage.

Ruth's weight problem also has psychodynamic meaning. Being overweight may lead to her feeling sexually unattractive and, therefore, less likely to be faced with dealing with her sexuality. Ruth's increasing difficulty in leaving home suggests a fear of meeting others who might threaten the stability of her marriage. This symptom is consistent with the dynamics of her being overweight.

The exacerbation of physical symptoms and anxiety are cited in the background information as being the catalyst for Ruth's seeking therapy at this time. A psychoanalytic approach to these symptoms would explore the "secondary gain" associated with each symptom. A symptom may protect the client from anxiety evoked by both sides of an intrapsychic conflict. For instance, a headache might serve to keep her sexually distant from her husband while also providing a pretext for avoiding social contacts that might threaten the marriage.

Analytic therapy provides a means for treating Ruth's symptoms, but only in the context of broader treatment of her psychological problems. Some symptoms can be treated directly, and at lesser expense, by nonanalytic therapies. When the client desires to obtain insight as well as symptom relief or when the "secondary gain" of the symptom leads to either failure of the direct approach or to the substitution of a new symptom for the old one, analytic therapy is indicated. Ruth gives evidence of multiple symptoms and of a desire to examine her life. Hence, consideration of analytic therapy rather than a symptom-focused behavioral approach is reasonable.

Ruth might also consider the alternative of brief therapy. I consider brief analytic therapy a specialty area in which selected clients opt to focus on highly specific goals. Although it shortens the duration of treatment, it also modifies the therapeutic contract and places stringent demands on client and clinician alike. Brief therapy as a specialty should not be confused with arbitrary restrictions on the length of treatment imposed by managed care. Such restrictions are generally inconsistent with insight-oriented analytic therapy. Insight in analytic therapy typically requires the client to experience therapeutic regression and the "working through" of distortions in the context of the therapeutic relationship, processes that cannot be terminated prematurely without danger of psychological harm to the client.

The therapy described in the remainder of this section includes a mixture of supportive and insight techniques. Hence, if it were necessary to limit Ruth's treatment to a fixed number of sessions, I would modify my approach to emphasize supportive interventions and minimize regressive techniques. Supportive therapy could be of value to Ruth, even within the constraint of an arbitrarily limited number of sessions, particularly if she could resume treatment periodically as needed. Ruth and I must agree on any limitation to the number of sessions at the onset of treatment, and it is my responsibility to ensure any limitation is understood throughout therapy.

Open-ended treatment, in which a third-party payer periodically approves or rejects additional sessions, is incompatible with both insight-oriented and supportive analytic therapy. Terminating therapy at the whim of an outside agency can be highly deleterious to the client. Such a termination is experienced as abandonment at best, and it may be equated unconsciously with betrayal or even malevolence on the part of the therapist.

Treatment Techniques

✍ **Psychoanalytically Oriented Psychotherapy Versus Psychoanalysis** The treatment approach I propose for Ruth is psychoanalytically oriented psychotherapy rather than psychoanalysis. This choice does not indicate a theoretical disagreement with the methods of classic analysis; psychoanalytic psychotherapy is a form of analytic treatment that has advantages and disadvantages compared with classical psychoanalysis. In classical analysis the analyst adopts a "blank-screen" approach in which expressions of the real analyst–client relationship are minimized to promote development of the client's transference relationship with the analyst. Transference leads the client to react to the analyst as if he or she were a significant person from the client's past life.

Psychoanalytic therapy does *not* require the blank-screen approach, is less frustrating to the patient, allows the therapist more flexibility in technique, is less costly, may be shorter in duration, and provides "support" for the patient's least maladaptive defenses. Hence, it is often the treatment of choice. The drawbacks of analytic psychotherapy as compared with psychoanalysis are directly related to the advantages. The variations in technique lead to a lowering of expectations, as many aspects of the client's personality will remain unanalyzed due to elimination of the blank screen and the consequent intrusion of aspects of the "real" relationship between therapist and client of their "as-if" transference relationship. If, for example, Ruth is in analysis with me, free-associating from the couch, and she states her belief that I disapprove of some feeling or behavior of hers, I can be reasonably sure that she is reacting to me as if I were some other figure in her life. In contrast, if she makes the same assertion in face-to-face psychotherapy, my actual nonverbal behavior (or prior self-disclosure of any sort) may have given her valid clues to my actual (conscious or unconscious) disapproval of her feelings or behavior. I can never know the exact degree to which her response is a transference response as opposed to a response to my real behavior in our real relationship. In psychoanalytically oriented psychotherapy with Ruth, I must keep in mind that every aspect of our interaction will have a mix of real and as-if components. To the degree that I participate in the real relationship by providing support, by giving advice, or by sharing an opinion or personal experience, I am limiting my ability to maintain an analytic stance to the material she presents.

Although significant therapeutic work is possible using this model, I must be very sensitive to the meanings Ruth will attribute to my real interactions with her. If I disapprove of a particular act or intention of hers, for example, I can reasonably expect her to assume that I approve of all her reported acts or intentions to which I have not expressed disapproval. Thus, although I am free to use the real as well as the as-if relationship in making therapeutic interventions, I am not free to vacillate in my therapeutic stance without risk of doing harm.

🐚 **The Therapeutic Contract**   I form as clear a therapeutic contract as possible with Ruth, explaining the goals, costs, and risks of the treatment as well as briefly describing the methods and theory of psychotherapy. As a psychoanalytic therapist, I believe the economics of treatment, both in terms of financial arrangements and also in the investment of time and energy in therapy, cannot be separated from the process and outcomes of therapy. Thus, I make my expectations regarding payment explicit, including the analytic rule that fees are charged for canceled sessions. This contractual clarity regarding fees has therapeutic implications in that Ruth's obligation to me for my services is specified at the outset of treatment. Thereafter, she can feel free of any additional requirement to meet my needs, and I can interpret any concerns that she does express about my needs in terms of the as-if relationship.

A treatment schedule of two or three sessions per week, each session lasting 50 minutes, is typical for psychoanalytically oriented therapy, but many of my clients are only seen weekly. Any planned vacations in the next 6 months or so, by either Ruth or me, should be noted, and therapy should not commence shortly before a vacation.

Other aspects of the contract include confidentiality (and its limitations), the degree to which I am available for emergencies or other between-session contacts, and an admonition to generally avoid making major life decisions during the course of treatment. The latter "rule" for clients in analysis is relevant to Ruth. She indicates that she wants a therapist to make decisions for her, and I have some concern about the possibility of her leaping to decisions while experiencing regression in the course of treatment. Unlike some analytically oriented therapists, I make myself available to clients by telephone between sessions. Ruth has some symptoms of depression, and I would encourage her to contact me should these symptoms worsen. With suicidal clients I establish a contract, often in writing, specifying that the client *will* contact me in the event of worsening symptoms.

🐚 **Free Association**   Free association is a primary technique in psychoanalysis and is the "basic rule" given to clients. In my therapy with Ruth I emphasize the technique of free association at certain times, such as when she comments that she doesn't know what to talk about. However, we have verbal interaction in addition to her free associations, even in the early phases of therapy. I often instruct her to express her associations to her dreams, to elements of her current life, and to memories of her past life, particularly new memories of childhood events that emerge in the course of treatment.

🐚 **Dreams, Symptoms, Jokes, and Slips**   Dreams are considered the "royal road" to the unconscious, and I encourage Ruth to report her dreams and to associate to them. As an analytically oriented therapist, I conceptualize each of her dreams as having two levels of meaning, the manifest content and the latent meaning. Analytic theory postulates that each dream is a coded message from her unconscious, a message that can be interpreted so as to understand the unconscious wish that initiated the dream and the nature of the repression that forced the wish to be experienced only in disguised form. Hypotheses about the latent meaning of dream symbols can be derived from theory, but the actual interpretation of her dream elements is based on her own unique associations to her dream symbols.

In addition to dreams, the hidden meanings inherent in Ruth's symptoms are subject to analysis. Her presenting symptoms, manifestations of resistance, memories, and spontaneous errors (slips of the tongue) are clues to her underlying dynamics. The wordplay involved in slips of the tongue is meaningful, as may be any intentional joke or pun made or recalled by her in a session.

Interpretations of Resistance and Content   My initial interpretations are of resistance, and I follow the rule of interpreting the resistance Ruth presents relative to a content area before actually interpreting the content. I recognize that every accurate interpretation is an assault on her defenses, and I know that she will react to the interpretation as a threat to her present adjustment. Hence, in choosing the timing of a particular interpretation, I am guided by her readiness to accept it as well as by my sense of its accuracy. I also follow the general rule that more inferential interpretations should be made in the later stages of therapy after a therapeutic alliance and trust have been established. Early interpretations should be minimally inferential, often only noting a correspondence. For example, commenting to Ruth that she wrote less in her autobiography about her mother than she did about her father is much less inferential than interpreting her overeating as a defense against sexuality.

Many interpretations, particularly in the later stages of therapy, relate to her transference reactions and are geared to helping her work through childhood-based conflicts in the context of her therapeutic relationship with me. This brief dialogue begins with the here and now and ends with an insight about the past:

RUTH: I worry I'm just hiding in my therapy. It's an indulgence; I should be using your time to fix my problems, not just to talk about anything I like.

THERAPIST: What's being hidden here?

RUTH: That I'm not really working. I tell myself I'm going to a doctor's appointment, but you just listen, and I just play around with my thoughts.

THERAPIST: Is it OK to play here, at your doctor's appointment?

RUTH: Of course not. This is work; we're not playing. You wouldn't see me if I were here to play, Dr. Blau.

THERAPIST: There was a time when your father didn't speak to you for weeks.

RUTH: That was about playing doctor too! Do I still think it's sinful to explore? My dad would be shocked at some of the thoughts I've explored here.

THERAPIST: How would he react?

RUTH: He'd be. Oh, I just remembered how he looked then. He got red in the face and stammered. His brow got sweaty. He punished me for my sin.

THERAPIST: For whose sin?

RUTH: Maybe for his own. I hardly knew anything about sex when he decided I was bad; maybe his thinking about me being sexual made him feel guilty or something.

THERAPIST: But you're the one who got punished.

RUTH: Yeah. I got punished for what he thought and felt, not for what I actually did.

In this example I follow a hunch that Ruth's concern about "playing" at her "doctor's" appointment might have associations to the childhood incident when she was punished for "playing doctor." Her acceptance of this association sets the stage for the final interpretive exchange and insight.

Even the best interpretations are only hypotheses that are presented to the client for consideration. Premature interpretations can be harmful, even if correct. As a therapist, I keep an open mind about the meaning of Ruth's thoughts, feelings, memories, dreams, and fantasies, and I rarely make interpretations about the actuality of past events, imagined or remembered. Although I use my hunches to promote the process of freeing repressed memories, I do not treat my hunches about the past as if they were facts to be imposed on the client's reality. Like other contemporary analytic therapists, I believe there are multiple interpretations that are equally true for each of Ruth's symptoms, dream images, and fantasies. I search for interpretations that convey useful truth, rather than striving for statements of *the* truth about elements of her life.

🕸 **Transference and Countertransference** Ruth's experience in therapy is both gratifying and frustrating. It is gratifying in that we spend each hour focusing on her life. Her needs, hopes, disappointments, dreams, fantasies, and everything else of importance to her are accepted as meaningful, and she need not share center stage with anyone else. It is her hour, and I listen to everything without criticizing her or demanding that she see anything my way or do anything to please me. My sustained, active attention to and interest in her are different from any other interpersonal interaction. Other people in her life insist on wanting things from her, or they want to criticize her, or at the very least they expect her to be as interested in them as they are in her.

But the sessions are also frustrating. Ruth wants help, and all I seem to do is listen and occasionally ask a question or comment on what she has said. Do I like her? Or am I only pretending to be interested because that's what I am paid for? When, she wonders, will the therapy start helping? When will she find out how to resolve her issues about her marriage and her boring life?

Given this mixture of gratification and frustration, it is not surprising that Ruth begins to see *me* as a source of both of those emotions. Moreover, it is not surprising that she will "transfer" onto me attributes of others in her life who have been sources of gratification and frustration to her. Hence, she begins to react to me as if I were her father, mother, or other significant figure.

The permissiveness of the sessions also allows Ruth to regress—to feel dependent and childlike and to express her thoughts and feelings with little censorship. I take almost all the responsibility for maintaining limits; she need only talk. Her regression is fostered to the degree that I maintain the classic analytic stance, and it is ameliorated to the degree that I interact with her in terms of our real relationship—for example, by expressing empathy.

Ruth's past haunts her present life and interpersonal relationships, and to an even greater degree it haunts her relationship with me. But the distortions projected onto me exist in a controlled interpersonal setting and, therefore, are amenable to interpretation and resolution. The therapeutic session provides a structure in which the nature of her conflicts can be exposed and understood, not only in the sense of intellectual insight but also in the analysis of their actual impact on her perceptions and feelings about me and the therapeutic relationship. My nonjudgmental acceptance of all aspects of Ruth's experience, including her darkest fears and impulses, provides a model from which she can begin to fully accept these parts of herself without condemnation or attachment. I believe such "radical acceptance" is healing, and I also find it a necessary foundation for positive change.

The therapeutic relationship provides gratification and frustration for the therapist as well as for the client. My therapeutic task includes monitoring not only the content of the sessions but also my feelings that grow out of this relationship. There are aspects of Ruth that I like and others that I dislike. I find her dependency both appealing and irritating. I enjoy the positive attributes she projects onto me, and I experience some hurt when she projects negative attributes onto me. Nevertheless, I must minimize indulgence in these reactions and concentrate instead on ensuring that my participation consistently promotes her self-understanding and individuation. Although she is free to demand anything and everything from me, I must deny myself almost all the rewards of a real relationship with her.

Understanding the theory of therapeutic techniques helps me keep my perspective, as does recollection of my own therapy. The therapy I have received is useful to me in understanding the psychotherapeutic experience from the client's point of view, and it helps me understand some of my conflicts that could impair my effectiveness as a therapist. Nevertheless, my adherence to the ideal role is imperfect. To some extent I inadvertently let my feelings and conflicts distort my perceptions of Ruth. My distortions include my projecting onto her attributes of significant figures in my own life; I experience countertransference. Although I can minimize countertransference, it can never be eliminated. Therefore, to minimize the negative impact of my countertransference on Ruth's treatment, I monitor my feelings about her and my reactions toward her, and I periodically discuss my treatment of her, including these feelings, with a trusted colleague. Voluntary consultation about my feelings and interventions is, in my opinion, an effective method for assessing and minimizing deleterious effects of countertransference. If I find myself uncomfortable discussing a particular aspect of Ruth's treatment, I suspect that countertransference is at work. Consultations must be conducted so as to protect her confidentiality; this usually includes her releasing the information and my altering information about her identity during the consultation. Should my countertransference have the potential to negatively affect Ruth's treatment, I would enter therapy myself and would either refer Ruth to a colleague or continue to treat her under supervision.

My scrutiny of my countertransference reactions to Ruth may be of value in helping me understand her; often my unconscious reactions give clues to that client's dynamics and to the reactions that others have to the client. Countertransference can be used in the service of the therapy if it can be understood and controlled. Monitoring my own countertransference feelings serves as a major source of clinical information about the client.

Some aspects of countertransference may be partially inseparable from the conscious motivation of the therapist to engage in the arduous work of psychotherapy. As I work actively with Ruth to break the spell cast on her in her past, I apply my understanding of the nature of the spell and of the "magic" needed to break it. As I engage in this struggle, I run the countertransference risk of becoming invested in the hero role, thereby fostering her dependence and prolonging her regression. But to some extent I have opted for this role by choosing the profession of psychotherapist. Thus, by participating in Ruth's life as the hero she has dreamed of, I am fulfilling my own not-so-unconscious needs. But if I am to stay a hero in the sense of being a good therapist, I must renounce the role of hero to Ruth at precisely the moment in therapy in which I have released her from the past's constricting spell.[2]

Jerry Corey's Work With Ruth From a Psychoanalytic Perspective

If you are using the *CD-ROM for Integrative Counseling*, refer to Session 10 ("Transference and Countertransference") and compare what I've written here with how I deal with transference and countertransference.

Basic Assumptions

As I work with Ruth within a psychoanalytic framework, I am guided by both the psychosexual perspective of Sigmund Freud and the psychosocial perspective of Erik Erikson. My work with Ruth is also influenced to some extent by contemporary psychoanalytic trends, which are often classified in terms of ego psychology and object-relations theory. I am moving beyond Freud to illustrate that contemporary psychoanalysis is an ever-evolving system rather than a closed and static model.

The *psychosexual* theory, as seen in traditional Freudian psychoanalysis, places emphasis on the internal conflicts of an individual during the first 6 years of life. This theory assumes that certain sexual and aggressive impulses are repressed during these formative years because, if they were to become conscious, they would produce extreme anxiety. Although these memories and experiences are buried in the unconscious, they exert a powerful influence on the individual's personality and behavior later in life.

The *psychosocial* theory, developed primarily by Erikson, emphasizes sociocultural influences on the development of personality. It assumes that there is continuity in human development. At the various stages of life, we face the challenge of establishing equilibrium between ourselves and our social world. At each crisis, or turning point, in the life cycle we can either successfully resolve our conflicts or fail to resolve them. Failure to resolve a conflict at a given stage results in fixation, or the experience of being stuck. It is difficult to master the psychosocial tasks of adulthood if we are psychologically stuck with unresolved conflicts from an earlier period of development. Although such a failure does not necessarily doom us to remain forever the victim of fixations, our lives are, to a large extent, the result of the choices we make at these stages.

The more recent work in the *psychoanalytic approach* is represented by the writings of Margaret Mahler, Heinz Kohut, and Otto Kernberg, among others. Contemporary psychoanalytic practice emphasizes the origins and transformations of the self, the differentiation between the self and others, the integration of the self with others, and the influence of critical factors in early development on later development. Predictable developmental sequences are noted in which the early experiences of the self shift in relation to an expanding awareness of others. Once self–other patterns are established, they influence later interpersonal relationships. Human development can best be thought of as the evolution of the way in which individuals differentiate self from others. One's current behavior is largely a repetition of the internal patterning established during one of the earlier stages of development.

In viewing Ruth's case, I make the assumption that her early development is of critical importance and that her current personality problems are rooted in repressed childhood conflicts. The psychoanalytic perspective on the developmental process provides me with a conceptual framework that helps me make sense of Ruth's current functioning. Borrowing from Kohut's thinking, I surmise that she was psychologically wounded during childhood and that her defensive structure is an attempt to avoid being wounded again. I expect to find an interweaving of old hurts with new wounds. Thus, I pay attention to the consistency between her emotional wounding as a child and those situations that result in pain for her today. Much of our therapeutic work is aimed at repairing the original wounding.

Assessment of Ruth

This assessment is based on a few initial sessions with Ruth, her intake form, and her autobiography. Her relationships with her parents are critically important from a therapeutic standpoint. She describes her father as "distant, authoritarian, and rigid." My hunch is that this view of her father colors how she perceives all men today, that her fear of displeasing her husband is connected to her fear of bringing her father displeasure, and that what she is now striving to get from her husband is related to what she wanted from her father. I expect that she will view me and react to me in many of the same ways she responded to her father. Through this transference relationship with me, Ruth will be able to recognize connecting patterns between her childhood behavior and her current struggles. For example, she is fearful of displeasing her husband, John, for fear he might leave. If he did, there would be a repetition of the pattern of her father's psychological abandonment of her after she had not lived up to his expectations. She does not stand up to John or ask for what she needs out of fear that he will become disgruntled and abandon her. She is defending herself against being wounded by him in some of the same ways that she was wounded by her father.

From a psychosexual perspective I am interested in Ruth's early childhood experiences in which she developed her views pertaining to sexuality. Her father's response when he caught her in an act of sexual experimentation needs to be considered as we work with her present attitudes and feelings about sex. As a child and adolescent, Ruth felt guilty and ashamed about her sexual feelings. She internalized many of her father's strict views of sexuality. Because her father manifested a negative attitude toward her increased sexual awareness, she learned that her sexual feelings were evil, that her body and sexual pleasure were both "dirty," and that her curiosity about sexual matters was unacceptable. Her sexual feelings became anxiety provoking and were thus rigidly controlled. The denial of sexuality that was established at this age has been carried over into her adult life and gives rise to severe conflicts, guilt, remorse, and self-condemnation.

Viewing Ruth from a psychosocial perspective will shed considerable light on the nature of her present psychological problems. Ruth never really developed a basic trust in the world. As an infant, she learned that she could not count on others to provide her with a sense of being wanted and loved. She did not receive affection throughout her early childhood, a deprivation that now makes it difficult for her to feel that she is worthy of affection. The task of early childhood is developing *autonomy,* which is necessary if one is to gain a measure of self-control and any ability to cope with the world. In Ruth's case she grew up fast, was never allowed to be a child, and was expected to take care of her younger brother and sisters. Although she seemed to be "mature" even as a child, in actuality she never became autonomous.

From the contemporary psychoanalytic perspective, Ruth will not feel truly independent until she feels properly attached and dependent. This notion means that to be independent she must allow herself to depend on others. Ruth, however, never felt a genuine sense of attachment to her father, whom she perceived as distant, or to her mother, whom she viewed as somewhat rejecting. For Ruth to have developed genuine independence, she would have needed others in her life whom she could count on for emotional support. But this support was absent from her background. During the school-age period she felt inferior in social relationships, was confused about her gender-role identity, and was unwilling to face new challenges. During adolescence she did not experience an identity crisis because she did not ask basic questions of life. Rather than questioning the values that had been taught to her, she compliantly accepted them. In part, she has followed the design established by her parents when she was an adolescent. She was not challenged to make choices for herself or to struggle to find meaning in life. In her adulthood she managed to break away from her fundamentalist religion, yet she could not free herself of her guilt over this act. She is still striving for her father's approval, and she is still operating without a clearly defined set of values to replace the ones she discarded. A major theme of Ruth's life is her concern over how to fill the void that she fears will result when her children leave home.

Psychoanalytic theory provides a useful perspective for understanding the ways in which Ruth is trying to control the anxiety in her life. She readily accepted her parents' rigid morality as one of her primary ego defenses because it served the function of controlling her impulses. Further, there is a fundamental split within her between the "good girl" and the "bad girl." Either she keeps in control of herself and others by doing things for them, or she gets out of control when she enjoys herself, as she did when she was "playing doctor." She feels in control when she takes care of her children, and she does not know what she will do once they leave home. Coupled with this empty-nest syndrome is her ambivalence about leaving the security of the home by choosing a career. This change brings about anxiety because she is struggling with her ability to direct her own life as opposed to defining herself strictly as a servant of others. This anxiety will be a focal point of therapy.

Goals of Therapy

The goal of our analytically oriented work will be to gradually uncover unconscious material. In this way Ruth will be able to use messages from the unconscious to direct her own life instead of being driven by her defensive controls. Therapy is aimed at promoting integration and ego development. The various parts of her self that she has denied will become more connected. The ideal type of identity is an autonomous self, which is characterized by self-esteem and self-confidence and is capable of intimacy with others.

Therapeutic Procedures

I suspect that a major part of our work will entail dealing with resistance, at least at the start of therapy. In spite of the fact that Ruth has come to therapy voluntarily, any number of barriers will make her progress slow at times. She has learned to protect herself against anxiety by building up defenses over the years, and she will not quickly surrender them. As we have seen, some of her primary defenses are repression and denial. The chances are that she will have some ambivalence about becoming aware of her unconscious motivations and needs. Merely gaining insight into the nature of her unconscious conflicts does not mean that her therapy is over, for the difficult part will be exploring and working through these conflicts.

I expect that I will become a significant figure in her life, for I assume that she will develop strong feelings toward me, both positive and negative. She will probably relate to me in some of the same ways that she related to her father. Working therapeutically with this transference involves two steps. One is to foster this development of transference; the second consists of working through patterns that she established with significant others in her past as these feelings emerge toward me in the therapy relationship. This second step is the core of the therapy process. *Working through* refers to repeating interpretations of her behavior and overcoming her resistance, thus allowing her to resolve her neurotic patterns. Although I do not use a blank-screen model, keeping myself mysterious and hidden, in this type of intensive therapy the client is bound to expect me to fulfill some of her unmet needs. She will probably experience again some of the same feelings she had during her childhood. How she views me and reacts to me will constitute much of the therapeutic work, for this transference material is rich with meaning and can tell Ruth much about herself.

The Therapeutic Process

The crux of my therapeutic work with Ruth consists of bringing her past into the present, which is done mainly through exploring the transference relationship. My aim is to do more than merely facilitate recall of past events and insight on her part; instead, I hope that she will see patterns and continuity in her life from her childhood to the present. When she realizes how her past is still operating, character change is possible, and new options open up for her.

ELEMENTS OF THE PROCESS   After Ruth has been in therapy for some time, she grows disenchanted with me. She does not see me as giving enough. She becomes irritated because I am not willing to share anything about my marriage or my relationships with my children. She says that I give her very analytical responses when she is simply trying to get to know something about me personally. She complains that she is the one doing all the giving and that she is beginning to resent it. Here is a brief sample of a session in which we talk about these feelings.

> RUTH: I want you to be more real with me. It feels uncomfortable for you to know so much about me when I know so little about you.
>
> JERRY: It's that I know a lot more about your life than you know about mine and that you're more vulnerable than I am.
>
> RUTH: You seem so removed and distant from me. You're hard to reach. This is not easy for me to say . . . uhm . . . I suppose I want to know what you really think of me. I'm often left wondering what you're feeling. I work hard at getting your approval, but I'm not sure I have it. I get the feeling that you think I'm weak.
>
> JERRY: I wonder if you have felt this way before?
>
> RUTH: Well, ah . . . you know you remind me of my father. No matter what I did to get his approval, I was never successful. Sometimes that is the way I feel around you.

I am consciously not disclosing much about my reactions to Ruth at this point because she is finally bringing out feelings about me that she avoided for so long. I encourage her to express more about the ways in which she sees me as ungiving and unreachable. It is through this process of exploring some of her persistent reactions to me that she will see more of the connection between her unfulfilled needs from the past and how she is viewing me in this present relationship. At this stage in her therapy Ruth is experiencing some very basic feelings of wanting to be special and wanting proof of it. By working with her transference reactions over a long period, she will eventually gain insight into how she has given her father all the power to affirm her as a person and how she has not learned to give herself the approval she so much wants from him. I am not willing to reassure her because I want to foster the expression of this transference.[3]

PROCESS COMMENTARY   I am not working with Ruth from the perspective of classical psychoanalysis. Rather, I am drawing from psychosocial theory and from concepts in the newer psychoanalytic thinking, especially from Kohut's work. I direct much of our therapy to the exploration of Ruth's old issues, her early wounding, and her fears of new wounds. The bruises to her self that she experiences in the here and now trigger memories of her old hurts. Especially in her relationship with me, she is sensitive to rejection and any signs of my disapproval. Therefore, much of our therapeutic effort is aimed at dealing with the ways in which she is now striving for recognition as well as the ways in which she attempted to get recognition in the past. In short, she has a damaged self, and she is susceptible to and fearful of further injury. We discuss her attachments, how she tried to win affection, and the many ways in which she is trying to protect herself from suffering further emotional wounds to a fragile ego.

Much of Ruth's work involves going back to early events in her life—recalling them and the feelings associated with them—in the hope that she can be free from the restrictions of her past. She comes to realize that her past is an important part of her and that old wounds will take time to heal.

One of the major ways Ruth gains insight into her patterns is by learning to understand her dreams. We regularly focus on their meanings, and she free-associates to some symbols. She has a very difficult time giving up control and simply allowing herself to say freely whatever comes to mind in these sessions. She worries about "saying the appropriate thing," and we examine this material in the sessions. Dream work is one of the major tools to tap her unconscious processes.

Ruth also discovers from the way she responds to me some key connections between how she related to significant people in her life. She looks to me in some of the same ways that she looked to her father for approval and for love. I encourage her recollection of feelings associated with these past events so that she can work through the barriers preventing her from functioning as a mature adult.[4]

Questions for Reflection

As you continue working with the therapeutic approaches described in this book, you will have many opportunities to apply the basic assumptions and key concepts of each theory to your own life. Some of these questions for reflection will assist you in becoming involved in a personal way. Other questions are designed to give you some guidance in beginning to work with Ruth. They are intended to help you clarify your reactions to how the consultant and I worked with Ruth from each of the therapeutic perspectives. Select the questions for reflection that most interest you.

1. Dr. Blau emphasizes the importance of understanding the "whys" of a client's experience and behavior. What advantages and disadvantages do you see in this focus?
2. Dr. Blau suggests that the psychosexual aspects of Ruth's relationships with her parents, and possibly her siblings, still represent key conflict areas in her present behavior. In what ways may her early experiences be having a significant impact on her life today? How might you explore these dynamics with her?

3. Do you share the emphasis of this approach on the importance of Ruth's father in her life? How might you go about exploring with her how conflicts with her father are related to some of her present conflicts?

4. What is one of the most significant themes (from the analytic perspective) you would focus on in your sessions with Ruth?

5. In what ways would you encourage Ruth to go back and relive her childhood? How important is delving into the client's early childhood in leading to personality change?

6. What defenses do you see in Ruth? How do you imagine you would work to lessen these defenses?

7. Dr. Blau discusses the importance of both the therapist's real relationship and the as-if relationship with Ruth. How might you differentiate between her transference reactions and her real reactions to you?

Notes

See the DVD/Online Program entitled Theory in Practice: The Case of Stan (Session 2: Psychoanalytic Therapy Applied to the Case of Stan) for ways of working with Stan's resistance and transference.

1. The source for the *DSM-IV-TR* is as follows: American Psychiatric Association (2000). *Diagnostic and statistical manual of mental disorders,* 4th edition, Text Revision. Washington, DC: Author.

2. Here Dr. Blau discusses his views of working with Ruth's transference and makes important comments pertaining to his ability and willingness to recognize, monitor, and deal with his own potential countertransference. If you are using the *CD-ROM for Integrative Counseling,* refer to Session 10 ("Working With Transference and Countertransference") to see my perspective on these issues.

3. Again, if you are using the *CD-ROM for Integrative Counseling,* refer to Session 10 ("Transference and Countertransference") and compare what I've written here with how I deal with transference and countertransference.

4. For a more detailed treatment of psychoanalytic theory, see G. Corey (2009), *Theory and Practice of Counseling and Psychotherapy* (8th ed., Belmont, CA: Brooks/Cole). The basic concepts introduced in William Blau's work with Ruth and in my version on psychodynamic work with Ruth are covered comprehensively in Chapter 4 ("Psychoanalytic Therapy").

CHAPTER THREE

Case Approach
to Adlerian Therapy

General Overview of Adlerian Therapy

The Adlerian approach focuses on assisting clients to better understand how they perceive themselves, others, and life and to better appreciate their strengths and assets while avoiding the counterproductive perceptions and behaviors that have led to the development and maintenance of symptomatic behaviors in their lives. Adlerian practitioners are not bound by any set of prescribed techniques. Rather, they may employ a variety of strategies and techniques that are suited to the unique needs of their clients. The concept of social interest, Adler's criterion for mental health, provides further direction for therapeutic interventions and evaluation of the therapy process. Social interest, *gemeinschaftsgefuhl* in the original German, meaning "a community feeling," involves a sense of belonging, of being connected to one's fellow humans and one's social and occupational communities on a basis of equality and mutual value or worth. The important criterion determining the relative health or pathology of any behavior is the issue of its usefulness to others and to the larger social community. Does the behavior contribute to the well-being of both the individual and others and foster relationships based on mutual respect and equality in personal value while accepting our shared imperfections?

A few of the therapeutic procedures commonly employed by Adlerian therapists to facilitate growth and change include encouragement, confrontation, relabeling, cognitive restructuring, humor, paradoxical intention, interpretation, homework assignments, and teaching new behavioral skills. Adlerians stress a democratic, collaborative approach to therapy, and the client and therapist typically discuss and decide upon termination. The emphasis on goal alignment provides a common frame of reference from which to assess the outcomes of therapy.

An Adlerian Therapist's Perspective on Ruth

by James Robert Bitter, EdD and William G. Nicoll, PhD

Introduction

Jerry Corey consulted with us on the case of Ruth and asked for our help conducting a thorough initial interview and developing a summary of impressions based on this initial interview. This initial interview generates a relatively clear picture of the client in relation to what Adler called the *life tasks* of (a) friendship and social relations, (b) work and occupation, and (c) love, intimacy, and sexuality. We also provided a lifestyle assessment, including a summary of the family constellation, a record of early recollections, and an interpretation of Ruth's pattern of basic convictions. We use a modified form of Adlerian counseling that we call *Adlerian brief therapy.*[1]

Lifestyle information is often collected and interpreted by two therapists, using a technique called *multiple therapy.*[2] The client is initially interviewed by one therapist, who then presents the data to a second therapist. The client experiences social interest in the very structure of therapy. The model of two therapists cooperating in a single effort is often therapeutic in and of itself.

This section provides a detailed and comprehensive assessment of Ruth's early background and her current functioning. We hope you will continue to use this material as you work with her case in other chapters. We begin with our narrative summaries from a general diagnosis and lifestyle assessment.[3] We co-construct these summaries with the client based on an interviewing model delineated in the *Individual Psychology Client Workbook,* which was developed by Robert L. Powers and Jane Griffith.[4] Here, we have provided some minimal data and our initial summaries from our assessment process. We follow these summaries with a process outline of *Adlerian brief therapy* and an example of its application with Ruth.

The Initial Interview

In addition to the information presented in Chapter 1 in Ruth's autobiography and intake interview, Ruth also indicated that she was the oldest of four children who are ordered as follows: Ruth, age 39, living with her husband in California; Jill (−4), age 35, an architect living in Chicago; Amy (−6), age 33, a social worker and homemaker in California; and Steve (−9), age 30, a clerk in a shipping office who still lives at home with Ruth's parents.

Ruth believes she is the one who is most affected by her unhappiness. Her family is kind and understanding. Ruth was a homemaker and mother until her children became adolescents. She then entered college part time and obtained a bachelor's degree. Through her contacts with others at the university she has become aware of how she has limited herself, how she has fostered her family's dependence on her, and how frightened she is of branching out from her roles as mother and wife. Ruth responded to questions about the three life tasks in the following way.

🥀 **Love and Intimacy**   "I have had only one relationship. John and I started dating after I graduated from high school. We got married, and we've been together ever since. John says he had been interested in me for a long time before we went out. He had seen me in church. We met formally at a church social. He stayed with me for a whole day. We talked, and he listened to everything I said. He was very attentive. When he walked me home, he asked if we could go to a movie. I said yes, and my parents didn't object. John was strong-minded, knew what he wanted, and had goals and dreams. I liked his dreams, especially since they included me. He was always calm and never seemed to get angry. He's still very patient, the way I think men should be. He's the only man I ever dated, and he has been good to me.

"I think being feminine means that you are nurturing and give a great deal of yourself to others. You must be able to balance family, which is your responsibility, and community. There is always a lot to do. I think being feminine also means that you're attractive to men. I do really well at the first part, but I doubt that I'm attractive to men, especially with my weight.

"John hardly ever complains, but he would probably like to have sex more often. I never really enjoyed sex that much. It's OK, but I don't get in the mood as often as John. If I have any complaint, it's that I would like to make more decisions in the family and even for myself, but I would probably not do well.

"If I could have anything going better in this area, I would like to feel more feminine and appreciated and loved. I would like to feel comfortable doing things for myself without feeling as if I'm letting John down or, worse, losing him."

🥀 **Work and Occupation**   "I have worked all my life in the home: first, my father's home and now, my own home. I have taken care of children and a home since I was a young teenager. I occasionally do volunteer work, but very little really. There's so much to do with the children and John. What I like most about being a homemaker, or housewife, is when people like what I do for them. Sometimes, though, it feels as if the kids don't even notice. They just expect everything. John notices more. I notice all the things that never get done, especially now that I'm getting my teaching credential. I guess school is my work for the moment. It's still hard, but I like it more than I liked high school. I'm learning a lot, but it takes a lot of time and energy, and I'm way behind at home.

"I want very much to finish my certification as a teacher and to teach in an elementary school, third grade. I want to help students who are struggling."

🥀 **Friendship and Community**   "I have developed some good friends recently at school. I feel that school has been a turning point for me, both for work and for having people to talk to. My classes have helped me meet people who seem to like me and with whom I feel comfortable, just talking.

"Most of my friends are women, but I don't have very many friends. I maybe have one or two long-term friends, but I have shared more with college friends than I have with my long-term friends. I think people like it that I listen well. I'm interested in what people have to say. I'm not a leader, but I like to be a part of things.

"I think when people first meet me, they are not impressed; but after they get to know me, they know that I'm dependable and that I care about people. I think I make a good friend, but this is new for me.

"I also know people who work around John, but we don't socialize much with them. I don't know what they think of me. I'm not nearly as community-oriented as my mother was.

"I would like to see the friendships I have started at school really grow and develop. I would like to have some of them as fellow teachers and get to work in the same school. That would be great, to have a friend just down the hall."

OUR SUMMARY   From this information, we developed a summary of our initial impressions. The summary is written in the third person to allow Ruth to stand back from her experience and to see herself through a narrative that puts her life in context and shows its dynamic movement.

Ruth has presented herself for therapy at a potential turning point in her life. She has spent many years doing what she prepared to do early in life. Ruth, the oldest of four children, was drafted into caring for her brother and two sisters at a young age. She used her mother as a role model of a "good homemaker" and continued her work when she married her husband, John. John and Ruth have four children, who are now adolescents. When her children became teenagers, she decided to seek work where she would continue to feel needed. Returning to school, she completed a bachelor's degree and is seeking a teacher's certificate. College and her fellow students opened a whole new world to Ruth. She began to see many new possibilities for herself, including a place in the world as a professional teacher and as a person with many more friends than she has been used to having. She is feeling both excited by the new possibilities and worried about losing the people and world she has known all her life.

Ruth feels pulled by both worlds; she is experiencing a conflict between satisfying her needs in the occupational life task and her needs in the family–intimacy life task. In one world (school), the opportunities seem limitless, exciting, and full of promise—even if new and somewhat overwhelming and risky. In the other world (home), her life is safe, known, familiar, and predictable, and she knows exactly what she needs to do to succeed and to feel safe and secure. She wants both worlds to fit together, but she is not always sure how to make that happen. She also wants to perform *perfectly* in both worlds. Even though part of her knows that the demand for perfection is impossible, she has not let herself off the hook. Mostly, she wants everyone involved to be happy with her and, above all, to avoid displeasing anyone. She wants John to be happy; she wants her children to be happy; she wants her instructors to be happy; she wants her new friends to be happy; and last, and least, she wants herself to be happy. When she cannot figure out how to make it all happen, she often finds herself becoming worried, anxious, and depressed. When she doesn't have time to become worried, anxious, or depressed, she settles for dizziness, headaches, heart palpitations, sleeplessness, and other physical disturbances, which act as a message to her family and herself that she needs some rest and needs some care.

Ruth has put everyone else in her life first. She comes from a family in which at least one other child achieved success easily, and she found it hard to please her mother and father. She could not guess what would make them happy, and she feared their disapproval and rejection. The family atmosphere was strict and controlled, and she found her place by caring for children and others in the way that she believed women were supposed to do. It is hard for her to put herself first at this point in life without fearing she will do something wrong, displease her husband and family, and thereby risk losing everything.

Ruth has a well-defined set of goals for therapy:

- Deal with the physical and emotional symptoms that express the conflict and demands she feels in her life.
- Find a balance between seeking what she wants and maintaining what she has.
- Get help with at least one daughter, whose rebellion acts as a constant reminder of "what can happen if Mom is not ever-present and vigilant."
- Discover what she can make of herself and her life with opportunities opening up and time running out. She is, after all, 39 years of age and "losing it" . . . fast!

Ruth's Lifestyle Assessment

The Family Constellation   During a lifestyle assessment, Ruth described her father as devoted to his work. When she was young, he was stern, and he was an authority figure in the community. He was respected and righteous. He was also cool and detached. With Ruth, he was often distant, strict, and ungiving. He was rather aloof from all of the children and insisted on respect. Jill is his favorite child; he likes her accomplishments.

With regard to discipline, he would yell at the children, or he would withdraw from a misbehaving child totally and not talk to the child for weeks. Ruth felt scared and, at times, disowned.

Ruth doesn't know what nationality her dad is, but she knows he is the oldest of four boys, and he came from a religious family. It was assumed early in his life that he would be a minister, and he prepared for it all his life. His family was poor, but always got by, and they were always proud.

Ruth's mother was a hard worker; she rarely complained out loud. She was very proper, always did the right thing, and was quite dignified. She was proud of her role as a minister's wife. She was self-sacrificing. She would go without so that her husband or the kids could have the things they needed. She would even give up things for herself so that people in the church could have food, clothing, or shelter.

It was very important to Ruth's mother that the children maintain a good image in the church and the community. As unselfish as she could be, she was emotionally ungiving, very serious, not very happy (or so it appeared), and very strict with the children.

She was devoted to seeing that the children grew up right, but she was not personally involved in their lives unless they got in trouble. Her favorite child is

Steve. He could do no wrong in her eyes. She did not want any of the children to bring shame on the family, and she wanted all of them to be hard workers.

Ruth's mother is Scots-Irish. She was also poor when she was little. She was the youngest of three girls, and she was the only one to marry. "She always told us how lucky she was to have a Christian life."

Ruth's parents have a stiff and formal relationship. Very little affection was demonstrated, and they rarely laughed. They did not argue: mother stood behind whatever father said or did. Ruth wanted to make them happy, but it was not an easy task.

Ruth's paternal grandmother took an interest in her. She seemed to understand Ruth, and she would often talk to Ruth and give her good advice. She was the one who first approved of John.

Ruth's description of her siblings can be drawn as follows:

Sibling Array

Ruth (39)	Responsible, hard-working, organized, dedicated, capable, trustworthy, self-critical, undemanding, scared, unable to please either parent.
	Ruth's perspective: I was lonely: I felt useful and needed; I wanted approval from my folks; I was a good girl, and I took care of my sister and brother.
Jill (−4)	Bright, pretty, accomplished, conforming, well- behaved. Got along with Dad; got along fairly well with Mom.
	Ruth's perspective: Jill was the most like me; she was good and was successful at life. Things came more easily to her. She won honors at school.
Amy (−6)	Immature, demanding, the family "troublemaker"; admiring of me, hard-working, independent. In trouble with Dad, and tried to please Mom, without success.
	Ruth's perspective: Amy was the most different from me; she seemed irresponsible by comparison.
Steve (−9)	Pampered, overprotected, in trouble with Dad but protected by Mom. Got Mom's attention. Sensitive, argumentative with me, not too accomplished.
	Ruth's perspective: Steve was also different from me; in Mom he found a shelter from life.

In Ruth's childhood neighborhood, Ruth and her siblings were mostly absent; she didn't play much. Children from church were sometimes invited to the house, but mostly siblings worked or played with one another, if at all. She didn't have any real friends of either sex: just her brother and sisters.

Ruth was expected to do well in school. It was hard for her. She had to work at it all the time. Even when she worked hard, she sometimes didn't do very well. Math and sciences were the hardest for her. English and history were her best subjects. She liked to read, and that helped. She would get so nervous when she was doing math or science that she couldn't concentrate. The teachers generally liked her (with one or two exceptions), but they always felt that she was not living up to her potential, and that's what they told her parents. She didn't socialize with other kids much. She was quiet and kept to herself. Other kids thought she was "weird."

When Ruth was 6 years old, she reports: "My father caught me 'playing doctor' with an 8-year-old boy. He lectured me and refused to speak to me for weeks. I felt guilty and ashamed." Ruth reached adolescence with minimal information from her mother, father, or peers. She remembers being scared at 12 when menarche occurred. "I didn't know what was happening. My mother gave me the things I needed and a booklet to read." She was not allowed to date until she completed high school; at age 19 she married the first person she dated. "I was lucky to find a good man. All I knew was my mother's version of how to be a good homemaker."

From Ruth's lifestyle information, we were able to co-construct with Ruth a narrative summary of the meaning she attached to her family constellation and family life. This summary constitutes a retelling of Ruth's life story with an emphasis on the meaning and patterns associated with her current life experiences.[5]

🕮 **Our Summary**   Ruth is the oldest of four children, raised in a family where hard work and perfection were expected; unfortunately, as she learned early in life, hard work was no guarantee that perfection could be achieved. Even after a huge effort, the slightest mistake could lead to a rebuke or a rejection that was deeply felt, leaving her lonely, cautious, and scared. Thus, Ruth approaches life with an emphasis on seeking to always do the "right" thing as she perceives others to define it while guarding against doing anything wrong, displeasing others and thereby inviting their rejection and loss of affection.

Her father set a masculine guiding line that was characterized by a harsh, strict, stern, and angry persona; his every stance was authoritarian, critical, and religiously perfectionistic. Indeed, her father was such a dominant authority in her life that it was easy for her to confuse God-fearing with father-fearing. Like a female version of Cain in the Bible, she was locked in a struggle for approval in which she would never be good enough and her sister Jill could do no wrong. The struggle to please her father gradually settled into strategies for avoiding his displeasure, and fear became the operative motivator in her life.

Ruth's mother set a feminine guiding line that was characterized by a serious devotion to principle, righteousness, duty, and her husband. Her behavior suggested that life was filled with hard work and sacrifice, a burden that women should suffer quietly, with dignity, and without complaint. Although she provided for the children's physical and spiritual needs, she did little to provide relief from the harsh stance that her husband took in the world.

Only Ruth's grandmother provided her with a different role model for womanhood. She demonstrated that it was possible for women to be interested in, involved with, and caring toward others.

The family atmosphere was characterized by formality and stiffness, a rigid consistency and discipline in which frivolity and, indeed, happiness were out of place. The family values included were hard work, perfectionism, and a belief that appearances were extremely important. No crack in the architecture could be tolerated.

🕸 **Record of Early Recollections**   Within an Adlerian lifestyle assessment, early recollections function as a projective technique. Each individual recounts 6 to 12 early memories that are chosen by the person to reflect images of self, others, the world, and, sometimes, ethical convictions. Early recollections are like little stories with morals (as in Aesop's fables) that serve as meaning-markers in the person's life. As such, early memories always reveal more about the person in the present than they do about the person's past. Indeed, sometimes an early memory is "real" to the person but can easily be shown to be historically inaccurate or even impossible.

To be useful as a projective device, our directions must remain minimal and neutral. We start by asking Ruth to think back to when she was very little (before the age of 9) and to tell us one thing that happened one time. In Ruth's interview, she is able to provide just five early recollections.

1. *Age 3.* "I remember my father yelling at me and then putting me in another room because I was crying. I don't remember why I was crying, but I know I was scared, and after he shouted, I was petrified."

   Most vivid moment: father yelling
   Feeling: scared, petrified

2. *Age 4½.* "I was in church, talking with a boy. My mother gave me dirty looks, and my father, who was conducting the service, gave me a stern lecture when we got home."

   Most vivid moment: the looks parents gave me
   Feeling: scared and confused

3. *Age 6.* "An 8-year-old neighbor boy and I had our clothes off and were 'playing doctor' when my father caught us in my bedroom. He sent the boy home and then told me in a cold and solemn voice that what I had done was very wrong. He did not speak to me for weeks, and I remember feeling very dirty and guilty."

   Most vivid moment: being caught by my father
   Feeling: scared, "bad," and guilty

4. *Age 7.* "I remember my second-grade teacher saying that I was not doing well in school and that I was going to get a bad report card. I tried so hard to do well because I didn't want to bring home bad grades. This teacher didn't like me very much, and I couldn't understand what I had done wrong. I thought I was trying my best. I was scared."

   Most vivid moment: the teacher telling me I was getting a bad report card
   Feeling: scared

5. *Age 8.* "I was in a church play, and I worked for months memorizing my lines. I thought I had them down perfect. My parents came to the play, and for a time I was doing fine, and I was hoping they would like my performance. Then toward the end I forgot to come in when I was supposed to, and the director had to cue me. My mistake was apparent to my father who later commented that I had spoiled a rather good performance by my lack of attention. I remember feeling sad and disappointed, because I had so hoped that they would be pleased. And I don't recall my mother saying anything about the play."

Most vivid moment: father commenting on my mistake

Feeling: embarrassed

⚘ **Our Summary**   These memories represent Ruth's convictions as she is now, so we summarize her position and stance in the first person. In many ways, the summary expresses Ruth's commentary on her life experiences.

"I live in a man's world that is often harsh, uncaring, and frightening. Helplessness and emotion will not be tolerated in this world and will lead to being separated from it. In a man's world, women must not speak, not even to other men. The rebuke of authority is both immediate and frightening. Men and their world are never available to women. A woman is wrong to want to know about men or explore them. Dabbling in a man's world can lead to banishment and total exile.

"Only achievement counts in the real world. No amount of hard work can make up for a lack of performance. No amount of pleasing can win over someone who is against you. Significant people always find out about mistakes: the most important people always seem to be present when a lack of attention leads to an error that ruins even a good effort. To err in the real world is embarrassingly human; to forgive is against policy."

From this summary, we fashion this list of basic convictions that serve as interfering ideas in Ruth's quest for a rich and fulfilling life:

- The power and importance of men are exaggerated, as is her fear of their disapproval. Pleasing seems to her the best route to safety in a man's world, but it leaves her unsure of her own identity and in constant fear of rejection.
- The inevitability of mistakes and failure is exaggerated and feared; the slightest human errors are to be avoided: 100% is passing, 99% is the start of creeping failure.
- Doing the right thing, being "good," is required just to survive; doing the wrong thing signals impending doom: caution is always warranted in an unpredictable world.
- Murphy's Law governs: What can go wrong will go wrong.
- Hard work is always demanded but will not necessarily produce the desired results or achievements.

Adlerian Brief Therapy With Ruth

Adlerian counseling has evolved substantially over the almost seven decades since Adler's death in 1937. Many different models have borrowed from

Adler's Individual Psychology concepts and have been integrated with Adlerian therapy. Even under the umbrella of Adlerian psychotherapy, different approaches to clinical practice currently coexist. Despite differences in style, all Adlerians share a focus on understanding lifestyle, the individual's socially constructed pattern of living, and a commitment to holistic, systemic, and teleological assessments and treatment.[6] We have successfully applied the Adlerian brief therapy model to our work with individuals, couples, and families.[7]

Five points define our therapeutic process: (a) time limitation, (b) focus, (c) counselor directiveness and optimism, (d) symptoms as solutions, and (e) the assignment of behavioral tasks. The two of us differ to some extent on the relative emphases that should be given to a definitive time limitation, counselor directiveness, and the assignment of behavioral tasks. We both agree, however, that *focused work* will tend to keep therapy brief, that nonorganic *symptoms are the client's solution* to a personal problem, and that *motivation modification* is the goal when both directive interventions and behavioral tasks are used.

Integrating a time limitation into therapy reflects the reality that we meet people in the middle of their lives, and we will say "goodbye" to them in the middle of their lives. We enter into a contract with our client that suggests we can make a difference in each other's lives in a relatively short period of time. There is optimism in the contract, a belief in the client's ability to change, grow, and improve her or his life situation. For the time we will be meeting, our focus is on being fully present for our clients. While we do not always define exactly the number and duration of sessions with a client, when we do, we are able to work more quickly, staying focused on desired outcomes.

Clarity of focus and practice is the central element that limits time in therapy. For the Adlerian brief therapist, two goals guide every session. First, the therapist seeks to develop a systemic, holistic understanding of the person in treatment. This is most often accomplished by some form of formal or informal lifestyle assessment process that seeks to elicit individual patterns and motivations and the rules of interaction that govern the individual's idiosyncratic patterns of perceiving, behaving, and coping. Second, the therapist wants to know what the individual wants from therapy: Toward what goals will they work together? Effective work requires that the therapist balance both goals. We ask ourselves recurrently: "Where are we going . . . and with whom?"

The process within sessions often resembles a meeting of minds and hearts. While both of us (Jim and Bill) recognize that "therapeutic relationship" and "client change" are intimately connected, Jim's focus emphasizes relational qualities in therapy (PACE) whereas Bill tends to organize his work around strategies for change (BURP). For a look at how the two of us think about therapist–client interactions, see Table 3.1.

Human beings have goals. They act purposefully and in goal-motivated patterns based on the interpretations they make about self, others, and life (their worldviews). A teleological understanding "makes sense" out of symptoms, patterns of behavior, feelings, convictions, values, and beliefs. A teleological orientation illuminates the client's present and intended future. In this

TABLE 3.1 Two Levels of Focus Within Adlerian Brief Therapy

JIM'S FOCUS   Jim likes to bring his attention to the rhythm of the therapeutic experience. This reflects his work with Virginia Satir and Erv and Miriam Polster and a focus on experiential therapy.

P*urpose*
Since every interaction, as well as every thought, feeling, and behavior, has a purpose, what is the purpose of what is happening right at this moment in therapy? What motivates the patterns that make up the person's life? What purpose do feelings serve? What meaning is attached to living?

A*wareness*
Awareness is the alpha and omega of experience. What awareness does the client enjoy? What experiences are blocked from client awareness? What meaning is lost? What purpose is served? How is awareness related to contact with others?

C*ontact*
What is the quality of contact between the therapist and the client? What kind of contact does the client make with others in her or his life, with the environment, and with oneself? What purpose is served by the contacts the client makes? How can contact augment client awareness? Which awarenesses would augment contact?

E*xperience*
What is the quality of life experience the person brings to therapy? Is it a thin life or one thick with meaning? Is it a fascinating or interesting life story? What experience exists between therapist and client? Would an experiment (only one form of experience) lead to a fuller appreciation of life and other experiences available to the person?

BILL'S FOCUS   Bill first listens to the "how" of behavior, especially what people do and what they feel. Next, Bill listens for the "what for," or the purpose or functions of behavior. Finally, Bill works with the client to reveal the "whys" of behavior and the rules of interaction.

B*ehavior redescription*
Clients, and counselors, often adopt the language of pathology, a language of possession: for example, "I am bipolar." "I have an anxiety disorder." By adopting a language of use, we move the client to focusing on behavioral interactions. We ask: When was the last time this occurred? What did you do? How did you feel? Who else was affected? What did they do? How did you respond?

U*nderlying rules*
Careful attention to the client's answers opens an avenue to the purpose(s) that symptoms may serve. The sequence of behaviors and interactions also begins to suggest the rules the person uses to function in life, to cope, and to maintain stability.

R*eorientation*
The therapist seeks a cognitive shift in the client's understanding of self and symptoms. Adlerians use tentative disclosures of purpose, reframing of rules and experience, relabeling concepts, paradox, and even humor. The therapist seeks to shift the client's "private logic" to common sense.

P*rescribing behavioral rituals*
Real change takes place *between* sessions, not *in* sessions. Rituals are regular, repeated actions that reaffirm and maintain new possibilities. We ask: What is the client going to do? What strategies and interventions will encourage the client to take "real" steps in his or her own behalf? How can the therapist use self to align with and augment client functioning?

sense, the past is merely a remembered (and often revised) context generated by the person in support of current goals and purposes. Real change, second-order change, always follows from some form of motivation modification, a re-orientation of client interpretations regarding the circumstances that brought him or her to therapy.

Adlerian brief therapists want to co-develop (with clients) functional solutions, expand limited choices, and create new possibilities. We want to activate underutilized resources—both internal and external. Actually, it is often possible to accomplish these therapeutic goals in a single session. Whether in one session or twelve, making a difference in clients' lives requires the therapist to pay attention to the flow of therapy as well as to the unique understandings that arise from that therapy.

The Flow of Adlerian Brief Therapy

Figure 3.1 presents a structural map for the flow of therapy that we adapted from Dreikurs's holistic approach to psychotherapy.[8] We use the word *flow* to indicate a fluid and dynamic movement, one that eschews mechanistic steps or stages. Indeed, there is nothing in the arrangement of the flow of the session that cannot be rearranged to fit the needs of the client or the therapy session.

🧘 **Meeting the Person**   The first contact we have with a client may be by phone or through a referral. We recognize that coming to therapy can be challenging, and we want to facilitate a smooth transition. We want the client to feel welcome. While client concerns are often rehearsed and tend to surface quickly, Adlerian brief therapists focus initially on the *client-as-a-person*. Through mutual respect, genuine interest, and even fascination, we hope the client will experience our full presence. This presence, real contact with the client, is supported even in the first few minutes of therapy by the use of our five senses. What the therapist sees, hears, and experiences, perhaps in the touch of a handshake, is especially important.

🧘 **The Subjective Interview**   Being fully present provides the client with the support that is needed to tell her or his unique story. Empathy, interest, and fascination enable the therapist to follow the client closely, staying with the next most interesting question or development. This concentration on *the next* brings focus to the interview and encourages a depth of disclosure and understanding between counselor and client. A client who can clearly articulate what is important to her or him has already begun to take some control of self and life. Toward the end of this part of the interview, Adlerian brief therapists ask: "Is there anything else you feel I should know to understand you and your concerns?"

During the subjective interview, motivational and behavioral patterns in the person's life begin to emerge. At first tentatively, Adlerian counselors begin to hypothesize about what works for the client. How do the patterns in a person's life reflect the individual's rules of interaction? How do the patterns and rules directly contribute to maintaining the concerns that are being identified? And in

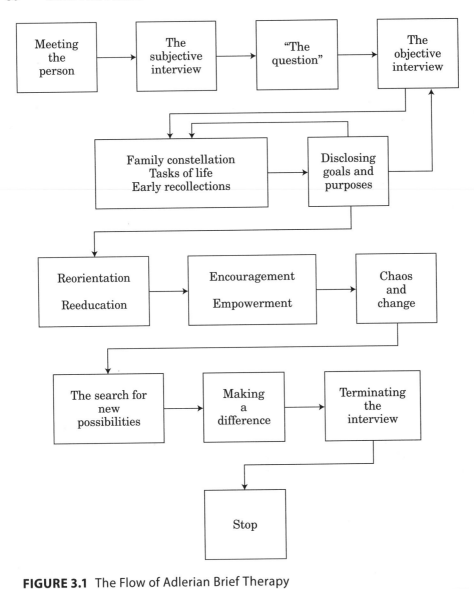

FIGURE 3.1 The Flow of Adlerian Brief Therapy

what way might the stated concerns actually be the person's best current solution to life's demands?

🕮 **"The Question"**   Based on Dreikurs's[9] formulation of "The Question," Adlerians attempt to differentiate organic symptoms or problems from ones that are psychogenic. Initially phrased by Adler[10] and later reframed by Dreikurs, The Question is: "What would you be doing, what would change, if you didn't have these symptoms or problems?" or "How would your life be different if you didn't have these issues, concerns, or problems?" When the answer is: "Nothing would be different, except the symptoms would be gone," then we suspect the problem is probably physiological or organic—even if it is masquerading as a psychological complaint. When the client indicates that life, work, friendships, or family relations would improve, we immediately suspect that the problem serves the purpose of helping the client retreat from the challenge of these life tasks.

When Ruth was asked "The Question," she said she would be happy at home and at work. She would have a job as an elementary school teacher and would work with a third-grade class. She would have energy for her children's activities and those of her husband, and she would see her family more often. Her answer suggests that she lives in doubt about her worth and value, and she fears possible failure and disapproval when she faces the test of her worth in the real world. Can she make it in the world of work as an elementary school teacher? Does she have a right to work and also be happy at home? Can she ever do enough for her husband and children to feel really loved by them? When Ruth faces these questions, she begins to doubt herself and her abilities, and her symptoms enable her to retreat from the answers she most fears.

The Objective Interview   The objective interview is essentially a lifestyle assessment of the client. We want to create a holistic picture of the individual, including information about when the problem or concern started, precipitating events, medical history, present or past medications, social history, and the reasons the person is seeking therapy. The most important aspects of the objective interview, however, started with the early systemic work of Adler: an investigation of *family constellation;* the *life tasks of friendships, occupation,* and *intimacy;* and *early recollections.*

Each of these areas of investigation will produce life stories that, taken together, yield patterns of living and coping: they "make sense" of the client's concerns. Listening to the client's interpretation of the place she or he holds in the family also helps us understand the client's overall sense of place in the world. The individual's experience of life's demands or tasks allows us to uncover client strengths, perceived weaknesses, and most important, coping styles. Early recollections reveal the person's convictions about self, others, life, the world and, sometimes, even ethical convictions. They also can reveal the client's stance in relation to the therapeutic relationship and the therapist.

Disclosing Goals and Purposes   Adlerians introduce goals and purposes as part of a meaningful dialogue about symptoms, behaviors, feelings, values, and convictions. Most goals and purposes function out of the client's awareness at a nonconscious level. To make goals conscious and explicit is to already change client process. Behavior is enacted in social engagements, and assessing the results of social interactions is the surest way to formulate a hypothesis or guess about an individual's motivation. When such disclosures follow from a "clarity of focus" obtained in the subjective and objective interviews, they often elicit a recognition reflex in the person.

🐚 **Reorientation and Reeducation**   Adlerian therapists use the concepts of reorientation and reeducation to emphasize that treatment is an educative process; it is about helping the client to change direction, cope more effectively, and meet life with a new understanding. Rather than merely decreasing or eliminating symptoms, Adlerian brief therapy aims at augmented social-emotional competence and mental health. We want clients to have a sense of belonging and a sense of being valued in their community as an antidote to isolation and withdrawal: we want to increase *community feeling* and *social interest.* While we do not have specific outcomes for therapy in mind before we meet the client, we believe that some general conditions can be identified that are better for human life: to think rationally, to feel fully within the human experience, to greet the world with optimism and hope, to have courage and confidence, to make a contribution, to have a sense of humor, to have friends and to be a true friend, and to be interested in the well-being of others.

🐚 **Encouragement and Empowerment**   Encouragement and empowerment are the foundation for all change through therapy. Adlerian counselors believe that courage follows from a sense of empowerment and that empowerment results from rediscovering the individual's internal and external resources. The discovery of strengths gets one through the difficult times and prepares the way for new possibilities. Functional solutions and real change are the result of facing life's challenges with courage rather than in retreat.

🐚 **Chaos and Change**   Change is seldom easy. It requires the person to move from what is familiar and known to what is unfamiliar and unknown. Disorientation and chaos are the most common experiences one has when change happens too fast or when the requirements are overwhelming. When a client is in chaos, the therapist must remain steady and focused if she or he is to help the client refocus. Careful and often delicate, small movements are needed during this time. We remind our clients that they are not alone—and not without strengths. We hold them *only* to decisions that can be implemented immediately, leaving longer-range issues for later.

🐚 **The Search for New Possibilities**   New possibilities tend to emerge rather than be created. They are what follows when a tight therapeutic focus is connected to the client in what we call "the relational present": the experience of being together with the therapist. In general, client-generated possibilities are more useful than therapist-generated possibilities because they reinforce a sense of personal strength, courage, and capability in the client. Still, when the relationship has been caring and collaborative throughout, most clients will accept therapist suggested options and prescriptions calmly and with hope.

🐚 **Making a Difference**   Adlerian counselors want to make a difference in the lives of their clients. In a single session, that difference may be only a small shift in understanding, a new clarity about patterns or meaning, an emotional realization, or a small experiment designed for more useful interactions. As therapists, we ask ourselves: "If I had only one session to be helpful in this person's life, what would I want to accomplish? And what would they want me to accomplish?" There is never any guarantee that a future session will occur.

⚗ **Terminating the Interview**   Terminating an interview session is merely an interruption of therapy. Of necessity, any therapeutic relationship, no matter how intense the involvement, is time-limited. Each session is followed by separation, the space in which clients may actually enact the new possibilities of their lives. In the beginning, these separations may be only days or a week, but over time, they will evolve into separations of months—or even years. Still, the relationship is always available and reconnection is only a phone call away. In this sense, we do brief, intermittent therapy, and we treat our therapy as a way-station in the ongoing journey through the client's life. The professional counselor–client relationship is never terminated, therefore; it is merely interrupted, much like the relationship with one's physician or dentist wherein we find ourselves returning when we require further assistance.

In the case of Ruth, the data for the initial interview and the lifestyle assessment were collected by Jim, her primary therapist. Those data were then presented to and discussed with Bill while Ruth listened and acted as a collaborating or clarifying agent to the discussion. The two therapists then generated their initial summaries, including *the pattern of basic convictions* and *the interfering ideas.* The session ended with the two therapists listening to Ruth give her initial impressions of the ideas and information contained in the summaries. Written copies of the summaries were sent to her the following day, so that she could read them before the next session.

REVIEWING THE PREVIOUS SESSION   Following this multiple therapy session, Ruth met with Jim alone. After they greet each other, they began this discussion.

> JIM: What was the last session like for you?
>
> RUTH: I was really amazed. The summaries that you came up with seemed just like me. Then when they came in the mail, I read them, and I wondered if my family knew me as well as I feel the two of you do.
>
> JIM: So what was it like for you to have two therapists instead of one?
>
> RUTH: It was very interesting. I was surprised that the two of you disagree sometimes. I liked the way you disagreed and stayed friends and didn't get mad or anything. That's hard for me. I don't like to disagree with John. [*Pause*] I think I'm afraid he'll get mad at me.
>
> JIM: What does he get mad at you about?
>
> RUTH: I know John pretty well, I guess, and there's not much we disagree about—except my schooling.
>
> JIM: If I were to hazard a guess based on what we learned in the lifestyle assessment, I would guess that there may be quite a lot you have not directly asked your husband—or even your children—because you

were concerned about displeasing them. Does that fit you? Do you find yourself "guessing," trying to read their minds so you won't upset them?

RUTH: Yes, I know I do that a lot.

JIM: What did you notice when Bill and I disagreed?

RUTH: Well, the two of you were just fine. You just listened, and then you asked me what I thought.

JIM: Actually, I was quite pleased that you and Bill had come to an understanding that I had missed. If we were all alike in the world, there wouldn't be much use in talking, would there? Do you think John would enjoy hearing your opinion even if it was different from his?

RUTH: Maybe.

JIM: I think you would really like to know what John thinks about your lifestyle summaries, and no amount of guessing is going to be the same as really hearing from him. The worst that might happen is that he wouldn't agree with them.

Here, in a relatively early session, the therapist uses the cooperation and mutual respect modeled in therapy to encourage Ruth to take a small chance with her husband. If she actually asks John to look at her lifestyle summaries and share his opinion with her, there will be some material for the next session whatever his response or her reaction to the response may be.

A SMALL REEDUCATION DURING MULTIPLE THERAPY Near the end of Ruth's counseling experience, she again meets with Bill and Jim together. This time the focus is on her value when she is engaged in meaningful work and when she is not. An early recollection is used to mark change and growth in her therapy.

BILL: Ruth, it's good to see you again. How long has it been? About 2 months or so since I last sat in with the two of you? How have things been going?

RUTH: I think our work together has been very good. We had some sessions that included John, and I really feel that he's supporting me in all of the transitions I'm making. In recent weeks, I walk away from here, and I sometimes wonder if I am doing enough in therapy. Much of what we talk about now seems so easy to me. I'm not leaving as I used to—practically exhausted and sure that I was working through a lot of stuff.

JIM: This is interesting. We haven't really talked about this before. How was it for you when you left here last time?

RUTH: Well, I think we did some good work together in that I learned something about staying with change in my life even when the going gets tough, but it was not actually hard to learn that. I used to leave here wondering if I would ever figure myself out. Last time, I felt, well, I can do what I need to do.

BILL: When I listen to Ruth, Jim, there's an idea that is repeated over and over. It's something like "Anything worth doing requires very hard work. Without the hard work, Ruth may doubt whether she is doing anything worthwhile." Did I get that right, Ruth?

RUTH [*With a look of recognition on her face*]: I think you did. That's been one of my beliefs since childhood.

BILL: Yes, it may have been, but I think we're inviting you to reconsider that notion. It may be a mistaken notion, especially now that you're older and more competent. Things do come easier to people as they gain competence.

RUTH: Maybe I have this therapy thing figured out.

JIM: My experience of you is that you have a lot of things figured out. There's been a lot of progress since you started about 9 months ago.

BILL: Let's try something—another early recollection. Ruth, see if you can think back to a time when you were very young. Something happened one time . . .

RUTH: Very young? Well, I remember something in second grade. Is that OK?

BILL: Yes, that's fine. You were about 7 or 8?

RUTH: Seven, I think. I was asked by a neighbor to help her little girl learn colors because she was in kindergarten. Her mother had colored four squares in the driveway with chalk. I think her name was Jan, the little girl, and we played all afternoon, bouncing a ball from one color to another. Her mother later told my mother that I had made all the difference in the world.

BILL: What stands out about that story. And how did you feel?

RUTH: The look of pride on my mother's face when she told me what Jan's mother had said. I like making a difference in someone's life.

JIM: It's a great memory! There's not an ounce of hard work in it. And it's a great early recollection for a future teacher to have. Can you sense how different this memory is from the ones you reported when you first came to see us?

RUTH: I don't actually even remember the early recollections I gave you originally. Is this one different?

BILL: Very different. I was just looking at them here in your file. I think the next time you get together with Jim, you should go back and review where you were when you started and where you are now.

A change in one's early recollections is not uncommon when change has also happened in one's life. The change may not be dramatic, as in a completely new memory. Sometimes, it is a shift in emphasis: something new stands out, or the client's reaction is different than originally reported. In Ruth's new memory here she is "making a difference" in someone's life (social interest), and she is now focused more on her own competence and experiencing the appreciation of others for her work. This is a significant change in her sense of belonging and a great place for a new teacher to start.

Jerry Corey's Work With Ruth From an Adlerian Perspective

With the detailed information about Ruth derived from the initial interview, the lifestyle assessment, and the sample therapy sessions provided by Drs. Jim Bitter and Bill Nicoll, I will continue counseling Ruth from an Adlerian orientation. In the following section, I demonstrate the Adlerian slant on working with Ruth regarding her mistaken beliefs.

Session 6 ("Cognitive Focus in Counseling") of the *CD-ROM for Integrative Counseling* illustrates Ruth's striving to live up to expectations and to measure up to perfectionistic standards. I draw upon Adlerian concepts in this particular therapy session with Ruth.

Basic Assumptions

As an Adlerian therapist, I view my work with Ruth as teaching her better ways of meeting the challenges of *life tasks.* One assumption that will guide my interventions with her is that although she has been influenced by her past, she is not necessarily molded by it. This premise of self-determination leaves little room for a client to take the role of a passive victim. I assume that my client has the capacity to influence and create events.

Ruth's childhood experiences are of therapeutic interest to me. They are the foundation and early context for the social factors that contributed to her psychological development. True to the Adlerian spirit, I function as a therapist on the belief that it is not her childhood experiences in themselves that are crucial; rather, it is her *attitude* toward these events. Since these early influences may have led to the development of *faulty beliefs* and assumptions in her style of life, I will explore with her what it was like at home as she was growing up. Our focus will be on understanding and assessing the structure of her family life, known as the *family constellation,* and her *earliest recollections* (both of which were reported in detail in the previous section by Drs. Bitter and Nicoll).

Because I operate from a phenomenological stance (dealing with the client's subjective perception of reality), I will want to find out how she views the major events and turning points of her life. I assume that she has created a unique style of life that helps to explain the patterns of her behavior. My attention will be on how she has developed her distinctive behaviors in the pursuit of her life goals.

Assessment of Ruth

Adlerian therapists typically use the lifestyle questionnaire in making an initial assessment of the client and in formulating the goals and directions for therapy. This questionnaire gathers information about the client's childhood experiences, especially as they relate to family influences, birth order, relationships of each of the other family members, early memories, and other relevant material that will provide clues about the social forces influencing the client's personality formation. The goal of assessment is to identify the mistaken logic in the major themes and patterns in the client's lifestyle that are connected to the presenting issue(s). In addition to the mistaken logic in Ruth's lifestyle, I will also identify assets (strengths and internal resources) she has developed that can be drawn upon to provide a direction for the course of Ruth's therapy. (Drs. Bitter and Nicoll drew heavily from the framework of Adlerian lifestyle assessment, so I will not repeat that discussion here.)

Goals of Therapy

The four major goals of an Adlerian approach to therapy with Ruth correspond to the four phases of the therapeutic process. These goals are (1) to establish and maintain an effective working relationship with Ruth, (2) to provide a therapeutic climate in which she can come to understand her basic beliefs and feelings about herself, (3) to help her reach insight into her mistaken goals and self-defeating behaviors, and (4) to assist her in developing alternative ways of thinking, feeling, and behaving by encouraging her to translate her insights into action.

Therapeutic Procedures

One of the aims of Ruth's therapy is to challenge her to take risks and make changes. Throughout the entire process *encouragement* is of the utmost importance. My assumption is that with encouragement Ruth will begin to experience her own inner resources and the power to choose for herself and to direct her own life. By now, Ruth will ideally have challenged her self-limiting assumptions and will be ready to put plans into action. Even though she may regress to old patterns at times, I will ask her to "catch herself" in this process and then continue to experiment with and practice new behavior.

Throughout her therapy I will use a variety of techniques aimed primarily at challenging her cognitions (beliefs and thinking processes). Adlerians contend that first people think, then feel, and then behave. So, if we want to change behavior and feelings, the best way is to focus on Ruth's mistaken perceptions and faulty beliefs about life and herself.[11]

The Therapeutic Process

The process of Adlerian therapy can be understood by recalling some basic ideas from contemporary psychoanalytic therapy. There is a link between these two approaches, especially on the issue of looking at how early patterns are related to our present personality functioning.

ELEMENTS OF THE PROCESS

🕮 **Uncovering a Mistaken Belief**   Ruth and I have been working together for some time, and she is beginning to see striking parallels between the role she assumed as an adolescent, by becoming the caretaker of her sisters and brother, and her contemporary role as "supermother" to her own children. She has discovered that all of her life she has been laboring under the assumption that if she handled herself unselfishly, she would be rewarded by being acknowledged and feeling a sense of personal fulfillment. As a child she wanted to be loved, accepted, and taken care of emotionally by her father, and she has worked very hard at being the perfect wife and the devoted mother to her own children. In this way she hopes her husband will love and accept her. Still, she has never really felt appreciated or emotionally nurtured by him, and now she is realizing that she has built her life on a personal mythology: If people loved her, she would be worthwhile and would find happiness through her personal sacrifices.

Helping Ruth Reach Her Goals   At this time in Ruth's therapy, we are exploring some other options open to her. Lately we have been talking a lot about her goals and about her vision of herself in the years to come. Ruth talks about feeling selfish that she is going to school since this means that she has less time to give at home. Ruth becomes aware that the guilt often stops her from reaching the goals that are meaningful to her. For part of our counseling session we explore some of Ruth's mistaken notions that get in the way of her doing what she would like to be doing.

> RUTH: I keep feeling I shouldn't be at school and should be at home. John keeps telling me how much he and the kids miss me. If only I could stop feeling guilty.
>
> JERRY: You say that John keeps telling you how much he and the kids miss you. It's really very nice to be missed; but you interpret his meaning to be "Ruth, you should stay at home. You're displeasing everyone."
>
> RUTH: That's true. That's what I think he is saying.
>
> JERRY: Well, it may be a mistaken notion you have. You could check it out. You could ask John what *he* means when he says he misses you. Maybe all he means is that he loves you [*Pause*], and believes that the kids love you too. You could ask.
>
> RUTH: Asking John how he really feels about my school and career and what I'm doing is extremely hard. [*Pause*] He could tell me that he hates my school and career goals, and they're threatening our relationship. But I am willing to give it a try.

I am hoping that Ruth, by confronting a mistaken notion, will find the courage to check a lifelong idea against a current reality. She will be scared, to be sure. Without some fear there is no need for courage. A week passes, and Ruth returns.

> RUTH: Guess what? John and I talked. We both cried. He was afraid that I wouldn't need him anymore. Afraid of losing *me*! Can you believe it? But he didn't want me to stop school.
>
> JERRY: I'm very happy for you. How great that a real risk worked out so well for you.
>
> RUTH: When John talked about the kids wanting their mother home, I started to feel guilty all over again. But at least now I notice those

times when my guilt stops me, and I'm working at not letting it control me. It's like you said: Guilt is what we "good" people do when we don't feel that we are living up to other people's expectations.

JERRY: Good! At this point in your life, guilt is a habit. Like any habit, it takes time to change it. Right now you're catching yourself when guilt is getting in your way. Eventually I suspect that you will be able to control your guilt instead of it controlling you.

From here we proceed to look at a week of Ruth's time and how she might balance personal needs with the needs of others. Planning special time for her family maintains Ruth's sense of belonging and her real need for social interest without short-circuiting the gift of time her family is giving her for school. It also provides her with a structure by which she can devote her full attention to the tasks or people at hand: quality time in both cases.

PROCESS COMMENTARY My major aim in our sessions is to both encourage and challenge Ruth to consider alternative attitudes, beliefs, goals, and behaviors. By seeing the link between her mistaken beliefs and her current feelings and behaviors, she is able to consider options and change. She takes a big risk in approaching her husband. Given her history with and interpretation of men, she anticipates a harsh, rejecting rebuke. What she gains, however, is an increased sense of her worth and value to this important man in her life. She also gains in courage and confidence.

Once Ruth has made some new decisions and modified her goals, I teach her ways in which to challenge her own thinking. At those times when she is critical of herself, I provide encouragement. Partly because of my faith in her and my encouragement, she comes closer to experiencing her inner strength. She becomes more honest about what she is doing, and she augments her power to choose for herself instead of merely following the values she uncritically accepted as a child.

A most important ingredient of the final stages of Ruth's therapy is commitment. She is finally persuaded that if she hopes to change, she will have to set specific tasks for herself and then take concrete action. Although she attempts to live up to what she believes is the role of the "good person," she eventually develops increased tolerance for learning by trial and error, and with this she becomes better at "catching herself" when she repeats ineffective behavior.[12]

Questions for Reflection

1. As you review the basic features of a lifestyle assessment (family constellation, early recollections, basic convictions, and interfering ideas) of Ruth, what associations do you have with your own childhood experiences?
2. As you think about your own family of origin, what most stands out for you? After reflecting on your early experiences in your family, attempt to come to some conclusions about the ways in which these experiences are operating in you life today.

3. What are three of your earliest recollections? Can you speculate on how these memories might have an impact on the person you are now and how they could be related to your future strivings?

4. List what you consider to be the major "basic mistakes" in your life. Do you have any ideas about how you developed these mistaken perceptions about yourself and about life? How do you think that they are influencing the ways in which you think, feel, and act today?

5. From what you learned about Ruth through the lifestyle assessment, what aspects of her life might you want to give the primary focus? What themes running through her life lend themselves especially well to Adlerian therapy?

6. One of the goals of Adlerian therapy is to increase the client's social interest. Can you think of ways in which you could work with Ruth to help her attain this goal?

7. Ruth describes herself as coming from a middle-class family. They were fundamentalist Christians, and the family values involved doing right, working hard, and living in a way that would reflect well on the family. Considering this background, how well do Adlerian concepts and therapeutic procedures fit for Ruth? How would the Adlerian approach fit for her if she were an Asian American? Latina? African American? Native American?

8. What major cultural themes do you see in Ruth's case? How would you address these themes using an Adlerian framework?

Notes

See the DVD/online program entitled *Theory in Practice: The Case of Stan* (Session 3: Adlerian Therapy Applied to the Case of Stan) for a demonstration of gathering Stan's early recollections.

1. See the following sources for a full discussion of Adlerian brief therapy: Bitter, J. R., & Nicoll, W. G. (2000). Adlerian brief therapy with individuals: Process and practice. *Journal of Individual Psychology, 56*(1), 31–44; Bitter, J. R., Christensen, O. C., Hawes, C., & Nicoll, W. G. (1998). Adlerian brief therapy with individuals, couples, and families. *Directions in Clinical and Counseling Psychology, 8*(8), 95–112; Nicoll, W., Bitter, J. R., Christensen, O. C., & Hawes, C. (2000). Adlerian brief therapy: Strategies and tactics. In J. Carlson & L. Sperry (Eds.), *Brief therapy strategies with individuals and couples* (pp. 220–247). Phoenix: Zeig/Tucker; Sonstegard, M. A., Bitter, J. R., Pelonis-Peneros, P., & Nicoll, W. G. (2001). Adlerian group psychotherapy: A brief therapy approach. *Directions in Clinical and Counseling Psychology, 11*(2), 11–24.

2. Multiple therapy is discussed in: Dreikurs, R., Shulman, B. H., & Mosak, H. H. (1982). *Multiple therapy: The use of two therapists with one patient.* Chicago: Alfred Alder Institute.

3. Based on material in Powers, R. L., & Griffith, J. (1987). *Understanding life style: The psycho-clarity process.* Chicago: AIAS; Shulman, B. H., & Mosak, H. H. (1988). *Manual for lifestyle assessment.* Muncie, IN: Accelerated Development.

4. *The Individual Psychology Client Workbook (with supplements)*, by Robert L. Powers and Jane Griffith, © 1995 by the Americas Institute of Adlerian

Studies, Ltd., 600 North McClurg Court, Suite 2502A, Chicago, IL 60611-3027.

5. For a more complete discussion on this topic, see Disque, J. G., & Bitter, J. R. (1998). Integrating narrative therapy with Adlerian lifestyle assessment: A case study. *Journal of Individual Psychology, 54*(4), 431–450.

6. An excellent overview of Adlerian therapy can be found in: Carlson, J., Watts, R. E., & Maniacci, M. (2006). *Adlerian therapy: Theory and practice.* Washington, DC: American Psychological Association.

7. Adlerian brief therapy is dealt with in detail in these two sources: Bitter, J. R., Christensen, O. C., Hawes, C., & Nicoll, W. G. (1998). Adlerian brief therapy with individuals, couples, and families. *Directions in Clinical and Counseling Psychology, 8*(8), 95–112; Bitter, J. R., & Nicoll, W. G. (2000). Adlerian brief therapy with individuals: Process and practice. *Journal of Individual Psychology, 56*(1), 31–44.

8. Dreikurs, R. (1997). Holistic medicine. *Individual Psychology, 53*(2), 127–205.

9. Ibid.

10. Adler, A. (1964). *Problems of neurosis: A book of case histories* (P. Mairet, Ed.). New York: Harper & Row. (Original work published 1929)

11. Here I demonstrate the Adlerian slant on working with Ruth cognitively, especially regarding her mistaken beliefs. Session 6 of the *CD-ROM for Integrative Counseling* reflects Ruth's striving to live up to expectations and to measure up to perfectionistic standards.

12. In Session 13 ("Evaluation and Termination") of the *CD-ROM for Integrative Counseling,* I encourage Ruth to make concrete plans regarding where she wants to go now that therapy has ended. For a more detailed treatment of Adlerian theory, see G. Corey (2009), *Theory and Practice of Counseling and Psychotherapy* (8th ed., Belmont, CA: Brooks/Cole). The basic concepts introduced by Jim Bitter and Bill Nicoll in their assessment of Ruth are covered comprehensively in Chapter 5 ("Adlerian Therapy"). Also see G. Corey (2009), *Student Manual for Theory and Practice of Counseling and Psychotherapy* (8th ed., Belmont, CA: Brooks/Cole). This manual contains a lifestyle assessment that you can take as an exercise. Completing the inventory will help you understand the comprehensive approach to assessment of Ruth used in this chapter by Drs. Bitter and Nicoll.

CHAPTER FOUR

Case Approach to Existential Therapy

General Overview of Existential Therapy

The principal goal of existential therapy is to challenge clients to recognize and accept the freedom they have to become the authors of their own lives. Therapists confront clients on ways in which they are avoiding their freedom and the responsibility that accompanies it. This approach places primary emphasis on understanding clients' current experience, not on using therapeutic techniques. Thus, counselors are not bound by any prescribed techniques and can borrow tactics from other schools of therapy. Interventions are used in broadening the ways in which clients live in their world.

The issues of termination and evaluation are typically resolved through an open exchange between client and therapist. Clients generally make the choice to enter therapy, and it is clients' choice and responsibility to decide when to leave therapy. If clients continue to rely on the therapist for this answer, they are not yet ready to terminate. However, therapists are given the latitude to express their reactions and views about the person's readiness for termination. The choices clients are making and the changes in their perceptions of themselves in their world are the basis for an evaluation of therapeutic outcomes.

An Existential Therapist's Perspective on Ruth

by J. Michael Russell, PhD, PsyD

Introduction

Existential counseling is rooted in existential philosophy. It is a way of thinking about people. It is not a specific method or set of techniques and not even a unified theory, but it draws from a group of philosophers and theorists who stress the idea that we are responsible for the meaning we choose to give to our circumstances. It is based on phenomenology, which is to say, it emphasizes subjective experience. However, unlike some other viewpoints and in common with psychoanalysis, it does not assume that clients know themselves particularly well, and it does not assume that they see very clearly the choices they make. Personal claims about experience are important, but they do not have any decisive and privileged status. On the contrary, from an existentialist perspective all of us are routinely self-deceived and inauthentic about our experience.

Various themes routinely come up in any sort of counseling, and some are particularly prominent in how existentialist counselors conceptualize their work. These are typically interconnected and all have to do with choice. One is that we all seem anxious about our sense of personal identity. We worry about who we want to be, who we don't want to be, how we are seen by others, how we see ourselves. The most common pitfall is when we try to regard "who we are" as fixed and finished so as to not have to face our choices. Mostly, who we are will depend on what we do in the future and how much we stick to resolves we make now. Hence, anxiety is a related theme since it alerts us to uncertainty about what we might do. We are anxious about identity. We can also turn this formulation around and consider that we try to pin down identity to stave off anxiety. So another closely related existential theme is about freedom. People often come to counseling because they would like more freedom. Just as often, clients want less freedom, or less of the sense of responsibility that goes with it.

Existential counseling seeks to enlarge clients' awareness of how they construct meaning in the world in which they live. The goal is for clients to have greater insight into how they think, what they feel, and what they can do. Clients learn what freedom entails and take responsibility for their own circumstances. Existentialism holds that we are responsible for the choices through which we give meaning to the circumstances in which we find ourselves, and these concerns take on particular force in light of the prospect of our own death, and the related experience of loss and isolation that can come with the death of significant others. Existential therapists help clients explore their uncertainty and anxiety about whether they are relating to others in an authentic or inauthentic and self-deceived way.

Assessment of Ruth

Existential issues—such as identity, freedom, and anxiety—practically jump off the pages of Ruth's autobiography. With respect to *identity,* she has defined herself as a superwoman, a good wife and a good mother, faced with the prospect of losing all of these familiar designations as she readies for her children leaving home. She also seems to identify with her family's view of her as overweight. She identifies with and then distances herself from her parents' religious values. These facets of the identity theme are pretty obvious. On a more subtle level, we can wonder to what extent she brings her panic attacks on herself. Does she tell herself she's prone to panic, and make this a self-fulfilling prophecy?

Ruth presents at least two very different perspectives on *anxiety* as an existential theme. We can see her as anxious because of her quest for identity. However, her efforts to establish a sense of identity may be seen as an attempt to manage a core of anxiety. From the first perspective, she is anxious because she is afraid she won't know who or how to be if she loses her roles as mother and wife or if new professional ambitions don't pan out. Insecurities like these build on some level of her awareness that it was never really possible to be safe and secure. In fact, she acknowledges that she has not always been the perfect mother or perfect wife, and there's enough hesitancy about pursuing a career as a teacher that we know that neither her past performance nor her future aspirations are concrete and fixed certainties. She's right to be anxious.

For many of the same reasons, we can see Ruth as ambivalent about *freedom*. She sought out a form of counseling that is insight-oriented. This suggests that she is interested in exploring options for change. But she also says she wants someone to tell her what to do, and evidently she has had plenty of directive people in her past, certainly including her father.

Virtually all of the existential issues pertain to Ruth, and they are interconnected. She may come to see that identifying herself as a wife and mother could be protecting her from a frightening kind of *isolation,* and a collapse of familiar *meaning.* Her concerns about *death* are likely to be a particularly valuable window for getting clearer about what might be meaningful for her, what choices she has, and how her anxiety has something to teach her.

What about a more formal diagnostic assessment of Ruth? Existentialists are likely to dislike labels generally and to dislike "medical" labels in particular. Up to a point, I agree; however, the same opportunity for using or abusing adjectives arises whether in everyday speech or technical psychological jargon. Whether we say Ruth is "dysthymic" or say she "sometimes gets the blues," the real question is whether our language helps or gets in the way. Should we say she "has a panic disorder" or say she's "really up tight"? Is it "an adjustment disorder" or is she "going through some changes"? If a diagnostic label fits loosely, it may enhance my capacity to understand my client. If it fits precisely, then I had better be open to learning from the experiences of other therapists of various orientations.

Each of the five of the *DSM* axes can sharpen my thinking about Ruth. I am not a slave to any of this vocabulary but neither do I dismiss it. Axis I considerations tend to highlight conditions that Ruth, herself, would like to be rid of. That certainly applies to her panic attacks and her depression. In my view, she tentatively qualifies for "panic attacks without agoraphobia" and for dysthymia. "Adjustment disorder" also fits, and it helps us to focus on specifics in her existential situation. She will experience her symptoms and circumstances as something that happens to her, and it remains to be seen to what extent she may learn to think of them as anything like choices. Surely she can, at least, consider what choices she has about how to deal with them.

I rather like Axis II terminology because I use it to enhance my understanding of a client without taking it so seriously as to try to reduce a person to a "disorder." I don't think Ruth fully meets the criteria for any full-fledged disorder, but I do think that some of the Axis II terms, applied loosely, can help me to understand her. "Dependent personality" fits somewhat. More interesting is "narcissism," not because Ruth shows anything close to a "narcissistic personality disorder" but because self-esteem issues are very relevant to her. About Axis III, the fact that a medical doctor has ruled out relevant medical conditions helps to assure me that insight-oriented psychotherapy may be appropriate for Ruth, but I suspect that further exploration of a medical perspective may be very much in order. A medical or physiological perspective and a meaning or existential perspective are incompatible, nor does applicability of one preempt the value of the other. As for Axes IV and V, assessing situational factors and stressors is part of what any therapist would consider. And, whether we want to admit it or not, all of us in fact make some sort of assessment of how well we think a client is functioning and how well we believe the client might function. I would rate Ruth's stressors as considerable, and I see her as fairly high functioning even if compromised by the issues and symptoms she brings to therapy.

So far I have addressed existential and diagnostic features of Ruth's case that can be made fairly explicit. In addition, a subtle dimension of assessment goes on all the time and shows up in the nuances of our interactions. Tone of voice, emotionality, eye contact, body language, sense of humor, level of sophistication in expression, and how I find myself responding to such traits, all figure into my overall "sizing a person up." For example, suppose my first impressions of Ruth were from her initial phone call in which she says she is "shopping for a therapist." I asked her to tell me more about what she was "shopping for," and she details some of the issues covered in the autobiography she will give me later. But in this telephone exchange there is a voice quality and even a playfulness I would not have picked up on in the autobiography. We set up an initial interview "to see whether we hit it off," with her first saying she wanted to be sure I didn't mind that she was "just shopping." I reply, "How else are you going to find your kind of bargain?" The fact that I find myself phrasing things is a somewhat playful way figures into my overall experience of her.

First impressions are often mistaken, but sometimes they are right on target, and usually there's some useful grain of truth implicit in our spontaneous responses. Putting it in a rather nonclinical way, I like her. I think we can work together.

In sum, my assessment of Ruth is: I am comfortable working with her, the existential perspective applies, and she meets some criteria for a formal diagnosis while other features of the *DSM* have some relevance.

Goals of Counseling

In spite of the fact that I sometimes use the term, I do not like the word "therapy." To my mind it too much suggests some kind of procedure that is going to happen to the client so that afterward she will be "fixed" or cured. Existential counseling isn't going to make you change. Insight doesn't make you change any more than does looking into a mirror, but it can broaden your options. I think of myself as a consultant in this process. My goal, first and foremost, is to be responsive to Ruth's goals.

THERAPIST: Tell me what you hope to get from having me as your counselor.

RUTH: Well, I'd certainly like to be rid of my panic attacks and not feel anxious. I'd like to lose some weight. I'd like to get a job—something besides being wife and mom. I guess I'd like to simply feel generally better about myself. I hope you can tell me how to do that and how long it's going to take. But I think there's something else that I'm wanting from counseling, and I don't quite know how to say what it is. I know I'm afraid that my life might not go on as usual, but in some ways I'm thinking being too "usual" is my problem! I'm tired of my usual routine, and I'm not sure that it means very much. And there's something that intrigued me about your description of yourself as an existentialist.

THERAPIST: Some of what you want is pretty specific, and you and I could target those objectives and go straight after them. Or, I could refer you to someone who focuses more on specific behavioral objectives. But I think there's also a side to you that your counseling class is tapping into, which is a more general kind of wanting to know yourself better. And that is more what I like to offer. Maybe we don't need to pin down how long that sort of search should go on.

🕮 **Process Commentary**   I do have some goals of my own, but I think of these as being in the service of my client. I would like Ruth to have an enlarged consciousness of herself as the free author of her own meaning, and a broader awareness of her choices. I would like her to develop a greater capacity to tolerate ambiguity, although she prefers what she calls "neat answers." She would like to be rid of her panic attacks, and I want this for her too. But I also want her to retain a certain amount of legitimate "existential anxiety." I think she can get past the incapacitating moments of panic. I would hope the enlarging of her awareness is not simply on an intellectual level, but also comes out in her capacity to feel a greater range of feelings and a broader range of possibilities for action. I think the process of pursuing these goals by means of thinking, feeling, and acting is intrinsically worthwhile, and I also believe she may be in a better position to deal with her options and choices because of this process of consulting with me. I would hope this shows up not only in how she thinks but also in terms of what she can let herself feel and do within our consulting room and outside. I would like to see her experience freedom in specific ways, such as taking on that substitute teaching job or trying out some changes in her eating behavior. I would like her to get much clearer about what she does or does not want in her marriage and look at what she could do to revitalize that relationship and also develop more independence. I'd like to see her have some specific experiences with altering her mood, so that she is more likely to see this type of option in various emotional situations in which she might find herself.

Counseling Process and Technique

There is no specific set of techniques for doing existential counseling. At our first meeting I looked through her autobiography while she read my consent form and description of services. I asked her to tell me more about some of the issues she mentioned in the autobiography, sometimes asking for elaboration, sometimes noting some connection between themes. While I often hint at the existence of choices, I virtually never impose an "existentialist" vocabulary of freedom and responsibility. Toward the end of this first session, after Ruth stated her hopes or goals in counseling, I proposed that we meet twice a week for half-hour sessions.

RUTH: Isn't that kind of unusual?

THERAPIST: You said being usual might be one of your problems.

We talked more about this twice a week idea and how the greater frequency of meetings might fit with her enthusiasm for "really getting into a phase of self-exploration." Half sessions meant half the fee, which she could afford. She liked the experiment. I said, "It's an experiment for me too."

Process Commentary   Why did I say that? One reason is that nonpretentious candor is in keeping with an existentialist's way of thinking. The short session idea really was an experiment. I am more self-disclosing than most therapists, and far more self-disclosing than ever would have been advocated in my psychoanalytic training. I hesitate to call that a "technique," although I do hope to be modeling candor and an openness to experimenting with options. I see existential counseling as an encounter between two people, not just one person scrutinizing the other. I certainly did not try to give Ruth the whole picture. While I might sometimes worry that my attention span isn't always everything I might wish, I would not burden Ruth with the fear that her therapist might really be drifting off! Still, it might be asked why I disclosed even as much as I did, risking repercussions from choosing a word like "experiment." It illustrates a level of openness I *do* advocate. More exactly, it felt right with Ruth and might not have felt right with some other client. I had recently mentioned my worries to a colleague who said, "Where is it written that sessions have to be 50 minutes."

Particularly in the early phases of time-indefinite insight-oriented counseling I am careful to not be "preachy" about believing we are all free persons responsible for making choices about the meaning of our circumstances. With exceptions for crisis situations that require immediate action and a shift in attitude, such lectures are generally pointless. The last thing I would want to do as an existential consultant is to get on a soapbox about existential freedom. My hope is that in the long run the client will attain a deep appreciation of personal responsibility.

For example, in our fourth session Ruth reported that she had talked with her father by phone and said nothing about being in counseling. She knew he would not approve. According to her, he "never" approves of anything she does. He certainly would never approve of "existential counseling." Basically, I encourage her to elaborate whenever her emotions are more evident. The bulk of what Ruth said in this meeting portrayed her as the doomed victim of a disapproving father. I certainly did *not* give her a lecture on how she has many choices.

In a subsequent session when Ruth was again bemoaning her critical father, I borrowed from Gestalt therapy the technique of role playing: talking to her father by talking to me, saying in a first-person way some of the things she did not say to her father on the phone. I elected to encourage her to talk directly to me—look me in the eyes—rather than either reporting in an abstract way or "talking to the empty chair." Ordinarily, in long-term work, I hesitate to employ any of these techniques, relying on supportive listening. Perhaps because of the pace of these half-hour sessions, this more "active" style on my part seemed right at the time. If I had consciously entertained a rationale, which I did not, it would involve a couple of objectives. One of these is that I would like Ruth to become more aware of her feelings and more aware of how she has considerable choice in whether or how she enters into what she feels— how she can "get into it." Another is that I'm sure her experience of her father is much more complex than her usual black-and-white portrait of him lets on. Expressing different sides of her in these role plays paves the way, in the long run, for a greater appreciation for ambiguity, complexity, and freedom.

When I do use a technique, it is usually a creative adaptation to unplanned events in which I am seeking to create a meaningful connection between events and themes. For example, I arrived at the seventh session out of breath, barely on time. Ruth talked more about her father, who approves of almost nothing, and her husband, who is supportive of her being in counseling, but with "strings attached." John doesn't like the resulting late dinners.

RUTH: Approval from men always seems so conditional!

THERAPIST: Anyone here remind you of a man? [*I like using humor appropriately, and Ruth laughed.*]

RUTH: Well, you are different. Like the way you were so out of breath, rushing to getting here today. It made me feel you really care.

THERAPIST: Well, thanks for the compliment. I'm not sure I'm all that unique, but I appreciate your letting me represent some different ways men might be experienced. You know, we've noticed before how ready you are to label yourself. Sometimes you'll say you are "just a mom," or "just a wife," or just someone who will never feel good about herself after so often being put down by Dad. Today I think we are getting a more complete picture not only about the simplified identity you give yourself, but also how you oversimplify other people in your life.

⚜ **Process Commentary**   There are several ingredients in this complex interpretive remark, and they illustrate a subtle promotion of existentialist thinking. It allows Ruth the space for a "positive transference" yet also suggests she is responsible for how she is construing our relationship. It connects with calling attention to how self-labeling can be self-deceiving. It suggests that these current expressions of attitude are choices and yet have a history. And it moves Ruth toward possible insight into how she renders her world static with her oversimplified labels of herself and others.

As another example of subtly promoting insight into existential responsibility, at a later meeting Ruth was venting anger about her daughter Jennifer, who had ditched school to go to the beach with friends.

RUTH: I can't get over how angry I am at Jennifer for ditching school. She's so irresponsible!

THERAPIST: Well, much as it's important for Jennifer to take school seriously, I wonder whether you are a bit jealous of how much she seems to be sort of a free spirit?

⚖ **Process Commentary**   Ruth's exceptionally "responsible" identity as a supermom and superwife is perhaps an evasion of another kind of flight from her responsibility for having made her life safe and "usual" without risk but without meaning and excitement. Jennifer reminds Ruth of something she has been missing.

Time-Limited Counseling

Up to now I have been trying to provide some sense for how I might work with Ruth in the early and middle phases of time-indefinite, insight-oriented existential counseling. As time goes on, I tend to put increasing emphasis on how Ruth and I interact, and focus less on past events and people not present in the consulting room or, at least, highlight comparisons between events outside and the "here and now, you and me." There is no way to neatly demarcate what counts as the early phase and what counts as the middle phase of existential counseling because there is no preconceived formula for when counseling should end. I do not share the popular criticism of counseling relationships that go on for a long time, and I do not understand why some therapists say that they don't have an agenda for the client but apparently believe they are supposed to be done with the work quickly and efficiently. I'll go on for as long as the client and I both feel there is vitality to the exchange. Ruth's situation changed in that she was presented with an unexpected opportunity to substitute full time for a teacher who would be taking a lengthy leave. This meant that our meetings would have to end in 8 weeks.

With time-limited existential counseling (and also, with the ending phase of long-term work) I become more active, more directive, and more focused on specific goals. My general objective remains the same, which is to address the client's goals while also promoting an enhanced awareness of one's freedom. What is different is the way specific changes are explored both in seeking solutions to specific problems and in promoting lasting habits of thinking that will plant seeds for continued growth. For example, Ruth's job opportunity came about because I had commented that going to an interview did not obligate her to accepting an offer. I phrased this with, "What's holding you back from just having an interview?" This lessened her reluctance to simply *try out* choices and possibilities, and I hope she will generalize learning from this event. To take another example, in these last weeks I renewed a suggestion I had made before—that Ruth get a second medical opinion about her excessive sweating. The previous (male) doctor's opinion seems to have been provided in a somewhat off-hand way. The second (female) doctor, a specialist in hyperhidrosis, proposed further evaluation of Ruth's hormone factors. As a result of further tests, Ruth was able to make progress with this physical symptom, and she did so without devaluing the time spent in counseling exploring the emotional significance of this symptom. She was also able to use this as an opportunity to review her habit of putting male (her father's) opinions too highly.

Topics of meaning and loss and death ran through many of Ruth's sessions, but they took on a particular importance with the transition to a time-limited format.

RUTH: I'd like to be able to leave the door open to seeing you again once this teaching job is over.

THERAPIST: The door is open to our working together again, down the road. And I like the way you are looking out for your options. But I also recommend that we not deprive ourselves of experiencing the ending of what we've been doing here. When we choose to avoid the reality of endings, we tend to lose sight of what's meaningful.

RUTH: I can see that. But don't worry. I'll be taking away plenty from our meetings.

THERAPIST: I'm sure you will. But in order to maximize that, I suggest that in these last times we get together we review some of the ground we have covered, and see if we can identify any particular accomplishments you would like to achieve either by the time we wrap up, or some time afterward. If we do that, it would be a good idea to be as specific as we can.

🖉 **Process Commentary**   As mentioned earlier, learning about our choices is not merely a matter of enlarging our thinking. It is also learning how to feel. And it is also experimenting with action. I tend to be a bit of a behaviorist toward the end of our counseling relationship because I would like Ruth to have a specific experience of the choices available to her. I hope these choices will be relevant both to the goals she brought to counseling and to my goal for her of an expanded consciousness of her part in giving meaning to the world she lives in. I asked her to think about some way she might summarize her time in counseling when we meet for the last time. Here, in part, is what she said at that last meeting.

RUTH: I think I've seen something about how eager I was to get myself and everyone else neatly packaged up into familiar labels. I've got a long way to go, but I think I see, for instance, how convenient it was to feel like the victim of my father's harsh judgments, my kid's lack of appreciation for my efforts, and my husband's lack of real supportiveness. I think I came here bemoaning what other people were doing to me, and I'm leaving with more of a sense of being responsible for what I do.

CONCLUDING COMMENTS   We do not learn such things once and for all, but Ruth is learning. For a more complete discussion of my views on topics such as the applications of existential theory to counseling practice, interventions and the therapeutic process, using the relationship, and case suggestions, see chapter 7 on existential psychotherapy in *Applying Counseling Theories: An Online, Case-Based Approach* (Rochlen, 2007).[1]

Jerry Corey's Work With Ruth From an Existential Perspective

In the *CD-ROM for Integrative Counseling,* Session 11 ("Understanding How the Past Influences the Present"), I demonstrate some ways I utilize existential notions in counseling Ruth. We engage in a role play where Ruth becomes the voice of her church and I take on a new role as Ruth—one in which I have been willing to challenge certain beliefs from church. This segment illustrates how Ruth explores finding new values. In Session 12 ("Working Toward Decisions and Behavioral Changes"), Ruth solidifies the process of making new decisions, which is also an existential concept.

Basic Assumptions

The existential approach to counseling assumes that the relationship the therapist establishes with the client is of the utmost importance in determining how successful therapy will be. Therapy is not something that I do to the person (in this case, Ruth); I am not a technical expert who acts on a passive client. I view therapy as a dialogue in the deepest and most genuine sense, an honest exchange between Ruth and me. We will be partners traveling on a journey, and neither of us knows where it will end. She and I may both be changed by the encounter, and I expect that she will touch off powerful associations, feelings, memories, and reactions within me. My hope is to understand her world from a subjective viewpoint and, at the same time, to let her know my personal reactions to her in our relationship.

Initial Assessment of Ruth

Ruth appears to be a good candidate for existential therapy. She is willing to question the meaning of life, to question the status quo, and to challenge some of her comfortable patterns. She is facing a number of developmental crises, such as wondering what life is about now that her children are getting ready to leave home. Her anxiety increases as she begins to expand her vision of the choices open to her. The process of raising questions has led to more questions, yet her answers are few. She is grappling with what she wants for herself, apart from her long-standing definition of herself as wife and mother. A major theme is posed by the question "How well am I living life?" One of Ruth's strengths is her willingness to ask such anxiety-producing questions. Another of her assets is her willingness to critically think about her existence. As a result of her examination of her life, she has already made some choices and taken some significant steps. She did diverge from her fundamentalist religion, which she no longer found personally meaningful; she is motivated to change her life; and she has sought out therapy as a way to help her find the paths she wants to travel.

Goals of Therapy

The purpose of existential therapy is not to "cure" people of disorders, nor to simply get rid of symptoms; rather, it is to help them become aware of what they are doing and to encourage them to act to make life-changing decisions. It is aimed at helping people like Ruth get out of their rigid roles and see more clearly the ways in which they have been leading a narrow and restricted existence. Therapy aims at helping clients to reflect upon and understand their existence. The basic purpose of Ruth's therapy is to provide her with the insights necessary to discover, establish, and use the freedom she possesses. In many ways Ruth is blocking her own freedom. My function is to help her recognize her part in creating her life situation, including the distress she feels. I assume that as she sees the ways in which her existence is limited she will take steps toward her liberation. My hope is that she can create a more responsible and meaningful existence.

Therapeutic Procedures

As an existential therapist, I do not rely on a well-developed set of techniques. Instead, I focus on certain themes that are part of the human condition, and I emphasize my ability to be fully present with Ruth by challenging her and by sharing my reactions with her as they pertain to our therapeutic relationship. My role is to help Ruth clarify what it is that brought her to me, where she is right now, what it is she wants to change, and what she can do to make these changes happen. I will borrow techniques from several therapies as we explore her current thoughts, feelings, and behaviors within the current situations and events of her life.[2]

When we deal with her past, I will encourage Ruth to relate her feelings and thoughts about past events to her present situation. Here are some of the questions I might pursue with her, any of which we might eventually explore in therapy sessions:

- In what ways are you living as fully as you might? How are you limiting yourself?
- To what degree are you living a life outlined by others?
- What choices have you made so far, and how have these choices affected you?
- What are some of the choices you are faced with now? How do you deal with the anxiety that is part of making choices for yourself and accepting personal freedom?
- What changes do you most want to make, and what is preventing you from making them?

In essence, Ruth is about to engage in a process of opening doors to herself. The experience may be frightening, exciting, joyful, depressing, or all of these at times. As she wedges open the closed doors, she will also begin to loosen the deterministic shackles that have kept her psychologically bound. Gradually, as she becomes aware of what she has been and who she is now, she will be better able to decide what kind of future she wants to carve out for herself. Through her therapy she can explore alternatives for making her visions become real.

The Therapeutic Process

At this point in her therapy, Ruth is coming to grips more directly with her midlife crisis. She has been talking about values by which she lived in the past that now hold little meaning for her, about her feelings of emptiness, and about her fears of making "wrong" choices. Here are some excerpts from several of our sessions.

ELEMENTS OF THE PROCESS

☙ **Helping Ruth Develop New Values**   In a later session Ruth initiates her struggles with religion:

> RUTH: I left my religion years ago, but I haven't found anything to replace it. I'm hoping you can help me explore this. You have so much more experience, and you seem happy with who you are and what you believe in. On my own I'm afraid I might make the wrong decisions.

> JERRY: If I were to give you answers, it would be a way of saying that I don't see you as capable of finding your own way. Maybe a way for you to begin is to ask some questions. I know, for me, one way of finding answers is to raise questions.

> RUTH: I know that the religion I was brought up in told me very clearly what was right and wrong. I was taught that once married, always married—and you make the best of the situation. Well, I'm not so willing to accept that now.

> JERRY: How is that so?

> RUTH: I'm afraid that if I stay in therapy I'll change so much that I'll have little in common with John, and I may eventually leave my marriage.

> JERRY: I'm aware that you've somehow decided that your changes will cause the breakup of your marriage. Could it be that your changes might have a positive effect on your relationship?

> RUTH: You're right, I haven't thought about it in that way. And I guess I've made the assumption that John won't like my changes. I more often worry that what I'm doing in therapy will eventually make me want to leave him, or he might want to leave me. Sometimes I have an impulse to walk away from my marriage, but I get scared thinking about who I'd be without John in my life.

> JERRY: Why not imagine that this did happen, and for a few minutes talk about who you would be without John in your life. Just speak whatever thoughts or images come to your mind, and try not to worry about how they sound.

> RUTH: All my life I've had others tell me who and what I should be, and John has picked up where my parents and church left off. I don't know what my life is about apart from being a wife and a mother. What would our kids think if John and I split up? How would it affect them? Would they hate me for what I'd done to the family? I know I'm tired

of living the way I am, but I'm scared to death of making any more changes for fear that it will lead to more turmoil. John and the kids liked the "old me" just fine, and they seem upset by the things I've been saying lately.

JERRY: In all that you just said, you didn't allow yourself to really express how you might be different if they were not in your life. It's easier for you to tune in to how the people in your life might be affected by your changes than for you to allow yourself to imagine how you'd be different. It does seem difficult for you to imagine being different. Why not give it another try? Keep the focus on how you want to be different rather than on the reactions your family would have to your changing.

✑ Dealing With Ruth's Anxiety   It is obvious that Ruth has trouble dealing with change. There is immediate anxiety whenever she thinks of being different. She is beginning to see that she has choices, and that others do not have to make her choices for her. Yet she is terrified by this realization, and for a long time it appears that she is immobilized in her therapy. She will not act on the choices available to her. So I go with her feelings of being stuck and explore her anxiety with her. Here is how she describes these feelings.

RUTH: I often wake up in the middle of the night with the feeling that the walls are closing in on me! I break out in cold sweats, I have trouble breathing, and I can feel my heart pounding. At times I worry that I'll die. I can't sleep, and I get up and pace around.

JERRY: Ruth, as unpleasant as these feelings are, I hope you learn to pay attention to them. They're telling you that all is not well in your life and that you're ready for change.

I know that Ruth sees anxiety as a negative thing, something she would like to be rid of once and for all. I see her anxiety as the possibility of a new starting point for her. Rather than simply getting rid of these symptoms, she can go deeper into their meaning. I see her anxiety as the result of her increased awareness of her freedom along with her growing sense of responsibility for deciding what kind of life she wants and then taking action to make these changes a reality.

✑ Exploring the Meaning of Death   Eventually we get onto the topic of death and explore its meaning to Ruth.

RUTH: I've been thinking about what we talked about before—about what I want from life before I die. You know, for so many years I lived in dread of death. I suppose that fear has kept me from looking at death.

JERRY: Why don't you talk about areas of your life where you don't feel really alive. How often do you feel a sense of excitement about living?

RUTH: It would be easier for me to tell you of the times I feel half dead! I'm dead to having fun. Sexually I'm dead.

JERRY: Can you think of some other ways you might be dead?

I am trying to get Ruth to evaluate the quality of her life and to begin to experience her deadness. After some time she admits that she has allowed her spirit to die. Old values have faded, and she has not acquired new ones. Ruth is gaining some awareness that there is more to living than breathing. It is important that she allow herself to recognize her deadness and feel it as a precondition for her rebirth. I operate under the assumption that by really experiencing and expressing the ways in which she feels dead she can begin to focus on how she wants to be alive. Only then is there hope that she can find new ways to live.

PROCESS COMMENTARY   Ruth's experience in therapy accentuates the basic assumption that there are no absolute answers outside of herself. She learns that therapy is a process of opening up doors bit by bit, giving her more potential for choices. This process happens largely because of the relationship between us. She becomes well aware that she cannot evade responsibility for choosing for herself. She learns that she is constantly creating herself by the choices she is making, as well as by the choices she is failing to make. As her therapist, I support her attempts at experimenting with new behaviors in and out of our sessions. Our open discussions, in which we talk about how we are experiencing each other, are a new behavior for her. These sessions provide a safe situation for her to extend new dimensions of her being. At the same time, I teach Ruth how she might use what she is learning in her everyday life. She is willing to get angry with me, be direct with me, and tell me how I affect her. We work on ways in which she might continue this behavior with selected people in her environment.

One of my aims is to show Ruth the connection between the choices she is making or failing to make and the anxiety she is experiencing. I do this by asking her to observe herself in various situations throughout the week. Through this self-observation process Ruth gradually sees some specific ways in which her choices are directly contributing to her anxiety. My goal in working with Ruth is not to eliminate her anxiety, but to help her understand what it means. From my perspective, anxiety is a signal that all is not well, that a person is ready for some change in life.

Perhaps the critical aspect of Ruth's therapy is her recognition that she has a choice to make. She can continue to cling to the known and the familiar. Or she can also accept the fact that in life there are no guarantees, that in spite of this uncertainty and this accompanying anxiety she will still have to act by making choices and then living with the consequences. Ruth chooses to commit herself to therapy.[3]

Questions for Reflection

1. What life experiences have you had that could help you identify with Ruth? Have you shared any of her struggles? How have you dealt with these personal struggles and issues? How are your answers to these questions related to your potential effectiveness as her therapist?

2. What are your general reactions to the ways in which Dr. Russell and I have worked with Ruth? What aspects of both of these styles of counseling might you use? What different themes would you focus on? What different techniques might you use?

3. Compare this approach to working with Ruth with the previous approaches, psychoanalytic therapy and Adlerian therapy. What major differences do you see?

4. What are your thoughts about Dr. Russell's view of assessment and diagnosis as applied to Ruth?

5. How would you work with Ruth's fears associated with "opening doors" in her life? Part of her wants to remain as she is, and the other part yearns for change. How would you work with this conflict?

6. Using this approach, how would you deal with Ruth's fears of dying? Do you see any connection between her anxieties and her view of death?

7. What are your thoughts and feelings about death and dying? To what extent do you think you have explored your own anxieties pertaining to death and loss? How would your answer to this question largely determine your effectiveness in counseling a person such as Ruth?

8. What are some of the other existential themes mentioned in this chapter that have personal relevance to your life? How do you react to the question "Can therapists inspire their clients to deal with their existential concerns if they have not been willing to do this in their own lives?"

Notes

See the DVD/online program entitled *Theory in Practice: The Case of Stan* (Session 4: Existential Therapy Applied to the Case of Stan) for exploring Stan's anxiety over death and the purpose of his life.

1. Russell, J. M. (2007). Existential psychotherapy. In A. B. Rochlen, *Applying Counseling Theories: An Online, Case-Based Approach* (pp. 107–125). Upper Saddle River, NJ: Pearson Prentice Hall.

2. In Session 9 ("An Integrative Focus") of the *CD-ROM for Integrative Counseling,* I illustrate what I am describing in my existential way of working with Ruth. As an existential therapist, I am free to draw techniques from many therapeutic modalities as an avenue of exploring with Ruth current situations and events of her life.

3. For a more detailed treatment of the existential approach, see G. Corey (2009), *Theory and Practice of Counseling and Psychotherapy* (8th ed., Belmont, CA: Brooks/Cole). Also see G. Corey (2009), *Student Manual for Theory and Practice of Counseling and Psychotherapy* (8th ed., Belmont, CA: Brooks/Cole). The combination of the textbook and manual will flesh out the existential perspective in my work with Ruth demonstrated in this chapter.

CHAPTER FIVE

Case Approach to Person-Centered Therapy

General Overview of Person-Centered Therapy

The person-centered approach seeks to provide a climate of understanding and acceptance through the client–therapist relationship that will enable clients to come to terms with aspects of themselves that they have denied or disowned. Other goals are enabling clients to move toward greater openness, trust in themselves, willingness to be a process rather than a finished product, and spontaneity.

Because this approach places primary emphasis on the client–therapist relationship, it specifies few methods. It minimizes directive intervention, interpretation, questioning, probing for information, giving advice, collecting history, and diagnosis. Person-centered therapists maximize active listening, reflection, and clarification. Current formulations of the theory stress the full and active participation of the therapist as a person in the therapeutic relationship.

In keeping with the spirit of person-centered therapy, it is the client who largely determines when to stop coming for therapy. Likewise, the therapist assumes that clients can be trusted to determine the degree to which therapy has been successful for them. As clients increasingly assume an inner locus of control, they are in the best position to assess the personal meaning of their therapeutic venture.

A Person-Centered Therapist's Perspective on Ruth

by David J. Cain, PhD, ABPP, CGP

Introduction

Assessment and diagnosis are viewed as ongoing processes by the person-centered therapist, not as formal procedures undertaken at the beginning of psychotherapy. The word *diagnose* is derived from a Greek word that means "to know" or "to discover." In my view, therapy is basically a process of self-discovery whose critical components are intrapersonal and interpersonal learning. The therapist's primary function is to facilitate learning in the client. Thus, the client's discovery of personal knowledge about self is much more relevant than what the therapist knows about the client or the psychiatric disorder the client is viewed as experiencing.

As a person-centered therapist, I would not undertake any formal assessment with a client unless the client requested it, nor would I attempt to establish a *DSM-IV-TR* diagnosis for the client. In more than 30 years as a practicing psychotherapist, I have found the practice of formal diagnosis to be fraught with more liabilities than assets. Although an extensive discussion of the pros and cons of diagnosis is beyond the scope of this book, I will mention what I believe to be some of the most significant limitations.

First, I have not found that establishing a diagnosis helps much with treatment. The *DSM-IV-TR* system of diagnosis does not provide treatment guidelines. With few exceptions (for example, exposure and cognitive restructuring for anxiety problems), the bulk of psychotherapeutic research has shown that all established approaches have roughly equivalent success with a wide variety of problems.

Second, all diagnostic categories are inevitably reductionist in that they reduce clients and their experiences to a list of symptoms. In reality there is considerable variability among individuals with the same diagnosis.

Third, the uniqueness of each person tends to be lost in the diagnostic process because the emphasis is placed on common characteristics. It is a biological and psychological fact that each person is unique. The act of categorizing tends to constrict the therapist's conceptual understanding of the client and de-emphasizes the importance of individual differences and the complexity of the person.

Fourth, diagnosis overly emphasizes what is wrong with clients and gives relatively little attention to their strengths and resources. Person-centered therapists have a stronger focus on client *growth* and development of personal resources than on problem solving and remediation of psychopathology.

And, finally, a diagnosis is made primarily from an external point of view (that of the clinician) rather than from the internal frame of reference of the client. Clients generally have relatively limited participation in the determination of their diagnosis, even though they are the best authorities on their experience.

I find that dimensions of the person other than diagnostic symptoms are more important in understanding and responding therapeutically to my client. Among the most relevant dimensions are the client's self-concept and worldview; incongruencies between the self-concept, behavior, and experience; the capacity to attend to and process experience, especially affect; learning style and ability to learn from experience; comportment or characteristic manner of living; implicit and explicit personal goals and strivings; a sense of purpose and personal meaning; and the sense of being grounded, whole, and integrated.

In my experience a critical endeavor of the client is the definition ("Who am I?") and redefinition of the self ("Who am I becoming?"). This process is facilitated by the therapist's and client's openness to the client's experience and its personal meaning and is hindered by limited diagnostic formulations of the client's psychopathology. In the optimal case, diagnosis is a continuous process of self-learning in which the client remains receptive to all sources of experience and relevant information. In contrast, diagnostic categorization on the part of therapists may create a false sense of security about what they "know" about the client and limit their creativity and adaptability in responding therapeutically. The danger here is that therapists may begin to interact with a static category rather than an evolving being, thus limiting their range of perceptions and variety of therapeutic responses and, consequently, the client's potential for change. Instead of attempting to identify the client's diagnostic category, two guiding questions that I hold throughout therapy are "What is it like to be you?" and "How are you living?"

The essential purpose of assessment is to enable the client to develop relevant and meaningful personal knowledge, especially knowledge about the "self" and how the self-concept affects behavior. One of the major factors characteristic of person-centered therapy is the responsibility placed on the client for self-direction. Although I may play a significant role in helping the client explore her- or himself, the client is more likely to be affected by, and to put to use, personal experiences and learning that are self-discovered. The excitement and deep satisfaction that come from self-exploration and self-discovery are potent factors that engage the client in the therapeutic process.

Assessment of Ruth

In working with Ruth, I will be especially attentive to how she views her *self*, including aspects that are evident and those that are implicit and unclear but forming. Several components of Ruth's self-concept emerge from her autobiography. In her own words Ruth identifies herself as the "good wife" and the "good mother" that "he [John] expects me to be." Thus, she strongly identifies herself with the roles of wife and mother, but she has defined and attempted to fulfill these roles in the image her husband wishes. By allowing her husband to define what she is and should be (if she is to be accepted), she has abdicated her role and power in defining the person she is and in making personal choices about her life. She has allowed her husband to determine her conditions of worth, and she lives in fear that if she does not live up to his conditions "he might leave me." Ruth's tendency to mold herself for others is a pervasive aspect of her functioning. As she says, "I've pretty much lived for others so far . . . I've been the superwoman who gives and gives." Defining herself as a giving and caretaking person are, of course, aspects of herself in which Ruth takes pride, and understandably so. At the same time, defining herself in this relatively narrow manner limits her view of who she might become.

Until she was 30, Ruth's identity and value system were strongly influenced by the fundamentalist religion of her parents, especially her father. She feared that she would be rejected by her parents if she did not live up to their expectations of who she should be. She states, "They haven't formally disowned me, but in many ways I think they have. I know I'll never win their approval as long as I remain away from the religion that's so dear to them." Ruth is intent on pleasing others, even at the cost of sacrificing her own needs and identity. In a real sense she is selfless, without a clear sense of who she is or can become. Some of the basic questions she is likely to address in therapy are "What do I want?" "What kind of person do I want to be?" "How do I want to live?" and "Can I be this person and maintain a good relationship with my husband and family?"

Other aspects of Ruth's self-concept are more peripheral. An important clue to her self-concept is the view she has of her body and its many symptoms. However she defines herself, it is important to realize that the self is embodied, that it is contained in and functions through a body. Thus, an essential part of her sense of herself has to do with how she sees and feels about her body. At present she views her physical self as overweight and unattractive. In her words: "I don't like what I see. I don't like who I am, and I certainly don't feel proud of my body." Ruth experiences many disturbing bodily symptoms that adversely affect her sense of her physical self. A large part of Ruth's manner of being is dominated by fear, anxiety, panic, and a sense that many daily life events and ongoing concerns are overwhelming. She is afraid that she will die. These fears and anxieties seem to manifest themselves in various forms of bodily symptoms (namely, insomnia, heart palpitations, headache, dizziness, and crying spells). Quite literally, much of Ruth's life is *sickening*—depressed, fearful, constricted, and avoidant.

Although Ruth feels some pride and satisfaction in being a caretaker, this role also results in ambivalence and dissatisfaction. She experiences considerable conflict over who she is, what she believes, and how she is living. By her own admission, she doesn't like who she is, her overweight body, and the fact that her life is devoid of any joyful or meaningful activity apart from her roles as wife and mother.

A potential aspect of her identity is that of a teacher, but she has not yet incorporated this role into her self-structure. She imagines that teaching will be fulfilling, but as yet she places her own desires behind those of her family. Her religious beliefs and values are changing and are in conflict with her earlier fundamentalist views. Other aspects of Ruth's identity will emerge during the course of therapy.

Ruth's future is vague and tentative. She is dimly aware of the person she might become, yet she is fearful that pursuing her interests and needs and developing her own identity will result in her losing her husband and family. But she has not given up. In recent years she has become a "questioner" and holds onto the glimmer of hope that she can "begin to live before it's too late." There is a yearning in Ruth to be more than she is—to expand herself and her life possibilities. She is entering a transitional phase in her life with considerable trepidation.

Key Issues

A key issue with Ruth is the incongruence between the person she is and the selves that are "trying" to emerge, though hesitantly and cautiously. Her incongruence manifests itself in a variety of ways—as cognitive dissonance, in her many physical symptoms, and in anxiety and stress—all of which have the tendency to impel her toward the solution of her discomfort. Her depression and physical symptoms tell her that something is wrong with her life, but fear is her main obstacle to becoming a more autonomous, fuller, and more gratified person. Fear of the loss of her husband's and children's support and love renders her hesitant to move from the safety of her current life, but her dissatisfaction with it and herself are drawing her forward.

A basic assumption of the person-centered therapist is that the human organism has a natural tendency to manifest its potential. Carl Rogers described the *actualizing tendency* as people's inherent inclination to develop all of their capacities: to differentiate, to expand, and to become more autonomous. This tendency for people to move in directions that maintain and enhance themselves can be deterred, however, by motives that interfere with their ability to manifest their growth needs. At such times they may fail to differentiate between actions that are gratifying (such as being liked) and those that develop their potential (namely, standing up for their values).

Ruth feels somewhat secure in her present life, even though it is boring and unfulfilling in terms of personal growth and meaning. Her capacity to move forward is limited by her lack of trust in her judgment ("I'm scared I'll make the wrong decisions.") and resourcefulness ("I'm trapped and don't see a way out."). As a consequence, she is inclined to look to others (God, husband, her therapist) for guidance and direction.

Paradoxically, Ruth is as much afraid of living as she is of dying. The anticipation of change terrifies her because it threatens the limited security and stability she experiences in her family and current lifestyle. Yet there are hopeful signs. Ruth is restless, dissatisfied, and afraid that her life is slipping by. She has a fragile desire for a better life and a tenuous vision of what she might become. She is "excited and afraid at the same time." If she can listen to the inner voices of her feelings and attend to the distress signals of her body, Ruth will begin to see more clearly who she is and what she wants and, in the process, will begin to find her own voice and path.

Therapeutic Process and Techniques

As I anticipate working with Ruth, my primary focus is on the quality of the relationship I hope to provide for her. My desire is to allow myself to be curious about her and receptive to anything she would like to share about herself and her life. To the best of my ability, I will be fully present and listen carefully to what she says while being sensitive to how she presents herself, including her nonverbal and implicit messages. As much as possible, I hope to leave any preconceptions and hypotheses I may have about her behind and to attend to her with fresh ears and eyes. It is my desire to create a trusting, supportive, safe, and encouraging atmosphere in which Ruth will experience me as genuinely interested in her, sensitive to her feelings, nonjudgmental, and accurately understanding of her expressed and intended meanings. I hope to communicate my belief in her resourcefulness and my optimism about her capacity to learn what she needs to learn and move forward in her life. If I am successful in these endeavors, Ruth will listen to herself, learn from her experiences, and effectively apply her learnings, and in the process, move from an external to an internal locus of control.

Any specific techniques, methods, or responses I may use will be dictated by Ruth's therapeutic needs and what best fits her at a given time. Because I view Ruth as a collaborator in the therapeutic process, I will take my cues from her regarding how I might best respond at the moment. At times I may collaborate more directly with Ruth to determine what might be helpful or check directly with her to ascertain if what I'm doing is helpful, trusting that she knows best how I can serve her at a given time. A variety of therapeutic responses or methods might be employed on Ruth's behalf with her participation in choosing the approaches that she feels might be most helpful. Careful listening and accurate understanding of my client's overt and tacit meanings always precede the introduction of therapeutic techniques or exercises. My basic question in employing any technique is, "Does it fit?"

One important aspect of my role is as a facilitator of learning. Life is constantly teaching us important lessons about ourselves, about others, and about life in general. At times, I view my role as helping my client "learn how to learn." My style of responding to Ruth will reflect my attempt to adapt to her personal learning style, which often can be inferred through observation or discussion.

Finally, I will be myself in the relationship. Thus, Ruth will have a good sense of who I am as a person. Consequently, she will experience my sense of humor, my openness and directness, and my serious and playful sides. She will find that I can be provocative and challenging as well as quietly attentive and gentle as she undertakes her personal journey. She will also see the pleasure I feel in working with her and seeing her become the person she wishes to be.[1]

THE BEGINNING PHASE OF THERAPY   I anticipate that Ruth will tend to be tentative as therapy begins, perhaps starting with her general sense of dissatisfaction with her life, herself, and her physical symptoms. She may find the relatively nondirective nature of our interaction somewhat disconcerting at first, preferring that I lead her in the "right" direction, ask questions, advise her on what she "should" do, and "push" her to do it. However, I believe she will gradually perceive that my reluctance to direct or advise her is based on my trust in her ability to determine her own direction and find a course of action that fits her. My message is, "This is your life, and you are the author of its future." I am confident that Ruth will discover that she has more personal strengths and resources than she is aware of at present.[2]

The beginning phase of therapy goes as follows:

THERAPIST: I'm interested in hearing anything you would like to share about yourself—anything that's troubling you—whatever is on your mind.

RUTH: Right now the thing that's bothering me the most is my weight. Whenever I get anxious or depressed, I tend to overeat. Lately I've gained about 10 pounds. I feel fat and dumpy. I hate the way I look.

THERAPIST: You sound angry with yourself for your eating and your appearance.

RUTH: I am. And my husband likes me better when I'm thinner. I've been trying to diet, but I just can't seem to stick with it.

THERAPIST: You're not pleasing your husband or yourself. And I guess you're getting discouraged about whether you're able to lose weight.

RUTH: It's not just losing weight. It's accomplishing anything I set out to do. I just can't seem to follow through. Usually I get off to a good start, but as soon as something goes wrong, I get discouraged.

THERAPIST: And when you get discouraged you . . . ?

RUTH: I start to give up and get depressed.

THERAPIST: And when you get depressed you . . . ?

RUTH: Eat.

THERAPIST: So you eat to ease those feelings.

RUTH: I guess so.

THERAPIST: If your feelings could talk, what might they say?

RUTH: I think they would say "You can't do anything right."

THERAPIST: Pretty harsh words. You start criticizing yourself.

RUTH: I do tend to get down on myself when I start to falter. Sometimes I think I need someone else to push me to accomplish my goals.

THERAPIST: Sometimes you'd just like someone to help you get through the tough times.

RUTH: I'm almost 40 and I'm still not sure what I want to do, much less if I can do it. I'd like to be a teacher, but my husband wants me to stay home and take care of him and the kids. I like being a mother and a wife, but I feel that life is passing me by.

THERAPIST: So there's a sense of urgency in your life. Life is moving on, and although you think you'd like to teach, you don't trust yourself to stick to it or your diet or anything else. And when you have a setback, you get discouraged, criticize yourself, and wish someone else could get you to stick to your goals. To ease the pain you eat. And all this is complicated by your fear that if you do teach you may alienate your husband.

RUTH: That about says it.

🕮 **Process Commentary** What quickly emerges are the emotions that impair Ruth's progress. She is fearful that she will fail, becomes angry and self-critical when she does, and then feels depressed and discouraged. She attempts to assuage these feelings by eating, only to find herself dissatisfied by her weight and herself again. Although she seems to like teaching and experiences some success at it, she is not yet clear that this career choice is right. Nor is she willing to take a step that might disrupt her family. As her therapist, I hope to enable her to view her feelings as "friendly" and potentially constructive messages that can help her develop a greater sense of clarity, direction, and confidence in her endeavors. So we continue.

THERAPIST: So what do you make of all that?

RUTH: I guess I do wish I could depend on someone else to help me when I'm stuck. I've always depended on my parents or John for guidance. I did break away from my church several years ago, but I don't think my parents will ever understand that or accept my beliefs about religion. John couldn't understand why I wanted to finish college and be a teacher. He thinks I should be happy being a homemaker and a mother.

THERAPIST: I guess you long to be understood and supported by your parents and husband, but sometimes they just don't. What makes sense to you doesn't always make sense to them. What you feel may be best for you and what they want for you are often in conflict. Yet you'd still like their approval and backing.

RUTH: I'm such a wimp. Sometimes I think I'll never be able to do what I believe in without worrying about what someone else thinks.

THERAPIST: What is clear is that what people think of you does matter—often a great deal. Then you feel like a wimp when you let others' opinions of you become more important than your own. But you did change your religious convictions, and you did finish college. You sometimes do finish what you start and do what you really want to do despite others' misgivings.

RUTH: Well, I do feel good about those things. It took me forever to finish college, but I did. And I think I did a pretty good job in my student teaching. I guess there's no reason I should expect them to agree with me. They have their own ideas about what is right.

THERAPIST: And so do you.

RUTH: Yes, I think I do. I'm pretty sure I want to be a teacher.

Ruth's dissatisfaction with her need for approval is becoming evident. When her self-initiated religious changes and completion of college are acknowledged and affirmed by the therapist, Ruth begins to see herself more positively apart from the views of others. She is beginning to recognize that she can give herself the credit she deserves for her accomplishments.

As therapy progresses, Ruth becomes increasingly aware of the incongruence she experiences between the person she is and the person she yearns to be. It is likely that she will feel guilty about what she perceives as selfishness when she attends more to her own needs, and she is fearful that her marriage and family will be disrupted. As Ruth expands and modifies her perceptual field, however, she comes to believe that her desires and goals are as deserving of attention as those of her family.

THE MIDDLE PHASE OF THERAPY Ruth may, at some point, wish to bring her husband into her therapy sessions to address the conflict she feels over taking a course of action that displeases him or her children. Whether John is supportive of her change or not, she will have to wrestle with her own conflict about doing what she wants and becoming a more separate, independent person.

Her marriage will probably go through a dramatic transition if she pursues her hopes. It may improve as she becomes a fuller person or become more conflicted if her husband is threatened by her development.

The middle phase of therapy highlights these ideas:

RUTH: John and I had another fight last night. He wants me to spend more time with him and the kids and less time with my friends and at the new church I've been attending. I feel a little guilty about being away from home more, but I really like some of the new people I've met.

THERAPIST: You feel torn between allegiances to your family and yourself.

RUTH: Yes. I love my kids and John, and I like taking care of them. But there's more that I want to do. And besides, the kids are old enough now to take care of themselves more. In fact, Rob just moved out last week, and Jennifer has started in a community college. Susan and Adam are involved in lots of activities at the high school. And John is involved in his bowling two nights a week. So it's not as if they need me around all the time.

THERAPIST: As you see that they have lives of their own, it seems that your family needs you less than they did. Or maybe you need them less as you have begun to do more things that are important to you.

RUTH: I think it's a little of both. I got a lot of satisfaction from making sure they were happy—you know, being a good mother and wife. But I realize that sometimes I got too involved and didn't let them do more for themselves because I wanted them to need me. Now I kind of like taking more time for myself. The kids are basically OK. Even Jennifer has begun to settle down. She just had to realize that when I said "no" I meant "no," not "maybe." She doesn't always like some of my rules, but she's more accepting of limits.

THERAPIST: Being a good mother and wife was very important to you, but sometimes you become more involved that you need to be. Now you've become clearer about the kind of mother you want to be and that includes setting limits and sticking to them. And you're less worried about how they'll ever survive without you.

RUTH [*laughs*]: Yeah, I must have thought I was supposed to be Mother Teresa or something. Actually, the kids aren't the problem. John is. He's having a hard time accepting the ways I've changed. He's used to having me spend more time with him and do little things for him that I don't have as much time to do now. Sometimes he complains that I'm not as interested in him as I used to be, or he just sulks. I think I've spoiled him, and he's having a hard time adjusting.

THERAPIST: Having a life of your own is risky to you and threatening to John. You seem to be struggling with your feelings about John's reactions to the ways you've changed.

RUTH: I am. But I'm not sure what I feel. Sometimes I think he's acting like a big baby. At other times I feel sorry for him. Or sad.

THERAPIST: What seems to be the main feeling?

RUTH: Kind of sad and annoyed. Doesn't make sense.

THERAPIST: Notice where in your body the feeling seems to be located.

RUTH: Mostly in my stomach.

THERAPIST: Can you describe the sensation in your stomach?

RUTH: Kind of queasy and scared.

THERAPIST: A queasy, scared feeling?

RUTH: Yeah.

THERAPIST: Just pay attention to that feeling for a while. See if there's a word or maybe an image that seems to fit that queasy, scared feeling.

RUTH: It's kind of like the panicky feelings I get sometimes.

THERAPIST: Panicky. Stay with it.

RUTH: It's like the feeling I get when I'm scared that I can't handle something. Sort of being afraid that I'll be overwhelmed.

THERAPIST: Um Hm. Scared. Overwhelmed.

RUTH: What comes to mind is the fight I had with my parents over leaving the church. I knew it was the right thing, but I was terrified of losing their support.

THERAPIST: So it's more like terrified.

RUTH: Like I'm frightened of having to be on my own. Like being abandoned! That's it.

THERAPIST: Abandoned. A sense that you're on your own and there's no one there to support you.

RUTH: Exactly. When I left the church, my parents were utterly disapproving of me. Whenever I wanted to do something they disapproved of, they would become distant and sometimes wouldn't even speak to me. It's the same with John. When I'm a good wife and focus my life around him and home, he's happy with me. But when I started doing things that meant a lot to me—like teaching and developing new friends—well, he got sulky and pulled away. So I guess I've been feeling abandoned by him too. It all makes sense.

THERAPIST: So it's fear of being abandoned and not being supported in being yourself.

RUTH: Yes, it all makes sense.

🖉 **Process Commentary**   Ruth is beginning to become more separate from her family, though she remains involved with them and concerned about their well-being. She is more acceptant and tolerant of the reality that taking care of her needs and desires may, at times, displease other family members. Ruth is also learning to allow her husband and her kids to take care of themselves more.

During the latter segment of this interview, Ruth was encouraged to focus on a feeling that was initially unclear. Using a process called experiential focusing, Ruth was encouraged to pay attention to where and how her feeling manifested itself in her body. Through a series of steps, Ruth was able to clarify the feeling and understand its relationship to her panic states and primary relationships. Such insights as these are often quite powerful because they clarify the way the problem is carried bodily. It's as if the body knows what's wrong in a more profound way than can be articulated verbally. As the problem is processed physically and cognitively, the insight derived has a convincing ring of truth. More important, Ruth has learned a process that will be invaluable in helping her make sense of her feelings by paying attention to them more closely.

Later in the therapy, Ruth continues addressing her marriage and its personal meaning.

RUTH: I sometimes feel a little guilty about taking more time for myself, but John has things to do on his own. And we still spend a lot of time together. It's just that he doesn't think I need him as much as I used to, and I think he feels insecure about this.

THERAPIST: Maybe you don't need him or his approval as much as you used to.

RUTH: Hmm. Well, I'm not sure. I think maybe I used to want him to approve of me more than I do now. And now he seems to want me to need him the way I used to. I think he doesn't feel as important to me as he did. He is important, but for different reasons. Now, I want us to be friends and more like equal partners. Before, he was more like my father—more controlling and demanding. It was as if he didn't think I could do anything without having him to guide me. And I guess I did let him take charge more then because I was so terrified of doing things on my own. In my mind he was more the head of the house. Now, I'm a little more confident and . . . well, I guess I don't want to need him like a little girl needs her parents. What I really want is his support.

THERAPIST: Looks to me like you've changed and grown quite a bit. Earlier in your marriage you wanted and allowed John to take charge more. You felt then that you needed his guidance because you weren't able to make decisions for yourself. And you became extremely anxious when John would withdraw and sulk. Now, as your confidence has grown, you want someone who will offer advice when you ask him but support you in your choices. Instead of a father, you want an equal partner.

RUTH: Yes! That's what I want. I want John to see that I'm different from him and to appreciate me for the person I am. When I want his input on something, I want him to understand that I may or may not do what he suggests. I think he still thinks that when I ask his opinion it means I'll do things his way. No wonder he gets frustrated or hurt sometimes. I think I need to make it clear that his ideas do matter to me but if I don't follow his suggestion it doesn't mean that I don't value him. I just want to do things my own way sometimes.

Ruth is growing stronger and more independent. She is clearer about the kind of relationship she wants with her husband and able to see her husband more objectively. As Ruth has progressed in therapy, she is beginning to see herself in a more positive and differentiated way. She is feeling more power and control in her life and is beginning to become more assertive. More of her satisfaction will be derived from her work and interests apart from, but not excluding, her roles of mother and wife. As she learns to listen to the messages of her feelings and her body, she will identify her needs more clearly and draw on her resources more effectively to satisfy them. Her depression, anxiety, and physical symptoms should diminish as Ruth learns to identify and effectively address the sources of her conflicts. Gradually, she will learn that there is someone in her life on whom she can always depend—herself.

THE FINAL PHASE OF THERAPY Here is a sample dialogue of the final phase of our therapy:

RUTH: Things have settled down a lot with John. Although it's been a difficult adjustment for him, he seems to accept me more the way I am now.

THERAPIST: And how are you now?

RUTH: I think the main thing is that I feel a lot more separate and independent. I still want my family and friends to like me and approve of what I do, but it's OK if they don't. The main thing is that I feel good about me, at least most of the time.

THERAPIST: You sure look better—more confident and settled. Your sense of independence and your ability to trust your decisions have made you stronger.

RUTH: I am. And I feel pretty good most of the time. Once in a while I'll get a panicky feeling, but I've learned to pay attention to my feelings, understand what's troubling me, and deal with it. Last week I was real anxious about my younger daughter, Susan. I didn't like the guy she's been going out with, and I told her why. Well, she insisted on seeing him, and I didn't know what to do. I talked it over with John, and we decided to let her continue to see this guy as long as we knew where she was and she made curfew. I think the main thing that helped me was realizing that she has pretty good judgment.

THERAPIST: Sounds like you've learned to trust your feelings and your judgment and to tolerate your anxiety about Susan because you trust her judgment. Maybe you haven't done such a bad job as a parent. You and John also seem to be working together more as parents—more as partners.

RUTH: Believe me, it hasn't been easy. It's still hard to sleep until I hear that door open when she comes home, but nothing awful has happened so far. As for John and me, most of the time we work out our differences. We still fight occasionally, but I don't worry anymore that he'll leave me. Even when I get stubborn about something he disagrees with, he tries to see my point of view. And sometimes we just agree to disagree.

THERAPIST: You've found that you can tolerate your anxieties much better than you thought you could. It seems, too, that you and John can deal with your differences without them becoming fatal.

RUTH: You know, I actually think he likes me better the way I am now. I may be harder to live with in some ways, but I'm not so dependent and scared. I'm more fun now, and John likes that. I like me a lot better too.

THERAPIST: You've become more of the person you've been struggling to be. There's a lot to like in you.

Ս **Process Commentary** Ruth now views others' acceptance and liking as desirable though not necessary to her well-being. More important, she has learned to like herself and feel at peace with who she is. She is more confident about herself as a wife and mother and is more able to tolerate the inevitable anxieties of parenting.

The process of person-centered therapy can be conceived of as a rebirth of the self, with the therapist serving as midwife. Many clients who seek therapy are conflicted about who they are and how they are living. Their sense of self lacks clarity and is often viewed in terms of important roles (namely, daughter, mother, wife, student) that are largely defined by their culture and significant others. To the degree that we buy into these roles, we tend to move away from and lose a sense of our natural inclinations and tendency to actualize our potential in a manner consistent with our true selves. In an attempt to find acceptance and approval and avoid conflict with others, especially with those most important to us, we try to bend and shape ourselves in a manner that often leaves us feeling incongruent, dissatisfied, conflicted, and at odds with ourselves and with others. Self-acceptance is usually a critical step in growth.

Person-centered therapy, as is evident in Ruth's case, provides the client with an opportunity to experience one's self and life in a clearer, more differentiated, and grounded manner. This process is assisted enormously by the therapist's ability to capture the essence of the client's experience, especially the person's current view of self, worldview, and explicit and implicit needs, goals, and strivings. The therapist helps the client recognize that his or her experiences are the basis for critical learning and the creation of personal knowledge, meaning, and choice about how one might live and who one might become. One of the critical processes of therapy is enabling clients to develop confidence in their perceptions, judgments, and sense of knowing. Because both affective and cognitive ways of knowing have strengths and limitations, a goal of person-centered therapy, as I conceive it, is to enable clients to draw effectively from both ways of knowing. When their knowledge of feelings is congruent with their cognitive knowledge, clients will usually experience a sense of clarity, peace, and confidence in their learning. They will often respond to such moments with comments like "Yes, that's it" or "That feels right." The cognitive and affective realms have been integrated, and they feel freer to act on their learning.

As Ruth became clearer about what she wanted in her life—as mother, wife, and individual—and began to re-create and accept herself, she also realized that this choice required that she stand up for herself and sometimes take a position that not all others would like, support, or approve. The therapist's genuine acceptance and affirmation help Ruth free herself from beliefs and feelings about how she "should" live. I believe Ruth learned to face life's most basic challenge: to be herself and find a way to live with others that allows her to maintain self-respect and integrity while accepting the reality that being herself will sometimes bring conflict with others.

Concluding Comments

A misconception about person-centered psychotherapy is that it is inevitably long-term therapy. It is not. In fact, like many therapeutic approaches, person-centered therapy is often effective in 10 sessions or less, and many clients have benefited from a single session. Therapies that are directive are thought to be briefer because they employ more teaching and guiding techniques. Such therapies assume that the therapist knows how to help the client relieve symptoms rapidly. In my view, such approaches fail to appreciate fully and draw from the resources and inherent wisdom in clients.

Although it may take a bit longer to help Ruth tap her own resources, find her own direction, and learn how to move forward, "slower may be faster." As Ruth learns how to process her experiences more effectively, she also develops attitudes and skills that can enable her to become more self-sufficient. The confidence Ruth gains from learning to trust her own experiences and decision-making capacity enables her to feel more grounded, centered, and optimistic.

Both personal and therapeutic experiences have convinced me that feeling understood and accepted by important others is conducive to our well-being. Regardless of one's therapeutic approach, the desire to hear our clients and to enter into their experiential world is almost inevitably helpful and never harmful.

Jerry Corey's Work With Ruth From a Person-Centered Perspective

It is clear that David Cain views the therapeutic relationship as the core of the therapeutic process. In the *CD-ROM for Integrative Counseling* I provide a concrete illustration of how I view the therapeutic relationship as the foundation for our work together. See Session 1 ("Beginning of Counseling"), Session 2 ("The Therapeutic Relationship"), and Session 3 ("Establishing Therapeutic Goals)" for a demonstration of these principles as they pertain to the person-centered approach.

Basic Assumptions

From a person-centered perspective I view counseling as being directed at more than merely solving problems and giving information. It is primarily aimed at helping clients tap their inner resources so that they can better deal with their problems, both current and future. In Ruth's case, I think I can best accomplish this goal by creating a climate that is threat free, one in which she will feel fully accepted by me. I work on the assumption that my clients have the capacity to lead the way in our sessions and that they can profit without my directive intervention. I assume that three attributes on my part are necessary and sufficient to release Ruth's growth force: genuineness, acceptance and positive regard, and empathy. If I genuinely experience these attitudes toward her and successfully communicate them to her, she will decrease her defensive ways and move toward becoming her true self, the person she is capable of becoming. Therapy is not so much a matter of my doing something to Ruth as it is establishing a relationship that she can use to engage in self-exploration and ultimately find her own way.

Assessment of Ruth

In talking to Ruth I can see that she is disappointed with where she is in life and that she is not being herself around her friends or family. Her therapy is based on this concern.

As I review Ruth's autobiography, I see her wondering: "How can I discover my real self? How can I become the person I would like to become? How can I shed my expected social roles and become myself?" My aim is to create an atmosphere in which she can freely, without judgment and evaluation, express whatever she is feeling. If she can experience this freedom to be whatever she is in this moment, she will begin to drop her masks and to reconsider her roles.

Goals of Therapy

My basic goal is to create a therapeutic climate that will help Ruth discover the kind of person she is, apart from being what others have expected her to be. When her facades come down as a result of the therapeutic process, four characteristics will likely become evident: (1) her openness to experience, (2) a greater degree of trust in herself, (3) her internal source of evaluation, and (4) her willingness to live more spontaneously. These characteristics constitute the basic goals of person-centered therapy.

Therapeutic Procedures

When clients begin therapy, they tend to look to the therapist to provide direction and answers. They often have rigid beliefs and attitudes, a sense of being out of touch with their feelings, a basic sense of distrust in themselves, and a tendency to externalize problems. As therapy progresses, they begin to express fears, anxiety, guilt, shame, anger, and other feelings that they have deemed too negative to incorporate into their self-structure. Eventually, they are able to distort less, express feelings previously out of awareness, and move in a direction of being more open to all of their experience. They can be in contact, moment by moment, with what they are feeling, with less need to distort or deny this experience.

The Therapeutic Process

ELEMENTS OF THE PROCESS During the early stages of her therapy, Ruth does not share her feelings but talks instead about externals. To a large degree she perceives her problems as being outside of herself. Somehow, if her father would change, if her husband's attitude would change, and if her children would present fewer problems, she would be all right. During one of our early sessions, she wonders whether I will be able to really understand her and help her if she does share her feelings.

🕮 **Exploring Our Relationship**   Ruth lets me know how difficult it is for her to talk personally to me, and she tells me that it's especially uncomfortable for her to talk with me because I'm a man. I feel encouraged because she is willing to talk to me about her reservations and her present feelings toward me.[3]

RUTH: I've become aware that I'm careful about what I say around you. It's important that I feel understood, and sometimes I wonder if you can really understand the struggles I'm having as a woman.

JERRY: I like it that you're willing to let me know what it's like for you to attempt to trust me. I hope that you won't censor what you say around me, and I very much want to understand you. Perhaps you could tell me more about your doubts about my ability to understand you as a woman.

RUTH: It's not what you've said so far, but I'm fearful that I have to be careful around you. I'm not sure how you might judge me or react to me.

JERRY: I'd like the chance to relate to you as a person, so I hope you'll let me know when you feel judged or not understood by me.

RUTH: It's not easy for me to talk about myself to any man; all of this is so new to me.

JERRY: What is it that you think I'd have a hard time understanding about you as a woman? You might want to talk more about what makes it difficult to talk to me.

RUTH: So far, no man has ever been willing to really listen to me. I've tried so hard to please my father and then to please John. I wonder if you can understand how I depended so much on my father, and now on John, to give me a feeling that I'm worthwhile as a woman.

JERRY: Even though I'm not a woman, I still know what it feels like to want to be understood and accepted, and I know what it's like to look to others to get this kind of confirmation.

It is important that we pursue what gets in the way of Ruth's trust in me. As long as she is willing to talk about what she is thinking and feeling while we are together in the sessions, we have a direction to follow. Staying with the immediacy of the relationship will inevitably open up other channels of fruitful exploration.

🏵 Becoming Aware of Feelings
In a later session Ruth talks about how hard it is for her to really experience her feelings. She is not very aware of the nature of her feelings because she blocks off any feelings that she deems inappropriate. She does not permit herself to freely accept the flow of whatever she might be feeling. Notice how she puts it:

RUTH: It's hard for me to feel. Sometimes I'm not sure what it is that I feel.

JERRY: From moment to moment you're not aware of the feelings flowing inside of you.

RUTH: Yes, it's difficult enough for me to know what I'm feeling, let alone express it to someone else.

JERRY: So it's also hard for you to let others know how they affect you.

RUTH: Well, I've had lots of practice in sealing off feelings. They scare me.

JERRY: It's scary not knowing what you're feeling, and it's also scary if you know.

RUTH: Sort of. . . . When I was a child, I was punished for being angry. When I cried, I was sent to my room and told to stop crying. Sometimes I remember being happy and playful, only to be told to settle down.

JERRY: So you learned early that your feelings got you in trouble.

RUTH: Just about the time I start to feel something, I go blank or get confused. It's just that I've always thought that I had no right to feel angry, sexual, joyful, sad—or whatever. I just did my work and went on without complaining.

JERRY: You still believe it's better to keep what you feel inside and not express feelings.

RUTH: Right! And I do that especially with my husband and my children.

JERRY: It sounds as if you don't let them know what's going on with you.

RUTH: Well, I'm not so sure they're really interested in my feelings.

JERRY: It's as if they really don't care about how you feel. [*Ruth begins to cry.*] Right now you're feeling something. [*Ruth continues crying, and there is a period of silence.*]

RUTH: I'm feeling sad and hopeless.

JERRY: Yet now you're able to feel, and you can tell me about it.

In this interchange it is important for Ruth to recognize that she can feel and that she is able to express feelings to others. My acceptance of her encourages her to come in more contact with her emotions. This is a first step for her. The more difficult task is for Ruth to increasingly become aware of and share her emotions with the significant people in her life.

※ **Exploring Ruth's Marital Problems**   In another session Ruth brings up her marital difficulties. She explores her mistrust of her own decisions and her search outside of herself for the answers to her problems.

> RUTH: I wonder what to do about my marriage. I'd like to have some time to myself, but what might happen to our family if I made major changes and nobody liked those changes?
>
> JERRY: You wonder what would happen if you expressed your true feelings, especially if your family didn't appreciate your changes.
>
> RUTH: Yes, I guess I do stop myself because I don't want to hurt my family.
>
> JERRY: If you ask for what you want, others are liable to get hurt, and there's no room in your life to think both about what's good for others and what's good for yourself.
>
> RUTH: I really didn't realize that it had to be either them or me. It's just that at 39 I'm just now thinking about who I am. Perhaps it's too late for me to question what I have in my relationships.
>
> JERRY: Well, I don't know that there's a given time when we should ask such questions. I feel excited for you and respect you for asking these questions now.
>
> RUTH: What I know is that my life has been very structured up to this point, and now all this questioning is unsettling to me and is making me anxious. I wonder if I want to give up my predictable life and face the unknown. I get anxious thinking about how my husband and kids will be if I keep making changes. What if they don't like my changes and it upsets them?
>
> JERRY: I'm touched by what you're saying, and I remember some of my own struggles in facing uncertainty. When you say you're anxious, it would help me to understand you better if you could tell me some of the times or situations in which you feel this anxiety.
>
> RUTH: Sometimes I feel anxious when I think about my relationship with John. I'm beginning to see things I don't like, but I'm afraid to tell him about my dissatisfactions lest he get angry.
>
> JERRY: Would you be willing to tell me some of the specific dissatisfactions you have with John?

Ruth then proceeds to talk about some of the difficulties she is experiencing with her husband. I encourage her to share with me some of the impulses that frighten her. I am providing a safe atmosphere for her to express this new awareness without reacting judgmentally to her. I also give her some of my personal reactions to what she is telling me. Then I ask her if she talks very often with John in the way she is talking to me. I am receptive to her and wonder out loud whether he could also be open to her if she spoke this way with him. We end the session with my encouraging her to approach him and say some of the things to him that she has discussed in this session.

PROCESS COMMENTARY We proceed with how Ruth's fear of others' anger keeps her from asking for what she really wants in her life. She then begins to seek answers from me, not trusting that she knows what is best for her. Ruth thinks I have the experience and wisdom to provide her with at least some answers. She continues to press for answers to what she should do about her marriage. It is as though she is treating me as an authority who has the power to fix things in her life. She grows very impatient with my unwillingness to give her answers. As she puts it, she is convinced that she needs my "validation and approval" if she is to move ahead.

We return to an exploration of Ruth's feelings toward me for not giving her more confirmation and not providing reassurance that she will make correct decisions. She tells me that if I really cared I would give her more direction and do more than I am doing. She tells me that all I ever do is listen, that she wants and expects more. I let her know that I do not like her telling me what I am feeling about her. I also tell her that I do care about her struggle but that I refuse to give her answers because of my conviction that she will be able to find better answers within herself. I hope she will learn that I can be annoyed with her at times yet not reject her.

Ruth continues to risk sharing more of her feelings with me, and with my encouragement she also begins to be more open with her family. Gradually, she becomes more willing to think about her own approval. She demands less of herself by way of being a fixed product, such as the "perfect person," and allows herself to open up to new experiences, including challenging some of her beliefs and perceptions. Slowly, she is showing signs of accepting that the answers to her life situation are not to be found in some outside authority but inside herself.[4]

Questions for Reflection

1. Knowing what you do of Ruth, how would it be for you to develop a therapeutic relationship with her? Is there anything that might get in your way? If so, how do you think you would deal with this obstacle? To what degree do you think you could understand her subjective world?

2. Dr. Cain indicates that he would not undertake any formal assessment or attempt to establish a *DSM-IV-TR* diagnosis for a client unless the client requested it. In working with Ruth, he emphasizes her self-assessment and her own definition of her problems. What are your thoughts about excluding formal assessment strategies before engaging in a therapeutic relationship? Do you believe Ruth is able to make a valid self-assessment?

3. Dr. Cain says, "If she can listen to the inner voices of her feelings and attend to the distress signals of her body, Ruth will begin to see more clearly who she is and what she wants and, in the process, will begin to find her own voice and path." To what degree do you agree with this assumption? How does your answer influence the way you would work with Ruth?

4. In the therapeutic relationship with Ruth, Dr. Cain's interventions were based mainly on listening and accurately responding to what she says. He did not make directive interventions but attempted to stay with her subjective

experiencing. What kind of progress do you see her making with this approach?

5. Ruth confronted me with her doubts about my ability to understand her as a woman. Do you think she would do better to see a female therapist? Would you recommend that I suggest a referral to a woman, especially since she brought up her concerns about my being a man? Do you think a male therapist would have a difficult time understanding her world and her struggles as a woman?

6. Ruth mentioned that it was especially difficult to trust a man and that she felt judged by men. How could you work with this theme therapeutically from a person-centered perspective?

7. With both this approach and existential therapy, the client–therapist relationship is central, and the focus is on clients' choosing their way in life. Do you agree that Ruth has this potential for directing her life and making wise choices? Would you be inclined to let her select the topics for exploration, or might you suggest topics? Would you be more directive than either Dr. Cain or I was?

Notes

See the DVD/online program entitled *Theory in Practice: The Case of Stan* (Session 5: Person-Centered Therapy Applied to the Case of Stan) for exploring the immediacy of the therapeutic relationship.

1. In David Cain's work with Ruth, he clearly views the therapeutic relationship as the core of the therapeutic process. The *CD-ROM for Integrative Counseling* provides a concrete illustration of how I also view the therapeutic relationship as the foundation for our work together. See the first three sessions: "The Beginning of Counseling," "The Therapeutic Relationship," and "Establishing Therapeutic Goals."

2. If you are using the *CD-ROM for Integrative Counseling,* compare David Cain's assumptions about his client's capacity to tap her internal resources with my interventions at the beginning phase of counseling.

3. In this section of my work with Ruth, I encourage her to explore our relationship, especially her reservations about talking about herself. What I describe here is similar to what is depicted in the *CD-ROM for Integrative Counseling,* Session 2 ("The Therapeutic Relationship"). What are some ways that I am attempting to build trust with Ruth?

4. For a more detailed treatment of the person-centered approach, see G. Corey (2009), *Theory and Practice of Counseling and Psychotherapy* (8th ed., Belmont, CA: Brooks/Cole). Chapter 7 ("Person-Centered Therapy") provides a foundation to understand Dr. Cain's work with Ruth from a person-centered perspective.

CHAPTER SIX

Case Approach
to Gestalt Therapy

General Overview of Gestalt Therapy

The goal of the Gestalt approach is enhancing awareness of here-and-now experiencing. This process of attending to present experience tends to provide the direction therapy takes; following the client's flow of awareness can lead in many directions.

Gestalt therapists seek a dialogue with their clients and employ experiments to sharpen "what is." Out of this dialogue experiments are created that deepen a client's exploration of what becomes salient for him or her. Experiments always grow out of the phenomenological context of the therapeutic relationship, and they are done collaboratively with the client and the therapist. Clients may engage in role playing by performing all of the various parts and polarities, thus gaining greater awareness of inner conflicts. Some examples of experiments include creating a dialogue with conflicting parts of oneself, exaggeration, focusing on body messages, reexperiencing past unfinished situations in the here and now, and working with dreams.

Clients are ready to terminate therapy when they become increasingly aware of what they are thinking, feeling, and doing in the present moment. When they have recognized and worked through their unfinished business, they are ready to continue therapy on their own. As with the other experiential therapies (existential and person-centered), the evaluation of therapeutic outcomes is rooted in clients' subjective experiences and perceptions about the changes that have occurred.

A Gestalt Therapist's Perspective on Ruth

by Jon Frew, PhD, ABPP

Introduction

Gestalt therapy is practiced with a theoretical foundation grounded in field theory, phenomenology, and dialogue. Individuals are inseparable from the environments they inhabit. Gestalt therapists are interested in the ongoing relationship between the individual and the environment (also referred to as the "field"). Phenomenology involves seeking an understanding based on what is given, obvious, or comprehensible through the senses rather than on interpretations or meanings defined objectively by the observer. The therapist encourages the client to describe his or her experience and to attend to moment-to-moment awareness of elements of the field. The emphasis is on the subjective world as the client perceives it.

Gestalt therapy has adopted Martin Buber's dialogical philosophy of relationship to capture the spirit of the I/Thou relationship between therapist and client.[1] The healing that occurs in psychotherapy is a result of the quality of the meeting that occurs between client and therapist. Practicing in a dialogical manner, Gestalt therapists attempt to be fully present, convey to the client that they comprehend and accept the other's experience, and vigilantly attend to the impact of each of their interventions.

The goal of Gestalt therapy is, quite simply, the restoration of awareness. The essential method involves following the aspects of the client's experience of self and of environment that become figural or salient for the client. Gestalt therapists will selectively bring aspects of their own moment-to-moment experience, what is figural for them, into contact with the client. In Gestalt therapy, we are not trying to get anywhere or make something in particular happen. Rather, our work is designed to heighten the client's awareness of the present moments as they unfold. Change occurs through attention to what is, not by striving toward preordained objectives.[2]

Assessment of Ruth

Gestalt therapy emphasizes healthy functioning and interruption in healthy functioning. As such, therapists do not use the language of "pathology," or "normal" and "abnormal." Instead, individuals are viewed as having the capacity to self-regulate in their dealings with the various environments they encounter throughout life. Contact with the environment can be satisfying or interrupted in a variety of ways. Gestalt therapists' assessment involves examining the process that occurs as the individual interacts with self and environment.

Instead of a *DSM-IV-TR* diagnosis, the Gestalt therapist assesses to determine a "functional diagnosis." The need–fulfillment cycle is one model used to assess a client's level of functioning in two primary and related areas: To what degree is the client aware of self and environment, and can the client move into contact with aspects of the environment in ways that meet needs, achieve self-regulation, and promote growth and change? The need–fulfillment model outlines a "cycle of experience," which begins with physical or emotional sensations and proceeds through awareness (a sharpened sense of meaning), excitement, action, and toward contact with the environment. A functional diagnosis allows the Gestalt therapist to assist clients to understand exactly how they experience interruptions in the natural process of need identification and fulfillment. This is eminently more useful to clients than telling them they are depressed or have panic attacks or have an adjustment disorder.

Assessment is an ongoing process embedded in the dialogue between client and therapist (not separate from or occurring before the therapy itself). Gestalt therapists assess in two ways.

First, hypotheses are formed as the therapist listens to clients talk about their lives outside the therapy session. For example, from Ruth's autobiography we learn that she is frequently flooded with powerful sensations (panic, dizziness) that do not lead to a sharpened awareness that could move Ruth into contact with her environment. Instead, she translates her sensations of fear into worry patterns about dying or losing control, and that cycle of experience ends without closure. The panic attacks continue because Ruth is unable to move from the sensation level into some type of action (for example, talking about her anxiety with another) and contact. Ruth also sets goals in her life, such as losing weight or getting a job, but does not engage in actions to reach those goals. She imagines that if she were different she would be happier, or in Gestalt therapy terms "be in more satisfying contact with the environment."

The second and primary way the Gestalt therapist assesses clients' level of awareness and contacting style is by attending to how clients are in contact with the therapist in the therapy session itself. Clients' diminished awareness and ways of making or interrupting contact will become manifest in the relationship with the therapist. The therapy relationship becomes a key vehicle for clients to learn more about how they experience themselves and how they can bring that awareness into contact with the therapist.

Gestalt therapy is practiced in both brief and longer-term contexts. The client's functional diagnosis can be determined relatively quickly through history taking and attending to the client's level of awareness and the quality of contact made in the therapeutic relationship. In a brief therapy model, the therapist supports the client's understanding of his or her characteristic ways of diminishing awareness and contact using the need–fulfillment cycle as a tool to aid in this understanding. Clients can do homework assignments between sessions and continue to examine their own awareness and contacting processes after the therapy is complete. In a longer therapy model, anachronistic patterns of contacting, which are artifacts of past creative adjustments, are examined and shift with more intensive and sustained support from the Gestalt therapist.

Key Issues and Themes

From her autobiography, certain key issues emerge about how Ruth makes contact with her environment. For much of her life Ruth has concentrated on what others want or expect her to be. Operating in that mode has taken Ruth away from paying attention to what she wants from others. Satisfactory contact begins with attention to self—what one is experiencing at the moment and what one is drawn toward in the environment. The payoff for Ruth in living for others has been security. By avoiding herself, she has kept others around her. She fears change in general and attending to her own wants and desires in particular because that could rupture the confluence with others on which she has come to depend. She has already lost her parents. She fears that any further demonstration of her needs and wants could drive her husband away.

The dread and doom of her anxiety experience could very well be a manifestation of this conflict between Ruth's natural inclination to begin to pay more attention to herself and what she needs from others and the learned but unaware response to block those kind of awarenesses, fearing they could lead to being abandoned and left unable to care for herself.

These points are drawn from her autobiographical information and must be viewed as purely hunches until the therapy with Ruth begins. The themes we will actually work with must arise in the session, within the dialogue between Ruth and the therapist, not from clever interpretations in the therapist's head.

Therapeutic Interventions

Gestalt therapy proceeds by watching and listening to clients as they describe what it is like to be in their experience as they sit with you during a therapy session. Assessment, "diagnoses," and identification of themes and issues follow from practicing in a phenomenological and dialogic way. In this dialogue with Ruth, my goals are to assist Ruth in identifying a "figure" or an experience that becomes salient for her, to heighten her awareness of that experience, and to explore how she might make contact with me about that figure of interest.

THERAPIST: What are you aware of, Ruth, as we begin today?

RUTH: Recently I've become aware that I live for others. I give and give until there is little left to give.

THERAPIST: How is it for you to give so much?

RUTH: Exhausting and frustrating. The expectations and demands of my husband and children never end, and I never feel like I am doing enough.

THERAPIST: What do you notice as you tell me this?

RUTH: I don't understand your question.

THERAPIST: You have been telling me about how much you give to others and how tiring that is. What are you experiencing right now?

RUTH: Well, I'm not tired.

THERAPIST: Take a minute and check in with yourself.

RUTH [*After a minute*]: I realize I don't do this very often.

THERAPIST: What are you discovering?

RUTH: I feel a little nervous, but it's different from the anxiety and panic I usually feel.

THERAPIST: Pay attention to the nervousness and tell me what you can about it.

RUTH: My stomach is fluttering, and I have lots of energy in my legs and arms. I did some theatre in college, and this feels like those moments before I would go on stage.

THERAPIST: From your description and the way you look right now, it sounds like you might be excited.

RUTH: Yeah, that fits—excited and apprehensive. I realize I don't know exactly what will happen next.

THERAPIST: You are looking at me very intently. Are you aware of that?

RUTH: I am now. [*Fidgets in her chair and looks away*] Do you have any ideas about how I can stop giving so much?

THERAPIST: I don't have any idea about that at this moment, Ruth. Tell me what you are aware of now.

RUTH: When you pointed out how I was looking at you, I got scared.

THERAPIST: Scared?

RUTH: Yeah, a wave of anxiety came over me.

THERAPIST: And now?

RUTH: Now I am having trouble looking at you. It's more comfortable to look out the window.

THERAPIST: Would you be willing to experiment for a few minutes?

RUTH: Sure, if you think it would help. What should I do?

THERAPIST: You agree to experiment without any information about what I have in mind?

RUTH: Sounds like me. I agree to a lot before I know what I'm getting into. To be honest, I'm not sure I want to experiment. What would be the objectives of this experiment?

THERAPIST: Experiments in Gestalt therapy don't have any particular pre-set goals. The purpose would be to help you learn more about yourself.

RUTH: Actually, I like the idea of not having goals. I never seem to reach the ones I set in my life.

THERAPIST: The experiment I am proposing would be to try switching back and forth between eye contact with me and looking away . . . to see what happens for you in each mode.

RUTH: That sounds easy enough. I would like to try it. [*Ruth spends more time looking away from the therapist at first but gradually increases time in eye contact.*]

THERAPIST [*After several minutes*]: So what do you notice?

RUTH: Looking away is easier, more comfortable. When I look at you, the anxiety returns.

THERAPIST: You are looking at me now. How is this for you?

RUTH: Like I said, I feel anxious, edgy [*She pauses, takes a deep breath*]. Actually, right now I feel lost and confused. I get this feeling a lot.

THERAPIST: Finish this sentence for me. Right now I'm lost and confused because _____.

RUTH: . . . because I know you must want something from me, but I don't know what it is. I know how to be a good mother and wife, but it's not clear what I should do here.

THERAPIST: I saw something shift in your expression. Did you notice that too?

RUTH: Yeah, the feeling has changed.

THERAPIST: What's going on now?

RUTH [*With a look of mild surprise*]: I'm frustrated. No, that's not all of it. I'm angry. [*She smiles.*]

THERAPIST: You seem amused by that.

RUTH: It's different. I never get angry except at myself.

THERAPIST: And this time?

RUTH: I'm angry at you.

THERAPIST: Will you say that again, and look at me when you do?

RUTH: Another experiment? OK, I'll try. I'm angry at you for not telling me what you want from me.

THERAPIST: What happens as you say that to me?

RUTH: I feel good, energized, and even powerful. [*Ruth sits silently, looking relaxed and content; then she looks away and begins to fidget.*]

THERAPIST: Where did you go?

RUTH: Images of my husband and father came in. I'm angry at them too. I don't know exactly what they want from me either. [*Ruth's expression changes again; she is quiet and tears begin.*]

THERAPIST: What's happening now?

RUTH: I'm so caught up in giving to others that I don't get what I want. I wouldn't know where to start to find out.

THERAPIST: We could start here. Is there anything you want from me now?

RUTH: When I started therapy with you, I wanted you to tell me what I should do.

THERAPIST: And now?

RUTH: I want you to be interested in how I feel and the things I think about.

THERAPIST: Look at me again Ruth. What do you see?

RUTH: I see a kind face. I see interest, even concern and care. It's very comfortable for me now to have this eye contact.

🐚 **Process Commentary**   Experienced basketball players talk about "letting the game come to them." They use this phrase in contrast to "forcing the action" or "trying to make something happen." Practicing Gestalt therapy in a dialogic, phenomenological way is very similar. Therapists take their time, follow their clients' lead, and let the dialogue unfold without rushing or pushing for results.

I began the session by inviting Ruth to check in with herself as she talked about issues in her life. That intervention brings her into the present moment and brings her to the awareness that she rarely attends to her immediate experience. The next several interchanges follow a cycle of experience as Ruth identifies a sensation that leads to an awareness and a sense of excitement about what will happen next.

A contact boundary phenomenon (or interruption) occurs at this point that is a key theme in Ruth's life. Instead of carrying on into action and contact that would be anchored in what Ruth wants, she scans the field (the environment) to ascertain what is wanted from her at that moment. When I point out how intently she is looking at me, her anxiety level increases, and she deflects by changing the subject.

I suggest an experiment. Notice how the experiment emerges "organically" from the moment-to-moment dialogue between us. She was already looking at me and looking away. The experiment simply allows us to explore that behavior more intentionally. As Ruth experiments with eye contact, the figure or theme of our session comes into sharper focus. When she looks at me, she experiences a set of feelings related to an assumption that I want something from her and that she doesn't know how to find out what it is.

Ruth's assumption that I want something from her could be defined as a projection, one of the boundary disturbances delineated in Gestalt theory. Typically, a Gestalt therapist would respond to this projection by requiring Ruth to own her own experience. When Ruth said that, I did not want anything from her. I could tell her that, to clarify the boundary condition, but I chose not to make that clarification. Instead, I stayed with Ruth's ongoing experience. As she perceived me as wanting something from her, what was that like for her?

Allowing Ruth to run with her perception of me as wanting something from her led her to another awareness. She was angry at me—and others—for not being clear about what I wanted. A brief experiment directed the anger outward rather than to her typical style of self-criticism. Telling me she was angry at me seemed to complete a cycle of experience (there are many in any therapy session). Ruth acted on the environment, and her contact with me led to a momentary sense of contentment. As that figure reached completion, another emerged. Ruth realized that she doesn't attend to what she wants. Invited to do that as we end the session, she identifies a specific want—my interest in her—and through eye contact sees accurately (without projection) that I am interested.

Like all of us, Ruth has characteristic ways of organizing and making meaning out of her moment-to-moment experience of herself and her environment. These ways of making sense out of experience are frequently shaped more by past experiences than by present needs and opportunities. The present moment is accessed through awareness, which is explored through the therapist's active interest in Ruth's ongoing experience.

As Ruth attended to herself and to contact with the therapist, one of her characteristic ways of perceiving relationships formed into an awareness. She saw the therapist as wanting something from her. As the session progressed, that figure eventually shifted to what she wanted from the therapist. This session demonstrates how change occurs through attention to "what is" and how the exact nature of change cannot be aimed for or predicted by a Gestalt therapist.

What Ruth perceives others to want from her and what she wants from others is a key theme, and I believe it will reappear in future sessions. Ruth's inclination to organize her experience of others as having expectations of her she must meet represents a creative adjustment she once made when the field conditions supported that interpretation and her efforts to give to others were reinforced. This probably began in relation to her parents and church. Currently, her relationships with her husband, children, and college professors replicate those same field conditions.

As my therapy relationship with Ruth proceeds, I continue to encourage her to be aware of her moment-to-moment experience. Present awareness, by definition, will counter her tendency to operate on automatic pilot in relation to me and others. Ruth will continue to learn, as she did in this session, how to accurately assess the present situation. Eventually, Ruth will be able to apply this ability to be in the present to other relationships in her life.

Jerry Corey's Work With Ruth From a Gestalt Perspective

In my version of Gestalt work with Ruth, I watch for cues from Ruth about what she is experiencing in the here and now. By attending to what she is expressing both verbally and nonverbally, I suggest experiments during our sessions. In the *CD-ROM for Integrative Counseling*, Session 7 ("Emotive Focus in Counseling"), I demonstrate how I create experiments to heighten Ruth's awareness. In this particular session I employ a Gestalt experiment, asking Ruth to talk to me as if I were John. During this experiment, Ruth becomes quite emotional. You will see ways of exploring emotional material and integrating this work into a cognitive framework as well.

Basic Assumptions

Approaching Ruth as a Gestalt therapist, I assume that she can deal effectively with her life problems, especially if she becomes fully aware of what is happening in and around her. My central task as her therapist is to help her fully experience her being in the here and now by first realizing how she is preventing herself from feeling and experiencing in the present. My approach is basically noninterpretive. I will ask Ruth to provide her own interpretations of her experiences. I expect her to participate in experiments, which consist of trying new ways of relating and responding.

I operate under the assumption that it is useful to invite clients to work in the present as much as possible. A basic premise of Gestalt therapy is that by experiencing conflicts directly, instead of merely talking about them, clients will expand their own level of awareness and integrate the fragmented and unknown parts of their personality.

Assessment of Ruth

Ruth has never learned that it is acceptable to have and to express feelings. True, she does feel a good deal of guilt, but she rarely expresses the resentment that she likely feels. Any person who is as devoted to others as she is probably feels some resentment at not having received the appreciation she believes is due her. Ruth does not allow herself to get angry with her father, who has punished her by withholding his affection and approval. She does not experience much anger toward John, despite the fact that here again she does not feel recognized. The same is true for both her sons and daughters. Ruth has made a lifetime career out of giving and doing for her family. She maintains that she gets little in return, yet she rarely expresses how this arrangement affects her. It appears that Ruth is keeping all of these feelings locked inside herself, and this is getting in the way of her feeling free. A lot of Ruth's energy is going into blocking her experience of threatening feelings, sensations, and thoughts. Our therapy will encourage her to express her moment-by-moment experience so that her energy is freed up for creative pursuits instead of being spent on growth-inhibiting defenses.

Goals of Therapy

My goal is to provide a context in which Ruth can expand her awareness of what is going on within herself and also how she interacts with others. With awareness, Ruth will be able to recognize denied aspects of herself and proceed toward the reintegration of the many facets within herself. Therapy will provide the necessary intervention to help her gain awareness of what she is thinking, feeling, and doing in the present. As Ruth comes to recognize and experience blocks to maturity, she can begin experimenting with different ways of being.

Therapeutic Procedures

I draw heavily on interventions aimed at intensifying here-and-now experiencing. These techniques are designed to help Ruth focus on what is going on within her body and to accentuate whatever she may be feeling. In this sense I am active in my sessions with Ruth. However, I take my cues from her, largely by paying attention to what she is saying and not saying. It is essential that I work within the context of what emerges for Ruth as we talk with each other rather than imposing my agenda of what I think Ruth should explore. From the cues I pick up from Ruth, I create experiments that enable her to heighten whatever she is experiencing.

Some of the experiments that Ruth might carry out may entail giving expression to unexpressed body movements or gestures, or they may involve talking in a different tone of voice. I may ask her to experiment with rehearsing out loud those thoughts that are racing through her—ones she usually keeps to herself. Ruth will be invited to try new behavior and see what these experiments can teach her. If Ruth learns how to pay attention to whatever it is she is experiencing at any moment, this awareness itself can lead to change.

JERRY: Ruth, as we sit here, what are you aware of?

RUTH: I'm having a hard time knowing what I want to talk about today. There are so many things going on, and I want to cover everything. I'm impatient and want to get to work.

JERRY: I can appreciate wanting to do a lot in a short time. Let me suggest that you sit for a few moments and listen to yourself. What is it that you'd most want for this hour?

RUTH: I just keep feeling guilty over all that I haven't been, especially as a mother. Right now I'm feeling pretty sad because of all the mistakes I've made with my kids.

JERRY: Does any child stand out for you?

RUTH: Jennifer! She's on my mind a lot. No matter what I try, nothing seems to work. I read books on parenting and that doesn't help. I just feel guilty!

JERRY: Ruth, rather than telling me about how guilty you feel over not having been the mother you think you should have been to Jennifer, how about simply listing all the ways that you feel this guilt?

RUTH: Oh, that's easy—there are so many ways! I feel guilty because I haven't been understanding enough, because I've been too easy on her and haven't set limits, because I've been away at college when she needed me during her difficult years. And in some ways I feel responsible for the problems she is faced with—I could go on!

JERRY: So go on. Say more. Make the list as long as you can. [*I am encouraging her to say aloud and unrehearsed many of the things she tells herself endlessly in her head. She continues to speak of her guilt.*]

RUTH [*Letting out a deep sigh*]: There! That's it!

JERRY: And what is that sigh about?

RUTH: Just relief, I suppose. I feel a little better. I just had a flash. You know, I resent Jennifer for expecting me to be the perfect mother. After all, I've gone out of my way for all of my kids. But Jennifer never gives me a clue that I do anything right for her.

JERRY: And what is it like for you to acknowledge that you resent the expectation that you have to be the perfect mother?

RUTH: Well, now I'm feeling guilty again that I have such negative feelings!

I am aware that Ruth is not going to rid herself forever of her guilt. If she does not let her guilt control her, however, she can make room for other feelings. Based on Ruth's bringing up her resentment, which I suspect is related to her guilt, I propose the following experiment:

JERRY: If you're willing to go further, I'd like you to repeat your list of guilts, only this time say "I resent you for . . ." instead of "I feel guilty over . . ."

RUTH: But I don't feel resentment—it's the guilt!

JERRY: I know, but would you be willing to go ahead with the experiment and see what happens?

RUTH [*After some hesitation and discussion of the value of doing this*]: I resent you for expecting me to always be understanding of you. I resent you for demanding so much of my time. I resent you for all the trouble you got yourself into and the nights of sleep I lost over this. I resent you for making me feel guilty. I resent you for not understanding me. I resent you for expecting affection but not giving me any.

[handwritten in margin: Externalization]

My rationale for asking Ruth to convert her list of guilts into a list of resentments is that doing so may help her direct her anger to the sources where it belongs, rather than inward. She has so much guilt partly because she directs her anger toward herself, and this keeps her distant from some people who are significant to her. Ruth becomes more and more energetic with her expression of resentments.

JERRY: Ruth, let me sit in for Jennifer for a bit. Continue talking to me, and tell me the ways in which you resent me.

RUTH [*Becoming more emotional and expressive*]: It's hard for me to talk to you. You and I haven't really talked in such a long time. [*Tears well up in her eyes.*] I give and give, and all you do is take and take. There's no end to it!

JERRY: Tell Jennifer what you want from her.

RUTH [*Pausing and then, with a burst of energy, shouting*]: I want to be more like you! I'm envious of you. I wish I could be as daring and as alive as you. Wow, I'm surprised at what I just said.

JERRY: Keep talking to Jennifer, and tell her more about how you're feeling right now.

With Ruth's heightened emotionality she is able to say some things to Jennifer that she has never said. She leaves this session with some new insights: Her feelings of guilt are more often feelings of resentment; her anger toward Jennifer is based on envy and jealousy; and the things she dislikes about Jennifer are some of the things she would like for herself.

EXPLORING THE POLARITIES WITHIN RUTH In later sessions Ruth brings up the many ways she feels pulled in different directions. What emerges for her is all the expectations that her parents had for her and the many expectations others still have for her. She reports that she doesn't always want to be the "perfect person." She resents having to be so good and never being allowed to have fun. As she talks, she becomes aware of the polarities within her that seem incompatible. We continue working with some of the splits within Ruth's personality. My aim is not to get rid of her feelings but to let her experience them and learn to integrate all the factions of her personality. She will not get rid of one side of her personality that she does not like by attempting to deny it, but she can learn to recognize the side that controls her by expressing it.

RUTH: For so many years I had to be the perfect minister's daughter. I lost myself in being the proper "good girl." I'd like to be more spontaneous and playful and not worry constantly about what other people would think. Sometimes when I'm being silly, I hear this voice in my head that tells me to be proper. It's as if there are two of me: one that's all proper and prim and the other that wants to be footloose and free.

JERRY: Which side do you feel most right now, the proper side or the uninhibited side?

RUTH: Well, the proper and conservative side is surely the stronger in me.

JERRY: I have an idea of an experiment that I'd like you to try. Are you willing?

RUTH: OK, I'm ready to work.

JERRY: Here are a couple of chairs. I'd like you to sit in this chair here and be the proper side of you. Talk to the uninhibited side, which is sitting in this other chair.

RUTH: I wish you would grow up! You should act like an adult and stop being a silly kid. If I listened to you, I'd really be in trouble now. You're so impulsive and demanding.

JERRY: OK, how about changing and sitting in the chair over here and speaking from your daring side? What does she have to say to the proper side over there?

RUTH: It's about time you let your hair down and had some fun. You're so cautious! Sure, you're safe, but you're also a very, very dull person. I know you'd like to be me more often.

JERRY: Change chairs again, talking back to the daring side.

RUTH: Well I'd rather be safe than sorry! [*Her face flushes*]

JERRY: And what do you want to say back to your proper side?

RUTH [*Changing chairs*]: That's just your trouble. Always be safe! And where is this getting you? You'll die being safe and secure.

This exchange of chairs goes on for some time. Becoming her daring side is much more uncomfortable for Ruth. After a while she lets herself get into the daring side and chides the prude sitting across from her. She accuses her of letting life slip by, points out how she is just like her mother, and tells her how her being so proper stops her from having any fun. This experiment shows Ruth the difference between thinking about conflicts and actually letting herself experience those conflicts. She sees more clearly that she is being pulled in many directions, that she is a complex person, and that she will not get rid of feelings by pretending that they don't exist. Gradually, she experiences more freedom in accepting the different parts within her, without the need to cut out certain parts of her.

A DIALOGUE WITH RUTH'S FATHER In another session Ruth brings up how it was for her as a child, especially in relation to her cold and ungiving father.

I ask her not merely to report what happened but also to bring her father into the room now and talk to him as she did as a child. She goes back to a past event and relives it—the time at 6 years old when she was reprimanded by her father for "playing doctor" with a friend. She begins by saying how scared she was then and how she did not know what to say to him after he had caught her in sexual play. So I encourage her to stay with her scared feelings and to tell her father all the things that she was feeling then but did not say. Then I say to Ruth:

> JERRY: Tell your father how you wish he had acted with you. [*As Ruth talks to her father, she strokes her left hand with her right hand. At a later point I hand her a pillow.*] Let yourself be the father you wished you had, and talk to little Ruth. The pillow is you, and you are your father. Talk to little Ruth.

> RUTH [*This brings up intense feelings, and for a long time she says nothing. She sits silently, holding "Ruth" and caressing her lovingly. Eventually, some words follow.*]: Ruth, I have always loved you, and you have always been special to me. It has just been hard for me to show what I feel. I wanted to let you know how much you mattered to me, but I didn't know how.[3]

PROCESS COMMENTARY   During the time that Ruth is doing her work, I pay attention to what she is communicating nonverbally. For example, she describes her heart, saying it feels as if it wants to break; the knots in her stomach; the tension in her neck and shoulders; the tightness in her head; her clenched fists; the tears in her eyes; and the smile across her lips. At appropriate moments I call her attention to her body and teach her how to pay attention to what she is experiencing in her body. At different times I ask her to try the experiment of "becoming" her breaking heart (or any other bodily sensation) and giving that part of her body "voice."

Ruth exhibits some reluctance to getting involved in these Gestalt experiments, but after challenging herself and overcoming her feelings of looking foolish, she is generally amazed at what comes out of these procedures. Without my interpretations she begins to discover for herself how some of her past experiences are related to her present feelings of being stuck in so many ways.

A theme that emerges over and over in Ruth's work is how alive material becomes when she brings an experience into the present. She does not merely intellectualize about her problems, nor does she engage in much talking about events. The emphasis is on participating in experiments to intensify whatever she is experiencing. When she does bring a past event into the present by actually allowing herself to reexperience that event, it often provides her with valuable insights. Ruth does not need interpretations from me as her therapist. By paying attention on a moment-to-moment basis to whatever she is experiencing, Ruth is able to see the meaning for herself.

Ruth's awareness is, by itself, a powerful catalyst for her change. Before she can hope to be different in any respect, she first has to be aware of how she is.

The focus of much of her work is on *what* she is experiencing at any given moment, as well as *how.* Thus, when she mentions being anxious, she focuses on *how* this anxiety is manifested in a knot in her stomach or a headache. I focus her on here-and-now experiencing and away from thinking about *why.* Asking why would remove Ruth from her feelings. Another key focus is on dealing with unfinished business. Business from the past does seek completion, and it persists in Ruth's present until she faces and deals with feelings that she has not previously expressed.

Questions for Reflection

1. Dr. Frew describes an assessment process that grows out of an I/Thou dialogue between Ruth and her therapist. What do you think of this approach to assessment?
2. Dr. Frew maintains that in Gestalt therapy the interventions are based on observing and listening to what is in the client's present awareness. He takes his time, follows Ruth's lead, and lets the dialogue unfold without rushing or pushing for results. What are your thoughts about using this approach to designing therapeutic interventions?
3. Gestalt interventions are useful in working with the splits and polarities within a person. As you can see, Ruth has problems because she is not able to reconcile or integrate polarities: dependent versus independent, giving to others versus asking and receiving, and the need for security versus the need to leave secure ways and create new ways of being. Are you aware of struggling with any of Ruth's polarities in your life now?
4. Can you think of some ways to blend the cognitive focus of Adlerian therapy with the emotional themes that are likely to emerge through Gestalt work with Ruth? Provide a few examples of how you could work with her feelings and cognitions by combining concepts and methods from the two approaches.
5. What main differences do you see between the way Dr. Frew worked with Ruth (as a Gestalt therapist) and the way Dr. Cain worked with her (as a person-centered therapist)? What about the differences in the way I counseled Ruth from these two perspectives?
6. Think about Ruth as being from each of the following ethnic and cultural backgrounds: Native American, African American, Latino, and Asian American. How might you tailor Gestalt experiments in working with her if she were a member of each of these groups? What are some of the advantages and disadvantages of drawing on concepts and interventions from Gestalt therapy in working with cultural themes in her life?
7. What specific areas of unfinished business are most evident to you as you read about Ruth? Do any of her unexpressed feelings bring to awareness any of your own business from the past? What potential unresolved areas in your own life might interfere with your ability to work effectively with Ruth? How might you deal with these feelings if they came up as you were counseling her?

Notes

See the DVD/Online program entitled *Theory in Practice: The Case of Stan* (Session 6: Gestalt Therapy Applied to the Case of Stan), which focuses on Stan reporting a dream in Gestalt fashion and his exploration of the personal meaning of his dream.

1. For a discussion of the dialogical philosophy of relationship, see M. Buber (1970), *I and Thou* (New York: Scribner's).

2. For a more detailed discussion of the key concepts of Gestalt therapy, see G. Corey (2009), *Theory and Practice of Counseling and Psychotherapy* (8th ed., Belmont, CA: Brooks/Cole). Chapter 8 ("Gestalt Therapy") outlines the basic elements of the therapeutic process.

3. The *CD-ROM for Integrative Counseling* has a vivid illustration of the power of Gestalt experiments. In Session 11 ("Understanding How the Past Influences the Present"), Ruth symbolically talks to her father. I ask her to bring the past event to life by talking directly to her father as the scared 6-year-old child.

CHAPTER SEVEN

Case Approach to Behavior Therapy

General Overview of Behavior Therapy

The main goal of behavior therapy is to eliminate clients' maladaptive behavior patterns and replace them with more constructive ones. Therapists identify thought patterns that lead to behavioral problems and then teach new ways of thinking that are designed to change the clients' ways of acting.

Some of the main behavioral techniques are systematic desensitization, in vivo exposure, relaxation methods, reinforcement, modeling, social skills training, self-management programs, mindfulness and acceptance approaches, behavioral rehearsal, coaching, and other multimodal techniques. Assessment and diagnosis are done at the outset to determine a treatment plan. "What," "how," and "when" questions are used (but not "why" questions).

This approach has the advantage of specifying clear and concrete behavioral goals that can be monitored and measured. Because therapy begins with an assessment of baseline data, the degree of progress can be evaluated by comparing clients' behavior on a given dimension at any point in the therapy with the baseline data. Moreover, assessment and treatment occur simultaneously. Clients are frequently challenged to answer the question, "Is what we are doing in here helping you make the changes you desire?" With this information, clients are in the best position to determine when they are ready to terminate.

A Multimodal Behavior Therapist's Perspective on Ruth

by Arnold A. Lazarus, PhD, ABPP

Introduction

Multimodal therapy is a broad-based, systematic, and comprehensive approach to behavior therapy that calls for technical eclecticism (that is, the use of effective techniques regardless of their point of origin). The multimodal orientation assumes that clients are usually troubled by a multitude of specific problems, which should be dealt with using a wide range of specific techniques. Whenever feasible, therapists should select empirically supported treatments of choice for specific disorders. The comprehensive assessment, or therapeutic modus operandi, attends to each area of a client's BASIC I.D. (B = behavior, A = affect, S = sensation, I = imagery, C = cognition, I = interpersonal relationships, and D = drugs and biological factors). Discrete and interactive problems throughout each of the foregoing modalities are identified, and appropriate techniques are selected to deal with each difficulty. A genuine and empathic client–therapist relationship provides the soil that enables the techniques to take root.

Multimodal Assessment of Ruth

In Ruth's case more than three dozen specific and interrelated problems can be identified using the diagnostic, treatment-oriented BASIC I.D. methodology:

Behavior: fidgeting, avoidance of eye contact, and rapid speaking; poor sleep pattern; tendency to cry easily; overeating; various avoidance behaviors

Affect: anxiety; panic (especially in class and at night when trying to sleep); depression; fears of criticism and rejection; pangs of religious guilt; trapped feelings; self-abnegation

Sensation: dizziness; palpitations; fatigue and boredom; headaches; tendency to deny, reject, or suppress her sexuality; overeating to the point of nausea

Imagery: ongoing negative parental messages; residual images of hellfire and brimstone; unfavorable body image and poor self-image; view of herself as aging and losing her looks; inability to visualize herself in a professional role

Cognition: self-identity questions ("Who and what am I?"); worrying thoughts (death and dying); doubts about her right to succeed professionally; categorical imperatives ("shoulds," "oughts," and "musts"); search for new values; self-denigration

Interpersonal relationships: unassertiveness (especially putting the needs of others before her own); fostering her family's dependence on her; limited pleasure outside her role as mother and wife; problems with children; unsatisfactory relationship with her husband (yet fear of losing him); looking to the therapist for direction; still seeking parental approval

Drugs and biological factors: overweight; lack of an exercise program; various physical complaints for which medical examinations reveal no organic pathology

Like Jerry Corey, I typically don't think in diagnostic terms. Indeed, a multimodal clinician sees the range of problems across the BASIC I.D. as the "diagnosis." It does not make sense to me to present one particular diagnosis. Many of the labels contained in the *DSM-IV-TR* would seem to apply to Ruth. These include:

300.4: dysthymic disorder

300.01: panic disorder

309.28: adjustment disorder with mixed anxiety and depressed mood

V61.1: partner relational problem

313.82: identity problem

If forced to pick one of these labels, I would say that adjustment disorder with mixed anxiety and depressed mood comes closest to covering her main difficulties.

Selecting Techniques and Strategies

The goal of multimodal therapy is not to eliminate each and every identified problem. Rather, after establishing rapport with Ruth and developing a sound therapeutic alliance, I would select several key issues in concert with her. Given the fact that she is generally tense, agitated, restless, and anxious, one of the first antidotes might be the use of relaxation training. Some people respond with paradoxical increases in tension when practicing relaxation, and it is necessary to determine what particular type of relaxation will suit an individual client (for example, direct muscular tension–relaxation contrasts, autogenic training, meditation, positive mental imagery, diaphragmatic breathing, or a combination of methods). I have no reason to believe Ruth would not respond to deep muscle relaxation, positive imagery, and self-calming statements.

The next pivotal area is her unassertiveness and self-entitlements. I will employ behavior rehearsal and role playing. Our sessions will also explore her right to be professional and successful. Cognitive restructuring will address her categorical imperatives and will endeavor to reduce the "shoulds," "oughts," and "musts" she inflicts on herself. Imagery techniques may be given prominence, and her homework assignment may include using a particular image over and over until she feels in control of the situation. For example, I may ask Ruth to picture herself going back in a time machine so that she can meet herself as a little girl and provide her alter ego with reassurance about the religious guilts her father imposed.

> THERAPIST: Can you visualize yourself stepping into a time machine and traveling back in time to meet up with yourself as a very young child?
>
> RUTH: OK, I think I can do that.
>
> THERAPIST: How far back in time would you like to travel? At what age would you wish to meet up with your alter ego, your much younger self?
>
> RUTH: I see myself as a 10-year-old child.
>
> THERAPIST: The special time machine and you are now journeying back into the past. [*Pause*] Now, please imagine yourself stepping out of the machine, and there you see a little girl. It is you, Little Ruth, at 10 years of age. She looks up at you but does not realize that she is looking at her adult self. But this Little Ruth senses something very special about you, and she will pay close attention to whatever you say to her. [*Pause*] Picture yourself giving Little Ruth a hug. [*Pause*] Now, what would you like to tell her about your father's preachings?
>
> RUTH: [*Big Ruth tells Little Ruth that her father is thoroughly misguided and not to heed the religious guilt he is imposing on her.*]

Most people resonate with this imagery and, with considerable emotion, they narrate the supportive, corrective, reparative, and encouraging points they would share with their alter ego. If they do not spontaneously go there, the therapist will prompt them in this direction. After 5 or 10 minutes (depending on how engrossed they remain in the image) clients are asked to reenter the time machine and go forward until they step out into the present. Many people have found this to be a robust and helpful procedure, and it can be practiced at home several times a day as well as in therapy sessions. The active mechanism behind this procedure is presumed to be a form of desensitization and cognitive restructuring.

If Ruth and her husband agree to it, some marital counseling (and possibly some sex therapy) may be recommended, followed by some family therapy sessions aimed at enhancing the interpersonal climate in the home. Indeed, if Ruth becomes a more relaxed, confident, assertive person, John and her children may need help to cope with her new behaviors. Moreover, I can try to circumvent any attempts at "sabotage" by him or the children.

If Ruth feels up to it, I will teach her sensible eating habits and will embark on a weight reduction and exercise regimen. Referral to a local diet center may be a useful adjunct.

As a part of the assessment process, I ask Ruth to fill out the 15-page Multimodal Life History Inventory.[1] This process enables me to detect a wide range of problems throughout the BASIC I.D. The following dialogue ensues:

THERAPIST: On page 12 of the questionnaire, you wrote "no" to the question "Do you eat three well-balanced meals each day?" and also to the question "Do you get regular physical exercise?" And on page 15, you wrote that you frequently drink coffee, overeat, eat junk foods, and have weight problems.

RUTH: Maybe I should go on a diet again.

THERAPIST: Well, the problem with going on a diet is that people soon come off it and gain weight, perhaps even more weight than they lost. I think the goal is to develop sensible eating patterns. To begin with, I have a list of foods a nutritionist gave me, stuff that we should avoid eating or cut down on. [*The list contains mainly foods with a high fat content, especially those with saturated fats, as well as foods with a high sugar content.*] For starters, would you be willing to take it home and see how many of these items you can cut out of your diet?

RUTH: Certainly.

THERAPIST: I wonder if we could make a pact?

RUTH: About what?

THERAPIST: That you would agree to take a brisk 1- to 2-mile walk at least three times a week.

RUTH: I can do that.

THERAPIST: By the way, there's an excellent diet center in your neighborhood. They have a program in which they train people to understand food contents and to easily calculate the amount of fiber and calories you require. They also run support groups. It's often easier to develop new eating habits when you're part of a group instead of trying to do it on your own.

RUTH: Yes, I know the place you mean. I've often thought of going there. Do you really think it would be a good idea?

THERAPIST: Yes, I really do.

Therapy Sessions With Ruth

After I draw up Ruth's Modality Profile (BASIC I.D. chart), the clinical dialogue proceeds as follows:

THERAPIST: I've made up a list, under seven separate headings, of what your main problems seem to be. For example, under behavior I have the following: fidgeting, avoidance of eye contact, rapid speaking, poor sleep pattern, tendency to cry easily, overeating, and various avoidance behaviors.

RUTH: That's what I do; they're all correct. [*Pause*] But I'm not exactly sure what you mean by "various avoidance behaviors."

THERAPIST: Well, it seems to me that you often avoid doing things that you'd like to do; instead, you do what you think others expect of you. You avoid following through on your plans to exercise and to observe good eating habits. You avoid making certain decisions.

RUTH: I see what you mean. I guess I'm a pretty hopeless case. I'm so weak and panicky, such a basic coward, that I can't seem to make up my mind about anything these days.

THERAPIST: One thing you seem to be very good at and never avoid is putting yourself down. You sure won't feel helpless if you start taking emotional risks and if you're willing to speak your mind. What does that sound like to you?

RUTH: Are you asking me if I'd like to be more outgoing and less afraid?

THERAPIST: That's a good way of putting it. What do you think would happen if you changed in that regard?

RUTH: I'm not sure, but I certainly don't think my father would approve.

THERAPIST: And how about your husband?

RUTH [*Looking downcast*]: I see what you're getting at.

THERAPIST: Would you agree that you first tended to march to your father's drum and then handed most of the control over to your husband? [*Ruth is nodding affirmatively.*] Well, I think it's high time you become the architect and designer of your own life.

Ruth does not feel overwhelmed, so I discuss the other items on her Modality Profile. If she had showed signs of concern ("Oh my God! I have so many problems!"), I would have targeted only the most salient items and helped her work toward their mitigation or elimination.

Whenever feasible, I select data-based methods of treatment. Thus, in dealing with her panic attacks, I first explain the physiology of panic and the fight-or-flight response. Emphasis is placed on the distinction between adaptive and maladaptive anxiety. For example, anxiety is helpful when it prompts Ruth to study for an exam, but it is maladaptive when its intensity undermines her performance. Her anxiety reactions are examined in terms of their behavioral consequences; secondary affective responses (such as fear of fear); sensory reactions; the images, or mental pictures, they generate; their cognitive components; and their interpersonal effects. In each instance I apply specific strategies. Behaviorally, for example, I encourage her to stop avoiding situations and instead to confront them. In the cognitive modality, she is enjoined to challenge thoughts like "I must be going crazy!" or "I'm going to die!" and to replace them with these self-statements: "My doctor confirmed that I'm physically healthy." "Being anxious won't make me crazy!" Because so many people who suffer from panic tend to overbreathe (hyperventilate), I teach Ruth how to breathe more slowly and use her diaphragm, thereby dampening her physical symptoms. The adjunctive use of drug therapy such as the new generation of antidepressants may also be considered, especially if her progress is unduly slow.

It is usually important to deal with "pivotal events"—critical incidents or significant memories that seem to play a central role. Thus, in an effort to extinguish the guilt and proscriptions associated with her father's general remonstrations, especially the way he berated her for "playing doctor," I would employ the time travel method discussed earlier.

THERAPIST: Let's use that time machine method again. You step into the device, and you step out and see 6-year-old Little Ruth. The 39-year-old Ruth, you at present, looks at the 6-year-old Ruth, 33 years into the past. [*Pause*] Can you picture that?

RUTH [*Nods affirmatively*]: Oh yes, I see her all right.

THERAPIST: What is she doing?

RUTH: She's holding a rag doll in her right hand and sucking two fingers of her other hand.

THERAPIST: Can you tell if your visit to her has come before or after her father caught her playing doctor?

RUTH [*Pausing*]: Judging by the guilty look in her eyes, it must be after.

THERAPIST: Now Little Ruth looks at you, at 39-year-old Ruth. She doesn't realize that you really are her, 33 years into the future, a grown woman, a wife, a mother, Little Ruth all grown up. But she senses something special about you, and she feels very close to you and trusts you. Can you get into that image?

RUTH [*Softly*]: Yes.

THERAPIST: Good. Now what do you want to say to Little Ruth?

RUTH: First, I want to tell her not to buy into all that stuff about religion, the gospel, and all that guilt [*Pause*].

THERAPIST: Talk to her, explain it to her. She'll hear you. She'll listen to you.

As this dialogue continues, Ruth is encouraged to offer her 6-year-old alter ego some good advice, encouragement, and nonjudgmental insights.

Ruth becomes deeply involved and grows very emotional, especially when challenging the painful notions and events that have tended to haunt her. At the end of the exercise I ask Ruth to step into the time machine again and to travel forward into the present. A detailed discussion then ensues, and Ruth experiences reparative effects.

A Conjoint Session With Ruth and John

The treatment trajectory depends mainly on Ruth's readiness for change (for example, her willingness to take risks, be assertive, and challenge her dysfunctional thoughts) and the extent to which her husband is invested in keeping her subservient. John feels threatened by Ruth when she starts expressing and fulfilling herself, and conjoint sessions are essential to persuade him that he will be better off in the long run with a wife who feels personally satisfied rather than bitter, frustrated, and bored. Thus, I suggest to her that she encourage John to attend at least one therapy session with her. I tell her that I intend to go out of my way to bond with John so as to gain his compliance. In this connection, I have the following dialogue with Ruth and John:

THERAPIST [*Addressing John*]: Thank you for agreeing to meet with me. As you know, I've been trying to help Ruth overcome various fears and anxieties, and I believe she has made considerable headway. But now we're at a point where I need your input and assistance. I wonder if we can start by hearing your views on the subject.

JOHN [*Glancing at Ruth*]: What do you want to know?

THERAPIST: Quite a number of things. I'd like to know how you view her therapy, whether you think it was or is necessary, and if you think she has been helped. I'd like to hear your complaints about Ruth—after all, no marriage is perfect.

JOHN [*Addressing Ruth*]: Can I be perfectly honest?

RUTH: John, that's why we're here.

THERAPIST: Please be completely frank and above board.

JOHN: What do I call you?

THERAPIST: Let's not be formal or stuffy. Call me Arnold.

JOHN: Well, Arnold, the way I see it is that Ruth has bitten off more than she can chew. Things were pretty good until she decided to go to college. I don't think she can manage a career and a home. It's putting too much pressure on her. I mean, you know, I think if you take things away from the family, everyone suffers. It's not as if she needs to work for the money. Heck, I've always made enough to support my family.

THERAPIST: That's very important. Have things changed for the worse inside the family since Ruth started studying? Has she neglected you and the kids? Is the family suffering?

JOHN: Well, not exactly. I mean, Ruth's always been a good wife and a devoted mother. But [*Pause*] I don't quite know how to put it. [*Pause*]

THERAPIST: Perhaps you're reacting to a feeling inside of yourself that there's the potential for some sort of penalty or withdrawal . . . that something will be taken away from you.

JOHN: Yeah, maybe.

THERAPIST: You're facing a turning point that many families encounter. The job of mothering is virtually done. Let's see. Your four children are now 19, 18, 17, and 16 years old. So the energy Ruth had to expend in taking care of them in the past must be replaced by something else. Now that the kids are almost grown up, she has more time on her hands. Her full-time homemaking has now become a part-time activity. As Ruth approaches 40, it seems that she needs to become more than a wife and mother. Not less, but more. It would be a mistake for her to do anything that would damage or undermine her relationship with you and the children. Let's say she aspired to become an executive who would spend 60 hours a week at work. Then there would be big trouble.

JOHN [*Smiling*]: You can say that again!

THERAPIST: Well, if she works as an elementary schoolteacher, the time that she used to devote to caring for your kids would be put to constructive use. But if she just hung around at home, you'd soon have a bitter, resentful, and frustrated woman on your hands. What would she do with all that free time except become a royal pain in the neck? Does that make sense?

JOHN: I guess I see what you're getting at.

THERAPIST: Besides, let's face it. Even though you make good money, with four kids to put through college, a bit of extra cash won't hurt. [*Talking to Ruth*] I hope you don't mind too much that John and I have been talking about you as if you weren't in the room. I meant no disrespect, but I really wanted to touch base with him.

RUTH: No, I understand. May I ask something?

THERAPIST [*Paradoxically*]: Only if you get down on bended knee.

RUTH [*Smiling*]: The 6-year-old strikes again! [*Turning to John*] John, have I ever neglected you or the children?

JOHN: Like I said, you've been a good wife and mother.

THERAPIST: Now the question is whether you can continue being a good wife and mother and also become a good teacher.

A follow-up session with Ruth after the conjoint meeting commences as follows:

THERAPIST: I'm curious to know if our threesome meeting seemed to have any positive effects. What do you think we accomplished?

RUTH: It's hard to tell. I mean John came away saying that you made sense, which I think is a very good sign. He seemed quite comfortable with you.

THERAPIST: Well, I hope that the "sense" I made adds up to getting him to realize that if you don't work but function as a full-time homemaker now that the children have grown up it will be to everyone's detriment. I want you, from time to time, to underscore that point. We need John to become fully aware that there's a positive payoff, a definite advantage for him if you work, and that it's in no way a reflection of his earning capacity. As I told him, the extra money will be useful, but it's not essential. Can you gently but firmly make those points over and over?

RUTH: I think that's what's needed for John to feel OK about it.

THERAPIST: And you? Do you feel OK about it? You've expressed quite a bit of conflict over this issue.

RUTH: I'm still afraid of many things, and I'm still not entirely confident that I can succeed.

THERAPIST: Well, should we look into this now?

RUTH: Susan—she's my 17-year-old—has me a little upset over an incident that occurred. Can we discuss this first?

THERAPIST: Sure.

Concluding Comments

The initial objective was to gain permission from "Big Daddy John" for Ruth to pursue a career. If John seemed motivated to enter couples therapy with a view to improving their marriage—really getting to know and appreciate each other, enhancing their levels of general and sexual communication—this would be all to the good. It would not surprise me if he also elected to seek personal therapy for some of his insecurities. As a multimodal therapist, I would expect to encounter no difficulties in treating Ruth individually, Ruth and John as a couple, and John as an individual.

The multimodal approach assumes that lasting treatment outcomes require combining various techniques, strategies, and modalities. A multimodal therapist works with individuals, couples, and families as needed. The approach is pragmatic and empirical. It offers a consistent framework for diagnosing problems within and among each vector of personality. The overall emphasis is on fitting the treatment to the client by addressing factors such as the client's expectancies, readiness for change, and motivation. The therapist's style (for example, degree of directiveness and supportiveness) varies according to the needs of the client and the situation. Above all, flexibility and thoroughness are strongly emphasized. I very much believe in "bibliotherapy" and would urge Ruth to read my user-friendly self-help book, *The 60-Second Shrink: 101 Strategies for Staying Sane in a Crazy World*. I might also give her a copy of my book, *Marital Myths Revisited: A Fresh Look at Two Dozen Mistaken Beliefs About Marriage*, as a gift.[2]

Most therapists would probably find Ruth capable of being helped and relatively easy to treat. Unlike some clients with severe personality disturbances, she displays no excessive hostility, no intense self-destructive tendencies, and no undue "resistance," and her interpersonal style appears to be collaborative rather than belligerent or contentious. Nevertheless, if one treats only two or three modalities (which is what most nonmultimodal counselors address), several important problems and deficits may be glossed over or ignored, thereby leaving her with untreated complaints that could have been resolved and with a propensity to relapse (for example, revert back to her timid, conflicted, anxious, depressed, and unfulfilled modus vivendi).

In this era, when brief therapy is the order of the day, instead of focusing or dwelling on one or two so-called pivotal issues (which is what many time-limited counselors attempt to do), multimodal therapists would address one major problem from each dimension of the BASIC I.D.[3] In Ruth's case, if we had only 6 to 10 sessions in which to work, the following issues might be selected:

Behavior: Address her avoidance response.

Affect: Implement anxiety-management techniques.

Sensation: Teach her self-calming relaxation methods.

Imagery: Use positive self-visualizations.

Cognition: Try to eliminate categorical imperatives ("shoulds," "oughts," and "musts").

Interpersonal relationships: Administer assertiveness training.

Drugs and biology: Recommend a sensible nutrition and exercise program.

The multimodal maxim is that breadth is often more important than depth. The clinician who sinks one or two deep shafts is likely to bypass a host of other issues. It is wiser to address as broad an array of problems as time permits. Through a "ripple effect," a change in one modality tends to generalize to others, but the greater the number of discrete problems that can be overcome, the more profound the eventual outcome is likely to be.[4]

Another Behavior Therapist's Perspective on Ruth

by Barbara Brownell D'Angelo, PhD

Introduction

Behavior therapy encompasses a wide variety of specific techniques, including biofeedback training, assertiveness training, desensitization, operant conditioning, modeling, and role playing. The common thread running through these techniques is a focus on finding solutions to current behavioral problems and complaints. The client identifies a specific complaint and, together with the therapist, devises a plan to address it. There is little mystery in the behavioral approach. In addition, since the treatment goals are well defined, it becomes clear early in the therapeutic process how well the therapy is progressing. The therapist's task is to fine-tune the program with constant attention to whether it is working. The behaviorist asks "what," "when," and "how" questions rather than "why" questions.

Basic Assumptions and Their Application

Behavior therapists make six basic assumptions.

1. Assessment is an ongoing process in behavioral therapy. It begins with the client's complaint, which is then analyzed to determine its antecedents and consequences. The client keeps a record of the frequency and intensity of occurrences, and this becomes the tool in devising a therapeutic plan and in deciding whether the therapy is working.

2. The therapeutic relationship is a source of powerful reinforcement and is essential if treatment is to succeed. The therapist must be supportive, attentive, and engender a feeling of confidence and trust in the client.

3. The major focus is on the present rather than the past. When the past is discussed, the emphasis is on discovering how it applies to the current situation.

4. Attention is directed toward observable behavior, although this can include not only actions but also feelings and thoughts. Anything that is identifiable, discernible, and quantifiable is fair game.

5. Therapist and client together conduct a careful evaluation of the antecedents and consequences of a behavior to determine how best to set up a program of behavioral change. Creativity is crucial because each person presents a unique challenge, and the most effective combination of techniques must be fine-tuned for each individual.

6. The client is encouraged to try new behaviors and, together with the therapist, to devise plans to put the program into effect. During the sessions, the therapist may model the desired behavior, role-play with the client, and may ask the client to practice the new behavior in the neutral office setting prior to trying it out in real life.

Let's look at how these assumptions can be applied in counseling Ruth.

⚖ Assessment   Traditional diagnostic categories are rarely useful to the behavior therapist because there is no direct relationship between the diagnosis and a specific treatment. The therapist may be required to submit a diagnosis, however, for the client to qualify for insurance to defray part of the cost of therapy or as a requirement of a managed care program. In such cases the diagnosis is made but is not a factor in decisions on treatment. There may also be unintended ramifications for clients should they be pinned with a diagnosis of mental disorder. The ethical issues involved with such diagnoses should be fully studied and understood to preclude clients from suffering future consequences. For example, disability, life, and health insurance plans may consider such diagnoses as negative factors in determining future eligibility for insurance.

Given these cautions, if Ruth chooses to participate in a third-party reimbursement process that requires a formal diagnosis, I think that an *adjustment disorder* is most fitting in her case. She evidences clinically significant emotional or behavioral symptoms in response to stressors such as having her children leave home, completing graduate school, and securing a teaching position.

As a behavior therapist, I rely on Ruth for direction by asking what is motivating her to seek therapy. I want to know from her which of her issues is causing her the most discomfort. Rather than theorizing about hidden meanings, I directly ask her what she would like to change.

THERAPIST: Tell me what brings you here today.

RUTH: I've been in therapy before, and it helped me a lot. I guess I had thought I could use what I'd learned and didn't need any more help.

THERAPIST: And now you're not so sure.

RUTH: Yeah, I'm just not following through on trying to get a job, and I'm feeling more and more upset with myself in general.

THERAPIST: What bothers you about this? Not having a job or the feeling of being upset?

RUTH: Both. I hate moping around, but I feel in my heart that if I got moving on a plan I wouldn't be so depressed. Then, too, I'm afraid if I really did get a job I couldn't be there for my family.

THERAPIST: It sounds as if you're not sure what you really want for yourself.

RUTH: You're right. I keep flip-flopping.

THERAPIST: OK. It's important that I understand how you see things. Before we look at this in more detail, could you tell me if you're concerned about any other issues?

RUTH: Well, yes. I was doing great on my weight-control program. I lost almost 12 pounds. And then I just stopped exercising and started stuffing again. I've already gained half of it back.

THERAPIST: So after initially being successful, you're finding yourself backsliding.

RUTH: Sad but true. I started to feel guilty about not getting breakfast for John and the kids. The exercise class was at eight in the morning, so I just dropped out.

THERAPIST: Your children.

RUTH: Four of them. They're all teenagers.

THERAPIST: And they expect you to make breakfast for them.

RUTH: Not really. But if I don't, then they'd just skip it altogether.

THERAPIST: It sounds as if you're carrying the full weight of responsibility for your family.

RUTH: I always have. I've always put their needs ahead of mine. It seems I can never find the time or energy to do anything I want to do—I mean, just for me.

Ruth touches on several specific areas she would like to target: getting a job, losing weight, and changing her role as supermom. Upon further discussion, it becomes clear that most of her difficulties are a result of her relationships with her husband and children. Her continuous sacrificing for them has created in her a reservoir of resentment, which has, in turn, immobilized her.

THERAPIST: Let me try to summarize what you've been saying. You would like to start putting yourself first, for a change.

RUTH: Yes, but I don't want to feel guilty about it.

THERAPIST: I understand. That's something we'll want to work on. This week, though, I'd like you to do some record keeping. It'll give us a good idea of what's really going on.

RUTH: You want me to write things down?

THERAPIST: Yes. We'll need some very concrete information to help us get a handle on this. Here's a small binder, divided into two sections. Let's write the day of the week at the top of each page. Now, whenever you do something for yourself, or do something that you really, truly want to do, write it down here. Whenever you do something for your husband or your children, describe it on this page. Also, make a note next to each entry about your feelings related to each episode. OK?

RUTH: All right. I think this is going to be interesting.

Ruth has identified her major complaint, but we don't know enough about it yet. After a week of keeping track, she will have a good record of the extent of the problem, and we will be on our way toward designing a program to deal with it. A second benefit of data collection is that her motivation is being put to a test. If she returns the following week with a blank binder and a bushel of excuses, I will wonder if she is truly motivated to make changes. A final reason for asking her to record her interactions is that it will give her a feeling of accomplishment and a sense that she is taking some positive action.

The Therapeutic Relationship Regardless of the therapeutic approach, the chemistry between therapist and client must be right if progress is to be made. Ruth has benefited from previous therapy, and she therefore has a positive expectation about seeking help. During the first session, we discuss her experiences with her previous therapist and her current expectations.

THERAPIST: You said you benefited from your previous therapy. Can you tell me what was particularly helpful?

RUTH: [*She then tells me what she found useful in her therapy and we have a dialogue about this.*]

Focus on the Present I want to concentrate on Ruth's current life and to encourage changes in the present. However, the past contains valuable lessons for the present, and we will therefore call on past experiences when necessary. A consistent pattern of self-denial characterizes Ruth's daily life. Even she was surprised to recognize the extent of it. At this point, I wish to determine the nature of the problem as she currently experiences it. I am not interested in searching for causative factors in her childhood but basically want to know "what is going on" with her today.

RUTH: Well, here it is—my week in review.

THERAPIST: You started on Tuesday. Let's see what you've got here.

RUTH: It started bright and early on Tuesday. Adam needed cotton balls for a school project, so I drove across town to the all-night grocery.

Then I made breakfast and packed lunches for everyone but Jennifer. She snubs brown-bagging.

THERAPIST: This brought you to 9 o'clock in the morning.

RUTH: Yes. I don't waste time. Then I cleaned up after everyone. I hate to say it, but I couldn't stand the messes in Susan's and Adam's rooms, so I picked up there too.

THERAPIST: And what were you feeling when you were in their rooms?

RUTH: I guess I felt disgusted . . . ticked off. I mean they're 16 and 17 years old, for heaven's sake. I felt like a servant, a totally unappreciated servant at that.

THERAPIST: No wonder. Balanced against these 26 entries on Tuesday, there was nothing that you did for yourself.

Now that Ruth is aware of the degree to which she sacrifices for her family and ignores her own needs, we want to begin thinking about making changes. I ask her for some ideas of what she might find enjoyable and ask her to recall activities from her past that gave her pleasure.

THERAPIST: This is a good time to do some brainstorming. Let's write down some of the things you think you might enjoy doing. Does anything come to mind?

RUTH: I used to sing in the choir. They say I have a pretty decent voice.

THERAPIST: OK, let's write, "Join the church choir."

RUTH: And right after John and I married, we went on long walks together. I remember that as having been fun.

THERAPIST: Good. Keep going. What else do you remember that was enjoyable?

RUTH: I used to love taking pictures and arranging them in artistic collages. I haven't done that in years.

THERAPIST: This is a nice start. You've come up with several things. During the next several days, keep your mind alert to ideas you can add to the list and jot them down. We'll go over them at our next meeting and make some selections.

☺ Attention Directed to Observable Behavior

Ruth has observed and recorded interactions with her family. In addition, she made notes on her thoughts and feelings about these interactions as they took place. Midway through the second session, we discuss some alternative behaviors she might try, but we also need to address the thoughts and feelings that are causing her such discomfort.

RUTH: This week I found myself getting overly concerned if all my kids were having breakfast. Of course, I put it on my shoulders to make sure they all ate. If I thought I could leave the family to their own devices, I would.

THERAPIST: Certainly it is important that your children have breakfast. But is this totally your responsibility?

RUTH: Unfortunately, I tell myself if they don't eat I am not doing my job!

THERAPIST: Let's try something. Close your eyes for a minute and imagine you've just set breakfast out for your family and you're getting into the car, heading for class.

RUTH: OK. Now what?

THERAPIST: Let this image become as real as possible to you, and tell me what you're saying to yourself.

RUTH: I'm saying, "What if Adam doesn't eat what I've put out for him?"

THERAPIST: All right. Now, tell me what you're feeling.

RUTH: A knot in my stomach . . . kind of a constricted feeling in my chest. I hate that feeling.

THERAPIST: OK. Now, just as an experiment, I'd like you to say—aloud: "I've done more than enough for them this morning. Adam will eat what he needs." Would you repeat that statement five times, and put some intensity into it.

Ruth repeats the statement aloud, and then I instruct her to repeat it silently until it seems natural to her. After several repetitions, I ask Ruth to focus on her feelings. After working on her feelings, further practice is desirable. I may also suggest that she take a step toward trying out a new behavior.

THERAPIST: Now, how do you feel about setting out breakfast for John and the kids and going to the exercise class? Is this something you'd be willing to do one time this week?

RUTH: I'll think about it and tell you how it goes next week. OK?

THERAPIST: Good. See you then.

Analyzing Antecedents and Consequences One of Ruth's short-term goals is to resume her morning exercise class. I want to assist her by making it easy for her to succeed and ensuring that she will feel positive about the experience. Setting the stage for success—arranging favorable antecedents—is crucial to carrying out the plan.

Then we work together to structure Ruth's situation so that she will find it easy to attend the exercise class. A related strategy is to build in as many rewards as possible. This is done by ensuring that the consequences of a behavior are rewarding.

Trying Out New Behaviors The therapy session provides a neutral setting where behaviors can be practiced without risk. Ruth needs assistance in developing a more assertive stance with her family. One aspect of assertiveness training involves learning new behaviors by way of role playing. In a role-playing exercise I pretend I am John and ask Ruth to talk to me as she would if I were John. Then we switch roles. Ruth takes on John's role, and I demonstrate a more assertive stance so that Ruth can consider alternative behaviors. Finally, we switch roles again, and Ruth practices relating to me as John in more assertive and effective ways.

Concluding Comments

Ruth is an exceptionally motivated client with positive expectations about the value of therapy. She shows willingness to take suggestions and follows through on homework assignments. These qualities are especially crucial if behavior therapy is to be effective because the burden of change is squarely on the shoulders of the client.

Maladaptive behavior develops over many years, beginning in early childhood, and continues to cause problems throughout an individual's life. Therefore, we must have patience when we encounter a person like Ruth because her behaviors are deeply entrenched. We cannot expect to erase the effects of years of maladaptive behaviors with a few suggestions. Rather, we should expect that she will cling to familiar patterns of behavior as she slowly comes to accept new ways of thinking and being.

As a behavior therapist I need to be somewhat eclectic to be effective. The focus is on overt behaviors but also includes thought patterns and emotions. All of these can be articulated and therefore manipulated by the client. Ruth was aware of the strong emotional reactions she felt when she put her own needs before her family's. Unless we address these powerful emotions, we set ourselves up for failure.

It is also important that Ruth have realistic expectations regarding therapy. Permanent change will not come immediately, and she should expect that living well is truly a lifelong process. This doesn't mean that therapy lasts forever. Therapy is seen as an aid in helping her establish more rewarding patterns of behavior. After 10 or 15 weekly sessions, I would recommend her tapering off to monthly meetings. This allows Ruth to become increasingly self-sufficient while guaranteeing therapeutic support for as long as she truly needs it. As she begins to obtain rewards from her positive changes, she will come to depend on her own abilities. My hope for Ruth is that she will learn more effective coping skills that will translate into improved relationships and greater self-acceptance.

Jerry Corey's Work With Ruth From a Behavioral Perspective

In the *CD-ROM for Integrative Counseling*, Session 8 ("Behavioral Focus in Counseling"), I demonstrate a behavioral way to assist Ruth in developing an exercise program. It is crucial that Ruth make her own decisions about specific behavioral goals she wants to pursue. This applies to my attempts to work with her in developing methods of relaxation, practicing assertive skills, and designing an exercise plan.

Basic Assumption

A basic assumption of the behavioral approach is that therapy is best conducted in a systematic manner. Although behavior therapy includes a variety of principles and therapeutic procedures, its common denominator is a commitment to objectivity and evaluation.

Assessment of Ruth

I very much like beginning with a general assessment of a client's current functioning. This assessment begins with the intake session and continues during
the next session if necessary.

Ruth and I come up with two problem areas on which she wants to focus.
First, she feels tense to the point of panic much of the time and wants to learn
ways to relax. Second, from the standpoint of her interpersonal relationships,
she does not have the skills to ask for what she wants from others, she has
trouble expressing her viewpoints clearly, and she often accepts projects she
does not want to get involved in.

Goals of Therapy

The general goal of behavior therapy is to create new conditions for learning.
I view Ruth's problems as related to faulty learning. The assumption underlying our therapy is that learning experiences can ameliorate problem behaviors.
Much of our therapy will involve correcting faulty cognitions, acquiring social
and interpersonal skills, and learning techniques of self-management so that
she can become her own therapist. Based on my initial assessment of her and
on another session in which she and I discuss the matter of setting concrete
and objective goals, we establish the following goals to guide the therapeutic
process:

- Learn and practice methods of relaxation
- Learn to manage stress effectively
- Learn assertion training principles and skills

Therapeutic Procedures

Behavior therapy is a pragmatic approach, and I am concerned that the treatment procedures be effective. I will draw on various cognitive and behavioral techniques to help Ruth reach her stated goals. If she does not make
progress, I must assume much of the responsibility because it is my task to
select appropriate treatment procedures and use them well. As a behavior
therapist, I am continually evaluating the results of the therapeutic process
to determine which approaches are working. Ruth's feedback in this area
is important. I will ask her to keep records of her daily behavior, and I will
encourage her to become active to accomplish her goals, including working
outside the session.

Our therapy will be relatively brief, for my main function is to teach Ruth
skills she can use in solving her problems and living more effectively. My ultimate goal is to teach her to become her own therapist. This I will do through
a variety of psychoeducational methods that she can practice in daily living.
For example, to manage her stress more effectively, I suggest that she read
Jon Kabat-Zinn's book, *Full Catastrophe Living: Using the Wisdom of Your Body
and Mind to Face Stress, Pain, and Illness*.[5] I also encourage her to purchase
Kabat-Zinn's audiotapes as a way for her to practice mindfulness-based stress
reduction.

The Therapeutic Process

ELEMENTS OF THE PROCESS   The therapeutic process begins with gathering baseline data on the specific goals Ruth has selected. In her case much of the therapy will consist of learning how to effectively manage stress and how to be assertive in situations calling for this behavior.

⚘ Learning Stress Management Techniques   Ruth indicates that one of her priorities is to cope with tensions more effectively. I ask her to list all the specific areas that she finds stressful, and I discuss with her how her own expectations and her self-talk are contributing to her stress. We then develop a program to reduce unnecessary strain and to deal more effectively with the inevitable stresses of daily life.

RUTH: You asked me what I find stressful. There are so many things. I feel as if I'm always rushing and never accomplishing what I should. I feel pressured much of the time.

JERRY: List some specific situations that bring on stress. Then maybe we can come up with some strategies for alleviating it.

RUTH: Trying to keep up with my schoolwork and with the many demands at home at the same time. Dealing with Jennifer's anger and defiance. Trying to live up to John's expectations. Getting involved in way too many community activities and projects and then not having time to complete them. Feeling pressured to complete my education. Worrying that I won't be able to find a good teaching job once I get my credential.

JERRY: I can see why you feel overwhelmed. We can't address all of them at once. I'd like to hear more about what being in these stressful situations is like for you. Tell me about one of these situations, and describe what you feel in your body, what you're thinking at the time, and what you actually do in these times of stress. [*I want to get a concrete sense of how she experiences her stress, what factors bring it about, and how she attempts to cope with it.*]

RUTH: Well, I often feel that I wear many hats—I just have so many roles to perform, and there's never enough time to do all that's needed. I lie awake at night and ruminate about the things I should be doing. It's hard for me to go to sleep, and then I wake up in the morning feeling tired. Then it's even harder for me to face the day.

JERRY: Earlier you mentioned that you have panic attacks, especially at night. I'd like to teach you some simple ways to use the relaxation response just before you go into a full-scale attack. You'll need to identify the cues that appear before a panic attack. I'd then like to teach you some simple and effective relaxation methods. Instead of wasting time lying there trying to sleep, you could practice a few exercises. It's important that you practice these self-relaxation exercises every day, for 20 minutes.

RUTH: I'm afraid I won't do it successfully.

JERRY: That depends on how you approach it.

We talk at some length because I am afraid Ruth will make this practice a chore rather than something she can do for herself and enjoy. She finally sees that it does not have to be a task that she does perfectly but is a means of making life easier for her. I teach her how to concentrate on her breathing and how to do some visualization techniques, such as imagining a very pleasant and peaceful scene. Then, following the guidelines described in Herbert Benson's book, *The Relaxation Response,* I provide her with these instructions:[6]

> JERRY: Find a quiet and calm environment with as few distractions as possible. Sit comfortably in a chair and adopt a passive attitude. Rather than worry about performing the technique, simply let go of all thoughts. Repeating a mantra, such as the word "om," is helpful. With your eyes closed, deeply relax all your muscles, beginning with your feet and progressing up to your face. Relax and breathe.

A week later, Ruth reports on how difficult it was to let go and relax.

> RUTH: I didn't do well at all. I did practice every day, and it wasn't as difficult as I thought. But it's hard for me to find a quiet place to relax. I was called to the phone several times, and then another time my kids wanted me for something. Even when I wasn't disturbed, I found my mind wandering, and it was hard to just get into the sensations of feeling tension and relaxation in my body.

> JERRY: I hope you won't give up. This is a skill, and like any skill it will take time to learn. But it's essential that you block off 20 minutes in a quiet place without disturbances to practice.

Ruth and I discuss how difficult it is for her to have this time for herself. I reinforce the point that this is also an opportunity to practice asking others for what she wants and seeing to it that she gets it. Thus, she can work toward another of her goals: being able to ask for what she wants.

🕮 **Learning How to Say No**   Ruth tells me that she gives to everyone but finds it difficult to ask anything for herself. We have been working on the latter issue, with some success. Ruth informs me that she does not know how to say no to people when they ask her to get involved in a project, especially if they tell her that they need her. She wants to talk about her father, especially the ways in which she thinks he has caused her lack of assertiveness. I ask her to recall a recent time when she found it difficult to say no and to describe that scene.

> RUTH: Last week my son Adam came to me late at night to type his term paper. I didn't feel like it at all because I had had a long and hard day, and besides, it was almost midnight. At first I told him I wasn't going to do it. Then he got huffy, and I finally gave in. What could I do?

> JERRY: You could have done many things. Can you come up with some alternatives?

I want Ruth to search for alternative behaviors to saying yes when it is clear that she wants to say no. She does come up with other strategies, and we talk about the possible consequences of each approach. Then I suggest some behavioral role playing. First, I play the role of Adam, and she tries several approaches other than giving in and typing the paper. Her performance is a bit weak, so I suggest that she play Adam's role, and I demonstrate at least another alternative. I want to demonstrate, by direct modeling, some behaviors she does not use, and I hope that she will practice them.

As the weeks progress, there are many opportunities for Ruth to practice a few of the assertive skills she is learning. Then she runs into a stumbling block. A PTA group wants her to be its president. Although she enjoys her membership in the group, she is sure that she does not want the responsibilities involved in being the president. In her session she says she doesn't know how to turn the group down, especially since no one else seems available.

We again work on this problem by using role-playing techniques. I play the role of the people pressuring her to accept the presidency, and I use every trick I know including her guilt. I tell her how efficient she is, how we are counting on her, how we know that she won't let us down, and so on. We stop at critical points and talk about the hesitation in her voice, the guilty look on her face, and her habit of giving reasons to justify her position. I also talk with her about what her body posture is communicating. Then we systematically work on each element of her presentation. Paying attention to her choice of words, her quality of voice, and her style of delivery, we study how she might persuasively say no without feeling guilty later. As a homework assignment, I ask her to read selected chapters of the book *Your Perfect Right*, by Alberti and Emmons.[7] There are useful ideas in this book that she can think about and practice between our sessions.

The next week we talk about what she has learned in the book, and we do some cognitive work. I especially talk with her about what she tells herself in these situations that gets her into trouble. In addition to these cognitive techniques, I continue to teach Ruth assertive behaviors by using role playing, behavioral rehearsals, coaching, and practice.

PROCESS COMMENTARY In this approach Ruth is clearly the person who decides what she wants to work on and what she wants to change. She makes progress toward her self-defined goals because she is willing to become actively involved in challenging her assumptions and in carrying out behavioral exercises, both in the sessions and in her daily life. For example, she is disciplined enough to practice the relaxation exercises she has learned from her reading and our sessions. She learns how to ask for what she wants and to refuse those requests that she does not want to meet, not only by making resolutions but also by regularly keeping a record of the social situations in which she was not as assertive as she would have liked to be. She takes risks by practicing in everyday situations those assertive skills she has acquired in our therapy sessions. Although I help her learn how to change, she is the one who actually chooses to apply these skills, thus making change possible.

Questions for Reflection

1. What are your thoughts about Dr. Lazarus's multimodal approach to assessment as a way to begin therapy?
2. What are some of the features you like best about Dr. Lazarus's approach? About Dr. D'Angelo's approach? About my approach in working with Ruth? What are some of the basic similarities in these three behavioral approaches? What are some basic differences? How might you have proceeded differently, still working within this model, in terms of what you know about Ruth?
3. Dr. Lazarus succeeded in getting Ruth to agree to take a brisk walk at least three times a week. As a behavior therapist, how would you deal with her if she told you that she had not kept her agreement?
4. What is your reaction to both Dr. D'Angelo's and my attempts to get Ruth out of therapy as fast as possible so that she can apply self-management skills on her own? What skills can you think of to teach her so that she can be more self-directed?
5. In what ways did Dr. Lazarus work with Ruth's past in helping her understand her present condition? Do you think that for change to occur in her current situation she must go back to her past and work out unfinished business? Explain.
6. What are your reactions to the manner in which Dr. Lazarus conducted the conjoint session with Ruth and John? If you were conducting such a behaviorally oriented session, what homework might you suggest to them as a couple? Do you have any suggestions for specific behavioral assignments for each individual?
7. Identify some specific coping skills that Dr. D'Angelo taught Ruth. Assuming that you were to teach her some new skills in dealing with her problems, how might you help her if she were to backslide by getting stuck in some old patterns?
8. Using other behavioral techniques, show how you might proceed with Ruth if you were working with her. Use whatever you know about her so far and what you know about behavior therapy approaches to show in what directions you would move with her.

Notes

See the DVD/online program entitled *Theory in Practice: The Case of Stan* (Session 7: Behavior Therapy Applied to the Case of Stan) that provides an illustration of how homework and behavior rehearsals can be used to promote assertive behavior.

1. For detailed information on the Multimodal Life History Inventory, see A. A. Lazarus & C. N. Lazarus (1991), *Multimodal Life-History Inventory* (Champaign, IL: Research Press). This is a comprehensive inventory that allows for an assessment of a wide range of problems throughout the BASIC I.D.
2. See A. A. Lazarus & C. N. Lazarus (1997), *The 60-Second Shrink: 101 Strategies for Staying Sane in a Crazy World* (Atascadero, CA: Impact Publishers). This self-help book deals with a range of topics including thinking

yourself healthy, building successful relationships, handling anxiety and stress, managing your weight, and communicating effectively. It makes a good companion for therapy clients. See also A. A. Lazarus (2001), *Marital Myths Revisited: A Fresh Look at Two Dozen Mistaken Beliefs About Marriage* (Atascadero, CA: Impact Publishers). This book makes a good adjunct for couples who are in marriage counseling.

3. For a more detailed description of the BASIC I.D., see A. A. Lazarus (1997), *Brief but Comprehensive Psychotherapy: The Multimodal Way* (New York: Springer). This is an excellent source of techniques and procedures for brief interventions. Lazarus shows how to deal with the whole person by developing assessments and treatment interventions for all the modalities of human experience.

4. For an overview of multimodal therapy, see G. Corey (2009), *Theory and Practice of Counseling and Psychotherapy* (8th ed., Belmont, CA: Brooks/Cole). Chapter 9 ("Behavior Therapy") describes the unique features of multimodal therapy as an assessment and treatment approach.

5. Refer to J. Kabat-Zinn (1990), *Full Catastrophe Living: Using the Wisdom of Your Body and Mind to Face Stress, Pain, and Illness* (New York: Dell). This is a practical guide to mindfulness meditation and healing. There are some excellent chapters on stress and how to manage it effectively.

6. Refer to H. Benson (1976), *The Relaxation Response* (New York: Avon). This is a readable and useful guide to developing simple meditative and other relaxation procedures. Particularly helpful are the author's summaries of the basic elements of meditation (pp. 110–111) and methods of inducing the relaxation response (pp. 158–166).

7. See R. E. Alberti & M. L. Emmons (2008), *Your Perfect Right: A Guide to Assertive Behavior* (9th ed., San Luis Obispo, CA: Impact Publishers). Therapy clients will learn about the principles and techniques of assertion training from this popular book.

CHAPTER EIGHT

Case Approach to Cognitive Behavior Therapy

General Overview of Cognitive Behavioral Approaches

The goal of cognitive behavior therapy is to eliminate clients' self-defeating outlooks on life and assist them in acquiring more tolerant and rational views. Clients are taught how they incorporated self-defeating beliefs, how they are maintaining this faulty thinking, what they can do to undermine such thinking, and how they can teach themselves new ways of thinking that will lead to changes in their ways of behaving and feeling.

Typically, REBT practitioners use a variety of cognitive, affective, and behavioral techniques. Procedures are designed to get clients to critically examine present beliefs and behavior. Cognitive methods include disputing irrational beliefs, carrying out cognitive homework, and changing one's language and thinking patterns. Emotive techniques include role playing, REBT imagery, and shame-attacking exercises. A wide range of active and practical behavioral procedures are used to get clients to be specific and committed to doing the hard work required by therapy. Cognitive behavioral approaches insist on client participation in homework assignments both during and outside the therapeutic sessions. Individuals will rarely change a self-defeating belief unless they are willing to act consistently against it.

Clients are ready to terminate when they no longer badger themselves with "shoulds," "oughts," and "musts" and when they replace their irrational and self-destructive beliefs with rational and constructive ones. Therapeutic outcomes can be evaluated by looking at the specific cognitive, affective, and behavioral changes demonstrated by the client.

A Rational Emotive Behavior Therapist's Perspective on Ruth

by Albert Ellis, PhD, ABPP

Introduction

REBT assumes that people like Ruth do not get disturbed by the unrealistic and illogical standards they learned (from their family and culture) during their childhood. Rather, they largely disturb themselves by the dogmatic, rigid "musts" and commands they creatively construct about these standards and values and about the unfortunate events that occur in their lives. Ruth is a good case in point. She has accepted some of the fundamentalist ideas of her parents, which many fundamentalist-reared children adopt without becoming disturbed. But Ruth rigidly insists that she has to follow them while simultaneously demanding that she must be herself and lead a self-fulfilling, independent existence. She could easily disturb herself with either of these contradictory commands. By devoutly holding both of them, she is really in trouble! As REBT shows, transmuting any legitimate goals and preferences into absolutist "musts" usually leads to self-denigration, rage, or self-pity. Ruth seems to have all of these disturbed feelings.[1]

Assessment of Ruth

Ruth has a number of goals and desires that most therapies, including REBT, would consider legitimate and healthy: the desire to have a stable marriage; to care for her family members; to be thinner and more attractive; to keep her parents' approval; to be a competent teacher; and to discover what she really wants to do in life and largely follow her personal bents. Even though some of these desires are somewhat contradictory, they would probably not get her into serious trouble if she held them as preferences because she could then make some compromises.

Ruth could choose to be *somewhat* devoted to her husband and children, and even to her parents, but also be determined to pursue a teaching career and to follow her own nonfundamentalist religious views and practices. She would then fail to lead a *perfectly* conflict-free and happy life but would hardly be in great turmoil. However, like practically all humans, Ruth has a strong (and probably partly innate) tendency to "sacredize" these important values. From early childhood onward, she rigidly concluded: "Because I want my parents' approval, I completely need it!" "Because I love my children, I have to be thoroughly devoted to them!" "Because I enjoy thinking for myself and doing my own thing, I have to do so at practically all times!" "Because I'd like to be thinner and more attractive, I've got to be!"

With grandiose, perfectionist fiats like these, Ruth's reasonable, often achievable, goals and standards are transmuted into absolutist "musts." She thereby almost inevitably *makes* herself—that's right, makes herself—panicked, depressed, indecisive, and often inert. Additionally, when she sees that she feels emotionally upset and is not acting in her best interests, she irrationally upsets herself about that. She strongly—and foolishly—tells herself "I must not be panicked" instead of "I wish I were not panicking myself, but I am. Now how do I unpanic myself?" She then feels panicked about her panic. And she rigidly insists, "I have to be decisive and do my own thing." Then she feels like a worm about her worminess! This self-castigation about her symptoms makes her even more disturbed and less able to see exactly what she is thinking and doing to create these symptoms. As a rational emotive behavior therapist, I assess Ruth's problems and her belief system about these problems as follows.

Ruth asks certain questions that lead to practical problems:

- How much shall I do for others, and how much for myself?
- How can I exercise and keep on a diet?
- How can I be a teacher and still get along well with my husband?
- How can I get along with my parents and still not follow their fundamentalist views?
- How can I benefit from therapy and live with the things I may discover about myself when undergoing it?
- How can I be myself and not harm my husband and kids?

Ruth could sensibly answer these questions by telling herself these things:

- If I do more things for myself, people may not like me as much as I want them to. Too bad!
- Exercising and dieting are really difficult. But being fat and ugly is even more difficult.
- If I get a teaching job, I may antagonize my husband. But I can stand that and still be happy.
- My parents will never like my giving up fundamentalism, and that's sad. But it's not awful.
- If I find out unpleasant things about myself in therapy, that'll be tough. But I can also benefit from that discovery.
- Being myself at the expense of my husband and kids is somewhat selfish. But I have a right to a reasonable degree of self-interest.

Instead, Ruth holds these irrational beliefs that lead to unhealthy feelings of anxiety and depression and to self-defeating behaviors of indecision and inertia:

- I must not do more things for myself and dare not antagonize others.
- Exercise and dieting are too hard and shouldn't be that hard!
- If my husband hates my getting a teaching job, that would be awful!
- I can't stand my parents criticizing me if I give up fundamentalism.
- I would be a thoroughly rotten person if therapy revealed bad things about me!
- I must never be selfish, for if I am, I'm worthless.

Ruth also holds certain irrational beliefs that lead to secondary disturbances (panic about panic, depression about depression):

- I must not be panicked!
- It's terrible if I'm depressed.
- I'm no good because I'm indecisive.

Key Issues and Themes

The key issues in most disturbed feelings and behaviors that I will look for are (1) self-deprecation, stemming from the irrational belief that "I must perform well and be approved of by significant others"; (2) the irrational insistence that "you [other people] must treat me kindly and considerately"; and (3) the irrational idea that "the conditions under which I live have to be comfortable and easy."

Ruth seems to have the first of these irrational beliefs because she keeps demanding that she be giving and lovable, that she be thin and beautiful, that she be a good daughter, that her "badness" not be uncovered in therapy, and that she make only good and proper decisions. With these perfectionist commands, she leads a self-deprecating, anxious existence. She also seems to have some unacknowledged irrational beliefs that her husband absolutely must not expect her to be herself, thus making her angry at him.

Finally, Ruth has low frustration tolerance and self-pity, resulting not from her desires but from her dire needs to lose weight without going to the trouble of dieting and exercising, to have a guarantee that she won't die, to have the security of marriage even though she has a boring relationship with her husband, to be sure that therapy will be comfortable, and to need a magical, God-will-take-care-of-me solution to her problems.

Because Ruth strongly holds the three basic irrational ideas (dogmatic "musts") that REBT finds at the root of most disturbances and because some of her demands—like those that she be herself *and* be quite self-sacrificial—are quite contradictory, I imagine that she will be a difficult customer and will require intensive therapy. Within a few sessions, however, she may be able to understand some of her *musts* and *demands* and start reducing them. Because she has already taken some big risks and worked at changing herself, I predict a good prognosis despite her strong tendency to create self-defeating beliefs.

Applying Therapeutic Techniques

REBT invariably includes a number of cognitive, emotive, and behavioral methods.[2] As I work with Ruth, I use these main methods.

Cognitive Techniques of REBT   I show Ruth how to discover her rational preferences and distinguish them from her irrational "musts" and demands. Then I teach her how to scientifically dispute these demands and change them back into appropriate preferences. I encourage her to create some rational coping statements and inculcate them many times into her philosophy; for example, "I want to be a caring mother and wife, but I also have the right to care for myself." I help her do REBT "referenting"—that is, making a list of the disadvantages of overeating and nondieting and thinking about them several times a day. I also have her do reframing to see that losing some of her husband's and children's love has its good as well as its bad sides. I encourage her to use some of REBT's psychoeducational adjuncts: books, pamphlets, cassettes, lectures, and workshops. I show her the advantages of teaching REBT to others, such as to her husband, children, and pupils, so that she will better learn it herself. I discuss with her the advantages of creating for herself a vital, absorbing interest in some long-range project, such as helping other people guiltlessly give up their parental fundamentalist teachings.

Here is one way I may work with Ruth to implement the cognitive technique of helping her dispute her irrational beliefs.

RUTH: Because I love my children, I have to be thoroughly devoted to them.

THERAPIST: That's an interesting conclusion, but how does it follow from the observation, which I assume is true, that you really do love your children?

RUTH: Well, isn't it right and ethical to be kind and helpful to one's children?

THERAPIST: Of course it is. You brought them into the world without them asking to be born, and you'd be quite unethical and irresponsible if you didn't devote considerable time and energy to them. But why must you be ethical? What law of the universe says you always have to be?

RUTH: My own law says so—and that of many other people.

THERAPIST: Fine. But why do you have to always keep your own laws? Actually, do you?

RUTH: Well, no. Not always.

THERAPIST: And do other people always keep their own and their culture's laws?

RUTH: No, not always.

THERAPIST: So obviously, although it's highly desirable and moral for you to care for your children, is it absolutely necessary that you do so?

RUTH: No, I guess not.

THERAPIST: But it still is highly desirable. What is the difference between something being preferable and desirable and being utterly necessary?

RUTH: I see. Quite a difference!

THERAPIST: Right. And no matter how much you love them, do you always have to be completely devoted to them?

RUTH: You're questioning my desire to be completely devoted?

THERAPIST: Yes, I am. How realistic would complete devotion be?

RUTH: Thoroughly unrealistic. I need time for other important things.

THERAPIST: So your dire need to be completely devoted to your children and also to your husband doesn't stem from your love for them, doesn't follow from any law of the universe, and is impractical and unrealistic. If you strongly believe you absolutely must be completely devoted to your children, what results will you probably get?

RUTH: I'll feel very anxious about doing what I supposedly must do and depressed in case I don't.

THERAPIST: Yes, your *must*urbation probably won't work.

I can have this kind of active, directive dialogue with Ruth in one of her early sessions and try to start her quickly on a new way of thinking about her demandingness.

Emotive Techniques of REBT   I will recommend that Ruth use some of the main emotive, evocative, and dramatic methods that I have found effective in REBT, such as these:

- She can forcefully and powerfully tell herself rational coping statements: "I do not (definitely not) need my parents' approval, though I would certainly prefer to have it!"
- She can tape a rigorous debate with herself, in which she actively disputes one of her irrational "musts." Then she can listen to her disputation and have some of her friends listen to it to see not only if its content is good but also if she is forceful enough.
- She can do rational emotive imagery, by imagining one of the worst things that could happen to her—for example, her father strongly berating her for her nonfundamentalist views. Then she can work on her feelings so that she first gets in touch with the horror and self-downing she unhealthily feels and then changes it to the healthy negative feelings of sorrow and regret.
- She can do some of the famous REBT shame-attacking exercises, whereby she publicly does something she considers shameful, foolish, or ridiculous and works on herself not to feel ashamed and self-damning while doing it.
- She can learn to receive unconditional acceptance from me, no matter how badly she is behaving in and out of therapy. I can show her how to always—yes, always—accept herself, whether or not she does well.
- We can do role playing, where I play her irate father and she plays herself, to see how she can cope with his severe criticism. In the course of it we stop the role playing from time to time to see what she is telling herself to make herself anxious or depressed while reacting to my role-playing her father's criticism.
- We can practice reverse role playing, where I stick rigidly to some of her irrational beliefs and encourage her to argue me out of them.
- She can use humor to rip up her irrational beliefs, especially singing to herself some of my rational humorous songs.

In this session with Ruth I use one of the emotive techniques of REBT.

THERAPIST: We've been disputing your irrational belief that because you love your children you have to be completely devoted to them. You could also use one of our popular emotional techniques, rational emotive imagery. Would you like me to show you how to use this exercise?

RUTH: Yes, I would.

THERAPIST: OK, close your eyes—just easily close them. Now vividly imagine one of the worst things that could happen to you. Imagine that you're not thoroughly devoted to your children—in fact, that you're somewhat neglecting them. Vividly imagine that they're complaining about this and that your husband and your mother are also chiding you severely for this neglect. Can you vividly imagine this happening?

RUTH: Definitely. I can clearly picture it.

THERAPIST: Good. Now, how do you honestly feel in your gut and in your heart? What is your honest feeling?

RUTH: Very guilty. Depressed. Self-critical.

THERAPIST: Good. Really get in touch with those negative feelings. Feel them. Strongly feel them!

RUTH: I really feel them. Quite strongly.

THERAPIST: Good. Now, keeping the same image—don't change it—make yourself feel only sorry and disappointed about what's happening but not guilty, not depressed, not self-downing. Only sorry and disappointed, which are healthy and appropriate negative feelings, instead of guilty, depressed, and self-downing, which are unhealthy and unhealthy negative feelings. You control your feelings, so you can change them. So let me know when you're only feeling sorry and disappointed.

RUTH: I'm having a hard time getting there.

THERAPIST: Yes, I know. But you can do it. You can definitely change your feelings. Anyone can.

RUTH [*After a pause of 2 minutes*]: I changed them.

THERAPIST: And now you feel only sorry and disappointed, not guilty or depressed?

RUTH: Yes, I do.

THERAPIST: Good! How did you change your feelings? What did you do to change them?

RUTH: I told myself "It's too bad that my children, my husband, and my mother are chiding me for neglecting the children, but I'm not sure I am being neglectful. Even if I am, that's bad, that's wrong of me, but that behavior doesn't make me a rotten person. I'll try to be less neglectful, while not being overly devoted to my children. But if I'm still criticized, it's just too bad—not the end of the world. I can take this criticism and still have a good life."

THERAPIST: Excellent! Now what I'd like to see you do is to help yourself by repeating this exercise every day for the next 20 or 30 days. Remember, it only took you about 2 minutes to change your unhealthy feelings of guilt and depression to healthy negative feelings of disappointment. So repeat this every day, using the same excellent coping statement you used this time or using several other similar coping statements that will occur to you if you keep doing this rational emotive imagery. If you do this, I think you'll see at the end of 10, 20, or 30 days, when you imagine this bad event with your children happening or when some other unfortunate activating event actually does occur, that you'll tend to feel automatically—yes, automatically—sorry and disappointed about your actions, but not damning your total self for doing this.

RUTH: You think that will really help me?

THERAPIST: Yes, I'm fairly sure it will. So will you try it to help yourself?

RUTH: Yes, I will.

THERAPIST: Great. Now, if you stop doing this exercise because you think it's too hard to continue it or something like that, you can always challenge your irrational belief that it must be easy and that you shouldn't have to do it to improve. You can also use reinforcement methods to encourage yourself to keep doing it.

RUTH: How do I do that?

THERAPIST: Very simply. What, for example, do you enjoy doing that you do practically every day of the week?

RUTH: Uh, reading.

THERAPIST: Fine. No reading, then, for the next 20 or 30 days, until after you do rational emotive imagery for the day and change your feelings of guilt and depression to those of disappointment. Is that OK?

RUTH: Yes, that's OK.

THERAPIST: And if that doesn't work, though it probably will, you can enact a penalty when you don't practice your rational emotive imagery.

RUTH: A penalty?

THERAPIST: Yes. For example, what do you hate doing—some task or chore that you usually avoid doing because you don't like it?

RUTH: Well, uh, cleaning the toilet.

THERAPIST: Good. If, during the next 30 days, your bedtime arrives and you haven't done your rational emotive imagery exercise, you can make yourself clean your toilet for an hour.

RUTH: That would work! I'm sure I'll do the exercise every day.

THERAPIST: Fine!

Rational emotive imagery, like several other REBT emotive techniques, can be taught to clients like Ruth and given as homework assignments, thus making therapy effective in a relatively brief period of time.

⚠ Behavioral Techniques of REBT   As with virtually all REBT clients, I use several behavioral methods with Ruth, including these:

- I show her how to select and perform in vivo desensitization assignments, such as registering for education courses despite her anxiety about her family's disapproval.
- I encourage her to do what she is afraid to do—for example, to talk to her husband about her career goals many times until she loses her irrational fears of his disapproval.

- I encourage her to reinforce herself with some enjoyable pursuits, such as reading or music, only after she has completed her difficult-to-do homework. And if she is truly lax about doing it, I urge her sometimes to penalize (but never damn) herself with an unpleasant chore, such as getting up an hour earlier than usual.
- I plan with her and supervise her carrying out practical goals, such as arranging for help with her household tasks.
- If she starts getting over her emotional hang-ups but has skill deficiencies, I help her acquire missing skills, such as assertiveness, communicating well, or decision making.

All of these behavioral methods of REBT can be given as homework assignments to be used between sessions and checked on during the following session. Therefore, the length of therapy can be appreciably shortened for clients who do their homework and are monitored by the therapist.

In one session I show Ruth how to use one of REBT's action-oriented techniques.

RUTH: How will I deal with my panic and, as you say, my panic about panicking?

THERAPIST: Good question. First, let's deal with your panic about your panic. Because of this secondary symptom, you often avoid situations where you might panic, even though it would be good to participate in them. Right?

RUTH: Yes. I especially avoid seeing or talking to my father, who's critical of my handling of the children and almost everything else. So I rarely call him, and when he calls, I get my family members to say I'm out when I'm really not.

THERAPIST: That's a good example. When avoiding these calls, what are you telling yourself?

RUTH: If he criticizes me, I'll panic, and that would be awful!

THERAPIST: Right. But every time you avoid speaking to your father, you reinforce your anxiety about talking to him and being criticized. You tell yourself, "If I speak to him, I'll be very anxious." So you increase your anxiety!

RUTH: You're right about that. Whenever I even think of talking to him, I panic.

THERAPIST: So the first thing you can do is to say to yourself, many times and very strongly, "Panicking is very uncomfortable, but it is not horrible. It's only inconvenient."

RUTH: That will cure me?

THERAPIST: Not exactly, but it will help a lot. In addition, deliberately arrange to talk to your father more. Do, as we say in REBT, what you're afraid of doing. Act, as well as think, against your phobia of panicking.

RUTH: But won't that make me panic more?

THERAPIST: It may at first. But if you keep doing what you're terrifying yourself about—talking to your critical father—and convince yourself at the same time that your panic is only inconvenient, not awful, you will significantly decrease your panic about your panicking.

RUTH: Will my original panic about my father's criticism decrease too?

THERAPIST: Most likely it will, and it may even disappear completely. For you were originally panicked about his criticism but then made yourself so panicked about your panic that this secondary symptom became more important than your primary one and actually helped keep it alive. So if you surrender the panic about panic, your original horror of criticism may well disappear too. If it doesn't, just go back to disputing, which we previously discussed, the irrational belief that criticism makes you a rotten person and that you can't stand it.

RUTH: So I'd better think and act against my panic?

THERAPIST: Yes, think and act, think and act against it. Against your original panic and your panic about your panic.

RUTH: Sounds good. I'll try it.

PROCESS COMMENTARY As can be seen in these typical excerpts, rational emotive behavior therapists have collaborative, Socratic dialogues with their clients and try to help them think, feel, and behave against their disturbances and, as they do so, to gain positive growth and self-fulfillment in accordance with their self-chosen goals, values, and purposes.

In using any or all of these REBT techniques with Ruth, I do not merely try to help her ameliorate her presenting symptoms (panic, guilt, and indecisiveness) but also try to help her make a profound philosophical change. The goals are for her to acknowledge her own construction of her emotional problems, to minimize her other related symptoms, and to maintain her therapeutic progress. By the time my therapy with Ruth ends, I expect that she will have strongly internalized and kept regularly using the three main insights of REBT:

1. "I mainly emotionally and behaviorally upset myself about unfortunate conditions in my life, and I largely do so by constructing rigid 'musts' and commands about these conditions."
2. "No matter when I originally started to upset myself and no matter who encouraged me do so, I'm now disturbed because of my present *mus*turbatory beliefs."
3. "To change my irrational thinking, my unhealthy feelings, and my dysfunctional behaviors, I'd better give up all magical solutions and keep working and practicing—yes, keep working and practicing—for the rest of my life."

Much of Ruth's main problem is learning to be "herself" and at the same time to resist conforming too much to social rules that tell her that she must be a "good woman," must be a "thin woman," and must be a "good fundamentalist." Although she theoretically has the right to avoid following these social rules, she will tend to feel guilty and she will tend to get into some amount of trouble with her family of origin and her current family if she decides to "truly" be herself. By using REBT and trying to follow her strong preferences without turning them into absolutist demands, she can probably determine how to largely be herself and at the same time largely, but not completely, avoid antagonizing her parents, her husband, and her children. REBT encourages her to lead a balanced life in these respects. But in being an individual, she will have to select the kind of balance she desires and accept the consequences of her own choices.

After working with Ruth for several sessions, I would say that she definitely has a panic disorder and is also dysthymic. I see her as someone with a personality disorder rather than as a "nice neurotic." She is very troubled and conflicted, but she has the ability and, I hope, the determination to work through her main problems. I enjoy working with clients like Ruth because I find them to be quite open to help. If she is willing to keep trying the antidisturbance theories and practices of REBT, I think that she has a good chance to change. She has already chosen not to follow some of the rigid rules of her family and her culture and is healthily sorry about the difficulties her rebellion entails. If I can help her continue to be sorry and regretful but to give up her severe guilt and self-deprecation about her rebelliousness, I think she will keep choosing her own pathways and not only she but also her close family members will considerably benefit. I sincerely hope so.[3]

A Cognitive Behavioral Approach to Family Therapy With Ruth

by Frank M. Dattilio, PhD, ABPP

Introduction

In the previous selection Albert Ellis demonstrates how he applies REBT, a form of cognitive behavior therapy, to individual therapy with Ruth. I have been influenced greatly by my former mentor, Aaron T. Beck, who pioneered cognitive therapy, as well as the late Joseph Wolpe, the father of behavior therapy. In addition to conducting individual therapy in my private practice, I have had a keen interest in applying the cognitive behavioral approach to couples and families.

There are many subtypes of cognitive behavior therapy. The two major versions that will be highlighted here are those practiced by Albert Ellis and Aaron T. Beck. Ellis's REBT emphasizes each individual's interpretation of the events that occur in the family environment. The basic theory contends that family members largely create their own world by the phenomenological view they take of what happens to them. The focus of therapy is on how particular problems of family members affect their well-being as a unit. Throughout the course of therapy, family members are treated as individuals, against the backdrop of the family system. Each of the members subscribes to his or her own specific set of beliefs and expectations. The role of the family therapist is to help members come to the realization that illogical or irrational beliefs and distortions serve as the foundation for their emotional distress and interactional conflicts and the impact that this has on the system as a whole. Beck's cognitive therapy, which also balances cognition and behavior, takes a more expansive and inclusive direction by focusing in greater depth on family interactional patterns and by remaining consistent with elements derived from a systems perspective. This theory has been elaborated on by Baucom, Epstein, Dattilio, and others.[4]

Basic Concepts and Assumptions

Consistent with systems theory, the cognitive behavioral approach to families includes the premise that members of a family simultaneously influence one another. Consequently, a behavior of one family member leads to behaviors, cognitions, and emotions in other members, which, in turn, elicit cognitions, behaviors, and emotions in response. As this process continues to cycle, the volatility of the family dynamics escalates, rendering members vulnerable to a negative spiral of conflict. As the number of family members involved increases, so does the complexity of the dynamics, adding more fuel to the escalation process.

Some of the more recent cognitive behavioral approaches place heavy emphasis on *schema*, or what has otherwise been defined as a set of core beliefs.[5] As this concept is applied to family treatment, the therapeutic intervention is based on the assumptions with which family members interpret and evaluate one another and the emotions and behaviors that arise in response to these cognitions. Just as individuals maintain their own basic schemata about themselves, their world, and their future, they also maintain schemata about families. I have found in my clinical experience that emphasis should be placed both on these cognitions among individual family members and on what can be termed the family schema. This consists of beliefs held jointly by the family that have formed as a result of years of integrated interaction among members. An example of such a belief in Ruth's family of origin might be that "It is unacceptable to talk about feelings and emotions openly." Not only is this an unwritten rule, it is also a strong belief among family members.

Individuals actually maintain two separate schemata about families. The first is the schema related to the parents' families of origin, which comprises the beliefs both partners learned during their upbringing and brought to the marriage. The second and more emphasized is the schema related to families in general. These schemata have a major impact on how an individual thinks, feels, and behaves within the family setting and also contribute to the development of rules and family patterns. An example in Ruth's present family is that emotions and feelings may be discussed, but only selectively.

Schemata are thus the long-standing and relatively stable basic assumptions people hold about how the world works and their place in it and are introjected into their current family constellation. In a familial situation such as Ruth's, for example, where it is understood that the father is the head of the household, all decisions regarding the family may be suspended until he has the final word. This pattern may disempower the mother in disciplining the children, and they may perceive her, in effect, as another sibling.

The family schema is very important when conducting family therapy. It also contains ideas about how spousal relationships should work, what problems should be expected in marriage and how they should be handled, what is involved in building and maintaining a healthy family, what responsibilities each family member should have, what consequences should be associated with failure to meet responsibilities or to fulfill roles, and what costs and benefits each individual should expect to have as a consequence of being in a marriage.

It is important to remember that the family schema is shaped by the family of origin of each partner in a relationship as well as by environmental influences such as the media and peer relationships. Beliefs funneled down from the family of origin may be either conscious or unconscious, and they contribute to a joint or blended schema that leads to the development of the current family schema (see Figure 8.1 for a diagram of Ruth's family schemata).

This family schema is then disseminated and applied during child rearing. When mixed with their individual thoughts, perceptions of their environment, and life experiences, the family schema contributes to the development of the family belief system. The family schema is subject to change as major events occur (death, divorce) and also continues to evolve over the course of ordinary day-to-day experience.

As this schema begins to form, distortions may develop, contributing to family dysfunction. Ten of the more common distortions found with both couples and families are listed here:

1. *Arbitrary inference.* A conclusion is made by family members in the absence of supporting substantiating evidence. For example, one of Ruth's teenage children who returns home half an hour after his curfew is judged by the family as having been "up to no good."
2. *Selective abstraction.* Information is taken out of context: certain details are highlighted, and other important information is ignored. John fails to answer Adam's greeting the first thing in the morning, and Adam concludes, "Dad must be angry at me."
3. *Overgeneralization.* An isolated incident or two are allowed to serve as a representation of similar situations everywhere, related or unrelated. Because John and the kids have left food out from time to time, Ruth develops the belief that her family is wasteful and takes everything, including her, for granted.
4. *Magnification and minimization.* A case or circumstance is perceived in greater or lesser light than is appropriate. John demands that the children wash their hands before eating, but he fails to do so himself. When confronted by the children, he minimizes it by saying, "Well, I don't miss very often—so I'm excused."
5. *Personalization.* External events are attributed to oneself when insufficient evidence exists to render a conclusion. Jennifer blames herself for her parents' repeated arguments, saying, "Maybe I never should have been born."

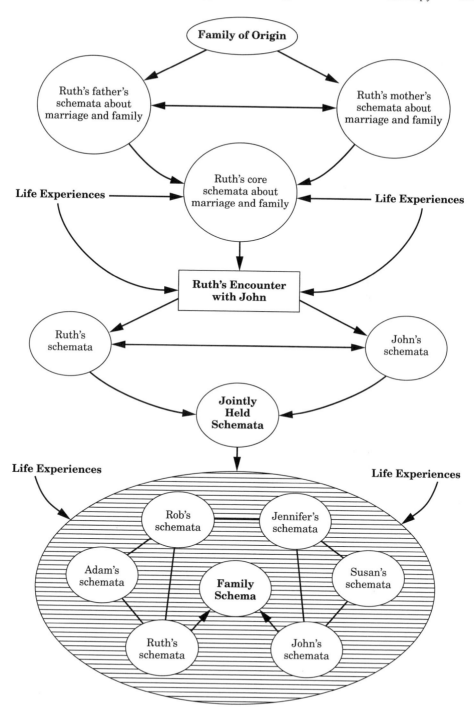

FIGURE 8.1 Ruth's Family Schemata

6. *Dichotomous thinking.* Experiences are codified as all or nothing, a complete success or a total failure. After repeated incidences in which Adam becomes involved in trouble at school, John and Ruth conclude, "We failed as disciplinarians."
7. *Labeling and mislabeling.* Imperfections and mistakes made in the past are allowed to serve as a stereotype of all future behaviors. Ruth and John failed to follow through on their word on one occasion and are consequently regarded by the children as being unreliable.
8. *Tunnel vision.* Family members sometimes see only what they want to see or what fits their current state of mind. John holds onto the rigid belief that the man is the "head of the household" because this is the way he perceived a father to be when he was growing up.
9. *Biased explanations.* In a polarized way of thinking that family members develop during times of distress, they assume that another member has an ulterior motive. John and the children distrust Ruth because she does not always admit to depressive thoughts when she indeed is experiencing them.
10. *Mind reading.* A family member has the magical gift of being able to know what others are thinking without the aid of verbal communication. Ruth anticipates that the family views her as a failure because she is unable to stand up for herself and demand what she wants.

These distortions become key targets in family therapy. Much of the intervention in therapy involves helping family members identify these distortions and then gather evidence to aid in reconstructing their thinking. It may also include practicing alternative patterns of behavioral interaction and dealing with their negative attributions.

Cognitive behavioral theory operates on a set of assumptions that Schwebel and Fine feel are central.[6] Here is a modified version of these assumptions:

Assumption 1. All members of a family seek to maintain their environment to fulfill their needs and wants. They attempt to understand their environment and how they can function most effectively in it, even if it sometimes means testing the boundaries. (For example, Adam may exceed his curfew by half an hour.) As family members gather data about how the family operates, they use this information to guide their behaviors and to aid in building and refining family-related cognitions. This leads to the development of an individual's construct of family life and family relationships. In Adam's case, he may begin to develop the concept that he can stretch the limits and not be chastised, thus inferring that rules may be broken.

Assumption 2. Individual members' cognitions affect virtually every aspect of family life. Five categories of cognitive variables determine these cognitions: (1) selective attention (John and Ruth's focus on the children's negative behaviors), (2) attributions (Ruth's explanations for why the children act up), (3) expectations (John's expectation that Ruth and the children will do as he asks without question), (4) assumptions (Adam's view that life is not fair), and (5) standards (Jennifer's thoughts about how the world should be).

Assumption 3. Certain "obstacles" to satisfaction lie within individual family members' cognitions (for example, Ruth's rigid view of the role of a wife and mother).

Assumption 4. Unless family members become more aware of their family-related cognitions and how these cognitions affect them in certain situations, they will not be able to identify areas that cause distress and replace them with healthy interaction.

Assessment of Ruth

My differential *DSM-IV-TR* diagnosis of Ruth would probably include the following:

> *Axis I:* (61.1) partner relational problem; (300.40) dysthymic disorder secondary to identity problem; (300.21) panic disorder without agoraphobia
>
> *Axis II:* (301.6) dependent personality disorder; (313. 2) identity problem
>
> *Axis III:* exogenous obesity
>
> *Axis IV:* problems related to social environment
>
> *Axis V:* GAF = 60 (on admission)

A family history is conducted to ascertain pertinent information about Ruth's family of origin. Although in most cases the family approach, like other modalities of family therapy, prefers to avoid "identifying a patient" and instead takes a balanced approach to dealing with family dysfunction, there are exceptions. It appears that this case is one. Ruth has already initiated individual psychotherapy, and it was decided to include her family as well. In a sense, therefore, she has already been designated as the "identified patient," and family treatment can initially center on her issues. However, typically, the CBT approach follows along much of the lines as the systems approach and prefers to consider the family as a whole as the identified patient.[7] Given Ruth's history and background, I elected to work on gaining a better understanding of her family of origin by having her invite members in for several visits. This will certainly lead toward developing a good grasp of her core schemata about herself and family life and will possibly provide me with insight into the development of her thinking style. Traditionally this should only involve Ruth, her parents, and any siblings. No other extended family members are invited—most importantly, her husband.

This session is exclusively designed for Ruth and the therapist to better understand the thinking styles of her origin and also to clear up any areas of conflict that remain from her past. If all were amenable, we could meet for three to five sessions of 2 hours each, focusing on the family schema and particularly on her emancipation from certain thinking styles that are deleterious to her. Although this is the ideal situation, such meetings are not always successful.

Ruth's family-of-origin meeting, which only included Ruth's biological parents, proved unsuccessful. Ruth's father, a very rigid man, decided to leave the family session abruptly, stating that he didn't believe in "this sort of stuff." Ruth's mother, being a rather passive individual, complied with her husband's demands to leave.

Initial Session With Ruth's Current Family

Because cognitive behavior family therapists attempt to identify both distorted schemata and maladaptive behavior patterns within the family dynamics, the next order of business in Ruth's case is to meet with her entire (immediate) family. As a result of the little that had been gathered from her family of origin and a separate interview with John, I now have some foundation for understanding the diverse philosophies that exist in each of their family backgrounds and can develop some insight into what schemata may have trickled down into the immediate family dynamics and affected Ruth's family schema.

During the initial family therapy session, I may ask various members of the family to describe their perceptions of the family and how things operate at home. It is often best to start with the youngest child and work up to the parents, so that the younger children are not influenced by what is said by their older siblings. As you will see in the excerpt from the initial session, I aim directly at ascertaining a solid understanding of the individual perceptions of the family and then attempt to conceptualize a joint consensus of the family schema. Once this is accomplished, the next step is to begin to educate the family in how the cognitive behavioral model of therapy works and then to begin to collaboratively identify cognitive distortions and erroneous thinking patterns that lead to maladaptive behavior patterns and dysfunction in the family.

> THERAPIST: I appreciate everyone coming in today. The aim of this meeting is to address some of the problems that exist in our family and explore some ways that may improve the way we interact with one another. Does that sound reasonable to everyone? [*Three members nod reticently in affirmation.*]
>
> JENNIFER: It doesn't to me! I think this sucks, and I don't want to be here.
>
> THERAPIST: So why did you agree to come?
>
> JENNIFER: I didn't. I was forced by my parents.
>
> THERAPIST: Listen, Jennifer, I want you to know that I never expect people to come here against their will. So if you feel so inclined, you are welcome to leave, provided that your parents and the rest of the family don't object. [*Pause*]
>
> JENNIFER: Well, so what do I do? Just leave now?
>
> THERAPIST: Yes, I suppose you could.
>
> JENNIFER: So where do I go?
>
> THERAPIST: I don't know. That's for you to decide.
>
> JENNIFER: Well, that's dumb. I'm not going to just sit outside in the car—bored!
>
> THERAPIST: OK, you're certainly welcome to stay if you choose, but I'm actually interested in hearing why you don't want to be here, particularly if being here would help the family.
>
> JENNIFER: Because this is all bull, and it's not my problem—it's Mom's. She just makes it everyone else's problem.

THERAPIST: Really? Does anyone else view things the same way Jennifer does? [*Brief pause*]

JOHN: No, I don't, totally. I think we all have some issues here that need to be discussed besides Mom, but Mom does have her problems.

THERAPIST: Anyone else have an opinion?

ROB: Yes, I'd like to say something. I think our family definitely has some problems in the way we think sometimes. Everyone is, like, all over the place, and there's no sense of . . . how would you say . . .

THERAPIST: Family unity?

ROB: Yeah! Sort of. I mean, like, Dad is sort of off in his own world—no offense, Dad—and Mom is doing her thing and trying to do for everyone else. It's sort of crazy.

THERAPIST: So, I'm hearing you say that things at home are somewhat chaotic at times, and you're uncomfortable with it?

ROB: Yes, but not at times. A lot of the time.

THERAPIST: OK! That's one perception. I'd also like to get back to something that Jennifer said about how Mom makes her problems everyone else's. Does that seem to be true for everyone here? Are we all in agreement with Jen's statement?

JOHN: No, I'm having a problem with Jennifer's statement. You know, Ruth and Jennifer really lock horns, and Jennifer will often take every opportunity she can to blame her mother, or anyone else for that matter—except, of course, herself.

THERAPIST: John, in addition to your concerns about Jennifer, you sound as though you're a bit protective of your wife.

JOHN: Well sure, but that's also the way I really see it.

THERAPIST: OK, but is there any agreement with any of what the kids are saying?

JOHN: Yeah, maybe some. I mean, look, Ruth has her problems, and we all know that. She's had a really rough upbringing, so I sort of see our roles as being to support her and not to give her a hard time.

THERAPIST: It seems to me that this is somewhat how your family has functioned for a long time until recently.

JENNIFER: Yeah! Until I screwed everything up, right? Right, Mom? That's it—say it.

RUTH [*Begins to sob*]: Oh, Jennifer, stop!

ADAM: I think Jennifer's problem is that she wants to grow up, and Mom won't let her. That's why she's mad at Mom and sort of miserable with everybody.

SUSAN: I sort of agree. I can see Mom starting to do a little of the same with me.

JOHN: What? Do what?

SUSAN: Uh-oh! Now I'm in deep shit! I opened my big mouth. [*Everyone chuckles*]

THERAPIST: No, that's OK, Susan. Say what you feel. The rule of therapy here is that we enjoy the freedom to say what's on our mind without fear of retribution.

SUSAN: Well, she's starting to be kind of overprotective with me the way she has with Jen.

JENNIFER: Yeah, and it's only with the girls. She's not like that so much with Adam and Rob.

THERAPIST: Ruth, how do you respond to everything you're hearing here today?

RUTH: Well, if I have to be honest, I guess it's true to some degree, but it's hard to listen to.

THERAPIST: OK, so you're protective of the girls, John is protective of you, and who is protective of Rob, Adam, and Dad?

ROB: Rob, Adam, and Dad. [*Everyone laughs*]

THERAPIST: Ah-ha! So the men take care of the men. That's interesting! Protecting one another appears to be a very important theme in your family.

JOHN: Well sure, you've seen that with both mine and Ruth's family.

THERAPIST: So I guess it would be fair to say, in a way, that this belief system was carried down to your family here [*Everyone agrees*]. We've just identified what's called a family schema or a core belief—that we protect each other in certain ways that sometimes differ. What belief exists in your family that calls for this behavior as opposed to the idea of everyone protecting themselves? [*Pause*]

SUSAN: Is it bad that we do this?

THERAPIST: Well, not necessarily, but the manner in which it has evolved in your family patterns here has caused some uneasiness. But let me get an answer to my question, because I think this is very important. [*Pause*]

JOHN: Well, I guess as the father, I feel the blame for some of it. While I support Ruth, I've kind of dumped on her by not taking more of an active role with the kids.

THERAPIST: Yes, and as a result of Ruth's upbringing, she has felt compelled to assume all of the responsibility for the family, perhaps in part to compensate for you. So there are several family-held distortions, as well as individual distortions about ourselves.

ADAM: What do you mean, distortions?

THERAPIST: Good question, Adam. Let me explain.

I then explain and review the cognitive distortions listed earlier in this chapter in a clear manner that the family members can understand, often using specific examples from their family.

THERAPIST: Let's try to identify some of the distortions together.

ROB: I have one that Mom does big-time.

THERAPIST: OK, let's hear it.

ROB: Well, it's the arbitration thing you said.

THERAPIST: Arbitrary inference?

ROB: Yeah, I guess that's it. Well, like if we're out past curfew, she freaks and starts accusing us of being up to no good, like we're guilty until proven innocent.

THERAPIST: Well, that's one that you may perceive Mom as doing, but do any of the other family members engage in the same distortion?

ADAM: Yeah, Jen does!

JENNIFER: Do not!

ADAM: Yes, you do.

SUSAN: Yes, you do, Jen. You're just like Mom in that way.

THERAPIST: Look, guys, we're just trying to identify cognitive distortions that you all engage in from time to time. This is not meant to be an antagonizing session. Also, you want to identify those distortions that you engage in yourselves as well as those that you witness with other family members.

JOHN: OK, I have one about myself. I sometimes find myself thinking much the way Ruth's father does, and I get annoyed when my decisions are questioned—as much as I hate to admit it. I guess I view compliance by the other members of my family as a gesture of respect, yet I tend to dump a lot onto Ruth.

At this point I have attempted to uncover some of the family's schemata and also to identify cognitive distortions. At the same time the family members are being oriented to the cognitive model in a subtle but clear way in which they will eventually be able to apply some of the techniques to themselves. The next step after identifying these distortions will be to teach them to begin to question and weigh the evidence that supports the internal statements that they make to themselves and to challenge any erroneously based assumptions.

THERAPIST: All right, that's a good one, John. So one of your beliefs that you're choosing to identify as being based on a distortion is that "the boss is never questioned, or it's disrespectful." In a sense, it's a matter of "do as I say, not as I do."

JOHN: Yeah, I guess. Boy, that sounds horrible when someone else actually says it in those terms.

THERAPIST: Well, don't worry so much about that, John. Let's just analyze it for a moment and see if we can challenge some of the basic tenets of that belief. Now, do you have any idea why you believe in that manner—that the man should be the boss and his requests or decisions should go unquestioned?

JOHN: Well, I know that I was closer to my father than I was to my mother. I also think that Ruthie's father had something to do with it early on. When we were first married he used to . . . sort of . . . drill me.

THERAPIST: Drill you?

JOHN: Yeah, you know, like take me aside and give me his lecture about how I need to act as the man of the house and family. Also, well, this may sound odd, but I kind of get the impression that this was sort of the way Ruthie was more comfortable with also, you know—like she kind of . . . oh, I forget the word you guys use all the time. It's a popular term . . .

THERAPIST: Enabled it?

JOHN: Yeah, yeah, enabled. That's it. She enabled me to be that way, subtly, I guess.

THERAPIST: I see. So, do you believe that you may enable Ruth as well with certain things, and perhaps you both enable the children?

RUTH AND JOHN [*In unison*]: Yes! Definitely.

THERAPIST: Might this be tied to the schema of taking care of one another? How does this all relate?

ROB: Well, I was thinking about that for a while when you were talking to Dad, and I think we're like a pack of wolves that sort of just look out for one another casually, and if one of us is in need, somebody will step in. But we never talk about it openly otherwise.

THERAPIST [*This was an interesting metaphor because wolves are animals that clearly tend to be protective of one another yet certainly are capable of protecting themselves as well.*]: OK, but how does this cause conflict?

ROB: I'm not sure.

SUSAN: I think that maybe the conflict comes when one person has one expectation and the other has a different expectation and it's never communicated. We just sort of . . . uh . . .

THERAPIST: Mind-read.

SUSAN: Yeah.

THERAPIST: OK, that's another distortion.

ADAM: Wow, we're one distorted family—cool! [*Everyone laughs*]

THERAPIST: Well, yes, you have your distortions, but all families do. It's not so unusual!

RUTH [*In jest*]: I don't know. When I listen to it all, it makes us sound as if we're the Adams family. [*Everyone laughs*]

THERAPIST: Good, Ruth! That was funny!

Here I am attempting to bolster some family cohesion through levity and at the same time trying to understand the family dynamics and how each member thinks and perceives various situations. Next, I will slowly introduce the idea of restructuring some of the thinking styles to bring about change.

THERAPIST: I think it might be important for us to take a look at some of the distortions you frequently engage in, now that you have identified a few of them, and see whether we may be able to challenge them, particularly those that interfere the most with your family dynamics. For example, John, would you be willing to volunteer so that I can demonstrate?

JOHN: Sure.

THERAPIST: You said, as I recall, that one of your beliefs is that as the father and one of the heads of the household "the boss is never questioned, or it would demonstrate disrespect"—something to that effect.

JOHN: Right.

THERAPIST: OK, now how well do you believe this statement can be substantiated?

JOHN: I don't know. It's just something I've come to know.

THERAPIST: So there's no substantiating evidence that renders it a sound principle. It's merely conjecture. So is it possible that it might be based on erroneous information?

JOHN: Possibly.

THERAPIST: Well, what do you know about the effect of this principle? In other words, what results have you received from it thus far?

JOHN: Well, not too good. In fact, no one obeys it, and I'm sort of scoffed at by my kids for believing it.

THERAPIST: All right, so perhaps you're seeing more evidence that says that it's not so effective than evidence supporting its use. So maybe it needs some modification, and you don't have to abandon the principle completely. I mean, respect is important, but to expect that no one will ever question what you say or do may be a bit unreasonable.

JOHN: Yeah, I see your point. But then how do I get it out of my head? I mean, it's ingrained there pretty heavily.

THERAPIST: Good question. Cognitive therapy utilizes a great many homework assignments. The basic theory contends that you must practice challenging negative self-statements, or what we call automatic thoughts, just as much as you have been using them in the past. One way to do this is by writing the corrected statement out each time you experience a negative self-statement, or in this case, a cognitive distortion. So, I'd like you to take a piece of paper and write across the top several headings, drawing a vertical line down the side of each to make columns like this:

Situation or Event	Automatic Thought	Cognitive Distortion	Emotion	Challenging Self-Statement	Alternative Response

Then, each time a situation occurs when you have a negative automatic thought, write it down. Starting with the left-hand column, record the situation or event in which you had the thought, and in the next column put exactly what the thought was. Next, attempt to identify what type of distortion you are engaging in and the emotional response that accompanies it. Then try to challenge that thought or belief by weighing the evidence that exists in favor of it. After that, write down an alternative response, using any new information you may have gathered. Does that make sense to you?

JOHN: Yes, but could we run through it once so that I'm sure I have it right?

THERAPIST: Certainly. Let's try an example.

JOHN: Something happened last week with Adam when he came in a little past curfew, and I said something about his being 5 minutes late. He started to, well, what I call challenge my authority by attempting to minimize what he had done, saying it had only been 5 minutes and was no big deal.

THERAPIST: So let's get everything down on paper.

Situation or Event	Automatic Thought	Cognitive Distortion
Adam arrives home 5 minutes late for curfew.	"He's defying me. He doesn't respect my position. If I don't chastise him, I'll be a lousy father."	Arbitrary inference Dichotomous thinking Personalization

Emotions	Challenging Self-Statement	Alternative Response
Upsets Angry	"Just because he comes home 5 minutes beyond his curfew doesn't mean that it's aimed directly at me. It also doesn't mean that he's intending to defy me."	"I could talk to him about it rather than jumping to conclusions and punishing him. Perhaps he just honestly lost track of time."

THERAPIST: That's excellent. Do you all see how we attempt to restructure some of our thinking?

ROB: Yeah, but what if Adam was really defying Dad? I mean, how do we know that it's correct?

THERAPIST: Good question, Rob. We gather information to support our alternative beliefs, and so one of the things that your dad could do is, as he said on the sheet, talk to Adam about what his intentions were in arriving home late. This could be applied to all of you at one time or the other as you recognize yourselves engaging in distorted thinking. We want to begin to examine your mode of thought and really question the validity of what you tell yourselves. This may make a monumental difference in how you interact.

Process Commentary

From this point I begin to monitor the family members in challenging their belief statements in the fashion just demonstrated. During this process, feelings and emotions are also addressed, as well as communication skills and problem-solving strategies. Regular homework assignments are also employed to aid family members in learning to challenge their distorted thoughts more spontaneously. Eventually, I will walk each family member through this specific technique to ensure its correct use. In addition, the use of behavioral techniques, such as the reassignment of family members' roles and responsibilities, becomes an integral part of the treatment regime in this particular case. Also, homework assignments are essential in facilitating change in the process of treatment.[8] The general concept behind this is that with the change and modification of dysfunctional thinking and behaviors there will be less family conflict.

Jerry Corey's Work With Ruth From a Cognitive Behavioral Perspective

In the *CD-ROM for Integrative Counseling* I work with Ruth from a cognitive behavioral perspective in a number of therapy sessions. Refer to the three sessions where I demonstrate my way of working with Ruth from a cognitive, emotive, and behavioral focus (Sessions 6, 7, and 8). See also Session 9 ("Integrative Perspective"), which illustrates the interactive nature of working with Ruth on thinking, feeling, and doing levels.

Basic Assumptions

In this section I combine elements from Ellis's rational emotive behavior therapy (REBT) and Beck's cognitive therapy (CT) in an integrative approach for my work with Ruth.[9] Beck's cognitive therapy shares with REBT an active, directive, time-limited, person-centered, structured approach. I draw on a range of cognitive, emotive, and behavioral techniques to demonstrate to my clients that they contribute to their own emotional disturbances by the faulty beliefs they have acquired. As a cognitive behavior therapist, I operate on the assumption that events or situations in life do not cause problematic emotions such as guilt, depression, and hostility. Rather, it is mainly our *evaluation* of the event and the *beliefs* we hold about these events that get us into trouble.

Initial Assessment of Ruth

As I review Ruth's intake form and her autobiography, it becomes evident that her beliefs are contributing to the majority of her problems. She has uncritically accepted certain values, many of which rely on guilt as a main motivation to control behavior. She is not making clear decisions based on self-derived values; rather, she is listening to intimidating voices in her head that tell her what she should do.

Ruth has an underlying dysfunctional belief that she must be perfect in all that she attempts. If she is not perfect, in her mind, there are dire consequences. She is continually judging her performances, and she is bound to think poorly of herself because of her unrealistically high standards. Indeed, there is a judge sitting on her shoulder and whispering in her ear. What I hope to teach Ruth are practical ways to talk back to this judge, to learn a new self-dialogue, and to help her reevaluate her experiences as she changes her behavior. This will be the focus of my therapy with her.

Goals of the Therapy

The basic goal of cognitive behavior therapy is to assist clients in learning how to replace self-defeating beliefs with constructive beliefs. To accomplish this goal, I will teach Ruth the A-B-C model of personality. This model is based on the premise that A (the activating event) does not cause C (the emotional consequences); rather, it is mainly B (her belief about the activating event) that is the source of her problems.

I collaboratively work with Ruth in formulating the goals for her therapy. During the initial session, she indicates that she does not want to act out the rest of her life according to her parents' design. Establishing a therapeutic contract with Ruth as a way to structure our working relationship is a way to reach agreed-upon goals.

Therapeutic Procedures

In working with Ruth as a cognitive behavior therapist, I employ a directive and action-oriented approach. Functioning as a teacher, I focus on what she can learn that will lead to changes in the way she is thinking, feeling, and behaving. Drawing on Beck's ideas from CT, I intend to focus on the inaccurate conclusions Ruth has reached by teaching her to look for the evidence that supports or contradicts her views and hypotheses. She will frequently hear the question "Where is the evidence for_____?" Through the use of open-ended questions and a Socratic dialogue, I will try to teach Ruth ways to systematically detect errors in her reasoning that result in faulty assumptions and misconceptions (cognitive distortions). After she has recognized her cognitive distortions, I will encourage her to carry out a range of homework activities, to keep a record of what she is doing and thinking, and to form alternative interpretations to replace her faulty assumptions. Eventually, through a process of guided discovery, I expect her to acquire insights into the link between her thinking and the ways she feels and acts. I also expect her to learn a range of specific coping skills to deal with current and future problems.

I will ask Ruth to read literature from a cognitive behavioral perspective as an adjunct to her therapy sessions. For instance, I'll strongly recommend that she study books such as Ellis and Harper's *A New Guide to Rational Living;* Ellis's *Rational Emotive Behavior Therapy: It Works for Me—It Can Work for You;* and Judy Beck's *Cognitive Therapy: Basics and Beyond.*[10]

Like any other form of learning, therapy is hard work. If Ruth hopes to successfully change her beliefs and thus change her behavior, it will be necessary for her to practice what she is learning in real-life situations. I will stress completing homework assignments, and I will ask her to fill out an REBT Self-Help Form. This form has her analyze activating events, her beliefs about these events, the consequences of those beliefs, her disputing and debating of her faulty beliefs, and the effects of such disputing.

In working with Ruth, I attempt to integrate the cognitive and affective (feeling) dimensions. Although I emphasize the cognitive aspects of therapy, I believe that changing entails actually experiencing feelings. However, experiencing feelings alone is not enough to bring about a substantive change in behavior. Much of our therapy will focus on examining Ruth's current behavior and trying on new ways of behaving both during the therapy hour and in her daily life.

The Therapeutic Process
ELEMENTS OF THE PROCESS

Working With Ruth's Faulty Beliefs   To assist Ruth in achieving a constructive set of beliefs and acquiring a self-enhancing internal dialogue, I perform several tasks as her therapist. First of all, I challenge her to evaluate the self-defeating beliefs she originally accepted without questioning. I also urge her to work toward giving up her faulty beliefs and then to incorporate functional beliefs that will work for her. Throughout the therapeutic process, I actively teach her that self-condemnation is the basis of many of her emotional problems, that it is possible for her to stop critically judging herself, and that with hard work, including behavioral homework assignments, she can greatly reduce many of her dysfunctional notions.

Ruth's *real* work, then, consists of doing homework in everyday situations and bringing the results into our sessions for discussion and evaluation. I am concerned that she not only recognize her self-defeating thought patterns but also take steps to challenge and change them.

We explore how her fear of failing stops her from doing so many things. She then says that she would love to square dance but has not because she is afraid of being clumsy and looking like a jerk. She would love to ski but avoids it for fear that she will fall on the "bunny hill." I am working with Ruth on her evaluation of events and her prediction that she will fail. I want her to see that even if she fails she can still learn to cope with the outcomes.

We continue for a couple of months, with Ruth agreeing to do some reading and also carrying out increasingly difficult homework assignments. Gradually she works up to more risky homework assignments, and she does risk looking foolish several times, only to find that her fantasies were much worse than the results. She gives her speech, and it is humorous and spontaneous. This gives her an increased sense of confidence to tackle some other difficult areas she has been avoiding.

Dealing With Ruth's Beliefs About Herself as a Mother   Ruth is feeling very guilty about failing one of her daughters. Jennifer is having troubles at school. and Ruth says Jennifer is "going off the deep end." Ruth partially blames herself for Jennifer's problems, telling herself that she must do better than her own mother.

RUTH: I don't want Jennifer to suffer the way I did. But in so many ways I know I'm critical of her, just as my mother was of me at that age.

JERRY: What are you telling yourself when you think of this?

I want Ruth to see that her self-defeating thoughts are getting her depressed and keeping her feeling guilty. My hope is that she will see that the key to eliminating needless anxiety and guilt lies in modifying her thinking.

RUTH: I feel guilty that I didn't help Jennifer enough with her schoolwork. If I had tutored her, she would be doing well in school.

JERRY: Do you see how your line of thinking gets you into trouble? What about Jennifer's role in creating and maintaining her own problems?

RUTH: Yes, but I've made many mistakes. Now I'm trying to make up for them so she can change.

JERRY: I agree that you may have made mistakes with her, but that doesn't mean it will be the ruination of her. Can you see that if you do so much for her and make yourself totally responsible for her, she doesn't have to take responsibility?

I am attempting to get Ruth to dispute her destructive thinking. She has continued this pattern for so long that she now automatically blames herself, and then guilt follows.

RUTH: Well, I try to think differently, but I just keep coming back to these old thoughts. What can I say to myself?

JERRY: When Jennifer does something wrong, who gets blamed?

RUTH: Me, most of the time.

JERRY: And those times that Jennifer does well, who gets credit?

RUTH: Not me. I dwell so much on what she's not doing that I don't often see what she does right.

JERRY: How is it that you're so quick to place blame on yourself and just as quick to discount any part you have in Jennifer's accomplishments?

RUTH: Because problems occupy my mind, and I keep thinking that I should have been better with her.

JERRY: I hope that you can begin to be kinder to yourself. Consider saying to yourself something like this: "Even though I've made mistakes in the past and will probably continue making mistakes, that doesn't mean I've ruined Jennifer or will. It doesn't mean I'm the same kind of mother to her that mine was to me."

RUTH: That sounds pretty good. . . . If only I could say those things and mean them, and feel them!

JERRY: Well, if you keep disputing your own thinking and learn to substitute constructive self-statements, you're likely to be able to say and mean these things—and you'll probably feel different too.

PROCESS COMMENTARY My major focus with Ruth is on her thinking. Only by learning to apply rigorous self-challenging methods will she succeed in freeing herself from the defeatist thinking that led to her problems. I place value on behavioral homework assignments that put her in situations where she is forced to confront her faulty beliefs and her self-limiting behavior. I also consistently challenge Ruth to question her basic assumption of needing the approval of others to feel adequate.

Questions for Reflection

1. What advantages do you see to the manner in which Dr. Ellis drew on cognitive, emotive, and behavioral techniques in working with Ruth's dysfunctional beliefs? Any disadvantages?
2. Assume that you suggested a technique to Ruth (such as keeping a journal or reading self-help books) and she refused, telling you that what you are asking was too much to expect. What might you say to her?
3. What common faulty beliefs do you share with Ruth, if any? To what degree have you challenged your own self-defeating thinking? How do you think this would affect your ability to work with her?
4 Working with Ruth in an active, directive, and challenging manner could raise some ethical issues, especially if you attempted to impose your values by suggesting what she should value. As you review Dr. Ellis's, Dr. Dattilio's, and my work with Ruth, do you have any concerns that any of us are "pushing values"?
5. Dr. Dattilio focused on Ruth's family schemata, including beliefs from her family of origin and those in her current family. What uses can you see in working with family schemata? What are some advantages of using a cognitive behavioral approach in counseling couples? Any disadvantages?
6. What might you do if Ruth came from a background where her "musts," "oughts," and "shoulds" arose out of her cultural conditioning? What if she insisted that she felt guilty when she dared to question her upbringing and that in her culture doing so was frowned upon?
7. In the example of my work with Ruth as a cognitive behavior therapist, I blended some of the concepts and techniques of Ellis (REBT) and Beck (CT). What are some aspects of REBT and CT that you might combine?
8. What ideas do you have for using cognitive behavior concepts and procedures in conjunction with Gestalt techniques? Can you think of examples in Ruth's case where you could use Gestalt techniques in working with her self-defeating thinking?

Notes

See the DVD/online program entitled *Theory in Practice: The Case of Stan* (Session 8: Cognitive Behavior Therapy Applied to the Case of Stan) for a demonstration of exploring Stan's faulty beliefs through the use of role reversal and cognitive restructuring techniques.

1. For a more detailed discussion of the basic assumptions, key concepts, and practical applications of rational emotive behavior therapy, see G. Corey (2009), *Theory and Practice of Counseling and Psychotherapy* (8th ed., Belmont, CA: Brooks/Cole). Chapter 10 ("Cognitive Behavior Therapy") outlines the

basic elements of Albert Ellis's REBT, Aaron Beck's cognitive therapy, and Donald Meichenbaum's cognitive behavior modification.

2. For a discussion of the cognitive, emotive, and behavioral techniques typically employed by rational emotive behavioral practitioners, see Albert Ellis (2001), *Overcoming Destructive Beliefs, Feelings, and Behaviors* (Amherst, NY: Prometheus Books).

3. For useful self-help books that present a straightforward approach to REBT based on homework assignments and self-questioning, see A. Ellis (2001), *Feeling Better, Getting Better, Staying Better* (Atascadero, CA: Impact Publications); and A. Ellis and R. Harper (1997), *A Guide to Rational Living* (Hollywood, CA: Wilshire).

4. See See D. H. Baucom and N. Epstein (1990), *Cognitive-Behavioral Marital Therapy* (New York: Brunner/Mazel). This work offers a wealth of assessment techniques, strategies, and case vignettes with couples. Also, for a comprehensive treatment of cognitive behavioral therapy with couples and families, refer to the edited work by F. Dattilio (1998), *Case Studies in Couple and Family Therapy* (New York: Guilford Press).

5. See F. M. Dattilio (2005), Restructuring family schemas: A cognitive-behavioral perspective. *Journal of Marital and Family Therapy* 31(1), 15–30.

6. See A. I. Schwebel and M. A. Fine (1994), *Understanding and Helping Families: A Cognitive-Behavioral Approach* (Hillsdale, NJ: Erlbaum). Modifications made with permission of the authors.

7. See F. M. Dattilio (1993), Cognitive techniques with couples and families, *The Family Journal, 1*(1), 51–65; F. M. Dattilio (2000), Cognitive-behavioral strategies, in J. Carlson & L. Sperry (Eds.), *Brief Therapy With Individuals and Couples* (pp. 33–70, Phoenix, AZ: Zeig, Tucker & Theisen); and F. M. Dattilio (2001), Cognitive-behavior family therapy: Contemporary myths and misconceptions, *Contemporary Family Therapy, 23*(1), 3–18.

8. See F. M. Dattilio (2002), Homework assignments in couple and family therapy, *Journal of Clinical Psychology, 58*(5), 535–547; and F. M. Dattilio, L. L'Abate, and F. Deane (2005), Homework for families, in N. Kazantzis, F. P. Dean, K. R. Ronan & L. L. L'Abate (Eds.), *Using homework assignments in cognitive-behavior therapy* (pp. 357–404, New York: Brunner-Routledge).

9. I do not repeat too much detail about the cognitive behavioral approaches, so it would be well it to review the perspectives of Drs. Ellis and Dattilio in this chapter.

10. Here are the complete references for the books I recommend for clients: A. Ellis and R. Harper (1997), *A New Guide to Rational Living* (Rev. ed., Hollywood, CA: Wilshire Books). The authors show how to apply the principles of REBT to problems of everyday living. A. Ellis (2004), *Rational Emotive Behavior Therapy: It Works for Me—It Can Work for You* (Amherst, NY: Prometheus). In this personal book, Ellis describes the many challenges he has faced in his life and how he has coped with them using REBT. J. Beck (1995), *Cognitive Therapy: Basics and Beyond* (New York: Guilford). Beck clearly outlines the principles and techniques of cognitive therapy, giving many clinical examples of how the internal dialogue of clients results in various emotional and behavioral problems.

CHAPTER NINE

Case Approach
to Reality Therapy

General Overview of Reality Therapy

The goal of reality therapy is to help clients get reconnected with the people—both old and new—they have chosen to include in their quality worlds and to teach clients choice theory. A main therapeutic goal is to teach clients how to improve the significant relationships in their lives. Therapists help individuals find more effective ways of meeting their needs for belonging, power, freedom, and fun. The approach challenges clients to make an assessment of their current behavior to determine whether what they are doing and thinking is getting them what they want from life.

Reality therapy is active, directive, and didactic. The therapist assists clients in making plans to change specific behaviors that they determine are not working for them. Skillful questioning and a variety of behavioral methods are often used to encourage clients to evaluate what they are doing. If clients decide that their present behavior is not effective, they develop a specific plan for change and make a commitment to follow through.

When clients are more effectively fulfilling their wants and needs and when they have gained (or regained) control of their world, they are ready to leave counseling. This approach has the advantage of being anchored in a specific plan for change. This plan is not nebulous, but specific, which allows for objective evaluation of outcomes.

A Reality Therapist's Perspective on Ruth

by William Glasser, MD

Introduction

Before showing how I would work with Ruth, I want to provide a brief introduction to a few key concepts of reality therapy. I continue to believe we choose all of our significant behaviors in an attempt to find happiness. Barring extreme poverty, physical illness, and the ravages of old age—none of which are chosen—when we are unhappy enough to seek therapy, I believe it is because we do not have a satisfying relationship. All of our chosen ineffective behaviors—neurosis, psychosomatic disease, and psychosis—are our self-destructive attempts to improve a present relationship or find a better one. Therefore, as you will see in the case of Ruth, reality therapy focuses on finding the unsatisfying present relationship.

We do not focus on the past because all relationship problems are in the present and must be solved in the present. We do not focus on the symptom because the symptom is always chosen to deal with the present unsatisfying relationship. The symptom will disappear when that relationship is improved. In contrast to most theoretical orientations, I believe that although we may be the product of our past we are not victims of our past unless we choose to be so. Approaching a client this way drastically shortens therapy because it quickly gets to the core of the problem, which is a present flawed or nonexistent relationship. A skilled reality therapist, using choice theory, can help most clients who are functional enough to walk into the office in about 10 sessions or less.[1]

Assessment of Ruth

Because psychological symptoms are chosen behaviors, in the description of my therapy with Ruth I use verb forms rather than nouns to describe how she chooses to behave. For example, you will see that I use "panicking" instead of "panic" to describe her symptoms. A panic disorder would be a consistent choosing of panicking behaviors as exemplified by Ruth. She will be taught to say, "I am choosing to depress" or "I am depressing" instead of saying, "I am depressed" or "I am suffering from depression." This way of describing symptoms or disorders makes sense when you understand choice theory.

As Ruth presents herself, it is obvious that she has not been able to satisfy her basic needs except her need for survival. She does not feel that she has love, power, fun, or freedom in her life, and her choices of anxietying, panicking, and psychosomaticizing are her ways of expressing her extreme frustration. These symptoms keep her anger from bursting forth, and they scream, "Help me!"

Key Issues and Themes

First of all, Ruth needs someone who will listen to her and not criticize her for what she says. She will, however, present her story and continually ask for criticism by saying things like, "It's wrong for me to complain; I have so much; I'm acting like a baby." She will make a whole family of comments like these. She knows how to "guilt," and the counselor must not get involved in the process. My most important task as her therapist is to listen to her and tell her that she has a right to express herself without criticism.

Then, it is important for Ruth to learn about her basic needs. She needs to try to give more to her marriage and improve the relationship with her husband. I can ask over and over, "How does your being miserable help you or anyone else?" Although Ruth can be kind to her parents and others when she talks to them, it is important that she tell them firmly that she is going to do what she believes is right for her life.

I would encourage Ruth in her choice to go to work, although I would discuss with her the choice to become an elementary schoolteacher. This is a very giving role, and she may not do well at this now. She may need to work among adults and to be appreciated for her adult qualities by her peers. She needs a job where she does not have to be a "good" person to be appreciated.

Ruth's weight, diet, or symptoms should not be discussed in detail because they are not the problem. If she wants to talk about them, I will listen, but I will not encourage her to explore these topics. Talking about her problems or failures will lead Ruth to choose to guilt, because she can only solve them through a better relationship. My approach will be to focus on her getting out of the house and finding a satisfying place in the adult world. If it is satisfying enough, her complaints and symptoms will be lessened, but she will still have to work on her relationship with her husband.

Ruth's finances will be discussed. What she earns for the first several years might be spent on herself and on doing things with her husband and children that are especially enjoyable to her. I would encourage Ruth not to save her money, give it to charity, or spend it on necessities unless that is what she really wants to do. Instead, I will constantly encourage her to do what is right for her, not what is right for others or "good" for the world. I think she needs to learn to be a little selfish.

From the first session I will bring up her relationship with her husband. But this will not be to find fault with what they are doing as much as it will be to try to guide Ruth to take the initiative and do something she believes will improve her marriage. Following choice theory, she can only control her own life; she cannot control her husband's life. If John is willing to come in for marriage counseling, I will employ what I call structured reality therapy, which is described in my book *Choice Theory*.[2]

Therapeutic Techniques

It is important that I be warm and uncritical and teach Ruth to be accepting of herself. In fact, I may say to her, "You need to realize that you are choosing your actions and only you can change what you are doing. You can't change anyone else." I will give Ruth my *Choice Theory* book to read, and we will discuss it in each session until she is well aware of these concepts and how they apply to the life she has and is still choosing to live. This information, coupled with a good client–therapist relationship, should substantially reduce the time for counseling.

It is best that plans be discussed, written out, and checked off. Ruth is competent, but her competence is never used for herself. She can be asked over and over, "How will satisfying your needs hurt anyone else?" and "How may doing this actually help others? Let's talk about this, because the answers to these questions are important for your life."

As much as possible, humor in the sessions will be helpful. Ruth is overdue for a laugh or two, and laughter will allow her to let go of her psychosomatic symptoms more quickly than anything else she can do. In therapy sessions I will emphasize her good points, which are many, and at each session she can be encouraged to tell what she did that was good for her and what she accomplished that she never thought she would be able to do.

It will be good for Ruth to consider the idea of inviting friends in and making a social life. She needs people. If her husband does not want to help, she can be encouraged to do this by herself. If she has a job, she might get hired help in to do the housework, which is something Ruth probably has never done or even dreamed of doing. The idea of spending money for enjoyment is worth a lot of therapy time.

Ruth can be encouraged to talk about her children and apply the ideas of choice theory to them. I will ask her what she thinks she needs to do to get along with her daughter Jennifer, and I will advise her to stop telling her daughter what to do. Also, Ruth can be challenged to stop criticizing Jennifer completely, no matter what Jennifer or any of her other children say or do. Instead, Ruth might go out with her daughter for a good time, tell her she likes her the way she is, and say, jokingly, that she should not model herself after an unhappy mother, only a happy mother.

I can teach Ruth that it is her life and that it is up to her, not anyone else, to make what she wants of it. Whenever she says that she can't do something, I can ask her why she can't, then ask her to give all the reasons why she could do it, and compare the two sets of reasons.

What Ruth needs is freedom. She has locked herself in a prison of her own making for most of her life, and there should be a discussion of who can let her out. If she is locked in, it is because she won't open the door.

A Sample Session With Ruth

I keep the sessions as light as I can. Ruth needs to learn to take her problems less seriously so it will be easier for her to convince herself that she can make better choices. Here is how I guide the therapy after about a month.

> RUTH: It was really bad last night, all horrible feelings.
>
> THERAPIST [*Interrupting*]: The sweats, the palpitations, the fear of impending doom, the whole kit and kaboodle of your midnight misery. I'll grant you this, if you've learned anything in your 39 years, it's how to panic. Don't you think it's time to learn something better to do at night?
>
> RUTH: How can you talk like that? Do you really believe I'm choosing this panic, that I enjoy these attacks? How can I possibly be choosing them? They come on while I'm sleeping, and they wake me up.
>
> THERAPIST: Tell me, if you're not choosing them, who is? You've read about choice theory. You choose all you do, just as I do, and just as everyone does. Of course, you're not enjoying this choice but—I know this is hard to believe—to you it's better than anything else you could choose in the middle of the night.
>
> RUTH: You're crazy! It's not better or worse, it's what I do as I sleep. Don't you listen to me? I'm asleep; it wakes me up.
>
> THERAPIST [*Not rising to the bait of arguing with her but continuing on*]: Suppose I called you in the middle of the night and woke you up before you woke up with your choice to panic. In fact, let's do it right now. Pretend you're sleeping, and I give you a call.

RUTH: I'm getting afraid to go to sleep, even to go to bed. The attacks are excruciating. You don't have any idea of how bad they are. You've never had one. If you had, you wouldn't be sitting there so smugly telling me I'm choosing this misery.

THERAPIST: If you want to be able to make better choices while you're asleep at night, you've got to learn to make better choices in the daytime. But, c'mon, let me call and wake you up. Will you do it, or do you have a better idea?

RUTH: Of course I don't have a better idea. If I did, would I be here listening to this nonsense? Go ahead and call me.

THERAPIST: OK, ring, ring!

RUTH: Hello, who is it? What time is it?

THERAPIST: It's me, Dr. Glasser. I got to thinking about you and your problems, and I decided to call you. Can we talk for a few minutes?

RUTH: I'm sleepy. Couldn't it wait until morning?

THERAPIST: Just one question—one, OK?

RUTH: OK, OK, I'm up now, so I might as well talk. What do you want to know?

THERAPIST: I want to know what you were thinking about tonight when you went to bed. Tell me as much as you remember.

RUTH: What I always think about—that my life is all messed up, and it's not getting better. I'm in a rut. There's nothing going on in my marriage, my body looks just awful, and my whole day is horrible. I can understand why people drink and take drugs if they feel the way I do all the time. What more is there to tell you? It's what I tell you every time we talk. That's what I think about, my awful day and my miserable life. What's the sense of repeating it now? What good will it do?

THERAPIST: If I call you tomorrow night, do you think the story will be the same?

RUTH: Of course it'll be the same. It's been the same for the last 10 years.

THERAPIST: No, it hasn't. It's different now.

RUTH: What are you talking about? How is it different?

THERAPIST: The panicking is new, and seeing me is even newer. That's different, a lot different.

RUTH: Yeah, it's even worse than it was. At least I didn't have the panic. And you're no bargain either. I never thought of it that way. Maybe if I get rid of you I'll get rid of the panic.

THERAPIST: If you want to quit, I won't try to stop you.

RUTH: Well, you don't seem to be doing me much good.

THERAPIST: You don't seem to be doing yourself much good either. Why don't you choose to do something for yourself? Do you want to keep going to bed afraid you're going to wake up scared to death and then come here and blame me because I'm not doing anything to help you? How's that going to help you?

RUTH: What can I do?

THERAPIST: You do a lot all day long, but you just don't do anything for yourself. Tomorrow, even if you have what you call a panic attack, don't tell me about it. It's your choice, and I can't do a thing about it. All I can help you do is have a better day and do some different things than you've been doing. Do you want to start tomorrow, start changing the way you live, or do you want to choose to go on as you are?

RUTH [*Softening now. She's been listening. The middle-of-the-night-call technique is getting her attention.*]: But how can I?

THERAPIST [*With emphasis*]: How can you not? Why keep waiting? I know you're afraid. We're all afraid to try new things because they might not work out. Let's stop wasting time and start right now to make a plan for you to do something for you. You won't hurt anyone if you start to take care of yourself. If you begin feeling better, you'll be doing your whole family a favor.

After this, we make a plan to do something that, for a change, will satisfy Ruth's needs, and we're on our way.

🐚 **Process Commentary**   I dare not wait much longer than a month to confront Ruth's resistance. She's not a weakling; it takes a lot of strength to panic as she has. But if I don't do this, and if I let her control me with her panicking as she has been trying to control everyone else, she won't change. To gain a sense of control, she has been willing to choose the suffering she complains about. We all do it once in a while; it's just that she does it a lot. I need to intervene, for that's my job as a therapist. There is no other way. As I told her, I've seen a lot of Ruths, and they have all changed. From my experience, her prognosis is very good if she's treated this way. Once she begins to put the energy into taking effective control of her life that she puts into panicking, she will make rapid progress.

I can't tell how long therapy will take. But if we focus on the marital relationship, do not pay attention to the symptoms, teach her that the only person's behavior she can control is her own, get her to put her energy into getting closer to her husband and children, and get her to find a satisfying job, it might not take much more than 10 initial sessions. After that I might see her once a month to keep her on course.

Another Reality Therapist's Perspective on Ruth

by Robert E. Wubbolding, EdD

Introduction

I will present several examples of interventions that typify the practice of reality therapy. These dialogues include specific questions that can be asked when using reality therapy. It is not my intention to imply that if the therapist merely asks a few questions the client will automatically make a rapid or dramatic change. The dialogues represent samples of the most important interventions, which are made repeatedly and rephrased in dozens of ways throughout the process of counseling.

🕮 Setting the Stage for Therapy

Because of the importance of informed consent, at the beginning of the first session or as soon as is appropriate I review with Ruth all pertinent details related to professional disclosure: my credentials, the nature and principles of reality therapy, confidentiality and its limits, her rights and responsibilities, and the general goals of counseling. I emphasize the common formulation used in reality therapy: "my job, your job, our job." "My job" is to function as an ethical professional who recognizes his limitations. "Your job" is to keep the scheduled appointments and to disclose as much as you choose. "Our job" is to work for changes in your life that will result in increased happiness (need satisfaction). I emphasize that if Ruth is willing to work hard this therapy will indeed be short term.

🕮 Exploring Ruth's Expectations

I then explore with Ruth the thoughts she had when she decided to come for counseling and the thoughts she had today before her first visit. She describes her uncertainties, her hesitancy, and her sense of failure. I encourage her to discuss her fears about counseling and about "opening Pandora's box" and becoming overwhelmed with what she might find. With empathic listening I begin to form a relationship with her. I show confidence that she can make progress, on one condition—that she is willing to work at feeling better. If she will expend some effort, she can gain a sense of control, which is now lacking.

One of my goals in the first session is to help Ruth relax about her problems. Our dialogue goes as follows:

THERAPIST: What thoughts went through your mind when you came here today?

RUTH: I was afraid and apprehensive. I have wondered what would happen. I often feel pain and am upset.

THERAPIST: How have you tried to fight off your pain, anxiety, fears, and overall upsetness?

RUTH: I have expended a great deal of energy to purge myself of my misery.

THERAPIST: And has this relentless effort paid off for you?

RUTH: When my efforts have not been successful, I have renewed them with more intensity and vigor.

THERAPIST: Is fighting your worries helping to lessen them?

RUTH: Well, I must admit that attacking my fears has not yet worked.

THERAPIST: If this approach is not working for you, I encourage you to think in terms of the opposite approach. Since fighting your fears does not help, now may be the time to admit to yourself, at least for a while, that you will continue to be upset. Could you consider embracing your problems? After all you've been through, it is no wonder you're upset. Who wouldn't be?

Presenting this alternative approach to clients often helps them to feel more confident in themselves. They realize that they are normal or at least are handling their problems in a normal way. For Ruth, my hope is that she will begin to consider that her fear, anxiety, and overall upsetness are reactions to her problems, but not the problem itself. If she can see these reactions as normal, she has a good chance of managing them in the future.

In the initial session and in subsequent sessions, we spend a lot of time exploring her "quality world" as it relates to counseling. She goes into detail about the statement that what she wants most from therapy is to be told "what I have to do and be pushed to do it, so that I can begin to live before it's too late." I again make a significant point that she already has a tremendous advantage: even now she believes she can do something, and she wants to begin to live. I ask her to define what it means for her to "live." She describes her feeling of being a doormat at home, being overweight, being lonely and isolated, and being spiritually alienated. As she describes her pain, I express excitement that she is able to put it into words and point out that being able to articulate this pain is a major step.[3]

RUTH: To be honest, I am upset that I need to seek professional help and that I can't work out my problems on my own.

THERAPIST: I would be surprised if you weren't upset about seeking outside help. It's a healthy way to feel. But actually, you deserve to be congratulated for taking this first big step. It must have taken courage.

RUTH: Well, I never thought of it as a big step.

THERAPIST: As you sit here now, do you believe counseling can help you? Do you believe things can improve for you in a short time?

RUTH: I came because I think it will help.

THERAPIST: I've read your history, and we've talked here for a while, and I believe you could feel better. I make no guarantees, but I think a better life is possible. And I base that thought not on an idle wish but on four pieces of specific information: You have taken a step by coming here, and you also have at least some belief that your life can be better. Moreover, you've already set a goal: to keep living. And finally, you're very open about what hurts. In other words, you can describe your pain.

RUTH: So there's hope.

THERAPIST: I agree. There is hope. I also believe you can feel at least a little better quickly, on one condition.

RUTH: What is that condition?

THERAPIST: That you're willing to put forth some effort, even hard work. And this work, strange as it sounds, means less effort in fighting off the pain.

RUTH: I'm willing to do that.

Working With Ruth's Depression

Ruth at times resists my optimistic attitude and my emphasis on her positive steps, insisting that they are minor successes and that she sometimes feels depressed. Because of her insistence, I determine how depressed she has become. Assessing the possibility of suicide reveals there is no risk. I decide to use paradoxical techniques with Ruth. At first she schedules some time for choosing to depress herself, perhaps 10 minutes every other day. I ask her to describe in detail what she can do to make the situation worse. She enjoys this discussion and laughs heartily as she goes into detail about how she can criticize herself publicly, procrastinate even more over her plans, increase her guilt, and exaggerate her fear of death. She comes to see how such ineffective thinking holds her back from a happier and need-satisfying life. But most important, she learns through this upside-down logic that if she can make her life more miserable she can also make it more enjoyable. It is important to reemphasize that I have determined early on that she is not suicidal or depressed to the point of being incapacitated. In such cases, paradoxical techniques are to be avoided.

I then encourage Ruth to describe what she wants that she is not getting and to say what she actually is getting from her husband, from each of her children, from her religion, from school, and, most important, from herself. (She has already described what she wants from me.) This exploration takes more than one session. She gradually develops more specific goals or wants related to her family, social life, self (for example, weight), professional life, and the spiritual aspect of her life (a much-neglected area in the counseling profession).

Exploring What Ruth Wants

An exploration of one aspect of Ruth's wants as they relate to her family—more specifically, her husband—is illustrated in this dialogue.

THERAPIST: You've described your relationship with your husband. Describe how you would like the relationship to be. To put the question another way, what do you want from him that you're not getting?

RUTH: I want him to be understanding.

THERAPIST: Could you be more specific about what you want that you're not getting?

RUTH: He takes me for granted. He only wants me to be a mother for his children. He's always busy at work and doesn't think of me as an independent person. And, you know, sometimes I think he's right.

THERAPIST: What do you want him to feel toward you?

RUTH: I would like him to appreciate me, to like me, to be friendly.

THERAPIST: And if he appreciated you, what would he do differently?

RUTH: He would show me more attention.

THERAPIST: Ruth, if he showed you attention tonight, what would you do?

RUTH: I'd be friendly. If he would share something about himself, I'd realize that he has confidence in me and has some feelings for me.

THERAPIST: Would you be interested in working toward having a better relationship with him?

RUTH: Of course.

THERAPIST: I think you've established a goal for your counseling. We'll be talking about what you can do to make the situation better for yourself.

In this dialogue Ruth has defined one want or goal. Using similar questioning, I help her clarify her wants as they relate to her children, religion, school, and other aspects of her life. The emphasis in formulating such goals is on helping her state her own role in the desired outcome.

During these early sessions Ruth also defines what she can control and what she cannot control. I ask her to evaluate whether she can "force" others to change and how much control she can exert over her past history. I gradually help her come to believe her life will be happier if she focuses on changing her own behavior in small increments.[4]

THERAPIST: You've defined what you want for yourself regarding your husband, children, and school. You've said that you want to feel that your life has some spiritual purpose—that it has lasting value. Would you describe the components of your life process that you have control of and what is beyond your control?

RUTH: I've tried hard to get my husband to change, and I've also tried to lose weight, to see some purpose to my life, to get rid of the night terrors, cold sweats, and all the pain I feel, and to get a professional identity and a life of my own.

THERAPIST: Can you really change any of these—the people or things on the list?

RUTH: I'm not sure. I'm so confused.

THERAPIST: Let's take them one by one. Can you force your husband to be the kind of person you want him to be?

RUTH: No, I've tried for years.

THERAPIST: Have your efforts gotten the result you wanted?

RUTH: No.

THERAPIST: Can you control your weight?

RUTH: I've lost and gained it back so many times.

THERAPIST: You have lost weight! So you know how to reduce your pounds, and you've succeeded many times.

RUTH: Well, I haven't looked at it as a success. It seems to me that regaining weight is a failure.

THERAPIST: But you have succeeded many times. You've taken charge of your eating for extended periods.

RUTH: I suppose you're right.

THERAPIST: What about gaining a sense of purpose—what I would call a sense of importance—that you are somebody, that you are worthwhile?

How much control do you have over specific plans to formulate this ideal and to work toward it?

RUTH: Well, the way you put it makes it sound as if I could do it and as if I do have some control.

THERAPIST: Ruth, in my counseling I try to translate my clients' ideas into actions—actions that they can take to fulfill their needs.

RUTH: So how do I begin?

THERAPIST: By taking small steps—one at a time. But let's not rush. In fact, I'd suggest that you not make any radical or extensive changes until we talk some more.

🙊 **Process Commentary**   I also ask Ruth to decide on her level of commitment. She is obviously not at the basic level: "I don't want to be here." For some parts of her life such as her weight, she may be at the second level: "I would like the outcome, but not the effort." "I'll try," the third level, is probably characteristic of much of her life. But I want to help her see her efforts to lose weight as successes. And so I lead her to the fourth and fifth levels: "I'll do my best" and "I'll do whatever it takes." If clients are willing to be open and work hard, they can benefit in a short time from reality therapy.

The real benefit in utilizing this system is not "the words" but "the music." This questioning format, often discouraged in counselor training programs, helps Ruth develop an internal perceived locus of control and realize that she has choices. She then gains a profound belief that life can be better, that she can feel better, and that she has more control than she ever dreamed of. It should be clear that reality therapy involves more than superficial planning and problem solving.

The underlying principle is that when Ruth improves her relationships, her pain will lessen and she will be happier. I will help her in the areas of her relationships with her husband, career, and education. I will work with Ruth's gaining increased acceptance of herself as both an imperfect and a worthwhile human being.

Helping Ruth Evaluate What She Is Doing

Interspersed throughout the entire process are dozens of questions related to self-evaluation: "Did your specific activities yesterday help you to the degree that you had hoped for?" "Are your wants realistically attainable?" "Is what you want really good for you?" More specifically, "Is your boring but comfortable life what you truly want?" "Is it good for you now?" "Are you spiritually the kind of person you want to be?" "What would you be doing differently if you were the type of person you wanted to be?" And the key question, "How are you getting closer to your husband and children?" We pick up the dialogue in a subsequent session.

THERAPIST: Let's focus on one aspect of what you have referred to as a source of great pain, which is your relationship with your husband. You mentioned in previous sessions that he ignores you, takes you for granted, and talks only minimally to you. And I gather that you want this situation to change.[5]

RUTH: I sure do.

THERAPIST: And you've also decided that your own actions are the only ones that are within your control.

RUTH: Yes.

THERAPIST: Now I want to ask you some important questions about the choices you've been making and what you've been doing in the relationship.

RUTH: OK.

THERAPIST: What happened last night? Describe exactly what you did last night from the time your husband came in to the time you went to bed.

RUTH: [*She describes the entire evening in detail. I help her to be precise.*]

THERAPIST: What did you want from him at that time?

RUTH: [*She describes what she would have liked from him.*]

THERAPIST: What could you say differently from what you said last night?

RUTH: I'll say, "Hello, how was your day?" and give him a hug. Then I'll say, "Let's read the mail and then fix supper together."

THERAPIST: Sounds good. So you'll take charge of the only part of the relationship that's within your ability to control?

RUTH: Yes, my own actions.

THERAPIST: Now let's suppose he doesn't respond the way you would like. What then?

RUTH: Well, I could tell myself: "I've done what I can do, and there's no guarantee that he'll change. I choose to feel satisfaction at having made better choices than those I've made in the past."

THERAPIST: And, if you make this kind of effort, there is a good chance that the relationship will improve.

🌸 **Process Commentary** In this session I put emphasis on helping Ruth evaluate her own behavior rather than her husband's actions. By questioning her, I indirectly reminded her that she has control only of her own actions and that if she takes action she will feel that she is doing her part. She was then helped to make short-range, attainable plans that have a high likelihood of success. In subsequent sessions she explores other choices—that is, her other unmet needs and their accompanying ineffective and effective behaviors as well as her perceptions regarding the inner sense of control she has gained and still wants to gain.

I encourage Ruth to make more attainable special plans to fulfill her need for fun. I select fun because it is the most obvious unmet need, the one she is most likely to be able to meet more effectively, and the easiest to work on. In view of the fact that she has said she wants to lose weight permanently, I encourage her to join a support group such as Weight Watchers. I suggest that she get to know the students in her classes and organize study groups. This will give her a sense of belonging and help her fulfill her need for power or achievement.

I ask Ruth to read 10 minutes a day (if she wants to) on a topic that is spiritually uplifting. A good starter is *A Set of Directions for Putting and Keeping Yourself Together.*[6] To be avoided is anything that encourages guilt, fear, or self-deprecation. She has expressed a deep need for "an anchor," and to neglect this part of her life would be unfortunate. She can at least be referred to a sensible clergyman who understands reality therapy.

Overall, I help her fulfill her needs for belonging and power and fun more effectively. This is accomplished by use of the "WDEP" system that includes the following process: W = determining wants, including level of commitment and perceived locus of control; D = examining the total behavior, including exploring what she is doing, thinking, and feeling; E = assisting her to make her own inner self-evaluations, especially regarding her wants and behaviors; and finally, P = helping her develop positive and realistic plans aimed at fulfilling her needs in ways that are different from previous choices.

I feel confident in applying reality therapy with Ruth. I also feel challenged by the multitude of Ruth's problems, but my knowledge of choice theory helps me to see that when she changes any behavior the good feeling and success generalize. Thus, I am confident that picking any symptom to work on will lead Ruth to increased satisfaction with her entire life. Her obvious high level of motivation and minimal resistance facilitate relatively steady and visible progress toward the fulfillment of her wants (goals).

Jerry Corey's Work With Ruth From a Reality Therapy Perspective

Introduction

Reality therapy is active, directive, practical, and cognitive behavioral in focus. As a reality therapist, I see my task as helping clients clarify their wants and perceptions, evaluate them, and then make plans to bring about change. My basic job is establishing a personal relationship with my clients that will give them the impetus to make an honest evaluation of how well their current behavior is working for them.

Because I make the assumption that changing feelings is more difficult than changing actions, the focus of therapy is on what Ruth is doing, and to some extent, what she is thinking. She will find that it is typically easier to get herself to *do* something different than to *feel* something different. Any discussion of her feelings is related to what she is doing and thinking.

Assessment of Ruth

Rather than focusing on Ruth's deficits, problems, and failures, I am interested in looking at her assets, accomplishments, and successes. Initially I ask her questions such as these: "What do you want? How might your life be different if you had what you wanted now? What do you consider to be your major strengths? What qualities do you most like about yourself? What have you done that you are proud of? What resources can you build on?" From Ruth's autobiography and intake form, I know that she has several strengths and inner resources. Now she needs to develop a clear plan for attaining her personal objectives.

Goals of Therapy

Ruth's present behavior is not working as well as it might. She is unproductively dwelling on unfortunate events from her past, and she is paying too much attention to feelings of guilt and anxiety and not enough to those things she is doing that create these feelings. In short, she is making herself anxious and guilty by what she is doing. I try to direct her attention toward these actions because they are the most easily controlled part of her life. I continue challenging her to make an honest assessment of how well her current behavior is getting her what she wants. Then we collaboratively make plans to bring about the changes she desires.

Therapeutic Procedures

I expect Ruth to make a commitment to carry out her plans. If she hopes to change, *action* is necessary. It is essential that she stick with her commitment to change and not blame others for the way she is or give excuses for not meeting her commitments. To facilitate this, we will develop a therapeutic contract that spells out what she wants from therapy as well as the means by which she will attain her goals.

If Ruth says that she is depressed, I will not ask *why* she is depressed, nor will I ask her to dwell on feelings of depression. Instead, I will ask what she has done that day to contribute to her experience of *depressing*. Changes in behavior do not depend on changing one's attitudes or gaining insights. On the contrary, attitudes may change, as well as feelings, once clients begin to change their behavior.

The Therapeutic Process

Ruth's therapeutic journey consists of my applying the procedures of reality therapy to help her meet her goals. Although the principles may sound simple, they must be adapted creatively to the therapeutic process. Although these principles are applied progressively in stages, they should not be thought of as discrete and rigid categories. Each stage builds on the previous stage, there is a considerable degree of interdependence among these principles, and taken together they contribute to the total process that is reality therapy. This process weaves together two components: the counseling environment and specific procedures that lead to changes in behavior.

ELEMENTS OF THE PROCESS

✆ **Establishing the Relationship**   During our initial sessions, my main concern is to create a climate that will be conducive to Ruth's learning about herself. The core of the counseling environment consists of a personal involvement with the client, which must be woven into the fabric of the therapeutic process from beginning to end. I convey this involvement through a combined process of listening to Ruth's story and skillful questioning. This process increases the chances that she will evaluate her life and move in the direction of getting what she wants.

In some of our early sessions, Ruth wants to talk about occasions when she experienced failure in her childhood and youth. She quickly wants to blame past negative experiences for her fears. She seems a bit stunned when I tell her that I do not want to go over her past failures and that if we are going to talk about the past at all I am more interested in hearing what went right for her. I do not encourage her to focus on feelings related to negative experiences. Part of her present problem is that she is already stuck in some negative feelings, and I do not want to reinforce her in continuing this pattern.

🖉 Challenging Ruth to Evaluate Her Behavior   After getting a picture of how Ruth sees her world, I encourage her to try something different—to take a hard look at the things she is doing and see if they are working for her. Questions that I pose to her are: "What are the things you've done today?" "What did you do this past week?" "Do you like what you're doing now?" "Are there some things you would like to be doing differently?" "What are some of the things that stop you from doing what you say you want to do?" Let me make clear that I do not bombard her with these questions one after another. The early sessions are, however, geared to getting her to consider this line of questioning. Rather than looking at her past or focusing on her attitudes, beliefs, thoughts, and feelings, I want her to know that we will be zeroing in on what she is doing today and what she will do tomorrow.

My assumption is that Ruth will change when she makes an assessment of the constructiveness or destructiveness of what she is doing. Here is a brief excerpt from a session.

> RUTH: So, what do you think I'm doing wrong? There are times I want to give up, because I don't know what to do differently. [*She very much wants me to make an evaluation for her.*]
>
> JERRY: You know how important it is for you to be the one who makes a judgment about your own behavior. It's your job to decide for yourself what is and isn't working. I can't tell you what you "should" do. [*For me to simply tell her that some of her present ways are ineffective will not be of much value to her.*]
>
> RUTH: Well, I do want to go out and get some practice with interviews for part-time or substitute teaching. But I keep telling myself that I'm so busy I just don't have time to set up these interviews.
>
> JERRY: And is that something you'd like to change? [*My line of questioning is to ascertain how much she wants what she says she wants. I am attempting to assess her level of commitment.*]
>
> RUTH: Yes, I want to change it. I want to be able to arrange for these interviews and then feel confident enough to have what it takes to get a part-time job.

We look at how Ruth stops herself (not why) and explore ways she might begin to change behavior that she calls "sitting back and waiting to see what happens." She says that she does not like her passivity and that she would like to do more initiating. One of the factors we talk about is how she lets her family get in the way of her doing some of these things she says she wants to do.

🐚 **Planning and Action**   We devote a number of sessions to identifying specific behaviors Ruth decides are not working for her. A few of these ineffective behaviors are procrastinating in arranging for job interviews; sitting at home feeling depressed and anxious and then increasing these feelings by not doing anything different; allowing her 19-year-old son, Rob, to come home after squandering money and then taking care of him; allowing her daughter Jennifer to control her life by her acting out; and continually taking on projects that she does not want to get involved in. Knowing that we cannot work on all fronts at once, I ask her what areas she wants to do something about.

We develop some plans to set clear limits with Ruth's family. She has a pattern of doing things for her children and then resenting them and winding up feeling taken advantage of. Part of her plan calls for sitting down with each of her children and redefining their relationships. I suggest that it would be a good idea to have at least one session with her family. The idea both excites and frightens her. Yet she actually surprises herself when she is successful in getting John and her four children to come in for a 2-hour session of family therapy. At this session we mainly negotiate some changes in roles after Ruth has told each family member specific changes she would like and has been striving for. One of her sons and one of her daughters are not at all excited about some of the proposed changes, and they want to know what is wrong with the way things are. What I had in mind when I suggested this family session was to give Ruth an opportunity to ask for what she wants and to witness her negotiating for these changes. The session helps me see how she relates to her family, and it helps her ask for what is important to her.

PROCESS COMMENTARY   Functioning within the spirit of reality therapy, I do not tell Ruth what she should change but encourage her to examine her wants and determine her level of commitment to change. It is up to her to decide how well her current behavior is working for her. Once she makes an evaluation about what she is actually doing, she can take some significant steps toward making changes for herself. She has a tendency to complain about feeling victimized and controlled, and my intention is to help her see how her behavior actually contributes to this perceived helplessness. In our sessions, we focus on what Ruth does from the time she wakes up to the time she goes to bed. Through a self-observational process, Ruth gradually assumes more responsibility for her actions. She sees that what she does has a lot to do with the way she feels.

After Ruth becomes clearer about certain patterns of her behavior, I encourage her to develop a specific plan of action that can lead to the changes she desires. Broad and idealistic plans are bound to fail, so we work on a concrete plan for change that she is willing to commit herself to. Through this process,

Ruth learns how to evaluate her own behavior and how to adjust her plans to experience success.[7]

Questions for Reflection

1. Dr. Glasser contends, "Although I believe we may be the product of our past, we are not victims of our past unless we choose to be so. Approaching a client this way drastically shortens therapy because it quickly gets to the core of the problem." What do you think of this viewpoint?

2. Dr. Glasser states, "All of our chosen ineffective behaviors—neurosis, psychosomatic disease, and psychosis—are our self-destructive attempts to improve a present relationship or find a better one." What are your reactions to this statement?

3. Both Dr. Glasser and Dr. Wubbolding seem very directive in pointing out the themes Ruth should explore, and they are also fairly directive in suggesting what she should do outside of the sessions. What are your reactions to this stance? As Ruth's counselor, would you be inclined to bring up topics for her to explore if she did not specifically mention them?

4. Do you have any concerns that reality therapy could be practiced in such a way that the therapist imposed his or her values on the client? Do you see this as potentially happening with the way Dr. Glasser, Dr. Wubbolding, or I worked with Ruth?

5. Dr. Wubbolding makes use of frequent questioning to help Ruth clarify what she wants. What are some of his questions that you most like? Why?

6. What differences do you see in the various styles and applications of reality therapy as practiced by Dr. Glasser and Dr. Wubbolding and my work with Ruth?

7. Apply the procedures of reality therapy to what you know of Ruth. Systematically show how you would get her to focus on what she is doing, on making an evaluation of her behavior, and on helping her formulate realistic plans.

8. Assume that you are a client in reality therapy. What do you think this experience would be like for you? How would you describe your current behavior? Can you come up with a plan for changing a particular behavior you really want to change?

Notes

See the DVD/online program entitled *Theory in Practice: The Case of Stan* (Session 9: Reality Therapy Applied to the Case of Stan) for an illustration of assisting Stan in designing an action plan.

1. For a more complete discussion of Dr. Glasser's latest thinking on how choice theory applies to the practice of counseling, see W. Glasser (2001), *Counseling With Choice Theory: The New Reality Therapy* (New York: HarperCollins).

2. W. Glasser (1998), *Choice Theory: A New Psychology of Personal Freedom* (New York: HarperCollins).

3. For a more detailed treatment of Dr. Wubbolding's perspective on applying reality therapy, see R. Wubbolding (2000), *Reality Therapy for the 21st Century* (Philadelphia, PA: Brunner Routledge [Taylor & Francis]). This is an easy-to-read, useful, and comprehensive book that represents significant extensions of reality therapy. The practical formulation of the WDEP system of reality therapy is developed. Many excellent questions and brief examples clarify ways of using its concepts.

4. Rather than have Ruth become overwhelmed by attempting to make sweeping changes in her life, Dr. Wubbolding suggests that Ruth select small aspects of her behavior that she can change.

5. You will notice that Dr. Wubbolding uses skillful questioning as a way to help Ruth evaluate what she is doing. In the *CD-ROM for Integrative Counseling,* Session 8 ("Behavioral Focus in Counseling"), you will note ways that I attempt to assist Ruth in specifying concrete behaviors that she will target for change.

6. See R. Wubbolding and J. Brickell (2001), *A Set of Directions for Putting and Keeping Yourself Together* (Minneapolis, MN: Educational Media Corporation). This is a practical and positive self-help book based on the concepts of reality therapy.

7. For an overview of the basic concepts of reality therapy, see G. Corey (2009), *Theory and Practice of Counseling and Psychotherapy* (8th ed., Belmont, CA: Brooks/Cole). Chapter 11 ("Reality Therapy") describes the WDEP system that both Dr. Wubbolding and I refer to in our work with Ruth. This chapter also contains a comprehensive discussion of Dr. Glasser's formulation of choice theory and reality therapy.

CHAPTER TEN

Case Approach
to Feminist Therapy

General Overview of Feminist Therapy

The major goal of feminist therapy is empowerment, which involves acquiring a sense of self-acceptance, self-confidence, self-esteem, joy, and self-actualization. Some other therapy goals are enhancing the quality of interpersonal relationships, assisting women to make decisions regarding role performances, and helping them to come to an understanding of the cultural, social, and political systems' influence on their current situation. Clients can expect more than adjustment or simple problem-solving strategies; they need to be prepared for major shifts in their way of viewing the world around them, changes in the way in which they perceive themselves, and transformed interpersonal relationships.

Feminist therapists carry out a range of information-giving functions and teaching functions. By focusing on external structures, they attempt to free clients from a "blaming the victim" stance. They are free to use techniques from many other therapy orientations, and they often employ techniques such as reframing and relabeling, bibliotherapy, advocacy, power intervention, social action, and gender-role analysis and intervention.

Feminist therapists emphasize the teaching aspects of therapy and strive to create a collaborative way of working with clients. Emphasis is placed on the demystification of the therapy process and on providing a context wherein informed consent can occur. Clients decide when they want to terminate, which usually occurs when clients feel an increased sense of personal identity and empowerment.

A Feminist Therapist's Perspective on Ruth

by Kathy M. Evans, PhD, Susan R. Seem, PhD, and Elizabeth A. Kincade, PhD[1]

Introduction

Feminist therapy is unique among counseling and psychotherapy theories. Feminist therapy views the "personal as the political," challenging a basic assumption of psychological thinking that distress is personal, due to individual pathology. It also takes into consideration the social and political milieu in which people live as a cause of distress. This was a pioneering approach that recognized that individuals are embedded in their social and cultural contexts, and that lasting psychological change must address these contextual issues as well as individual issues. Feminist therapy emerged from three aspects of the women's liberation movement of the 1960s: consciousness-raising groups, battered women shelters, and the anti-rape movement. Eschewing patriarchal structures that foster a "father knows best" attitude, women met and worked together to change personal, political, social, and cultural beliefs and values about women and their roles.

Consciousness-raising groups consisted of women who met together to discuss their experiences as women. These groups were leaderless, nonhierarchical, and functioned on the feminist values of egalitarianism, the equitable distribution of power, and shared responsibility. Women realized that what they initially believed was their unique individual problem was common among women as a group.

In battered women shelters and the anti-rape movement, women worked together to combat the patriarchal culture that resulted in male violence against women. Traditional approaches of counseling, operating from an androcentric perspective, viewed the etiology of rape and battery as women's masochism. In sharp departure to this, feminists viewed male violence, supported by sociocultural values, as the cause.

Feminist therapists work to change the dominant culture's structure and power that is harmful to individual clients, and they have had a profound effect on the field of counseling and psychology, especially with regard to gender bias and gender-role stereotyping. As a result, there have been significant changes in how the profession views diagnosis, case conceptualization, and treatment. For feminist therapists there is no lasting individual change without social change.

It is important to note that awareness of women as an oppressed group developed from the privileged class of women, who for the most part were White, middle class, and educated. Contemporary feminist therapy, however, acknowledges other forms of oppression, such as racism, homophobia, ageism, and classism, in addition to sexism and the effect of multiple oppressions on people. Privilege can harm all individuals, not just those who are oppressed. Historically, feminist therapy focused exclusively on women both as therapists and clients, yet presently it is considered as an appropriate modality for both women and men.

In the past, feminist therapists disagreed about whether feminist therapy was based on a series of political and philosophical assumptions or grounded in psychological theory. Recent literature and research suggest that feminist therapy is based on psychological theory and not just a set of philosophical assumptions.[2] Current feminist therapy more closely resembles existential and humanistic modes of therapy than the evidence-based or empirically validated approaches. This does not mean that feminist therapy techniques are not grounded in empiricism, but rather, that feminist therapy emphasizes the relational intersections in therapy including those of the client and the greater societal context. This emphasis influences the treatment choices made by feminist practitioners.

Approaches to Feminist Therapy

Feminism holds that gender inequity exists and that this is a source of oppression to individuals and societies. In addition, this oppression is painful and harmful. This inequality is based in power, and for the most part the power balance is in favor of men. Furthermore, feminist philosophy seeks to answer the question, "What is the source of gender oppression?" How one answers this question largely determines the interventions used with clients. Various feminist philosophies answer this question differently.

At one end of the continuum is the belief that oppression is due to patriarchy, or male domination. In this model, enduring change requires political and social change rather than merely individual change. At the other end of the continuum is the belief that oppression is largely caused by socialization, our internalized individual and self-replicating cultural beliefs. Within this model, individual change *is* possible and necessary as this forces societal beliefs and positions to change.

Although there are philosophical differences among feminist practitioners, the basic tenets and beliefs of feminist therapy are the same: Therapist and client work together to understand and remove the psychological, sociopolitical, and cultural factors that result in client distress. Feminist therapy holds two overarching goals. The immediate goal is to relieve an individual client's distress. The ultimate goal is to alleviate sociopolitical oppression. This long-term goal requires feminist therapists to consider social change as a part of the therapeutic process.

Basic Tenets of Feminist Therapy

Feminist therapy holds a number of common tenets that cut across diverse theories. These common tenets are (a) the personal is political, (b) the importance of egalitarian relationships, and (c) privileging the female experience.

The personal is political reflects the belief that individual experiences do not occur in a vacuum. Feminist therapy assumes that the *primary* source of client distress lies within the social and political context, not within the individual. Pathology is reframed, and external causes are separated from internal causes. Individuals are not blamed or pathologized for feeling, thinking, and behaving in ways that are a function of living in an oppressive society. However, this focus on external causes of distress does not negate the importance of examining intrapsychic factors that interact with external forces.

Feminist therapy posits that *relationships should be egalitarian.* Therefore, the counseling relationship should not replicate the power imbalance individuals experience in society. Most traditional therapies operate from dominant cultural values that place the counselor in the role of expert. In contrast, feminist therapy is viewed as a collaborative process in which counselor and client are considered as being of equal worth. Counselor expertise is based on specialized knowledge; clients are experts on themselves and their lived experiences.

Traditional psychological theory and therapies are based on androcentric norms; feminist therapy *privileges the female experience.* Historically, psychological theory compared female experience to male experience, and females were often seen as deviant. In feminist therapy, female experience is valued in understanding distress. Women are understood in the primary context of their female experience, not the male experience. Feminist therapy does not negate the male experience, but rather values the female experience for both women and men.

Initial Assessment and Evaluation

Although none of the three of us takes a single approach to feminist therapy, we agreed that we would each discuss Ruth's case from a different point of view based on the question "What is the basis of gender oppression?" Susan will present the radical feminist perspective that patriarchy is the source of oppression. Kathy presents the cultural perspective that oppression is due to undervaluing women's unique ways of being in the world. Elizabeth takes the socialist perspective that the core of oppression is a complicated blend of economic philosophy and gender disparity. We will discuss our theoretical and therapeutic differences in conceptualizing Ruth's case when appropriate. When we agree, we will present one point of view. The final dialogue with Ruth will be a combination of our three approaches.

🕮 **Traditional Diagnosis and Assessment**   As traditionally practiced, diagnostic systems such as the *DSM-IV-TR* reflect the dominant culture's definitions of pathology and health. Many feminist therapists avoid using these diagnostic systems. However, if we as feminists were to use a formal diagnostic system to diagnose Ruth as part of her assessment, we would use the *DSM-IV-TR* with knowledge of its major weaknesses.[3]

The *DSM-IV-TR* assumes androcentric and monocultural models of mental health and functioning. Sexism, racism, classism, ableism, heterosexism, and ageism are all embedded in its descriptions. For example, overcompliance with traditional female gender-role socialization is viewed as pathological (see dependent and borderline personality disorders). Furthermore, some female gender-role stereotyped descriptors exist in certain diagnostic labels (for example, histrionic personality disorder). In contrast, diagnostic categories that have higher prevalence rates for men (such as antisocial personality disorder) have clear behavioral descriptors. Additionally, the *DSM-IV-TR* infers an intrapsychic focus that contradicts a political analysis. It disconnects personal experiences from the political arena and ignores the environmental context.

Traditionally, psychological distress is viewed as private and results in an individual solution rather than a social or political one. In fact few diagnostic labels locate the source of a client's problem in the environment. Misdiagnosis and blaming the victim may occur when sociopolitical factors are minimized or ignored. Moreover, counselor bias and subjectivity may influence the diagnostic process. The fact that a number of authors from different theoretical orientations arrived at a number of variant diagnoses for Ruth points to the role that clinical bias or subjectivity may play in diagnosis.

🕮 **Feminist Assessment and Evaluation**   Historically, feminist therapists eschewed diagnosis because they could not formally diagnose internalized oppression. However, a feminist sensitivity to diagnosis can result in the use of formal diagnostic systems without replicating patriarchal assumptions and attitudes. Diagnosis, as traditionally practiced, is an act of power that exacerbates the power imbalance between counselor and client. In contrast, feminist assessment and diagnosis require a cooperative and phenomenological approach.

After reviewing the summary of Ruth's intake interview and her autobiography, all three of us agreed that our work with Ruth would examine the multifaceted social, political, and economic context of her life. This examination would move beyond understanding Ruth within her family and seek to comprehend her personal relationships within the context of the larger society.

Ruth's exposure to sexism and other forms of oppression constitute an insidious long-term trauma. Our evaluation of Ruth consists of listening for connections between the personal and the political in her story. We work to understand Ruth as a gendered being who is assigned a subordinate status by the dominant male culture. Thus, we use gender and power as categories of analysis for Ruth and her life experience. This type of analysis creates avenues for the exploration of gender-role concerns and issues of power without punishing Ruth for participation in her socialization process and subordinate societal status.

Ruth's people pleasing, living for others, difficulty acting on her own behalf, being a superwoman, and being a good wife and good mother are viewed as evidence of her compliance with traditional female gender-role socialization and with her second-class status, not as indications of her pathology or dependency. Ruth's symptoms of panic are viewed as a result of role conflict. Women are often forced to choose between their own growth as individuals and traditional female gender-role behavior. This choice results in internal conflict that surfaces as anxiety. Ruth expresses her awareness of living for others and feeling obligated to stay in her marriage. She communicates her acute awareness of dissatisfaction with her life as it is but also clearly articulates her fear of change. Thus, Ruth's symptoms of panic, her feelings of conflict, and her identity confusion are viewed as coping strategies for or adaptations to surviving oppression, discrimination, and gender-role stereotyping. Her symptoms might also be a protest against her oppression. Ruth's behaviors and feelings are adaptive rather than pathological, and we would not give her a diagnostic label at this time.

We would also look closely at Ruth's anger. Women are not supposed to have legitimate power in patriarchal societies, and they often feel powerless. Feeling powerless often leads to feelings of rage at having little or no control over one's life. Additionally, patriarchal norms do not support and often punish direct expression of female anger. Therefore, women have learned to convert anger into symptoms that are acceptable. Based on this assumption, we explore with Ruth her feelings about being powerless. We encourage Ruth to express her anger at her treatment as a woman. We view anger as potentially positive energy and help Ruth use this energy to take either individual or social action to obtain power in her life.

We differ in our assessment work with Ruth in that Susan, working from a radical feminist perspective, pays particular attention to the meaning and presence of female gender-role compliance and noncompliance for Ruth, including past and current rewards and penalties. She examines with Ruth how her second-class status as a woman influences her psychological distress. One focus of assessment, therefore, is to identify how Ruth has internalized oppressive sociocultural forces. Kathy adds to this perspective by helping Ruth identify her stage of feminist identity development and assessing such things as anger, self-examination, acceptance, and role confusion. As a socialist feminist, Elizabeth addresses the economic issues of payment and the sociopolitical implications of a *DSM-IV-TR* diagnosis.

Any assessment would be done in collaboration with Ruth, and we would encourage Ruth to ask questions or pose alternative options. If, as a result of our assessment, a formal label is given, the diagnosis and its possible consequences will be discussed with Ruth. In that discussion we would share with Ruth the process by which we arrived at such a formal diagnosis. Also, Ruth would share in decisions about how this information would be used.

Therapeutic Procedures

All therapy demands a firm relational foundation, otherwise client changes tend to be ephemeral or superficial. The necessary conditions for feminist therapy are the establishment of an egalitarian relationship and a deep and thorough understanding of Ruth's story, or the narrative of her experience.

🕸 Establishing and Modeling Egalitarian Relationships   An egalitarian relationship is essential if Ruth is to achieve a sense of her own power. It is important to work with Ruth to remove artificial power boundaries in the counseling relationship. Feminist counselors consider the first contact with clients as an interview: an opportunity for counselor and client to get to know each other and make a mutual decision about whether or not they will work together. Feminist therapists work to demystify counseling. To that end, we ask Ruth why she is seeking counseling and what she wants to gain from it. We share with her that we are feminist therapists who approach counseling from a feminist perspective and explain what this means without jargon, with respect for Ruth's intelligence.

In addition, since Ruth has little experience with mutually satisfying relationships in which she is viewed as an equal participant, it is important that Ruth experience and learn how to establish egalitarian relationships in her own life. Thus it is important to model an egalitarian relationship in the counseling relationship. This modeling begins with the first session. Ruth is invited to actively participate in the assessment process, in the contracting of counseling, and in setting counseling goals. Further, feminist therapy has the goal of helping Ruth develop interdependence in relationships and enabling her to develop skills to negotiate her needs and wants in relationships.

Kathy, working from her perspective as a liberal, African American feminist therapist, acknowledges the power differential between Ruth and herself, which is based in American conceptions of race. By seeking help from Kathy, the balance of power between Kathy and Ruth shifts so that it is more equal in that Ruth (a White woman with supposedly more power in our society) needs

Kathy's help (which gives Kathy more power). Kathy would explore Ruth's experiences with people of color and would tell her about herself as a professional and as a person. She would let Ruth know that if she wishes to see a counselor more similar to herself she understands.

Elizabeth, examining the case from the socialist feminist perspective also focuses on power but does so by acknowledging that clients pay for counseling and that this interferes with establishing an egalitarian relationship. In addition, as a socialist feminist she is aware of how titles are used to take power away from people. Those we call by a title usually hold economic power or social status different from our own.

All three of us hold that self-disclosure, when it is in service to Ruth, is a very powerful and important part of establishing and maintaining an egalitarian relationship. We share with Ruth our belief that although we possess expertise in counseling techniques and psychological theory Ruth has her own specialized knowledge—she is the expert in her life and experiences.

🐦 **Understanding Ruth's Story**   It is important that Ruth's story is accepted and validated by her therapist. Feminist therapy embraces values that may conflict with some of Ruth's cultural and religious values, and we accept this. We do not lecture Ruth about oppression; rather, we guide her through an exploration of her life experiences that involve oppression. We tell Ruth that we believe each woman experiences her gender, race, ethnicity, and culture differently, and we listen for evidence of all these factors in Ruth's story.

Further, we help Ruth understand herself in relation to her sociopolitical context. Part of understanding Ruth's story and educating her about the complex sources of her distress entails knowing her beliefs, thoughts, and feelings about being a White, 39-year-old, middle-class woman who comes from a fundamentalist religious background. We provide Ruth with information about women in general, and we self-disclose about our own beliefs and experiences when appropriate. In addition, we engage in self-examination of our own strengths and limitations, biases and prejudices, and worldview regarding this client.

Interventions and Therapy Goals

Feminist therapy is based on a model of egalitarianism, choice, and empowerment. These three elements produce feminist therapists who work with clients in the context of the client's environment, which includes various economic, cultural, and family situations that often preclude long-term therapy. Short-term interventions, such as assertion training, cognitive restructuring, and short-term dynamic models are woven into feminist therapy practice. Additionally, as one of the goals of feminist therapy is empowerment for the client, feminist therapists assume that clients will leave counseling empowered to act on their own. When and how they do this is a collaborative effort between therapist and client. This means that the therapist and client are aware of changing needs in the therapeutic relationship and negotiate for more or fewer sessions when mutually agreed upon.

To model healthy boundaries in counseling and further strengthen the relational context, feminist therapists share relevant information about themselves and their values and beliefs with their clients. Clients are invited to discuss information and beliefs with their therapist. Goals for counseling are devised collaboratively. Further, feminist therapists educate their clients about the theory and process of feminist therapy, which empowers clients to make informed choices about therapy. Therapy is demystified, and clients are taught therapeutic skills. Feminist therapists model egalitarian behaviors that will help clients negotiate relationships within and outside of counseling.

Despite ideological differences in conceptualizing women's oppression, the three of us use these interventions with our clients and believe these specific interventions would be useful with Ruth. These interventions are (a) gender-role and power analysis, (b) increasing assertiveness, (c) bibliotherapy, (d) reframing Ruth's concerns and symptoms, (e) social and political action, and (f) working with weight and body concerns.

✪ Gender-Role and Power Analysis

Gender-role analysis is used to increase Ruth's insight about how societal gender-role expectations adversely affect women and how women and men are socialized differently. Ruth needs to examine the gender-role messages (verbal, nonverbal, and modeled) she has experienced in her lifetime from society as a whole, from her family of origin, and from her religion. As a result, Ruth learns that her conflicts about her life and identity are due to the fact that she wants to step outside her traditionally defined female gender role. Ruth identifies the positive and negative consequences of following those gender-role messages. She gains awareness about her strengths and how and why these may not be valued in a patriarchal society.

We help Ruth recognize and value her strengths, some of which are part of her learned gender role. These strengths include her ability to nurture and to balance a multitude of roles and a willingness to question the values and beliefs she was taught. Through therapy Ruth learns how she has internalized certain gender-role messages in conscious and unconscious ways. She is supported in developing a woman-identified sense of femininity rather than a male-identified one. Ruth is encouraged to acquire a full range of behaviors that are freely chosen rather than prescribed by gender-role stereotypes.

Working from the radical feminist stance, Susan explores with Ruth several definitions of power, resulting in a definition that best fits her. Together, Ruth and Susan explore the kinds of power to which Ruth has access. Ruth has been encouraged to exert her power in indirect and helpless ways rather than in direct and competent ways. In therapy with Susan, Ruth is encouraged to change her internalized messages about her use of power and to freely explore various ways she can use her power.

Kathy's perspective differs somewhat. As a liberal feminist therapist, her goal is for Ruth to examine her changing relationships with her husband and children, her parents, and her relationship with God. Kathy seeks to assist Ruth in realigning the balance of power in her familial relationships so that she can develop her own female style of self without subservience.

Elizabeth believes Ruth underestimates her power and is, perhaps, afraid of it. This is shown through Ruth's fears that her choices will destroy her family. As women, we are not trained to accept power or to admit that we have any.

It might well be that Ruth's problems with her daughter are a manifestation of the loss of the only power she has been "allowed" to have within her dominant culture. In addition, as a socialist feminist therapist with an awareness of the economic exploitation of women, Elizabeth wonders aloud with Ruth why she is considering substitute teaching (a role that traditionally exploits married women) and has not sought to become a full-time teacher. Elizabeth would explore with Ruth whether she does not pursue full-time teaching because she fears the responsibility and freedom of her own classroom.

Increasing Assertiveness

Assertiveness training has been a part of feminist therapy since its inception. For women, assertiveness is frequently equated with aggression, and young girls do not learn how to stand up for their rights as human beings. Assertiveness training seeks to teach women how they can assert their own rights, without being aggressive. Because of the goals Ruth has set for herself, we are inclined to work with her on being more assertive.

Our conceptualization of Ruth is that she feels confused and guilty when she wants to step out of her prescribed gender role. Part of the goal of counseling is to help Ruth define a sense of self without taking a subservient role. Group therapy allows members to interact with others in a cooperative manner while at the same time learning new ways of being. An assertiveness group for women is indicated for Ruth. In this group she will learn that she is not alone and that being assertive does not mean she will alienate others. She will learn new skills and be able to help other women as well as receive help from others in the group.

Bibliotherapy

An important goal of feminist therapy is to help Ruth begin to understand how her own situation is connected with the common experience of all women. To that end, bibliotherapy helps Ruth understand that her personal pain is not unique to her and that many women experience similar struggles. It is important that Ruth has an opportunity to discuss her reactions to the readings during counseling sessions and to explore how they apply to her life.

We suggest two types of readings to Ruth. The first are readings from mental health professionals who write about issues similar to hers. The next are essays and fiction by women who have explored and experienced concerns similar to hers. For example, readings in White female experience and in feminist Christianity can help Ruth retain the essence of her faith yet at the same time be more comfortable with the changes she may decide to make in her life. We suggest to Ruth several writers who explore the juxtaposition of Christianity and feminism and describe feminist and Christian ethics. These readings would help to create a sense of connection and possibilities for Ruth without overtly threatening her status quo. As feminist therapists who have benefited from the struggles and experiences of other women, we share with Ruth that reading about the lives and works of others has been a source of strength and learning for us.

Reframing Ruth's Concerns and Symptoms

Feminist therapists believe many of the symptoms clients bring to counseling are symptoms of living in a male-dominated culture that does not value the female experience. Although all people are harmed by living in a male-dominated culture, women have learned to view their experiences negatively, and Ruth is no exception. She obviously sees her symptoms as signs of weakness and believes something is innately wrong with her. Feminist therapists view Ruth's symptoms as indicative of the stress between cultural and personal conflicts. This reframing, however, does not negate her actual symptoms. Consequently, we work with Ruth to teach her how to gain control of her symptoms through cognitive and behavioral techniques such as stress and relaxation management, thought stopping, and positive self-statements. In addition, even though Ruth comes to an understanding that the cause of her problems lies within society and cultural mores, she is not absolved from taking responsibility for making changes in her life.

As a radical feminist therapist, Susan views many of the symptoms women bring to counseling as passive forms of female rebellion against femininity as defined by the patriarchy. She reframes Ruth's distress with her role in life and her family. She sees Ruth's panic symptoms as ways Ruth is trying to communicate to herself her desire to step outside the constricted traditional female gender role. Susan explores with Ruth the possibility of suppressed rage being manifested in symptoms that allow her to still be feminine yet also revolt against male-defined femininity. Ruth is encouraged to acknowledge and express her anger. Her feelings and thoughts are reframed as evidence of her revolt against being placed in a subservient role, which no long brings her satisfaction. Susan would engage in a dialogue with Ruth about the ways in which she wants to define herself as mother and wife that might meet her need to be interdependent and nonsubservient.

The liberal feminist perspective seeks to help women understand gender roles and works toward creating a society with more equal power between the genders. Kathy works with Ruth on reframing her experience as a woman in American society and as a cultural being. Together, Kathy and Ruth explore the centuries of cultural and religious mandates regarding women and the inequities of the traditional system of marriage and family. They look at Ruth's family system and how it keeps her from taking care of herself while taking care of everyone else. Interventions include asking Ruth to listen to and identify those messages from her parents and church that continue to be replayed in her head and cause most of her conflicts. They engage in reframing or replacing these internalized messages with ones that fit with her current circumstances.

Elizabeth chooses to focus on Ruth's strengths. Ruth is managing a family and is juggling various roles. Together they work to identify and honor her strengths. She is asked to do some simple homework consisting of two lists: things she values about herself and things she does not value. This gives Ruth and Elizabeth a starting point for focusing on what Ruth views as important in her therapy. It helps identify what she has been taught to value and not value about herself. Negative beliefs can then be gently confronted through self-disclosure, assigning readings, and presenting her with conflicting evidence of her own behavior. For instance, Elizabeth would congratulate Ruth on having raised a daughter who can stand up for herself and make her own choices, even when she knows that this will displease others.

Taking Social and Political Action A primary goal of feminist therapy with Ruth is to help her understand how her distress as an individual woman is connected to women as a cultural group. Consequently, we are interested in sharing with Ruth our involvement in social action that is geared toward changing the oppressive and painful features of society that do not value women and their work. We encourage Ruth to engage in social action to reduce her sense of isolation, to help use her anger constructively and feel better about herself, and to effect some change on the structures of society. We suggest that Ruth become part of a Christian women's support group with a feminist perspective. Perhaps she could start such a group herself if one does not yet exist in her community. She could start out by attending a women's support group and getting to know something about how these groups work and branch out later.

We also recommend that Ruth engage in some sort of collective work focused on women's oppression. Social action is a way of refocusing and reframing anger. We often tell clients who doubt the usefulness of anger, or who fear their own strong emotions, that such emotions can be positive. If it were not for anger, women's shelters would not exist. If women had not been angry, sexual abuse would not have been addressed, and people would be in pain and more children abused. This puts social action in perspective. For Ruth, being involved in social action would be a way of healing past pains. We might suggest that she volunteer at the local women's shelter either on the hot line or as a support person. Being a support person would allow her to use her nurturing skills to help other women. This, in turn, would help her feel more competent. This is a potent therapeutic modality for both societal and individual change.

Working With Weight and Body Image Western culture is unmerciful to women. We are bombarded daily with images of women considered to be perfect. Not conforming to this iconic image can severely affect self-esteem because women in our society are judged by how they look, not by what they can do. Ruth has been socialized to believe that food is comforting, and, in fact, it may be the only comfort she has when presented with emotions that women are not encouraged to express. Stuffing her emotions to conform with cultural expectations reinforces her position of powerlessness. As a result, Ruth has developed a body size that is unacceptable to that same culture. She is left in the untenable position of being punished for the only solution she could find to comply with cultural mandates. The goal of feminist therapy is to assist Ruth in discovering ways to love her body. Ruth's relationship with food is also reframed as seeking comfort, and we will help Ruth discover other ways to get her needs met.

From a radical feminist perspective that views patriarchy as the cause of oppression and psychological distress, Ruth's weight is viewed as a refusal against the role of woman as body. It is a demonstration of Ruth's nonconscious wish to defy the male cultural dictate that women are to be beautiful sex objects. Ruth's weight is an obvious, but indirect, demonstration of her disallowed wish to be seen as a person, not as an object for males. Thus, Susan's work with Ruth's weight would be reframed as a protest, as a message rather than as further evidence that something is wrong with her and that she lacks willpower. Additionally, Ruth's weight may be a way to avoid seeing herself as a sexual being; it may be a way to neuter herself in her eyes and in the eyes of the males in her life. Helping Ruth to understand the power of fat would allow Ruth to make some choices about how she wants to define herself as a woman and her sexuality.

The socialist feminist perspective differs from both the radical and liberal perspectives in that it focuses on how our society twists consuming and eating into issues of power. Elizabeth believes food is a form of economic consuming. We walk into a grocery store and have myriad choices, and it can all be ours. This is one of the few venues where women can exercise choice and be powerful. Just buying and consuming food is a way of feeling powerful. Therefore, Ruth's weight issues are related to power and maladaptive ways of gaining power. In addition, weight gain is related to depression. This is often a vicious cycle. Ruth eats to make herself feel more powerful. However, eating undermines her self-esteem because women who do not "fit" the cultural model of beauty are disparaged.

Overall, the work in feminist therapy and weight issues is aimed at increasing self-esteem and personal power, emphasizing Ruth's strengths, and increasing her repertoire of coping behaviors. We might refer her to a feminist nutrition counselor and to a weight loss support group with an empowerment focus rather than a strict weight loss focus. It is important that Ruth be referred to adjunct modalities that support her emerging sense of self. Ruth needs to be empowered to accept and celebrate her body, her mind, and her life.

Glimpses of Ruth's Therapy

🖎 **Establishing and Nurturing the Egalitarian Relationship**   This is the beginning of the first session. The therapist's focus on power in the relationship reinforces trust building. This discussion models a healthy relationship between peers, values Ruth's life experience, and allows Ruth to begin making healthy decisions for herself.

THERAPIST: You mentioned that this is your first time in counseling. Would it help you if I tell you a little about myself and about the process of counseling?

RUTH: Yeah. I guess so. I really don't know what to expect. It's a big step for me to admit that things aren't going right. Before I came in today I thought I would just ask you to tell me what to do, but now I don't know. I'm confused about what I want. Is that all right?

THERAPIST: I agree that it is scary and confusing when you realize that you can't solve all your problems yourself. I know this from personal experience. I can't tell you what to do because I haven't lived your life, but I do think that together we will be able to work out a counseling plan for you. I have found with other people who are anxious about counseling that a good place to start is for me to tell you how I work with my clients. Then you can tell me a bit more about why you are here, and we can talk about how we can go about counseling and what will work best for you. How does that sound?

RUTH: You mean I don't have to do all the talking right away?

THERAPIST: No. Not right now.

RUTH: OK. I guess I was just expecting to tell my problems and have you tell me how to solve them.

THERAPIST: The way I see counseling is that it's the two of us working together to find out what is best for you. You are the expert in your life. I am the expert in counseling. I work from a feminist perspective. This means two things. First, I will work hard to understand your concerns from your perspective. I value your knowledge about yourself and your difficulties. Second, I bring a social and political perspective to my understanding of you and your life. I believe the causes of the problems many women bring to counseling are external. In general women are not valued by our society, and this creates psychological distress.

RUTH [*Looking perplexed and somewhat dubious*]: I'm not sure I understand.

THERAPIST: I understand this sounds confusing at first. After all, if women are not valued, wouldn't you have noticed? I believe that you have noticed, and that is part of what your pain is about, even if you haven't recognized it yet. For example, you mentioned a concern about your weight when we first talked. Look at current fashion magazines and ask yourself who decides what looks good and if it really does look good. Then ask yourself what happens to those of us who don't fit the model. I believe that what happens when we don't fit the ideal is that we feel bad about ourselves.

RUTH: I never thought that my concerns might be connected to being a woman. That's something I'm going to have to think about because all I know is that I feel scared and anxious and worried all the time about what I'm going to do, and I think something is wrong with me.

THERAPIST: Yes, I agree. It is scary to be here. I am not surprised that you're anxious.

RUTH: Also, I don't know if I feel comfortable working with someone who is a feminist. I know my husband will not be happy because he is always putting down feminists.

THERAPIST: That's an important concern for you. It sounds like your husband is important to you, and you don't want to upset him. I am wondering, however, if you can share with me some more of your concerns about working with a feminist counselor?

RUTH: I am afraid you will tell me that all my problems are because of my husband and that all I need to do is divorce him and leave my kids. Don't feminists believe that men are the cause of all problems?

THERAPIST: For the most part, individual men are not the problem, but the fact that our culture places men first might be. With regard to feminism, I can't speak for all feminist therapists, but only for myself. I encourage clients to take responsibility for making changes that will help them feel better about themselves. I will work with you to help you figure out what is best for you.

RUTH: So you're a feminist therapist because of your belief that a lot of women's problems are caused by the way women are treated and valued?

THERAPIST: Yes.

RUTH: You won't force your beliefs on me?

THERAPIST: No, I won't.

RUTH: OK, I guess I am willing to work with you.

THERAPIST: You don't sound sure.

RUTH: Yes, I am. Well, not exactly sure. I know my father says that feminists are the cause of the destruction of the family.

THERAPIST: It sounds like you have two concerns. One is about doing what the important people in your life think is right, and the other is that you are concerned that feminism might harm you and interfere with your relationships with those people. Does that sound right to you?

RUTH: Maybe I do want to figure myself out without others telling me what to do or how to be. This is new for me.

THERAPIST: You are telling me very clearly that you do not want to be influenced in ways that don't fit with who you are.

RUTH: Yes. I want to be able to figure out what I believe without others telling me what to believe.

THERAPIST: I think your desire to figure things out for yourself is a strength. Let me propose this: How about if we work together for four sessions. That way you can get a feel for me and how I work. We will set aside our fourth session to discuss whether or not you are feeling that I am hearing, understanding, and helping you.

RUTH: So I could leave if I wanted to?

THERAPIST: Yes. Although if you leave, I would like us to be able to talk about why so I can understand your decision.

RUTH: I like that.

THERAPIST: All right, it sounds like we have developed our first plan— together.

Power and Gender-Role Analysis in Family Relationships   This is Ruth's fifth session. It occurs after the therapeutic relationship has been established and Ruth and the therapist have negotiated 10 more sessions. This section reflects a melding of therapeutic influences. Elizabeth, influenced by cognitive approaches, and Susan, influenced by psychodynamic theory, collaborated on the response. Thus, Ruth is both challenged to confront dysfunctional beliefs and helped to explore emotions and relationships. This section highlights how feminist therapists integrate different styles and perspectives into their reper-toire of counseling skills.

RUTH: I am so glad I am here today. I just need to talk to you.

THERAPIST: It sounds like something has come up for you. Last week you said you were learning to manage stress better and your episodes of panic seemed to have subsided.

RUTH: Oh, but this is different [*Pauses and looks somewhat less excited*]. My church has its own school. They know I have my Bachelor's in Educa-tion now. They want to hire me full time. How can I do that? I would be away from home all day. Even when I was going to school I was still only gone part time. Will my family think I am a lousy mother be-cause I won't be at home? I am not even a certified teacher yet. What should I do?

THERAPIST: Wow, this sounds like something you are really split about. On one hand you would like to continue as you always have and not have change in your life; on the other hand you have been working toward this change for many years.

RUTH: Yeah. That's the funny thing. I didn't just go to college without a goal. I actually knew that I wanted to teach. I knew that someday it would be real. But, now that it is, I don't know what to do.

THERAPIST: The school must like you and respect you if they want to hire you for the fall.

RUTH: I have been tutoring and volunteering on and off ever since I changed churches. I like the kids and the teachers. I just thought I was lucky because they let me volunteer, but I guess I must have done well.

THERAPIST: So, what stops you from accepting the position?

RUTH: John and the kids. You know, John keeps telling me he wants me back like I was before I went back to college. Last week I asked him to pick up the two younger children from band practice at school while I went to a committee meeting. He told me that he couldn't and then was sarcastic. He said, "Maybe you'd like it better if I divorced you. Then you could go to meetings all the time."

THERAPIST: Are you afraid to accept the position because John talks about divorce?

RUTH: Yeah. He plays the divorce card frequently.

THERAPIST: And it sounds like you back down from doing what you want to do when John plays the divorce card.

RUTH [*Thinks a bit*]: I guess you could see it that way. But he does have the upper hand. I don't want to lose him and the kids. I don't really dislike my life, but I'm just not satisfied. I don't know. Now I'm confused all over again.

THERAPIST: Let's talk about your relationship with John. I think this might help you figure out what to do about the job offer.

RUTH: OK. I think you might be right. It is my fears about my family that are confusing me. I never imagined myself as a working mother. I know I really want to teach, but I am afraid that if I take the full-time job, it won't be good for my family.

THERAPIST: This is a concern many women have. It's hard not to feel selfish when you choose something you really want. We women are told that if we do anything for ourselves, someone else will suffer.

RUTH: I want the family together. That's probably what I am doing wrong here. By pursuing the job I am pulling the family apart. You're right. I am being selfish and my family will suffer.

THERAPIST: That certainly is a piece of what John is telling you. Traditionally this is what women do in our society. It is our job to keep the family together. This gives John a lot of power. We want to do what is best for ourselves and for others. If we do the wrong thing, people with power will tell us that we are selfish, not good enough, or bad.

RUTH: My father was like that.

THERAPIST: I guess I'm not surprised, given what we've talked about over the past few weeks. Can you tell me more about this?

RUTH: Oh, if I did something that he didn't like, he would tell me I was bad or not speak to me for several days. I felt awful and so wrong.

THERAPIST: It sounds like that was quite painful for you. When you acted on your own behalf, you felt unloved and punished by your father.

RUTH: I hadn't thought about it like that.

THERAPIST: Those feelings are pretty powerful, particularly to women who depend on men for their livelihood, as you have with John. Your life is changing a great deal right now, and there is much uncertainty. Your kids are getting ready to move on with their own lives in a few years, so they are less invested. John implies that a divorce would be OK with him.

RUTH [*With anger toward the therapist*]: John would be lost without me! He still can't do the laundry. I know that's funny—and you'd probably call it stereotypical—but I have done everything for him. If he left me, he'd fall apart.

THERAPIST: Take a moment and feel this emotion you are expressing. What would you name it?

RUTH [*Thinks for a moment*]: Anger. I am angry with you for suggesting that John would leave me. I know he wouldn't!

THERAPIST [*Nodding in agreement*]: You are right. I don't know John, but I do know that you could easily convince me that John has more invested in this relationship. What does that mean?

RUTH: That I don't have to be afraid that he would leave me?

THERAPIST: Yes. If he has more invested in the relationship, you have more power.

RUTH: Power is scary.

THERAPIST: You are a powerful woman. You passionately care for your family and for your chosen profession.

RUTH: What do I do about the job?

THERAPIST: What do you want to do?

RUTH: I think I want the job.

THERAPIST: Use your power in the relationship to help John change and do the right thing for you and for your family. Your interest in teaching is an extension of being a good and caring parent. In addition, you will be setting a good model for children to follow. This is just another part of being a parent.

Working With Body Image/Acceptance

This is Ruth's eighth session. The therapist helps Ruth question the cultural definition of weight and age.

RUTH: I know it sounds silly, but I just feel old, fat, and ugly these days. I don't even try to diet anymore because it never works. Since I have trouble sleeping, I have dark circles under my eyes. I look like hell.

THERAPIST: You're pretty disgusted with yourself.

RUTH: Oh, I just can't stand myself anymore. I gave my full-length mirror to the girls. They are slim and trim and young; they like looking at themselves.

THERAPIST: They look more like how an attractive woman should look.

RUTH: Yeah, they are beautiful. What I wouldn't do to have their bodies right now!

THERAPIST: You know, it seems like even though we get better in so many ways as we get older, in our society the only way we are appreciated and valued is for how we look.

RUTH: You know, you're right, and it's not fair. I do think I have a lot to offer even if I'm not thin and young.

THERAPIST: You certainly do, but you came in here today saying that you felt old, fat, and ugly—that you look like hell. I know this is important to you because you usually don't use strong language to describe your feelings.

RUTH [*Smiles slightly*]: It sometimes seems that I feel better about one thing and then worse about something else. I guess this morning I was only thinking about how I looked in the mirror and not about how valuable a person I am. One really doesn't have anything to do with the other, does it?

THERAPIST: No. But that's the way we are trained to think. And if a woman looks like hell, she feels like hell because she is devalued in our society. Ruth, what do you like about yourself?

RUTH: I like that I am a loving and caring person, that I am a good mother most of the time, and that I usually get things done. I'm proud of finishing my degree and finally having taken some action on the job front.

THERAPIST: And what don't you like?

RUTH: That I struggle with my daughter, that I eat and can't stop, and that I'm so fat that I'm unattractive.

THERAPIST: We've talked about your relationship with your daughter a great deal, but we haven't really talked about your weight [*Ruth nods*]. Maybe being overweight is serving some other purpose. Maybe being fat is a way you are able to get people to recognize your strengths and protect yourself from being ogled by men. Your fat is a way of using your power. Can you think of an example of this in your life?

RUTH [*Looks dubious but thinks*]: Well, where I am teaching some of the college boys help out. They make really disgusting comments about the college girls who volunteer. I get embarrassed for the college girls when this happens. I am sort of glad that they don't even seem to notice me [*Ruth pauses*]. You know, I never would have thought about it that way in a million years. I never thought about how I might use my fat to get what I want or even to get respect. That's an interesting idea.

THERAPIST: Our bodies are the single most powerful asset we have in our society. We all use that power a little differently, but we often use that power to get what we want—even if we are not completely aware of it.

RUTH: It seems really manipulative to me, and I don't want to be manipulative.

THERAPIST: You want to become powerful in other ways.

RUTH: Absolutely.

THERAPIST: The way I see it you can do a couple of things to help with this problem. Let me share my ideas, and you see how they fit for you.

RUTH: OK.

THERAPIST: You might try to adjust your thinking about your weight by discovering ways in which being fat affords you power in your relationships and begin to love yourself just the way you are.

RUTH: That won't be easy.

THERAPIST: I know. It wasn't easy for me either. The hardest thing I did was to actually get a full-length mirror in my bathroom. I forced myself to look at my body and learn to love it.

RUTH: How?

THERAPIST: First you discover what you like and admire about your physical self. Then you look at the areas you are indifferent toward. Then think about what those areas do for you. For example, my legs support me when I stand. They get me where I am going and help me run from trouble. Many women worry about their hips and belly, which grow with each child. A way to reframe it is to think about the children they were able to nourish and protect in the uterus.

RUTH: So you just looked at your body and started to think about how each part contributes to your life instead of how fat and ugly it is [*Ruth smiles*].

THERAPIST: That's pretty much it.

RUTH: And it worked?

THERAPIST: It worked for me. I don't know if it will work for you. You're the expert on you.

Jerry Corey's Work With Ruth From a Feminist Perspective

Introduction

The CD-ROM for Integrative Counseling is especially useful as a demonstration of interventions I make with Ruth that illustrate some principles and procedures of feminist therapy. In Session 1 ("Beginning of Counseling") I demonstrate ways to engage Ruth as a collaborative partner in the therapeutic venture. Session 2 ("The Therapeutic Relationship") highlights the importance of creating a good working relationship and demystifying the therapy process. In Session 3 ("Establishing Therapeutic Goals") I show how I work collaboratively with Ruth in formulating clear and personal goals that will guide the course of therapy. Clearly, Ruth is the expert on her own life and my job is to assist her in attaining the goals we jointly identify as a focus of therapy. In Session 4 ("Understanding and Dealing With Diversity") Ruth brings up gender differences, but she also mentions our differences in religion, education, culture, and socialization. Together we explore how any of our differences might affect our therapeutic task. Such open exploration is essential if therapy is to be effective.

Basic Assumptions

The basic assumptions, goals of therapy, and therapy strategies of feminist therapy have been spelled out in detail earlier in this chapter by Drs. Evans, Seem, and Kincade. In my description of counseling Ruth from a feminist perspective, I will emphasize how I would enlist her as a collaborator. I'll also describe working with Ruth and John in conjoint counseling. In working with Ruth from a feminist perspective, it is essential that the interventions I make be done within the context of her social and cultural world, and that I attend to the environmental factors that are contributing to the problems that bring Ruth to therapy.

Assessment of Ruth

I strive to include Ruth in the assessment and treatment phase. Collaborating with Ruth in all aspects of her therapy will provide a rich therapeutic experience. I am not eager to give Ruth a diagnosis, for I don't see how a diagnostic category will assist her in formulating a picture of what she wants from therapy. Assessment will be an ongoing process in which the two of us will consider what is the most appropriate focus of our work together.

Goals of Therapy

Functioning within a feminist therapy model, my primary goal is to intervene with Ruth in ways that increase the chances of her recognizing, claiming, and embracing her personal power. After the first few sessions, Ruth and I collaboratively establish these goals to guide the therapy process:

- Trusting her own intuition rather than relying on outside experts
- Learning that taking care of herself is as important as taking care of others
- Accepting her body rather than punishing herself for not having the perfect body
- Identifying internalized gender-role messages and replacing them with her own constructive beliefs
- Acquiring skills to bring about changes at home and school
- Defining for herself the kind of relationship she wants with her husband and her children

Therapeutic Procedures

I spend time talking with Ruth about how therapy works, and I enlist her as an active partner in our relationship. As a part of the informed consent process, we discuss ways of getting the most from the therapy process, clarifying expectations, identifying Ruth's goals, and working toward a contract that will guide her therapeutic journey. This educational process assists Ruth in being an informed client and is the basis for evaluating how useful the therapy is in terms of reaching her personal goals.

The Therapeutic Process

ELEMENTS OF THE PROCESS Ruth says that she loves reading, and she is very open to reading selected books on topics that are directly pertinent to therapy issues. As a supplement to our sessions, I encourage Ruth to keep a journal and talk with her about bibliotherapy. Ruth and I explore a range of possibilities for extending the therapeutic value of our sessions. She also agrees to join a women's support group that is available through the Women's Center at her college. Although at first she was reluctant to take the time for herself to join this group, she is finding that she can identify with other women in her group. Ruth is able to bring her experiences in her support group, her reading, and her journal writing into her therapy sessions.

The Therapeutic Relationship Guided by the principle that the therapeutic relationship should be egalitarian, I take three steps to reduce the power differential between us. Certainly I do not want to misuse the power that is inherent in being a therapist.

First, I monitor the ways I might misuse my power in the professional relationship, such as by diagnosing unnecessarily, by giving advice too freely, by hiding behind an "expert" role, or by minimizing the impact of the power imbalance between Ruth and myself.

Second, I call to Ruth's attention the power that she has in this collaborative relationship. I expect her to take responsibility for herself, to become aware of the ways she relinquishes her power in her relationships with others, and to take increasing charge of her life.

Third, I consistently attempt to demystify the counseling process. I do this by sharing with Ruth my own perceptions about what is going on in our relationship, by making her an active partner in determining any diagnosis, and by engaging in appropriate and timely self-disclosure.

Role-Playing Ruth's Marriage

In one session Ruth and I do some role playing in which I play John. She tells me (John) how frightened she is of making demands on me for fear that I might leave. Out of that session Ruth begins to be aware of how intimidated she has allowed herself to become. She continues to set John up to punish her by giving him the power to make her feel scared and guilty. As a homework assignment I ask her to write a letter to John saying all the things she really wants him to hear, but not to mail it. The writing is geared to getting her to focus on her relationship with her husband and what she wants to be different. (In an earlier session I gave her a similar assignment of writing a detailed letter to her father, which she agreed not to send to him but to bring in for a session with me.) I make the observation to Ruth that in many ways she is looking to John for the same things she wanted from her father as a child and adolescent. Further, she assumed the role of doing whatever she thought would please each of them, yet she typically ended up feeling that no matter how hard she tried she would never succeed in gaining their approval. I try to show her that she will have to change her own attitudes if she expects change in her relationships, rather than waiting and hoping her father or her husband might change. This is a discovery for her, and it represents a different direction for her life.

Holding a Joint Session With John

Ruth expresses her interest in having John come to a few counseling sessions with her, yet she is ambivalent about it. Initially she gives a list of reasons why she is sure that he will never come to any kind of counseling. After some discussion with me, she does agree to ask him to attend at least one session (which we will also role-play first). To her surprise, John agrees to join her. Here are a few excerpts from this initial joint session:

RUTH: I brought John here today even though I don't think he really wanted to be here. [*Notice that she speaks for him.*]

JERRY: John, I'd like to hear from you about what it's like for you to be here today.

JOHN: When Ruth asked me, I agreed because I thought I might be of some help to her. I couldn't see any harm in giving it a try.

RUTH: Now that he's here, I don't know what to say.

JERRY: You could begin by telling him why you wanted him here.

RUTH: It's that our marriage just can't go on this way much longer. Things are no longer satisfactory to me. I know that for many years I never complained—just did what was expected and thought that everything was fine—but the truth is that things are not fine by me.

JOHN [*Turning to me*]: I don't know what she means. Our marriage has always seemed OK by me. I don't see the problem.

JERRY: How about telling Ruth this?

I want Ruth and John to talk to each other directly rather than talking about each other. My guess is that at home they are very indirect. By having them speak to each other in this session, I get a better sense of how they interact.

RUTH: See what I mean! Everything is fine by John—I'm the one with the problems! Why is he so content while I'm so discontent?

JERRY: Tell John. You're looking at me. He needs to hear from you, not me.

RUTH: Why, John, am I the only one who is complaining about our marriage? Can't you see anything wrong with the way we're living? Do you really mean that everything is just fine by you?

JERRY: Ruth, let me make a suggestion. You are asking John questions. Instead of asking him these questions, tell him what it is like for you to be in this relationship with him.

RUTH [*Again turning and addressing me*]: But I don't think he ever hears me! That's the trouble—I just don't think he cares or listens to me when I talk about our life together.

JERRY: So here is an opportunity to test out your assumptions. I hope you are willing to hang in with him and keep on talking.

RUTH [*With raised voice and a great deal of emotion*]: John, I'm tired of being the perfect wife and the perfect mother, always doing what's expected of me. I've done that for as long as I can remember, and I want a change. I feel that I'm the one holding together our family. Everything depends on me, and all of you depend on me to keep things going. But I can't turn to any of you for emotional support. I take care of everybody and everything, but I don't feel cared for.

JERRY: Tell John how that affects you and what you want from him.

RUTH: I'm tired of the way things are with us [*Pause*]. There are times that I need to know that I matter to you and that you appreciate me.

JOHN: Well, I do appreciate your hard work. I know you do a lot in the home, and I'm proud of you.

JERRY: How does it feel to hear John say that to you?

RUTH: But you never say that you appreciate me. I need to hear that from you. I need to feel your emotional support.

JERRY: Yet right now he is telling you that he appreciates you and is proud of you. So, how is it for you to hear what he just said?

I am calling to Ruth's attention that in this brief interaction, for one short moment, her husband responded to her in a way that she says she would like him to. Yet she does not acknowledge what he did say, which is what she says she'd like to hear more of.

RUTH: I like it when you tell me that you appreciate me. It means a lot to me.

JOHN: I'm just not used to talking that way. You know how I feel about you.

JERRY: John! That's just the problem. You don't often tell Ruth how you feel about her and what she means to you, and she is not very good at asking for that from you.

RUTH: Yeah, I agree. I'm missing affection from you. It's so hard for me to talk about my life with you—about you and me—about our family—oh! [*Ruth's tears up, she lets out a sigh, and then she grows quiet.*]

JERRY: Don't stop now, Ruth. Keep talking to John. Tell him what your tears and the heavy sigh are about.

My hunch is that Ruth often feels defeated and stops there, seeing herself as misunderstood. I am encouraging her to stay with herself and continue to address John. Even though John is looking very uncomfortable at this point, he sounds receptive.

JOHN: Sometimes I find it hard to talk to you because I feel I can never do enough. How can I be sensitive when you don't tell me what you want?

JERRY: John, she is telling you right now what she wants. How is it for you to hear what Ruth is saying to you?

JOHN: She is right. I should listen more often.

JERRY: So, are you willing to listen to Ruth a bit more right now?

JOHN: Yes.

RUTH: You may not know how important going to college really is for me, John. I so much want to finish and get my credential. But I can't do that and be responsible for the complete running of our house. I need for the kids to pitch in and do their share instead of always expecting me to do everything. I need some time to myself—time just to sit and think for a few minutes—when I'm at home. And I'd like to be able to sit down with you after dinner and just talk for a bit. I miss talking to you. The times we do talk, the topic is household maintenance.

JERRY: What are you hearing, John, and how does it sound to you?

JOHN: Well, we do talk about chores. I just don't understand what she wants me to say.

John continues for a time with a critical voice. Yet eventually he does admit that the children don't help as much as they could and that he might be willing to do a bit more around the house. He adds that the way he grew up men were supposed to work outside of the house and women were supposed to stay home and take care of the family. He admits that he doesn't know how to begin making changes to these well-established patterns.

RUTH: Well, I'd really like your help at home. What about spending time with me? Is that possible?

JOHN: Yes. Too often I just want to relax after working all day. I want it to be positive at home after a long day.

JERRY: It sounds as if both of you would like to talk to each other. Would you be willing to set aside some time during the next week when you can have some uninterrupted conversation?

Together we develop a realistic contract that specifies when, where, and how long they will spend uninterrupted time with each other. John agrees to come in for another joint session. I let him know that it will be important that we explore messages that he has embraced unthinkingly and determine if there are ways he might modify his version of what constitutes a "natural" role for women and men. I point out to both of them that they have bought into a fixed vision of whose responsibility it is to maintain the family. This is expressed when Ruth requests that John and the children help her with household chores, for instance. When Ruth asks for help, it is implied that household maintenance is exclusively her job. They may want to begin to question these stereotyped gender-role expectations and consider redefining their roles. At a future session we will focus on what both John and Ruth have learned about roles and division of responsibilities, deciding if these values are functional in their marriage.

In the meantime I ask Ruth to monitor what she actually does at home for 2 weeks and to keep these notes in her journal. I suggest that she write down a specific list of the changes she wants at home. We pursue our individual sessions, working mainly on what she wants in her life for herself, and at times what she wants in her family situation.

PROCESS COMMENTARY   Ruth and I spend several sessions working with her part in creating and maintaining the difficulties she is experiencing in her marriage. I challenge her to stop focusing on John and what he can do to change and, instead, to change her own attitudes and behaviors, which may lead to changes in her relationship with him. Ruth begins to see how difficult it is for her to make requests of John or to ask him for what she needs emotionally. Although she initially resists the idea of telling him directly what she wants with him and from him, she eventually sees some value in learning to ask for what she wants. Ruth has decided in advance that he (and others) will not take care of her emotionally, and with this expectancy she has blocked off possibilities of feeling emotionally nourished by others. She often becomes aware of slipping into old patterns, many of which were developed as a child, yet she becomes increasingly able to avoid these traps and to behave in more effective ways.

Ruth and I spend considerable time in our sessions talking about messages she received about gender roles. Up to this time she had not really given much thought to the impact her socialization continues to have on her, nor had she reflected on how she (and John) have uncritically accepted stereotyped gender roles. Much time is devoted in our sessions to reviewing and critically examining decisions she made about herself as a wife and mother. Ruth is realizing that her definition of herself is rather restricted, and now she is beginning to think about how she wants to expand her options.

Questions for Reflection

1. How might you integrate concepts and techniques from the other therapy orientations you've studied with feminist therapy? Are there any theories that you think would not fit with a feminist perspective? If so, which ones, and why?

2. What themes from the feminist approach would you most want to incorporate in counseling Ruth?

3. Feminist therapists believe in the value of educating clients about the therapy process and stress the importance of an egalitarian relationship. What other counseling approaches share this orientation? What are your thoughts about demystifying therapy and establishing a collaborative relationship with a client such as Ruth?

4. Feminist therapy takes a dim view of traditional diagnosis and assessment. What other therapies share this view? At this point, what are your thoughts about the use of the *DSM-IV-TR* as a basis for making an assessment and arriving at a diagnosis? To what extent do you think that traditional diagnosis contributes to blaming the victim?

5. Feminist assessment and diagnosis requires a cooperative and phenomenological approach. If you accept the feminist perspective on assessment and diagnosis, what problems might you expect to encounter in an agency that required you to come up with a diagnosis during an intake session?

6. What would you say to Ruth if she is enrolled in a managed care program that permits only six therapy sessions, and then only if a suitable diagnosis is submitted to the health provider program?

7. Feminist therapy focuses on gender-role and power analysis. What ways might you employ these interventions in your work with Ruth and John during a conjoint session? To what degree have you thought about how your gender-role socialization has influenced your views of what it means to be a woman or a man? How might your views influence your work with a client like Ruth?

8. Assume that Ruth were to say to you: "I know I am dependent on my husband, and that he wants me to give up my professional ambitions as long as our children still live at home. I really don't want to make waves in our marriage, so what I want from you as a counselor is to help me to be happy in doing what is expected of me." How might your own values work for or against you if Ruth tells you she is seeking adjustment more than change in her life?

9. As you read about the basic tenets of feminism, to what extent do you think it is appropriate for a therapist to teach clients ways of challenging the status quo and a patriarchal system? What modifications, if any, might you make in applying feminist therapy to clients who embrace cultural values that keep women in a subservient role?

10. Ruth's weight and her body image are of central concern to her. Contrast the psychoanalytic view with the feminist perspective of the meaning of Ruth's overweight condition. Do you see any way to integrate these two perspectives in working with Ruth's concern about her weight?

Notes

See the DVD/online program entitled *Theory in Practice: The Case of Stan* (Session 10: Feminist Therapy Applied to the Case of Stan), which deals with Stan's exploration of his gender-role identity and messages he has incorporated about being a man.

1. We made a commitment to feminist collaboration in writing for this chapter and the order of our names holds no meaning. This is truly a collaborative piece with each of us contributing equally to its content and effort.

2. A more detailed description of feminist therapy can be found in chapter 12 of G. Corey (2009), *Theory and Practice of Counseling and Psychotherapy* (8th ed., Belmont, CA: Brooks/Cole).

3. The source for making a traditional diagnosis is the *DSM-IV-TR.* American Psychiatric Association (2000), *Diagnostic and Statistical Manual of Mental Disorders* (4th ed., text revision, Washington, DC: Author).

CHAPTER ELEVEN

Case Approach to Postmodern Approaches

General Overview of Postmodern Approaches

A major goal for postmodern therapists is to create a context in which clients can create new stories that highlight their ways of being. Therapy provides the opportunity for clients to take apart (or deconstruct) the dominant story they bring to therapy. Clients are encouraged to rewrite these stories by looking at their past and rewriting their future.

Postmodern therapists view clients as the experts on their own life. The therapist is not the expert but assumes the role of a curious, interested, and respectful partner in the therapeutic relationship. The therapist and clients together establish clear, specific, realistic, and personally meaningful goals that will guide the therapy process. The therapist explores with clients the impact their problems have on them and how they are taking action to reduce this impact. Through the use of questions that challenge clients to separate themselves from problem identities, therapists assist clients in re-authoring their stories and in constructing a more appealing story line. It is essential that the story being authored in the therapy context be carried out into the social world where clients live.

Because this approach emphasizes the collaborative nature of therapy, clients are the primary agents in deciding when they have achieved their goals and when they are ready to terminate the therapeutic relationship. This approach to therapy emphasizes a time-effective format. It is appropriate to end therapy when the client finds solutions that work.

A Social Constructionist's Perspective on Ruth

by Jennifer Andrews, PhD

Introduction

Social constructionism proposes that reality is created in language between people, and the expertise I offer Ruth has to do with language and meaning. I construct questions in our interviews that will assist Ruth in discovering more choices and developing a sense of being in charge of her life. Thus, when Ruth tells me that she has just accepted a job as a substitute teacher, I want to know what this means to her. I do not know the correct path for Ruth in her life. I do not make assumptions about substitute work or insert my values into her decisions. Rather, I focus on her expertise about teaching. I try to use ordinary everyday language in a conversational style while remaining curious about Ruth's situation and her ideas about it.

Prior to any assessment, I read Ruth's autobiographical notes and her intake summary. After reflecting on this material I had the following thoughts:

> What an amazing woman. With four adolescents, approaching launching, she had the foresight to start an alternative life plan for herself 4 years ago. She is rehearsing her new life in her mind's eye while her current life is demanding and very much in progress. How did she manage to break away from her church 9 years ago? How did she decide to become a teacher? I wonder if the same process is at work in this situation where she sees herself perhaps outgrowing a situation and she needs for something to be different. Her concerns about her husband seem to be legitimate. If she is accurate about his wanting her to remain the way she was, then her changes are probably difficult for him to support. I wonder if he would join her for some couples work. Her complaints about anxiety and panic need to be addressed. I need to listen to her very carefully. It seems that she has made some relationships through her college program. I wonder how she perceives some of her new friends seeing her. I am likely to ask her what they would tell me about her. If she is able to have multiple voices in her head instead of just the ones that diminish her, she may experience some support for her changes. I wonder what actions she has taken about her weight problem. Many other thoughts occur to me as I anticipate my first interview with Ruth.

Assessment of Ruth

I am therapeutically interested in how people describe their lives. Frequently the stories people tell about their problems and the meanings they attribute to their stories are a reflection of how others value them. For instance, when Ruth describes herself as a "superwoman who gives and gives until there is little left to give," I become curious about how she came to believe she is a superwoman and ask her how that description helps or hinders her in achieving her goals. If I ask her if a "superwoman" gives to herself, she may give some thought to what self-care means to her. Furthermore, the meaning of "superwoman" can change and, subsequently, her reality of giving to herself can change.

Operating from a social constructionist perspective, I experience a dilemma when I am required to assess and diagnose clients. As part of the community of therapists, I understand the need to speak a common language, and I use the *Diagnostic and Statistical Manual* (DSM-IV-TR), which classifies mental disorders in a language that is common to other mental health practitioners.[1] In communicating with insurance companies or creating case notes, I am required to use the *DSM-IV-TR*. My assessments and provisional diagnoses are generally arrived at in collaborative conversation with the client. I explain the use of the diagnostic manual and the requirement for diagnoses for record keeping and reimbursement. Because Ruth will be using her husband's health care insurance for reimbursement, I read the descriptions from the *DSM-IV-TR* to her and ask her which she thinks is a better description of her complaint: "Would you say that you are more depressed or more anxious? Or do you think you are experiencing a combination of these moods? How long would you say this has been a problem?" With this therapeutic approach, a written record is never a surprise to a client, and, generally, the client appreciates becoming an informed participant in creating his or her records.

Traditionally mental health workers are concerned with the first two sections of the *DSM-IV-TR*, which help them diagnose the client with clinical disorders or personality disorders. For example, Ruth could be described as having a "dependent personality disorder" (301.6), a "panic disorder" (300.01), or an "eating disorder" (307.50). A social constructionist would regard these diagnoses as having been derived from an expert posture and as disrespectful of the client. The third section of the *DSM-IV-TR* is concerned with medical conditions such as heart condition, diabetes, or a broken leg.

The *DSM-IV-TR* also offers two more sections that are descriptive of subjects that are compatible with my thinking. Axes IV and V are concerned with psychosocial and environmental problems and the overall ability of the client to function in his or her daily life. It is in Axis IV that we can truly experience ourselves as having systemic lenses. I show Ruth the Severity of Psychosocial Stressors Scale and ask her where she sees herself regarding the severity of the stressors in her life over the last year. I then show Ruth Axis V, the Global Assessment of Functioning (GAF), and we go through the ratings until she arrives at the code she feels most closely describes her situation. I respect her opinions and stay out of the "one-up" position of knowing more about her than she knows about herself. We continue to discuss this at different times during the course of therapy to monitor gains she is making.

After discussing the assessment criteria, we agree on some provisional diagnosis. I include Ruth in this formal process as fully as possible. We agree to a diagnosis of "generalized anxiety disorder with panic attacks" (293.83) on Axis I. At my suggestion we consider a V-code (62.89) "phase of life problem," and she agrees to include this too. She wonders about a V-code (61.20) for the parent–child relationship problem with her daughter but then says it isn't serious enough to list here. She also declines listing her relationship with her husband as a problem. I explain Axis II, but Ruth doesn't think that an Axis II diagnosis applies to her. We agree to list the weight problem on Axis III, and she comments that she wants to take this up with her medical doctor, to treat it seriously. On Axis IV she creates a list that includes problems related to the social environment, adjustment to life-cycle transition (for example, launching children, graduation from BA program, seeking credentials), self-concept, self-esteem, and related concerns about aging and health. On Axis V she locates herself between a 60 and 62 because she is having panic attacks.

Key Issues

Traditional therapeutic approaches have assumed the presence of some internal structure that we have called the "self." More recent ideas claim that the self is relational, fluid, and ever changing depending on what we are doing and with whom we are doing it. We do not have scientific evidence supporting either position, but the latter view is a more optimistic one for therapists. If the self is mutable and relational, change can be accomplished more easily than if we see the self as a permanent structure that is relatively unchangeable. It makes sense to me that Ruth is having a hard time knowing who she is at the moment. She is in a transitional stage of development, moving from the identity of wife and mother to a new identity she hasn't yet fully articulated. How interesting that she is having this crisis at 39 years of age. She tells me there is something about becoming 40, which says that she is at midlife, no longer a youth with all of her potential ahead of her. She says that she hasn't achieved her goals, and she feels like a failure.

Times of transition can be characterized by feelings of confusion, despair, humiliation, and shame. The person in transition is no longer certain about having a place of belonging, or a place in the world. In primitive societies people in this state become invisible; they cover themselves in ashes and have out-of-body and hallucinogenic experiences. They truly do not know who they are. The identity crisis is over when they reincorporate into the community. Usually this happens with ceremony and ritual. At this time they step into changed identities, new commitments, and new descriptions of who they are and what they will become. The community welcomes them back with this new identity and supports the changes.

Ruth is not living in a primitive community; here the transition is unofficial and the rituals are partial. For example, even though graduation and credentialing are formal rituals that herald her new identity, she does not experience a major change in her life. Through conversation about her new relationships with colleagues and new friends, Ruth can expand her sense of what she has accomplished. Our exchange goes as follows:

THERAPIST: If one of your colleagues was here right now and I asked her how she sees your teaching ability, what would she say?

RUTH: My friend Carole would say that I am a good teacher and a wonderful team member. Carole can count on me, and she admires my ability to be a mom to four kids and be the kind of student I have been.

This is an example of how I work to situate new behaviors and punctuate Ruth's competencies. As Ruth gives herself compliments through these imagined conversations, she begins to accept the credit she so richly deserves. Therapy can become a ritual space where having these conversations connects her with her developing ideas about her own future.

I believe that "reality" is not objective, not "out there." It is very much a result of individual experience, which includes all of Ruth's past experiences. Her ideas about religion, marriage, personal appearance, and parenting can be seen as internal filters through which all of the current situations are experienced. I can only learn about Ruth's unique experience by asking her about it and listening carefully to what she says.

The Therapeutic Process

At our first session I am very interested in what it is that Ruth wants for her future. The conversation proceeds:

RUTH: I want to become a teacher. My children are getting older, and I can see that they will all be off on their own in only a few years. So I started to think about what will happen to me when they leave home.

THERAPIST: So you started to make plans for your own future.

RUTH: Yes, but it isn't that simple. I feel guilty about taking so much time for myself. I wish I could do this without feeling guilty.

THERAPIST: You would like to feel more comfortable about realizing your personal goals.

RUTH: That's true, but it is more complicated because my own goals also involve my marriage and my relationship with my husband.

THERAPIST: Your marriage is important to you.

RUTH: Yes, very important. My relationship with John needs some work, as well as my relationship with Jennifer, my daughter. She is 18, and this is a crucial time. She'll be leaving home soon, and I want her to remember that we had a good home life.

THERAPIST: Ruth, what other goals do you have for yourself?

RUTH: I would like to lose a significant amount of weight. I would like to be seen as a good-looking teacher, not an overweight, middle-aged wannabe. I have tried over and over to lose weight, but rather unsuccessfully.

THERAPIST: I wonder if you can tell me about anything that you undertook where you were successful.

RUTH: Yes, 9 years ago I decided to leave the church that my parents belong to.

THERAPIST: How did you do that?

RUTH: Oh, it was very difficult. It took years of planning and trying and failing repeatedly before I finally left for good.

THERAPIST: I am interested in how you knew that last time was "for good."

RUTH: The last time I left, it was irreversible. I knew in my bones that I could not go back. I am no longer a member of that church.

THERAPIST: I hear that a time came when you could not return to the church of your childhood. I am still curious about how you knew that you had outgrown the church.

RUTH: I knew for years before, but I didn't have the courage to stand up to my mother and father.

THERAPIST: So you finally got the courage to stand up to your parents and that made the separation permanent.

RUTH: Yes, but you know that I still hear them inside my head. They continue to protest in my mind, but it doesn't matter now. There's no turning back at this point.

THERAPIST: I guess that we all have voices that continue to talk to us. I agree that the voices from our childhood can remain powerful and resonant even when we have outgrown their authority.

RUTH: Well I sure have those voices!

THERAPIST: Your parents were good teachers. Their lessons took root. Do you think the lessons have outlived their usefulness to you?

RUTH: I haven't thought about it that way. I guess those early lessons come at a time when we are the most impressionable. Hard lessons to shake off.

THERAPIST: What did you learn from your parents that is likely to influence your teaching methods?

RUTH [*Laughs*]: I have already employed some of those methods with my own children.

THERAPIST: If you think of these internal voices as early lessons, do you suppose you might feel less guilty?

RUTH: Thinking about it as early lessons, rather than the truth, makes it easier already.

THERAPIST: Is there anything in this example that will make current changes you are considering a bit easier for you?

RUTH: I will really think about that one.

At our first session I ask Ruth to think about the fact that we have limited sessions from her insurance plan. Therefore, it would make sense to prioritize what to work on. As a part of prioritizing her goals, I ask her who in her life would support the changes she wants to make.

RUTH: [*Without hesitation*]: John would support me in the changes that I want. He would be happy for me that I finished school, and he would like my new friends.

THERAPIST: So John's responses to you are very important when you think about the future.

RUTH: Definitely.

THERAPIST: I don't know what I can do to help John change. I wonder whether we should invite John to join us for a session or two. Think about what would be the pros and cons of such a meeting. Perhaps you can talk with John about it too.

RUTH: I'll for sure consider this and probably bring it up to John.

THERAPIST: Ruth, what would you like to consider here that you can work on without needing anyone else to change?

RUTH: I wish that I didn't need so much approval from other people. It would be nice to be comfortable when I make a decision and not have to worry about what everyone else thinks about it.

THERAPIST: Ruth, there are probably other things that may come up during the week that we can add to your goals. We can talk more about them next week.

A week passes, and Ruth returns. She tells me that the disadvantage to having John attend a meeting would be that she would have to share the time and she was just getting to want more for herself. On the other hand, she could have a safe forum to deal with many of her concerns about her future and their future. When she brought this up with John, they began to talk about some of the issues that concern her. Ultimately she thought that having him attend was preferable and that she could share her time for one or two sessions. We continued to talk about her priorities for change, and we planned to have John attend the next session.

The next week Ruth and John appear in my office. Ruth introduces John, and after some polite socializing and getting acquainted, I reflect on an exercise that many couples have found to be useful for their relationship. I describe how I can be driving home alone in my car and having a rather accurate conversation with my husband. After many years I have incorporated a version of him and our relationship that is fairly reliable, and I can rehearse a conversation with him. I further point out that when working with a couple in therapy, I often reflect upon what different interests and ideas he might be considering if he were in conversation with this couple. I ask for permission to interview the "Ruth inside John" and the "John inside Ruth." I explain that they may "pass" on any question they prefer not to answer, and I assure them of my intention of being respectful. Ruth offers to go first. I suggest to John that he listen in a way that a good friend would be listening, and I provide reassurances that the person who is in the listening position will have ample opportunity to talk before the session is over.

THERAPIST: Hello John inside of Ruth. Is it OK with you if we chat for a short while with you responding as-if you are John?

RUTH [*Answering as John*]: Yes.

THERAPIST: John, I was wondering what your ideas are about the plans Ruth is making for a teaching career?

RUTH [*As John*]: I know that Ruth has been working really hard to become a teacher, and I think that probably she is a good teacher. But I don't care for the commitment of time that she has to put into this thing, and it doesn't stop. And now she is talking about getting a job, and we'll see less of her.

THERAPIST: John, are you telling me that you would like to see more of Ruth?

RUTH [*As John*]: Yes, I feel like she has run out on our agreement about our family responsibilities.

THERAPIST: What other thoughts do you have about Ruth's plans?

RUTH [*As John*]: I don't see where she has put me into her schedule. I can't tell you when the last time was that we were intimate. She is always writing papers.

THERAPIST: Thank you John in Ruth. I would like to ask John a few questions now [*Speaks directly to John*]. John, as you listened to Ruth's version of you talk about how she believes you feel about her plans, what occurred to you? What percent was she accurate?

JOHN: I would say that she was about 50% accurate.

THERAPIST: Really? What part did she get right, and what part perhaps did not quite fit?

JOHN: Well, I do want to see more of her. And I do feel that she sort of changed the rules about how we participate in the family. But she totally doesn't get that I am really proud of her. At first I wasn't too upset about school because I didn't seriously think that she had it in her. But then as the years went by I could see that she was going to do it. I felt proud of her, yet I also felt angry that she traded us in for a degree. Sometimes I'm worried that she will leave me.

THERAPIST: Ruth, as you hear John tell us his thoughts and feelings about your plans, what occurs to you?

RUTH: I knew he was upset and not supportive of my returning to school, but it was upsetting to hear him say I traded him and the children in for a degree.

THERAPIST: Was there anything else that he said that surprised you, and why was it surprising?

RUTH: I never had the sense that he was proud of me because he never gave me any indication of being proud.

THERAPIST: What did you hear that made you feel most hopeful?

RUTH: At first it was sad to hear him say he was afraid I would leave him, but then it felt good to know that he does still care about me and our marriage.

THERAPIST: Now, John, I am inviting you to talk with me as if you were Ruth [*After a nod of consent from John*]. What effect did you think continuing your education and mapping out a teaching career would have on the family and your relationship with John?

JOHN [*As Ruth*]: I thought improving myself through education would be a way to improve the relationship [*Pause*]. We would be more equal, and I would be able to contribute more income for the family's future.

THERAPIST: So some people might agree that you had honorable intentions. What would you say is most important for you and the future of the marital relationship now?

JOHN [*As Ruth*]: That my husband would stop trying to stop me from being the kind of person that has become important to me.

THERAPIST: How has he contributed to your becoming this way or taking this position?

JOHN [*As Ruth*]: Small things. Like, there was a time he kissed my neck when I fell asleep reading my textbook at night or when he brought me coffee and hugged me early in the morning.

THERAPIST: What are some of the small things you do that you know John appreciates?

JOHN [*As Ruth*]: When I come into the den to watch television with him.

THERAPIST: I'm curious. What was it about these times that was important?

JOHN [*As Ruth*]: He knows that I think watching television is a waste of time. But the other night I came in and snuggled next to him, and we both talked about how we felt connected.

THERAPIST: What else have you tried to do to help the situation so far?

JOHN [*As Ruth*]: I have made special efforts to express my appreciation for John's extra help at home and with the children.

THERAPIST: What difference do you think his experiencing that appreciation has on the relationship now and perhaps promises for the future?

JOHN [*As Ruth*]: That's a tough question. I would hope that he realizes that I still love him. Early in our relationship, he used to tell me that I looked at him with loving eyes. We were intimate and had fun together.

THERAPIST: Can you imagine the difference it will make when you are both appreciating one another and seeing each other through your loving eyes?

JOHN [*As Ruth, with tears in his eyes*]: I would really like to have that happen.

THERAPIST: Is it OK if we stop at this point and allow Ruth to comment? [*John agrees, and I then turn to Ruth.*] How well would you say John performed being you? For example, on a scale of 1 to 10, where 1 would indicate he was completely off base and 10 would mean he was 100% on target, where would you rate John's internalized experience of you and the relationship?

RUTH: I am having a very strange reaction to what John imagined that I would say. I haven't really thought about it, but as he spoke I thought, "Yes, that is what I would like to say." It is almost like John has answered from the best part of me. I would like to have John come back again and have both of us continue to talk here with you together. [*John expresses his interest in returning.*]

THERAPIST: I want to thank you both for the special way you each were willing to participate in this relational exercise. From what you have both said, it seems that each of you has had a struggle during this difficult time of so many changes. And I am pleased to be a witness to what your relationship may look like as you continue your conversations and struggle together. Thank you again for this opportunity. When would you prefer to meet again?

🌿 **Process Commentary** During the initial interview, I want to hear at least a few things about people's lives that are not related to the presenting problems—their interests, their living situation, and so forth. I want to be as clear as possible as to what Ruth expects from our meeting together. I want to be able to provide a unique kind of listening, what has been referred to by some colleagues as "generous listening." This is not listening for symptoms that will help provide a diagnosis, for surface clues to deep meaning or underlying themes, for couple or family dynamics, for self-defeating cognitions, or for so-called facts related to some theory of personality. This kind of listening attempts to open up more possibilities rather than close possibilities. In my inquiry and responses, I attempt to utilize Ruth's and later John's vocabulary and worldview rather than mine. I am interested not only in how the problems affect Ruth's life and relationships but in how her personal values, abilities, accomplishments, and possible resources affect her life and relationships.

I often recall an old saying attributed to Native American meetings that reflects important aspects of this therapeutic process: "Show Up"; "Be Present"; "Tell the Truth"; and finally, "Don't Be Attached to Outcome." I attempt to connect and cultivate a genuine curiosity in the present. I am interested in both Ruth's and John's lived experience and realities ("truths") that evolve in conversations external to and within our meetings. I attempt to be aware of how certain ideas and practices that are found in our society may have some influence on Ruth and her relationships. In couples therapy I listen particularly for things Ruth tells herself that may be associated with pressures from the culture in which she was brought up. I strive to avoid leading either Ruth or John to any predetermined resolution of problems or preferred way of being in the world.

During the later phase of therapy, I am concerned about the multiple voices that Ruth experiences about her future. This includes voices about gender, culture, self-limitations, and assets available to her. The internalized dialogues that she has carried from the past and her present relationships are important ideas to bring into the therapy. These multiple voices enhance the possible choices that Ruth can make.

The session in which John joined us was valuable because Ruth could experience John's ideas directly instead of the version of John that is her internalized reality. In this exercise I am trying to be more client-focused than theory-focused and therefore I feel free to use therapeutic interventions that may be particularly helpful to Ruth.[2] There were a number of possible advantages of introducing "an internalized other" exercise in this couples session:

- Each partner has a greater opportunity to understand and appreciate the other's personal perspective and story.
- An attitude of reflection and contemplation is fostered and escalating, more-of-the-same interactions are avoided or minimized.
- Each partner can eavesdrop on the other's "best self," and defensiveness is minimized.
- Each partner has the opportunity to experience what it is like to "stand in the other's shoes."

I feel optimistic about Ruth's future. It is to her credit that she is already involved in a process of change. Therapy is just another tool she is using to assist her in the endeavor that she began years ago. She is on a path to change that is irreversible. Ruth's case is a good example of a client taking charge of her life and developing new choices or possibilities for her future and relationships.

A Solution-Focused Brief Therapist's Perspective on Ruth

by David J. Clark, PhD

Introduction

Ruth called for an appointment and told me that she was interested in working with me because she had read about brief therapy in her class work. She had never been in therapy and was concerned that it would take a long time and interfere with her family life. We set an appointment for the following week.

Solution-focused brief therapy is based on the notion that there are times when a person's particular problem has not been an issue. This exception to the problem is called "a solution," and it is considered to be happening already in the client's life. My task as a therapist is to be a detective who looks for these exceptions. My tools for this investigation are my questions within a collaborative relationship with the client.

Basic Assumptions

The solution-focused approach represents a different perspective from most of the traditional therapy approaches with respect to thinking about and doing brief therapy. Applied to the case of Ruth, this model assumes that she has the internal and external resources she needs to make the kind of changes she wants to make. My work with Ruth is not a problem-solving approach but one that helps her to discover her internal strengths and the external resources to utilize them. Here are some basic assumptions underlying my approach and interrelated guidelines I use in counseling Ruth from a solution-focused perspective.

1. I strive to keep the conversation nonpathological and to redescribe problems in such a way as to open up possibilities. When Ruth describes herself and her life with a problem focus, these descriptions continue to reinforce her beliefs about herself, keeping her stuck in old actions. I find it helpful to offer a new description that invites Ruth to think about the exceptions to her problems.

As Ruth describes the situation that brings her to therapy, I kindly and respectfully suggest a new description that employs hope. Suggesting a new perception does not change the diagnosis or minimize the problem. It simply normalizes and redefines the presenting problem so that Ruth may begin to perceive solutions to it. Problems are not viewed as pathological manifestations but as ordinary difficulties and challenges of life. I view diagnosis as being important and a sign of the underlying fact that something has gone off track.

2. There is a focus on looking for exceptions to the problems that Ruth brings up for discussion. I tend to ask, "What is different about the times when you do

not feel quite as depressed?" Changing the direction in therapy from a problem focus to a solution focus can dramatically change Ruth's beliefs about her life situation.

3. This approach does not highlight Ruth's deficits, problems, and failures. Instead, emphasis is on her strengths, assets, accomplishments, abilities, competencies, skills, and successes. When a strength becomes evident in the therapy session itself, I comment on it as a method of reinforcement. Compliments are often perceived as real when they relate to here-and-now interactions. Ruth provides some evidence of her strengths in her autobiography and intake form.

4. Rather than trying to promote insight, I focus on Ruth's ability to survive a problem situation. For me, it is important to refrain from urging Ruth to engage in totally unfamiliar activities. She is more likely to take on activities that she has some degree of comfort with and that fit within her realm of experience.

5. I view Ruth as a person who has complaints about her life rather than as a person with symptoms. In solution-focused therapy, empathy, compassion, and genuine concern are essential for establishing a therapeutic partnership. In addition, it is especially important to help Ruth understand that she has strengths and coping styles that have been successful in dealing with troublesome situations in the past. This provides Ruth with a positive message that can translate into productive actions.

6. I operate on the assumption that complex problems do not necessarily require complex solutions. I invite Ruth to think in simpler ways. Ruth's life situation tends to appear the most complicated when she truly believes that her problem will be solved only when someone else changes his or her behavior. Here are some questions I am likely to pose to Ruth:

- What would it do for you when the behavior of _____ changes?
- Suppose that happened. What would you be doing on the day the change occurs that could be different from what you did yesterday?
- Suppose _____ never changes but you are ready to step back into life on a small scale. What behaviors would others see as they watched you go through your day that would tell them you were getting back into life?

In some situations Ruth may feel overwhelmed by how complicated her problems are. Her beliefs may seem to center around the need for a problem to be totally solved in order for her life to move forward. I am likely to answer by saying, "I understand how hard it is to envision this happening and how easy it is to imagine how it might not ever happen. But I'm still interested in what you would like to be doing instead."

7. It can be helpful to temporarily adopt Ruth's worldview to lessen her resistance. I reframe resistance by considering certain behaviors as doing something important for Ruth, and I assist her in the discovery of actions and behaviors that would be less dangerous and interfering than the ones she currently uses. Asking Ruth to discuss how her present behaviors offer support, relief, and gratification can help resolve resistance.

8. I assist Ruth in viewing her problem (such as depression) as external to herself and to her life. This can help her see the problem as a separate entity

that influences but does not always control her life. I might ask Ruth, "Consider a scale from 1 to 10, where 1 indicates depression has total control of you and your life and 10 indicates you are in control of it. Where would you say you are today?" By asking how the problem has been affecting Ruth's relationships, she can feel more capable of intervening in her own life. This may increase her self-rated level of confidence and her degree of hopefulness. Ruth can learn to think of her new actions as giant steps that move her away from her problem's influence on her life, which will empower her.

9. I focus only on what is possible and what Ruth is able to change. I assist Ruth in thinking about and establishing useful goals in therapy: ones that are realistic, attainable, meaningful, and measurable. When Ruth states, "I just want to be happier," I respond with, "When you are happier, someday, what would _____ be seeing you do differently?"

10. My tendency is to go slowly and encourage my clients to ease into solutions gradually. An effective method of measuring small amounts of success efficiently is one that suggests a need for change on the basis of a client's reported position on a scale. I ask, "What needs to happen between now and the next time we meet for you to maintain the 3 and or to move up a little bit to, say, a 3.5?" I want to teach Ruth to see how each new strategy is an experiment rather than a technique that guarantees success. Whatever happens as a result of a new strategy is simply part of an experiment toward change.

Assessment of Ruth

When Ruth arrived at my office, an early intervention was to get her thinking about what kind of changes she most wanted in her life.

> THERAPIST: Have you thought about how you would know that therapy was no longer needed?
>
> RUTH: I am not sure I understand. Could you ask that question another way?
>
> THERAPIST: Ruth, if we were to work together for 2 or 3 months and if therapy went really well, what would be happening that would make you say, "It was a really good thing that I went to see Dave"?

This is a typical beginning of a first solution-focused therapy session. I immediately start to work toward a goal. Asking Ruth to focus on what positive difference therapy could make starts her thinking in the direction of a goal. As she focuses on the future and constructs positive outcomes, she is inventing and rehearsing these events.

Ruth thinks a while and answers, "I would be getting along better with my husband and with my daughter, Jennifer. I would be confident in going forward in my teaching career. I would be losing weight sensibly and feel better about myself." She pauses and adds, "I would be more sure of my decisions." Ruth's enthusiastic answer is important to me because in solution-focused brief therapy we see the work as interactional. In having a specific and positive vision for what she can achieve through therapy, Ruth communicates her willingness and interest in having change occur.

If Ruth presents a request for third-party payment by her health care provider, I may have specific paperwork responsibilities, which include the *DSM-IV-TR* diagnosis.[3] Solution-focused brief therapy tends to eschew formal diagnosis, yet this is typically a requirement for third-party payment. These issues would be discussed with her. We agree that Axis I would be an Adjustment Disorder with mixed anxiety and depressed mood (309.28). To acknowledge her concern with her weight problem, I agree to a provisional diagnosis on Axis I of an Eating Disorder (NOS: 307.50). For the distress with her husband and daughter, we choose V-codes for relational problems: Parent-Child Relational Problems (V61.20) and Partner Relational Problem (V61.10). I defer diagnosis on Axis II and III. Axis IV, Psychosocial and Environmental Problems, highlight the transition Ruth is going through, including the decisions about work, completing her credentials, and making peace with John about these changes.

The *DSM-IV-TR* also has a fifth axis. This is called the Global Assessment of Functioning (GAF). This scale gives an overall description of how the client is functioning. The GAF describes the general functioning of the individual regarding his or her psychological, social, and occupational pursuits. The range of the GAF scale is from a low of 1, which indicates that the client is persistently suicidal or homicidal, to a high of 90, which indicates that the client is free of any symptoms. Ruth has bouts of anxiety and depression as described on the scale, and we estimate that her score would fall between 70 and 75. Here again, Ruth and I collaborate to find the score that we agree is a description of her situation.

The Therapeutic Process

A key concept of solution-focused brief therapy is that we are always looking for positive exceptions or difference. We call these positive exceptions "news of difference." When we find news of difference, we ask many questions about the difference because we believe that this information can lead to change. Consequently, we are not as interested in hearing about the problem as we are in hearing about times when the problem is not a problem—the exceptions.

Most of the time clients want to talk about their problems, which we call "problem-talk." This is rarely helpful in bringing about change. Only when we ask questions about difference do clients shift to focus on that. We call the resulting conversation about difference or exceptions to the problem "change-talk." It is through change-talk that clients are able to co-create real and enduring change. Once we are having this kind of conversation, we ask important questions to create opportunities for change, such as "What has to happen for that (the change) to happen more often?" Here is an example of a conversation with Ruth aimed at having her think about changes.

THERAPIST: The day people call for an appointment is usually a day that they feel low. They have decided that they cannot solve their problem on their own, and they are ready to invite a stranger to help.

RUTH: Well, yes, I was really at a loss to know how to deal with my problems by myself.

THERAPIST: On a scale of 1 to 10, where 1 represents how you were feeling when you made the call for an appointment and 10 represents how you will be feeling when you are done with therapy, where would you say you are right now?

RUTH: I'm about a 3 today.

THERAPIST: If we assume that you were a 1 when you called, how did you move from a 1 to a 3?

RUTH: When I made the appointment, I started to focus on what I would say when I got here, and when I got clearer about that, I felt better.

THERAPIST: What difference do you notice in yourself when you are at a 3?

RUTH: I feel a little more sure of myself, and I feel hopeful that I can get better.

THERAPIST: What does your husband notice when you are at a 3?

RUTH: He notices that I am less wishy-washy. I sound more definite when I say something.

THERAPIST: How is that helpful? [*Another way of asking about difference*]

RUTH: Well, he takes me more seriously when I sound focused.

THERAPIST: And what difference does that make?

RUTH: I want to continue in getting my teaching credential. John wants me to stay home. I don't think he believes I am competent. When I sound focused, I think he sees me as more competent.

THERAPIST: And when he sees you as more competent, does he treat you differently?

RUTH: John seems to respect me more when I feel more sure of myself. I think he starts to take me seriously.

THERAPIST: When you are at a 3, how does your relationship with your daughter change?

RUTH: Jennifer acts less confrontational when I feel better.

THERAPIST: What difference does that make to your relationship?

RUTH: It is a lot easier for us to be around each other? We are less irritable.

These questions I am posing to Ruth are called relational questions because they punctuate the effect that different behaviors have on other people and, reciprocally, how their changes influence her responses. During the therapeutic process I continue with questions that look for differences. I want to know if Ruth responds differently to John when he sees her as more competent. I point out the fact that change is reciprocal and interactional. When Ruth changes, John's reactions to her change, and she then changes in reaction to his response to her. I never think of the person as an individual. I believe people are always in relationship to themselves (internal dialogues), other people, a life context, a community context, or a cultural context.

An acronym, EARS, outlines the therapeutic process I follow: *Elicit, Amplify, Reinforce, Start over.* I listen to the client and elicit news of difference by inquiring about what is different. I amplify the difference by asking more questions about the difference: "How was that helpful?" or "What difference does that make?" I reinforce the difference by letting the client know that I am impressed. This may be by a nod of the head or a simple expression like, "wow" or "really," and then I start over: "What else is different?" Although this process is simple, it is not easy. With certain therapeutic models, counselors are lured into asking questions about the problem or engaging in discussions about feelings. This line of inquiry tends to distract from the direct path of learning what differences will have an impact on clients and what has to happen for those events to happen more often.

The format of a solution-focused session, which I employ with Ruth, involves a reliable pattern with which she will become familiar. The first part of the session, about 35 minutes, is spent in change-talk conversation such as this, and the questions I pose to Ruth lead to news of difference.

THERAPIST: What will be signs to you that changes are happening, even in small ways?

RUTH: There would be less tension at breakfast.

THERAPIST: What would be there instead of tension?

RUTH: John and Jennifer would be having a pleasant conversation, and they would be friendlier to me.

THERAPIST: How do you explain that these changes would happen?

RUTH: I think that they would see that I was more relaxed and would follow my lead.

THERAPIST: When was the last time something like that happened, even a little bit?

RUTH: Last Sunday morning we all had brunch together, and it was less tense.

THERAPIST: How do you explain that things were better last Sunday?

RUTH: We all had plans to go to church together, and we had separate events planned for the afternoon. We were looking forward to the day.

THERAPIST: What has to happen for these kinds of differences to happen more often?

RUTH: I guess if we really start to make more separate plans for ourselves, then the kids could be more independent and the tension would lessen.

THERAPIST: When these better experiences continue to happen, what difference will this make in your life?

RUTH: My life would start to look more like what I'm hoping for, and I could get on with my teaching career without worrying so much about the family.

After this we take a break during which time I leave the room for about 5 minutes to think about the session and to develop some compliments, a bridging statement, and a homework task. The compliments must be genuine and represent something that Ruth can feel good about. A second benefit of the break is that it sets an expectancy. Ruth will eagerly wait for me to return, and she is anxious to hear my comments. I take notes during the session and survey my notes for the compliments. When I decide what they are, I write them down and read them to Ruth. I generally select only two or three of the many potential compliments that I have listed.

Frequently, when I give compliments, clients nod their head in agreement with me. This subtle agreement puts the client into a "yes set." In other words, the client is starting to agree with me. Doing this with Ruth makes it more likely that when I assign a homework task she will follow it. I look at my notes to see where desired changes are already occurring, and I am likely to assign something Ruth is already doing as a homework task. Homework is also linked to the original assessment of Ruth's position with me. When I return from the break, I introduce the message and the homework assignment.

> THERAPIST: Ruth, I am impressed with your ability to take charge of your life. Not many people are able to do what you did 10 years ago. It took a lot of courage to leave the church in which you were brought up. And more recently, your decision to go to school and become a teacher shows courage and determination. Now you are completing your education to launch another big change in your life. In view of the fact that last Sunday was a better morning because you all had plans for the day, I am wondering if you might do some homework?
>
> RUTH: What do you have in mind?
>
> THERAPIST: Between now and the next time we meet, could you, on two separate occasions, deliberately plan for a meal when everyone has some different plans and notice if the better mood is still present? Next time we meet we can discuss what you noticed.
>
> RUTH: I can certainly give that a try.
>
> THERAPIST: OK! I'll plan to see you again at this time in 2 weeks.

In this case, I looked for something Ruth told me about in the session that worked and built an introduction to the homework task. This introduction makes sense of the task and is called a bridging statement, or segue. An alternative homework assignment might be: "Ruth, since you find yourself at a 3 and you feel better at a 3, I'm wondering if you can intentionally notice how you rate yourself on days when you are feeling good about an interaction with John or Jennifer. I suggest that you make some notes about your ratings and what was happening at the time that you rated it. Next time we meet we can discuss your experience with this task." Because I am asking her to do something, I call this a "rehearsal task."

One procedure that is part of solution-focused brief therapy is the "miracle question." There may be times when Ruth cannot think of any exceptions to a problem she is experiencing. She might report that a certain problem is always there. In these instances, I look for "hypothetical solutions." These are solutions that have not yet happened, but because I ask the question, Ruth is likely to think of an exception. Even though it hasn't happened in Ruth's daily life, it can happen in her consciousness as she invents it in her mind. Typically the miracle question sounds like this:

> THERAPIST: Suppose that after we finished here and you went back to your life and finished your day, that tonight while you were asleep a miracle happened and the problem that brought you here was solved. Wouldn't that be nice? Tomorrow morning when you wake up you don't know that the miracle happened because you were asleep when it happened. Now, what would be the first clue to you that would make you think that a miracle must have happened? What would be the first indication that the problem was solved?

> RUTH: In the morning when I first see John, he will smile at me and say "good morning."

Ruth comes up with a response to the miracle question, and I regard this response as news of difference. I can use this in our conversation or in homework assignments. The response is an exception to the problem even though it is only hypothetical, and it is Ruth's material, not mine.

🕮 **Process Commentary**   Solution-focused therapy is typically completed in less than six sessions, and outcome research demonstrates that 78% of clients are satisfied with the results of the therapy.[4] With Ruth, sessions four through six are essentially maintaining and reinforcing gains or achieved solutions. My major focus with Ruth is on her lived experience (thinking, feeling, behaving, and relational context). We work together in a collaborative relationship, setting useful goals for the course of therapy. The purpose of asking questions about exception periods, coping strategies, and pretreatment change is to initiate conversations about client-based strategies, strengths, and resources. All of this is referred to as "solution-talk." I operate from a relational, pragmatic, and minimalist perspective. My primary emphasis is on describing what Ruth and others did differently during the exceptional period. I then prescribe more of what she has found that works. I place value on related observational and behavioral homework tasks with an emphasis on the so-called common factors of outcome research.[5] At times, I utilize outcome–process measurements such as those discussed by Duncan, Miller, and Sparks.[6]

A Narrative Therapist's Perspective on Ruth
by Gerald Monk, PhD

Introduction

Ruth contacted me because she has heard that I work from a narrative perspective, which she thinks might be a good fit for her. Ruth wants me to help her get clarity about what she might do with her life. What she wants most of all is certainty about what will make her happy without cost to others. She wants to know whether she should continue to stay married to John. She wonders whether she will survive without him at worst, or be miserable on her own at best. She is not sure that John will survive without her, and that worries her.

Ruth is fearful of the judgment that she will incur from God, her father, and her children if she were to live a life that is not influenced by servitude, compliance, and emotional caregiving toward her husband and her soon to be grown children. She is frightened by attacks of anxiety, periods of depression, the prospect of dying and going to hell, her aging body, and her weight gain.

Basic Assumptions

A narrative approach involves entering a therapeutic situation with a range of specific assumptions. These assumptions have been largely pieced together into what is called narrative therapy by Michael White and David Epston.[7]

At the heart of this practice is the notion that we live our lives according to the stories that people tell about us and the stories that we tell ourselves. The story is not merely viewed as a means by which real experiences are accounted for. Rather, the story constructs "real experiences" and actually shapes our reality. Narrative practitioners contend that we construct what we see as well as describe what we see.

Significant therapeutic importance is placed on how people story their experiences and perform these stories in their lives. Narrative therapists work from the premise that narratives do not encompass the full richness of our lives. Rather, particular lived experiences, or narratives, are not selected out for expression. These lived experiences are often overlooked, never noticed or understood, and are overshadowed by dominant problem-saturated stories. It is these overlooked lived experiences that are the material of interest in the narrative approach. Although a client is often strongly positioned by a problem-saturated story, a narrative therapist recognizes that this person will also have desirable lived experiences. These experiences are viewed as the basis from which an alternative, more preferred story line can be developed.

Narrative therapists maintain that problems are identified within sociocultural and relational contexts rather than existing within individuals.[8] The therapeutic endeavor concentrates on the socially constructed dialogue and the narrative accounts that clients present. Narrative practitioners maintain that one's identity or personhood is developed, sustained, and transformed in and through relationships, both immediate and within the society at large. Their recognition of sociocultural contexts and language in generating problems invites narrative therapists to challenge traditional Western psychology, which defines adjustment in terms of dominant cultural values. Therefore, although traditional psychotherapy privileges Western, White, middle-class values as the "valid" means to mental health, narrative approaches recognize the potential negative effects of therapies that pathologize and categorize human beings when they do not conform to stereotypical health standards. Instead, they hold knowledge tentatively and assist people to identify resources to attain preferred outcomes.

Consistent with its opposition to models of health, narrative approaches employ a nonexpert stance in relation to clients. Narrative therapists seek to understand clients' lived experience and avoid efforts to predict, interpret, or pathologize. Within this process, narrative practitioners are committed to collaborating with clients in assisting them to experience a heightened sense of agency or ability to act in the world.

Narrative therapists consider problems through a political lens, whether an overt cultural problem such as racism or a more covert pressure such as "healthy" relationships. This sociopolitical conceptualization of problems invites the exploration of cultural practices that produce dominant, oppressive narratives. In other words, this approach encourages us to reflect on where we get our restrictive notions and how these ideas produce a negative effect on us or others. Accordingly, narrative therapists "deconstruct" or "unpack" the cultural assumptions that contextualize client problems to demonstrate the effects of oppressive social practices on their clients. This practice invites narrative therapists to identify how dominant cultural practices or certain mainstream belief systems attempt to define and regulate people.

Narrative Techniques

Narrative techniques are constructed on the assumptions just described. I will discuss the techniques of externalizing, mapping the effects, deconstruction, co-authoring alternative stories, several kinds of questions, and building an audience as a witness to the emerging preferred story.

🕮 **Externalizing Conversation**   "The person is not the problem. The problem is the problem." This catch phrase, coined by Michael White, is associated with narrative therapy because of its emphasis on separating the problem from the person rather than demanding that the person own the problem. This is perhaps narrative therapy's most distinctive feature. The method employed to separate the person from the problem is referred to as *externalizing conversation*. Externalizing conversations create space between clients and problems to counteract oppressive, problem-saturated stories, thereby altering clients' relations to problems. Externalizing requires the therapist to identify discourses (cultural ideas and beliefs) that are problematic and oppressive and to identify the effects of these discourses on clients. This externalization allows clients to locate problem stories within a community context rather than within themselves.

Although externalizing descriptions are typically developed in consultation with clients, narrative practitioners actively contribute in this process by identifying externalizing descriptions that fit with the problem's central themes and the wider sociocultural milieu. In fact, narrative practitioners use externalizing conversations to interrupt the tendency of the community or individuals to pathologize people into positions of helplessness, guilt, and shame. For example, a therapist's externalizing language is captured in these questions: "To what extent is this notion of the perfect wife contributing toward the distress that you currently feel?" "How do you manage to fulfill all of the demands placed upon you when fear continues to undermine your confidence?"

🕮 **Mapping the Effects of the Problem Story**   The full effects of the problem story have seldom been grappled with by the person seeking help. Clients often fear that they might be overwhelmed by their difficulties. When externalized descriptions of problems are embedded in the conversation, their effects on clients are examined in a more dispassionate light. Clients feel less shamed and blamed. When the problem influences are examined in a systematic fashion, people feel listened to and that their concerns are taken seriously. They become more mindful of the burden they have been operating under, and after hearing and using externalized descriptions, they are more motivated to move away from the harmful effects of the problem. The externalized problems are understood in terms of the length of time they have been around (length), the extent to which they have had an impact on the person's life (breadth), and the strength and intensity of their influence (depth).[9]

Here are some examples of questions exploring the length, breadth, and depth of the problem-saturated story:

Length Questions
- How long has this problem been around?
- When did it start?
- If things keep going like this, what length of time do you think you might be wrestling with this problem?

Breadth Questions
- How widely spread is this difficulty?
- To what extent is it troubling you on a day-to-day basis?
- How are your present difficulties affecting your mental health, relationships with yourself, friends, children, husband, wife, siblings, physical well-being, your work, leisure time, spiritual well-being, plans for your future, ability to have fun?

Depth Questions
- What level of distress has this problem been causing you?
- At what times is this problem most difficult to handle?
- When is it less difficult?
- On a scale of 1 to 10, how impactful is the problem right now if 10 indicates the problem is in charge of you and 1 indicates that you are completely in charge of it? What score would you give it at its worst? At its best?

Deconstructive Practices Frequently, people are unaware of how discourses restrict their knowledge, volition, and ways of being in the world. Alternative, more preferred ways of living may remain out of reach, unavailable, or unattainable. Deconstruction questions provide opportunities for the client to examine the cultural restraints that hold them back. Deconstruction questions involve challenging taken-for-granted assumptions about how life must be lived, feelings that must be felt, and behaviors that must be performed. Here are some examples of deconstruction questions:

- What ideas do you have about being female that explain why you acted that way?
- Where and how did you learn these ideas?
- Who in your life keeps reminding you that you should continue to live by these ideas?
- What areas of your life keep reinforcing these ideas about how you should think, feel, and act?

⌘ **Co-Authoring a Preferred Story**   The biggest challenge in constructing a non–problem-saturated story, or what is called an "alternative story," lies in the contrast between the fragility of the emerging story and the intensity and strength of the problem story. Problem stories typically take hold over a long period of time. Clients often experience problem stories as true accounts of what is taking place in their lives. Just as the problem story has grown in strength, so must the alternative story develop sufficient plot strength to be vibrant and potent enough to challenge and stand up to the authority of the problem-saturated story. A range of specific questions designed to elicit the alternative story open up new possibilities for clients who have lost sight of the competencies and abilities that have once been expressed but are often eclipsed by chronic problem issues. The alternative story needs to be fleshed out in sufficient detail in the counseling sessions so that it remains compelling and strong. The alternative story has a beginning in the early life of the client. It is the task of the practitioner to rediscover with clients their demonstrated abilities and strengths in their early life. These rediscoveries are essential to the process of making desirable changes in their present life.

A narrative practitioner makes notes of these competencies, or makes a mental note to return to these later when a preferred client narrative will be constructed. These lived experiences provide the material for the emerging history of the preferred story. Moments of creativity, capacity, and capability are woven together into a story that will endure in the face of the problem-saturated stories that are ready to reconsume the client. Unique outcome, unique account, redescription, and unique possibility questions are all examples of questions that help elicit the client's preferred story.[10]

⌘ **Unique Outcome Questions**   Client competencies are the unique outcomes (sparkling moments that stand apart from the problem story) that provide the material that can be storied into an enlivening narrative. In other words, in collaboration with the client, the practitioner locates desirable experiences the client can reflect on that can be used to assemble a new plot for the alternative story. For example:

- Tell me about moments recently where this anxiety and distress has subsided even for a short time?
- Have you had any brief flashes of clarity amidst the confusion? Tell me about these momentary insights.
- In our interview together, are there things you are saying to me that hint at some possible creative solutions to the dilemma that you face? Say more about this.

⌘ **Unique Account Questions**   These questions assist clients in giving an account of how they were able to accomplish the desirable, favored moments. These questions provide opportunities to promote encouragement and optimism and help to build a sense of competence and capacity for people struggling with issues that attempt to incapacitate them. Here are two examples:

- How were you able to speak out and stand up for yourself when it seemed like everything and everybody else were wanting you to go along with their ideas for you?
- What is it about you that gives you the strength to ask for new possibilities for your life when you have been instructed to conform to certain pre-scriptions of how to be a woman?

⚘ Redescription Questions   Redescription questions invite people to reflect on new emerging or submerged preferred identities. Another way of saying this is that redescription questions provide an opportunity for clients to explore other ways of being in the world that are in contrast to the ways they are currently adopting. They get at people's preferences for their personal development and the kinds of new relationships they are establishing. Here are some examples:

- What does this action, series of thoughts, or feeling responses tell you about yourself that you have not previously been in touch with?
- Now that you are prepared to question and reexamine the direction your life is taking, what does this behavior suggest to you about the personal qualities and abilities you are exhibiting right now?

⚘ Unique Possibility Questions   Unique possibility questions move the focus into the future. They encourage people to reflect upon what they have currently achieved, and based on these successes, they invite people to consider what their next steps might be. Here are some examples:

- Given your present discoveries and understandings, what do you think your next steps might be?
- When you are acting from this preferred identity, what actions will it lead you to do more of?
- Now that you have observed people responding in a supportive manner to your self-caring, what plans do you have for yourself to not let go of your ability to nurture yourself?

⚘ Building an Audience   Identities or ways of being are not performed in a vacuum. We are forever presenting ourselves to an audience. An audience are those significant others in families and communities whose opinions and viewpoints have immense influence on a client. Sometimes this audience is critical and scathing. When significant others are consistently negative, they act as powerful definers of how we perceive ourselves and the dominant stories we carry about our lives. Thus, dominant problem stories are often cultivated under the gaze of scornful or judgmental observation.

Emerging alternative stories that carry with them the possibility of a pre-ferred self-description must be nurtured by an audience of significant others who will notice and take delight in this desired self-depiction. An appreciative audience can verify the changes being made as real and sustainable. A com-mon form of narrative questioning might begin with the request that the client identify a person in his or her life who would be least surprised to learn of the changes he or she is now making. Clients can be asked what this valued person might say or do if informed about the emerging new story.[11]

Preparing for a Therapeutic Conversation With Ruth

Narrative therapy is essentially a therapy of questions conducted by persons who work from a nonexpert position of respectful and persistent curiosity and naive inquiry. Ruth will be asked if it is OK to ask her a series of questions about her life circumstances. Ruth will be given the assurance that she does not have to answer any questions she finds intrusive or distressing. I view Ruth as the senior author in the therapeutic conversation. She is the expert on her own life and will be consulted in regard to what she would like to achieve, how long she would like to attend sessions, and who she would like to include in future meetings. Therapy is generally a playful and optimistic activity where Ruth is viewed as somebody who already has a variety of resources, abilities, and insights that she can capably bring to bear on her problem concerns. Together we discover her talents and capacities, which provide the basis for narratives of strength and resiliency, and we seek to understand the problem-saturated stories that restrain Ruth from attaining the level of personal satisfaction she would like to achieve.

In working with Ruth I am attentive to learning about the problem-saturated stories that are shaping her troubles. Through a systematic process of careful listening and curious and persistent questioning, the therapeutic task is to co-construct enlivening alternative client narratives with Ruth. This is done within a spirit of partnership and collaboration. In the narrative conversation, I address seven domains in assisting Ruth with her concerns, although in practice they may not be followed in a specific order. I want to assist Ruth in some of the following ways:

- Story the problem-saturated narratives that feature prominently in her life.
- In a focused and systematic way, consider and experience the effects of the problem narratives on her life.
- Determine the extent to which she would like something different than her present circumstances.
- Deconstruct discourses that have a negative impact on her.
- Story a range of preferred alternative narratives that lie outside the problem-saturated stories.
- Reflect on how preferred narratives invite Ruth to construct new, more preferred identities.
- Build an audience to the emergence of Ruth's preferred identities.

Like many other narrative therapists, I view Ruth's concerns within the context of her life. I see us as two cultural beings doing the best we can to sustain ourselves in the face of a world that is challenging, fast changing, and unpredictable. As we work together, we are both making sense of our lives and producing meanings that take us forward, whatever they might be.

Initial Assessment and Evaluation

I begin my interview with Ruth by inviting her to tell me the concerns she has and what she is hoping to accomplish in our meetings together. I want to understand what help she would like from me. I explain the philosophy and practices underpinning narrative therapy because I want to be as transparent as I can be about what I am here to do. From a narrative perspective, I am not at all invested in producing a *DSM-IV-TR* diagnosis to guide my work with Ruth. I am concerned about the inadvertent effects of labeling Ruth's experience in this way, and I am opposed to the pathologizing tendencies that the *DSM-IV-TR* promotes. The *DSM-IV-TR* focuses on inadequacy and personal failure rather than on solutions and attention to resources and competence. It is seldom useful in helping me know what to do. I believe that Ruth is in a continual state of reinventing her identity, and such labeling invites a static perspective about her future directions. It also fails to address the significance of interpersonal and cultural factors that shape Ruth's experience.

However, if I worked under a managed health care system requiring a *DSM-IV-TR* diagnosis, we would look at Axes I, III, IV, and V only, and I would explain that this may or may not be helpful to Ruth. I would not engage in an Axis II diagnosis because of its totalizing descriptions of people. In a collaborative manner, we would probably choose what I would call a "cultural description" (what others may call a diagnosis) that Ruth was comfortable with. I would emphasize to Ruth the somewhat subjective, arbitrary nature of the exercise and the significant variation in diagnoses that are made by practitioners using this system.

Therapeutic Processes and Procedures

🕮 **Telling Problem-Saturated Narratives**   Ruth tells me about a number of her concerns including her feelings of confusion, depression, inadequacy, distress, and anxiety. While Ruth still has concern with the panic attacks, the yoga class she is taking has decreased their frequency. Ruth also expresses concerns about her weight problems. However, right now Ruth is requesting very specific help—she wants advice about what she should do in relation to her marriage. She doesn't want marital counseling, but she wants to explore her own feelings about whether "she still loves John." She wants to get as clear as possible about whether she should try and salvage her marriage with John or leave him. She thinks some of the difficulties she is having with Jennifer (her daughter) relate to her current lack of communication and cooperation with John.

Despite entering into counseling, Ruth can barely believe she is asking herself these questions, let alone telling somebody else. Ruth feels like she is really letting John down by exploring her confusion, uncertainty, and ambivalence about their relationship. She wants lots of assurance that what she is doing is not evil and full of betrayal.

RUTH: I can't believe I am telling you about my inner thoughts about my future. It is scary to say these things out loud.

THERAPIST: Tell me more about that.

RUTH: Well, I felt like I would always be married to John. Even though we have had some terrible times together, I have never, until very recently, faced the prospect that I could leave John. The fear of judgment from my children, from John, from my father, and fear of some kind of divine punishment—that I would go to hell—has stopped me from even considering anything but staying together. But right now I have been honest enough to accept the fact that I hate the kind of life I have been living and shudder to think that I may continue to live this life until the day I die.

THERAPIST: Ruth, tell me about your life right now and how it got to be this way. [*An invitation to tell the problem-saturated story*]

Ruth talks about how desperately unhappy she is. She talks about the fact that while John was OK about her pursuing a teaching credential, he has continued to be somewhat resentful about her developing her own professional interests. She feels like she can't really talk to John about how alone she feels. She lies alone at night wishing she were living somebody else's life. She talks some more about how scared she is to make any life changes. She is worried that things could get even worse.

I ask Ruth to tell me the story of her relationship with John from when they first met. She described the euphoria of falling in love and the profound sense of security she felt being with him. Ruth felt protected from the world. John was so strong, so secure within himself, so confident. He was also a good provider. Their relationship worked well for her for the first 15 years, but in the last 5 years things have started to deteriorate. She described feeling taken for granted by John and by the children as they reached adolescence. Ruth feels like a chauffeur, a housemaid, a cook, a counselor, a financial planner, and a caregiver/nurse. She reports feeling unfulfilled and unsupported. Ruth talks about her fear of speaking honestly to John about the depth of the despair she feels.

THERAPIST: What's stopping you from speaking to John about your present feelings?

RUTH: I really don't know. I guess I am just terrified that my world is going to come crashing around my ears if I tell people how I really feel.

THERAPIST: How long do you think fear and terror has stopped you from expressing your heartfelt thoughts? [*I introduce externalizing conversation into the interview.*]

RUTH: When I think about it, I have always been scared of speaking out. From as early as I can remember, I have been frightened about so many things.

Ruth speaks at length about how fear has silenced her in many different areas of her life on so many occasions. I am very curious about Ruth's relationship with fear. I enter the next phase of the narrative conversation.

Exploring the Effects of the Problem Narratives on Her Life   I begin by exploring with Ruth the effects of being silenced by fear. I ask Ruth what contributions fear and terror have made to her life. What has it added? What has it taken away? What has the fear cost her? What has the impact of fear had on her health? Her relationships? Her career? Her spirituality? Her ability to enjoy her life? Theses questions help us map the effects of the problem.

Ruth talks about some of her fear. She is afraid of what is involved in pursuing her career. She feels that the fear she is feeling stops her from taking risks to build new friendships. Ruth speaks about being afraid of what Jennifer might do if she is more honest with her daughter. Most of all, fear is causing her misery because she feels she can't speak openly with John about how she is feeling about her life. Ruth agrees that this state of affairs is far from ideal!

THERAPIST: Do you think there might be a relationship between being silenced and living with fear and the depression, anxiety, panic attacks, and confusion you speak of? [*Exploring themes and plotting connections within the problem story*]

RUTH: I think there is a relationship between these feelings and being able to speak openly about what is going on.

THERAPIST: Ruth, tell me how big you think fear is right now as you think about talking to John about what is really going on. Out of 10, how much do you think fear is silencing you from sharing your thoughts and feelings with John? [*Further mapping the effects of the problem according to depth*]

RUTH: I guess it's just about 10 because I just feel so terrible. I feel so unhappy. He has no real idea about how unhappy I am.

✇ Making a Decision to Create an Alternative Narrative   At this stage, I encourage Ruth to begin creating an alternative narrative.

THERAPIST: Ruth, you have been speaking fully about the kind of life you have led with fear, and at times terror, dominating the quality of your relationships with your family and friends, your career, and diminishing your ability to play, have fun, and create a life of your own design. I am wondering if you feel ready to take on this pervasive fear, or do you feel that fear might still be serving you well?

RUTH: I know that being so afraid has closed in on my life in so many ways. I feel ready to take this on, but it would be too overwhelming to become so honest with myself and everybody else in lots of areas of my life all at once.

THERAPIST: So you would like to challenge fear and express yourself more openly, but you want do so in small steps. Is that right?

RUTH: Sure.

✇ Understanding the Discursive Constraints   As Ruth is motivated to diminish the fear and anxiety that has dominated so much of her life, I ask her if she is willing to explore some of her life experiences that have contributed to the fear and anxiety she has felt. Ruth has made a link between the desire to step outside of her duties as a wife and a mother and the fear of doing so. She remembers the consequences as a young child of wanting to play and have fun, and the tensions and judgments that arose in the family if she participated in activities that weren't related to caring for others.

THERAPIST: Ruth, where did you learn how to be a woman, a wife, a parent?

RUTH: I don't know. I haven't really thought about it.

THERAPIST: Well, I am just wondering where you got the ideas of being very caring and putting your own needs aside to focus on other people's needs, sometimes at the expense of your own.

RUTH: I guess I mainly got the ideas from my Mom and the way my Dad treated my Mom, and the way he still treats her.

THERAPIST: Do you think you live your life according to the ways your Mom modeled how you should be a woman, mother, and wife?

RUTH: I'm not sure. I don't think I have really examined whether I live the same kind of life that my mother does. I know she would never have considered developing a career or going to college. In that way, we are quite different.

THERAPIST: Yes, that does seem to be a real difference. I am wondering if you can identify areas where you are the same?

RUTH: Well, I think Mom sees relationships in pretty traditional terms. The man is the head of the household, the primary income earner, the protector, if you like. The woman's job is to rear the children, to look after and take care of the house, and I guess to take care of the husband.

THERAPIST: How many of these ideas have you taken on board that your mom trained you in?

RUTH: Well, I guess for the first 15 years I've followed in Mom's footsteps. That is the kind of woman I have been for virtually all my married life. Now, this is the problem. I feel like I want to stop doing that. I don't want to keep feeling responsible for John's happiness at the expense of my own. I don't want to keep living my life through John. But this is what I hate. I feel so guilty for wanting to establish my own career. And yet I feel really resentful of John when he doesn't support me and help me with the kids. I am also sick of being some kind of domestic slave. Sometimes I feel really clear about wanting a very different life, and then I start feeling really guilty and bad. I get so confused, and then I get depressed again.

THERAPIST: What areas of your life keep reinforcing these ideas about how you should think, feel, and act?

RUTH: Well, I think my Mom and Dad sure reinforce the kind of mother I should be. Dad has been really opposed to me training as a teacher. He feels it is taking me away from my duties as a parent. Mom is asking me whether I still cook for John and the children since I started my teacher training. I guess those are some obvious examples. There are lots of other subtle ones. Anyway, I just get this really yuk feeling when I am wanting to do career stuff, develop new friendships, and want John to get more involved in helping with the kids and around the house.

As Ruth and I work together, we mutually identify a number of cultural influences that are shaping Ruth and her experiences. My task here is to work with her to deconstruct some of the cultural discourses that might play a central role in producing the conflicts, depression, anxieties, tensions, ambiguities, and fears Ruth experiences. On the white board, Ruth and I work together and identify the following cultural discourses as being influential in her defining herself as a woman:

- As a woman, you are a worthy person if you live your life to serve others.
- As a woman, you are a selfish and unworthy person if you consider your own needs and want to have a lot of fun in your life.
- It is a woman's job to dedicate her life to being the socioemotional caregiver to her husband and children.
- A wife can gain her sense of pleasure and satisfaction through the achievements of her husband.
- A woman's job is to stand by her husband no matter what the cost.
- A woman should put aside her own career aspirations to fulfill the needs of a man.

As Ruth looks at this list, she agrees that these are the very beliefs held by her husband, and by her to some extent. These are also common cultural ideas about women that circulate in many societies.

THERAPIST: Ruth, do you think there is any relationship between the fear and anxiety you experience and the efforts you are making to continue to fulfill these prescriptions about the kind of life you should be leading?

RUTH: Oh, yes, there is. I guess I have believed that these ideas about womanhood were true and it was my job to fulfill them. I have really started to question these beliefs in the last 5 years. I think I have been faithfully living by these ideas for virtually all my life. But I really don't know whether this is going to help. I guess I want some specific advice about what I should do.

THERAPIST: OK, let's figure out what you are already doing to challenge these beliefs before I give you any suggestions. Is that OK with you?

RUTH: Sure, but I don't see what I am doing to challenge these beliefs. I feel like a complete weakling living the kind of life I am leading. I wish I were more courageous.

THERAPIST: Ruth, I would really like to ask you some questions about your ability to challenge others and speak about things that you care about.

RUTH: OK, but I really don't think there is anything much to say about courage. I don't have any.

✎ **Building the Alternative Story**   At this point, we turn to the storying of Ruth's preferred narrative.

THERAPIST: Ruth, I am really intrigued that you are not aware of the occasions where you have been courageous and have challenged the kind of fear that had closed in so much on your life. I am really excited to start making some connections with you about the many moments you have mentioned already in this session where you are being an active participant in your life. For example, tell me about what it was like to make a decision to come to counseling.

RUTH: What do you mean?

THERAPIST: Well, you knew you were going to start examining your life in a way you haven't done before, and that must be pretty scary.

RUTH: You're right. I was terrified to make the appointment. I was thinking to myself, "What if I find out things about myself that I don't like?" You know, I am still really scared about where this is going to go.

THERAPIST: Would it be true that last year you would have been seriously challenged by fear and not made an appointment, and yet recently you decided you could make an appointment and start talking with me as openly as you have? [An identified unique outcome]

RUTH: Yeah, but I have been feeling so desperate, I just had to go ahead and do something. I have been feeling like I am going crazy.

THERAPIST: OK, I hear that. However, despite feeling desperate, how did you prepare to face fear so directly and start talking about your life so openly with me? [Unique account question]

RUTH: I dunno, I just said to myself one day, "I can't stand this anymore, I have got to do something."

THERAPIST: What do you think you might have said to yourself in the face of "Oh, my God, my life could completely change in ways I can't predict. I have got to do something." Did you say, "I can do this?" What did you say?

RUTH: I really don't know. I think I just said, "Ruth you have got to do something." I don't want to keep doing what I have been doing.

THERAPIST: OK, you knew you wanted something more, and you were prepared to go for it in spite of the fear.

RUTH: Yes, I guess so.

THERAPIST: OK, so we have one example of your ability to demonstrate courage and face fear. You were saying earlier that you feel like fear is about 10 and that you are almost completely silenced by it. Is that right?

RUTH: Yes.

THERAPIST: Well, as I am having you reflect more on these issues, I am wondering if there are even just a few occasions where you speak up about feelings you are having in day-to-day interactions with John.

RUTH: I usually don't tell John what I am feeling, and frankly I don't think he is interested most of the time.

THERAPIST: Can you think of an occasion in the last week where you have said to John something you feel strongly about and you didn't let fear silence you?

RUTH: Well, I guess there was an occasion on Tuesday when I said to John I needed his support when the children are rude. I told him in no uncertain terms that I wanted him to speak up and challenge the children when their tone of voice is rude.

THERAPIST: What was it like to tell him that?

RUTH: It felt good, but I'm not sure it made much difference.

THERAPIST: In that moment, how much were you in charge of yourself, and how much was fear in charge?

RUTH: I felt pretty confident saying that. It is more difficult to talk about my feelings for him and about our marriage.

THERAPIST: What would you rate fear in that moment?

RUTH: Oh, about a 3.

THERAPIST: Earlier you said you were excited about what could be in your life even though fear was really huge. You have been willing to talk openly and honestly with me to gain more understanding of yourself.

🕸 Developing the Alternative Story

In this phase of the narrative interview, I am storying lived experiences with Ruth about her courage, her ability to be decisive, to take risks in the face of not knowing, and being willing not to be controlled or stifled by fear. We speak together about a number of unique outcomes, occasions when Ruth has demonstrated courage in the face of serious fears. These include making a decision to train as a teacher, completing university studies, taking huge risks by leaving her parents' fundamentalist church, the courage to speak about shaming experiences about playing doctor when she was a child, her ability to care for her siblings when she was a child, and her ability to reflect now on her right to have fun and joy in her life.

We speak about the strengths and abilities required to raise four children, to "make a marriage work," and her ability to know that she has a right to be excited about her life. All of these lived experienced are linked together into a narrative of resilience and strength. To thicken the plot of the story of risk-taking, courage, determination, and having the right to enjoy life, I need to story with Ruth the courageous events that had recently happened and link them to events featured throughout her life. This includes eliciting occasions from as early as she can remember when Ruth displayed acts of courage. These memories are folded into the narrative that honors her own journey throughout her life. Ruth feels very excited and more potent as she reflects on these events.

It is not enough just to construct a lasting preferred narrative of strengths and abilities. We also need to reflect on how these actions influence Ruth's evolving and changing identity. In other words, I am interested in assisting

Ruth to revise her understandings of herself as she reflects on these preferred narratives. I continue to move into exploring the unique account questions to further thicken the plot of this emerging story.

> THERAPIST: Ruth, we have spent some time reflecting on the many, many instances when you have demonstrated courage in the face of fear and the unknown. What explanation do you give of your ability to have a history of courage, determination, and a willingness to take risks? [*Unique account question*]
>
> RUTH: Well, to tell you the truth, it comes as a bit of a shock to think that I have been kind of brave at different stages in my life. It is surprising to put all of those experiences together and realize there really is something to all of this.
>
> THERAPIST: What does this say about the kind of person you are?
>
> RUTH: Well, I guess it says that I can be gutsy sometimes.
>
> THERAPIST: Do you like that description about yourself?
>
> RUTH: I do, but it still feels a little strange to describe myself in these terms.
>
> THERAPIST: OK, I understand that. You want to get used to that?
>
> RUTH: Yeah, I do.
>
> THERAPIST: What title would you give this story of courage that we have been exploring together? [*A question to concretize the alternative story*]
>
> RUTH: It is really hard for me to think of this. I am not really creative in that way.
>
> THERAPIST: Would you like to have a name for this story? The story tends to be much more present for you when you name it. Are you willing for us to name it together?

Ruth and I go back and forth, and we eventually come across a title that is fitting for Ruth. We call it "Ruth's coming out." I then explore with Ruth the impact of the redescribing questions.

> THERAPIST: What does it mean for you now to think of yourself as gutsy when you consider facing John and telling him what is honestly going on for you?
>
> RUTH: Well, I think it helps. I will still feel scared, but I really want to be more honest with John. I think I am prepared to face him. We keep getting stuck in an argument, and I keep ending up feeling blamed. So often I feel like I have done something wrong, and I end up feeling guilty. To tell you the truth, I don't feel very hopeful for our relationship. All he really wants me to do is to go back to the kind of person I was before.

Recruiting an Audience I explore with Ruth the possibilities of recruiting an audience who will provide support for her as she moves more fully into her preferred story of "Ruth's coming out." Depending on how our work goes together with Ruth, John, and their children, it might be possible for Ruth's own family to appreciate her growing confidence, stronger voice, and ability to take more risks and be more honest. What is more realistic at this juncture is to engage Ruth to consider people in her life now who can support her, applaud her efforts, and cheer her on.

> THERAPIST: I have been wondering as we have been working together, who would be least surprised to hear your "Ruth's coming out" story? You know, if they were to hear about this whole story of you who takes risks, challenges others, faces fear, who might say, "Sure, I'm not the least surprised to hear that Ruth did that"?
>
> RUTH: Well, the only person I can think of now is my maternal grandmother. She would not be surprised by my "coming out story."
>
> THERAPIST: What would your grandmother say to you if she were sitting in the room with us now?
>
> RUTH: Well, she might say, "Ruth you have got what it takes. Trust yourself. It will all work out."
>
> THERAPIST: What is it like to hear that?
>
> RUTH: It is really good. It encourages me.

Ruth and I talk some more about the people in her life and what they would say to her if they listened in on our conversation. Ruth identifies two of her friends that she would like to bring into the loop and be much more open with about what is going on in her relationship with John. She thinks she will get some support from these friends.

Future Challenges

In future sessions, we will come back to these cultural ideas that have been so influential in producing anxiety, depression, and confusion in Ruth's life. Ruth is coming to awareness that many of the troubles she is experiencing are not caused by personal deficits or difficulties in communicating. Rather, they are about the discursive clashes that invade her world. These culture clashes pull men and women in different ways. Here are a few examples of discursive clashes:

- It is a woman's job to dedicate her life to being the socioemotional caregiver to her husband and children versus men and women sharing the family responsibilities for providing for the emotional and psychological needs of its members.
- A woman's job is to stand by her husband no matter what the cost versus men and women have the right to an equitable and respectful relationship.
- A woman should put aside her own career aspirations to fulfill the needs of a man versus a woman has a right to develop her own career aspirations within a marriage and be supported by her partner.

There are flashes of awareness in Ruth that John is not a bad person intent on thwarting her plans. Rather, she is beginning to see that John is subject to cultural messages about how to be a man and a husband just as much as she is shaped by the cultural messages about how to be a woman and a wife. Knowing this doesn't mean it is going to be easy for Ruth to accept John's traditional beliefs about important familial matters when they are in opposition to her changing viewpoints. The difference for Ruth involves her knowing that the challenges she is experiencing with John aren't about her going crazy. It is about something much bigger than her.

Concluding My Work With Ruth

Ruth is already changing her sense of herself, and she knows a little more about what is possible in her life. She is connected more with her ability to take risks and express herself more openly and honestly, and she is more understanding about her confusion and anxieties about what she wants and what she is to do. There is also a qualitative shift in the extent to which she feels frightened. She is more trusting of herself in the face of the consequences of her decisions. However, there is a lot more to do.

Ruth doesn't know for sure whether she should continue to stay married to John, but she is now prepared to explore what it will mean to stay together as intimate partners. She is more confident in her ability to survive and less burdened by worrying about John's future. Issues about her relationship with the children remain a concern to her. She is more trusting of herself to handle her father's reactions to her, including blaming and judgment, and recognizes that this relationship will always be a struggle for her. Our work together has provided a strong foundation to address these ongoing concerns. Her story, "Ruth's coming out," is important to her and reminds her of her new emerging identity as a gutsy Ruth. Ruth is motivated to do more in future counseling sessions. For instance, she wants marital counseling, she wants a closer yet more respectful relationship with her children, and she wants to address her problems with body image and weight.

Ruth and I have established a strong collaborative partnership, and she is beginning to believe in her own expertise. She feels more sure of herself, knowing that many of the struggles she faces are less to do with some kind of personal deficits, malfunctions, and dysfunctions occurring within her and more to do with the clash of cultural expectations required of her as a woman, mother, and partner. As she enters into the next stage of her personal work, she is becoming less willing to internalize inadequacy and more willing to externalize and challenge the cultural prescriptions that have constrained the kind of life she wishes to lead.

At this point, Ruth doesn't have all the answers to her questions, nor may she ever have such answers. She still doesn't know whether she will leave John, defy the God that her father introduced to her, change her body shape, or ever be completely free of sadness and anxiety. However, she is certain that whatever she is yet to come up against, she has the strength and courage to step forward into the unknown.

Jerry Corey's Work With Ruth: A Commentary

Introduction

In this chapter three different contributors have presented postmodern approaches to counseling with Ruth: Dr. Andrews (social constructionist), Dr. Clark (solution-focused brief therapy), and Dr. Monk (narrative therapy). Because of these detailed descriptions, I will deviate from the usual format of discussing at length my particular approach within this theory and will make only brief mention of a few aspects of working with Ruth from the solution-focused and narrative perspectives. Then I will show how I might build on earlier work from these theories in thinking about Ruth's case.

Basic Assumptions

Narrative therapy emphasizes the value of devoting time to listening to clients' stories and to looking for events that can open up alternative stories. I make the assumption that Ruth's life is inhabited by powerful cultural stories. Her life story influences what she notices and remembers, and in this sense her story influences how she will face the future. Although I am somewhat interested in Ruth's past, we will certainly not dwell on her past problems. Instead, our focus will be on what Ruth is currently doing and on her strivings for her future.

I make the assumption that many of Ruth's problems have been produced by the contradictory cultural messages she has received from society about what kind of person, woman, mother, and partner she should be in the world. Part of our work together will be to look for personal resources Ruth has that will enable her to create a new story for herself. In short, from the narrative perspective my commitment is to help Ruth rewrite the story of her life. The collaboration between Ruth and me will result in her reviewing certain events from her past and rewriting her future. Drawing on contributions from solution-focused brief therapy and narrative therapy, I am more concerned with Ruth's strengths than I am with discussing her problems. A problem-focused approach to therapy is likely to cement unhelpful modes of behavior.

Many of the various theories stress the central role of a working relationship and a collaborative spirit in therapy (Adlerian therapy, the humanistic approaches, the cognitive behavioral approach, and feminist therapy). Working within a postmodern approach, I am influenced by the notion that our collaboration will be aimed at freeing Ruth from the influence of oppressive elements in her social environment and empowering her to become an active agent who is directing her own life.

The Therapeutic Process

In the first instance, the heart of the therapeutic process from the postmodern perspective involves identifying how societal standards and expectations are internalized by people in many ways that may constrain and narrow the kind of life that they might otherwise lead. Second, it focuses on how identifying a client's resistances to limiting cultural restraints provide the basis for the construction of an alternative story. Ruth's preferred story will be constructed based on her ability to embrace what she might regard as desirable cultural meanings and her ability to resist limiting cultural prescriptions. Ruth's autobiography provides me with significant clues to the unfolding story of her life.

Narrative therapy and solution-focused brief therapy can help Ruth feel motivated, understood, and accepted. A method of supporting Ruth with the challenges she faces is to get her to think of her problems as external to the core of her selfhood. A key concept of both solution-focused therapy and narrative therapy is that the problem does not reside in the person. Even during the early sessions, I encourage Ruth to separate her being from her problems by posing questions that externalize her problem. I view Ruth's problems as something separate from her, even though her problems are influencing her thoughts, feelings, and behaviors. She presents many problems that are of concern to her, yet we cannot deal with all of them at once. When I ask her what one problem most concerns her right now, she replies, "Guilt. I feel guilty so often over so many things. No matter how hard I work at what is important to me, I generally fall short of what I expect of myself, and then I feel guilty." Ruth feels guilty because she is not an adequate daughter, because she is not the mother she thinks she should be, because she is not as accomplished a student as she demands of herself—when she falls short of "perfect performances" in these and other areas, guilt is the result.

My intention is to help Ruth come to view her problem of guilt as being separate from who she is as a person. I ask her how her guilt occurs and ask her to give examples of situations where she experiences guilt. I am interested in charting the influence of the problem of guilt. I also ask questions that externalize the problem, such as "What is the mission of this guilt, and how does it recruit you into this mission?" "How does the guilt get you, and what are you doing to let it become so powerful?" "How has guilt dominated and disrupted your life?" "What does guilt whisper in your ear?"

In this narrative approach, I follow up on these externalizing questions with further questions aimed at finding exceptions: "Has there ever been a time when guilt could have taken control of your relationship but didn't? What was it like for you? How did you do it?" "How is this different from what you would have done before?" "What does it say about you that you were able to do that?" "How do you imagine your life would be different if you didn't have this guilt?" "Can you think of ways you can begin to take even small steps toward divorcing yourself from guilt?"

My questioning is aimed at discovering moments when Ruth hasn't been dominated or discouraged by the problem of guilt. When we identify times when Ruth's life was not disrupted by guilt, we have a basis for considering how life would be different if guilt were not in control. As our therapy proceeds, I expect that Ruth will gradually come to see that she has more control over her problem of guilt than she believed. As she is able to distance herself from defining herself in terms of problematic themes (such as guilt), she will be less burdened by her problem-saturated story and will discover a range of options. She will likely focus more on the resources within herself to construct the kind of life she wants.

PROCESS COMMENTARY In close alliance with the work of Drs. Andrews, Clark, and Monk, my approach places emphasis on Ruth's assets rather than her liabilities. Looking at her strengths is not unique to the postmodern approaches, for other theories also emphasis the resources of the client. Building on a client's strengths is part of Adlerian therapy, the humanistic therapies, cognitive behavioral therapies, feminist therapy, and reality therapy. Likewise, most of these approaches pay primary attention to what is happening currently and the client's future strivings rather than exploring the past. However, postmodern approaches to working with Ruth are distinct to the extent that they encourage her to create a richer life story by exploring new cultural meanings that are desirable to her. In this sense, therapy is a new beginning.

Questions for Reflection

1. In reflecting on the separate contributions of Drs. Andrews, Clark, and Monk, what are some basic assumptions that all of these therapists share?
2. What are some of the main differences you notice in reviewing each of the therapeutic styles in this chapter?
3. What are your thoughts about the manner in which diagnosis is viewed by the postmodern approaches? What do you think about working with Ruth to collaboratively establish a diagnosis?
4. What are some of your reactions to the specific techniques used by each of the therapists in this chapter? What are some of the techniques that you would want to incorporate into your therapeutic style? What kind of questions do you find particularly useful?
5. What are some of the advantages to the approach of externalizing the problem from the client? How might you attempt to do this with Ruth? Are there any disadvantages to this approach?
6. To what degree might you want to incorporate solution-talk as opposed to problem-talk? How would you deal with Ruth if she insisted that she came to see you so she could talk about her problems?
7. Asking clients to think of exceptions to their problems often gets them to think about a time when a particular problem did not have such intense proportions. What are some of the advantages you can see in asking Ruth to talk about a time when she did not have a given problem? How might you build on times of exceptions?
8. What are some ways that Gerald Monk's narrative therapy with Ruth shares common ground with the feminist approach?
9. In what ways are some of the basic ideas of narrative therapy compatible with a multicultural perspective on counseling practice? What applications do you see for using narrative therapy with culturally diverse client populations?
10. In considering all of the therapists in this chapter, what fundamental differences separate postmodern approaches from some of the traditional therapies?

Notes

See the DVD/online program entitled *Theory in Practice: The Case of Stan* (Session 11: Solution-Focused Brief Therapy Applied to the Case of Stan) for an illustration of techniques such as identifying exceptions, the miracle question, and scaling.

See the DVD/online program entitled *Theory in Practice: The Case of Stan* (Session 12: Narrative Therapy Applied to the Case of Stan), which focuses on Stan's creating a new story of his life.

1. American Psychiatric Association. (2000). *Diagnostic and statistical manual of mental disorders* (4th ed., text revision). Washington, DC: Author.

2. Anderson, H., & Goolishian, H. (1992). The client is the expert: A not-knowing approach to therapy. In S. McNamee & K. J. Gergen, (Eds.), *Therapy as social construction* (pp. 25–39). Newbury Park, CA: Sage.

3. American Psychiatric Association. (2000). *Diagnostic and statistical manual of mental disorders* (4th ed., text revision). Washington, DC: Author.

4. DeShazer, S. (March 23, 2002, personal communication). Teaching and training of solution-focused behavioral therapy with Steve DeShazer. Family Studies Center at Purdue University, Calumet, Indiana.

5. Miller, S. D., & Duncan, B. L. (2000). Paradigm lost: From model-driven to client-directed, outcome-informed clinical work. *Journal of Systemic Therapies, 19,* 20–31.

6. Duncan, B. L., Miller, S. D., & Sparks, J. A. (2004). *The heroic client* (Appendix IV, pp. 222–223). San Francisco: Jossey-Bass.

7. Michael White and David Epston are the principal founders of narrative therapy. See M. White & D. Epston (1990), *Narrative means to therapeutic ends* (New York: Norton).

8. See an excellent overview of these ideas in J. Freedman & G. Combs (1996), *Narrative therapy: The social construction of preferred realities* (New York: Norton). See also G. Monk, J. Winslade, K. Crocket, & D. Epston (1997), *Narrative therapy in practice: The archaeology of hope* (San Francisco: Jossey Bass).

9. Winslade, J., & Monk, G. (2007). *Narrative counseling in schools: Powerful and brief* (2nd ed.). Thousand Oaks, CA: Corwin Press.

10. White, M. (1989). The process of questioning: A therapy of literary merit? In *Selected Papers* (pp. 37–46). Adelaide, Australia: Dulwich Centre.

11. See Recruiting an Audience, in M. White (1995), *Re-authoring lives: Interviews and essays* (Adelaide, Australia: Dulwich Centre).

CHAPTER TWELVE

Case Approach to Couples and Family Therapy

General Overview of Couples and Family Systems Therapy

Depending on the specific orientation of a couples or family systems practitioner, this approach has a variety of goals. For a therapist working with couples, these goals may include teaching communication skills, increasing attitudes of acceptance, identifying and modifying core beliefs, teaching more effective interpersonal skills, and relationship education and enhancement. For a therapist working with families, some goals might include resolving the presenting problems of the client and the family; resolving a family crisis as quickly and efficiently as possible; creating an environment where new information can be infused into a system, allowing the family to evolve on its own; restructuring a system so that autonomy by all family members is encouraged; changing the rules and patterns of interaction among family members; teaching communication skills; and teaching problem-solving skills.

A diversity of techniques may be employed, depending on the therapist's theoretical orientation. Because the therapist joins with the couple or family, intervention strategies are best considered in conjunction with the personal characteristics of the therapist. The central consideration is what is in the best interests of the couple or the family. Outcomes are evaluated on the basis of the particular orientation of the therapist, yet a primary criterion is the degree of relational change that occurs between the couple or among members of a family. In all couples and family therapy models, change needs to happen relationally, not just intrapsychically.

A Couple Therapist's Perspective on Ruth

by Mia Sevier, PhD

Introduction

Let's assume that Ruth has made considerable progress in individual therapy but is increasingly discontented in her marriage. Although historically both Ruth and John have avoided overt conflict, recently they have experienced obvious tension in their relationship with blow-ups including yelling, tears, and slamming of doors. Ruth is talking more and more about her relationship problems in individual therapy, so her therapist suggests couple therapy. Ruth agrees. John is reluctant to seek therapy, but he has also felt frustrated and angered and agrees to try couple therapy. The individual therapist refers to me, as Ruth wishes to continue her personal work, and having a separate couple therapist can allow for an "unbiased" approach to both spouses.

In couple treatment, Ruth will experience a shift in therapy perspective from individual work. Behaviorally oriented approaches to couple therapy assume that both partners contribute more or less equally to their relationship. Hence, in treating the couple, I'll attend to Ruth's issues but will balance this with a new focus on John's issues. Given that I'll be treating their relationship, we'll primarily work on how Ruth and John interact and influence one another.

I'll be working from an *integrative behavioral couple therapy* (IBCT)[1] approach with Ruth and John. We will focus primarily on building acceptance in their relationship with a secondary focus on creating direct behavior change.

Traditional behavioral therapies[2] for couples focus on changing how partners behave in relationships. The assumption is that couples lack skills or are not carrying out rewarding behaviors. In traditional approaches, Ruth and John would be encouraged to take action and do rewarding things for one another. Later in therapy, they would learn structured, constructive, and direct ways to communicate, including using I-statements, taking turns as speakers and listeners, and paraphrasing. Therapy would conclude with problem-solving training to teach Ruth and John structured ways to solve relationship problems, such as brainstorming, negotiating, and agreeing. IBCT was developed because research showed that the traditional approach has limitations.[3] A pure behavior change focus during therapy may not be sufficient for lasting relationship change because couples may stop using their behavioral skills over time, or perhaps because some problems are unsolvable, or at least not amenable to direct change.

Behavioral therapy as a field is moving toward including acceptance and mindfulness in treatment and teaching clients to be aware, nonjudgmental, and accepting of current experiences. IBCT shifts the focus from changing specific behaviors to building emotional acceptance. When acceptance is developed in relationships, the context in which partners behave is improved and behavior changes follow. IBCT may include a focus on direct behavior change, but would do so in a secondary and less structured way than more traditional approaches. Building acceptance, as demonstrated here, is the primary goal.

Acceptance in relationships includes a deep understanding of the self, the partner, and the unique dynamics of the relationship and shifts the context in which partners behave. With acceptance, potentially unpleasant partner behavior makes sense, is tolerable, and can even be used to create greater closeness. Acceptance softens the negative emotional impact of unpleasant partner behavior. Each partner can tolerate, or even embrace, behavior that could be a source of conflict or emotional distancing. Individuals shift from unsuccessfully trying to change their partner toward embracing the partner for how he or she is. For example, John is displaying increased anger toward Ruth around her focus on career pursuits rather than the family. If Ruth starts to understand that John becomes angry when he feels he is being abandoned and that he is sensitive to this because of the unavailability of his mother in childhood, she may be able to tolerate his anger, or may even react to his anger with sympathy and support. This reaction would be an example of acceptance in their relationship.

As an IBCT therapist, I'll model acceptance in my interactions with Ruth and John. I will encourage open discussion in a nonblaming, tolerant, and warm manner. I will not accept verbally or physically aggressive behavior or substance abuse, but on other subjects I will allow each partner to determine what is generally acceptable, or not, in the context of his or her own values through mutual exploration.

Assessment

The first step is to develop a clear understanding of Ruth and John's issues and the way they relate. Although there are commonalities across couples, such as a common theme of one partner wanting closeness while the other wants independence, or a common pattern of one partner demanding change while the other withdraws, I'm assuming Ruth and John are unique. Ruth and John come in for assessment sessions and answer standardized questionnaires on relationship satisfaction, commitment, communication, and domestic violence. These answers will guide and supplement my interviews as I determine which issues are problematic and why these issues are problematic for Ruth and John.

We have one session conjointly, two individual sessions, and one conjoint feedback session. In individual sessions, I build equal alliances and gather information that each spouse might not initially share in front of the other. I inform each that everything said is open for sharing unless I'm told otherwise, in which case we'll discuss and decide how to proceed. If requested, I might be willing to keep information from a partner if it is unrelated to their relationship functioning. However, I am unwilling to keep certain subjects a secret, such as an ongoing affair, unless the partner agrees to terminate the affair. Because John was initially reluctant to come to therapy, I strategically invite him in first. I use this time to connect with John and encourage him to recognize how therapy might help him. Later, I meet with Ruth with similar goals of cementing our relationship and assessing her individual needs and history.

IBCT therapy works from a collaborative model, and the feedback session allows me to share my impressions and clarify any misperceptions I may have. The feedback session also serves as a formal introduction to the therapy perspective, allowing each partner to learn of my views of salient relationship issues. In my assessment, I gathered information to identify a theme in their relationship. Although Ruth and John likely fight about many different subjects, such as housework, decisions about finances, and attending their children's sport events, there is a common theme across their arguments. In addition, I share my opinions about the process of how Ruth and John get polarized into opposing positions and how they each have gotten more and more distant from one another over time so that they both feel trapped and hurt in their relationship.

THERAPIST [*Directed to John about Ruth*]: I've noticed a repeated theme across your arguments, and I'd like to hear what you think about this. I'm noticing that most fights seem to relate to mutually not feeling loved or appreciated. It seems that you each have different definitions of what expressions of love look like. Hence, it might be hard to feel appreciated by the other. The signs used to be crystal clear, but recently you are both missing signals of appreciation and love from one another.

RUTH [*Nods in agreement*]: Um-hum.

JOHN [*Surprised*]: I don't understand. Can you say more?

THERAPIST [*Facing John*]: Well, in the past, John, you felt loved when Ruth cooked you meals and placed clothing out for you in the morning. Sex with Ruth helped you feel even more connected and loved. This all might have helped you recognize that Ruth appreciated you.

JOHN: Yes, I do like those things.

THERAPIST: Given what you were telling me during our individual session about how your mom disappeared and left your family for some time while you were a child, I could see why Ruth's availability in the house would feel like a clear sign of love.

JOHN [*Nods in agreement*]: OK.

THERAPIST [*Facing Ruth*]: Along these lines, Ruth, you feel loved by John when he seems pleased with you and expresses approval of your actions. You feel his affection when he smiles at you across the table and thanks you for your work around the house and with the children. Does this seem right?

RUTH: Yeah. That is true. I feel appreciated when John thanks me.

THERAPIST: And Ruth, given what you told me about your family, that your mother was very critical and your father was very aloof, I could see how you might really look forward to clear signs of approval, and might be very sensitive to any criticism.

RUTH: Um-huh. . . . John's disapproval of my schooling is hard to take.

THERAPIST: Yes. We will want to talk more about that later. To give you feedback, I was also thinking that returning to school might be something that is difficult for you to do on many levels. You also told me how your parents expected you to be a homemaker. This seems like a huge change for you to now pursue a career. I imagine you feel a lot of anxiety about breaking out of the role your parents prescribed for you.

RUTH: Yes. They never wanted me to be a professional!

THERAPIST: Doing this might be frightening and take a lot of courage on your part.

RUTH: Yes.

JOHN [*Interested*]: This is new information for me!

THERAPIST: So you didn't know about Ruth's parents' expectations?

JOHN: No.

THERAPIST [*Addressing both*]: I suspect you'll both get to know each other better as we work together. Here's more about how I think the two of you have ended up stuck and suffering in your relationship. When it comes to feeling loved by the other, you two have drifted further and further apart over time. As Ruth spends more energy on her career, she is spending less time on the household. Given that this is how John felt loved before, he might miss Ruth's homemaking. John began to make requests, which Ruth could not meet, and then he became more critical. Ruth, in turn, misses John's approval as that is how she felt his affection and she is very sensitive to the criticism. The more John criticizes, the more anxious Ruth feels and, hence, is even less available. The more unavailable Ruth is, the more John feels unloved and expresses his disapproval. This is a vicious cycle that you are doing together; neither one of you is solely responsible. Understandably, neither of you feels satisfied and, unfortunately, both of you suffer, feeling neglected and unappreciated.

🕮 **Process Commentary** A major goal of the feedback session is to explain, expand upon, and help Ruth and John adopt a common understanding of their relationship. By formally addressing the couple by name and describing their behaviors in a direct and honest way, I hope to begin to help each partner step back from his or her emotional struggles and begin to form a more intellectual and mutual understanding in collaboration with me. Oftentimes feedback can have a therapeutic effect by encouraging awareness of partners' experiences. Until now, Ruth and John have been alone in their hurt and suffering. Helping Ruth and John begin to recognize the "mutual trap" that they are in together can plant the seeds of empathy. In addition, differences between Ruth and John are presented as natural and understandable. Although Ruth and John may have been vilifying each other around their differences in views of affection and love, saying "He's an uncaring jerk," or "She is a failed wife," my goal will continue to be to make differences acceptable. The rest of therapy revolves around deepening Ruth and John's understanding of who they are and how they function together in the relationship.

Major Interventions

🕸 **Unified Detachment** As Ruth and John finish the formal assessment phase of therapy, they are encouraged to bring in salient incidents or issues that they wish to discuss. After several weeks of work together, I begin to help Ruth and John step away from the heated emotionality of their arguments, recognize their roles and repeated patterns, and gain a sense of mutual understanding about their fights. My goal is to help them shift toward being intellectually descriptive rather than emotionally aroused or evaluative.

RUTH: We had a big fight last night. John started it when he came home from work.

JOHN: I didn't start it. It was her night to cook, and the dinner was not on the table when I got home late. All I did was point that out to her.

RUTH: You didn't just "point it out," you were mean about it!

JOHN [*With increasing volume*]: Ruth, I did just point it out to you.

THERAPIST: OK, it looks like we have something to focus on today. Let's slow this down and explore. I suspect you both have different views, and I suspect you are both right! This might be that sensitive area of "love me, no you don't." Let's start with John and then later, Ruth, I'm going to focus on your perspective.

JOHN: Well, I'd had a difficult workday. I finally got home and was surprised there wasn't any dinner waiting.

THERAPIST: So you were surprised, and maybe even a little disappointed that there was no dinner.

JOHN: Yeah, that's right. But I was calm and asked Ruth where the meal was. Then she blew up.

THERAPIST: I'd like to stop here for a moment. Ruth, let's hear your perspective.

RUTH: I'd had a hard day too. I'd had an exam and had decided to send the kids over to my mother's for dinner. I already felt guilty about asking for help. That's why there wasn't any food.

THERAPIST: OK, so you'd had a hard day too. What happened next?

RUTH: Well, I heard John calling me, and I remembered I'd forgotten his meal. I right away felt really bad. I knew he was going to be angry with me. I got downstairs, and he asked me where the meal was. I was feeling all worked up, my heart was pounding, and I felt really guilty. So I sort of shouted that it was in the freezer.

THERAPIST: So you might have been reacting to what you were saying to yourself, as well as the reality of the situation?

RUTH: Yes, I can't stand it when I know I am going to be criticized.

THERAPIST: OK, so we have a risky situation, where you both might feel unloved. This sounds like that common pattern. It could start with either of you. Perhaps Ruth was already feeling criticized from earlier in the day with her mom. Let's say that here it starts with John feeling somewhat unloved, which moves to Ruth feeling criticized, and then Ruth snaps at John, and then John criticizes more strongly. Then it all just escalates from there until Ruth runs away, slams a door, and cries. Both of you end up hurt and feeling unappreciated. Does this fight fit into this pattern?

JOHN: Yeah, I think so.

RUTH: Yeah, I guess we are doing our unloved abandonment versus criticized boxing match thing again.

THERAPIST [*Laughs*]: That's a great way to describe it. Watch out when that starting bell rings because the gloves are coming off! We can use that name. Let's keep talking about the sequence of events from both of your perceptions to learn more.

⚵ Process Commentary   Debriefing recent troublesome interactions can be a useful way to build a sense of understanding and emotional distance from repeated conflict patterns. We examine their fight in a step-by-step manner to start to identify common behaviors and triggers for fights. As Ruth and John become familiar with their patterns, they can notice when they are falling into problematic interactions and take steps to stop these interactions. By naming their process, humor and metaphors can be used to building a unified sense of detachment. The goal is to create a mutual intellectual understanding and distance from conflict patterns instead of getting caught up in emotionally destructive ways of behaving.

Empathic Joining Intervention

This intervention is designed to create mutual understanding and empathy around vulnerabilities or emotional triggers. When using these types of interventions, I work to shift Ruth and John from defensive and hard emotions to softer and more vulnerable emotions that might allow them to join together rather than continue to argue and grow apart.

JOHN [*Angrily*]: Ruth doesn't care about our family. How dare Ruth stop caring and step away from the family. It is just not right! [*Ruth looks defensive.*]

THERAPIST [*Toward John*]: I hear your anger here. Clearly, we know that this type of situation can trigger your anger. Today, I'm wondering and maybe sensing something else behind your frustration. I'm wonder if it hurts you to see Ruth focused more on earning her degree than on the family and on you.

JOHN [*Confused*]: Of course, it hurts! She is hurting us!

THERAPIST: So you might end up with many very painful feelings from all of this. Angry. Hurt. Maybe even a sense of sadness or loss. Maybe some feelings of abandonment. . . . I wonder if this situation at all seems familiar to you from an earlier time. Does this remind you of when your mom left the house?

JOHN [*Softens, voice trembles*]: Maybe . . . I worry . . . maybe sometimes I wonder if Ruth is going to leave us.

RUTH [*Surprised, concerned, takes his hand, speaks softly*]: John, I would never leave you.

🕸 **Process Commentary**   Although this shift happens more quickly than what typically occurs, there is a clear shift from hard emotions to vulnerable ones. Until now John has only been expressing his frustration and anger with Ruth. These "hard" emotions are often easier to express and might even serve a protective function for John, but they have created distance in the relationship. John starts to explore and share the "soft" emotions underlying his expressions of anger. Because soft emotions reveal vulnerabilities, their expression encourages Ruth to respond empathically. Indeed, in this ideal situation, Ruth is touched by John's expressions of sadness and loss and is able to reach out in a supportive way. By helping couples explore vulnerabilities, we can move past unpleasant behavior and toward acceptance with understanding and connection.

Tolerance Building

The final set of intervention strategies, which usually are not tried until later in treatment, are designed to help relieve the emotional pain that comes from experiencing unpleasant behavior from a partner. Several strategies could help Ruth and John become less reactive to behavioral triggers from their partner. In the following segment, I work on exposing and desensitizing Ruth to perceived criticism from John.

THERAPIST: Let's try something different today. As we've been discussing and Ruth has been acknowledging, clearly at times Ruth is highly reactive to perceived criticism. Now this might seem a little strange, but to help you both learn what happens, I'm wondering if you, John, could intentionally say something to Ruth that might sound critical. What do you both think about this?

RUTH: It makes me a little uncomfortable just thinking about it, but I guess I could give it a try.

JOHN: What if I accidentally upset her?

THERAPIST: That's OK. That is part of the process. I want you to observe what happens to Ruth when you say critical things. Ruth, if you do get upset, that's OK. In fact, it would be normal and expected. It will be good for you two to experience these things while I'm here to help.

RUTH: All right, fine. Go ahead John. Give it your best shot.

JOHN: Well, as long as you are OK with it. . . . Hum . . . Ruth, you didn't take the dishes out of the dishwasher this morning. When I went to find a clean glass, there were none in the cabinet. [*Ruth looks a little uncomfortable.*]

THERAPIST: John, go ahead and continue.

JOHN: And last night I went by the store to pick up milk. So this morning, not only were the dishes not done, neither was the shopping.

RUTH [*Laughs uncomfortably*]: Oh, boy! I'm feeling anxious and angry just now, even knowing that it isn't really real! I'm all hot inside.

THERAPIST: Yes, this is naturally upsetting to you. I wonder if we can work more on this so it feels less upsetting to have John say things that seem critical.

JOHN: Wow, I had no idea I affected her like that. Sometimes I'm not purposely being critical, I'm just asking for things or saying how things are. But I can see how upsetting it can be.

⚘ **Process Commentary** I introduce the exercise carefully to allow Ruth and John some insight into its usefulness. If Ruth can begin to tolerate John's criticism, she may become desensitized, or less reactive, to it and less likely to continue an argument. We could also work with John on his "triggers" for arguments, including feeling abandoned. There are many ways to help Ruth and John tolerate previously upsetting behaviors and emotions. For example, we could build tolerance by giving a partner a homework assignment to fake a negative trigger behavior at home sometime during the next week. We would do this in the presence of both partners, so each knows the assignment. This can serve to desensitize couples to triggering behaviors as the recipient will not know if his or her partner is faking or really engaging in the behavior. In addition, the faking partner can observe the impact of the behavior in a reserved manner and learn more about it. Another strategy under tolerance building is to explore positive aspects of seemingly negative behaviors. For example, we can talk about how part of Ruth's sensitivity to criticism about household tasks reflects her strong desire to care for her loved ones and that she truly cares. Problematic behaviors can have a positive side as well as the negative. Finally, I could suggest that Ruth and John learn additional ways to take care of themselves such as by learning to self-sooth or to reach out to friends or other outside resources to manage emotions or get appropriate needs met outside of the relationship, instead of relying solely on their marriage.

Conclusion

Through work in integrative behavioral couple therapy, Ruth and John develop acceptance in their relationship and behavior changes naturally follow. Overall, Ruth and John have started to approach each other with more warmth, and the tension and hostility that they entered therapy with has faded away. As they've become unified in a common understanding, and developed more empathy for one another, they have naturally started to change their behavior and to do things to please one another. For example, John is less likely to say critical things about Ruth's desire for a career, and he occasionally praises her and thanks her. Ruth learned to be less sensitive to criticism from John and is more sensitive of his feelings as she steps out of the housewife role.

At this point, if each partner still wanted additional behavior change from one another, I could implement some of the more traditional behavioral approaches of communication or problem-solving training. However, I would do so in an informal way, with fewer rules and more direct informal coaching than traditional approaches. This shift in focus away from pure direct behavior change toward acceptance reflects the overall shift in behavior therapies toward integrating strategies, including mindfulness, which indirectly bring behavior changes.

To work effectively with Ruth and John, I'll want to carefully consider cultural factors in therapy. I will explore what values each member brings and will respect cultural variations that are different from my own. Within the IBCT interventions are various cultural assumptions, such as comfort with expressing vulnerable emotions in empathic joining or using nonrelationship sources for tolerance building. As a culturally competent therapist, I'd be thoughtful in shifting between the cultural perspective of the therapy and of Ruth and John to avoid blindly imposing cultural expectations.[4]

It was a pleasure to work with Ruth and John because they were motivated, cooperative, and thoughtful in their work. In terminating therapy, we summarize the progress that has been made, clarify our common understanding, and discuss possible risky situations in the future. Although Ruth or John may occasionally slip up and feel angered or hurt, I'd expect them to recover more quickly and even use the argument, after it is over, as a subject of discussion to reach out in supportive ways and grow closer. In our last few sessions, Ruth and John discuss an interest in bringing their children to therapy, and a family approach is explored as a possibility.

A Family Systems Therapist's Perspective on Ruth

by Mary E. Moline, PhD, Dr. PH

Introduction

Family therapy perspectives call for a conceptual shift from practicing individual therapy, for the family is viewed as a functioning unit that is more than the sum of the roles of its various members. The family provides a primary context for understanding how individuals function in relationship to others and how they behave. Actions by any individual family member will influence all the others in the family, and their reactions will have a reciprocal effect on the individual. The transactions that occur between the individual and other family members shape the person's concept of self, relationships with others, and worldview.

For a family with members who demonstrate a poor sense of self, a developmental approach might be integrated with a systems model. In the case of Ruth a systemic family approach requires an assessment of her family system, including her husband, her children, and her parents. An even more comprehensive systemic assessment could include examining her relationships (interactions) with other important units such as church, work, and friends. No rules dictate how much of her system of relationships the therapist must work with; rather, this will depend on the therapist's clinical judgment. Conceptually (or symbolically), however, the therapist will make interventions with Ruth that will enable her to deal with her husband, children, and parents, even though they may not be physically present in the therapy session.[5]

Confidentiality and Dealing With Secrets

A decision family therapists often make prior to a client's first visit is whom they will see. Many insist that a client's entire family be seen during the first visit. Given the variety of systemic approaches available, the therapist may decide to see only the concerned client in the beginning and later invite others in his or her system to attend therapeutic sessions. In that case, the matter of confidentiality must be addressed. The therapist needs to decide if what a client reveals in an individual session will be kept secret. It should be noted that many systems therapists avoid seeing the concerned client first, partially because of the problems involved with deciding how to deal with this client's disclosures in family sessions.

In my view, a safe rule in working with couples or families is not to keep secrets. This definitely applies in those situations where the law mandates that the therapist reveal information indicating that clients are likely to harm themselves or others and in child abuse cases. Even in those situations where the law does not mandate revealing a secret, it is advisable to inform clients of any policies that apply to dealing with secrets. If secrets are kept, the therapist will certainly have a difficult time doing effective therapy with various parts of a family system. Therapists can easily forget what they may not say when the entire family gets together. For this reason, many family therapists refuse to become entangled in keeping secrets, and they let this be known from the outset.

If you decide to work within the framework of refusing to keep secrets, I suggest that you have this policy in writing and that you encourage your clients to discuss its ramifications. This contract informs your clients of the risks involved with the therapy process. Of course, clients in family therapy should be clearly informed about the legal limits of confidentiality from the beginning, just as would be the case for individual therapy.

Considering the Cultural Perspective

Family therapists are concerned about how the family is influenced by their ethnic and cultural perspective. What might be observed as an ineffective hierarchical structure in a White, middle-class family may be quite normal if observed in a Latino, middle-class family. For example, in a Latino family, having the grandmother take on the parent role for the grandchildren may be culturally normal. However, a grandmother in Ruth's family taking on the parent role might create problems in the system. If the grandmother in Ruth's family is Ruth's mother-in-law and she is forming a coalition with Ruth's husband regarding the rearing of their children, this might disempower Ruth's role as the parent. Thus, it is important to consider the family's cultural perspective before determining whether certain behavior is to be considered a problem. What might be considered enmeshment in one family may be normal for another family.

Key Themes and Issues

Ruth's problems could be viewed from a developmental approach, with the theme of family stages becoming central to the treatment process. Or Ruth's family could be assessed from a structural perspective, in which case the boundaries of the system (rules for communicating) are also quite important. It may even hold true that the themes or issues to be examined determine the theoretical approach. In Ruth's case I would approach treatment from a structural intergenerational model, which is my integration of models developed by Murray Bowen and Salvador Minuchin. My rationale for working from this integrated perspective is that Ruth's primary concern regarding change is how her going back to school and seeking a teaching job are likely to affect her husband and children.

I view treatment in three phases. I approach the first two phases from an intergenerational (Bowen) model. The first phase involves having Ruth's husband, John, attend sessions, and the second phase includes assessing John's and Ruth's families of origin. The third phase entails bringing Ruth's entire family in for assessment and intervention. I approach these family sessions from a structural model. A more detailed explanation of these models is given in the section that deals with an assessment of Ruth.

Ruth appears to be unable to define herself separately from her husband and her children. Her struggle with her identity leads me to examine her process of *differentiation* (identity) as a central issue. Other key issues that I would assess and treat pertain to the ways in which anxiety is perpetuated through rigid (inflexible) patterns of three-person systems (known as *triangulated interaction*) across multiple family generations and to the ways in which her current family structures communication. I borrow the concepts of differentiation and triangulation from Bowen's approach to family therapy.[6]

Differentiation Ruth appears to be struggling with developing a sense of self that is separate from her family and possibly from her family of origin. Her decision to develop an identity separate from her parents, husband, and children is known in Bowen's terminology as the "process of differentiation." The less differentiated people are, the more they invest their energies in relationships to the degree that they do not have a separate identity. Ruth is so concerned about what her husband and children will think if she pursues her own goals that she becomes immobilized. The goal for Ruth from a systemic perspective is to increase her level of differentiation. This does not mean that she will selfishly follow her own directives; rather, it implies that she can determine the direction of her life.

What keeps Ruth from having a sense of self is that she usually interacts with others by triangulation. This is a process by which a person (A) does not directly communicate information with another person (B) but goes through another individual (C). Gossip is a form of triangulation. It is an indirect and often ineffective form of communication. For example, Ruth may wish to communicate that she is upset with her father, but she chooses to tell her mother instead. In turn, her mother relays the message and adds, "How dare you make my daughter angry!" This results in a confused and poorly delivered message. Ruth needed another person to deliver her thoughts to her father because she was unable to do so herself. Her indirect communication is a manifestation of her lack of differentiation. Her style of communication keeps her emotionally fused to others, such as her parents, husband, and children. In her case, the more fused she has become with others, the less she has been able to understand what she values and believes. To some degree, her value system has become identical to those of the people with whom she is fused. Fortunately, it appears that she is at least examining a desire to become a separate individual from John and that she is considering what the consequences will be if she does acquire a new sense of identity.

🌸 **Anxiety**   Ruth's fused relationship with John gives her a sense of well-being. When she attempts to change her relationship to others in her system (parents, husband, and children), however, the level of stress (anxiety and emotional distress) increases in the system. Her inability to reduce anxiety and emotional distress is exhibited by physical symptoms such as panic attacks, difficulty breathing, and inability to sleep. Her referring physician has determined that there is no organic or physical causation. Depending on the outcome of her medical evaluation, she may be given medication as a way to control her symptoms so that she will be more amenable to psychotherapy. Generally, I do not recommend medication for removing anxiety symptoms because of my belief in the value of working through the issues that are leading to panic attacks rather than merely numbing these symptoms.

Ruth is anxious that her movement away from homemaking to teaching may threaten her family. Such anxiety is typical of clients who exhibit little clear sense of self. A differentiated person makes decisions confidently about the direction of his or her life and is willing to face the consequences of those decisions as necessary. The anxiety that is manifested in Ruth's family system pertains to the intensity, duration, and types of tensions that are occurring between the members. Anxiety is occurring because John and the children fear the possible changes taking place with Ruth. They may assume that her changes imply that she no longer loves them. One way of examining this anxiety and how it is manifested is to work with Ruth from a natural systems (Bowen) perspective. The goal is to explore the processes within the family system that bring about Ruth's symptoms, including the manner in which family members form triangles.

🌸 **Transgenerational Patterns of Interaction**   A triangle (three-person relationship), according to Bowen's theory, is the smallest stable unit of human relations. Triangulation consists of redirecting a conflict between two people by involving a third person, which stabilizes the relationship between the original pair. In other words, if two people are threatened by conflict, a third person is introduced in an attempt to create an overt appearance of togetherness. Actually, the conflict and the focus on the third person serve the purpose of reducing the tension between the two people.

This concept can be applied to Ruth's case. To assess her panic attacks and determine her level of differentiation, the therapist can assess the patterns of interaction in her current family as well as the relational patterns that have occurred in previous generations and have been transmitted from generation to generation. As mentioned, this involves examining the triangular process.

Looking at the situation between Ruth and John provides examples of triangular relationships. Because this couple is not able to discuss emotionally charged issues, there has been a tendency to focus on a particular child within the family. Jennifer, who is seen as the rebel, gets considerable attention. John may not have learned how to share the feelings of loneliness that he experiences when he considers Ruth working outside the home. Likewise, she cannot share how angry she feels about his not accepting her need for a career apart from her role in the family. Instead of dealing directly with each other about their concerns as a couple, they argue about their daughter Jennifer.

Consider this example as yet another illustration of the nature and functioning of triangles. Jennifer comes home and tells her mother she is angry that there is no food on the table. She also begins to complain about all the time her mother spends at school and accuses her of neglecting the children. If Ruth allows herself to become anxious about Jennifer's response, she may not be able to sit her down and tell her about her need to go to school. If her identity (self) is influenced strongly by Jennifer's values, she may go to John and say, "Jennifer is at it again. She doesn't appreciate me at all." Then she may begin to experience physical symptoms, including shortness of breath. In his attempt to reduce her anxiety, John may approach Jennifer and say, "You've made your mother very upset. You will stay home tonight."

This example provides a further illustration of the nature of interlocking triangles. These indirect relationships do not solve family problems; rather, they increase the chances that symptoms will be maintained. Ruth and Jennifer do not discuss their upset feelings toward each other; instead, John takes on their anxiety.

Every family system forms triangles, but when one triangle becomes the consistent or persistent pattern of communication, symptoms arise. Ruth's symptoms include panic attacks. Jennifer may not be allowed to have peer relationships, and any of her attempts to define herself separately from the triangle will lead to anxiety among key family members. Jennifer may be rebellious and act out or may turn her angry feelings inward and become depressed. It is likely that she will develop psychosomatic symptoms because that is her mother's pattern of relieving stress.

I am particularly interested in observing Ruth's relationship with John. To help her attain her goal of determining her own direction without experiencing anxiety, I want to observe and understand the patterns that characterize their relationship. How and why do they avoid emotionally charged topics? With whom in the family do they form alliances? How are triangular relationships in Ruth's current family a manifestation of patterns that go back over one or two generations in Ruth's and John's families?

Whatever the marital relationship patterns are, it is most likely that they will become apparent by studying patterns that have been passed on over several generations. This method of interacting and relating is often referred to as the family emotional system. An exploration of both John's and Ruth's families of origin may determine patterns of closeness, conflict, and distance that emerge from generations of interaction. I would work with those themes that emerge from an intergenerational perspective. The goal of therapy from this perspective, which is the reduction of anxiety expressed in the system so that all the members of the family can improve their sense of self, fits Ruth's case well.

Rigid Boundaries   Observed from a structural paradigm, a theme in Ruth's case is that the family structure appears to have rigid boundaries. Boundaries are the rules that define who participates and how members of a family interact with one another and with "outsiders." Ruth says on the phone that she is concerned about "losing" her children. They are appropriately trying to join peer groups outside the home, which worries her. They are at an age (16 to 19) when it is time for them to gain an identity outside of the family.

It appears that Ruth's family does not have mutually agreed-upon rules that would help it through this developmental stage. This is understandable, for her family of origin was characterized by rigid rules. Now her current family may be struggling with making the transition from a family with children to a family with adolescents and adults. Thus, the rules may be: "Adolescents will not challenge their parents." "The parents will decide what adolescents do with their time." These rules may be appropriate for children but not for adolescents. If a family keeps these rules and adolescents agree to abide by them, the family has rigid boundaries. Its rules for communication are closed. They do not change, even when the need to do so is appropriate to a developmental stage.

In working with Ruth's family I want to ascertain who is interacting with whom and by what rules. I will be raising this question: Are coalitions of two people who join together against another occurring in this family? If Ruth is having a difficult time defining herself within this system, perhaps her children and her husband are having the same difficulty. I want to ascertain whether rules for communication are closed (no opportunity for change) or open (constantly changing) and whether relationships are distant or enmeshed. It is probable that it is not just John who is having difficulty with Ruth's need to change but that her children are having the same trouble. If she is having a hard time defining herself outside this system, it may be that her children and her husband are having the same struggle. I will examine her family system from a structural family therapy perspective, mainly founded by Salvador Minuchin. Structural family therapists focus on the interactions of family members to determine when, how, and to whom individuals presently relate as a way to understand the organization or structure of a family. The structural approach pays particular attention to concepts such as the family as a system, boundaries, power, and transactional patterns. For a detailed account of structural family therapy, see Minuchin's book, *Families and Family Therapy.*[7]

Assessment of Ruth

Family therapists bring to the therapeutic process their own perceptions and interactive processes, which have been influenced by their family's intergenerational system, as does the client. Together they form a new system. As within any system, a change in one part will influence the other. Therefore, a treatment approach that comprehensively addresses the family as well as the "identified" client is required. Because a family is an interactional unit, it has its own set of unique traits. It is not possible to accurately assess an individual's concern without observing the interaction of the other family members, as well as the broader contexts in which the person and the family live. To focus primarily on studying the internal dynamics of an individual without adequately considering interpersonal dynamics yields an incomplete picture. Ruth is embarking on a journey that will affect those closest to her: her husband, her children, her family of origin (parents and siblings), her peers, and her therapist. In addition, assessments made about her will evolve and change as the therapeutic process progresses.

The assessment and treatment process has three phases. In Phase 1, I will have John accompany Ruth for the first visit. I will ask him to assist her in assessing her presenting problem by asking them about their marital history and about their children. My decision to include him is based on my limited phone conversation with her, in which she said she was aware not only that it frightened her to think of making changes in her life but also that John was resisting her changes and preferred that she remain her "old self."

It is my goal to assess Ruth and John's relationship and try to determine what influence each has on the other. What kind of relationship do they have that prevents her from changing and him from wanting change? Do they lack the ability to negotiate a different relationship, and if so, why? To address these questions and as a means of enhancing their relationship, I will encourage John to become interested in couples therapy and in therapy with the entire family. If he chooses to become involved in the process, I will continue to work with both Ruth and John and examine their families of origin (Phase 2). To assess patterns that affect the presenting problem, it is necessary to assess a client's family over a span of three generations.

Phase 3 entails bringing the entire family in for assessment. If there are changes in Ruth and John, I predict that other parts of the system will react. In our telephone conversation, Ruth indicated that she was concerned that her professional involvement would threaten her family. From my perspective it is important to include John and, later, the entire family because they appear to be part of the reason Ruth's changes have been difficult. There are many ways to approach this case from a systemic perspective.

Establishing a Diagnosis

In addition to the descriptive assessment of Ruth's family, I might be asked to provide a formal diagnosis for Ruth, depending on the setting in which I work. Just as the assessments made about Ruth are subject to change as the therapeutic process progresses, any diagnosis should be considered tentative at the initial phase of therapy.

Ruth was referred to me because of her general anxiety symptoms, which interfered in many areas of her functioning. I justify her diagnosis of "panic disorder without agoraphobia" on the ground that her anxiety is not due to direct physiological effects of a substance or a general medical condition. She said that she had concerns about having additional anxiety attacks and that she sometimes felt that she was "going crazy."

Although Ruth's main reason for seeking therapy was her generalized anxiety, her relationship problems with her parents and with her spouse could certainly be underlying factors contributing to the symptoms of anxiety and panic. The diagnoses of parent–child relational problem and also partner relational problem seem appropriate due to a number of her behavioral patterns. Her relationships with her parents are characterized by impaired communication, rigid discipline, and overprotection, all of which are associated with clinically significant impairment of the way she functions as an individual and in her family. Likewise, her relationship with her husband is marked by ineffective communication and fear of losing his support, which also affect her functioning.

My initial assessment and tentative diagnosis of Ruth logically lead to several specific treatment goals.

Treatment Goals

The individual goal for this case is the reduction of Ruth's symptomatic behaviors (panic attacks). The family system goals include (1) reducing triangles that have prevented her and others from obtaining a confident position in the system; (2) restructuring her immediate system so autonomy by all family members will be encouraged; (3) changing patterns of interaction, not only among family members but also between her and John, so that the relationship can become more flexible and able to cope with changes as the family moves to the next developmental stage; (4) reducing the presenting symptoms; and (5) creating an environment in which all members of the system feel secure and, indeed, are reinforced as they make needed changes.

Phase 1: Session With Ruth and John

My goals for our first session are (1) to obtain a working and therapeutic relationship with Ruth and John; (2) to assess John's willingness to be involved in the treatment process; (3) to encourage John's participation as a critical actor in this family act; and (4) to explore family-of-origin dynamics to shift the focus from symptoms (Ruth's panic attacks) to process (who says what to whom and under what circumstances). This shift will help put Ruth's problems in a larger context, minimize blame, and thereby reduce anxiety, especially hers. Another goal is to confirm or refute my stated hypotheses (described in the section on themes and issues).

After introductions, I begin with Ruth's and John's concerns regarding this session. I address them individually.

> THERAPIST: How were you feeling before you got here, and how is it to be here?
>
> RUTH: I'm a little nervous to have John here with me.

THERAPIST: Could you explain what you mean by a little nervous?

RUTH: I guess I'm afraid that he may be here to make sure I continue to do things his way.

THERAPIST: What do you mean by "doing things his way"?

RUTH: That he'll be upset if I talk about wanting to make changes such as going to work. And that he'll try to pressure me not to.

THERAPIST: John, to what degree do you think Ruth's concerns are realistic?

JOHN: Well, to some degree her concerns are realistic. At first when she asked me to come here, I was angry because I thought she was inviting me because I was the one with a problem. Then I decided that I'd give it a try.

I am interested in their answer to the question "How were you feeling before you got here?" This question brings out in the open each person's reactions and gets dialogue going that makes it possible to discover what each needs to be more relaxed before treatment can begin. Their answers to this question tell me that John and Ruth are willing to be honest with each other. Neither hesitated, and yet both were nervous in sharing their concerns. His honesty and her willingness to share their reactions are signs that the prognosis for change in their relationship is good. Her anxiety may be reduced as they learn to negotiate a new relationship.

Other questions I pursue during the beginning of the first session are (1) "Who said what to whom to convince you both to come to this session?" and (2) "What do you both hope to have happen during this session, and what do you expect from me?" These questions help me ascertain how each sees the meaning of their being here. If it appears that John has a desire to be a part of the therapeutic relationship, I continue to gather background information on both of them. This is done in the form of a genogram.

A *genogram* is an organized map, or diagram, that demonstrates one's family over three generations. It is a method by which therapist and client shift from examining a symptomatic individual (Ruth) to a family system conceptualization of the problem, and it often gives an indication of a solution. In obtaining this transgenerational history, I acquire a history of the nuclear family (Ruth and John's family), a history of her extended family, and a history of his extended family.

One goal in developing a genogram is to determine the following: (1) *relationship patterns* that have been repeated from one generation to the next, which explain the context in which the presenting problem or symptoms developed; (2) the occurrence, if any, of *emotional cutoffs*, which are a means by which people attempt to distance themselves from a fused, or overclose, relationship; (3) *triadic relationships* (triangles), which denote conflict, fusion, or emotional cutoffs; and (4) *toxic issues* such as religion, gender independence, money, politics, and divorce, which create in the client emotional reactivity with other parts of the system.

In doing the genogram work with Ruth and John, I will gather the following information about their current family, their family of origin, their mother's family, and their father's family: occupations; educational background; date of birth of self and present children; dates of marriage, separation, or divorce; names of former spouses and children; miscarriages, stillbirths, and adopted and foster children; where all children now live; dates and types of severe illnesses; passages such as promotions and graduations; demographic data; cultural and ethnic data; socioeconomic data; military service; religion; addictions such as drugs, alcohol, and sex; abuse of old people, children, or adults; and retirement or unemployment dates. This information forms a database that will be used to demonstrate family interaction patterns. After gathering this information I prepare a summary that gives useful information in understanding Ruth and John's relationship.[8]

🕊 **Summary**   Through the process of using the genogram to understand the family system, I learn that John has unresolved feelings toward his mother. It is my new assumption that John's triadic relationship (fused with his father and emotionally cut off from his mother) has kept him from forming a healthy individuated relationship with Ruth or with any other woman. His parents were unable to resolve their conflicts, and so one parent moved closer to him, just as the other was emotionally cut off in an effort to reduce the stress and anxiety in the marital dyad. John and Ruth discovered that they were continuing the same pattern that was evident in John's family of origin. Their identities were blended (fused) to the extent that they were unable to discuss the emotionally laden issue of gender independence, and therefore they chose not to relate to each other. In an attempt to dissipate their anxiety, they triangled Rob into their relationship (see Figure 12.1). John, like his father before him, chose to tell his son about his unresolved feelings toward his wife. Rob began to distance himself from his mother, most likely for reasons he cannot completely understand. This triangle left Ruth feeling isolated and without support. She felt that her family really did not appreciate her. But an emotional revelation during therapy helped give Ruth and John a new perspective on the family's problems.

In addition, a new option for interacting was opened up. John found he was able to break the *family rule* of not discussing emotionally charged issues, especially with a woman, a rule that prohibited Ruth from exploring with him how each of them felt as she was trying to become a more independent person

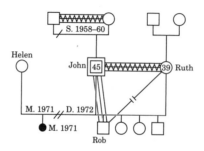

FIGURE 12.1 Multigenerational Triangles, Showing Repeated Structural Patterns With Emphasis on John's Family

within this system. When she decided to make some changes, she inadvertently influenced him to change. This is a good example of how change in one part of the system will result in other parts of the system being changed.

Phase 2: Ruth's Genogram

I assign Ruth to gather information from her parents and siblings and any other family member willing to discuss her family's story. I ask John to collect the same information from his family. I tell them that the purpose of gathering such data is not to help them change others in the system but to assist them in making individual changes that can also result in a healthy relationship. After Phase 1, both John and Ruth say they feel a strengthened sense of commitment to their marriage.

Ruth finds in going to her parents' home and separately approaching each of them that her mother is freer to discuss the family and their issues than her father. However, her father does give her some illuminating details about himself. The process of gathering information is an intervention within itself. Ruth is breaking the family taboo about asking questions of her superiors and also is inquiring about their own feelings in regard to others.

Mother's Family Ruth discovers that her mother is relieved to tell her about the family. Her mother, Edith, says she is the eldest of three siblings. She explains that she felt burdened by the role of caretaker for her brother and sister. She also says her father was abusive toward her and punished her severely if she did not obey him. He was not a religious man and was a heavy drinker. Edith decided at an early age not to try to relate much to her father. Her family members never discussed their feelings about one another. Conflict arose when religion was brought up or when she talked of going on to college. Her father and mother sat down with her and explained that they could not afford to send her (but they did send her brother) and that she would not be permitted to bring the subject up again.

Edith tells Ruth that she never heard a supportive word from any member of the family. Also, there was a rumor that Edith's mother had been sent to a hospital for what was known then as a nervous breakdown. This incident was never discussed among family members, and Ruth had never heard about it. She asks why her mother never spoke about this incident, and Edith weeps, saying that she was never allowed to discuss it. This is the first time Ruth has seen her mother cry, much less express emotions. In addition, her mother shares that she sees Ruth as the most stable person in the family. This is the first positive remark Ruth can remember receiving from her mother.

Father's Family Ruth's father, Patrick, is less cooperative. He asks her a number of questions about her need to know family information. I advised her it was best not to tell the family that her questions were part of a therapeutic process. She chooses to say that they are part of an educational experience, which is true. Her father begins by saying that he is uncomfortable with giving her any information about his family. This is the first time he has admitted a feeling to her. When she asks about his reasons, he says families should keep

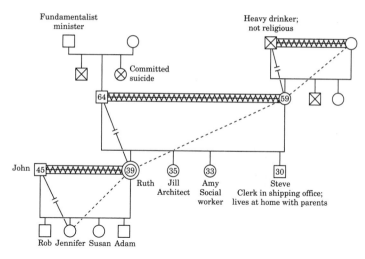

FIGURE 12.2 Multigenerational Triangles and Repeated Structural Patterns in Ruth's Genogram

their lives private. He believes only God should know what really goes on inside a family. Ruth does not react to her father but simply accepts whatever he feels comfortable revealing.

Patrick goes on to tell her that his older brother died at birth and that his youngest sister committed suicide. Her death left him as the only child of a fundamentalist minister and a mother that he knew little about. This is the first time her father has ever shared anything about himself. It allows Ruth to see her father in a different light. She also gains a sense about herself that she never had before. She discovers that she can handle discussing emotionally laden issues with her father. In the past she would never have permitted herself to do so. She also feels more grown up with her father. It is as if he is treating her as an equal for the first time. Her genogram evolves as shown in Figure 12.2.

🙋 **Ruth's Interpretation of Her Genogram**   Ruth develops her own insight regarding her place and process in the family. Here are some of her discoveries:

- A toxic issue in this system over the years is a female notion of independence from the family.
- Over three generations the eldest daughters have been emotionally cut off from their fathers and have remained distant with their mothers, and the mothers and fathers have stayed in conflicted marriages.

One hypothesis regarding this pattern is that what controls anxiety in this couple's relationship is for the husband and wife to deflect their attention to the eldest daughter. The toxic issue that evokes the process is the desire of the eldest daughter to move physically and emotionally away from the fused triad (mother/father/daughter).

Ruth begins to understand that when she became the focus of attention in her family, her parents' communication with each other increased. When she tried to move out on her own (emotionally and physically), her parents would focus on her. They were unable to work out their personal conflicts and instead chose to argue about her. When Ruth complied and the family appeared calm, her mother and father approved of her and had little more to say to each other. In a therapy session we discuss Ruth's understanding of patterns carried on from one generation to the next:

THERAPIST: Ruth, what are you learning from the work you're doing with your family?

RUTH: I'm beginning to realize that whenever I made an independent move, I began to feel guilty. My movement created a great deal of reactivity from my parents, and in my desire to reduce their anxiety I decided not to have a career. In some ways, I believe, I was keeping them together.

THERAPIST: Do you see any correlations between what you did in your family of origin and what you're currently doing in your own family?

RUTH: I'm seeing that I've continued the pattern. If John even hints at being uncomfortable with my making decisions independently from the family, I feel guilty, and I feel responsible for reducing his stress. Also, I'm continuing this pattern with my children. I make them feel guilty if they try to become independent from the family.

THERAPIST: Do you still believe John doesn't want you to become your own person?

RUTH: Not anymore. It is becoming clearer to us how we've brought the patterns of our own families of origin into our marriage. We're getting along much better. In fact, John has actually encouraged me to take courses next semester.

THERAPIST: Have your panic attacks continued during this time?

RUTH: I still get anxious, but now that I'm beginning to see what this is all about, I haven't had a panic attack for quite a while now.

This work accomplished with John and Ruth is a condensed example. It could take months before someone would come to these conclusions. For a time I might meet weekly with the family, and then at a later time meet less frequently.

Phase 3: Presenting Ruth With the Idea of Family Therapy

Ruth reports that since she and John began to come to therapy, Adam has been acting out more at home and at school. Adam and Ruth are having more arguments, usually centering on her request to have him clean up his room or do his homework. Before she entered treatment, they were very close, going to the movies and attending school events. John is frustrated with Adam, who has been having trouble at school. According to John, Adam does not clean his room when asked.

I recommend to Ruth that she consider bringing her entire family into the therapeutic process. She and John, having explored their intergenerational dynamics in depth, have made some significant changes. According to both of them, their relationship has improved, and she is feeling far less guilt and anxiety about her decision to return to school. However, she complains that their children are still resisting change, and especially her changes. Adam and Jennifer have told her that they prefer the "old Mom" and do not want their lives to become unsettled.

Based on our discussion, Ruth decides to ask her family to join her in therapy. The entire family is asked to attend the first session. All of the children agree to participate, which can be considered a good sign. But Rob, the elder son, is reluctant. He feels that he does not have any problems, and he does not understand why he should attend.

With the family's permission, I ask Jerry Corey to attend the meeting as my co-therapist. The luxury of having female and male co-therapists can be most therapeutic. Because I have been working with John and Ruth, we have a relationship that the children might perceive as a coalition, with their parents against them. Having a neutral person as part of a therapeutic team can counterbalance this situation. Choosing a co-therapist of the opposite gender allows for working with transference and also provides opportunities for the co-therapist to model behaviors during the session.

THE FIRST SESSION   Jerry asks the family members to be seated wherever they want. I thank the family for coming and address each member by first name. I say that the purposes of this first meeting are to establish the goals for treatment and to assess with them whether further sessions might be helpful to the family. We also discuss the limits of confidentiality and the reporting laws for the state.

The Presenting Complaint   It is apparent that there is some confusion over why everyone needs to be present. Therefore, we ask Ruth to explain her concerns to the family and her hopes for these sessions.

> RUTH: Since John and I have been in therapy, I've seen this family change. Adam, you've been more moody. We've been arguing more, and you seem unwilling to take any suggestions of mine to get your homework done or to clean your room. I believe our marriage is improving, but my relationship with the children, especially Adam, is getting worse.

Jerry and I observe that Ruth and Adam sit next to each other. John sits next to me, and Jennifer sits between Adam and Susan. Rob, who is 19, sits away from the rest of the family. Jerry and I ask each member for his or her observations regarding the family. We also ask them: "If you could get something from this session for yourself, what might that be? Would you like to have a different relationship with anyone in your family?"

The Family Interaction   Here are some excerpts of a dialogue among the family members, Jerry, and myself during this first session with the family. Those present in the family include Ruth, John, Rob, Jennifer, Susan, and Adam.

JOHN: Since Ruth and I began to improve our relationship through counseling, Adam has become less obedient and cooperative, especially with Ruth. Yesterday, Adam yelled at Jennifer, and when I tried to punish him, Ruth told me to leave him alone and let them work it out by themselves. I disagree with her new idea of how to discipline these children.

ROB [Interrupting and in anger]: You should listen to Mom. She knows more about what is going on in this family than you.

JERRY COREY: Rob, you sound angry at your father. If that is true, can you tell him why you are upset, and would you share that directly with your father? [Jerry has Rob face his father.]

ROB [Looking at Jerry as if he was odd, but he faces Dad directly]: You are on everyone's case, and you don't have a clue as to what is going on in this family. Mom is more reliable and has backed off from telling us continually what to do. She's not on my case as much as she was before.

JERRY: Rob, would you tell your mother what you mean by "being on your case"?

ROB: Mom would always want to know where I was going and what I was doing. She would clean my room without my permission.

JERRY: Rob, you're talking about your mother as though she weren't in the room. How about talking directly to her over there?

ROB: You're asking me to do something I'm not comfortable with. Why can't I just explain myself to you?

JERRY: You have said you're uncomfortable with the way things are in this family. You would like more of a voice in how you are treated in your family. One way for that to happen is to talk directly to your parents so they receive clearly the messages you want them to understand. Try this out and see if it doesn't give you a stronger position in the family.

ROB: That's kind of hard for me to do. It's not something that I usually do.

MARY MOLINE: I can understand that, Rob. But I believe you are up to the task. Jerry and I are not just asking you to deal directly with your family, but for each of you to talk directly to one another. It also helps Jerry and me to better understand your position in this family.

ROB: OK. I also want to say something about Dad. I feel he's too hard on Adam.

JERRY: So, Rob, there sits your dad. Can you tell him directly what you mean by your statement that he's too hard on Adam?

ROB [Reluctantly]: Dad, you're always upset when Adam starts arguing with his sisters or me. And you're getting on my case lately. If I'm not home by 10, you get all bent out of shape, just like Mom used to do.

JERRY: John, how is it for you to hear what Rob is saying to you?

JOHN [Looking to Jerry]: I don't believe I have to take this. I never corrected my father.

MARY: John, would you please sit closer to Rob and tell him directly how it is for you to hear what he is saying to you?

JOHN [*Moves his chair closer to Rob*]: Well, it does make me upset. Don't you know how much your mother and I care for you?

ROB [*Facing his father and looking surprised*]: No, I don't know you care.

MARY: It seems that the two of you have more to talk about. I'm hoping that you two will continue this dialogue before the next session. Is that possible?

Both agree to meet outside and before the next session. They agree to go out for lunch and discuss their relationship. They agree to report at the next family session what occurred.

MARY: I would like to make sure that we get to each person in the family before this session is over. [*She turns to Jennifer.*] What would you like to say about being here and what you would like for yourself in these sessions?

JENNIFER [*Looking to Ruth and Susan*]: Susan and I like the idea of coming here, because the family seems so different since Mom and Dad went to counseling. But we feel that Mom has abandoned the family.

JERRY: Would you tell your mother what you mean by "abandoning the family"?

JENNIFER: Well, Mother, you don't do our wash anymore. We have to make our own lunches. You're arguing more with Adam and me. I want to stay out of the house when the bickering begins, especially between you and Adam.

MARY: Ruth, how do you respond to what Jennifer just said to you?

RUTH: It's hard to hear Jennifer disapproving of my going to college or my wanting her and the children to become more independent from me. I think that's why it's so difficult for me to get a job outside the home. I'm torn between making myself happy or my family happy.

MARY: How do you respond to what your mother just said, Jennifer?

JENNIFER: I'd rather not respond right now.

MARY: That's OK, you don't need to answer now. I hope we can get back to what's going on between you and your mother later in this session. [*She turns to Susan.*] How, specifically, would you like things to be different for yourself with each member of your family?

SUSAN: Jennifer and I would like more of Mom's time.

JERRY: Instead of talking for Jennifer, perhaps you could talk for yourself. Later Jennifer can say what she would like to be different.

MARY: Susan, is there anything that you want to add?

SUSAN: Well, I'd like to say that I agree with Rob that Dad is not as nice as he used to be since Mom got into counseling. He's nicer to Mom but seems more upset with all of us and . . .

JOHN [*Interrupting*]: How can you say that I'm not nice to you? I do the best I can, and nobody appreciates that!

JERRY: Is that what you were trying to tell your father, Susan? Did he hear you right?

SUSAN [*Turning to Jerry*]: No.

JERRY: Would you mind telling your father what you'd like from him?

SUSAN [*With tears in her eyes*]: Dad, it's not that we don't appreciate how hard you work. It's just that I don't hear anything nice from you anymore.

MARY: Susan, if you could have one thing different with your father, what would that be?

SUSAN: That we could do something together without getting into a fight.

MARY: How would that be for you, John?

JOHN: Well, if I could find the time, I'd like to do more with Susan. But I don't know what a father does with a 17-year-old.

MARY: Why don't you ask her?

JOHN [*Looking at Susan, after a long pause*]: Well, what do you think?

SUSAN: We could go to a movie.

MARY: Is that something you'd like to do with Susan?

JOHN: Yeah, if we could ever agree on a movie.

MARY: It sounds good, and I hope the two of you will make the time to talk with each other about what both of you want. [*She turns to Adam.*] Adam, what would you like to say about yourself?

ADAM: I think it's unfair that my family picks on me.

MARY: Who in this room picks on you, and would you tell them directly?

ADAM: Susan, you've been picking on me. And Jennifer just sits around and smiles. And, well . . . [*Fidgeting and looking to the floor*] Dad and Mom have been upset with me a lot lately and . . .

JOHN [*Interrupting*]: When have I been upset with you that you didn't deserve it?

RUTH [*Interrupting and turning to John*]: I think you ought to let Adam finish.

MARY: Ruth, how about letting John speak for himself. [*She looks to John.*] What would you like to say to Adam?

JOHN: I feel that everyone is picking on me, and it's getting me mad!

JERRY: John, I can understand that you might feel as if you're being picked on. But another way to look at this is to consider that what they're telling you is a sign that they trust you enough to be open and honest with you about their feelings. Maybe these are things that they haven't been able to express to you until now.

JOHN: Well . . . I don't know . . . But I do want my kids to be able to talk to me.

JERRY: If you could be more open with them, that would allow them to be more open with you. A short time ago Adam said some things to you, and you seemed to be very emotionally moved. Is there anything you'd like to say to Adam?

JOHN: It's very difficult to hear what you had to say, Adam. [*He turns to Jerry laughingly.*] Did I do it right this time?

JERRY: I hope you'll continue to talk. [*He addresses all the family members except Ruth.*] Several of you have mentioned that your mother's counseling has affected your lives. Some of you have even said that you felt abandoned by her. Would each of you be willing to talk to your mother?

SUSAN: Mom, it's hard to see you being different. I was so used to you taking an interest in us, even though at times I complained. You did so much for us, but I guess you have a life of your own too.

ROB: I think you're right on, Susan!

ADAM: Mother, I miss you not sticking up for me more. I don't like fighting with you, but at times I find myself starting a fight with you.

MARY: Do you think the fighting and missing your mom are related?

ADAM [*Thinking for a while*]: Maybe!

JENNIFER: I like talking like this. We never do this at home, and we're not even fighting right now.

MARY [*Turning to Ruth*]: How is it for you to hear that?

RUTH: It feels good to see my family talking about themselves and realizing that I don't have to take so much care of them anymore.

JERRY: Our time is almost up, but before we close I'd like to ask each of you if there are reasons you might want to return.

All of the family members feel that it is important to return because they like what has happened during the session. They are agreeable to attending another session the following week. Jerry then explains to them the value of doing some homework before the next session. Because the family members are open to this idea, he suggests the following assignments:

- For Ruth: Avoid interfering when one of the children is attempting to interact with John.
- For Susan and John: Decide on an activity that you're willing to do together before the next session.
- For Rob and John: Take some more time to let your father know what you'd like with him. You agree to go out together and talk. Rob, it's important that you don't tell your father how he should be different, but instead talk about yourself with him.
- For Jennifer: Take the initiative to ask your mother to do something with you before next week, such as going shopping or spending 20 minutes together.
- For Ruth and John: Continue to discuss what you would like to do with each other and what you would like to do separately. When you do start to focus on the children, try to talk instead about yourselves.

The family members are asked if they have any objections to these assignments and if they would be willing to follow through with them by the following week, at which time they will meet again with both therapists. All feel that they can complete the assignments.

It is important that families work on issues outside of therapy as well as during therapy. In this way they can observe that they have the strength to make their own changes. By taking this responsibility they empower themselves. The only family member not given an assignment is Adam. This is an attempt to keep the other family members focusing away from him and keep him from continuing to be identified as a "patient" in this family.

PROCESS COMMENTARY The co-therapists set out to observe the structure of the family by (1) allowing the members to sit where they wanted to and (2) attempting to get a clearer picture of the family's transactional patterns. We assume, in observing the structure of this family, that Ruth's change has produced stress among the siblings. There was stress between Ruth and John, but including John in the beginning session reduced it. Ruth appears to have rigid boundaries with Adam. Her ability to make changes has strengthened her boundary with Adam, and he is reacting to those changes. No longer does she feel the need to give in to his demands. But conflicts have increased in their relationship. Her changes are resulting in new strains on this relationship. If Adam can have a closer relationship with his siblings or other peer groups, he may be able to better adjust to this change. Jennifer also appears to be having difficulty with the changes, not only with Ruth but also with the fact that the spousal subsystem is becoming stronger. We repeat: If change occurs in any one part of the system, change will occur in the other parts. In other words, changes in Ruth and changes in Ruth and John's relationship have affected the equilibrium of this family. Whenever possible, therefore, it is important to have the whole family enter treatment so that the changes that occur are productive for the system as well as each individual within it.

In this family there is an enmeshment among members. They lack a clear sense of their individuality and roles in the family. Families such as this one are prone to conflict and confusion, and the behavior of one member or unit, in this case both Ruth and John, immediately affects the other members of the family.

Ruth and John are learning new behaviors. She is learning not to maintain her role as peacemaker, and he is learning to be more supportive of her. As a result, the other family members are being forced to learn to deal with one another. Up to this session they have been increasing the conflict among themselves and with Ruth to bring her back into her previous role as mediator. In family therapy terms this is known as an attempt to maintain homeostasis, which involves prompting a return of the family to the former status.

This system (family) is relatively functional. Its members were able to make some strides in communicating in the session, especially considering that they generally have not expressed their own feelings with one another. John and Ruth's exploration of transgenerational patterns has assisted them in learning how to express these feelings, and that change helped them facilitate the children's flexibility, difficult as it has been at times. Intergenerational patterns of not expressing feelings and allowing independent thought are not likely to continue. Because these patterns do not change overnight, the family still has considerable work to do. The committed effort aimed at modifying these patterns will not only free this family to be more honest and open but will benefit future generations.

The family has an excellent chance of making these structural changes:

- Becoming more direct with one another
- Taking the focus off of Adam as a problem
- Reducing the coalition that Adam and Ruth have against John
- Reducing the enmeshed (overclose) relationship Ruth has with Adam so she can have a closer relationship with John and so Adam can have appropriate closer relationships with his siblings and other peers

The chances are that the entire family will not always be included in future therapy sessions. Instead, therapy may include parts of the system (John and Rob), the spousal subsystem (Ruth and John), or the sibling subsystem (Rob, Jennifer, Susan, and Adam). Ruth and John will need to continue strengthening their independence from each other and their togetherness.

Questions for Reflection

1. What differences do you see between working with Ruth in individual counseling and using couple or family therapy? Do you think that including her husband or family in a few sessions will promote or inhibit her progress in individual therapy?
2. Can you see any complications arising from having Ruth both in individual and couple therapy at the same time, and if so, what are they? How could you address any potential problems? In the family therapy approach, do you see any disadvantages in not meeting with her individually in therapy?
3. What possible ethical issues are involved if you do not suggest couple or family therapy for Ruth, given clear indications that some of her problems stem from conflicts within her family?
4. Can you think of areas in your relationships with others where you demonstrate the attitude of acceptance? In what ways might learning to be accepting of a significant other benefit a relationship?
5. Integrative behavioral couple therapy assumes that with acceptance partners often spontaneously change their behaviors. Can you identify some specific behaviors that Ruth and John changed, even though therapy did not focus directly on asking for behavioral changes?
6. If you were conducting family therapy in this case, whom would you consider to be your primary client? Would your client be the family as a system? Ruth? John? Jennifer? Adam? Susan? Rob? Can you see any ethical binds if you develop an alliance with certain members of this family?
7. How do you think your own relationships with an intimate partner or in your family of origin might either help or hinder you in working with this family? Can you see any possible sources of problems or potential countertransferences? If you become aware that you have unfinished business with either your family of origin or your present family, what course would you probably take?
8. If you were working with Ruth's family, with whom might you be most inclined to form an alliance? With which person do you think you would have the most difficulty in working, and why?

9. If you and Ruth were from different cultures, what factors would you as a family therapist want to address with both her and the members of her family? What role might cultural factors play in understanding the structure of this family? How might the interventions you make vary depending on the cultural background of the family involved in the therapeutic process?

10. Do you have any bias toward Ruth because of her desire to change her role within the family? Does her thinking fit with yours regarding female roles in the family? Regarding male roles in the family? What do you think about the way that values around gender roles were handled by both therapists in this chapter?

Notes

1. Integrative behavioral couple therapy was developed by Andrew Christensen and Neil Jacobson. For further discussion and a treatment manual for therapists, see N. Jacobson & A. Christensen (1998), *Acceptance and Change in Couple Therapy: A Therapist's Guide to Transforming Relationship*s (New York: Norton). For a self-help book for couples, see A. Christensen & N. Jacobson (2000), *Reconcilable Differences* (New York: Guildford Press).

2. See N. S. Jacobson & G. Margolin (1979), *Marital Therapy: Strategies Based on Social Learning and Behavioral Exchange Principles* (New York: Brunner/Mazel), for a detailed treatment manual for the traditional behavioral couple therapy approach.

3. It is important to study whether the therapy provided is effective. Research shows this type of intervention to be effective, yet the positive effects fade over time for many couples after therapy ends. For a fuller discussion, see N. S. Jacobson, K. B. Schmaling, & A. Holtzworth-Monroe (1987), Component analysis of behavioral marital therapy: Two-year follow-up and prediction of relapse. *Journal of Marital and Family Therapy, 13,* 187–195.

4. Culture in couples work is an important topic that has recently received increasing attention by theoreticians and practitioners. A colleague and I (Jean Yi) are currently writing a chapter on culturally competent practice within empirically supported couple therapy.

5. As a basis for understanding the guest contributors' presentations of family therapy perspectives on working with Ruth, refer to G. Corey (2009), *Theory and Practice of Counseling and Psychotherapy* (8th ed., Belmont, CA: Brooks/Cole). Chapter 14 ("Family Therapy") contains a comprehensive overview of the approaches to family therapy along with a comprehensive list of references and recommended readings on family therapy.

6. Bowen, M. (1978). *Family therapy in clinical practice.* New York: Jason Aronson.

7. Minuchin, S. (1974). *Families and family therapy.* Cambridge, MA: Harvard University.

8. For detailed information about constructing genograms, consult M. McGoldrick, R. Gerson, & S. Shellenberger (1998), *Genograms: Assessment and Intervention* (2nd ed., New York: Norton).

CHAPTER THIRTEEN

Counseling Ruth From Multicultural and Integrative Perspectives

Introduction

This chapter focuses on how to work with Ruth from various multicultural and integrative perspectives. Different contributors show how they would counsel Ruth assuming she is a Latina, an Asian American, or an African American, and another describes his integrative perspective in counseling Ruth. The multicultural and integrative perspectives are not separate theories; these perspectives can be incorporated into any of the theories considered in previous chapters. Each contributor in this chapter draws from his or her own integrative approach when counseling Ruth.

Jerome Wright, PhD, a colleague and friend who teaches social work practice and cultural diversity courses conceived of a way to encourage his students to appreciate the subtle aspects of working with cultural themes in the lives of clients. He gave Ruth's case to his students and asked them to form small study groups to research the cultural variables that would apply if she were from each of these ethnic groups: Asian American, Latina, and African American. The students were also asked to think of issues that would be involved if she were being counseled from a feminist perspective and special issues to consider if she were a lesbian. Each of the study groups had the freedom to present its findings in any way it deemed fit, as long as the members did so as a group. Some did role-playing situations, others invited guest speakers who represented the group they were studying, and others found interesting ways to involve the class in their presentation. I was impressed with the value of this approach in teaching multicultural awareness to counseling students. Issues such as race, ethnicity, gender, age, socioeconomic status, religion, lifestyle, and sexual orientation are crucial when establishing a therapeutic relationship with clients.

Becoming immersed in the study of cultural diversity is not without its dangers, however. Accepting stereotypes and applying general characteristics of a particular group to every individual within that group is problematic. Indeed, the differences among individuals within a given ethnic group can be as great as the differences between populations. Knowledge about the client's culture provides counselors with a conceptual framework, but knowledge of a client's cultural values is only the beginning. Counselors also need to be aware of how their own culture influences their behavior, assumptions, and biases, and how these factors are likely to influence the manner in which they work with clients who differ culturally from them. Counseling across cultures is personally demanding, but it can also be rewarding.

As counselors who work with diverse client populations, it would be impossible for us to have a comprehensive and in-depth knowledge of the cultural background of all of our clients. I believe clients will teach us about those aspects of their culture that are important for us to attend to in our work together. Universal human themes unite people just as much as their differences enrich us all. We all need to receive and give love, to make sense of our psychological pain, and to make significant connections with others. However, we need to be aware of specific cultural values as we counsel people from various backgrounds. Any difference that has the capacity to create a gap in understanding should be explored, including differences such as age, gender, culture, ability, socioeconomic status, religion, and sexual orientation.

The Many Faces of Ruth

Let's assume that Ruth is an Asian American. Depending on her degree of acculturation, I want to know something about the values of her country of origin. I may anticipate that she has one foot in her old culture and another foot in her new one. She may experience real conflicts, feeling neither fully Asian nor fully American, and at some points she may be uncertain about the way to integrate the two aspects of her life. She may be slow to disclose personal material, but this is not necessarily a reflection of her unwillingness to cooperate with the counseling venture. Rather, her reluctance is likely to reflect a cultural tradition that has encouraged her to be emotionally reserved. Knowing something about her case and about her background, I am aware that shame and guilt may play a significant role in her behavior. Talking about family matters is often considered to be something shameful and to be avoided. Furthermore, in her culture stigma and shame may arise over experiencing psychological distress and feeling the need for professional help.

As another example, consider the importance of accurately interpreting nonverbal behavior. Let's assume now that Ruth is a Latina and that she is cautious in attempting to maintain eye contact because her therapist is a man. I would probably err if I assumed that this behavior reflected resistance or evasiveness. Instead, she is behaving in ways that she thinks are polite, for direct eye contact could be seen as disrespectful. Also, I would need to be patient while developing a working alliance with her. As is true of many ethnic groups, Latinos and Latinas have a tendency to reveal themselves more slowly than do many Anglo clients. Again, this does not mean that Ruth is being defensive, but it can reflect different cultural norms. She may not relate well to a high level of directness, because in her culture she has learned to express herself in more indirect ways.

If Ruth were a Native American and if I were unfamiliar with her culture, I could err by interpreting her quiet behavior as a sign that she was stoic and unemotional. Actually, she may have good reason to be emotionally contained, especially during the initial meeting with a counselor of a different cultural background. Her mistrust does not have to be a sign of paranoia; rather, it can be a realistic reaction based on numerous experiences that have conditioned her to be cautious. If I did not know enough about her culture, it would be ethically imperative either that I learn some of its basic aspects or that I refer her to a counselor who was culturally skilled in this area. I don't burden myself with the unrealistic standard that I should know everything. It would be acceptable to admit to her that I lacked knowledge about her culture and then proceed to find a way to remedy this situation. Openness with a client can certainly be the foundation for a good relationship. Ruth can provide me with some information regarding what would be important for me to know about her cultural background.

If Ruth is a member of certain ethnic, cultural, and racial groups, she is likely to have encountered her share of discrimination based on being different. This factor will need to be addressed if her counselor is of a different ethnic or racial group. As an African American, Latina, Native American, Asian American, or Pacific Islander, Ruth will share the experience of institutional oppression. She will know what it means to struggle for empowerment. Chances are that being both a woman and a member of one of these diverse groups she will experience a compounding of the problems that have previously been described in her case. This experience is bound to be reflected in the dynamics of our therapeutic relationship. I will need to somehow demonstrate my good faith and my ability to enter her world and understand the nature of her concerns. If I ignore these cultural realities, chances are that Ruth will not stay in therapy with me very long. However, I cannot emphasize enough the guiding principle of letting her provide me with the clues for the direction of therapy. In our initial encounter I will want to know what it was like for her to come to the office and why she is there. Rather than having prior conceptions of what we should be doing in this venture, I will ask her what she wants and why she is seeking help from me at this time in her life. If cultural issues are present, I expect that they will emerge very soon if I am listening sensitively to her and attempting to understand her world.

In this chapter various contributors write about their work with Ruth assuming that she is an African American, a Latina, or an Asian American. The last piece in this chapter focuses on counseling Ruth from an integrative perspective. These four different contributed pieces are designed to assist you in thinking about applying multicultural and integrative perspectives in counseling Ruth. As you read about the themes in Ruth's life in the following pages, be aware of how cultural variations can easily be woven into the fabric of the counseling process.

Ruth as an African American: A Spiritually Focused Integrative Perspective

by Kellie Kirksey, PhD

Introduction

Ruth, an African American female, is seeking counseling in a private practice setting. By entering therapy Ruth is engaging in a healing modality that is not typically embraced by her culture. She might well have heard a number of negative messages about seeking counseling such as these:

- Therapy is for crazy people.
- Don't tell your business to strangers.
- What happens at home, stays at home.
- Talk to your preacher or minister if you have a problem.
- You can't trust the system.
- If you are a Christian, you have Jesus and there is no need for an intercessor.

These are challenging perceptions, and historically, in many cases, these beliefs were the basis for survival.

When Ruth phoned to make her initial appointment, she requested an African American, Christian, female therapist. I don't market myself as a Christian counselor, but I see spirituality and faith as important variables in the healing process. Ruth makes an appointment, and we schedule an intake interview. I introduce myself and begin by asking her to discuss her perceptions of what counseling is and is not. During the intake process, I talk about what counseling entails and how we will go about meeting our goals. I acknowledge the courage it took for her to come in and tell her this is a significant step in the healing process. I also let her know that the initial session is about laying the groundwork for counseling, and that asking questions is a part of the assessment and consequent treatment process.

I invite Ruth to explore her beliefs and attitudes about seeking professional help and encourage her to talk openly about any concerns or fears she has about beginning counseling. I tell her that I am not the keeper of answers to her life problems, but simply a collaborator in this process. I operate from the assumption that individuals who come to me already have many of the answers within themselves. Although I have expertise in facilitating the therapeutic process, I view clients as the experts on their own lives.

Assessment of Ruth

Ruth was referred for counseling by her primary care physician due to anxiety, panic attacks, and general feelings of sadness and frustration with her life. She reports being brought up in a strict home where it was not acceptable to express emotions. As an adult, she has consistently repressed her feelings and experienced guilt when she attempted to express her dissatisfactions in life. This way of responding to the world was modeled to her by her mother and grandmother. She has recently returned to school where she is the only African

American woman in her program. Her inability to express her honest reactions when she encounters discriminatory and racist comments in the classroom is causing her significant distress.

It is critical to ask Ruth about her race and ethnicity. I pay careful attention to how she defines herself. She tells me she is "Black like me." I respond by telling her, "I was born in Cleveland, my husband is Haitian, although we are both Black, our cultures are worlds apart, and this affects how we see the world." The questions I pose to Ruth assist me in knowing more of who she is and how she sees herself in relation to her cultural group and the world. I am interested in hearing her talk about both the specific challenges and the strengths she experiences in belonging to her racial and ethnic group. Ruth mentions resiliency as a particular strength of her race. This information is important as we move into the treatment phase.

I ask Ruth about her religious or spiritual background at the initial session. I want to learn what kind of religious practices, if any, were used in her home as she was growing up. I explore the following questions: (1) Is religion an important part of your daily life? (2) What religion is practiced in your home? (3) What aspects of your religion/spiritual practice provide the most support for you? (4) Define your spiritual connection. Ruth's answers let me know how relevant religion and spirituality might be to our therapeutic work together.

This conversation reveals Ruth's ambivalent feelings toward counseling. She states if she were truly living by the Word of God, she wouldn't need a stranger to help her deal with her personal issues. Because of her ambivalence, I lean away from a traditional multiaxis diagnosis and focus on building a collaborative relationship in which she feels free to co-create a new healthy life story.

Goals of Therapy

We will use a collaborative integrative approach to meet the following treatment goals:

1. Establish a therapeutic relationship built on trust and mutual respect.
2. Explore and deconstruct the cultural and societal messages that have played a role in her feelings of unworthiness and victimization.
3. Create a new, healthy narrative that supports her in being more authentic in her life.
4. Increase her ability to trust her inner wisdom and spiritual connection.

Key Issues and Themes

Ruth is entering therapy with a host of personal concerns, one of which is her lost sense of self, both culturally and as a woman in society. She has lived most of her life as a people-pleaser and has given into the myth of the strong African American woman. Viewing herself as "superwoman," she has assumed the role of caretaker to everyone. In doing this she has become self-sacrificing and overextended physically and emotionally. Ruth's challenge is to learn that she can take care of herself, have healthy interpersonal boundaries, and speak her truth as an African American woman.

As a woman of African descent who has been raised to never disclose family business, it is important that I acknowledge her courage in breaking the silence and doing something that generations before her have been hesitant to do. It is vital that she understands my office is a safe and nonjudgmental zone and that she can trust me. I inform her about the limitations of confidentiality as a way of furthering this safety.

Ruth's anxiety is a major presenting concern; it has led her to control others, repress her feelings, and engage in unhealthy eating patterns. She tends to pacify her fear and frustration with food, leading to binge eating and weight gain. We will work on mindfulness strategies to assist her in becoming more aware of her automatic emotional eating and in making more life-affirming decisions.

Ruth's feels that in the midst of being there for others she has lost sight of herself. She has never allowed herself to explore what it means to be an African American woman in society. As she is confronted with discrimination and bias on the college campus, she is more determined to explore those social and cultural issues that have defined her existence.

Therapeutic Process and Procedures

Ruth's primary task in therapy is for her to teach me who she is. I remind her that she is the expert on her life and let her know that her answers for improving her life already live within her. Our joint partnership involves being intentional in discovering those answers and putting them into practice.

The therapeutic goals that Ruth and I have collaboratively developed will be accomplished through the use of the psychoanalytic, cognitive behavioral, existential, and postmodern therapy approaches. I draw from the psychoanalytic approach during the initial stage of counseling to identify repressed emotion. This approach is used to bring unconscious material to the forefront and to assist Ruth in accessing early experiences. I ask her to bring in old photos that will stimulate a discussion of childhood experiences that may be affecting her current level of functioning.

I begin to weave in the cognitive behavioral perspective by allowing Ruth to witness the language she uses in relation to herself. I keep a list of statements she makes so we can reflect on the negative patterns she uses. Once she realizes how often she calls herself "foolish or stupid," she begins to be more aware of her negative, self-defeating thoughts and how this affects her behavior. Cognitive behavioral strategies assist her in recognizing the negative self-talk that contributes to her sense of fear and panic. These strategies give her a framework for being more proactive in her life and help her see that changing her thoughts lead to behavioral change.

Existential theory, as well as some postmodern ideas, will be woven into Ruth's treatment. These approaches facilitate increased awareness on a variety of levels, including mind, body, and spirit. I encourage and challenge Ruth to be more mindful of who she is, what she is doing, and where she is going. The existential approach is coupled with cognitive behavioral work by increasing her awareness of her negative self-talk and then introducing affirmations. When Ruth makes statements such as "I am no good," I give her positive affirmation cards with phrases such as "I am worthy." Unable to read the statement, we move on to discuss the anxiety around feeling worthwhile. Once she begins to explore some of her existential concerns, it becomes easier to work on shifting how she sees herself.

Because Ruth has indicated the church is a guiding force in her life, I invite her to call on her spiritual connection to assist us in our work together. I view her spiritual connection as whatever source she goes to for spiritual strength, comfort, and direction. She tells me that her spiritual connection is God, and we then proceed with our work, claiming in a clear voice that we invite God into our session to guide and protect us on this journey of healing and self-discovery.

I tailor my therapeutic style to the specific needs of my clients. I realize that my ability to facilitate growth in my clients is consistent with my willingness to challenge my own personal struggles. In working with African American clients, I tend to lend special attention to generational transmission or those tendencies, traits, and habits that are consciously or unconsciously passed along. The use of genograms (family maps) is helpful in the early phase of therapy as we explore these generational patterns.

The Beginning Phase of Therapy

Ruth is quite talkative in our initial sessions. She feels comfortable because she respects her doctor who referred her and she is relieved to have a place to be heard. Ruth has spent an enormous amount of time in classes and at home holding back her true feelings. She is relieved to have a safe place to speak her mind. She is encouraged to take note of the pace of her breathing. I talk to her about the role breath work has in decreasing anxiety. I demonstrate diaphragmatic breathing and ask her to practice at home. I also encourage her to get a journal and begin to express her pent-up emotions. She reports feeling like she has already made progress and is glad she has something to do between sessions.

🖉 **Process Commentary**   The breathing activity is a way of assisting Ruth in becoming more aware of her body, what she is doing with her body, and what her body can do for her. As she continues her breathing activity, she will more quickly be able to relax and decrease her anxiety level. I will continue to work with Ruth on body awareness and incorporate movement.

During the beginning phase of therapy we initiate affirmations and continue this practice until the very end. These affirmations are born out of Ruth's own story. As I observe Ruth expressing phrases such as "I'm so stupid" or "I hate my life," I begin to write down her affirmation on an index card. The affirmations are meant to cancel out her negative self-talk, increase awareness of inner dialogue, and replace a defeatist statement with a life-supporting phrase. The first card she receives has a separate statement on each side. I pass the card to Ruth with the words "I matter" and "I am worthy" written in black marker, highlighted in pink.

THERAPIST: Would you read those words out loud please? [*Ruth is silent and does not respond.*] How are you feeling as you look at those words?

RUTH [*Tears begin to stream down her face*]: I feel sad because I wish I felt this way about myself.

THERAPIST: As I listened to you share your experiences, I heard some harsh words coming from you . . . about you.

RUTH: Yeah, it's all I heard growing up!

THERAPIST: Would you consider using kinder words as you refer to yourself?

RUTH: It just comes up before I can stop it!

THERAPIST: I want to challenge you to begin monitoring what you tell yourself. We know scripturally that "as a woman thinketh so is she." I'm challenging you to guard your thoughts and intentionally create something new in your mind. This entire process is about renewing your mind . . . forgiving yourself and others and moving forward.

RUTH: Easier said than done.

THERAPIST: That's why this is a practice, we practice new and different skills . . . try it on . . . see what it feels like.

Throughout our sessions I continue to discuss the importance of using positive self-statements, and I encourage Ruth to actively work on modifying her cognitions. We begin to create a list of negative messages that she has both received from others and that she has told herself. Some of these automatic thoughts are related to her race, gender, and current stage in life. As she begins to work on her list, she notices how her negative thoughts contribute to her poor self-image. I remind her that in our future sessions we will explore positive, rational, coping statements to cancel negative self-statements.

The Middle Phase of Therapy

Once I have a sense that we have established a solid therapeutic bond, we begin to go into more existential work, focusing on Ruth's anxiety and how she feels about her place in the world as an African American woman. It can be expected that intense emotions will surface as she begins to really speak from her heart.

THERAPIST: Ruth, how are you today?

RUTH: Sick and tired!

THERAPIST: OK. Expand on that for me. Tell me more about being sick and tired.

RUTH: Well, it's this school thing. I am going to finish. I know I'll succeed. It's just getting past all the mess that goes along with it! Sometimes it's the smallest things that get to me.

THERAPIST: Give me an example.

RUTH: Well, the other day I was in the college bookstore and an older White lady said to me, "You are such an articulate colored woman." For one, I thought I was hearing things, and for another thing, can't I speak like I have some sense and be Black? I was about two seconds from telling her off!

THERAPIST: I'm glad you curbed that impulse. What stopped you?

RUTH: I knew she didn't know better. She was old and had probably only seen someone like me on TV. There just aren't too many of us around the college, and I get tired of it sometimes.

THERAPIST: What feelings were stirring up inside of you after she made her comment?

RUTH: I mostly felt frustrated and sad. I can't say I was angry. A part of me could have cried because it just doesn't make sense that this old woman doesn't know that her comment was offensive. She didn't even know that we are called African American now . . . huh, she could have at least said Black.

THERAPIST: There's some more in there Ruth. It's your session, and now is a good time to let some of those feelings out. Remember how we talked about taking out the trash . . . let's get rid of some of those toxins.

RUTH: I just get tired of the people at the college sometimes. I want to be there and I will get my degree, but it would be nice to see more people that look like me. But no, I just get to be the poster child for all things Black. When we talk about diversity or multicultural issues in class . . . all the eyes roll toward me. Can't they see that they have some culture too! I don't get it. Then there's the conversations about family dynamics and poverty . . . well, I usually sit there feeling the heat. I think they see me as the older Black woman who was probably on welfare, crack, and has a different daddy for each of her kids . . . but somehow I made good and turned my life around, that I am the exception. It's like they think they know me because they have seen people that look like me.

THERAPIST: Do you really think that's what they think of you? And does it matter?

RUTH [*Heavy sigh*]: No. Who knows what they think. I don't care what they think. I just want to be able to go to school and do my thing. I don't want it to matter, but sometimes I feel like all I do is fight that stereotype.

THERAPIST: So do you?

RUTH: Do I what?

THERAPIST: Do you fight that image? Do you work to tear down that stereotype?

RUTH: Fight it how? Every time I raise my hand my professor shuts me down. See, in his world slavery has been abolished and racism doesn't exist. They think it's something we should just get over. I try to tell them it's alive and well and I live some aspect of it everyday. If they really hear what I'm saying, then just maybe they have to be more accountable for their own biased views. I know my professor thinks I'm paranoid or hypersensitive when I tell him that we still get followed in stores or that my work seems to be scrutinized more than anyone else's in class. This is my world, so don't minimize my reality! I don't expect them to understand, but don't make it seem like I'm making this all up just to get pity. I don't want it and don't need it.

THERAPIST: When I was in school, I imagined that the next generation wouldn't have to deal with all this bias and judgment. But here we are, and it is still happening. It makes me so sad to hear you saying the same things we said 20 years ago, yet I am elated that you are in the trenches doing this.

RUTH: It's not easy.

THERAPIST: If it were easy, everyone would do it. Stay in your lane. God put you in this situation for a reason. Whenever you feel that heat rise inside of you, take a deep, slow breath, choose your battles, and share your truth. Let people know who you are as an individual. Telling your own story can break down the false images.

RUTH: They don't need to know my business. I don't need to tell them about myself.

THERAPIST: So you let the heat rise inside of you. Does that make you feel good?

RUTH: You know it doesn't or I wouldn't be here. Sometimes I speak up and become the angry Black woman who is sick of the foolishness, and there I go feeding into the stereotype.

THERAPIST: It's important to be aware of how we deliver our message. Sometimes we go right to our victim mode and that makes us defensive, and the anger can rise. It's not effective. That's the behavior that they've seen from us on TV. Don't perpetuate the myth . . . break it! What if you allowed yourself to detach from the victim and then speak, but just from your perspective?

RUTH: You got yours Doc, you don't know what its like.

THERAPIST: I have had to deal with some of what we are talking about, Ruth. It's a tough road. I had to realize that I couldn't do it alone, and you can't either. Going back to school is difficult under any circumstance. And here you are doing all types of things you never imagined yourself doing. Be proud of yourself, tell your story . . . it's powerful! It could be healing for others to hear more about who you really are.

RUTH: I guess I can give it a try. What I've been doing is not really working, and I can't continue to leave class tense and stressed out.

THERAPIST: That's a good attitude. You can also do some mental rehearsal and see yourself speaking more from your heart . . . not from your anger and frustration.

RUTH: OK, I can try that.

THERAPIST: I see a couple of things going on here. You're feeling isolated and alone at the college, and it's a struggle dealing with all the stereotypes. I can understand that. Your job is to consider who you can connect with to help you through this. You may need to step out of your comfort zone and actively seek out other people that are in a similar situation and start a support network. I know your college has an Office of Multicultural Affairs. Go to one of the meetings. There could be someone in another department who is feeling isolated and would like to connect with another student of color. It can be as simple as having coffee and conversation with this person.

RUTH: OK. That's a thought. I might be able to look into that.

🕮 **Process Commentary**   I want to validate Ruth's feelings about being the only African American woman in her program. Her feelings of isolation, loneliness, and frustration are very real. It is helpful to simply allow her to be heard without interrupting the flow of her emotions. My use of self-disclosure may help her feel understood and less isolated. Because I am able to relate to Ruth's situation, it is likely that she will begin to feel it's appropriate and useful to express what she genuinely feels.

Encouragement is essential for Ruth. She doesn't receive a great deal of support and encouragement regarding her endeavors in her everyday life. Therapy is a place where she can be understood, encouraged, and affirmed. Teaching her to affirm and validate herself is a crucial aspect of our work together. She also has a pattern of doing everything on her own and then feeling overwhelmed and isolated. By connecting with the Office of Multicultural Affairs, she will begin to build community and gain more strength and resiliency through her interactions with others.

Final Stages of Therapy

As we enter the final stages of therapy Ruth is well aware that she can create a new story for herself. She knows that playing the victim is unproductive and leads to increased anxiety. No longer is she triggered by the behaviors and attitudes of others. As our time together comes to an end, we discuss the gains she has made through her work in therapy. She feels proud that she is now able to express her views at home and in the classroom without feeling overwhelmed or victimized. She feels stronger in her cultural identity and no longer feels the need to defend herself. Through her work in session, she has developed the habit of checking in with herself, tuning into her body, and doing what is necessary to return to a state of inner calm. She began the practice of writing her frustrations and success stories in her journal. This practice has helped her deal more effectively with frustrations as they arise. Trusting her inner voice and setting clear boundaries are also gains that she has made. Ruth can now say no without being riddled with guilt. She now finds herself more able to express her opinions in class without being emotionally triggered. She has come to the conclusion that people don't have to understand her walk as an African American woman. She can simply meet people where they are and stand in her truth and integrity as a woman of African descent.

Ruth continues to work on issues such as building community, allowing herself to be vulnerable in relationships, and honoring her body as a temple through exercise and healthy nutrition. She has made amazing gains in these areas and continues to use cognitive behavioral strategies to support her continued growth.

As we transition from our weekly sessions, I tell Ruth that she can schedule at any time for maintenance of her change, or to address any major problems that might arise in the future. I thank her for allowing me the honor of sharing this journey with her and tell her that I, too, am changed because of our work together. We say a prayer together, hug, and bid each other peace on our journeys.

Concluding Comments

Ruth showed great courage in staying faithful to her counseling process. This is still a new healing path for the majority of African American women. By taking this step she is validating a new way of wellness for herself and others. She has even given testimony in her new nondenominational church about the many tools God will use for the healing of our spirits.

Through having a safe place to discuss her feelings, she is able to give herself permission to live more authentically. She realizes that her behaviors in life were motivated by fear that she would be misunderstood and judged if she were to express herself. Counseling provided Ruth with the opportunity to explore and claim those things that she has been doing well in her life. She had been so preoccupied with what was going wrong, that she could not recognize all the blessings and positive choices interwoven between the challenges. In therapy, she began to question her old patterns and to validate herself through positive self-talk and increased awareness of behaviors that have been effective for her. She has been able to draw on the strength and resiliency of our ancestors. In discussing the middle passage (the slave trade), Ruth felt proud when she realized that she is the descendant of those who survived.

Once she was able to connect with her spiritual side and say out loud that God is a kind, loving, and supportive God, she began to feel a greater sense of self-worth. She is now able to use her spirituality to affirm that she does not need to be all things to all people. She is realizing that it is natural to express a full range of emotions including tears, anger, disappointment, sadness, and most important, love.

Ruth has begun to move through her life in a more mindful way. She has started to walk in the evening with her husband and is making healthier food choices. Her self-image has improved, and she is now living a more authentic life. She understands that life is a journey and she will encounter challenges along the way, but because of the time and effort she has devoted to her therapy, she now has a vast array of tools to cope effectively with whatever obstacles life brings her way.

Ruth as a Latina: An Integrative, Culturally Grounded Perspective

by Andrés J. Consoli, PhD, and Robert C. Chope, PhD

Introduction

In this contribution we offer an integrative, culturally grounded perspective on Ruth as a Latina. We base our contribution on the following counseling principles:

1. Every counseling encounter is a cross-cultural one, typically across multiple dimensions, and requires both cultural competence and cultural humility.
2. The therapeutic alliance is central to effective counseling.
3. As treatment progresses, so does the alliance, from an empathic and respectful bond to a secure base for deliberate risk taking.
4. Counseling needs to be tailored to fit clients' strengths and difficulties.
5. Counseling is best aimed at enlisting clients' self-healing capacities.
6. Counseling should transcend *traditional* approaches and focus on the main forces of change: motivation, learning, meaning-making, and facilitative context.

Throughout this discussion we give our combined input on aspects of Ruth's therapy. However, Ruth's therapy sessions are conducted by a single therapist, a bilingual Latino professional who is an immigrant from a country other than the one Ruth's parents came from.

Initial Interview and Assessment of Ruth

Ruth is a Latina born in the United States to immigrant parents who impressed upon her the importance of "fitting in" the "American culture" to avoid experiencing the segregation they once experienced themselves in the predominantly Caucasian community in which they live.[1] Ruth reports that she met John, a Caucasian, at a church function, and he seemed to be a "shoe in" based on what her parents had wanted for her. She describes John as a color-blind individual when it comes to racial and ethnic differences and one who embraces traditional values concerning gender roles. She credits her recent college courses with awakening in her an interest in her Latina roots.

⚙ **Initial Interview**   We start the session by discussing confidentiality and its limitations. We then acknowledge the information we have about Ruth already and encourage her to discuss what is going on in her life that has prompted her to seek counseling. We honor her risk taking in seeking counseling, and we inquire about how we can best be of help. We foster her inquisitiveness and cultural wonderings. We acknowledge her self-abnegation and dedication to her family. We are attentive to her ambivalence about embarking on the counseling experience, and we understand the stigma she has previously associated with counseling. We are particularly attentive to the potential dissonance between her view of self as "living for others" and seeking counseling for "herself."

Throughout the initial interview we seek to enact collaboration and convey a message of appreciation for her perspectives on the matters at hand. We welcome the questions she raised in her autobiography and encourage her to frame such questions as hypotheses that we can work on in a collaborative way. The following exchange takes place near the end of the first session.

THERAPIST: Ruth, we have a few minutes left in our session, and I want to check in with you and ask what it has been like for you to be in counseling today?

RUTH: I didn't know I had so much to say! I guess you got it all out of me. You are good!

THERAPIST: I thank you for the compliment. I wonder about other explanations you may have about how much you had to say.

RUTH: You seem very interested in me. I am not used to this kind of attention.

THERAPIST: Say more about what it was like for you to be here today and receive complete attention.

RUTH: That's it! You are persistent. You don't let me off the hook easily.

THERAPIST: Ruth, you are very perceptive. Now if I were not persistent, what would happen? [*And after exploring this a bit further.*] In closing, I sense your hesitations about coming to counseling, where are you now with respect to pursuing counseling?

RUTH: Glad you asked. It is hard for me to commit to something.

We notice ourselves feeling pulled to make a decision for her, and we refrain from that. We ask Ruth what she needs to make this decision. She commits to a next appointment and asks for a reminder call the night before.

⚘ **Assessment**   We ask Ruth to complete a life history questionnaire covering presenting complaints; view of self with respect to strengths and shortcomings; goals and expectations for counseling; family, cultural, educational, employment, and medical history; prior counseling experiences; and current expectations for counseling. We organize the information from the clinical interview into a *DSM-IV-TR* multiaxial assessment and supplement it with two additional dimensions. The first dimension involves paying close attention to our reactions while working with Ruth: What do we feel inclined to do when we are in her presence? To what extent might this reflect how others could feel in her presence? The second dimension consists of a systematic identification of her personal strengths and accomplishments.

Ruth's assessment indicates a "dysthymic disorder," a "generalized anxiety disorder," and a "binge eating disorder" based on long-standing, chronic dissatisfaction with herself coupled with worries or apprehensive expectations and maladaptive coping strategies. We do not have a clear sense of an Axis II diagnosis and are cautious about it due to the danger of pathologizing what are otherwise traits congruent with traditional gender expectations. As we are not medically trained, we record nothing on Axis III unless as self-report or as a quote from Ruth's personal physician. She presents several psychosocial challenges that, while noted in Axis IV here, must be listed on Axis I should they become the principal focus of clinical attention: phase of life problems; parent-child and partner relational problems; problems on occupation and identity; and religious or spiritual problems. Finally, we record a current GAF of 55 (moderate symptoms and difficulties) in Axis V, and 65 for the past year. The GAF difference indicates a worsening of symptoms and difficulties, creates a sense of urgency for the work, and underscores the need for therapy.

Following the *DSM-IV-TR* cultural formulation we indicate that Ruth self-describes as "Latina" and possesses moderate Spanish speaking capacity. She quotes her mother describing Ruth's problems as *"nervios"* and *"ataques de nervios."* She has not used traditional healers or *curanderos/as,* and lives in a predominantly Caucasian community.

In conceptualizing Ruth's strengths and difficulties we consider the assimilation strategy emphasized by her parents as one of survival but also one that helps us understand Ruth's self-perception as "weird," especially in a predominantly Caucasian community, and Ruth's feelings of anxiety, depression, guilt, and shame. Ruth's own cultural identity development and family scripts help us understand her personal struggles and some aspects of her present disputes with her daughter, who is close to Ruth's age when she married and became a mother. In short, we wonder *with* Ruth about how cultural dimensions can help us understand her circumstances while providing a platform for change. Based on our assessment of Ruth, we collaboratively establish the beginning goals of treatment.

Goals of Therapy

We work with Ruth in discerning the meaning of the assessment results. We establish immediate goals addressing urgent matters, such as safety and stabilization, followed by short- and long-term goals for counseling. We explore Ruth's time availability, commitment level, readiness for counseling, and resources to accomplish the treatment goals. We arrive at a mutually agreed-upon counseling contract for 20 sessions, once a week.

We are particularly mindful of Ruth's suicidality in light of her statement, "I worry about death—about my dying—a lot," and her diagnoses, and we address this straightforwardly with her. Two important goals of therapy are symptom reduction and creating a strong support network that affirms and sustains her personal and career aspirations.

Key Issues and Themes

We anticipate Ruth may have some significant difficulties in following through with counseling, and that she may be hesitant, in much the same way as she has been with her exercise routine and job offer. An area of concern pertains to her perception of the lack of support from her spouse with respect to possible changes in her. Another concern is the anticipated catastrophic response she thinks she would receive from her father if he were to learn about her being in counseling.

We pay particular attention to her tendency to treat us in the therapeutic relationship in much the same way that she is accustomed to being in her other relationships. She wants us to be the engine that drives the therapy and set the goals and expectations for it: "Tell me what I have to do and push me to do it." She may express worries that she is not a good enough client. She is especially concerned that her therapy will become "boring and stale," much as she thinks of her life. From time to time she may look after us, perhaps even complimenting us regularly.

In light of her nascent cultural interest, Ruth is attentive to our degree of comfort when discussing cultural matters so as to discern the safety of such explorations. Our knowledgeable, receptive, respectful, and inviting stance toward cultural matters plays a significant role in establishing a solid relationship, as does our office décor.

We entertain three cultural constructs with Ruth, though we would not be imposing these onto her. The first one pertains to her gender role and has been termed *"marianismo"* in the Latina literature. *Marianismo* is a female gender socialization process modeled after the Virgin Mary. Women are expected to be selfless, self-sacrificing, nurturing, pious, and spiritually stronger than men while living under the 10 commandments of *The María Paradox*.[2] The second one captures her devotion to her family and has been termed *"familismo,"* where Ruth embraces a collectivistic worldview and is willing to endure sacrifices for the sake of her immediate and extended family.

The third cultural construct addresses the importance of fostering Ruth's *confianza* in us, a multilayer concept that implies confidence, trust, security, intimacy and familiarity, and facilitates treatment adherence. We remain attentive to our gender differences. We ask Ruth about her degree of comfort in working with us and are watchful about our limited understanding of what it is like to be a Latina woman. We establish peer consultation with a female Latina colleague when we determine this is needed.

In light of her anxiety and depressive features as well as a possible eating disorder, we wonder with Ruth whether perfectionism, intolerance of uncertainty, and overcontrolling play a role in her struggles with initiative and lack of satisfaction with realized outcomes, resulting in feelings of inadequacy and guilt. It becomes apparent that Ruth's worries are expressed in fears of catastrophic failures lurking around every developmental milestone despite having accomplished much in life already, which she alternatively acknowledges, "I've been the superwoman," or minimizes by saying, "I haven't done enough." We encourage her to explore unrealistic expectations she may have about her participation and progress in therapy and about us as her therapist.

Therapeutic Process and Techniques

We believe that our therapeutic endeavor is directly influenced by Ruth's ongoing assessment and by the therapy goals that we collaboratively develop. This includes addressing the "greatest catalyst" triggering her consultation: "her physical symptoms and her anxiety." We want to get a sense of the working alliance early in therapy because this is among the best predictors of treatment adherence. Because of our commitment to strengthening the therapeutic relationship, we ask Ruth to complete the client version of the Working Alliance Inventory (WAI) by the third session.[3] We also complete the therapist version of this instrument. We use the results to monitor and work on the alliance over time, administering the WAI at regular intervals.

We continue to monitor Ruth's mood difficulties through repeated usage of the Beck Depression Inventory FastScreen,[4] paying close attention to her responses to items 2 (hope) and 7 (suicidality), and Ruth's worrying through the Worry Questionnaire.[5] We work with Ruth on her mood and anxiety difficulties. She will challenge her debilitating moods and anxiety-inducing, catastrophic cognitions. Through her therapy we anticipate that Ruth will construct an alternative story, one that is life affirming, to replace the problem-saturated story she tells herself over and over. We recognize the formative nature of her upbringing, and we believe that Ruth's current circumstances may shed equal light on her difficulties in finding joy in her life today. In our sessions, we invite Ruth to reflect upon what she is doing in her daily life that leads her to conclude that she has a "boring and stale" life.

> RUTH: If I speak up, I am afraid people will think I'm weird, I am afraid of saying the wrong thing, of getting dizzy, or losing control. . . . It is easier if I don't say anything.
>
> THERAPIST: And then what happens?
>
> RUTH: Same all, same all, I think of my parents telling me not to stick out, to fit in but then I feel guilty for not saying anything or for having said something and now what people are going to think of me.
>
> THERAPIST: And then?
>
> RUTH: Back to boring and stale . . . it is safer that way. But then I feel bad about myself; I turn to food and feel guilty for overeating.
>
> THERAPIST: Ruth, you are indeed in a difficult position, with plenty of reasons for continuing the way you are, a budding desire for things to be different, yet a nagging fear of what may happen if you do act differently. At the same time, I am struck by the fact that you are here, in counseling, with me, and you have taken much risk in looking at yourself, your values, and your actions. How do you reconcile it all?
>
> RUTH: ¡La que no arriesga no gana! [*The one who doesn't take risks doesn't win.*]
>
> THERAPIST: Ruth, I am delighted you are even taking the risk of using your Spanish. How does this *dicho* [saying] capture your work in counseling?
>
> RUTH: I know I have to if I am to turn things around. I feel safe here.
>
> THERAPIST: I am curious as to how you and I have made it safe here for you to explore being different.
>
> RUTH: I don't feel judged by you.
>
> THERAPIST: And that's from my end. What is it that you contribute?
>
> RUTH: Honesty . . . and that frees me. I don't feel the need to be perfect here. I just am.

THERAPIST: I am wondering about ways in which you are already doing some of this elsewhere.

RUTH: Well, I was talking to John the other day as we discussed . . .

As our alliance becomes stronger we work with Ruth on curtailing avoidance strategies and co-creating relevant exposure exercises with response prevention within the session and eventually outside the session. Whenever Ruth has a tendency toward avoiding a life situation, we suggest that she ask herself this question: "Am I better off avoiding this challenge, or would it be better for me to take a different action?"

We explore with Ruth her relationship to her body, exercise, and food. She might think more about the range of activities that give her pleasure and bring joy into her life. This would include inviting Ruth to talk about the quality of her sexual life, even though such a conversation may be somewhat awkward initially. With our gender differences, we appreciate that it may take some time for Ruth to be more open with us. We discuss her exercise and relaxation repertoire, the role that food plays in her life, and the familial and cultural scripts that are shaping her views of self and others. We might suggest a referral to a dietician and a personal trainer to get her going on a relevant exercise routine. However, we would make this recommendation at a time when we think there is a good chance that she would be open to considering these referrals.

We entertain the possibility of internalized oppression, self-hating ways of relating to self born out of assimilative processes with respect to her "Latina roots" and are watchful of such matters in relation to her body image and expectations of self. We maintain a stance that is not neutral about these matters. Our stance is characterized by a broad latitude of acceptance. It may turn out that our work with Ruth centers on her accepting herself and learning to love herself in spite of her imperfections. We also ask her to question what she learned about the standards of beauty while encouraging her to watch relevant movies such as *Real Women Have Curves*.

We discuss with Ruth the importance of support groups that scaffold her explorations and expansive values. This may be accomplished by participating in a relevant book club, taking further courses that could pertain to understanding more about ethnic identity, or volunteering at a civic or social service organization. The latter is an important alternative considering her career aspirations and the need to build her resume and letters of reference.

Overall, we balance the treatment focus between symptoms and cultural and relational themes. We enlist Ruth in seeking cultural expressions capturing her strengths and dilemmas. She finds herself spending increasing amounts of time talking with her parents, siblings, and even her children about their ethnic roots. These novel explorations are captured in a cultural genogram that she constructs over time and with the help of her parents. She volunteers further *dichos* and song lyrics that support her explorations on gender and personal realizations even when such explorations challenge prior held values. While initially John appeared somewhat puzzled by her cultural interests, She has enticed John on his own cultural explorations, which have made for some lively discussions during family gatherings. She rejoices in the feelings of excitement and curiosity she and her family are experiencing.

Twenty sessions later, Ruth's counseling is well on the way and her symptoms have decreased. She is ready to involve other people in treatment such as her husband or the daughter with whom she is having difficulties. It is also an opportune time to explore her career aspirations more directly through a new counseling contract. We turn to these aspirations now.

Ruth, as a newcomer to the job market needs all the support she can muster, and her counselor can help with that. She wants to be recognized for who she is and for who she might become without alienating her family. At the same time, she will need the support or, at the very least, the tacit acceptance of her family in this undertaking. It may be appropriate to enlist her family and extended family members to create the necessary support system that will nurture her aspirations. However, this may prove to be a challenge because neither Ruth's husband nor her father is likely to encourage her intention to seek a career outside of the home. Bringing other family members into the process increases the chances for support while gaining allies to her career aspirations. Extended family members can offer some practical advice, which we would assist her in thinking about so that she could determine if she wanted to follow the advice she is getting.

Ruth's siblings can offer a wealth of emotional support and human resources. And in looking for work, apprenticeships, volunteering, or part-time projects, family members can be used to generate ideas. In short, we want to work with Ruth in establishing, maintaining, and fostering a strong network. She can let everyone in her family address book know what kind of work she is looking for by sending out a broadcast letter. She is likely to find that these human connections will be a most important asset in her job search.

We assist Ruth in honing in on her interests, skills, and talents. She may not be as interested or committed as she once was with respect to becoming an elementary school teacher, and this may account for her "dragging her feet" at pursuing it. Therefore, some exploration of career interests may be appropriate. Ruth has accrued both specific and transferable skills, and we will engage her in figuring out what these are. She would need to work on a resume and cover letters based on her talents. This is an area in which we would offer suggestions and feedback on her actions.

In light of Ruth's limited work experience outside the home, she might try several part-time positions for a while, creating a portfolio career path. We help Ruth stay focused and flexible, regularly reviewing her decisions while treating goals as hypotheses. We prepare her for job interviews while emphasizing creativity, as creative questioning has become a significant part of the job search process. She may benefit from reading books like *How Would You Move Mt. Fuji?*[6] We work with Ruth in maintaining vision, flexibility, and adaptability along with realistic expectations. We anticipate that this will be a challenging aspect for her in light of her perfectionism and fear of failure.

Concluding Comments

As goals are achieved, we discuss the transition in the therapeutic relationship. We eschew the finality of the word "termination" and embrace the concept of "transition." We remain open to seeing Ruth for future counseling sessions if she determines this would be in her best interests. The scientific literature highlights the likelihood of lapses and relapses among people living with anxiety, depression, eating difficulties, ethnic identity exploration, and career indecision. In light of this, we encourage a follow-up appointment with Ruth 6 months after her final session.

Ruth as an Asian American: A Multicultural, Integrative Perspective

by Alvin N. Alvarez, PhD, and Grace A. Chen, PhD

Introduction

Recognizing the diversity within the Asian American community is the first step in working with Ruth as an Asian American. One of the fastest growing racial groups, the Asian American community encompasses 43 distinct ethnic groups (Thai, Chinese, Vietnamese, Filipino, Pakistani, and so forth). Despite presumptions of their academic and financial success, certain Asian ethnic groups have the lowest levels of academic achievement and highest levels of poverty in the country. Although large-scale Asian immigration began with the Chinese in the mid-1800s, currently 69% of Asian Americans are foreign born, and 76% of all Asian Americans arrived after 1980, according to the 2000 U.S. Census.[7] Linguistically, 79% of Asian Americans speak a language other than English at home. Working with a refugee from Laos with limited academic and socioeconomic resources is significantly different from working with a third-generation Japanese American who comes to counseling with a greater likelihood of both economic resources and a familiarity with Western culture. Consequently, recognizing Ruth as an Asian American should merely be a catalyst for an additional assessment of her ethnicity, generational status, socioeconomic status, acculturation level, and linguistic fluency. For the purposes of this case, we will assume that Ruth is a Chinese American immigrant, who arrived when she was 10, is fluent in English, has college-educated parents, and comes from a middle-class background.

Our work with Ruth as an Asian American is grounded in a number of fundamental tenets of multicultural counseling. Namely, we assume the following: (a) the therapist's and the client's cultural backgrounds shape their expectations of the process and outcome of counseling; (b) the effectiveness of counseling is directly related to the therapist's awareness and knowledge of Asian Americans and her or his ability to work with the client in a culturally congruent manner; (c) counseling occurs within a larger sociocultural and sociopolitical context; and (d) interventions may occur at the level of the individual, group, or system.

Assessment of Therapist

A central tenet of multicultural counseling holds that cultural competence is reflected in the therapist's awareness, knowledge, and skills with Asian Americans.

It is critical for therapists to receive training on counseling Asian Americans as well as to reflect on their limitations and biases in working with Asian Americans *prior* to delivering services. In this particular case, we believe that the therapist will need to evaluate his or her knowledge of Chinese Americans and their history in the United States, their cultural values, expectations about help-seeking, conceptualization of psychological well-being, family and gender roles, and communication patterns. Moreover, the therapist will need to assess her or his own socialization experiences around Chinese Americans and consider how that shapes the therapist's expectations and assumptions of such clients. It is imperative for therapists to engage in a candid assessment of their own comfort with and ability to raise issues of race and culture in a counseling session. We believe that the ability to address and name the cultural dimensions in a client's life is a significant contributor to the success of multicultural counseling. Finally, it is also our belief that this self-reflection on the part of the therapist should occur regardless of whether the dyads are of the same race and ethnicity or not. In the current case, Grace Chen, who is second-generation Chinese American, will be working with Ruth. Although this decision was based on increasing the racial, ethnic, and gender match between therapist and client, self-assessment is still essential because the meaning of these social identities for Grace and Ruth may differ significantly.

Assessment of Ruth

Our assessment of Ruth is a formative and informal assessment based on the information currently available and subject to revision as counseling proceeds. We believe that an informal assessment of Ruth's presenting concerns is valuable for (a) organizing the information that has been obtained, (b) developing a coherent, yet tentative conceptualization of her presenting issues, (c) prioritizing and developing therapeutic goals, and (d) implementing relevant interventions. Nevertheless, we are reluctant to develop a more formalized diagnostic assessment, such as the *DSM-IV-TR,* unless we were required to do so in compliance with institutional or financial expectations. Consistent with multicultural counseling principles, our hesitance in this area stems from our awareness of the sociopolitical context and stigma associated with diagnostic labels and their potential effects on the therapeutic relationship.

With this in mind, our informal assessment of Ruth's presenting concerns is centered on the following areas: (a) depression symptoms: suicidal ideation, melancholic mood, binge eating; (b) anxiety symptoms: physical tension, obsessive worrying, insomnia; (c) phase of life issues: career exploration and change, changing role in the family; and (d) multicultural considerations: cultural influences and pressures, racial and gender stereotypes, and exploring religious identity.

Key Issues

From a multicultural counseling perspective, distinctions between race and ethnicity need to be acknowledged in order to work effectively with Ruth. The racial category of Asian Americans is a sociopolitical construct historically rooted in a system created to exclude "non-White" individuals from many privileges and rights in the United States. Racial stereotypes, such as the model minority, are often reflected in media portrayals of Asian Americans. Thus, Ruth's racial identity is a psychological construct based on how she experiences racial categorization, which is imposed on her by American society. However, one's ethnic background is usually associated with a particular culture's values, beliefs, traditions, and language. For Ruth, her ethnic identity is based on how she views herself in relation to her Chinese culture. Although racial and ethnic identities are interconnected, recognizing the differences between the two is important in understanding Ruth as an Asian American of Chinese descent. Therapists who focus only on ethnicity or only on race may overlook a significant aspect of identity when they do not consider how both race and ethnicity affect Asian Americans.

It is important also to consider where spirituality fits in Ruth's self-identity as her religious confusion seems to be a significant piece of her presenting concern. Ruth has multiple social identities—being Chinese American, a woman, a spiritual person, and an Asian American. Working with Ruth from a multicultural perspective means the therapist needs to assess the saliency of Ruth's various social identities to understand what aspects of her self-identity have meaning for her and, equally important, which social identities are not salient for her.

Another key issue to consider is how Ruth's distress manifests itself in her physical and mental health. A common response to difficulty or lack of opportunity to express emotions, particularly among Asian Americans, is for individuals to convert their anxiety and depression into bodily symptoms. Because Ruth seems to have little social support, it is important to be aware that her physical health is also negatively affected by her current concerns.

Goals of Therapy

Consistent with the collaborative stance inherent in multicultural counseling, as her therapist, I (Grace Chen) work *with* Ruth in identifying and prioritizing the goals of counseling. To initiate the process, I focus on the following immediate goals: (a) establishing a safe, trusting therapeutic relationship with Ruth; (b) providing psychoeducation about counseling, given Ruth's limited experience with counseling and the potential cultural stigma associated with counseling; and (c) conducting a suicide assessment, given Ruth's comments about death.

In the near term, Ruth and I work on symptom reduction, with anxiety as a major presenting concern. In addition to working toward symptom relief, I focus on helping Ruth understand her presenting concerns within a cultural context. Specifically, I work with her in obtaining insight into how the cultural intersections of ethnicity, race, gender, and religion influence (a) her identity as a Chinese American woman, (b) her familial obligations and relationships, (c) her expectations of academic and career achievement, and (d) her body image and sexuality. In the long term, I work on empowering Ruth with the ability to recognize, deconstruct, and determine the cultural dimensions of her identity. Thus, I work toward developing Ruth's self-affirming racial, ethnic, gender, and religious identities and her ability to respect and balance her needs as an individual with the needs of the group (in this case, parents, partner, and children).

Therapeutic Process and Techniques
BEGINNING PHASE

🕮 **Psychoeducation About Counseling**   In the beginning phase of counseling, it is critical to address Ruth's expectations of counseling. Multicultural counseling research has consistently demonstrated that high rates of premature termination are a risk for Asian Americans in counseling. Cultural stigmas—such as "counseling is for crazy people"—reflect both attitudes toward mental health and toward therapists. Cultural expectations about self-disclosure and saving face for oneself and one's family are also potentially limiting factors. An example is the message, "You don't talk about personal problems with outsiders." When we take into consideration matters such as cultural prohibitions, Ruth's own expectations of counseling, her limited experience with counseling, and the referral by her physician, it is essential that Ruth and I explore her commitment and intrinsic motivation to stay in counseling. Until her intrinsic motivation to remain in counseling increases, the potential for premature termination will remain, and it may be difficult to address therapeutic issues in depth. During our initial session I explicitly address Ruth's expectations about counseling and our respective roles in the therapeutic endeavor.

THERAPIST: Ruth, I know you mentioned that you've been to a counselor a few times as part of a class. But I'm wondering what it's like for you to come on your own to talk with me?

RUTH: Well, to be honest, it's kind'a strange, and I always thought only crazy people came in here. Sorry about that!

THERAPIST: No need to apologize. I think a lot of people think that, particularly if they are not familiar with the counseling field.

RUTH: Oh, absolutely! If my father found out I were here, he would flip out.

THERAPIST: What do you think is behind all of that?

RUTH: Well, you're not supposed to be talking about your business with a stranger. It's just such a shameful thing. Plus to talk to a therapist, well you gotta be really crazy if you need to do that.

THERAPIST: So, you're crossing a lot of lines by coming in here?

RUTH: Yeah, I never thought of it that way. But I guess that's why I'm kind'a nervous about all of this.

THERAPIST: Well, I guess I wanted us to talk about it directly because I think it's important to give you credit for taking such a big step that is outside of your comfort zone.

RUTH: Thanks, I appreciate that. I was wondering if you thought I was nuts or something.

THERAPIST: No, I don't think you're nuts at all. From what I can see, the things that are happening in your life and your reaction to them are pretty normal.

RUTH: Really?

THERAPIST: Absolutely. But since you're fairly new to counseling, I'm wondering if it would be helpful for us to talk more about who comes to counseling, what they do here, what I do in all of this, and how this all works.

RUTH: That sounds good!

THERAPIST: So, let's start with any questions you might have about all of this. What do you want to know?

🕮 **Acculturation and Enculturation**   A central issue from a multicultural perspective involves the degree to which Ruth identifies with her social identities—factors including ethnicity, race, gender, and religion. Multicultural counseling is based on the premise that culture, broadly defined, influences how clients view counseling and the help-seeking process. Culture also influences notions of psychological well-being, expectations of oneself and the counselor, expectations of the process and outcome of counseling, as well as symptom manifestation. Yet culturally competent counselors also recognize the heterogeneity in how individuals identify with their various cultures. In other words, the psychological salience of an individual's culture and the degree to which that individual identifies with that culture, varies from one person to another. For instance, although Ruth is biologically Chinese American, she may not identify with being Chinese, and her cultural worldview and identity may be more aligned with White Americans. Similarly, although Ruth's religious identity has been salient for her throughout most of her life, her relatively recent ambivalence about her beliefs suggests that her identification with her religion may be shifting. Hence, I incorporate questions about race, ethnicity, religion, and gender in our initial meetings to better understand Ruth's cultural frames of reference.

THERAPIST: I noticed that your parents emigrated here from Hong Kong.

RUTH: Yes, we came here when I was little—around 10 or so.

THERAPIST: What was that like for you? Growing up here in the states in a Chinese family?

RUTH: Well, you know my dad was a Baptist minister. So, he was pretty strict. You know, the traditional Chinese dad . . . didn't say much but you knew he expected certain things from you.

THERAPIST: You used the phrase "traditional Chinese dad." Even though I might have a sense of what you're getting at, I'm wondering if you could tell me what that means for you.

RUTH: Hmm. My parents have always been proud to be Chinese, and they expected us to be the same . . . so, we had to know how to speak Cantonese, how to read and write in Chinese, and we were expected to celebrate Chinese holidays.

THERAPIST: So, being Chinese is important to your parents.

RUTH: Oh yeah. Big time.

THERAPIST: Well, how about for you? How important is being Chinese to you?

RUTH: As a kid, I really hated being Chinese. Everyone doing the "ching-chong chinamen" song and pulling their eyes when I walked by! Kids made fun of the food I brought for lunch. I hated standing out, and I just wanted to be normal. You know what I mean? I guess I wanted to be like the White kids. But when I got older, I realized that there's a lot about me that's pretty Chinese and it isn't all bad.

Recognizing the saliency of Ruth's ethnic identity early in the counseling process, I continue to explore the cultural dimensions of Ruth's concerns.

🌿 **Therapist Disclosure** Because of the ethnic, racial, and gender match between Ruth and me, I determine that my self-disclosure about my experiences as a Chinese American woman is likely to be a powerful intervention. In seeking to define her identity, Ruth may not have any relationships with other Chinese American or Asian American women that would allow her to talk about such shared experiences. Moreover, depending on the region, it may be quite challenging to find other Chinese American women or a venue where such discussions could take place. I might well serve as an initial model for what it means to be a "Chinese American woman." I think that appropriate and timely self-disclosure can be quite powerful to deepen the therapeutic relationship. By acknowledging both our similarities and differences I hope to create a therapeutic alliance that Ruth can use in better understanding her struggles.

THERAPIST: Ruth, we talked a lot about being Chinese and being a Chinese American woman.

RUTH: Yeah, we sure have.

THERAPIST: And one of the things that strikes me is that being Chinese and being women are things we both share.

RUTH: I've thought about that too. I feel like you understand me better because we're the same.

THERAPIST: Well, I figured you might feel more comfortable talking about being a Chinese American woman around me. That's to be expected. Of course, even though we have similar backgrounds, I do want to be careful to avoid assuming that I know exactly how you feel as a Chinese American woman because we've had different life experiences. It's important that we continue talking openly about your experience as a Chinese American woman.

Once I clarify that I respect Ruth's unique experiences as a Chinese American woman, then it seems more appropriate for me to self-disclose my own experiences as a Chinese American woman. For instance, Ruth talked about having some apprehension of how she'll be perceived as a teacher as an Asian American woman. She is afraid that students may expect her to be a pushover as a "passive Asian female," which actually reflects her fear that she fulfills that stereotype. I can validate Ruth's fear and share with her that I also have had to deal with people stereotyping me as a "passive Asian female."

MIDDLE PHASE

🌀 **Symptom Reduction**   In response to Ruth's expressed hope for the therapist to "tell her what to do," I explain to Ruth that there is no "right" way for her to live life. At the same time, it is important to address Ruth's expectation that counseling will give her concrete suggestions. Thus, I begin the process of symptom reduction to provide Ruth with psychological relief as well as a tangible outcome from coming to counseling. This is consistent with what scholars have referred to as the concept of "gift-giving" in multicultural counseling. The "gift" in this case may involve providing Ruth with an understanding of anxiety, recognizing her symptoms and triggers, as well as expanding her coping repertoire with deep breathing exercises, meditative practices, muscle-relaxation techniques, distraction exercises, and thought-stopping techniques. Insofar as Ruth experiences positive outcomes from such gifts, it is more likely that she will remain committed to counseling. Additionally, it is important for the therapeutic relationship that Ruth feels that I am responding to her direct requests for help. Through discussions about how counseling involves various techniques, Ruth understands that utilizing concrete techniques are only part of how she can use counseling.

🌀 **Cultural Analysis**   After engaging Ruth's commitment to counseling, one focus of the middle phase of counseling involves a cultural analysis of her presenting concerns. In contrast to the individual and intrapsychic focus of traditional Western psychotherapy, multicultural counseling is based on the belief that it is facilitative for clients to recognize the role of culture and larger systems of oppression in their lives. I strive to shift Ruth's understanding and attributions of her presenting concerns from a purely intrapsychic and self-blaming focus to an understanding of her presenting concerns within a cultural context. For instance, it is important for me to help Ruth recognize that her inability to define who she is apart from her roles of daughter, wife, and mother is normative given traditional Chinese gender roles based on patriarchy and sexism. Ruth and I discuss the development of her identity as a collective rather than a strictly individualistic process. I will work with Ruth to recognize that her lack of a self-determined identity is culturally influenced rather than a reflection of a deficiency on her part.

> THERAPIST: Ruth, you've talked about being a daughter, a wife, and a mother. It makes me wonder what your family taught you about what women were supposed to do in their lives.
>
> RUTH: Well, my mom didn't work, and she mostly just looked after us kids.
>
> THERAPIST: So, that seems pretty traditional to me.
>
> RUTH: I guess so.
>
> THERAPIST: Did you know any other Chinese women who had careers or went to college?
>
> RUTH: Well, in my mom's generation, no way! But some of my friends went to college, but they were still expected to raise families and watch over the kids after college.

THERAPIST: What's the underlying message for women in your family?

RUTH: I guess that your family and being a mom is number one.

THERAPIST: It doesn't seem like you've had much support or encouragement to be anyone other than a mom or a wife.

RUTH: Exactly. Even John doesn't like all these courses I've been taking.

THERAPIST: And how is that for you?

RUTH: Well, I know he makes sense about how important it is to take care of the kids. But sometimes I just get really upset because it feels like it's always about him and the kids. What about me?

Discussing cultural influences in Ruth's life provides a better understanding of her presenting concerns in that Ruth feels torn between two cultures that sometimes have competing values. For instance, for this case, we assume her husband is a Chinese immigrant from Hong Kong who is more traditional. He does not want Ruth to work because he's concerned about how he would look as a husband and father who is expected to provide for the family. If Ruth starts working, John fears that others will think it is because he is not able to support his family. Consequently, he would "lose face" in the community. Ruth understands his fear but doesn't know if that is enough reason for her to give up her dream to teach. She struggles with balancing her own needs with the cultural expectations her husband has for their family. I acknowledge her dilemma by sharing with Ruth that balancing cultural values is a common struggle for Asian Americans. Fulfilling her own needs is a mainstream American value that is strongly encouraged, whereas "saving face" and focusing on the family is an important Chinese cultural value.

✥ Emotional Expression   As the prior scene suggests, the middle phase of counseling may elicit a great deal of anger and frustration from Ruth as she awakens to the effects of gender and cultural socialization on her life. In racial identity terms, this dissonance-inducing period will be a time of confusion, anger, and resentment. Therefore, I work to provide a space and a relationship where Ruth's anger and resentment can be expressed, normalized, and validated. In a family where gender roles and a cultural system devalue self-assertion and the expression of negative emotions from women, counseling becomes a rare opportunity for Ruth to express herself without judgment.

LATER PHASE Throughout counseling, my interventions are aimed at helping Ruth feel more empowered to make decisions for herself. To continue this process, I focus on enhancing Ruth's social support system by exploring venues—including support groups, cultural groups, and student organizations—as a way for Ruth to meet with other Asian American women or women of color. Similarly, bibliotherapy in areas such as women's studies or Asian American literature may further expose Ruth to the struggles that she shares with other women. In particular, the cultural and gender dimensions of body image will be explored in conjunction with a referral to a nutritionist. Additionally, I encourage Ruth to discuss with her pastor and other members of her church how gender, race, and ethnicity may be integrated into her religious views. Career counseling may also be vital in helping Ruth to recognize the influence of ethnicity, race, and gender on her choices to enter education. I also address the value of being active in the community to (a) solidify Ruth's connections with other Asian American women, (b) provide Ruth with a constructive outlet for addressing racism and sexism, and (c) increase her sense of self-efficacy in dealing with societal oppression.

Concluding Comments

In the later phase of counseling, Ruth's growth is manifested in a personally meaningful definition of herself that integrates her personal identity with that of her social identities as a Chinese American, as a woman, and as a Christian. Ruth also recognizes that this growth is only the beginning of a continually evolving process. Questions remain about her relationships with John and her children and how these relationships may need to be redefined. Similarly, Ruth's relationship with her own parents and the role of religion, gender, and family obligation continue to be relatively unexplored areas, but Ruth faces these concerns with a renewed and self-affirming sense of self. Consequently, in honor of that strength, Ruth and I candidly examine these remaining concerns in her life and her plans to address these issues in the future. We discuss and anticipate times of relapse as well as steps to maintain progress such as follow-up and maintenance sessions, couples counseling, and family therapy.

As illustrated by the case of Ruth, multicultural counseling is complementary to treatment rather than being in competition with other theoretical and treatment approaches. Our emphasis on the cultural dimensions of Ruth's presenting concerns does not diminish the significance of addressing and treating her phase of life concerns or her symptoms of anxiety or depression. We believe that multicultural counseling can be integrated with other theoretical approaches insofar as therapists remain cognizant of the cultural factors that influence their own assumptions and practices, as well as the counseling experience and presenting concerns of their clients. In effect, multicultural counseling challenges therapists to situate themselves and their clients within a cultural context.

An Integrative Therapist's Perspective on Ruth

by John C. Norcross, PhD, ABPP

Introduction

Rivalry among systems of psychotherapy and counseling has a long and undistinguished history, dating back to Freud. In the infancy of the field, therapy systems, like battling siblings, competed for attention and affection. Psychoanalysts, Adlerians, existentialists, behaviorists, to mention a few, have traditionally operated from within their own particular theoretical frameworks, often to the point of being blind to alternative conceptualizations and potentially more effective methods.

Fortunately, the ideological cold war has waned and integration has become a therapeutic mainstay. Virtually all psychotherapists now acknowledge the inadequacies of any one theoretical system and the potential value of others. Indeed, many young students of psychotherapy express surprise when apprised of the ideological cold war of the preceding generations.

Psychotherapy integration is characterized by dissatisfaction with single-school approaches and the concomitant desire to look across and beyond school boundaries to see how clients can benefit from other forms of behavior change. Integration refers not only to combining diverse systems of psychotherapy, but also to blending psychotherapy with medication, spirituality, exercise, social support, sociopolitical advocacy, self-help, and other curative forces. Improving the effectiveness, efficiency, and applicability of psychotherapy is the raison d'etre of integration.

Eclecticism—or the increasingly favored term, integration—is now well established as the most frequent orientation of mental health professionals. And this integrative fervor will apparently persist: A recent panel of psychotherapy experts portended its escalating popularity well into 2010.[8]

Many roads lead to an integrative Rome. The most popular roads or pathways to psychotherapy integration are *common factors, technical eclecticism, theoretical integration,* and *assimilative integration.*[9] My own integrative approach borrows from each of these roads in tailoring or customizing psychotherapy to the unique needs of the individual client, in this case, Ms. Ruth Walton. Different folks need different strokes. We strive to create a new therapy for each client by tailoring it to the particulars of the client according to general principles identified by research and experience. Remember: the integrative mandate is to improve treatment effectiveness, not to entertain the therapist or simply borrow techniques from different schools.

Initial Consultation

We start in our initial contact with Ruth and with our nascent relationship. As every counselor knows and as the research demonstrates,[10] the therapy relationship is pivotal to the ultimate success of psychotherapy. I immediately begin with standard open-ended questions:

THERAPIST: Ms. Walton, what brings you here today?

RUTH: Well, I don't know where to start. There's so much that has been troubling me, especially these anxiety attacks.

We begin with Ms. Walton's story and with respect. I address the client as Ms. Walton until or if she grants me permission to call her Ruth. In return, I request that she address me as "John" if she is so inclined (and not all clients are). We also begin with the client's presentation of her narrative and concerns. My primary task in the early sessions is to cultivate a warm, empathic, and supportive relationship, one in which Ruth will feel understood and prized. Using these Rogerian facilitative conditions increases Ruth's comfort and decreases her ambivalence.

Following about 30 minutes of Ruth's concerns and basic history, I inquire about her history of psychotherapy. Upon learning that this is her first experience and upon hearing the anxiety in her voice about pursuing therapy, I begin to explore and define our relationship.

THERAPIST: How would a psychotherapist be most useful to you? What would he or she do? And not do?

RUTH: Well, I am not sure. I suppose I most want a therapist to tell me what I have to do and push me to do it.

Ruth's answer naturally segues into an exploration of our respective roles and her active collaboration in psychotherapy. She intellectually understands the importance of an active client but, emotionally, feels inadequate to the task.

RUTH: I probably won't make a very good client. I set goals but then cannot move on them.

THERAPIST: As you say that Ruth, I am struck by how often this hour you have put yourself down, saying self-deprecating and defeatist things. Are you aware of that too?

RUTH: Oh, not really. It seems that I cannot help myself. I probably do it automatically.

THERAPIST: What would you say to a therapy agreement that I politely note those times you put yourself down? Would you find that helpful in here?

RUTH: Yes.

THERAPIST: And once you become aware of it, I am certain that you will be able to control it.

Thus, psychotherapy begins with both an explanation and an experience of the way we might proceed. To ensure that therapy proceeds with Ruth's informed consent and active collaboration, we jointly develop three between-session goals. First, Ruth will consider her preferences for a therapist. What would the therapist do and what should he or she avoid? Might Ruth be better served in her first counseling experience with a female therapist? Second, at my request, Ruth agrees to complete a life history inventory to systematically cover the essential ground. We will review her responses next session. And third, Ruth will prioritize her treatment goals. Among the desirable changes, which would she like to focus on at the outset?

All of these goals are designed to jump-start the therapy process and to activate Ruth's collaboration, despite her inexperience and understandable ambivalence about psychotherapy. Instead of only talking to Ruth about empowerment, we design therapy to actualize it. Instead of only offering Ruth support and affirmation, we contract for Ruth to offer it to herself.

Assessment of Ruth

As an integrative therapist, I am less concerned about formal diagnoses and more concerned with understanding Ruth in all of her uniqueness and complexity. At our second session, we review Ruth's completed life history inventory and realize that we desire additional information on the breadth of her psychological suffering. I offer Ruth the opportunity to take a broadband psychological test, typically the Minnesota Multiphasic Personality Inventory or the Millon Clinical Multiaxial Inventory, on the office computer between sessions. She agrees, commenting, "I probably will look like a big mess and a bad client on it." I smile and playfully comment, "There you go again." This leads into a productive 10 minutes in which Ruth observes impressive early gains in catching and reducing her self-depreciation outside of our sessions. I congratulate Ruth on her early success and, in addition, on recognizing the success.

It is difficult to diagnose a person on paper and by long distance, but the severity and chronicity of Ruth's problems exceed those associated with an adjustment disorder. The clinical history, her autobiography, her life history inventory, and the psychological test results converge on a series of diagnosable disorders. On Axis I, these would probably entail "panic disorder without agoraphobia," "dysthymic disorder" (chronic dissatisfaction and mild depression), marital dissatisfaction or partner relational problem, partner-child relational problem (particularly with Jennifer), and a question of binge eating or an atypical eating disorder. But I would be careful not to over diagnose her eating behavior without additional information. On Axis II, Ruth probably suffers from a "dependent personality disorder" (living for others) and, on Axis III, overweight/obesity. Her physician has ruled out medical origins for her anxiety and depression. Ruth is also beset by myriad Axis IV psychosocial problems, including problems with primary support group and occupational problems.

Most clients crave a coherent picture of their disorders and their origins. I offer Ruth a formulation on how her multitudinous problems are interconnected. For example, depression and anxiety are highly correlated, and in turn, both are perpetuated by dependency and unassertiveness. Relational problems and parenting conflicts are part and parcel of this constellation of problems. Following the assessment, I offer some tentative statements about the multiple, intertwined origins of her disorders. Such feedback usefully mentions the formative experiences of childhood (without encouraging pessimism or victimhood), leading to skill deficits and thinking patterns, intersecting genetic vulnerabilities (in cases of family psychiatric history), and culminating in a vicious cycle of life choices and behavioral enactments.

Ruth's autobiography contains several hints of an abusive father and definite reasons to explore the possibility of physical and sexual abuse as a child. Ruth's autobiography does not indicate any abuse, nor does it specifically disavow abuse. I wonder about a history of sexual abuse given her father's punitive punishments and the dynamics of her family of origin. I sensitively inquire about this possibility along with Ruth's own adult sexual functioning in the next session or two as our alliance solidifies.

With all clients, I conduct an assessment of their strengths. Ruth is encouraged to nominate her personal strengths, and I comment on some that she may have missed. She raised four children and is dedicated; she devoted herself to others and is responsible; she broke from a fundamentalist church to pursue her own values and is courageous; she described her life situation and is reasonably aware; she self-described herself as a late-blooming questioner and is open to the process. And she is here, in psychotherapy, despite her father's vehement objections and her husband's skepticism.

But assessment falls short for treatment purposes if we stop with disorders and strengths. It is frequently more important to know the person who has the disorder than the disorder the person has. What about Ruth as a person? What are her treatment goals, her treatment preferences, her readiness to change, and her personality style? Ruth has been so busy tending to others and concentrating on her problems that we do not hear much from her as a person.

Decades of empirical research have identified several cross-diagnostic client characteristics that serve as powerful indicators for treatment selection. Three of these are the client's preferences/goals, stage of change, and resistance level. For selecting the relationship and treatment to offer Ruth, these are as important, if not more important, than her disorders.

Ruth's Preferences and Goals   Ruth is hesitant initially to give voice to her preferences, consistent with her core dependency and deference to authorities. With encouragement, she brings a list into the second session as part of her between-session homework.

RUTH: It was hard to decide what I want from a therapist. In fact, it seems a little presumptuous. After all, you are the expert, right?

THERAPIST: Right, I am the expert on psychotherapy and behavior change. You are the expert on Ruth and what she wants. We will work together as a team pursuing your goals. I hear that it was difficult— and maybe new—to figure out what you want. Yes?

RUTH: Oh, yes. But it feels good.

THERAPIST: Feels frightening *and* good. That's how many of your changes will feel at first.

RUTH: Well, I wrote on my list that I would like to stay with you. I feel comfortable with you, and I don't know whether I would feel that with a woman therapist. And I would like you to push me a bit. I really liked doing things between appointments and our agreement for you to point out when I put myself down.

THERAPIST: I am heartened that you are finding your own voice, Ruth, and I will remember to end sessions with us developing between-session goals. Sounds like that will fit both of us just fine.

RUTH [*Smiling*]: Yes. And you know, almost nobody has ever asked me what I want.

THERAPIST: That's how therapy is really a special relationship. It is all about you, your life, your growth.

Ruth decides to focus in early sessions on her panic attacks and her dependency. "The other stuff is less important, but I do want to get to them." It would be naive to assume that clients always know what they want and what is best for them. But if clinicians had more respect for the notion that their clients often sense how they can best be served, fewer mismatches would ensue.

Ruth's Stage of Change
People enter the consulting room literally in different places or stages. Change unfolds over a series of stages: precontemplation, contemplation, preparation, action, and maintenance.[11] Ruth presents in the contemplation stage: aware of her problems and seriously thinking about overcoming them, but not yet taking specific action. People can remain stuck in the contemplation stage for years, as in Ruth's case. This is contemplation: knowing where you want to go, but not quite ready yet to go there.

Ruth presents for psychotherapy as a chronic contemplator seeking to move into action. She has failed resolutions to begin an exercise program, dragged her feet in becoming an elementary school teacher, and in general taken a post-dated check from life. In her autobiography she wonders, "What if I open Pandora's box and too much comes out and I get even more overwhelmed than I already am?"

Psychotherapy is more effective when the treatment strategy and therapy relationship are tailored to the client's stage of change and then evolve as the client moves along the stages during the course of treatment. With contemplators, my role as therapist is akin to a Socratic teacher who encourages clients to achieve their own insights into their condition. As Ruth enters the action stage, my stance is more like that of an experienced, supportive coach who has been through many crucial matches and can provide a fine game plan. The treatment methods of choice during contemplation are more exploratory, but those same methods are contraindicated once Ruth enters the action stage. Then, specific cognitive and behavioral methods are demonstrably more effective. The stages of change systematically guide me in tailoring the treatment and my relationship with Ruth.

Ruth's Resistance Level
A person's tendency to react against external influence is an indicator for how directive a therapeutic stance to take. Research has reliably found that directive methods work best among clients who have relatively low resistance, while nondirective methods work best with clients with high levels of resistance. Ruth, with a lifelong history of dependency and low reactance, will respond best to a directive stance on the part of the therapist. Moreover, this is in line with her treatment goals and therapist preferences.

Proceeding in a directive fashion in synch with Ruth's preferences and in accord with the outcome research is likely to enhance her eventual outcome. At the same time, we must be careful not to reenact, in conscious and unconscious ways, Ruth's unassertive and subservient relationship with the powerful therapist. Thus, I will broach this concern early with Ruth and contract for an evolving relationship in terms of our respective roles.

> THERAPIST: I am comfortable in following your preference for a directive therapist with an action plan and using between-session goals, Ruth. Your preference also agrees with the research. My concern is that doing so may reinforce in here your tendency to behave dependently and defer to others. Does that make sense?

RUTH: Yes. I haven't thought about that way before. Hmm.

THERAPIST: Might I suggest this. In the short run, I can be more directive, in charge, so that you can become less panicky and depressed. Once that happens, in the longer run, then we ask and teach you to become more assertive, more in charge in our sessions. How does that sound?

This distinction between mediating goals and ultimate goals is almost always enthusiastically received. The mediating goal is to reduce symptomatic distress; the ultimate goal is to restructure interpersonal behavior. Psychotherapy can be more directive in the short term to work toward more mature and assertive relationships in the long term.

These three client characteristics—treatment goals/preferences, stage of change, resistance level—in addition to diagnoses are evidence-based means of accelerating treatment and enhancing eventual success. These cross-diagnostic characteristics also underscore the potential for integration. Therapists will be directive *and* less directive according to the client's level of resistance; therapists will incorporate awareness-enhancing *and* action-oriented methods depending on the client's stage of change. In this respect, ostensibly rival or contradictory therapy methods are, in fact, complementary when tailored to the individual client.

Goals of Therapy

Adherents of single theoretical perspectives frequently but unknowingly dictate therapy goals to their clients. They behave like the legendary Greek innkeeper, Procrusteus, who owned a single hotel bed and stretched short guests and trimmed tall guests to fit that bed. Clients are all too often fit to the one-size, Procrustean bed when they receive the same assessment and the identical treatment.

By contrast, adherents to an integrative perspective favor fitting the therapy to the client and creating a new therapy for each client. It is Ruth's therapy, and her goals should predominate. I value clinical theory and therapists' preferences, but they should assume lower priority than the client's goals.

Ongoing assessment will, of course, refine Ruth's goals, and her early success will lead us to further goals. Ruth's immediate goals are to reduce her panic attacks and dependency; phrased more positively, to increase calm/relaxation and assertion/autonomy. That is where we begin, that is where Ruth's commitment and action lie, and that is where initial success awaits us.

Therapeutic Process and Procedures

Early on I introduce panic control therapy (PCT), a multicomponent treatment that includes elements of cognitive therapy, behavior therapy, and exposure therapy. I educate Ruth about the nature and physiological aspects of panic, train her in slow breathing, initiate cognitive restructuring directed at negative cognitions related to panic, and ask her to repeatedly expose herself to feared physical sensations associated with panic. The efficacy of this treatment has been demonstrated in numerous clinical trials; on average, about 80% of

PCT clients are panic free posttreatment, compared with 40% of clients receiving relaxation training alone and 30% of clients on a waiting list.[12] This treatment also fits well with Ruth's preferences for active methods, between-session goals, and a directive therapist stance.

Within 8 to 10 sessions, Ruth is free of panic and brimming with confidence. She succeeds without short-term anxiolytic medication, which she would accept "only as a last resort." She is ready to dive headlong into her dependency, which, not surprisingly, is comorbid with panic disorder. We begin with education about her unassertive, approval-seeking style through bibliotherapy. I offer Ruth a selection of assertion self-help resources rated highly by mental health professionals,[13] again, in the existential tradition, asking her to actively choose instead of passively accepting a prescription. She selects one, and we begin with assertion training: exploring differences between assertion and aggression; cognitive restructuring for her inevitable guilt when assertive; role-playing specific responses in session; tape recording her during role plays to fine tune her voice and words; and jointly developing homework assignments with family members.

"We are really cooking," Ruth enthusiastically asserts in session 15. Her panic is eliminated, and despite some anxious moments in challenging assertion situations, she is successful in asserting herself. I punctuate her success, comment on her newfound self, and reintroduce our agreement that she begin to exercise more direction in our therapy session.

Assertion is a goal not only outside therapy but within it as well. Now that Ruth has gained more confidence and our relationship is firmly established, one method to engender assertion in the therapy hour is to request that Ruth ask for something in each session. Our exchange goes likes this.

THERAPIST: If you agree, let's spend a few moments on your asserting yourself in here, with me. Your therapy is going terrifically well, but we can always improve on something. What would you like to do differently—perhaps something I could do less of or something we can do more of to your liking?

RUTH: It's going well. . . . I can't think of anything.

THERAPIST: I appreciate that it is difficult and also appreciate that you would not want to offend me. Yet it is your therapy, and one of your goals is for you to be assertive in here, not only at home. What are you experiencing now as I say that?

RUTH: Fear, fear that you might dislike me or abandon me if I complain.

Ruth's underlying identity or schema as inadequate is activated, which requires extensive emotional processing, cognitive restructuring, and active practice over the next five or six sessions. The emotion-focused work follows in the experiential or Gestalt tradition, including a few sessions with two-chair dialogues. The active practice occurs in her life and in our sessions, as we agree that Ruth will ask in every session for "something different," not necessarily a complaint about therapy or me. She is able to do so, requesting that we spend more time role-playing assertive responses and that I not ask at the end of each session, "When would you like to schedule our next session?" She informs me that she understands why I do it—"it helps clients to take control of their therapy"—but she finds it annoying because I already know that she desires weekly sessions. I thank her for her candid feedback, agree that I have taken a good idea too far, and pledge to stop asking each session. Voila!

Ruth's emerging self is now confronted with endless choices in her life and in therapy. Should she remain in school? What about her marriage? What would she like to tackle in therapy? I participate in these discussions, of course, but ultimately Ruth will decide, knowing that I support her and her decisions. Here is how Ruth probably opts to tackle other areas on her own schedule.

• *Marital dissatisfaction:* Now that her distressing symptoms have remitted and her assertion skills are enhanced, Ruth opts to invite her husband in for several conjoint sessions to improve their communication and to clarify expectations about her education and occupation. "I am finishing school, and whether he likes it or not, I will become a teacher." Ruth startles her husband and me (ever the optimist) by asking her husband in the third conjoint session to devote the next session to their sex life. Voila again!

Sequencing Ruth's various goals in psychotherapy turns out to be crucial. I had casually suggested to Ruth earlier in therapy that perhaps it was time to invite her husband in for conjoint sessions. Ruth insightfully observed that, if we had done so early, she would have communicated as a submissive spouse requesting permission rather than as an assertive partner negotiating the relationship. Her wisdom shows us the way.

• *Discipline with Jennifer:* At the intersection of her assertion work and conjoint sessions, Ruth declares that she is determined to parent more assertively and insists that her husband back her up. Ruth consumes a self-help book on effective parenting in a few days and then invites Jennifer into three sessions, each a month apart. Using communication and structural family methods, I assist them in expressing feelings, repairing ruptures, and arranging a contingency contract. Jennifer will follow the signed behavior contract with her mother; compliance brings privileges (such as more freedoms) and violation brings punishments (such as being grounded). Both Ruth and Jennifer report sustained improvement in their relationship and household compliance. Relationship voila!

• *Weight reduction and body image:* Ruth tackles this goal reluctantly and with some honest resignation about the futility of quick weight-loss schemes. I suggest that perhaps our goal could first be to initiate an exercise plan and to confront gender-linked stereotypes about body image. With the money saved by moving from weekly to biweekly therapy sessions, Ruth decides to join a women only exercise club, where she makes friends and consults a dietician monthly. We also spend several sessions examining, in the feminist tradition, the detrimental impact of social pressures on women's body image. Ever the eager student, Ruth pursues another self-help resource on overeating and gender.

• *Toward growth and pleasure:* As therapy winds down—our sessions now every three weeks—and as Ruth consolidates her progress, I wonder about her future. I gently suggest that the best protection to slipping back into panic, depression, dependency, stagnant relationships, and inactivity is self-nurturance. Ruth thinks on this for a few weeks and then, at our next session presents a self-nurturance list. This includes ongoing exercise at the gym, regular participation in her new church (which she finds comforting and calming), and a "girl's night" out with school friends at least once a month.

In 35 to 45 sessions, Ruth's efforts and success are remarkable. She transforms herself from a panicky, tired, underappreciated farm horse into a reassured, vibrant, affirming Pegasus. What psychotherapists do (and do not do) matter, but they matter less than Ruth's actions. I revel in the pride of her treatment success and remind myself of the blessings of being a psychotherapist. I express my admiration of and to Ruth, and of her ability to use what I offered. I anticipate the mutual sadness, the sweet sorrow of our termination.

Concluding Comments

The case of Ruth vividly demonstrates the value of psychotherapy integration. Her treatment combines individual sessions, conjoint couples sessions, sex therapy sessions, and mother-daughter sessions. Her integrative psychotherapy entails relationship stances and treatment methods associated with the psychodynamic, experiential, person-centered, cognitive, behavioral, exposure, systemic, and feminist traditions. Her integrative treatment blends psychotherapy, self-help, exercise, social support, and spirituality. Clinical wisdom is integrated with research evidence in devising that treatment plan and in enhancing the probability of her success.

Her case also usefully warns us of the danger of imposing narrow theories and singular treatments onto complex clients. Had Ruth been offered only medication, only individual therapy, only conjoint therapy, or only self-help, it seems doubtful that she would progress as quickly or as far. Beware of the propensity of theories to approach the proverbial elephant and discover only the elephant's trunk, leg, or tail. Let us discover, celebrate, and treat all of our clients in their glorious complexity.

In closing, a final word on the centrality of a systematic, evidence-based integration in clinical work. Integration is more than borrowing techniques from various therapeutic approaches; it is a thoughtful and research-informed approach that seeks to improve treatment effectiveness. Gone are the days of haphazard eclecticism; we now can use clinical experience and research evidence to direct us to what works best for clients and their unique context. Research can increasingly tell us how to effectively tailor treatment to individual clients beyond their diagnoses; three examples illustrated with Ruth are her preferences/goals, stage of change, and resistance level.

Each psychotherapist will establish his or her own integrative style on the basis of values, personalities, and life experiences. Let us also incorporate the research evidence into the integrative mix. In the end, our ethical responsibility is to the client's welfare; we strive to create for each client a new therapy that works.

Questions for Reflection

1. If your cultural background and life experiences are very different from Ruth's, will this present any particular problems in establishing a therapeutic relationship? If you do differ from her on any of these dimensions—gender, race, culture, ethnicity, socioeconomic status, age, value system, religion, or sexual orientation—would you feel a need to discuss these differences with her? How might your differences affect your counseling with Ruth? Might any of these differences incline you to refer her to another therapist? What are the ethical considerations in referring Ruth to another therapist?

2. In examining your own belief system and life experiences, do you think you would have any difficulty working therapeutically with any particular racial, ethnic, or cultural group? If you expect that you might have difficulty, what are your concerns, and what might you do about them?

3. What specific aspects about each culture do you feel a need to understand to develop a therapeutic alliance and work effectively with a client? If you do not have this knowledge, how could you go about acquiring it?

4. How important is it that you be like your client in each of the following areas: age, gender, race, ethnicity, culture, socioeconomic status, religion, values, sexual orientation, education, marital status, and family status?

5. Are you aware of referral sources for clients from various ethnic and cultural backgrounds? If so, what are they? If not, how could you find out about such referrals?

6. What are some key questions you could ask clients to learn more about their cultural background? Why do you think it is important to learn how clients identify themselves culturally?

7. Considering that cultural competence involves knowledge of your own biases and stereotypes, awareness of other cultural groups and practices, and the skills to form relationships across cultures, what competency area do you think you most need to improve, and how might you go about accomplishing this goal?

8. How diverse have your own life experiences been? What cultural groups might you be most anxious in working with, and where did this anxiety originate?

9. As Ruth's therapist, how would you respond to the issue of discrimination? What could you do to become more prepared to address this topic?

10. What direct experiences, assumptions, and beliefs do you have about Asian Americans? About African Americans? About Latinas/Latinos? How might this influence your conceptualizations, assessments, and interventions with such individuals?

11. As you consider the three selections on Ruth as an African American, as a Latina, and as an Asian American, what common themes do you notice? In what ways are the contributors of all of these pieces addressing both multicultural and integrative themes?

12. What potential challenges do you think you will face in combining concepts from both the multicultural and integrative perspectives in your work with a client who is culturally different from you?

13. Dr. Norcross mentions some of the advantages of an integrative approach as opposed to practicing within the framework of a single-school approach. What are your thoughts about the potential advantages of using an integrative perspective as a basis for your counseling practice? What possible disadvantages do you see in psychotherapy integration?
14. Dr. Norcross states that treatment goals, stage of change, and resistance level are important client characteristics to consider when working with Ruth. Would you consider these factors if you were working with Ruth? Explain.
15. Each of the contributors in this chapter draws from his or her own integrative approach when counseling Ruth. What have you learned from these contributors that you might use if you were counseling Ruth?

Notes

1. To maintain a broad stance, we will not identify a country of origin for Ruth's parents although we recognize the importance of such information with an actual client.
2. Gill, R. M., & Vásquez, C. I. (1996). *The María paradox: How Latinas can merge Old World traditions with New World self-esteem.* New York: G. P. Putnam.
3. Horvath, A. O., & Greenberg, L. S. (1989). Development and validation of the Working Alliance Inventory. *Journal of Counseling Psychology, 36,* 223–233.
4. Beck, A. T., Steer, R. A., & Brown, G. K. (2000). *BDI-FastScreen for medical patients.* San Antonio, TX: Harcourt.
5. Meyer, T., Miller, M., Metzger, R., & Borkovec, T. (1990). Development and validation of the Penn State Worry Questionnaire. *Behaviour Research and Therapy, 28,* 487–495.
6. Poundstone, W. (2003). *How would you move Mt. Fuji? Microsoft's cult of the puzzle—How the world's smartest companies select the most creative thinkers.* Boston: Little, Brown.
7. Reeves, T. J., & Bennett, C. E. (2004). *We the people: Asians in the United States, Census 2000 special reports CENSR-17.* Washington, DC: U.S. Department of Commerce.
8. Results of the Delphi poll on the future of psychotherapy are presented in J. C. Norcross, M. Hedges, & J. O. Prochaska, J. O. (2002). The face of 2010: A Delphi poll on the future of psychotherapy. *Professional Psychology: Research and Practice, 33,* 316–322.
9. See J. C. Norcross & M. R. Goldfried (2005), *Handbook of Psychotherapy Integration* (Oxford, NY: Oxford University Press), for a fuller discussion and clinical examples of integration.
10. Research on the therapy relationship and its association to treatment success are summarized in J. C. Norcross (2002), *Psychotherapy Relationships That Work* (Oxford, NY: Oxford University Press).
11. For definitions of the stages of change and its clinical applications, consult J. O. Prochaska, J. C. Norcross, & C. C. DiClemente (1995), *Changing for Good* (New York: William Morrow). The relation between systems of

psychotherapy and stages of change is considered in detail in J. O. Prochaska, & J. C. Norcross (2007), *Systems of Psychotherapy: A Transtheoretical Analysis* (6th ed., Belmont, CA: Brooks/Cole).

12. Barlow, D. H., Gorman, J. M., Shear, M. K., & Woods, S. W. (2000). Cognitive-behavioral therapy, imipramine, or their combination for panic disorder: A randomized controlled trial. *Journal of the American Medical Association, 283,* 2529–2536.

13. J. C. Norcross and colleagues (2003), *Authoritative Guide to Self-Help Resources in Mental Health* (New York: Guilford Press) compiles psychologists' self-help ratings and recommendations.

CHAPTER FOURTEEN

Bringing the Approaches Together and Developing Your Own Therapeutic Style

Jerry Corey's Integrative Approach to Working With Ruth

This chapter is devoted to my integrative approach in counseling Ruth. I demonstrate how I would work with the themes of Ruth's life from a variety of therapeutic perspectives. Let me emphasize that no one single approach has a monopoly on the truth. There are many paths to the goal of providing Ruth with insight and mobilizing her resources so that she can take constructive action to give new direction to her life. These therapeutic perspectives can actually complement one another.

For an illustration of my work with Ruth from an integrative perspective, see Session 9 ("An Integrative Perspective") of the *CD-ROM for Integrative Counseling*.[1] This segment of the CD-ROM is a useful supplement to this chapter.

Each therapy approach has something unique to offer in understanding Ruth. I will use a combination of approaches to work with Ruth on a thinking, feeling, and behaving basis. Table 14.1 shows what I am likely to borrow from each of the therapies as I conceptualize Ruth's case. As I describe how I would proceed with her based on the information presented in her autobiography and the additional data from the various theoretical perspectives chapters, I make parenthetical comments that indicate from what theoretical orientations I am borrowing concepts and techniques in any given piece of work. Thus, in addition to seeing a sample of my style of working with Ruth, you will have a running commentary on what I am doing, why I am using particular techniques, and what direction I am going in. As you read, think about what you might do that is similar to or different from my approach.[2]

TABLE 14.1 Major Areas of Focus in Ruth's Therapy

Orientation	Areas of Focus
Psychoanalytic Therapy	My focus is on ways in which Ruth is repeating her past in her present relationships. I have a particular interest in how she brings her experiences with her father into the session with me. I concentrate on her feelings for me because working with transference is a major way to produce insight. I am also interested in her dreams, any resistance that shows up in the sessions, and other clues to her unconscious processes. One of my main goals is to assist her in bringing to awareness buried memories and experiences, which I assume have a current influence on her.
Adlerian Therapy	My focus is on determining what Ruth's lifestyle is. To do this, I examine her early childhood experiences through her early recollections and family constellation. My main interest is in determining what her goals and priorities in life are. I assume that what she is striving toward is equally as valid as her past dynamics. Therapy consists of doing a comprehensive assessment, helping her understand her dynamics, and then helping her define new goals.
Existential Therapy	My focus is on challenging the meaning in Ruth's life. What does she want in her life? I am interested in the anxiety she feels, her emptiness, and the ways in which she has allowed others to choose for her. How can she begin to exercise her freedom? I assume that our relationship will be a key factor in helping her take actual risks in changing.
Person-Centered Therapy	I avoid planning and structuring the sessions because I trust Ruth to initiate a direction for therapy. If I listen, reflect, empathize, and respond to her, she will be able to clarify her struggles. Although she may be only dimly aware of her feelings at the beginning of therapy, she will move toward increased clarity as I accept her fully, without judgment. My main focus is on creating a climate of openness, trust, caring, understanding, and acceptance. Then she can use this relationship to move forward and grow.
Gestalt Therapy	My focus is on what is emerging in Ruth's awareness. I am guided by the shifts in her awareness, and together we create experiments that grow out of her awareness and her struggles. The emphasis is on our dialogue and the quality of our contact in the therapy sessions. I ask Ruth to bring her feelings of not being accepted into the

present by reliving them rather than by merely talking about past events. I am mainly interested in helping her experience her feelings fully, not in developing insight or speculating about why she behaves as she does. The key focus is on how Ruth is behaving and what she is experiencing.

Behavior Therapy	My initial focus is on doing a thorough assessment of Ruth's current behavior. I ask her to monitor what she is doing so that we can have baseline data. We then develop concrete goals to guide our work. I draw on a wide range of cognitive and behavioral techniques to help her achieve her goals: stress reduction techniques, assertion training, role rehearsals, modeling, coaching, systematic desensitization, and relaxation methods. I stress learning new coping behaviors that she can use in everyday situations. She practices these in our sessions and elsewhere.
Cognitive Behavior Therapy	My interest is focused on Ruth's internal dialogue and her thinking processes. I uncover the ways in which she is creating her problems through self-indoctrination and retention of beliefs that are not rational or functional. By use of Socratic dialogue I try to get her to detect her faulty thinking, to learn ways of correcting her distortions, and to substitute more effective self-statements and beliefs. I use a wide range of cognitive, behavioral, and emotive techniques to accomplish our goals.
Reality Therapy	Our focus is guided by the principles of choice theory. Key questions are "What are you doing now?" and "Is this behavior helping you?" Once Ruth has evaluated her own current behavior and has decided what she wants to change, we collaboratively make plans. I get a commitment from her to follow through with these plans.
Feminist Therapy	My interest is to provide a context for Ruth to evaluate how oppression may be operating in her life today. As a woman she has learned to subordinate her wishes to care for her family, which makes it difficult for her to identify and honor what she wants out of therapy. Because oppression profoundly influences Ruth's beliefs, choices, and perceptions, we will examine the cultural context of her gender-role socialization and how that is influencing her behavior now.
Postmodern Approaches	Rather than focusing on problems, I ask Ruth to look for exceptions to her problem or for times when she

(continues)

TABLE 14.1 Major Areas of Focus in Ruth's Therapy *(continued)*

Orientation	Areas of Focus
Postmodern Approaches (continued)	functioned without a specific problem. I also strive to get her to externalize her problem from the person that she is. The crux of Ruth's therapy is to conceive of the kind of life she would like to have, a life without the problems that are bringing her into therapy. The emphasis is on finding solutions rather than talking about problems.
Family Systems Therapy	My focus is on the degree to which Ruth has become differentiated from her significant others. We also examine ways in which anxiety is perpetuated by rigid interactional patterns and by her family's structure, and ways in which she can balance her role as a mother with taking care of herself.
Multicultural Perspectives	At the initial stage of counseling, and throughout the rest of the counseling process, I keep in mind how Ruth's culture is affecting her current behavior. I want to understand Ruth's subjective world and work within this framework. For the duration of therapy, she is asked to assess what she is getting from our work together, and I will make adjustments based on her input. From this perspective, counseling is focused on both her inner world and how the outer world is influencing her.

Initial Stages of Work With Ruth

I read Ruth's autobiography before our initial session, and I feel excited about working with her. I like her ability to pinpoint many of her concerns, and the information she provides is rich with possibilities. From her autobiography alone I do not have a clear idea of where our journey together will take us, for a lot will depend on *how far* Ruth wants to go and what she is willing to explore. However, reading Ruth's autobiography has given me many ideas of how I want to proceed, which I describe next.[3]

Our Beginning I assume that Ruth, too, has some anxiety about initiating therapy. I want to provide her with the opportunity to talk about what it is like for her to come to the office today. That in itself provides the direction for part of our session. I surely want to get an idea of what has brought her to therapy. What is going on in her life that motivates her to seek therapy? What does she most hope for as a result of this venture? I structure the initial session so that she can talk about her expectations and about her fears, hopes, ambivalent feelings, and so forth. Because Ruth's trust in me will be an important part of the therapy process, I give her the chance to ask me how I will work with her. I do not believe in making therapy into a mysterious adventure. I think Ruth will get more from her therapy if she knows how it works, if she knows the nature of her responsibilities and mine, and if she is clear on what she wants from this process.

🕮 **The Contract**   I begin formulating a working contract that will give some direction to our sessions. As a part of this contract, I discuss what I see as my main responsibilities and functions, as well as Ruth's responsibilities in the process. I want her to know at the outset that I expect her to be an active party in this relationship, and I tell her that I function in an active and directive way (which is characteristic of most of the cognitive, behavioral, and action-oriented therapies).

I see therapy as a significant project—an investment in the self, if you will—and I think Ruth has a right to know what she can expect to gain as well as some of the potential risks. I begin by getting some sense of her goals. Although she is vague at first, I work with Ruth to help her define her goals as specifically and concretely as possible.

🕮 **Ruth's Self-Presentation**   As a way of beginning the counseling process, I see value in first letting Ruth give her presentation of self in the way she chooses. How she walks into the office, her nonverbal language, her mannerisms, her style of speech, the details she chooses to reveal, and what she decides to relate and not to relate provide me with a valuable perspective from which to understand her. I am interested in how Ruth perceives the events in her life and how she feels in her subjective world. (This is especially important in the existential and person-centered models and in the postmodern approaches.) If I do too much structuring initially, I will interfere with her typical style of presenting herself. So I give everything to listening and letting her know what I am hearing.

I want to avoid the tendency to talk too much during this initial session. Being fully present in the therapy session and giving Ruth my sincere attention will pay rich dividends in terms of the potential for therapy. If I listen well, I will get a good sense of what she is coming to therapy for. If I fail to listen accurately and sensitively, there is a risk of going with the first problem she states instead of waiting and listening to discover the depth of her experience.

🕮 **Gathering Data**   I did not begin the session by asking Ruth questions pertaining to her life history, but after Ruth talks about what brought her to therapy at this particular time I ask questions to fill in the gaps. This method gives a more comprehensive picture of how she views her life now, as well as events that she considers significant in her past. Rather than making it a question-and-answer session, I like the idea of using an autobiographical approach, in which Ruth writes about the critical turning points in her life, events from her childhood and adolescent years, relationships with parents and siblings, school experiences, current struggles, and future goals and aspirations, to mention a few. I ask her what she thinks would be useful for her to recall and focus on and what she imagines would be useful to me in gaining a better picture of her subjective world. In this way she does some reflecting and sorting out of life experiences outside of the session, she takes an active role in deciding what her personal goals will be for therapy, and I have access to rich material that will give me ideas of where and how to proceed with her.

Therapy Proceeds

I favor integrating cognitive work into therapy sessions and recommend some books to Ruth to supplement her therapy. These may include novels, books that deal with central areas of concern to her personally, and something on the nature of therapy. For example, I suggest that she read some books about women facing midlife crises, about parent–child relationships, about enhancing one's marriage, about sex, and about special topics related to her concerns. I find that this type of reading provides a good catalyst for self-examination, especially if these books are read in a personal way—meaning that Ruth would apply their themes to her life.

🕸 **Clarifying Therapy Goals**   During the beginning stages, I assist Ruth in getting a clearer grasp of what she most wants from therapy, as well as seeing some steps she can begin to take in attaining her objectives. Like most clients, Ruth is rather global in stating her goals in her autobiography, so I work with her on becoming more concrete. When she looks in the mirror, Ruth says she does not like what she sees. She would like to have a better self-image and be more confident. I am interested in knowing specifically what she does not like, the ways in which she now lacks confidence, and what it feels like for her to confront herself by looking at herself and talking to me about what she sees.

Ruth reports that she would like to have more fun in her life. She can be helped to pinpoint specific instances in which she is overly serious and not having fun. We can further define what she would like to be doing that she considers to be fun. We consistently move from general to specific; the more concrete she is, the greater are her chances of attaining what she wants.[4]

🕸 **Importance of the Client–Therapist Relationship**   One of the most significant factors determining the degree to which Ruth will attain her goals is the therapeutic relationship that she and I will create. Therapy is not something the therapist does to a passive client, using skills and techniques. Although I have expertise with respect to therapeutic interventions, Ruth is clearly the expert on her own life. I operate on the premise that therapy will be productive to the extent that it is a collaborative venture. Furthermore, Ruth will get the most from her therapy if she knows how the therapeutic process works. I strive to demystify the therapy process by providing information, securing her informed consent, sharing with her my perceptions of what is going on in the relationship, and by making her an active partner in both assessment and treatment phases. I am concerned with the potentially harmful uses of power dynamics in the client–therapist relationship, and I strive to build mutuality and a sense of partnership into the therapeutic endeavor.

Therapy is a deeply personal relationship that Ruth can use for her learning. The person I am is just as important as my knowledge of counseling theory and the level of my skills. Although I value using techniques effectively and have a theoretical base from which to draw a range of techniques, this ability becomes meaningless in the absence of a relationship between Ruth and me that is characterized by mutual respect and trust. Some of the questions that I am concerned with in forming our relationships are: To what degree can I be real with Ruth? To what degree can I hear what she says and accept her in a nonjudgmental way? To what degree can I respect and care for her? To what degree can I allow myself to enter her subjective world? To what degree am I aware of my own experiencing as I am with her, and how willing am I to share my feelings and thoughts with her? An authentic relationship is vital at the initial stages of therapy, and it must be maintained during all stages if therapy is to be effective.[5]

Working With Ruth in Cognitive, Emotive, and Behavioral Ways

My integrative style is a blend of concepts and techniques from many therapeutic approaches. As a basis for selecting techniques to employ with Ruth, I look at her as a *thinking, feeling,* and *behaving* person. Although I may have to describe the various aspects of what I am doing separately here, keep in mind that I tend to work in an integrated fashion. Thus, I would not work with Ruth's cognitions, then move ahead to her feelings, and finally proceed to behaviors and specific action programs. All of these dimensions would be interrelated. When I am working with Ruth on a cognitive level (such as dealing with decisions she has made or one of her values), I am also concerned about the feelings generated in her at the moment and about exploring them with her. And in the background I am thinking of what she might actually *do* about the thoughts and feelings she is expressing. This *doing* would involve new behaviors that she can try in the session to deal with a problem and new skills that she can take outside and apply to problems she encounters in real-life situations. (As a basis for this integrative style, I am drawing on the cognitive and emotional insight-oriented approach of psychoanalysis; on the experiential therapies, which stress the expression and experiencing of feelings; on the cognitive therapies, which pay attention to the client's thinking processes, affecting behavior and beliefs; and on the action-oriented therapies, which stress the importance of creating a plan for behavioral change.)[6]

⚕ **Exploring Ruth's Fears Related to Therapy**   Ruth begins a session by talking about her fears of coming to know herself and by expressing her ambivalent feelings toward therapy:

> RUTH: Before I made the decision to enter therapy, I had worked pretty hard at keeping problems tucked away. I lived by compartmentalizing my life, and that way nothing overwhelmed me. But the reading I'm doing, writing in my journal, thinking about my life, talking about my feelings and experiences—all this is making me uncomfortable. I'm getting more and more anxious. I suppose I'm afraid of what I might discover.

From an existential perspective, I see this anxiety as realistic, and even useful. I surely do not want to merely reassure Ruth that everything will turn out for the best if she will only trust me and stay in therapy. I want to explore in depth with her the decision she must now make. Looking at her life in an honest way is potentially frightening. There are risks attached to this process. Although she has security now, she is paying the price in terms of boredom and low self-respect. Yet her restricted existence is a safe one. The attractions of getting to know herself better and the possibilities for exercising choice and control in her life can be exciting, yet also frightening. At this point I hope Ruth will look at this issue and take a stand on how much she wants for herself and the risks she is willing to take in reaching for more.

🕉 **Ruth Decides to Continue**   Being in therapy is a series of choices. Not only does therapy open Ruth up to new possibilities by expanding her awareness and thus widening the brackets of her freedom to choose, but she makes choices all during the therapy process itself. I respect her choices, and I support her when she is struggling with difficult ones. I also push her gently and invite her to ask for more and to take more risks. Ultimately, she is the one who decides many times during our sessions the depth to which she is willing to go.

🕉 **Ruth Works to Become Free**   In one session Ruth expresses her desire to be liberated. I suggest that she imagine all the ways she has felt unfree and write down the messages she has heard. I ask her to write to herself as her father, and then again as her mother.

Here is the idea of "homework assignments" (borrowed from the cognitive and behavioral therapies), but I am stressing the feelings that go with such an exercise. In this way Ruth can review some earlier experiences, and I hope she will stir up some old feelings associated with these memories, which we can deal with in future sessions.

At the following session Ruth brings her journal and says she would like to talk about what it was like to write herself letters (as her father and as her mother), saying all that was expected of her. I ask her to share what this was like, and I pay attention to her body as well as her words. (Like the Gestalt therapist, I think the truth of one's messages are conveyed in voice inflections, postures, facial features, and the like. If I listen only to her words, I am likely to miss a deeper level of meaning. Like the person-centered therapist, I value listening to what she is feeling and expressing.) Although I think it is important that I reflect and clarify, I deem it crucial that I bring myself into a dialogue with Ruth. If I am having reactions to what she is saying or if she is touching something within me, sharing my present experience with her can facilitate her work. My own disclosure, at timely and appropriate moments, can lead to a deeper self-exploration on Ruth's part. I must take care not to disclose merely for its own sake; nor is it well to take the focus off of her. But even a few words can let her know that I understand her.

Ruth is talking about her mother's messages to her. As I listen to her, I notice that there is a critical tone and a sharpness to her voice, and she makes a pointing gesture with her finger. I get an idea that I want to pursue.

JERRY: Would you sit in this red rocking chair? Actually rock back and forth, and with a very critical voice—pointing your finger and shaking it—deliver a lecture to Ruth, who is sitting in this other chair.

RUTH: I want you to work hard and never complain. Look at how I've slaved, and look at how moral I've been. Life is hard and don't forget that. You're put on earth here to see if you can pass the test. Bear all your burdens well, and you'll be rewarded in the next life—where it counts!

There are many possibilities of places to go from here. (So far I have been using a Gestalt technique of asking her to "become" her mother in the hope that she can actually feel what this brings up in her as she relives the scene.) I ask her to sit in the other chair and be Ruth and respond to her mother's lecture. The dialogue continues with exchanges between her mother and Ruth, and finally I ask her to stop and process what has gone on. This technique can also be done with her father, and will likely be done in further sessions because her relationship with her father continues to have a powerful influence in her way of being and behaving.

I give Ruth a different kind of journal assignment at this session. Earlier I had suggested that she write about all the ways she has felt unfree in life. Her personal writing was a catalyst that stimulated some useful exploration in her therapy sessions. Now I ask Ruth to think about the times in her life when she felt the most free. I ask her, "If you were to awaken and a miracle happened when you were asleep, what would your life be like if you were really free?" By using this *miracle question* (a solution-focused technique), I am inviting Ruth to design the kind of free existence she would hope for. As an alternative, I might use the Adlerian "acting as if" approach: "Ruth, I know that you experience yourself as being unfree most of the time, but I'd like you to try an experiment. For one week I would like you to consciously act as if you were free. For this period of time operate on the assumption that you are the free person now that you'd like to be. Let me suggest that you write in your journal about your experience when you are acting as if you are really free."

I assume that it is not a matter of Ruth feeling completely unfree or completely free, rather her sense of freedom may exist on a continuum. When she describes a time when she felt relatively free, I would then pursue with her what she did to contribute to feeling free. What's more, I will ask her to come up with small steps she can take and is willing to take to move in the direction of increasing her sense of freedom. The various journal assignments are useful for helping Ruth carry out her own therapy at home; she can then bring into her therapy session topics she wants to pursue.

We Work on Ruth's Cognitions   Gestalt techniques are very useful for assisting Ruth to get an experiential sense of the messages and values she has swallowed whole without digesting. My goal is to help her externalize these introjections so that she can take a critical look at them. I have an investment in getting her to look at this process and make her values truly her own.

I ask Ruth to identify as many family rules as she can that she recalls having grown up with as a child. She recollects parental messages such as these: "Don't think for yourself." "Follow the church obediently, and conform your will to God's will." "Never question the Bible." "Live a moral life." "Don't get close to people, especially in sexual ways." "Always be proper and appropriate." We spend time identifying and dealing with gender-role messages Ruth still struggles with such as these: "Your main concern should be your family." "Don't put your career needs before what is expected of you as a woman." "Defer to what men want." "Always be ready to nurture those who need care and attention."

In addition to working with Ruth's feelings, I find it essential to work with her *cognitive structures*, which include her belief systems, her thoughts, her attitudes, and her values. (In behavior therapy attention would be given to beliefs and assumptions that have an influence on her behavior; in rational emotive behavior therapy attention would be paid to irrational beliefs and self-indoctrination; in Adlerian therapy we would look at her basic mistakes; in reality therapy the focus would be on values; and in feminist therapy we would do an assessment of the impact of gender-role messages.) I focus on the underlying messages Ruth pays attention to now in her life. I assume that her self-talk is relevant to her behavior.

🕮 **Ruth Brings Up Her Spirituality**   Although I do not have an agenda to impose religious or spiritual values on Ruth, I do see it as my function to assess the role spirituality plays in her life currently and to assess beliefs, attitudes, and practices from her earlier years. Several times Ruth initiated a discussion about the void she feels in the area of religion. She was brought up with a strict fundamentalist religion and was taught that she should never question the religious and moral values that were "right." Eventually Ruth rejected much of the guilt-oriented aspects of her religion. However, even though she cognitively confronted many of the religious beliefs she was taught, on an emotional level she still feels a sense of unease and has yet to find what she considers a viable alternative to the religion of her parents.

Ruth lets me know that mainly what she remembers from her church experiences is feeling a sense of guilt that she was not good enough and that she was always falling short of being the person that her church and parents thought she should be. Not only was she not enough in the eyes of her parents, but she was also not enough for God.

Ruth is engaged in a struggle to find spiritual values that will help her find meaning in her life. Although formal religion does not seem to play a key role for Ruth now, she is struggling to find her place in the universe and is seeking spiritual avenues that provide her with purpose. She is floundering somewhat and realizes that this is a missing dimension in her life. She also lets me know that she is pleasantly surprised that I am even mentioning religion and spirituality, because she was not sure that it was appropriate to bring matters such as religion and spirituality into counseling. She says that it was good for her to be able to initiate a discussion about her past experiences with religion and her present quest to find a spiritual path that has meaning to her. Ruth tells me about her intention to further explore in her sessions ways that she can enhance her spiritual life.

Ruth Brings Up Her Father We devote several sessions to discussion of how Ruth's father played a central role in the moral and religious values that she believed she had to accept to stay in his "good graces." Eventually, Ruth gets the insight that she does not want to live by the religious dogma that her father preached, nor does she want to accept for herself the messages he continues to give her about the "right path for living."

As we explore the messages that Ruth was reared with, one theme seems to emerge. She has lived much of her life in ways that were designed to get her father's approval. She feels that unless she gets her father's acceptance and approval, she will never have "arrived." She reasons that if the father who conceived her could not love her, then nobody ever could. If this man does not show her love, she is doomed to live a loveless life! I proceed by using cognitive behavioral concepts and techniques to get her to critically evaluate some invalid assumptions she continues to make.

As much as possible, without pushing Ruth away, I challenge and confront her thinking and her value system, which appear to be at the root of much of her conflict. I am not imposing my values on her; rather, it is a matter of getting her to look at beliefs and values she has accepted to determine if she still wants to base her life on them. Does she want to spend the rest of her life in a futile attempt to "win over" her father? Does she want to continue making all men into her father? What will it take for her to finally gain her father's acceptance and love—if this is possible? What might she think of the person she had to become to gain his acceptance? I take this line of questioning in an attempt to get her to *think*, to *challenge* herself, and to *decide* for herself her standards for living.[7]

Dealing With Ruth's Past in Understanding Her Decisions I have been talking about some of the early decisions Ruth made in response to messages she received from her parents. I very much value the exploration of a client's early childhood experiences as a basis for understanding present pressing issues. (The psychoanalytic approach emphasizes a reconstruction of the past, a working through of early conflicts that have been repressed, and a resolution of these unconscious conflicts. Family approaches encourage clients to work through conflicts with their parents.) I accept that Ruth's childhood experiences were influential in contributing to her present development, although I do not think these factors have determined her or that she is fixed with certain personality characteristics for life unless she goes through a long-term analytic reconstructive process. (I favor the Gestalt approach to working with her past.) I ask her to bring any unresolved conflicts from her past into the here and now through use of her imagination and role-playing experiments. In this way her past is being dealt with in a powerful way as it is being manifested in her current problems.

Overall, Ruth is a willing and motivated client. She is insightful, courageous, able to make connections between current behavior and past influences, willing to try risky behaviors both in the session and out of the session, and willing to face difficult issues in her life. Even under such favorable (and almost ideal) circumstances, I still think Ruth will experience some resistance. She debates about whether to continue therapy; at times she blames her parents for her present problems; and at other times she chooses to stay comfortable because of her fear of plunging into unknown territory. In short, I work with whatever resistance she shows by pointing out its most obvious manifestations first and encouraging her to talk about her fears and explore them. An effective way to deal with resistance is to recognize it and deal with it directly. This can be done in a gentle yet confrontational way, along with providing support to face issues that she might otherwise avoid.[8]

Working Toward Redecisions   I try to structure situations in the therapy session that will facilitate new decisions on Ruth's part. Her redecisions have to be made on both the emotional and cognitive levels. (In encouraging Ruth to make new decisions, I draw on cognitive, emotive, and behavioral techniques. I use role-playing procedures, fantasy and imagery, mindfulness approaches, assertion-training procedures, Gestalt techniques, feminist therapy social action strategies, solution-focused therapy techniques, narrative approaches, and family systems therapy methods, to mention a few.) She can spend years getting insights into the cause of her problems, but what is more important is her willingness to commit herself to some course of action aimed at changing herself and also bringing about environmental change.

Encouraging Ruth to Act   In many ways I look at therapy as a place of safety where clients can experiment with new ways of being to see what behavioral changes they really want to make. The critical point consists of actually taking what is learned in the sessions and applying it to real-life situations. I consistently encourage Ruth to carry out homework assignments geared to having her challenge her fears and inhibitions in a variety of practical situations. Thus, if she says that she is yearning for a weekend alone with her husband yet fears asking for it because she might be turned down and the rejection would hurt, I challenge her: "If you don't bother to ask, chances are you won't have this weekend you say you want with John. You've often brought up in your sessions that you don't ask for what you want, and then end up feeling depressed and unloved. Here's your chance to actually do something different."

At various times I gently ask Ruth to decide if she *really* wants to make changes in her life or merely wants to *talk about* making changes. Because she sincerely wants to be different, we use session time in role playing and behavioral rehearsal, and then I ask her to experiment with her new learning in different life situations, especially with her family. For me, translating what is learned in the sessions into daily life is the essence of what therapy is about.[9]

Evaluating Ruth's Therapy Experience

My style of counseling places emphasis on continuing assessment by both the counselor and the client from the initial to the final session. In my work with Ruth I bring up from time to time the topic of her progress in therapy. We openly discuss the degree to which she is getting what she wants from the process (and from me). If she is not successfully meeting her objectives, we can explore some factors that might be getting in the way of her progress. I could be a restricting factor. This is especially true if I am reacting to her strictly from a technical approach and am withholding my own reactions from her. If I am being inauthentic in any way in the sessions, I am certain this will show up in a failure on her part to progress to the degree to which she might have.

I also explore with Ruth some of the circumstances in her life that may be contributing to what appears to be slow or nonexistent progress. She has done a lot of changing, which may itself be creating new problems in her home relationships, and she may feel a need to pull back and consolidate her gains. There may be a plateau for a time before she is ready to forge ahead with making other major life changes. Still another factor determining her progress or lack of it lies within her—namely, her own decision and commitment of how far she wants to go in therapy. Is she willing to make some basic changes in her personality and create a new identity for herself? Is she willing to pay the price that changing entails? Does she merely want to solve some pressing problems on the surface while remaining personally unchanged? These are but a few of the factors we have to consider in understanding any failure in the therapy process.

How do Ruth and I determine the degree to which she is progressing? What criteria do we use to make this determination? I look at Ruth's work in the sessions and what she is doing outside of them as a measure of the degree to which therapy is working. Another important index is our relationship. If it is one of trust and if she is dealing with difficult personal issues in her therapy and also working on these issues outside of the sessions, then therapy is working. Also, her own evaluation of how much progress she sees and how satisfied she is by the outcomes is a major factor in assessing therapeutic results.

When is it time for Ruth to terminate therapy? This, too, is a matter that I openly evaluate at appropriate times and we explore in a collaborative way. Ultimately, I see termination as her choice. My hope is that once Ruth attains a degree of increased self-awareness and specific behavioral skills in meeting present and future problems, she might well be encouraged to end formal therapy and begin to become her own therapist. To keep her beyond this point could result in needlessly fostering her dependence on me, which is not too unlike the problem that brought her to therapy in the first place.[10]

How Would You Work With Ruth Using Your Own Approach?

Try your hand at achieving some synthesis among the various approaches covered in the previous chapters by drawing on each of them in a way that seems meaningful to you—one that fits your own personality and your view of people and the nature of therapy. Here are some questions to help you organize the elements of your approach.

1. What would you be thinking and feeling as you approach your initial session with Ruth? Use whatever you know about her from the material presented about her and her autobiography in the first chapter, from the 12 chapters on her work with various therapists, and from my integrative approach in working with her in this chapter.

2. Briefly state how you see Ruth in terms of her current dynamics and most pressing conflicts. How would you feel about working with her as a client? How do you view her capacity to understand herself and to make basic changes?

3. How much direction do you see Ruth needing? To what degree would you take the responsibility for structuring her sessions? Where would you be on a continuum of highly directive to very nondirective?

4. If you were applying brief therapy with Ruth, what kinds of interventions would you most be interested in making?

5. What major themes do you imagine that you would focus on in Ruth's life, especially if you were working within the context of short-term therapy?

6. In what ways might you go about gathering life-history data to make an initial assessment of her problems and to determine which therapy procedures to use?

7. How might you help Ruth clarify her goals for therapy? How would you help her make her goals concrete? How would you assess the degree to which she was meeting her goals?

8. How much interest would you have in working with Ruth's early childhood experiences? Her current issues? Her future aspirations and strivings? Which of these areas do you favor? Why?

9. What value do you place on the quality of your relationship with Ruth? How important is the client–therapist relationship as a determinant of therapeutic outcomes?

10. Would you be more inclined to focus on Ruth's feelings? Her thought processes and other cognitive factors? Her ability to take action as measured by her behaviors?

11. How supportive might you be of Ruth? How confrontational might you be with her? In what areas do you think you would be most supportive? Most confrontational?

12. How much might you be inclined to work toward major personality reconstruction? Toward specific skill-development and problem-solving strategies? Toward social action strategies?

13. How might you explore Ruth's major fears, both about therapy and about her life?

14. What life experiences have you had that would most help you in working with Ruth? What personal characteristics might hinder your work with her?

15. How might you proceed in dealing with Ruth's parents and the role she feels that they have played in her life? How important would it be to focus on working through her attitudes and feelings toward her parents?

16. To what degree would you strive to involve Ruth's current family in her therapy?

17. How much might you structure outside-of-therapy activities for Ruth (homework, reading, journal writing, and so forth)?

18. What specific techniques and concepts might you derive from the psychoanalytic approach? From the experiential approaches? From the cognitive, behavioral, and action-oriented approaches? From the postmodern

approaches? From systemic approaches? From the multicultural approaches?

19. Would you orient Ruth's therapy more toward insight or toward action? What balance might you seek between the cognitive aspects and the feeling aspects?

20. How might you make the determination of when Ruth was ready to end therapy?

An Exercise: Themes in Ruth's Life

A few of the major themes that have therapeutic potential for further exploration are revealed in these statements that Ruth made at one time or another:

1. You seem so distant and removed from me. You're hard to reach.
2. In spite of my best attempts, I still feel a lot of guilt that I haven't done enough.
3. I just don't trust myself to find my own answers to life.
4. I'm afraid to change for fear of breaking up my marriage.
5. It's hard for me to ask others for what I want.
6. I feel extremely tense, and I can't sleep at night.
7. All my life I've tried to get my father's approval.
8. It's hard for me to have fun. I'm so responsible.
9. I've always had a weight problem, and I can't seem to do much about it.
10. I'm afraid to make mistakes and look like a fool.
11. My daughter and I just don't get along with each other.
12. I give and give, and they just take and take.
13. I've lived by the expectations of others for so long that I don't know what I want anymore.
14. I don't think my marriage is the way it should be, but my husband thinks it's just fine.
15. I'm afraid to tell my husband what I really want with him because I'm afraid he'll leave me.
16. I fear punishment because I've given up my old religious values.
17. I wear so many hats that sometimes I feel worn out.
18. There's not enough time for me to be doing all the things I know I should be doing.
19. I'm afraid of my feelings toward other men.
20. When my children leave, I'll have nothing to live for.

Look over this list of Ruth's statements and select the ones that you find most interesting. Here are three suggestions for working with them. For each of the themes you select, (1) show how you would begin working with Ruth from each of the 12 perspectives; (2) take only two contrasting approaches and focus on these; or (3) combine several therapeutic models and work with Ruth using this synthesis.

Attempt to work with a few of Ruth's statements after reading about my integrated way of working with her in this chapter. This would make interesting and lively material for role playing and discussion in small groups. One person can "become" Ruth while others in the group counsel her from the vantage point of several different therapeutic perspectives. Practicing a variety of approaches will assist you in discovering for yourself ways to pull together techniques that you consider to be the best.

Concluding Comments

Developing a counseling style that fits you is truly a challenge. It entails far more than picking bits and pieces from theories in a random and fragmented manner. As you take steps to develop an integrated perspective, think about these questions. Which theories provide a basis for understanding the *cognitive* dimension? Which theories help you understand the *affective* dimension? Which theories address the *behavioral* dimension? As you are aware, most of the therapeutic approaches you have studied focus primarily on one of these dimensions of human experience. The task is to wisely and creatively select therapeutic procedures that you can employ in working with a diverse population. Knowing the unique needs of your clients, your own values and personality, and the theories themselves is a good basis for beginning to develop a theory that is an expression of yourself.

It requires knowledge, skill, art, and experience to be able to determine what techniques will work best with particular clients and with certain problems. It is also an art to know *when* and *how* to use a particular therapeutic intervention. Because building your personalized approach to counseling is a long-term venture, I do hope that you will be patient with yourself as you continue to grow through your reading, thinking, and experience in working with clients and through your own personal struggles and life experiences.

Notes

See the DVD/online program entitled *Theory in Practice: The Case of Stan* (Session 13: An Integrative Approach to Working With Stan), which deals with termination and takes an integrative view of Stan's work.

1. In addition to the video, see Chapters 15 and 16 of Corey (2009), *Theory of Counseling and Psychotherapy* (8th ed., Belmont, CA: Brooks/Cole), which address the topic of an integrative perspective in more detail.
2. In G. Corey (2009), *The Art of Integrative Counseling* (Belmont, CA: Brooks/Cole), the parallel topics presented provide a useful resource for a more in-depth presentation of how to develop an integrative approach.
3. The *CD-ROM for Integrative Counseling* provides a demonstration of my work with Ruth during the initial stage of counseling (Session 1, "Beginning of Counseling").
4. Refer to Session 3 ("Establishing Therapeutic Goals") in the *CD-ROM for Integrative Counseling* for a demonstration of ways I assist Ruth in identifying concrete goals that will guide our work together.
5. Refer to Session 2 ("The Therapeutic Relationship") in the *CD-ROM for Integrative Counseling* for a demonstration of some issues that are essential to developing a therapeutic alliance.

6. In the *CD-ROM for Integrative Counseling,* Session 6 deals with the cognitive focus, Session 7 deals with the emotive focus, and Session 8 deals with the behavioral focus.

7. In the *CD-ROM for Integrative Counseling,* Session 11 ("Understanding How the Past Influences the Present"), Ruth explores her feelings toward her father via a role play.

8. In Session 5 ("Understanding and Dealing With Resistance") in the *CD-ROM for Integrative Counseling,* Ruth expresses some resistance toward continuing counseling.

9. In Session 12 ("Working Toward Decisions and Behavioral Change") in the *CD-ROM for Integrative Counseling,* Ruth explores some of her early decisions and begins to make new decisions.

10. In Session 13 ("Evaluation and Termination") in the *CD-ROM for Integrative Counseling,* Ruth and I review what she has learned in counseling and also discuss future directions after terminating counseling.

TO THE OWNER OF THIS BOOK:

I hope that you have found *Case Approach to Counseling and Psychotherapy*, Seventh Edition, useful. So that this book can be improved in a future edition, would you take the time to complete this sheet and return it? Thank you.

School and address:_____

_____

Department:_____

Instructor's name: _____

1. What I like most about this book is: _____

_____

_____

2. What I like least about this book is:_____

_____

_____

3. My general reaction to this book is:_____

_____

_____

4. The name of the course in which I used this book is:_____

_____

5. Were all of the chapters of the book assigned for you to read?_____

   If not, which ones weren't? _____

6. Did you use CD-ROM for Integrative Counseling with this book? If so, what was your reaction to the CD-ROM program?

7. In the space below, or on a separate sheet of paper, please write specific suggestions for improving this book and anything else you'd care to share about your experience in using this book.

_____

_____

BROOKS/COLE
CENGAGE Learning™

BUSINESS REPLY MAIL
FIRST-CLASS MAIL   PERMIT NO. 34   BELMONT CA

POSTAGE WILL BE PAID BY ADDRESSEE

Attn: Counseling Editor

Brooks/Cole
10 Davis Drive
Belmont CA 94002-9801

Il.l...l..lll...ll....l.lll.l..l..l.lll......lll...ll

FOLD HERE

OPTIONAL:

Your name: _____ Date: _____

May we quote you, either in promotion for *Case Approach to Counseling and Psychotherapy*, Eighth Edition, or in future publishing ventures?

Yes: _____   No: _____

Sincerely yours,

Gerald Corey